Praise for the Award-
BEN BOVA

"Bova proves himself equal to the task of
showing how adversity can temper character in
unforeseen ways."
—*The New York Times*

"With Isaac Asimov and Robert Heinlein gone,
Bova, author of more than seventy books, is one of
the last deans of traditional science fiction.
And he hasn't lost his touch."
—*The Kansas City Star*

"Bova gets better and better, combining plausible
science with increasingly complex fiction."
—*Daily News* (Los Angeles)

"[Bova's] excellence at combining hard science
with believable characters and an attention-grabbing
plot makes him one of the genre's most accessible
and entertaining storytellers."
—*Library Journal*

MERCURY

AND

PROMETHEANS

BEN BOVA

A TOM DOHERTY ASSOCIATES BOOK
NEW YORK

This is a collection of fiction and nonfiction. All of the characters, organizations, and events portrayed in the novel and short stories are either products of the author's imagination or are used fictitiously.

MERCURY AND PROMETHEANS

Mercury copyright © 2005 by Ben Bova

Prometheans copyright © 1986 by Ben Bova

All rights reserved.

A Tor Book
Published by Tom Doherty Associates, LLC
175 Fifth Avenue
New York, NY 10010

www.tor-forge.com

Tor® is a registered trademark of Tom Doherty Associates, LLC.

ISBN 978-0-7653-8549-9

Our books may be purchased in bulk for promotional, educational, or business use. Please contact your local bookseller or the Macmillan Corporate and Premium Sales Department at 1-800-221-7945, extension 5442, or by e-mail at MacmillanSpecialMarkets@macmillan.com.

First Edition: January 2016

Printed in the United States of America

0 9 8 7 6 5 4 3 2 1

CONTENTS

MERCURY

To the memory of my friend and colleague,
the star-seeker Robert Forward;
and to A.D., of course;
but most of all to the beauteous Barbara.

History will remember the inhabitants of [the twentieth] century as the people who went from Kitty Hawk to the moon in sixty-six years, only to languish for the next thirty in low-Earth orbit. At the core of the risk-free society is a self-indulgent failure of nerve.

—Buzz Aldrin,
Apollo 11 astronaut

A species with all its eggs in one planetary basket risks becoming an omelet.

—Stephen Webb
Where Is Everybody (Copernicus Books, 2002)

PROLOGUE:
THE LONG SEARCH

When, in disgrace with Fortune and men's eyes,
I all alone beweep my outcast state . . .

As he had every night for more than twelve years, Saito Yamagata wearily climbed the winding dark stone stairway to the top of Chota Lamasery's highest tower. He could feel the cold winter wind whipping down from the low entrance to the platform at the top. It was going to be a long, bitterly cold night. No matter. Yamagata was seeking atonement, not comfort. Atonement—and something more.

Once he had been a giant of global industry. Yamagata Corporation had even reached beyond the Earth to build the first solar-power satellites. Men trembled at his slightest frown; fortunes were made when he smiled. Then he had been struck down by an inoperable brain cancer and died.

That had been Yamagata's first life. Yamagata's only legitimate son, Nobuhiko, had personally administered the lethal injection that allowed the doctors to pronounce him clinically dead. More carefully than an ancient Pharaoh, Yamagata was preserved in a stainless steel sarcophagus filled with liquid nitrogen to await the day when his tumor could be safely removed and he might be brought back to life.

By the time he was cured and revived, Nobu was physically the same age as his father. Yamagata burst into laughter when he first saw his son: it was like looking into the mirror when he shaved. With great wisdom, he thought,

Yamagata declined to resume his position at the head of the corporation. Nobu had done well, and to demote him now would shame his son intolerably. So the elder Yamagata retired to this lamasery carved into the distant Himalayas to contemplate his first life. However, he did not live as the lamas did; he had comfortable furniture and decorations carried laboriously up the mountains to his bare stone cell. He maintained contact with the outside world through the latest electronic communications systems, including a satellite relay lofted especially for him alone. To the despair of the grand lama, who earnestly wanted to teach Yamagata the way to enlightenment, he brought in his own cook and even managed to gain weight. And he began to write his memoirs.

Perhaps because he dwelt on his former life, Yamagata found it impossible to stay entirely away from the corporation he had founded. He spoke to his son often over the videophone system in his quarters. He began to offer advice to Nobu. He envisioned a grand plan for Yamagata Corporation, a plan that extended far beyond the Earth. He led the corporation into the Asteroid Wars.

It took the slaughter of the *Chrysalis* habitat to shock Yamagata into realizing what he had done. More than a thousand helpless men, women, and children were massacred senselessly, needlessly.

I did not order the attack, he told himself. Yet he found that he could not sleep. Even his cook's most tempting preparations became tasteless, unappetizing to him. In his mind's eye he kept seeing those terrified, innocent people screaming in helpless horror as their space habitat was torn apart.

It took Yamagata many weeks to realize that he felt more than guilt. For the first time in his lives he felt shame. He was ashamed of what he had set in motion. I did not order the attack, he repeated to himself. Still, it was the inevitable consequence of the war that I willingly started.

Unsure of himself for the first time in his life, racked by a sense of shame he had never felt before, Yamagata begged for a private audience with the grand lama, hoping the old man could soothe his inner turmoil.

"There has been a tragedy," he began, hesitantly.

The grand lama waited for him to continue, sitting in silent patience on the low couch of his chamber, his head shaved bald, his ascetic face bony, hollow-cheeked, his dark mahogany eyes squarely on Yamagata.

"There is a war going on in space," Yamagata continued. "Far from here. In the Asteroid Belt."

"Even here, such rumors have been whispered," said the grand lama, his voice little more than a soft murmur.

"A few days ago more than a thousand people were killed," Yamagata stumbled on. "Slaughtered. In a space habitat."

The lama's lean face went gray.

His heart pounding, Yamagata finally blurted, "It may have been my fault! I may have caused their deaths!"

The grand lama clutched at his saffron robe with both hands. Yamagata thought the old man was having a heart attack. He stood before the lama, stiff with shame and guilt, silent because he had no words to express what he felt.

When at last the grand lama recovered his self-control he looked into Yamagata's eyes with a stare that pierced to his very soul.

"Do you accept responsibility for these murders?" he asked, his voice now hard as iron.

It was not easy for a man of Yamagata's pride and power to stand there humbly asking forgiveness from this aged, robed lama. He feared that the old man would expel him from the lamasery, shame him, accuse him of polluting the very air they were breathing.

"I do," he whispered.

The grand lama said, "For more than four years you have

lived among us, but not as one of us. You have used our sanctuary and our way of life for your personal convenience."

Yamagata said nothing. It was true.

Slowly, in words as hard and unyielding as the stones of the mountain aerie itself, the grand lama told Yamagata that he must seek true atonement or suffer the deadly weight of guilt forever.

"How do I do that?" Yamagata asked.

The lama was silent for many moments. Then, "Become one of us, not merely among us. Accept our way. Seek your path to atonement. Seek enlightenment."

Yamagata bowed his acceptance.

Heavy with remorse, Yamagata started out on the path to atonement. He sent his cook back to Japan, got rid of his comfortable furniture and electronic equipment, moved into a bare cell, and tried to live as the lamas did. He fasted with them, prayed with them, slept on a hard wooden pallet. And every night, winter or summer, he climbed the high tower to spend hours alone in contemplation, trying to meditate, trying to find true atonement in his soul.

The grand lama died, since the sect did not believe in rejuvenation treatments, and was replaced by a younger man. Still every night Yamagata climbed his weary way and sat cross-legged on the cold stone floor of the tower's platform, waiting for—what? Forgiveness? Understanding?

No. Yamagata realized over the slow passage of the years that what he truly sought was enlightenment, a satori, a revelation of the path he must follow.

Nothing. Night after night, year after year, not a glimmer of a hint. Yamagata prayed to the deaf heavens and received nothing in return. He wondered if the fault was in him, if he was not worthy of a sign from the vast universe. Deep in his soul, though, he thought that perhaps all this meditation and mortification was nothing more than cleverly packaged nonsense. And this troubled him, because he realized that as long as he harbored such thoughts, he would never find the path he so desperately sought.

So he hunkered down against the stone rail as the cold night wind gusted by, his teeth chattering despite the padded coat he had wrapped around himself, his fur hat pulled down over his ears, his chin sunk on his chest, his inner voice telling him that he was a fool for going through all this pain and humiliation. But doggedly he remained there, waiting, hoping, praying for a revelation.

It was a bitterly cold night. The moaning wind was like daggers of ice that cut through him mercilessly. Yamagata sat alone and miserable, trying to ignore the freezing wind, trying to find the path to atonement. Nothing. Only darkness and the glittering points of thousands of stars staring down at him from the black bowl of night.

He stared back at the stars. He could make out the Big Dipper, of course, and followed its Pointers to the North Star. Polaris was a thousand light years distant, he remembered from an astronomy lecture many years ago.

The nearest star was Alpha Centauri, but it was too far south to be seen from these frigid mountains.

Suddenly Yamagata threw his head back and laughed, a hearty, full-throated roar of delight that he hurled back into the teeth of the keening night wind. Of course! he said to himself. The answer has been all around me for all these years and I was too blind to see it. The stars! My path must lead to the stars.

BOOK I

THE REALM OF FIRE

No, Time, thou shalt not boast that I do change:
Thy pyramids built up with newer might
To me are nothing novel, nothing strange;
They are but dressings of a former sight.

ARRIVAL

aito Yamagata had to squint against the Sun's over-whelming glare, even through the heavily tinted visor of his helmet.

"This is truly the realm of fire," he whispered to himself. "Small wonder our ancestors worshiped you, Daystar."

Despite his instinctive unease, Yamagata felt physically comfortable enough inside his thickly insulated spacesuit; its cooling system and the radiators that projected from its back like a pair of dark oblong wings seemed to be working adequately. Still, the nearness, the overpowering brightness, the sheer *size* of that seething, churning ball of roiling gases made his nerves flutter. It seemed to fill the sky. Yamagata could see streamers arching up from the Sun's curved limb into the blackness of space, huge bridges of million-degree plasma expanding and then pouring back down onto the blazing, searing surface of the photosphere.

He shuddered inside the cramped confines of his suit. Enough sight-seeing, he told himself. You have proven your courage and audacity for all the crew and your guests to see and remember. Get back inside the ship. Get to work. It is time to begin your third life.

Yamagata had come to Mercury to seek salvation. A strange route to blessedness, he thought. I must first pass through this fiery inferno, like a Catholic serving time in purgatory before attaining heaven. He tried to shrug philosophically, found that it was impossible in the suit, so instead he lifted his left arm with the help of the suit's miniaturized servomotors and studied the keyboard wrapped around his wrist until he felt certain that he knew which keys he must touch to activate and control his suit's propulsion unit. He could call for assistance, he knew, but the loss of face was too much to risk. Despite the lamas' earnest attempts to teach him humility, Yamagata still held to his pride. If I go sailing out into infinity, he told himself, then I can call for help. And blame a suit malfunction, he added, with a sly grin.

He was pleased, then, when he was able to turn himself to face *Himawari,* the big, slowly rotating fusion torch ship that had brought him and his two guests to Mercury, and actually began jetting toward it at a sedate pace. With something of a shock Yamagata realized this was the first time he had ever been in space. All those years of his first life, building the power satellites and getting rich, he had remained firmly on Earth. Then he had died of cancer, been frozen, and reborn. Most of his second life he had spent in the lamasery in the Himalayas. He had never gone into space. Not until now.

Time to begin my third life, he said to himself as he neared *Himawari.* Time to atone for the first two.

Time for the stars.

LANDFALL

Even with three subordinates assisting him, it took Yamagata nearly an hour to disencumber himself of the bulky, heavily insulated spacesuit. He was dripping wet with perspiration and must have smelled ripe, but none of his aides dared say a word or show the slightest expression of distaste. When they had helped him into the suit Yamagata had thought of a Spanish toreador being assisted in donning his "suit of lights" for the bullring. Now he felt like a medieval knight taking off his battered armor after a bruising tournament.

Going outside the ship in the spacesuit had been little more than a whim, Yamagata knew, but a man of his wealth and power could be indulged his whims. Besides, he wanted to impress his subordinates and guests. Even though his son Nobu actually ran Yamagata Corporation and had for decades, the elder Yamagata was treated deferentially wherever he went. Despite the years of patient instruction that the lamas had spent on him, Yamagata still relished being fawned upon.

Money brings power; he understood that. But he wanted more than that. What he wanted now was respect, prestige. He wanted to be remembered not merely as a wealthy or powerful man; he wanted to go down in history for his vision, his munificence, his drive. He wanted to be the man who gave the stars to the human race.

Yamagata Corporation's solar power satellites were bringing desperately needed electrical power to an Earth devastated by greenhouse flooding and abrupt climate shifts. Under Nobuhiko's direction, the corporation was helping to move Japan and the other nations crippled by the global warming back onto the road toward prosperity.

And freedom. The two went hand in hand, Yamagata knew. When the greenhouse cliff struck so abruptly, flooding coastal cities, collapsing the international electrical power grid, wrecking the global economy, Earth's governments became repressive, authoritarian. People who are hungry, homeless, and without hope will always trade their individual liberties for order, for safety, for food. Ultraconservative religious groups came to power in Asia, the Middle East, even Europe and America; they ruled with an absolute faith in their own convictions and zero tolerance for anyone else's.

Now, with the climate stabilizing and some prosperity returning, many of the world's peoples were once again struggling for their individual rights, resuming the age-old battle that their forebears had fought against kings and tyrants in earlier centuries.

All to the good, Yamagata told himself. But it is not enough. The human race must expand its frontier, enlarge its horizons. Sooner or later, humankind must reach out to the stars. That will be my gift to humanity.

Can I do it? he asked himself. Do I have the strength and the will to succeed? He had been tough enough in his earlier lives, a ruthless industrial giant before the cancer had struck him down. But that had been for myself, he realized, for my corporation and my son's legacy. Now I am striving to accomplish greatness for humanity, not merely for my own selfish ends. Again he smiled bitterly. Foolish man, he warned himself. What you do now you do for your own purposes. Don't try to delude yourself. Don't try to conceal your own ambitions with a cloak of nobility.

Yet the question remained: Do I have the determination, the strength, the single-minded drive to make this mad scheme a success?

Finally freed of the suit with all its paraphernalia and boots and undergarments, Yamagata stood in his sweat-soaked sky-blue coveralls, which bore on its breast the white flying crane symbol of his family and his corporation. He dismissed his subordinates with a curt word of thanks. They bowed and hissed respectfully as Yamagata turned and started up the corridor that led to his private compartment and a hot shower.

Yamagata was a sturdily built man, slightly over 175 centimeters tall, who appeared to be no more than fifty-some years old, thanks to rejuvenation therapies. In his youth he had been as slim as a samurai's blade, but the years of good living in his first life had softened him, rounded his body and his face. The cancer ate away much of that, and his years in the lamasery had kept him gaunt, but once he left the Himalayas to begin his third life he soon reverted to his tastes in food and drink. Now he was slightly paunchy, his sodden, stained coveralls already beginning to strain at the middle. His face was round, also, but creased with laugh lines. In his first life Yamagata had laughed a lot, although during those years of remorse and penance he had spent with the lamas in their stone fortress high in the Himalayas there was precious little laughter.

Freshly showered and dressed in a crisply clean open-necked shirt and fashionable dark trousers, Yamagata made his way to the ship's bridge. He thought about dropping in on his two guests, but he would see them later at dinner, he knew. As soon as he stepped through the open hatch into the bridge the Japanese crew, including the captain, snapped to respectful attention.

Waving a hand to show they should return to their duties, Yamagata asked the captain, "Are we ready to send the landing craft to the planet?"

The captain tried to keep his face expressionless, but it was clear to Yamagata that he did not like the idea.

"It is not necessary for you to go down to the surface, sir," he said, almost in a whisper. "We have all the necessary facilities here on the ship—"

"I understand that," said Yamagata, smiling to show that he was not offended by the captain's reluctance. "Still, I wish to see the surface installation for myself. It's near the north pole, I understand."

"Yes, sir. Borealis Planitia."

"Near the crater Goethe," said Yamagata.

The captain dipped his chin to acknowledge Yamagata's understanding of the geography. But he murmured, "It is very rugged down there, sir."

"So I have been told. But personal comfort is not

everything, you know. My son, Nobuhiko, enjoys skiing. I cannot for the life of me understand why he would risk his life and limbs for the joy of sliding down a snowy mountain in all that cold and wet, but still he loves it."

The captain bowed his head. But then he added one final warning: "Er . . . They call it 'Dante's Inferno' down there. Sir."

DATA BANK

The closest planet to the Sun, Mercury is a small, rocky, barren, dense, airless, heat-scorched world.

For centuries astronomers believed that Mercury's rotation was "locked," so that one side of the planet always faced the Sun while the other side always looked away. They reasoned that the sunward side of Mercury must be the hottest planetary surface in the solar system, while the side facing away from the Sun must be frozen down almost to absolute zero.

But this is not so. Mercury turns slowly on its axis, taking 58.6 Earth days to make one revolution. Its year—the time it takes to complete one orbit around the Sun—is 87.97 Earth days.

This leads to a strange situation. Mercury's rotation rate of nearly fifty-nine Earth days is precisely two-thirds of the planet's year. A person standing on the surface of the planet would see the huge Sun move from east to west across the dark airless sky, but it would slow down noticeably, then reverse its course and head back east for a while before resuming its westerly motion. At some locations on Mercury, the Sun rises briefly, then dips down below the horizon before finally rising again for the rest of the Mercurian day. After sunset the Sun peeks back up above the horizon before setting for the length of the night.

Counting the Mercurian day from the time the Sun appears directly overhead (local noon) to the next time it reaches that point, it measures one hundred seventy-six Earth days. From the standpoint of noon-to-noon, then, the Mercurian day is twice as long as its year!

The Sun looms large in Mercury's sky. It appears twice as big as we see it from Earth when Mercury is at the farthest point from the Sun in its lopsided orbit and three times larger at the closest point.

And it is *hot*. Daytime temperatures soar to more than 400° Celsius, four times higher than the boiling point of water, hot enough to melt zinc. At night the temperature drops to -135°C because there is no atmosphere to retain the day's heat; it radiates away into space.

With a diameter of only 4,879 kilometers, Mercury is the smallest planet in the solar system except for distant-most Pluto. Jupiter and Saturn have moons that are larger than Mercury. The planet is slightly more than one-third larger than Earth's own Moon.

Yet Mercury is a dense planet, with a large iron core and a relatively thin overlay of silicon-based rock. This may be because the planet formed so close to the Sun that most of the silicate material in the region was too hot to condense and solidify; it remained gaseous and was blown away on the solar wind, leaving little material for the planet to build on except iron and other metals.

Another possibility, though, is that most of Mercury's rocky crust was blasted away into space by the impact of a mammoth asteroid early in the solar system's history. Mercury's battered, airless surface looks much like the Moon's, testimony to the pitiless barrage of asteroids and larger planetesimals that hurtled through the solar system more than three billion years ago. Caloris Basin is a huge bull's-eye of circular mountain ridges some 1,300 kilometers in diameter. This gigantic impact crater is the center of fault lines that run for hundreds of kilometers across the planet's rocky surface.

An asteroid roughly one hundred kilometers wide smashed into Mercury nearly four billion years ago, gouging out Caloris Basin and perhaps blasting away most of the planet's rocky crust.

Despite the blazing heat from the nearby Sun, water ice exists at Mercury's polar regions. Ice from comets that crashed into the planet has been cached in deep craters near the poles, where sunlight never reaches. Just as on the Moon, ice is an invaluable resource for humans and their machines.

DANTE'S INFERNO

Yamagata rode the small shuttle down to the planet's airless surface in his shirtsleeves, strapped into an ergonomically cushioned chair directly behind the pilot and copilot. Both the humans were redundancies: the shuttle could have flown perfectly well on its internal computer guidance, but *Himawari*'s captain had insisted that not merely one but two humans should accompany their illustrious employer.

The shuttle itself was little more than an eggshell of ceramic-coated metal with a propulsion rocket and steering jets attached, together with three spindly landing legs. Yamagata hardly felt any acceleration forces at all. Separation from *Himawari* was gentle, and landing in Mercury's light gravity was easy.

As soon as the landing struts touched down and the propulsion system automatically cut off, the pilot turned in his chair and said to Yamagata, "Gravity here is only one-third of Earth's, sir."

The copilot, a handsome European woman with pouty lips, added, "About the same as Mars."

The Japanese pilot glared at her.

Yamagata smiled good-naturedly at them both. "I have never been to Mars. My son once thought of moving me to the Moon, but I was dead then."

Both pilots gaped at him as he unstrapped his safety harness and stood up, his head a bare centimeter from the cabin's metal overhead. Their warning about the Mercurian gravity was strictly pro forma, of course. Yamagata had instructed *Himawari*'s captain to spin the fusion torch vessel at one-third normal gravity once it reached Mercury after its four-day flight from Earth. He felt quite comfortable at one-third *g*.

Leaning between the two pilots' chairs, Yamagata peered out the cockpit window. Even through the window's tinting, it looked glaring and hot out there. Pitiless. Sun-baked. The stony surface of Mercury was bleak, barren, pockmarked with craters and cracked with meandering gullies. He saw the long shadow of their shuttle craft stretched out across the bare, rocky ground before them like an elongated oval.

"The Sun is behind us, then," Yamagata muttered.

"Yes, sir," said the pilot. "It will set in four hours."

The copilot, who still had not learned that she was supposed to be subordinate to the pilot, added, "Then it will rise again for seventy-three minutes before setting for the night."

Yamagata saw the clear displeasure on the pilot's face. The man said nothing to his copilot, though. Instead, he pointed toward a rounded hillock of stony rubble.

"There's the base," he informed Yamagata. "Dante's Inferno."

Yamagata said, "They are sending out the access tube."

A jointed tube was inching toward them across the uneven ground on metal wheels, reminding Yamagata of a caterpillar groping its way along the stalk of a plant on its many feet. He felt the shuttle rock slightly as the face of the tube thumped against the craft's airlock.

The pilot watched the display on his panel, lights flicking on and off, a string of alphanumerics scrolling across the screen. He touched a corner of the screen with one finger and a visual image came up, with more numbers and a trio of green blinking lights.

"Access tube mated with airlock," he announced, reverting to the clipped jargon of his profession. To the copilot he commanded, "Check it and confirm integrity."

She got up from her chair wordlessly and brushed past Yamagata to head back to the airlock. He appreciated the brief touch of her soft body, the hint of flowery perfume. What would she do if I asked her to remain here at the base with me? Yamagata wondered. A European. And very independent in her manner. But I have a dinner appointment with my two guests, he reminded himself. Still, the thought lingered.

After a few silent moments, the pilot rose from his chair and walked a courteous three steps behind Yamagata to the airlock's inner hatch. The copilot stepped through from the opposite direction, a slight smile curving her generous lips.

"Integrity confirmed," she said, almost carelessly. "The tube is airtight and the cooling system is operational."

Yamagata saw that the outer airlock hatch was open, as

well, and the access tube stretched beyond it. He politely thanked the two pilots and headed down the tube. Despite her insouciance, at least the copilot had the sense to bow properly. The tube was big enough for him to stand without stooping. The flooring felt slightly springy underfoot. It curved gently to the left; within a few paces he could no longer see the two pilots standing at the shuttle's hatch.

Then he saw the hatch to the base, which was closed. Someone had scrawled a graffito in blood-red above the curved top of the hatch: *Why, this is hell, nor am I out of it.*

Yamagata grunted at that. As he reached out his hand to tap the electronic panel that controlled the hatch, it swung open without his aid.

A lean, pale-skinned man with dark hair that curled over his ears stood on the other side of the hatch, wearing not the coveralls Yamagata expected, but a loose-fitting white shirt with flowing long sleeves that were fastened tightly at his wrists and a pair of dark baggy trousers stuffed into gleamingly polished calf-length boots. A wide leather belt cinched his narrow, flat middle.

He smiled politely and extended his hand to Yamagata. "Welcome to Goethe base, Mr. Yamagata. I can't tell you how pleased I am to have you here. I am Dante Alexios."

Yamagata accepted his hand. His grip was firm, his smile gracious. Yet there was something wrong with his face. The two sides of it seemed slightly mismatched, almost as if two separate halves had been grafted together by an incompetent surgeon. Even his smile was slightly lopsided; it made him appear almost mocking, rather than friendly.

And his eyes. Dante Alexios's dark brown eyes burned with some deep inner fury, Yamagata saw.

Dante's Inferno indeed, he thought.

SUNPOWER FOUNDATION

A lexios showed Yamagata through the cramped, steamy base. It was small, built for efficiency, not human comfort. Little more than an oversized bubble of honeycomb metal covered with rubble from Mercury's surface to protect it from the heat and radiation, its inside was partitioned into cubicles and larger spaces. Goethe base was staffed with a mere two dozen engineers and technicians, yet it seemed as if hundreds of men and women had been packed into its crowded confines.

"We thought about establishing the base in orbit around the planet," Alexios explained as they walked down a row of humming consoles. Yamagata felt sweaty, almost disgusted at the closeness of all these strangers, their foreignness, their body odors. Most of them were Europeans or Americans, he saw; a few were obviously African or perhaps African-American. None of them paid the slightest attention to him. They were all bent over their consoles, intent on their tasks.

"My original plan was for the base to be in orbit," Yamagata said.

Alexios smiled diplomatically. "Economics. The great tyrant that dictates our every move."

Remembering the lessons in tolerance the lamas had pressed upon him, Yamagata was trying to keep the revulsion from showing on his face. He smelled stale food and something that reminded him of burned-out electrical insulation.

Continuing as if none of this bothered him in the slightest, Alexios explained, "We ran the numbers a half dozen times. If we'd kept the base in orbit we'd have to bring supplies to it constantly. Raised the costs too high. Here on the surface we have access to local water ice and plenty of silicon, metals, almost all the resources we need, including oxygen that we bake out of the rocks. Plenty of solar energy, of course. So I decided to plant the base here, on the ground."

"*You* decided?" Yamagata snapped.

"I'm an independent contractor, Mr. Yamagata. These people are my employees, not yours."

"Ah yes," Yamagata said, recovering his composure. "Of course."

"Naturally, I want to do the best job possible for you. That includes keeping the project's costs as low as I can."

"As I recall it, you were the lowest bidder of all the engineering firms that we considered, by a considerable margin."

"Frankly," Alexios said, smiling slightly, "I deliberately underbid the job. I'm losing money here."

Yamagata's brows rose in surprise.

"I'm fairly well off. I can afford a whim now and then."

"A whim? To come to Mercury?"

"To work with the great Saito Yamagata."

Yamagata searched Alexios's strangely asymmetrical face. The man seemed to be completely serious; not a trace of sarcasm. He dipped his chin slightly in acknowledgment of the compliment. They had come to the end of the row of consoles. Yamagata saw a metal door in the thin partition before them, with the name D. ALEXIOS stenciled on it. Beneath it was a smeared area where someone had tried to wipe out a graffito, but it was still faintly legible: *He who must be obeyed.*

It was somewhat cooler inside Alexios's office, and a good deal quieter. Acoustic insulation, Yamagata realized gratefully, kneading his throbbing temples as he sat in a stiff little chair. Alexios pulled up a similar chair and sat next to him, much closer than Yamagata would have preferred. The man's unbalanced face disturbed him.

"You need a drink," Alexios said, peering intently into Yamagata's perspiring face. "Tea, perhaps? Or something stronger?"

"Water would be quite welcome, especially if it's cold." Yamagata could feel his coveralls sticking to his sweaty ribs.

The office was tiny, barely big enough for a quartet of the spartan little chairs. There was no desk, no other furniture at all except for a small bare table and a squat cubicle refrigerator of brushed aluminum. Alexios went to it and pulled out an unmarked ceramic flask.

Handing it to Yamagata, he said, "Local product. Mercurian water, straight from the ice cache nearby."

Yamagata hesitated.

With a crooked grin, Alexios added, "We've run it through the purifiers, of course, although we left a certain amount of carbonation in it."

Yamagata took a cautious sip. It was cold, sparkling and delicious. He pulled in a longer swallow.

The room's only table was on Alexios's far side, so there was no place to set the bottle down except on the floor. Yamagata saw that it was tiled, but the plastic felt soft to his touch.

"Now then," he said as he deposited the bottle at his foot, "where we do we stand? What are your major problems?"

Alexios leaned back in his chair and took a palm-sized remote from the table. The partition on Yamagata's right immediately lit up with a flat screen display.

"There's Mercury," Alexios began, "the gray circle in the middle. The blue oblongs orbiting the planet are the first four solar power satellites, built at Selene and towed here."

Yamagata said, "With six more on their way here from the Moon."

"Correct," said Alexios. Six more blue oblongs appeared on the screen, clustered in the upper right corner.

"So it goes well. How soon can we be selling electrical power?"

"There is a problem with that."

Despite the fact that he knew, intellectually, that no project proceeds without problems, Yamagata still felt his insides twitch. "So? What problem?"

Alexios replied, "The point of setting up powersats in Mercury orbit is that they can generate power much more efficiently. Being almost two-thirds closer to the Sun than Earth is, we can take advantage of the higher power density to—"

"I know all that," Yamagata snapped impatiently. "That is why I started this project."

"Yes," Alexios said, his smile turning a trifle bitter. "But, as they say, the Lord giveth and the Lord taketh away."

"What do you mean by that?"

"The very intensity of sunlight that improves the solar panels' efficiency so beautifully also degrades the solar cells very quickly."

"Degrades them?"

The image on the wall screen changed to a graph that showed a set of curves.

"The blue curve, the one on the top, shows the predicted power output for a solar cell in Mercury orbit," Alexios explained.

Yamagata could see for himself. A yellow curve started out closely following the blue, then fell off disastrously. He looked along the bottom axis of the graph and gasped with dismay.

"It gets that bad after only six weeks?"

"I'm afraid so," Alexios said. "We're going to have to harden the cells, which will cut down on their efficiency."

"How much?"

"I have my people working on that now. I've also taken the liberty of transmitting this data back to your corporate headquarters on Earth so that your experts can double-check my people's calculations."

Yamagata sank back in the little chair. This could ruin everything, he thought. Everything!

As quickly as he gracefully could, Yamagata returned to *Himawari* riding in orbit around Mercury. He sat in gloomy silence in the little shuttle craft, mulling over the bad news that Alexios had given him. From his seat behind the two pilots, however, he couldn't help watching the European woman. It wouldn't do to pay any attention to her in front of her superior, he reasoned. Still, she was a fine-looking woman with strong features. The profile of her face showed a firm jawline, a chiseled nose, high cheekbones. Nordic, perhaps, Yamagata thought, although her hair was a dark brown, as were her eyes. Her coveralls were tight, almost form-fitting. Her form pleased Yamagata's discerning eye immensely.

Later, he thought, I'll dig her name out of the personnel files. Perhaps she would not be averse to joining me for an after-dinner drink this evening.

He had almost forgotten her, though, by the time he reached his stateroom aboard the fusion torch ship. His quarters were spacious and well-appointed, filled with little luxuries such as the single peony blossom in the delicate, tall vase on the corner of his desk, and the faint aroma of a spring-time garden that wafted in on the nearly silent air blowers.

Yamagata peeled off his sweaty coveralls, took a quick shower, then wrapped himself in a silk kimono of midnight blue. By then he had worked up the courage to call his son, back at corporate headquarters in New Kyoto.

Earth was on the other side of the Sun at the moment, and his call had to be relayed through one of the communications satellites in solar orbit. Transmission lag time, according to the data bar across the bottom of Yamagata's wall screen, would be eleven minutes.

A two-way conversation will be impossible, Yamagata realized as he put the call through on his private, scrambled channel. I'll talk and Nobu will listen; then we'll reverse the process.

It still startled him to see his son's image. Nobuhiko Yamagata was physically almost exactly the same age as his father, because of the years Saito had spent in cryonic suspension.

"Father," said Nobu, dipping his head in a respectful bow. "I trust you had a good journey and are safely in orbit at Mercury." Before Saito could reply, Nobu added jokingly, "And I hope you brought your sunblock lotion."

Saito rocked back with laughter in his contoured easy chair. "Sunblock lotion indeed! I didn't come out here for a tan, you know."

He knew it would take eleven minutes for his words to reach Nobu, and another eleven for his son's reply. So Saito immediately launched into a description of his visit to Goethe base on Mercury and the problem with the solar panels on the powersats.

He ended with, "This Alexios person claims he has sent the data to your experts. I am anxious to hear what they think about it."

And then he waited. Yamagata got up from his chair, went to the bar and poured himself a stiff Glenlivet, knocked it back and felt the smooth heat of the whisky spread through him. He paced around his compartment, admired the holograms of ancient landscapes that decorated the walls, and tried not to look at his wristwatch.

I know how to pass the time, he said to himself. Sliding into his desk chair, he opened a new window on the wall display and called up the ship's personnel files. Scanning through the names and pictures of the pilots aboard took several minutes. Ah! He smiled, pleased. There she is: Birgitta Sundsvall. I was right, she's Swedish. Unmarried. Good. Employee since . . .

He reviewed her entire dossier. There were several photographs of the woman in it, and Yamagata was staring at them when his son's voice broke into his reverie.

"Alexios has transmitted the data on the solar cells' degradation, Father," Nobuhiko replied at last.

Yamagata immediately wiped the personnel file from the screen, as if his son could see it all the way back on Earth.

Nobu went on, "This appears to be quite a serious problem. My analysts tell me that the decrease in power output efficiency almost completely wipes out any advantage of generating the power from Mercury orbit."

Yamagata knew it would be pointless to interrupt, and allowed his son to continue, "If this analysis stands up, your Mercury project will have to be written off, Father. The costs of operating from Mercury are simply too high. You might as well keep the sunsats in Earth orbit, all things considered."

"But have we considered all things?" Yamagata snapped. "I can't believe that this problem will stop us. We did analyses of cell degradation before we started this project. Why are the actual figures so much worse than our predictions?"

Yamagata realized he was getting angry. He took a deep breath, tried to remember a mantra that would calm him.

"Please call me," he said to his son, "when your people have more definite answers to my questions." Then he cut off the connection and the wall screen went blank.

Technically, the Mercury project was not being funded by Yamagata Corporation. Saito had officially retired from the corporation soon after he'd been revived from his long cryonic sleep. Instead, once he left the lamasery and returned to the world, he used his personal fortune to establish the Sunpower Foundation and began the Mercury project. As far as Nobu and the rest of the world were concerned, the Mercury project was devoted to generating inexpensive electrical power for the growing human habitations spreading through the solar system. Only Saito Yamagata knew that its true goal was to provide the power to send human explorers to the stars.

Saito—and one other person.

PAHS

Even after a dozen years of living with the lamas, Yamagata could not separate himself from his desire for creature comforts. He did not consider the accommodations aboard his ship *Himawari* to be particularly sumptuous, but he felt that he had a right to a certain amount of luxury. Sitting at the head of the small dining table in his private wardroom, he smiled as he recalled that the great fifteenth-century Chinese admiral Zheng He had included "pleasure women" among the crews of his great vessels of exploration and trade. At least I have not gone that far, Yamagata thought, although the memory of the Sundsvall woman still lingered in the back of his mind.

Seated at his right was Bishop Danvers, sipping abstemiously at a tiny stemmed glass of sherry. He was a big man, with heavy shoulders and considerable bulk. Yet he looked soft, round of face and body, although Yamagata noticed that his hands were big, heavy with horny calluses and prominent knuckles. The hands of a bricklayer, Yamagata thought, on the body of a churchman. On Yamagata's left sat Victor Molina, an astrobiologist from some Midwestern American university. The ship's captain, Chuichi Shibasaki, sat at the far end of the table.

Bishop Danvers had come along on *Himawari* because the New Morality had insisted that Mercury Base must have a chaplain, and the project manager had specifically asked for Danvers to take up the mission. Danvers, however, showed no inclination to leave the comforts of the ship and actually go down to the planet's surface. Hardly any of the ship's mainly Japanese crew paid the scantest attention to him, but the bishop did not seem to mind their secularist indifference in the slightest. Sooner or later he would go down to Goethe base and offer the men and women there his spiritual guidance. If anyone wanted some. What would the bishop think of pleasure women? Yamagata wondered, suppressing a grin.

Danvers put down his barely touched glass and asked in a sharp, cutting voice, "Victor, you don't actually expect to find living creatures on Mercury, do you?"

Victor Molina and Bishop Danvers knew each other, Yamagata had been told. They had been friends years earlier. The bishop had even performed Molina's wedding ceremony.

Molina was olive-skinned, with startling cobalt blue eyes and a pugnacious, pointed chin. His luxuriant, sandy hair was tied back in a ponytail, fastened by a clip of asteroidal silver that matched the studs in both his earlobes. He had already drained his sherry, and answered the bishop's question as one of the human waiters refilled his glass.

"Why not?" he replied, a trifle belligerently. "We've

found living organisms on Mars and the moons of Jupiter, haven't we?"

"Yes, but—"

"And what about those enormous creatures in Jupiter's ocean? They might even be intelligent."

The bishop's pale eyes snapped angrily. "Intelligent? Nonsense! Surely you can't believe—"

"It isn't a matter of belief, Elliott, it's a question of fact. Science depends on observation and measurement, not some a priori fairytales."

"You're not a Believer," the bishop muttered.

"I'm an observer," Molina snapped. "I'm here to see what the facts are."

Yamagata thought that Dr. Molina could use some of the lamas' lessons in humility. He found himself fascinated by the differences between the two men. Bishop Danvers's round face was slightly flushed, whether from anger or embarrassment Yamagata could not tell. His hair was thinning, combed forward to hide a receding hairline. He refuses to take rejuvenation treatments, Yamagata guessed; it must be against his religious principles. Molina, on the other hand, looked like a young Lancelot: piercing eyes, flowing hair, strong shoulders. Yamagata pictured him on a prancing charger, seeking out dragons to slay.

Before the discussion became truly disagreeable Yamagata tried to intervene: "Everyone was quite surprised to find creatures living in the clouds of Venus, and even on that planet's surface," he said.

"Silicone snakes, with liquid sulfur for blood," Captain Shibasaki added, taking up on his employer's lead.

Bishop Danvers shuddered.

"Incredible organisms," Molina said. "What was that line of Blake's? 'Did He who made the lamb make thee?' " He stared across the table at the bishop, almost sneering.

"But none of those creatures have the intelligence that God gave us," Danvers countered.

"Those Jovian Leviathans just might," said Molina.

The table fell silent. At a nod from Yamagata, the two waiters began to serve the appetizers: smoked eel in a seaweed salad. Yamagata and the captain fell to with chopsticks. The two others used forks. Yamagata noted that neither of the gaijin did more than pick at the food. Ah well, he thought, they'll feel more at home with the steak that comes next.

Bishop Danvers wouldn't let the subject drop, however.

"But surely you don't expect to find anything living down on the surface of Mercury," he said to Molina.

"I'll grant you, it's not the most likely place to look for living organisms," Molina admitted. "The planet's been baked dry. Except for the ice caches near the poles there's not a drop of water anywhere, not even deep underground."

"Then what makes you think—"

"PAHs," said Molina.

"I beg your pardon?"

"PAHs," Molina repeated.

The bishop frowned. "Are you being deliberately rude to me, Victor?"

"I believe," Yamagata intervened, "that our noted astrobiologist is referring to a certain form of chemical compound."

"Polycyclic aromatic hydrocarbons," Molina agreed. "P-A-H. PAHs."

"Oh," said Bishop Danvers.

"You have found such compounds on the surface of Mercury?" Yamagata asked.

Nodding vigorously, Molina replied, "Traces of PAHs have been found in some of the rock samples sent for analysis by the people building your base down there."

"And you believe this indicates the presence of life?" Danvers challenged. "A trace of some chemicals?"

"PAHs are biomarkers," Molina said firmly. "They've been found on Earth, on other planets, on comets—even in interstellar clouds."

"And always in association with living creatures?" Yamagata asked.

Molina hesitated a fraction of a second. "Almost always. They can be created abiologically, under certain circumstances."

Danvers shook his head. "I can't believe anything could live on that godforsaken world."

"How do you know god's forsaken this planet?" Molina challenged.

"I didn't mean it literally," Danvers grumbled.

"How strong is this evidence?" Yamagata asked. "Does the presence of these compounds mean that life is certain to be found on Mercury?"

"Nothing's certain," Molina said. "As a matter of fact, the PAHs deteriorate very rapidly in the tremendous heat and totally arid conditions down there."

"Ah," said the bishop, smiling for the first time.

Molina's answering smile was bigger, and fiercer. "But don't you see? If the PAHs deteriorate quickly, yet we still find them present in the rocks, *then something must be producing them constantly.* Something down there must be continuously creating those complex, fragile compounds. Something that's alive."

The bishop's face blanched. Yamagata suddenly foresaw his sunpower project being invaded by armies of earnest environmentalists, each eager to prevent any activity that might contaminate the native life-forms.

GOETHE BASE

Dante Alexios sat rigidly in his chair and tried not to let his satisfaction show on his face. The wall screen in his office clearly showed the earnest, intent expression on Molina's face.

He wants to come down to the base, Alexios said to himself, delighted. He's asking me for permission to come down here.

"My mission is sanctioned by the International Astronautical Authority," Molina was saying, "as well as the International Consortium of Universities and the science foundations of—"

"Of course," Alexios interrupted, "of course. I have no intention of interfering with your important research, Dr. Molina. I was merely trying to explain to you that conditions down here on the surface are rather difficult. Our base is still fairly rugged, you know."

Molina's intent expression softened into a smug smile. "I've been in rugged places before, Mr. Alexios. You should see the site on Europa, with all that radiation to protect against."

"I can imagine," Alexios replied dryly.

"Then you have no objection to my coming down to your base?"

"None whatsoever," said Alexios. "Our facility is at your disposal."

Molina's bright blue eyes sparkled. "Wonderful! I'll start the preparations immediately."

And with that, Molina ended the transmission. Alexios's wall screen went suddenly blank. He didn't bother to thank me, or even to say good-bye, Alexios thought. How like Victor, still as impetuous and self-centered as ever.

Alexios got up from his chair and stretched languidly, surprised at how tense his body had become during his brief conversation with the astrobiologist.

Victor didn't recognize me, Alexios said to himself. Not the slightest flicker of recall. Of course, it's been more than ten years and the nanosurgery has altered my face considerably. But he didn't even remember my voice. I'm dead and gone, as far as he's concerned.

All to the good, Alexios told himself. Now he'll come down here on his fool's errand and destroy himself. I'll hardly have to lift a finger. He's eager to rush to his own annihilation.

Alexios dreamed troubling dreams that night. The steel-hard determination that had brought him to Mercury and lured Victor Molina to this hellhole of a world softened as he slept, thawed slightly as he sank into the uncontrollable world of his inner thoughts, the world that he kept hidden and firmly locked away during his waking hours.

In his dream he was standing once again at the base of the skytower, craning his neck to follow its rigidly straight line as it rose beyond the clouds, up, up, farther than the eye could follow, stretching up toward the stars.

Lara was standing beside him, her arm around his waist, her head resting on his strong shoulder. The diamond ring on her finger was his, not Victor's. She had chosen him and rejected Molina. Alexios turned to her, took her in his arms, kissed her with all the tenderness and love his soul could contain.

But she pulled away from him, suddenly terrified. Her lovely face contorted into a scream as the proud tower began to slowly collapse, writhing like an immense snake of man-made fibers, coiling languidly, uncontrollably, unstoppably, as it slowly but inexorably crashed to the ground. All in silence. In utter silence, as if he had suddenly gone completely deaf. Alexios wanted to scream, too, but his throat was frozen. He wanted to stop the tower's collapse with his bare hands, but he could not move, his feet were rooted to the spot.

The immense collapsing tower smashed into the workers' village and beyond, crushing houses and cinderblock work buildings, smashing the bodies of men, women, and children as it thundered to the ground, pulverizing dreams and plans and hopes beyond repair. The whole mountainside shook as dust rose to cover all the work, all the sweat and labor that had raised the tower to its full height. Alexios's mouth tasted of ashes and a bitterness that went beyond human endurance.

Lara had disappeared. All around him, as far as the eye could see, there was nothing but devastation and the mangled bodies of the dead.

My fault, he told himself. The sin of pride. My pride has ruined everything, killed all those millions of people. Covered with ashes, his soul crushed along with everything else, he screamed to the vacant sky, "My fault! It's all my fault!"

He awoke with a start, covered with cold sweat. In the years since the skytower's destruction, Alexios had learned that the catastrophe was not his fault, not at all. The soul-killing guilt he had once felt had long since evolved into an implacable, burning hatred. He thirsted not for forgiveness, nor even for the clearing of his name. He lived for vengeance.

THERMOPHILES

Victor Molina also dreamed that night as he slept on the airfoam bed in his stateroom aboard *Himawari,* in orbit around the planet Mercury.

He dreamed of the Nobel ceremony in Stockholm. He saw himself dressed in the severely formal attire of the ritual as the king of Sweden handed him the heavy gold award for biology. The discoverer of thermophiles on the planet Mercury, Molina heard the king announce. The courageous, intrepid man who found life where all others said it was impossible for life to exist. Lara sat in the front row of the vast audience, beaming happily. Victor reminded himself to add a line to his Nobel lecture, thanking his wife for her love and support through all the years of their marriage.

Then he began his lecture. The huge audience hall, crammed with the elite of every continent on Earth, fell into an expectant silence.

Thermophiles are organisms that live at temperatures far beyond those in which human beings can survive, he told the rapt and glittering audience. On Earth, microscopic thermophiles were discovered in the latter part of the twentieth century, existing deep underground at temperatures and pressures that were, up until then, considered impossible as habitats for living organisms. Yet these bacterial forms not only exist, they are so numerous that they actually outweigh all the living matter on the surface of the Earth! What is more, they survive without sunlight, shattering the firmly held belief that all life depends on sunlight as its basic source of energy. The thermophiles use the heat of Earth's hellish core to derive their metabolic energy.

A British cosmologist, Thomas Gold, had earlier predicted that a "deep, hot biosphere" existed far below the surface not only of Earth, but of Mars and any other planet or moon that had a molten core. Scornfully rejected at first, Gold's prediction turned out to be correct: bacterial life forms have been found deep below the surface of Mars, together with the cryptoendoliths that have created an ecological niche for themselves inside Martian surface rocks.

While astrobiologists found various forms of life on the moons of Jupiter and even within the vast, planet-girdling ocean of that giant planet itself, the next discovery of true thermophiles did not occur until explorers reached the surface of Venus, where multicelled creatures of considerable size were found living on that hothouse planet's surface, their bodies consisting largely of silicones, with liquid sulfur as an energy-transfer medium, analogous to blood in terrestrial organisms.

Still, no one expected to find life on Mercury, not even thermophilic life. The planet had been baked dry from its very beginnings. There was no water to serve as a medium for biochemical reactions; not even molten sulfur. Mercury was nothing but a barren ball of rock, in the view of orthodox scientists.

Yet the surprising discovery of polycyclic aromatic hydrocarbons on the surface of Mercury challenged this orthodox view. PAHs are quickly broken down in the high-temperature environment of Mercury's surface. The fact that they existed on the surface meant that some ongoing process was generating them continuously. That ongoing process was life: thermophilic organisms living on the surface of Mercury at temperatures more than four times higher than the boiling point of water. Moreover, they are capable of surviving long periods of intense cold during the Mercurian night, when temperatures that sink down to -135° Celsius are not uncommon.

Now came the point in his lecture when Molina must describe the Mercurian organisms. He looked up from the podium's voice-activated display screen, where his notes were scrolling in cadence with his speaking, and smiled down at Lara. His smile turned awkward, embarrassed. He suddenly became aware that he had nothing to say. He didn't know what the creatures looked like! The display screen was blank. He stood there at the podium while his wife and the king and the huge audience waited in anticipation. He had no idea of what he should say. Then he realized that he was naked. He clutched the podium for protection, tried to hide behind it, but they saw him, they all saw he was naked and began to laugh at him. All but Lara, who looked alarmed, frightened. Do something! he silently begged her. Get out of your chair and do something to help me!

Suddenly he had to urinate. Urgently. But he couldn't move from behind the podium because he had no clothes on. Not a stitch. The audience was howling uproariously and Molina wanted, needed, desperately to piss.

He awoke with a start, disoriented in the darkness of the stateroom. "Lights!" he cried out, and the overhead panels began to glow softly. Molina stumbled out of bed and ran barefoot to the lavatory. After he had relieved himself and crawled back into bed he thought, I wish Lara were here. I shouldn't have made her stay at home.

TORCH SHIP *HIMAWARI*

T he ship's name meant "sunflower." Yamagata had personally chosen the name, an appropriate one for a vessel involved in tapping the Sun's energy. Earlier generations would have said it was a fortunate name, a name that would bring good luck to his enterprise. Yamagata was not superstitious, yet he felt that *Himawari* was indeed the best possible name for his ship.

While all except the ship's night watch slept, Yamagata sat in the padded recliner in his stateroom, speaking to a dead man.

The three-dimensional image that stood before Yamagata was almost solid enough to seem real. Except for a slight sparkling, like distant fireflies winking on a summer's evening, the image was perfect in every detail. Yamagata saw a short, slightly chubby man with a shock of snow white hair smiling amiably at him. He was wearing a tweed jacket with leather patches on the elbows and blue jeans, with a soft turtleneck sweater of pale yellow and an incongruous velvet vest decorated with colorful flowers.

Robert Forward had died nearly a century earlier. He had been a maverick physicist, delving into areas that most academics avoided. Long before Duncan and his fusion propulsion drive, which made travel among the planets practical, Forward was examining the possibilities of antimatter rockets and laser propulsion for interstellar travel.

Yamagata had hired a team of clever computer engineers to bring together every public lecture that Forward had given, every seminar appearance, every journal paper he had written, and incorporate them into a digitized persona that could be projected as an interactive holographic image. Calling themselves "chip-monks," the young men and women had succeeded brilliantly. Yamagata could hold conversations with the long-dead Forward almost as if the man were actually present.

There were limits to the system, of course. Forward never sat down; he was always on his feet. He paced, but only a few steps in any direction, because the image had to stay within the cone of the hologram being projected from the ceiling of Yamagata's stateroom. And he always smiled. No matter what Yamagata said to him, Forward kept the same cheerful smile on his round, ruddy face. Sometimes that smile unnerved Yamagata.

As now. While Yamagata showed the disastrous efficiency curves to Forward's image, the physicist's hologram continued to smile even as he peered at the bad news.

"Degraded by solar radiation, huh?" Forward said, scratching at his plump double chin.

Yamagata nodded and tried not to scowl at the jaunty smile.

"The numbers check out?" Forward asked.

"My people back at New Kyoto are checking them."

"You didn't expect the degradation to be so severe, eh?"

"Obviously not."

Forward clasped his hands behind his back. "Wellll," he said, drawing the word out, "assuming the numbers check out and the degradation is a real effect, you'll simply have to build more power satellites. Or larger ones."

Yamagata said nothing.

Forward seemed to stand there, frozen, waiting for a cue. After a few seconds, however, he added, "If each individual powersat can produce only one-third the power you anticipated, then you'll need three times as many power-sats. It's quite simple."

"That is impossible," said Yamagata.

"Why impossible? The technology is well in hand. If you can build ten powersats you can build thirty."

"The costs would be too high."

"Ah!" Forward nodded knowingly. "Economics. The dismal science."

"Dismal, perhaps, but inescapable. The Foundation cannot afford to triple its costs."

"Even if you built the powersats here at Mercury, instead of buying them from Selene and towing them here from the Moon?"

"Build them here?"

Forward's image seemed to freeze for an eyeblink's span, then he began ticking off on his chubby fingers, "Mercury has abundant metals. Silicon is rarer than on the Moon but there's still enough easily scooped from the planet's surface to build hundreds of powersats. You'd save on transportation costs, of course, and you'd cut out Selene's profits."

"But I would have to hire a sizeable construction crew," Yamagata objected. "And they will want premium pay to work here at Mercury."

Forward's smile almost faded. But he quickly recovered. "I don't know much about nanotechnology; the field was in its infancy when I died. But couldn't you program nano-machines to build powersats?"

"Selene makes extensive use of nanomachines," Yamagata agreed.

"There you are," said Forward, with an offhand gesture.

Yamagata hesitated, thinking. Then, "But focusing thirty laser beams on a starship's lightsail . . . wouldn't that be difficult?"

Forward's smile returned in full wattage. "If you can focus ten lasers on a sail you can focus thirty. No problemo."

Yamagata smiled back. Until he realized that he was speaking to a man who had lived a century earlier and even then was known as a wild-eyed theoretician with no practical, hands-on experience.

NANOMACHINES

N anomachines?" Alexios asked the image on his office wall.

"Yes," replied Yamagata with an unhappy sigh. "It may become necessary to use them."

"We have no nanotech specialists here," said Alexios, sitting up tensely in his office chair. It was a lie: he himself had experience with nanotechnology. But he had kept that information hidden from everyone.

"I am aware of that," Yamagata replied. "There are several in Selene who might be induced to come here."

"We're crowded down here already."

Yamagata's face tightened into a frown momentarily, then he regained control of himself and put on a perfunctory smile. "If it becomes necessary to build more power satellites than originally planned, your base will have to be enlarged considerably. We will need to build a mass launcher down there on the surface and hire entire teams of technicians to assemble the satellites in orbit."

Alexios nodded and tried to hide the elation he felt. It's working! he told himself. I'm going to bleed him dry.

Aloud, he said to Yamagata, "Many of my team are quite distressed by nanomachines. They feel that nanotechnology is dangerous."

Strangely, Yamagata grinned at him. "If you think *they* will be unhappy, imagine how Bishop Danvers will react."

Sure enough, Yamagata heard an earnest rap on his stateroom door within a half hour of his conversation with Alexios.

"Enter," he called out, rising from his comfortable chair.

Bishop Danvers slid the door open and stepped through, then carefully shut it again.

"How kind of you to visit me," said Yamagata pleasantly.

Danvers's usually bland face looked stern. "This is not a social call, I'm afraid."

"Ah so?" Yamagata gestured to one of the plush armchairs arranged around his recliner. "Let's at least be physically comfortable. Would you like a refreshment? Tea, perhaps?"

The bishop brushed off Yamagata's attempts to soften the meeting. "I understand you are considering bringing nanomachines here."

Yamagata's brows rose slightly. He must have spies in the communications center, he thought. Believers who report everything to him.

Coolly, he replied, "It may become necessary to use nanotechnology for certain aspects of the project."

"Nanotechnology is banned."

"On Earth. Not in Selene or anywhere else."

"It is dangerous. Nanomachines have killed people. They have been turned into monstrous weapons."

"They will be used here to construct a mass driver on Mercury's surface and to assemble components of power satellites. Nothing more."

"Nanotechnology is evil!"

Yamagata steepled his fingers, stalling for time to think. Do not antagonize this man, he warned himself. He can bring the full power of Earth's governments against you.

"Bishop Danvers," Yamagata said placatingly, "technology is neither evil nor good, in itself. It is men who are moral or not. It is the way we *use* technology that is good or evil. After all, a stone can be used to help build a temple or to bash someone's brains in. Is the stone evil?"

"Nanotechnology is banned on Earth for perfectly good reasons," Danvers insisted.

"On a planet crowded with ten billion people, including the mentally sick, the greedy, the fanatic, I understand perfectly why nanotechnology is banned. Here in space the situation is quite different."

Danvers shook his head stubbornly. "How do you know that there are no mentally sick people among your crew? No one who is greedy? No fanatics?"

A good point, Yamagata admitted silently. There could be fanatics here. Danvers himself might be one. If he knew this project's ultimate aim is to reach the stars, how would he react?

Aloud, Yamagata replied, "Bishop Danvers, every man and woman here has been thoroughly screened by psychological tests. Most of them are engineers and technicians. They are quite stable, I assure you."

Danvers countered, "Do you truly believe that anyone who is willing to come to this hellhole for years at a time is mentally stable?"

Despite himself, Yamagata smiled. "A good point, sir. We must discuss the personality traits of adventurers over dinner some evening."

"Don't try to make light of this."

"I assure you, I am not. If we need nanomachines to make this project succeed, it will mean an additional investment that will strain the resources of the Sunpower Foundation to the utmost. Let me tell you, this decision will not be made lightly."

Danvers knew he was being dismissed. He got slowly to

his feet, his fleshy face set in a determined scowl. "Think carefully, sir. What does it gain a man if he wins the whole world and suffers the loss of his immortal soul?"

Yamagata rose, too. "I am merely trying to provide electrical power for my fellow human beings. Surely that is a good thing."

"Not if you use evil methods."

"I can only assure you, Bishop, that if we use nanomachines, they will be kept under the strictest of controls."

Clearly unhappy, Bishop Danvers turned his back on Yamagata and left the stateroom.

Yamagata sank back into his recliner. I've made an enemy of him, he realized. Now he'll report back to his superiors on Earth and I'll get more static from the International Astronautical Authority and god knows what other government agencies.

Ordinarily he would have smiled at his unintentional pun about god. This time he did not.

Bishop Elliott Danvers strode back toward his own stateroom along the sloping corridor that ran the length of *Himawari*'s habitation module. He passed several crew personnel, all of whom nodded or muttered a word of greeting to him. He acknowledged their deference with a curt nod each time. His mind was churning with other thoughts.

Nanotechnology! My superiors in Atlanta will go ballistic when they learn that Yamagata plans to bring nanomachines here. Godless technology. How can God allow such a mockery of His will to exist? Then Danvers realized that God would not allow it. God will stop them, just as he stopped the skytower, ten years ago. And he realized something even more important: I am God's agent here, sent to do His work. I haven't the power to stop Yamagata, not unless God sends a catastrophe to this wicked place. Only some disaster will bring Yamagata to his senses.

Despite his bland outward appearance, Elliott Danvers had led a far from dull life. Born in a Detroit slum, he was always physically big for his age. Other kids took one look at him and thought he was tough, strong. He wasn't. The real bullies in the 'hood enlarged their reputations by bloodying the big guy. The wiseguys who ran the local youth club made him play on the local semipro football team when he was barely fourteen. In his first game he got three ribs cracked; in the next contest they broke his leg. When he recovered from that the gamblers put him in the prizefight ring and quietly bet against him. They made money. Danvers's share was pain and blood and humiliation.

When he broke his hand slugging it out with a young black kid from a rival club, they tossed him out onto the street, his hand swollen monstrously, his face unrecognizable from the beating he'd taken.

One of the street missionaries from the storefront New Morality branch found Danvers huddled in the gutter, bleeding and sobbing. He took Danvers in, dressed his wounds, fed his body and spirit, and turned his gratitude into a life of service. At twenty he entered a New Morality seminary. By the time he was twenty-two, Elliott Danvers was an ordained minister, ready to be sent out into the world in service to God. He was never allowed to return to his old Detroit neighborhood. Instead he was sent overseas and saw that there were many wretched people around the globe who needed his help.

His rise through the hierarchy was slow, however. He was not especially brilliant. He had no family connections or well-connected friends to help push him upward. He worked hard and took the most difficult, least rewarding assignments in gratitude for the saving of his life.

His big chance came when he was assigned as spiritual counselor to the largely Latin-American crew building the skytower in Ecuador. The idea of a space elevator seemed little less than blasphemous to him, a modern-day equivalent to the ancient Tower of Babel. A tower that reached to the heavens. Clearly technological hubris, if nothing else. It was doomed to fail, Danvers felt from the beginning.

When it did fail, it was his duty to report to the authorities on who was responsible for the terrible tragedy. Millions of lives had been lost. Someone had to pay.

As a man of God, Danvers was respected by the Ecuadorian authorities. Even the godless secularists of the International Astronautical Authority respected his supposedly unbiased word.

Danvers phrased his report very carefully, but it was clear that he—like most of the accident investigators—put final blame on the leader of the project, the man who was in charge of the construction.

The project leader was disgraced and charged with multiple homicide. Because the international legal system did not permit capital punishment for inadvertent homicide, he was sentenced to be banished from Earth forever.

Danvers was promoted to bishop, and—after another decade of patient, uncomplaining labor—sent to be spiritual advisor to the small crew of engineers and technicians working for the Sunpower Foundation building solar power satellites at the planet Mercury.

He was puzzled about the assignment, until his superiors told him that the director of the project had personally asked for Danvers. This pleased and flattered him. He did not realize that the fiery-eyed Dante Alexios, running the actual construction work on the hell-hot surface of Mercury, was the young engineer who had been in charge of the skytower project, the man who had been banished from Earth in large part because of Danvers's testimony.

FIELD TRIP

Victor Molina licked his lips nervously. "I've never been out on the surface of another world before," he said.

Dante Alexios put on a surprised look. "But you told me you've been to Jupiter's moons, didn't you?"

The two men were being helped into the heavily insulated spacesuits that were used for excursions on Mercury's rocky, Sun-baked surface. Half a dozen technicians were assisting them, three for each man. The suits were brightly polished, almost to a mirror finish, and so bulky that they were more individual habitats than normal spacesuits.

Molina's usual cocky attitude had long since vanished, replaced by uncertainty. "I was at Europa, yeah," he maintained. "Most of the time, though, I was in the research station *Gold,* orbiting Jupiter. I spent a week in the smaller station in orbit around Europa itself but I never got down to the surface."

Alexios nodded as the technicians hung the life-support package to the back of his suit. Even in Mercury's light gravity it felt burdensome. Both men's suits were plugged into the base's power system, mainly to keep the cooling fans running. Otherwise they would already be uncomfortably hot and sweaty inside the massive suits.

He knew that Molina had never set foot on the surface of another world. Alexios had spent years accumulating a meticulous dossier on Victor Molina, the man who had once been his friend, his schoolmate, the buddy he had asked to be his best man when he married Lara. Molina had betrayed him and stolen Lara from him. Now he was going to pay.

It took two technicians to lift the thick-walled helmet over Molina's head and settle it onto the torso ring, like churchmen lowering a royal crown on an emperor. As they began sealing the helmet, two other techs lowered Alexios's helmet, muffling all the sounds outside. Strange, Alexios thought. We don't really notice the throbbing of the base's pumps and the hiss of the air vents until the sound stops. Through his thick quartz visor he could see the technicians fussing around Molina's suit, and the serious, almost grim expression on the astrobiologist's face. Once we pull down the sun visors I won't be able to see his face at all, Alexios knew.

He moved his arm with a whine of servomotors and pressed the stud on his left wrist that activated the suit's radio.

"Can you hear me, Dr. Molina?"

For a moment there was no reply, then, "I hear you." Molina's voice sounded strange, preoccupied.

The woman in charge of the technicians at last gave Alexios a thump on the shoulder and signaled a thumbs-up to him. He switched to the radio frequency for the base's control center:

"Molina and Alexios, ready for surface excursion."

"You are cleared for excursion," came the controller's voice. Alexios recognized it; a dour Russian whom he sometimes played chess with. Once in a while he even won.

"Cameras on?" Alexios asked, as he started clumping in the heavy boots toward the airlock hatch.

"Exterior cameras functioning. Relief crew standing by."

Two other members of the base's complement had suited up at the auxiliary airlock and were prepared to come out to rescue Alexios and Molina if they ran into trouble. Neither the main airlock nor the auxiliary was big enough to hold four suited people at the same time.

The inner airlock hatch swung open. Alexios gestured with a gloved hand. "After you, Dr. Molina."

Moving uncertainly, hesitantly, Molina stepped over the hatch's sill and planted his boots inside the airlock chamber. Alexios followed him, almost as slowly. One could not make sudden moves in the cumbersome suits.

Once the inner hatch closed again and the air was pumping out of the chamber, Molina said, "It's funny, but over this radio link your voice sounds kind of familiar."

Alexios's pulse thumped suddenly. "Familiar?"

"Like it's a voice I know. A voice I've heard before."

Will he recognize me? Alexios wondered. That would ruin everything.

He said nothing as the panel lights indicated the airlock chamber had been pumped down to vacuum. Alexios leaned a hand on the green-glowing plate that activated the outer hatch. It swung outward gradually, revealing the landscape of Mercury in leisurely slow motion. Molten sunlight spilled into the airlock chamber as both men automatically lowered their sun visors.

"Wow," said Molina. "Looks freaking hot out there."

Alexios got a vision of the astrobiologist licking his lips. Molina stayed rooted inside the chamber, actually backing away slightly from the sunshine.

"It's wintertime now," Alexios joked, stepping out onto the bare rocky surface. "The temperature's down below four hundred Celsius."

"Wintertime." Molina laughed shakily.

"When you step through the hatch, be careful of your radiator panels. They extend almost thirty centimeters higher than the top of your helmet."

"Yeah. Right."

Molina finally came out into the full fury of the Sun. All around him stretched a barren, broken plain of bare rock, strewn with pebbles, rocks, boulders. Even through the heavily tinted visor, the glare was enough to make his eyes tear. He wondered if the suit radio was picking up the thundering of his pulse, the awed gushing of his breath.

"This way," he heard Alexios's voice in his helmet earphones. "I'll show you where the crew found those rocks you're interested in."

Moving like an automaton, Molina followed the gleaming armored figure of Alexios out across the bare, uneven ground. He glanced up at the Sun, huge and menacing, glaring down at him.

"You did remember your tool kit and sample boxes, didn't you?" Alexios asked, almost teasingly.

"I've got them," said Molina, nodding inside his helmet. Something about that voice was familiar. Why should a voice transmitted by radio sound familiar when the man was a complete stranger?

They plodded across the desolate plain, steering around the rocks strewn haphazardly across the landscape. One of the boulders was as big as a house, massive and stolid in the glaring sunlight. The ground undulated slightly but they had no trouble negotiating the gentle rises and easy downslopes. Molina noticed a gully or chasm of some sort off to their right. Alexios kept them well clear of it.

It was hot inside the suit, Molina realized. Cooling system or not, he felt as if the juices were being baked out of him. If the radiators should fail, he said to himself, if the suit's electrical power shuts down—I'd be dead in a minute or two! He tried to push such thoughts out of his mind, but the sweat trickling down his brow and stinging his eyes made that impossible.

"You're nearing the edge of our camera range," came the

voice of the controller back at the base. He sounded almost bored.

"Not to worry," Alexios replied. "We're almost there."

Less than a minute later Alexios stopped and turned slowly, like a mechanical giant with rusty bearings.

"Here we are," he said brightly.

"This is it?" Molina saw that they were in a shallow depression, most likely an ancient meteor crater, about a hundred and fifty meters across.

"This is where the construction team found the rocks you're interested in."

Molina stared at the rock-strewn ground. It wasn't as dusty as the Moon's surface was. They had walked all this way and their boots were barely tarnished. He saw their bootprints, though, looking new and bright against the dark ground.

"What was your construction crew doing all the way out here?" he heard himself ask.

Alexios did not reply for a moment. Then, "Scouting for locations for new sites. Our base is going to grow, sooner or later."

"And they found the rocks with biomarkers here, at this site?"

He sensed Alexios nodding solemnly inside his helmet. "You can tell which rocks contain the biomarkers," Alexios said. "They're the darker ones."

Molina saw that there were dozens of dark reddish rocks scattered around the shallow crater. He forgot all his other questions as he unclipped the scoop from his equipment belt and extended its handle so he could begin picking up the rocks—and the possible life-forms in them.

LARA

I t was not easy for her to leave their eight-year-old son on Earth, but Lara Tierney Molina was a determined woman. Her husband's messages from the Japanese torch ship seemed so forlorn, so painful, that she couldn't possibly leave him alone any longer. When he suddenly departed for Mercury, he had told her that his work would absorb him totally and, besides, the rugged base out there was no place for her. But almost as soon as he'd left, he began sending pitifully despondent messages to her every night, almost breaking into tears in his loneliness and misery. That was so unlike Victor that Lara found herself sobbing as she watched her husband's despondent image.

She tried to cheer him with smiling responses, even getting Victor, Jr., to send upbeat messages to his father. Still, Victor's one-way calls from Mercury were full of heartbreaking desolation.

So she made arrangements for her sister to take care of Victor, Jr., flew from Earth to lunar orbit aboard a Masterson shuttlecraft, then boarded the freighter *Urania* that was carrying supplies to Mercury on a slow, economical Hohmann minimum energy trajectory. No high-acceleration fusion torch ship for her; she could not afford such a luxury and the Sunpower Foundation was unwilling to pay for it. So she coasted toward Mercury for four months, her living quarters a closet-sized compartment, her toilet facilities a scuffed and stained lavatory that she shared with the three men and two women of the freighter's crew.

She had worried, at first, about being penned up in such close quarters with strangers, but the crew turned out to be amiable enough. Within a few days of departure from Earth orbit, Lara learned that both the women were heterosexual and one of them was sleeping with the ship's communications officer. The other two males didn't come on to her, for which Lara was quite grateful. The entire crew treated her with a rough deference; they shared meals together and became friends the way traveling companions do, knowing that they would probably never see each other again once their voyage was over.

Lara Tierney had been born to considerable wealth. When the greenhouse floods forced her family from their Manhattan penthouse, they moved to their summer home in Colorado and found that it was now a lakeside property. Father made it their permanent domicile. Lara had been only a baby then, but she vaguely remembered the shooting out in the woods at night, the strangers who camped on Father's acreage and had to be rooted out by the National Guard soldiers, the angry shouts and sometimes a scream that silenced all the birds momentarily.

By and large, though, life was pleasant enough. Her father taught her how to shoot both rifles and pistols, and he always made certain that one of the guards accompanied Lara whenever she went out into the lovely green woods.

At school in Boulder, her friends said she led a charmed life. Nothing unhappy ever seemed to happen to her. She was bright, talented, and pleasant to everyone around her.

Lara knew that she was no beauty. Her eyes were nice enough, a warm gold-flecked amber, but her lips were painfully thin and she thought her teeth much too big for her slim jaw. She was gangly—her figure hardly had a curve to it. Yet she had no trouble dating young men; they seemed attracted to her like iron filings to a magnet. She thought it might have been her money, although her mother told her that as long as she smiled at young men they would feel at ease with her.

The most popular men on campus pursued her. Victor Molina, dashing and handsome, became her steady beau— until Molina introduced her to a friend of his, an intense, smoldering young engineer named Mance Bracknell.

"He's interesting," Lara said.

"Mance?" Molina scoffed. "He's a weirdo. Not interested in anything except engineering. I think I'm the only friend he has on campus."

Another student warned, "You know engineers. They're so narrow-minded they can look through a keyhole with both eyes."

Yet she found Bracknell fascinating. He was nowhere near handsome, she thought, and his social skills were minimal. He dressed carelessly; his meager wardrobe showed he had no money. Yet he was the only male in her classes who paid no attention to her: he was far too focused on his studies. Lara saw him as a challenge, at first. She was going to make him take his nose out of his computer screen and smell the roses.

That semester, she and Molina shared only one class with the young engineering student, a mandatory class in English literature. Bracknell was struggling through it. Lara decided to offer her help.

"I don't need help," Bracknell told her, matter-of-factly. "I'm just not interested in the material."

"Not interested in Keats? Or Shakespeare?" She was shocked.

With an annoyed little frown, Bracknell replied, "Are you interested in Bucky Fuller? Or Raymond Loewy?"

She had never heard of them. Lara made a deal with him. If he paid attention to the literature assignments, she would sign up for a basic science class.

Molina was not pleased. "You're wasting your time with Mance. For god's sake, Lara, the guy doesn't even wear socks!"

It took most of the semester for her to penetrate Bracknell's self-protective shell. Late one night after they had walked from one end of campus to the other as he flawlessly—if flatly—recited Keats's entire poem *The Eve of St. Agnes* to her, Bracknell finally told her what his dream was. It took her breath away.

"A tower that goes all the way up into space? Can it be built?"

"I can do it," he answered, without an eyeblink's hesitation.

He wanted to build a tower that rose up to the heavens, an elevator that could carry people and cargo into orbit for mere pennies per kilogram.

"I can do it," he told her, time and again. "I know I can! The big problem has always been the strength-to-weight ratio of the materials, but with buckyball fibers we can solve that problem and build the blasted thing!"

His enthusiasm sent Lara scurrying to her own computer, to learn what buckyball fibers might be and how a space elevator could be built.

Her friends twitted her about her fascination with "the geek." Molina fumed and sulked, angry that she was paying more attention to Bracknell than to him.

"How is he in bed?" Molina growled at her one afternoon as they walked to class together.

"Not as good as you, Victor dear," Lara replied sweetly. "I love him for his mind, not his body."

And she left him standing there in the autumn sunshine, amidst the yellow aspen leaves that littered the lawn.

It took months, but Lara realized at last that she was truly and hopelessly in love with Mance Bracknell and his dream of making spaceflight inexpensive enough so that everyone could afford it.

Even before they graduated, she used her father's connections to introduce Bracknell to industrialists and financiers who had the resources to back his dream. Most of them scoffed at the idea of a space elevator. They called it a "skyhook" and said it would never work. Bracknell displayed a volcanic temper, shouting at them, calling them idiots and blind know-nothings. Shocked at his eruptions, Lara did her best to calm him down, to soothe him, to show him how to deal with men and women who believed that because they were older and richer, they were also wiser.

It took years, years in which Bracknell supported himself with various engineering jobs, traveling constantly, a techno-vagabond moving from project to project. Lara met him now and then, while her parents prayed fervently that she would eventually get tired of him and his temper and find a young man more to their liking, someone like Victor Molina. Although she occasionally saw Molina as he worked toward his doctorate in biology, she found herself thinking about Bracknell constantly during the months they were separated. Despite her parents she flew to his side whenever she could.

Then he called from Ecuador, of all places, so excited she could barely understand what he was saying. An earlier attempt at building a space elevator in Ecuador had failed; probably it had been a fraud, a sham effort aimed at swindling money from the project's backers. But the government of Ecuador wanted to proceed with the project, and a consortium of European bankers had formed a corporation to do it, if they could find an engineering organization capable of tackling the job.

"They want me!" Bracknell fairly shouted, his image in Lara's phone screen so excited she thought he was going to hyperventilate. "They want me to head the project!"

"In Ecuador?" she asked, her heart pounding.

"Yes! It's on the equator. We've picked a mountaintop site."

"You're really going to do it?"

"You bet I am! Will you come down here?"

"Yes!" she answered immediately.

"Will you marry me?"

The breath gushed out of her. She had to gulp before she could reply, "Of course I will!"

But Bracknell's tower had collapsed, killing millions. He was disgraced, tried for mass homicide, exiled from Earth forever.

And now Lara Tierney Molina, married to Bracknell's best friend, mother of their eight-year-old son, rode a shabby freighter to Mercury to be with her husband.

Yet she still dreamed of Mance Bracknell.

GOETHE BASE

As soon as the technicians peeled him out of the cumbersome spacesuit, Molina grabbed his sample box and rushed to the makeshift laboratory he had squeezed into the bare little compartment that served as his living quarters at Mercury base.

From the equipment box that blocked the compartment's built-in drawers he tugged out the miniature diamond-bladed saw. Sitting cross-legged on the floor, he wormed the safety goggles over his eyes, tugged on a pair of sterilized gloves, then grabbed one of the rocks out of his sample box and immediately began cutting microthin slices out of it.

He got to his knees and lifted out the portable mass spectrometer from his equipment box. Despite Mercury's low gravity it was so heavy he barely was able to raise it clear of the box. "Portable is a relative term," he muttered as he looked around for an electrical outlet. The spectrometer's laser drew a lot of power, he knew.

"So what if I black out the base?" he said to himself, almost giggling, as he plugged the thick power cord into a wall outlet. His quarters were hardly a sterile environment, but Molina was in too much of a hurry to care about that. I'll just work on a couple of the samples and save the rest for the lab up in *Himawari,* he told himself. Besides, he reasoned, these samples are fresh from the site; there hasn't been enough time for any terrestrial organisms to contaminate them.

Time meant nothing now. Hours flew by as Molina sawed sample microslices from the rocks and ran them through the spectrometer. When he got hungry or sleepy he popped cognitive enhancers and went back to work revitalized. Wish I had brought the scanning, tunneling microscope here, he thought. For a moment he considered asking Alexios if there was one in the base, but he thought better of it. I've got one up in the ship, he told himself. Be patient.

But patience gave way to growing excitement. It was all there! he realized after nearly forty hours of work. Pushing a thick flop of his sandy hair back from his red-rimmed eyes, Molina tapped one-handed at his laptop. The sample contained PAHs in plenitude, in addition to magnetized bits of iron sulfides and carbonate globules, unmistakable markers of biological activity.

There's life on Mercury! Molina exulted. He wanted to leap to his feet and shout the news but he found that his legs were cramped and tingling from sitting cross-legged on the floor for so long. Instead, he bent over his laptop and dictated a terse report of his discovery to the astrobiology bulletin published electronically by the International Consortium of Universities. As an afterthought he fired off a copy to the International Astronautical Authority. And then a brief, triumphant message to Lara.

He realized that he hadn't called his wife since he'd left Earth, despite his promise to talk to her every day. Well, he grinned to himself, now I've got something to tell her.

I'll be famous! Molina exulted. I'll be able to take my pick of professorships. We can live anywhere we choose to: California, Edinburgh, New Melbourne, any of the best astrobiology schools on Earth!

He hauled himself slowly to his feet, his legs shooting pins and needles fiercely. Hobbling, laughing aloud, he staggered around his cluttered compartment, nearly tripping over the equipment he had scattered across the floor until his legs returned to normal. A glance at the digital clock above his bunk, which displayed the base's time, showed him that the galley had long since closed for the night. What matter? He was hungry, though, so he put in a call for Alexios. He's the head of this operation, Molina told himself. He ought to be able to get them to produce a meal for the discoverer of life on Mercury.

Alexios did better than that. He invited Molina to his own quarters to share a late-night repast, complete with a dust-covered bottle of celebratory champagne.

Alexios's living quarters were no larger than Molina's compartment, the astrobiologist saw, but the furnishings were much better. The bed looked more comfortable than Molina's bunk, and there was a real desk instead of a wobbly pullout tray, plus a pair of comfortably padded armchairs. Their supper—cold meats and a reasonably crisp salad—was augmented by a bowl of fruit and the champagne. It all tasted wonderful to Molina.

"Living organisms?" Alexios was asking. "You've found living organisms?"

"Not yet," said Molina, leaning back in the luxurious chair as he munched on a boneless pseudochicken wing.

Alexios raised his dark brows.

"As a point of fact," Molina said, gesturing with his plastic fork, "there might not be living organisms on Mercury."

"But I thought you said—"

Falling into his lecturer's mode of speech, Molina intoned, "What I've discovered here is evidence of biological activity. This shows conclusively that there was once life on Mercury. Whether life still exists here is another matter, calling for much more extensive exploration and study."

Alexios's slightly mismatched face showed comprehension. "I see. You're saying that life once existed here, but there's no guarantee that it is still extant."

"Precisely," said Molina, a trifle pompously. "We'll have to bring in teams to search the planet's surface extensively and bore deeply into the crust."

"Looking for organisms underground? Like the extremophiles that have been found on Earth?"

Nodding, Molina replied, "And Mars. And Venus. And even on Io."

Alexios smiled thinly. "I wonder what Bishop Danvers will think about this? The thought of extraterrestrial intelligence seems to bother him."

"Oh, I don't expect we'll find anything intelligent," said Molina, with a wave of one hand. "Microbes. Bacterial forms, that's what we're looking for."

"I see." Alexios hesitated, then asked, "But tell me, if you bring in teams to scour the surface and dig deep boreholes, how will that affect my operation? After all, we're planning to scoop ores from the surface and refine them with nanomachines so that we can—"

"All that will have to stop," Molina said flatly.

"Stop?"

"We can't risk contaminating possible biological evidence with your industrial operation. And nanomachines—they might gobble up the very evidence we're seeking."

Alexios sank back in his chair. "Mr. Yamagata is not going to be pleased by this. Not one bit." Yet he was smiling strangely as he spoke.

TORCH SHIP *HIMAWARI*

B ut that could ruin us!" Yamagata yowled, his usually smiling face knotted into an angry grimace.

Alexios had come up to the orbiting ship to present the troubling news personally to his boss. He shrugged helplessly. "The IAA regulations are quite specific, sir. *Nothing* is allowed to interfere with astrobiological studies."

The two men were standing in *Himawari*'s small observation blister, a darkened chamber fronted by a bubble of heavily tinted glassteel. For several moments they watched in silence as the heat-blasted barren surface of Mercury slid past.

At last Yamagata muttered, "I can't believe that any kind of life could exist down there."

Alexios raised his brows slightly. "They found life on the surface of Venus, which is even hotter than Mercury."

"Venus has liquid sulfur and silicone compounds. Nothing like that has been found here."

"Not yet," Alexios said, in a barely voiced whisper.

Yamagata frowned at him.

"We won't have to stop all our work," Alexios said, trying

to sound a little brighter. "We still have the power satellites coming in from Selene. Getting them up and running will be a considerable task."

"But how will we provide the life-support materials for the crew?" Yamagata growled. "I depended on your team on the surface for that."

Alexios clasped his hands behind his back and turned to stare at the planet's surface gliding past. He knew his base on Mercury was too small to be seen by the unaided eye from the distance of the *Himawari*'s orbit, yet he strained his eyes to see the mound of rubble anyway.

"Well?" Yamagata demanded. "What do you recommend?"

Turning back to look at his decidedly unhappy employer, Alexios shrugged. "We'll have to bring in the life-support materials from Selene, I suppose, if we can't scoop them from Mercury's regolith."

"That will bankrupt us," Yamagata muttered.

"Perhaps the suspension will only be for a short time," said Alexios. "The scientists will come, look around, and then simply declare certain regions to be off-limits to our work."

Even in the shadows of the darkened observation blister Alexios could see the grim expression on Yamagata's face.

"This will ruin everything," Yamagata said in a heavy whisper. "Everything."

Alexios agreed, but forced himself to present a worried, downcast appearance to his boss.

Fuming, trying to keep his considerable temper under control, Yamagata repaired to his private quarters and called up the computer program of Robert Forward. The long-dead genius appeared in the middle of the compartment, smiling self-assuredly, still wearing that garish vest beneath his conservative tweed jacket.

Between the smile and the vest, Yamagata felt too irritated to sit still. He paced around the three-dimensional image, explaining this intolerable situation. Forward's holographic image turned to follow him, that maddening smile never slipping by even one millimeter.

"But finding life on Mercury is very exciting news," the image said. "You should be proud that you helped to facilitate such a discovery."

"How can we continue our work if the IAA forces us to shut down all activities on the surface?" Yamagata demanded.

"That won't last forever. They'll lift the suspension sooner or later."

"After Sunpower Foundation has gone bankrupt."

"You have four powersats in orbit around Mercury and six more on the way. Can't you begin to sell energy from them? You'd have some income—"

"The solar cells degrade too quickly!" Yamagata snapped. "Their power output is too low to be profitable."

Forward seemed to think this over for a moment. "Then spend the time finding a solution for the cell degradation. Harden the cells; protect them from the harmful solar radiation."

"Protect them?"

"It's probably solar ultraviolet that's doing the damage," Forward mused. "Or perhaps particles from the solar wind."

Yamagata sank into his favorite chair. "Solar particles. You mean protons?"

Forward nodded, making his fleshy cheeks waddle slightly. "Proton energy density must be pretty high this close to the Sun. Have you measured it?"

"I don't believe so."

"If it's the protons doing the damage you can protect the powersats with superconducting radiation shields, just as spacecraft are shielded."

Yamagata's brows knit. "How do you know about radiation shielding? You died before interplanetary spacecraft needed shielding."

"I have access to all your files," Forward reminded him. "I know everything your computer knows."

Yamagata rubbed his chin thoughtfully. "If we could bring the powersats' energy output up to their theoretical maximum, or even close to it . . ."

"You'd be able to sell their energy at a profit," Forward finished his thought. "And go ahead with the starship."

Nodding, Yamagata closed the Forward program. The physicist winked out, leaving Yamagata alone in his quarters. He put in a call for Alexios, who had returned to the base on the planet's surface.

"I want to find out what's causing this degradation of the solar cells," Yamagata said sternly. "That must be our number one priority."

Alexios's mismatched image in the wall screen looked as if he had expected this decision. "I already have a small team working on it, sir. I'll put more people on the investigation."

"Good," said Yamagata. To himself he added silently, Let's hope we can solve this problem before the IAA drives me into bankruptcy.

EARTH

The International Consortium of Universities was less an organization than a collection of powerful fiefdoms. It consisted of nearly a hundred universities around the world, no two of which ever agreed completely on anything.

Moreover, each university was a collection of departments ranging from ancient literature to astrobiology, from psychodynamics to paleontology, from genetic engineering to gymnastics. Each department head tenaciously guarded her or his budget, assets, staff, and funding sources.

It took a masterful administrator to manage that ever-shifting tangle of alliances, feuds, jealousies, and sexual affairs.

Jacqueline Wexler was such an administrator. Gracious and charming in public, accommodating and willing to compromise at meetings, she nevertheless had the steel-hard will and sharp intellect to drive the ICU's ramshackle collection of egos toward goals that she herself selected. Widely known as "Attila the Honey," Wexler was all sweetness and smiles on the outside and ruthless determination within.

Today's meeting of the ICU's astrobiology committee was typical. To Wexler it seemed patently clear that a top-flight team of investigators must be sent to Mercury to confirm Dr. Molina's discovery and organize a thorough study of the planet's possible biosphere. Indeed, everyone around the long conference table agreed perfectly on that point.

Beyond that point, however, all agreement ended. Who should go? What would be their authority? How would they deal with the industrial operation already planted on Mercury's surface? All these questions and more led to tedious hours of wrangling. Wexler let them wrangle, knowing precisely what she wanted out of them, realizing that sooner or later they would grow tired and let her make the effective decisions. So she smiled sweetly and waited for the self-important farts—women as well as men—to run out of gas.

The biggest issue, as far as they were concerned, was who would lead the team sent to Mercury. Rival universities vied with one another and there was much finger-pointing and cries of "You got the top spot last time!" and "That's not fair!"

Wexler thought it was relatively unimportant who was picked as the lead scientist for the team. She worried more about who the New Morality would send as their spiritual advisor to watch over the scientists. The spiritual advisor's ostensible task was to tend to the scientists' moral and religious needs. His real job, as far as Wexler was concerned, was to spy on the scientists and report what they were doing back to Atlanta.

There was already a New Morality representative on Mercury, she knew: somebody named Danvers. Would they let him remain in charge of the newcomers as well, or send in somebody over his head?

A similar meeting was going on in Atlanta, in the ornate headquarters building of the New Morality, but there were only four people seated at the much smaller conference table.

Archbishop Harold Carnaby sat at the head of the table, of course. Well into his twelfth decade of life, the archbishop was one of the few living souls who had witnessed the birth of the New Morality, back in those evil days of licentiousness and runaway secularism that had brought down the wrath of God in the form of the greenhouse floods. Although his deep religious faith prohibited Carnaby from accepting rejuvenation treatments such as telomerase injections or cellular regeneration, he still availed himself of every mechanical aid that medical science could provide. He saw nothing immoral about artificial booster hearts or kidney dialysis implants.

So he sat at the head of the square table in his powered wheelchair, totally bald, wrinkled and gnomelike, breathing oxygen through a plastic tube inserted in his nostrils.

His brain still functioned perfectly well, especially since surgeons had inserted stents in both his carotid arteries.

"Bishop Danvers is a good man," said the deacon seated at Carnaby's left. "I believe he can handle the challenge, no matter how many godless scientists they send to Mercury."

Danvers's dossier was displayed on the wall screen for Carnaby to scan. Apparently someone in Yamagata's organization had specifically asked for Bishop Danvers to come to Mercury. Unusual, Carnaby thought, for those godless engineers and mechanics to ask for a chaplain at all, let alone a specific individual. Danvers must be well respected. But there was more at stake here than tending souls, he knew.

The deacon on Carnaby's right suggested, "Perhaps we could send someone to assist him. Two or three assistants, even. We can demand space for them on the vessel that the scientists ride to Mercury."

Carnaby nodded noncommittally and focused his rheumy eyes on the man sitting at the foot of the table, Bishop O'Malley. Physically, O'Malley was the opposite of Carnaby: big in the shoulders, wide in the middle, his face fleshy and always flushed, his nose bulbous and patterned with purple-red veins. O'Malley was a Catholic, and Carnaby did not completely trust him.

"What's your take on the situation, Bishop?" Carnaby flatly refused to use the medieval Catholic terms of address; "your grace" and "my lord" had no place in his vocabulary.

Without turning even to glance at the dossier displayed on the wall behind him, O'Malley said in his powerful, window-rattling voice, "Danvers showed his toughness years ago in Ecuador. Didn't let personal friendship stand in the way of doing his duty. Let him handle the scientists; he's up to it. Send him an assistant or two if you feel like it, but keep him in charge on Mercury."

"He's done good work since Ecuador, too," Carnaby agreed, his voice like a creaking hinge.

The two deacons immediately fell in line and agreed that Danvers should remain in charge.

"Remember this," Carnaby said, folding his fleshless, blue-veined hands on the table edge in front of him, "every time these secularists find another form of life on some other world, people lose a portion of their faith. There are even those who proclaim that extraterrestrial life proves the Bible to be wrong!"

"Blasphemy!" hissed the younger of the deacons.

"The scientists will send a delegation out to Mercury," Carnaby croaked on, "and they will confirm this man Molina's discovery. They'll trumpet the news that life has been found even where no one expected it to exist. More of the Faithful will fall away from their belief."

O'Malley hunched his bulky shoulders. "Not if Danvers can show that the scientists are wrong. Not if he can give them the lie."

"That's his real mission, then," Carnaby agreed. "To do whatever is necessary to disprove the scientists' claim."

The deacon on the left, young and still innocent, blinked uncertainly. "But how can he do that? If the scientists show proof that life exists on the planet—"

"Danvers must dispute their so-called proof," Carnaby snapped, with obvious irritation. "He must challenge their findings."

"I don't see how—"

O'Malley reached out and touched the younger man on his shoulder. "Danvers is a fighter. He tries to hide it, but inside his soul he's a fighter. He'll find a way to cast doubt on the scientists' findings, I'm sure."

The deacon on the right understood. "He doesn't have to disprove the scientists' findings, merely cast enough doubt on them so the Faithful will disregard them."

"At the very least," Carnaby said. "It would be best if he could show that those godless secularists are lying and have been lying all along."

"That's a tall order," said O'Malley, with a smile.

Carnaby did not smile back.

MERCURY ORBIT

Captain Shibasaki allowed himself a rare moment of irony in the presence of his employer.

"It's going to become crowded here," he said, perfectly straight-faced.

Yamagata did not catch his wry attempt at humor. Standing beside the captain on *Himawari*'s bridge, Yamagata unsmilingly watched the display screen that showed the two ships that had taken up orbits around Mercury almost simultaneously.

One was the freighter *Urania,* little more than a globular crew module and a set of nuclear ion propulsion units, with dozens of massive rectangular cargo containers clipped to its long spine. *Urania* carried equipment that would be useless if the scientists actually closed Mercury to further industrial operations. It also brought Molina's wife to him, a matrimonial event to which Yamagata was utterly indifferent.

The other vessel was a fusion torch ship, *Brudnoy,* which had blasted out from Earth on a half-*g* burn that brought its complement of ICU scientists and IAA bureaucrats to Mercury in a scant three days. Yamagata wished it would keep on accelerating and dive straight into the Sun. Instead, it braked expertly and took up an orbit matching *Himawari*'s.

Yamagata could actually see through the bridge's main port the dumbbell-shaped vessel rotating slowly against the star-strewn blackness of space.

"*Urania* is requesting a shuttle to bring Mrs. Molina over to us," Captain Shibasaki said, his voice low and deferential. "They are also wondering when they will be allowed to offload their cargo containers."

Yamagata clasped his hands behind his back and muttered, "They might as well leave the containers in orbit. No sense bringing them down to the surface until we find out what the scientists are going to do to us."

"And Mrs. Molina?"

"Send a shuttle for her. I suppose Molina will be glad to see his wife."

Hesitantly, the captain added, "Two of the scientists from *Brudnoy* are asking permission to come aboard and meet you, as well."

"More mouths to feed," Yamagata grumbled.

"Plus two ministers from the New Morality. Assistants to Bishop Danvers."

Yamagata glowered at the captain. "Why didn't they send the Mormon Tabernacle Choir while they were at it?"

It took every ounce of Shibasaki's will power to keep from laughing.

Molina had rushed up to *Himawari* immediately after he had finished his preliminary examination of the rocks down at Mercury base. Once aboard the orbiting ship, he shut himself into the sterile laboratory facility that Yamagata had graciously allowed him to bring along and spent weeks on end studying his precious rocks.

The more he examined them, the more excited he became. Not only PAHs and carbonates and sulfides. Once he started looking at his samples in the scanning tunneling microscope he saw tiny structures that looked like fossils of once-living nanobacteria: ridged conical shapes and spiny spheroids. Life! Perhaps long extinct, but living organisms once existed on Mercury! Perhaps they still do!

He stopped his work only long enough to gulp a scant meal now and then, or to fire off a new set of data to the astrobiology journal. He stayed off the cognitive enhancers. Not that the pills were habit-forming or had serious side effects; he simply had run through almost his entire supply and decided to save the last few for an emergency. He slept when he could no longer stay awake, staggering to his quarters and collapsing on his bunk, then going back to his laboratory once his eyes popped open again and he showered and pulled on a clean set of coveralls.

It was only the announcement that his wife would be arriving aboard *Himawari* within the hour that pulled him away from his work. For weeks he had ignored all incoming messages except those from the International Consortium of Universities. He accepted their praise and answered their questions; personal messages from his wife he had no time for.

Dumbfounded with surprise, it took him several moments to register what the communications technician was telling him. "Lara? Here?" he asked the tech's image on his compartment's wall screen.

Once he was certain he had heard correctly, Molina finally, almost reluctantly, began to strip off his sweaty clothes and headed for the shower.

"What's Lara doing here?" he asked himself as the steamy water enveloped him. "Why did she come? What's wrong?"

To Molina's surprise, Yamagata himself was already waiting at the airlock when he got there, scant moments before his wife arrived.

"I should be very angry at you," Yamagata said, with a smile to show that he wasn't.

"Angry?" Molina was truly surprised. "Because there's life on Mercury?"

"Because your discovery may ruin my project."

Molina smiled back, a trifle smugly. "I'm afraid that momentous scientific discoveries take precedence over industrial profits. That's a well-established principle of the International Astronautical Authority."

"Yes," Yamagata replied thinly. "So it seems."

The speaker set into the metal overhead announced that the shuttle craft had successfully mated to *Himawari*'s airlock. Again Molina wondered worriedly why Lara had come. He saw the indicator lights on the panel set into the bulkhead beside the hatch turn slowly from red to amber, then finally to green. The hatch clicked, then swung inward toward them.

One of the shuttle's crew, a Valkyrie-sized woman in gunmetal gray coveralls, pushed the hatch all the way open and Lara Molina stepped daintily over the coaming, then, with a smile of recognition, rushed into her husband's waiting arms.

He held her tightly and whispered into her ear, "You're all right? Everything is okay back home?"

"I'm fine and so is Victor, Jr.," she said, beaming happily.

"Then why didn't you tell me you were coming? What made you—"

She placed a silencing finger on his lips. "Later," she said, glancing toward Yamagata.

Molina understood. She wanted to speak to him in private.

Yamagata misunderstood her glance. "Come," he urged. "Dinner is waiting for us. You must be famished after having nothing but the freighter's food."

* * *

She's not truly beautiful, Yamagata thought as he sat at the head of the dinner table, but she is certainly lovely.

He had seated Mrs. Molina at his right, her husband on his left. Next to them, Bishop Danvers and Alexios sat opposite one another, and the two cochairmen of the ICU's scientific investigation team sat next to them. Captain Shibasaki was at the end of the table.

Yamagata saw that Lara Molina was slim as a colt; no, the picture that came to his mind was of a racing yacht, trim and sleek and pleasing to the eye. Her features were nothing extraordinary, but her amber-colored eyes were animated when she spoke. When she was silent, she kept her gaze on her husband, except for occasional glances in Alexios's direction. Alexios stared unabashedly at her, as if she were the first woman he'd seen in ages.

Molina was in his glory, with his wife hanging on his every word and two of the leading astrobiologists of Earth paying attention to him, as well. His obvious misgivings about his wife's unexpected arrival seemed far behind him now.

"Chance favors the prepared mind, of course," he was saying, wineglass in hand. "No one expected to find any trace of biological activity on Mercury, but I came out here anyway. Everybody said I was being foolish; even my lovely wife told me I was throwing away months that could be better spent back at Jupiter."

His wife lowered her eyes and smiled demurely.

"What brought you to Mercury, then?" Alexios asked. He had not touched his wine, Yamagata noted.

"A hunch. Call it intuition. Call it a belief that life is much tougher and more ubiquitous than even our most prestigious biologists can understand."

The elder of the ICU investigators, Ian McFergusen, russet-bearded and heavy-browed, rumbled in a thick Scottish accent: "When a distinguished but elderly scientist says something is possible, he is almost always right. When he says something is impossible, he is almost always wrong."

Everyone around the table laughed politely, Molina loudest of all.

"Clarke's Law," said the younger ICU scientist.

"Indeed," Yamagata agreed.

"But surely you must have had more than a hunch to bring you all the way out here," Alexios prodded, grinning crookedly.

Yamagata saw that Mrs. Molina stared at Alexios now. Is she angry at him for doubting her husband's word?

Molina seemed not to notice. He drained his wineglass and put it down on the tablecloth so carefully that Yamagata thought he must be getting drunk. One of the waiters swiftly refilled it with claret.

"More than a hunch?" Molina responded at last. "Yes. Of course. A man doesn't leave his loving wife and traipse out to a hellhole like this on a lark. It was more than a hunch, I assure you."

"What decided you?" Alexios smiled, rather like the smile on a cobra, Yamagata thought.

"Funny thing," Molina said, grinning. "I received a message. Said that the team working on the surface of Mercury was finding strange-looking rocks. It piqued my curiosity."

"A message? From whom?" asked Bishop Danvers.

"It was anonymous. No signature." Molina took another gulp of wine. "I kind of thought it was from you, Elliott."

"Me?" Danvers looked shocked. "I didn't send you any message."

Molina shrugged. "Somebody did. Prob'ly one of the work crew down on the surface."

"Strange-looking rocks?" Alexios mused. "And that was enough to send you packing for Mercury?"

"I had the summer off," Molina replied. "I was in line for an assistant professorship. I thought a poke around Mercury would look good on my curriculum vitae. Couldn't hurt."

"It has certainly helped!" Danvers said.

"I think it probably has," said Molina, reaching for his wineglass again.

"I'm sure it has," said Alexios.

Yamagata noticed that Alexios stared straight at Lara Molina as he spoke.

EXPLANATIONS

essages?" Molina blinked with surprise.

He and Lara were alone now in the stateroom that Yamagata had graciously supplied for them. It was larger than Molina's former quarters aboard the ship. The Japanese crewmen who had moved Molina's belongings to this new compartment laughingly referred to it as the Bridal Suite. In Japanese, of course, so neither of the gaijin would be embarrassed by their little joke.

"I couldn't leave you alone out here," Lara said as she unpacked the travel bag on the stateroom's double-sized bed. "You looked so sad, so lonely."

Molina knew he had never sent a single message to his wife until his triumphant announcement of his discovery. He also knew that he had promised to call her every day he was away from her.

"You got messages from me?" he asked again.

She turned from her unpacking and slid her arms around his neck. "Don't be shy, Victor. Of course I got your messages.

They were wonderful. Some were so beautiful they made me cry."

Either I've gone insane or she has, Molina thought. Has she been hallucinating? Blurring the line between her dreams and reality?

"Lara, dearest, I—"

"Others were so sad, so poignant . . . they nearly broke my heart." She kissed him gently on the lips.

Molina felt his body stirring. One thing he had learned over nearly ten years of marriage was not to argue with success. Accept credit when it comes your way, no matter what. It had been a good guide for his scientific career, as well.

He kissed her more strongly and held her tightly. Wordlessly they sat on the edge of the bed. Molina pushed his wife's half-unpacked travel bag off the bed; it fell to the floor with a gentle thump in Mercury's low gravity. They lay side by side and he began undressing her.

I'll figure out what this message business is all about tomorrow, Molina told himself as the heat of passion rose in him. Tomorrow will be time enough.

Dante Alexios had returned to Goethe base on Mercury's surface after dinner aboard *Himawari*. Lara hasn't changed a bit, he thought. She's as beautiful as she was ten years ago. More beautiful, even.

Did she recognize me? he wondered as he undressed in his tiny compartment. Not my face, surely, but maybe she remembers my voice. The nanomachines didn't change my voice very much.

He stretched out on his bed and stared at the low ceiling. The room's sensors automatically turned the lights out, and the star patterns painted across the ceiling glowed faintly.

Victor looked puzzled that his wife had flown out here,

Alexios said to himself. Wait until she tells him about the messages she got from him. That'll drive him crazy, trying to figure it out. Who would be nutty enough to send love letters to Lara and fake his image, his voice, for them?

It had been easy enough to do. Alexios had secretly recorded Molina's face and voice from his university dossier. It was simple to morph that imagery into the messages that Alexios composed. He had poured his heart into those messages, told her everything he wanted to say to her, everything he wanted to her to know. Plagiarized from the best sources: Shakespeare, Browning, Rostand, Byron, and the rest.

He told Lara how much he loved her, had always loved her, would always love her. But he said it with her husband's image, with Victor's voice. He didn't dare use his own. Not yet.

Ian McFergusen was a burly man of delicate tastes. His fierce bushy beard and shaggy brows made him look like a Highland warrior of old, yet he had dedicated his career to the study of life. He was a biologist, not a claymore-swinging howling clansman.

Still, he was a fighter. Throughout academia he was known as a tough, independent thinker. A maverick, a burr under the saddle, often an inconvenient pain in the ass. He seldom followed the accepted wisdom on any subject. He asked the awkward questions, the questions that most people wished to shove under the rug.

McFergusen had studied all the data about the evidence for Mercurian biology that Molina had sent Earthward. Alone now in his compartment, as he sipped his usual nightcap of whisky, neat, he had to admit that the data were impressive. Molina may have made a real find here, McFergusen said to himself.

But something nagged at him. As he drained the whisky

and set the empty glass on his night table, he fidgeted uneasily, scratched at his beard, knitted his heavy brows. It's all too convenient, he told himself, too convenient by far. He began pacing across his narrow compartment. Molina gets an anonymous tip. He's given a clutch of rocks that the construction workers have found. All in the same location.

The rocks contain PAHs and all the other biomarkers, that's sure enough. But it's all too easy. Too convenient. Nature doesn't hand you evidence on a platter.

He shook his shaggy head and sat heavily on the bunk. Maybe I'm getting too old and cranky, he said to himself. Then a new thought struck him. Maybe I'm just jealous of the young squirt.

GOETHE BASE

So far," Alexios was saying, "the scientists have not discovered any other sites that contain biomarkers."

Yamagata had come down from *Himawari* to the surface base for this meeting, the first time he had been to Mercury's surface in more than a month. For nearly five weeks now the IAA scientists had been combing the planet's surface with automated tracked vehicles, searching for more rocks that contained signs of life.

"Yet still they prevent us from expanding this base," Yamagata grumbled. He was too troubled to sit in the chair Alexios had offered him. Instead he stood, hands clasped behind his back, and stared at the display screen that took up one whole wall of Alexios's modest office. It showed the barren, rock-strewn surface outside the base: the Sun was up and the hard-baked ground looked hot enough to melt.

The bleak landscape matched Yamagata's mood perfectly. If the scientists didn't lift their ban on industrial activities on Mercury's surface soon, Sunpower Foundation would go bankrupt. It angered Yamagata to be so frustrated. Despite all the teachings that the lamas had tried to instill in him, he found it impossible to accept what was happening, impossible to be patient. Yamagata wanted to round up McFergusen and his entire crew and send them packing back to Earth. Now. This day.

Standing respectfully beside him, Alexios said quietly, "At least we're putting the time to some good use. The preliminary tests on the shielded powersat look quite good."

Yamagata turned toward him. Alexios was slightly taller than he, a fact that added to his displeasure.

"Just as you suspected, the power degradation is caused by the solar proton influx," Alexios went on calmly.

"And the superconducting shields protect the cells?"

Alexios called out, "Computer: show results of shielding test."

The landscape disappeared from the wall screen, replaced by a set of graphs with curving lines in red, green, yellow, and blue. As Alexios explained them, Yamagata saw that the superconducting shields performed much as the Forward persona had predicted.

"The high positive potential of the structure around the cells deflects the protons," Alexios said, "and the magnetic field created by the superconducting wire keeps the electrons off."

"Otherwise the electrons would discharge the high positive potential," Yamagata muttered, showing his employee that he understood the physics involved.

"Exactly." Alexios nodded. "So we can shield the powersats and get them up close to their nominal power output, if . . ." His voice trailed off.

"If?" Yamagata snapped.

"If we can afford enough superconducting wire."

"It's expensive."

"Very. But most of the elements needed to make super-conducting wire exist in Mercury's soil."

"You mean regolith," said Yamagata.

Alexios bowed slightly. "Excuse me. Of course, regolith. Soil would imply living creatures in the ground, wouldn't it?"

"We can manufacture the superconductors here, out of local materials?"

"I believe so. If we use nanomachines it should be relatively inexpensive."

"Once we are allowed to work on the surface again," Yamagata muttered.

Alexios stifled the satisfied little smile that began to form on his lips. Forcing his face into a sorrowful mask, he agreed, "Yes, we must get permission from the IAA before we can even begin to do anything."

Yamagata fumed. Instead of a mantra, he silently cursed the International Astronautical Authority, the International Consortium of Universities, all their members past and present, and all their members' mothers back to five generations.

Ian McFergusen looked around at the barren, sun-blasted rocky ground and shook his head. Nothing. Every site we've investigated has turned up nothing. Only that one site next to the base Yamagata's people have built.

Thanks to the virtual reality equipment that the ICU team had brought with them, McFergusen could sit in the laboratory they had set up aboard *Brudnoy* and still experience precisely what the tracked robot vehicle was doing down on the surface of Mercury. The first time he had used VR equipment, back when he was part of the third Mars expedition, it had seemed little less than a miracle to him. He could see, feel, hear what the robot machines were experiencing thousands of kilometers away, all while sitting in the comfort of a secure base. Now, so many years later, virtual reality was just another tool, no more wondrous than the fusion engines that propelled interplanetary torch ships or the tunneling microscopes that revealed individual atoms.

Sitting on a lab stool, his head and lower arms encased in the VR helmet and gloves, McFergusen picked up a rock in his clawlike pincers and brought it close to his sensors. A perfectly ordinary piece of volcanic ejecta, he thought. With the strength of the robot he broke the rock apart, then brought the broken edges to his sensor set and scanned their exposed interiors for several minutes.

Nothing. No PAHs, no sulfides, no iron nodules. If I bring it up to the ship's tunneling microscope, McFergusen thought, I won't find any nanometer-sized structures, either. He tossed the broken fragments of the rock back to the ground in disgust.

For long moments he simply sat there, his body aboard the torch ship *Brudnoy,* his eyes and hands and mind on the blazing hot surface of Mercury.

How can there be such rich specimens at one site and nothing anywhere else? Of course, he reminded himself, we have an entire planet to consider. In these few weeks we've barely tested a few dozen possible sites. Perhaps we're looking in the wrong places.

Yet, he reasoned, we concentrated our searches on sites that are similar to the one where Molina found his specimens. We should have found *something* by now.

Unless . . .

McFergusen did not want to consider the possibility that had arisen in his mind. We've got to widen our net, he told himself, search different kinds of sites.

That won't be easy, he knew. Not with Yamagata breathing down our necks. Lord, he's been sending messages to IAA headquarters daily, demanding to know when we'll allow him to start digging up the regolith again.

None of it is easy, McFergusen said to himself. It never is. Then that nagging suspicion surfaced in his mind again. How could Molina have been so lucky?

Luck plays its role in science, he knew. It's always better to be lucky than to be smart. But so damnably lucky? Is it possible?

Victor Molina was in his lab, flicking through the tunneling microscope's images of the latest rock samples brought up from the surface. Nothing. These samples were as dead and inert as rocks from the Moon. No hydrates, no organic molecules, no long-chain molecules of any sort. Baked dry and dead.

He leaned back in his chair and rubbed his eyes wearily. How can this be? Even the samples of dirt scraped off the ground showed no biomarkers of any kind.

Sitting up straight again, he reminded himself that the dirt samples from the surface of Mars tested by the old *Viking* landers a century ago showed no signs of biological activity, either. Not even a trace of organic molecules in the soil. And Mars not only bears life today but once bore intelligent life, before it was wiped out in an extinction-level meteor impact.

He turned and looked at the set of rocks he himself had tested when he'd first arrived at Mercury. They were carefully sealed in airtight transparent plastic containers. McFergusen wants me to let him send them back to Earth for further testing. Never! I'm not letting them out of my sight. They'll go back to Earth when I do, and they'll be tested by third parties only when I'm present.

Molina felt a fierce proprietary passion about those rocks. They were his key to a future of respect and accomplishment, his ticket to Stockholm and the Nobel Prize.

It took a few moments for him to realize that someone was knocking at his laboratory door, rapping hard enough to make the door shake. With some irritation he called out, "Enter."

Bishop Danvers slid the door back and stepped into the lab, a look of stern determination on his fleshy face. The door automatically slid shut.

"Hello, Elliott," Molina said evenly. "I'm pretty busy right now." It was a lie, but Molina was in no mood for his old friend's platitudes.

"This is an official visit," Danvers said, standing a bare two paces inside the doorway.

"Official?" Molina snapped. "What do you mean?"

Without moving from where he stood, Danvers said, "I'm here in my capacity as a bishop in the New Morality Church."

Despite himself, Molina grinned. "What are you going to do, Elliott, baptize me? Or maybe bless my rocks?"

"No," said Danvers, his cheeks flushing slightly. "I'm here to interrogate you."

Molina's brows shot up. "Interrogate? You mean like the Inquisition?"

Danvers's face darkened, his heavy hands knotted into fists. But he quickly regained control of himself and forced a thin smile.

"Victor, the New Morality has placed a heavy burden on my shoulders. I've been tasked with the responsibility of disproving your claim of finding life on Mercury."

Molina smiled and relaxed. "Oh, is that all."

"It's very serious!"

Nodding, Molina said, "I understand, Elliott." He gestured to the only other chair in the room. "Please, sit down. Make yourself comfortable."

The plastic seat of the tubular metal chair squeaked as Danvers settled his bulk into it. The bishop looked tense, wary.

"Elliott, how long have we known each other?" Molina asked.

Danvers thought a moment. "I first met you in Ecuador, more than twelve years ago."

"It's closer to fourteen years, actually."

"To be sure. But I haven't seen you since the trial at Quito, and that was about ten years ago."

Nodding again, Molina said, "But we were friends back in Ecuador. There's no reason why we shouldn't still be friends."

Danvers gestured to the analytical equipment lining the laboratory's walls. "We live in two different worlds, Victor."

"Different, maybe, but not entirely separate. There's no reason for us to be adversaries."

"I have my responsibilities," Danvers countered, somewhat stiffly. "My orders come straight from Atlanta, from the archbishop himself."

Molina let out a little sigh, then said, "All right, just what do they want you to do?"

"As I told you: they want me to disprove your claim that life exists on Mercury."

"I've never claimed that."

"Or once existed, ages ago," Danvers added.

"That seems irrefutable, Elliott."

"Because of the chemicals you've found in those rocks?" Danvers pointed to the clear plastic containers.

"That's right. The evidence is unmistakable."

"But as I understand it, McFergusen and his team haven't found any corroborating evidence."

"Corroborating evidence!" Molina smirked. "You're learning how to talk like a scientist, Elliott."

Danvers grimaced slightly. "Your fellow scientists seem terribly puzzled that they haven't been able to find anything similar to what you've discovered."

With a shrug, Molina replied, "Mercury may be a small planet, Elliott, but it's still a planet. A whole world. Its surface area must be similar to the continent of Eurasia, back on Earth. How thoroughly do you think a handful of scientists could explore all of Eurasia, from the coast of Portugal to the China Sea? In a few weeks, no less."

"Yet you found your rocks the first day you set foot on Mercury."

"So I did. I was lucky." Suddenly Molina came up with a new thought. "Perhaps, in your terms, God guided me to those rocks."

Danvers rocked back in his chair. "Don't make a joke of God. That's blasphemy."

"I didn't mean to offend you, Elliott," Molina said softly. "I was simply trying to put my good fortune in terms you'd understand."

"You should try praying, instead," said Danvers. "As far as your fellow scientists are concerned, they don't believe in your luck. Or God's grace."

TORCH SHIP *BRUDNOY*

want it clearly understood," McFergusen said, in his gravelly Highland brogue, "that this is strictly an informal meeting."

Informal, Molina repeated silently. Like a coroner's inquest or a session of the Spanish Inquisition.

The Scottish physicist sat at the head of the table, Molina at its foot. Along the table were ranked the other scientists that the IAA had sent, together with Bishop Danvers, who sat at Molina's right. They were using the captain's conference room; it felt crowded, tight, and stuffy. Too many people for a compartment this size, Molina thought.

"Although the ship's computer is taking a verbatim record of what we say," McFergusen went on, "no report of this meeting will be sent back to IAA headquarters until each person here has had a chance to read the record and add any comments he or she wishes to make. Is that clear?"

Heads nodded up and down the table.

McFergusen hesitated a moment, then plunged in. "Now then, our major problem is that we have been unable to find any specimens bearing biomarkers."

"Except for the ones I found," Molina added.

"Indeed."

"How do you account for that?" asked the woman on Molina's left.

He shrugged elaborately. "How do you account for the fact that, during some war back in the twentieth century, the first cannon shell fired into the city of Leningrad killed the zoo's only elephant?"

Everyone chuckled.

Except McFergusen. "We have been scouring the planet for some six weeks now—"

"Six weeks for a whole planet?" Molina countered. "Do you really believe you've covered everything?"

"No, of course not. But you found your specimens on your first day, didn't you?"

Feeling anger simmering inside him, Molina said, "You forget that I came here because of a tip from one of the construction workers. I didn't just blindly stumble onto those rocks."

"A tip from whom?" asked one of the younger men.

"I don't know. It was an anonymous message. I've questioned the workers down there on the surface and none of them admits to sending me the message."

"An anonymous tip that no one admits to sending,"

grumbled McFergusen. "It strains credulity a bit, doesn't it?"

The woman on Molina's left, young, slightly plump, very intense, asked, "Why you?"

"Why me what?"

"Why did he—or she—send that message to you? You're not a major figure in planetary studies. Why not to Professor McFergusen," she gestured toward the older man, "or the head of the IAA?"

"Yes," picked up one of the others. "Why wasn't the message sent to the head of the astrobiology department of a major university?"

"Why is the sky blue?" Molina snapped. "How the hell should I know?"

"We know why the sky is blue," McFergusen murmured, a slight smile on his bearded face.

"Rayleigh scattering," said the young woman on the other side of the table.

"The question remains," McFergusen said, in a voice loud enough to silence the others, "that you received an anonymous message that led you directly to the specimens you discovered, and no one else has been able to find anything similar."

"And no one else has tested your specimens," said the woman on Molina's left.

Seething, Molina hissed, "Are you suggesting that I *faked* my findings?"

"I am suggesting," she said, unfazed by his red-faced anger, "that you allow us to independently test your specimens."

"It's possible to make an honest mistake," Bishop Danvers said softly, laying a placating hand on Molina's arm.

"Look at Percival Lowell, spending his life seeing canals on Mars that didn't exist."

"Or the first announcement of pulsar planets."

McFergusen said gently, "No one is impugning your honesty, Dr. Molina. But we can't be certain of your results until they are checked by a third party. Surely you understand that."

Reluctantly, Molina nodded. "Yes. Of course. I'm sorry I got so excited."

Everyone around the table seemed to relax, ease back in their chairs.

"But," Molina added, pointing straight at McFergusen, "I want to be present when the tests are made."

"Certainly," McFergusen agreed. "I see no problem with that. Do any of you?"

No one objected.

"Very well, then. We can test the rocks tomorrow. Dr. Baines, here, is the best man for the job, don't you agree?"

Molina nodded.

"I will attend the procedure myself," McFergusen said, almost jovially. "With you, Dr. Molina."

Molina nodded again and muttered, "Thank you," through gritted teeth.

GOETHE BASE

You've got to help me," Victor Molina said, his voice trembling slightly. "You've *got* to!"

Dante Alexios sat stiffly in his straight-backed chair and struggled to keep any emotion from showing on his face. "*I* have to help you?"

"None of the others will. You're the only one who can."

The two men were in Alexios's bare little office. Molina was on his feet, pacing like a caged animal back and forth.

Alexios sat unmoving, except for his eyes, which tracked Molina's movements like a predator sizing up its intended victim.

Molina paced to the wall, turned around, strode back to the opposite wall, turned again.

"I've got to find more samples!" he blurted. "They won't believe me if I don't. I've got to go out on the surface and find more rocks that contain biomarkers."

As evenly as he could manage, Alexios said, "But the IAA team is looking for samples all over the planet, aren't they? They've stopped us from doing any further activities—"

"The IAA team! McFergusen and his academics! A bunch of incompetent fools! They sit up there safe and comfortable in their ship and send teleoperated rovers to snoop around the surface for them."

"Virtual reality is a powerful tool," Alexios goaded.

Standing in front of him, bending over so that their noses nearly touched, Molina cried, "They won't allow me to use their VR system! I let them examine my rocks but they won't let me touch their equipment! It's not fair!"

Alexios slowly rose to his feet, forcing Molina to back off a few steps. "And that's why you've come to me."

"You have tractors sitting here at the base doing nothing. Let me borrow one. I've got to get out there and find more specimens."

Alexios's oddly irregular face slowly curled into a lopsided smile. "It's against safety regulations for anyone to go out on a tractor alone."

Molina's already-flushed face turned darker. Before he could say anything, though, Alexios added, "So I'll go out with you."

"You will?" Molina seemed about to jump for joy.

With a self-deprecating little shrug, Alexios said, "I have little else to do, thanks to the IAA."

He could have said, *Thanks to you,* but Molina never thought of that possibility.

Instead he asked, "When? How soon?"

"As soon as you're ready."

"I'm ready now!"

In truth, it took more than a day for Molina to be ready. He shuttled back up to *Himawari* to gather the equipment he wanted, and by then it was time for dinner. So he spent the night aboard Yamagata's torch ship with his wife. Alexios slept in his quarters alone, trying not to think of Molina in bed with Lara. He slept very little, and when he did his dreams were monstrous.

Molina arrived at the base early the next morning, with four crates of equipment. Alexios hid his amusement and walked him to the garage where the base's tractors were housed. A baggage cart trundled behind them on spongy little wheels, faithfully following the miniature beacon Alexios had clipped to his belt.

The garage was empty and quiet. "Mr. Yamagata came in here just once since the IAA embargoed us," Alexios said, his voice echoing off the steel ribs of the curving walls. "He wasn't happy to see all this equipment sitting idle."

Molina said nothing. The tractors were simple and rugged, with springy-looking oversized metal wheels and a glassteel bubble up front where the driver and passengers sat. The two men loaded Molina's equipment into the cargo deck in back, then closed the heavy cermet hatch.

"I'll get into my suit now," said Molina.

Alexios could see dark stains of perspiration on his coveralls. It couldn't be from the exertion of lifting those crates in this light gravity, he thought. Victor must be nervous. Or maybe he's afraid of going outside again.

He went with Molina and suited up also.

"But you won't have to leave the tractor," Molina objected as a team of technicians began to help them into the bulky suits.

"Unless you get into trouble," said Alexios.

"Oh."

"You wouldn't want to wait a half hour or more while I wiggled myself into this outfit."

"No, I imagine not."

At last they were both ready, the cumbersome, heavily insulated suits fully sealed and checked out by the technicians.

Alexios called base control with his suit radio. "Dr. Molina and I are going out on tractor number four. We will go beyond your camera range."

The controller's voice sounded bored. "Copy you'll go over the horizon. Sunup in one hour, seventeen minutes."

A flotilla of miniature surveillance satellites hugged the planet in low orbits, so every square meter of Mercury's surface was constantly covered by at least two of the minisats. They provided continuous communications links and precise location data.

"Sun in one seventeen," Alexios acknowledged.

"You are clear for excursion," said the controller.

It wasn't easy to climb up into the tractor's cab in the awkward suits, despite the low gravity. Alexios heard Molina grunt and puff until he finally settled in the right-hand seat.

"Comfortable?" Alexios asked.

"Are you kidding?"

Laughing lightly, Alexios engaged the tractor's electric engine and drove to the open inner airlock hatch.

"Do you have a specific route for us to follow or will we simply meander around out there?" Alexios asked as the inner hatch closed and the air was pumped out of the lock.

Molina struggled to fish a thumbnail-sized chip from his equipment belt and clicked it into the computer in the tractor's control panel. The display screen showed a geodetic map of the area with a route marked clearly by a red line.

Alexios studied the display for a moment, then tapped a gloved finger against it. "That's a pretty steep gully. We should avoid it."

Molina's voice in his earphones sounded irked. "That's the most likely spot to find what I'm looking for."

The outer hatch slid open. The barren landscape looked dark and foreboding, the horizon frighteningly near, thousands of stars gleaming steadily beyond it. Alexios saw the glowing band of the Milky Way stretching across the sky.

As he put the tractor in gear, he checked the status of the electrical power systems on the control panel displays. Fuel cells at max, backup batteries also. Once the Sun came up, he knew, the solar cells would take over.

They bounced over the hatch's edge and onto the rugged, uneven rocky surface.

"I'm afraid we can't take the tractor down into that gully," Alexios said.

Silence from Molina for a moment, although Alexios could hear his breathing in his helmet earphones. Then, "All right. Get as close to it as you can and I'll go down on foot."

Alexios felt his brows rise. Victor has guts, he said to himself. Or, more likely, he's driven by a demon.

Alexios knew all about being driven by demons.

SURFACE EXCURSION

Molina sat in silence inside the heavy pressurized suit, jouncing slightly as the tractor trundled along the route he had selected. They passed the shallow crater where he had found his specimens. In the tractor's headlights it looked gray and lifeless.

A relentless anger simmered through him, overwhelming the uneasiness he felt about being out on the surface of this deadly world, where a slight mistake could kill you.

Once he allowed McFergusen and his dilettantes to examine his samples, they wouldn't let go of them. Just one more test. Oh, yes, we thought of another way to probe the samples. You don't mind our keeping them another day or two, do you?

Molina saw that the results they were getting matched his own almost exactly. Within the margin of measurement error, at least. So why are they still sawing away at my rocks? What do they think they'll find that I haven't already found? They can't take the credit for discovering them away from me. What in hell are they trying to do?

He thought he knew the answer. They're trying to prove I'm wrong. They're doing their damnedest to discredit me. They'll keep poking and probing and studying until they find some error in my analysis, some mistake I've made.

Never! he told himself. There's no mistake. No error. The biomarkers are there and no matter what they do they can't make them go away.

But still they're hammering away at it, trying to show I'm wrong. Molina seethed with barely controlled fury. He tried to remember that age-old saw: *Extraordinary claims require extraordinary evidence.* Who said that originally? Fermi? Sagan?

What fucking difference does it make? he raged inwardly. The evidence is there. It's real, goddammit. They can't make it disappear.

But they won't be satisfied until more specimens with biomarkers are found. All right. They can't find them, sitting up there in orbit with their virtual reality thumbs up their asses. So *I'll* find them down here. I'll bring back more specimens and shove them under their noses and then they'll *have* to admit I'm right.

"We're coming up on that gully." Alexios's voice in his earphones startled him back to the here and now.

Blinking away his angry ruminations, Molina saw off to their right a long, fairly straight gorge paralleling their course, a split in the bare rocky surface. It didn't look very deep on the geodetic map, but now as he stared through the glassteel bubble of the tractor's cab, it seemed as yawning as the Grand Canyon.

It's just an illusion, he told himself. With no light except the stars, everything looks dark and deep and scary.

"Where do you want me to pull up?" Alexios asked.

Strange how familiar his voice sounded through the earphones, Molina thought. I couldn't have heard it before; I just met the man a few weeks ago. And yet—

"Where should I stop?" Alexios asked again.

"Get as close to the edge as you can," Molina said, feeling his insides fluttering with anticipation and more than a little fear.

Alexios drove the tractor up to the rim of the gully, so close that Molina was momentarily alarmed that they would topple into it. When he finally stopped the tractor, Molina could peer down into its shadowy depths.

"Better wait until the Sun comes up," Alexios suggested.

Nodding inside his helmet, Molina started to get up from his seat. "I'll get my equipment out of the back."

Alexios pressed the keypad on the control panel that popped the hatch on Molina's side of the bubble, then opened the hatch on his side. "I'll give you a hand."

They worked by starlight, hauling the cases of equipment out of the tractor's cargo bay. One of the metal boxes stuck to the tractor's deck.

"Frozen," Alexios muttered. "It must have had some moisture on its bottom when you put it in."

Molina realized that it was more than a hundred below zero in the nighttime darkness.

"It'll thaw quickly enough when the Sun comes up," said Alexios.

Impatient, Molina climbed up onto the deck and opened the crate there. He began hauling out the equipment it held: sample scoops, extensible arms, handheld radiation meters. One by one, he handed them to Alexios, who laid them in a neat row on the ground.

Alexios lifted his left arm so he could see the miniature display screen on his wrist. "Still another half hour to sunrise."

Molina was already setting up a winch and buckyball cable. Alexios saw a power drill among the equipment arrayed on the ground and helped the astrobiologist to firmly implant the steel-tubed frame into the hard, rocky ground. Then they fastened the winch to it and connected its power cable to the tractor's electrical outlet.

Wordlessly they lowered Molina's equipment to the bottom of the gully. It was a fair test of the winch, although none of the paraphernalia weighed as much as Molina and his suit.

Despite the coldness of the night, Alexios was sweating from his exertions. Good, he thought. The suit's well insulated. He straightened up and saw a pearly glow on the horizon.

"Look," he said to Molina, pointing.

For a moment Molina felt confused. Mercury has no atmosphere, he knew. There can't be a gradual dawn, like on Earth. Then he realized that what he was seeing was the Sun's zodiacal light, the sunlight scattered off billions of dust motes that orbited the Sun's equator, leftover bits of matter from the earliest times of the solar system's birth that hovered close to the star like two long oblate arms, too faint to see except when the overwhelming glare of the Sun itself was hidden, as it was now.

Molina grunted, then said, "I'd better get into the rig."

Inside his helmet, Alexios shook his head. You never were the poetic sort, Victor. Not a romantic neuron in your entire brain. But then a sardonic voice in his head reminded him, But he got Lara, didn't he?

By the time he had helped Molina into the climbing harness, the rim of the Sun was peeping above the horizon, sending a wave of heat washing across the desolate landscape. Alexios heard his suit ping and groan as its cermet expanded in the sudden roasting warmth. The air fans whirred like angry insects. The visor of his helmet automatically darkened.

"Ready?" he asked Molina.

He heard the man gulp and cough. Then he replied, "Yes, I'm ready."

The gully was filling with light as the Sun climbed higher against the black sky. Alexios stood by the winch as it unreeled its cable and Molina slowly, carefully, picked his way down the steep slope of the crevasse.

It's not all that deep, Alexios saw, peering down into the ravine. Ten meters, maybe twelve. Just deep enough. He watched as Molina reached the bottom and unhitched the cable from his climbing harness.

"Good hunting," Alexios called to him.

"Right," said Molina faintly. His voice was already

breaking up slightly, relayed from the bottom of the crevasse to one of the commsats orbiting overhead and then to Alexios's suit radio.

In pace requiescat, Alexios added silently.

Once he'd removed the climbing cable from his suit, Molina took in a deep, steadying breath and looked up and down the gully. It was like a long, slightly irregular hallway without a roof. One steep wall was bathed in sunlight, the other in shadow. But enough light reflected off the bright side so that he could see the uneven floor and even the shadowed side fairly well.

This must be a fault line, he told himself. Maybe it cracked open when a meteor impacted. He attached his sampling scoop to the metal arm and extended it to its full length. Not much dust on the ground, he saw. The bottom here must be exposed ancient terrain. If I can get some ratio data from the radioactives I'll be able to come up with a rough date for its age.

It was all but impossible to kneel in the heavy, cumbersome suit, but slowly Molina lowered himself to his knees. Inside the suit he could hear its servomotors whine in complaint. He chipped out a small chunk of rock, then fumbled through the sets of equipment lying on the ground until he found the radiation counter. No sense trying for argon ratios, he told himself. The heat's baked all the volatiles out of these rocks eons ago.

The radiation signature of uranium was there, however. Weak, but clearly discernable in the handheld's tiny readout screen. Then he tried the potassium signature. Stronger. Unmistakable. Molina weighed the sample, then did some rough calculating on the computer built into his suit's wrist. This sample is at least two and half billion years old, he concluded. If I can dig deeper, I should find older layers of rock.

He looked down the length of the slightly uneven corridor of rock. The floor seemed to drop away farther down. Maybe I can get to older strata without digging, he thought. I don't have a really powerful drill with me, anyway.

It took a mighty effort to get back on his feet again, even with the servomotors doing their best. Molina blinked sweat from his eyes and called up to Alexios:

"I'm going down the arroyo about a hundred meters or so."

It took a moment for the radio signal to bounce off the nearest commsat.

"Which direction?" Alexios asked.

Molina pointed, then realized it was foolish. He tapped at his wrist keyboard, then peered at the positioning data that came up on its display.

"North," he said into his helmet microphone. "To your left as you face the rim."

A silence longer than the time for the signal to be relayed off the satellite. Then, "Very well. If you go any farther, let me know and I'll bring the tractor and rig to your position."

"That won't be necessary," Molina answered immediately.

Again a delay. Finally, "Very well. I'll wait here."

Molina started slogging along the rock-walled chasm. That voice, he said to himself. Why should it sound so familiar?

Alexios climbed back into the tractor's bubble of a cab and sat awkwardly in the driver's seat. The chair was bare metal, designed to accommodate the bulky suits that the tractor crew had to wear.

No sense standing in the open, Alexios thought. The glassteel doesn't afford that much protection against radiation, but every little bit helps. He remembered an old adage he had heard from a mercenary soldier out in the Belt: "Never stand when you can sit. Never stay awake when you can sleep. And never pass a latrine without using it."

No latrines out here, Alexios knew. Nor out in the Belt, either. You piss into the relief tube built into your suit and you crap when you can find a toilet inside a pressurized vessel.

The Sun was halfway above the horizon now, already frighteningly large and glaring.

Alexios smiled. In another fifteen minutes or so it will dip back down and plunge this whole region into darkness again. What's Victor going to do when the light goes away and he's stuck down in that crevasse?

FALSE DAWN

Dante Alexios sat in the cab of the tractor and watched the Sun drop toward the horizon, a twisted smile on his slightly mismatched face. Although Molina hadn't spoken to him since he announced he was heading farther up the gully, he could hear Victor's breathing through the open microphone in the astrobiologist's helmet.

Alexios turned off the suit-to-suit link and called in to the base on another frequency.

"Alexios to base control."

The reply was almost immediate. "Control here."

"Do you have our position?"

A slight delay. Alexios could picture the controller flicking his eyes to the geographic display.

"Yes, your beacon is coming through clearly."

"Good. Anything happening that I should know about?"

A slight chuckle. "Not unless you have a prurient interest in what the safety director and her assistant are up to."

Alexios laughed, too. "Not as long as they keep their recreations confined to the privacy of their quarters."

"So far. But there's a lot of heavy breathing going on at their workstations."

"I'll speak to her when I get back."

"Her? What about him?"

"Her," Alexios repeated. "The woman's always in control in situations like this."

"That's news to me," said the controller.

There was nothing else significant to report. One of the powersats was getting some experimental shielding; otherwise, the base was running in standby mode until the IAA gave them clearance to resume their work.

Alexios clicked off the link to the base and sat back as comfortably as he could manage inside the suit. How long will it take Yamagata to go bankrupt? he wondered. And when the Sunpower Foundation does go bust, will Yamagata simply siphon more money out of his corporation? Will his son allow that? A battle between father and son would be interesting.

The Sun was dipping lower. Turning, he could see bright stars spangling the blackness on the other side of the sky. Alone with the stars. And his thoughts.

Lara. She was Molina's wife. Had been for just about ten years now. They have a child, a son. Victor, Jr. His son, out of her body.

The pain Alexios felt was real, physical. He realized his jaws had clamped so tightly that he could hear his teeth grinding against one another.

With a physical effort, he forced himself to relax and tapped the keypad to reopen the suit-to-suit link.

"—dark down here," Molina was saying. "My helmet lamp isn't all that much help."

"The Sun's going down for a while," said Alexios.

"How long?"

Alexios had memorized the day's solar schedule. "Fifty-eight minutes, twelve seconds."

"A whole hour?" Molina's voice whined like a disappointed child's.

"Just about."

"What the hell am I supposed to do down in this hole in the dark for an hour? You should have told me about this!"

"I thought you knew."

"I can't see fucking shit down here!"

"You have the helmet lamp."

"Big help. It's like trying to find your way across the Rocky Mountains with a flashlight."

"Have you found anything?"

"No," Molina snapped. "And I won't, at this rate."

You won't at any rate, Alexios replied silently. Aloud, he asked, "Do you want to come back to the tractor?"

A long silence. Alexios could picture Molina angrily weighing the alternatives in his mind.

"No, dammit. I'll wait here until the frigging Sun comes up again."

"I'll move the tractor down to your location."

"Good. Do that."

With no atmosphere to dilute their brightness, the stars provided adequate light for Alexios to reel up the winch's cable, disassemble the rig and pack it all back onto the tractor's rear deck. Then he drove carefully along the rim of the crevasse to the spot where Molina sat, waiting and fuming, for enough sunlight to resume his search. A waste of time, Alexios knew. Victor won't find what he's looking for.

By the time he had drilled the holes in the ground for the rig's supporting frame and set the winch in place, the Sun was rising above the bare, too-near horizon once again. This time it would remain up for weeks. Even through the heavy tinting of his visor Alexios had to squint at its powerful glare. The Sun was tremendous, huge, a mighty presence looming above him.

The hours dragged on. Alexios listened to Molina panting and grumbling as he searched for rocks that might harbor biomarkers.

"Christ, it's hot," the astrobiologist complained.

Alexios flicked a glance at the outside temperature readout on the tractor's control panel. "It's only three-eighty Celsius. A cool morning on Mercury."

"I'm broiling inside this damned suit."

"You'd broil a lot faster outside the suit," Alexios bantered.

"There's nothing here. I'm going farther up the gully."

"Check your suit's coolant systems. If the levels are down in the yellow region of the display, you should come back."

"It's still in the green."

Alexios called up the suit monitoring program and saw that Molina's coolant systems were on the edge of the yellow warning region. He's got about an hour left before they'll dip into the red, he estimated.

Nearly an hour later, Alexios called, "Time to come back, Dr. Molina."

"Not yet. There's a bunch of rocks up ahead. I want to take a look at them."

"Safety regulations, sir," Alexios said firmly. "Your life-support systems are going critical."

"I can see the readouts as well as you can," Molina replied testily. "I've got a good hour or more before they reach the red line, and even then there's a considerable safety margin built in."

"Dr. Molina, the safety regulations must be followed. They were formulated for your protection."

"Yeah, yeah. Just let me take a look at—hey! Damn! Ow!"

"What happened?" Alexios snapped, genuinely alarmed. "What's wrong?"

"I'm okay. I fell down, that's all. Tripped over a crack in the ground."

"Oh."

Alexios heard grunting, then swearing, then quick, heavy breathing. The sound of panic.

"Christ, I can't get up!"

"What?"

"I can't lift myself up! I'm down on my left side and I can't get enough leverage in this goddamned suit to push myself up onto my feet again."

Alexios could picture his predicament. The suit's servomotors were designed to assist the wearer's normal arm and leg movements. Basically they were designed to allow a normal human being's muscle power to move the suit's heavy sleeves and leggings. Little more. Molina was down on the ground, trying to lift the combined weight of his body plus the suit back into a standing position. Even in Mercury's light gravity, the servos were unequal to the task.

"Can you sit up?" he asked into his helmet mike.

A grunt, then an exasperated sigh. "No. This damned iron maiden you've got me in doesn't bend much at the middle."

Alexios thought swiftly. He can last about two more hours in the suit, maybe three. I can leave him there and let him broil in his own juices. He left me when I needed him; why should I save his life? It's not my fault—he *wanted* to go down there. He insisted on it.

Base control wasn't on the suit-to-suit frequency. The suit radios could be picked up by the commsats, of course, but you had to plug into the commsat frequency and Victor didn't know that. He rushed out here without learning all the necessary procedures, Alexios thought. He depended on me to handle the details.

Just as I depended on him to help me when I needed it. And he walked away from me. He took Lara and left me to the wolves.

Inside his helmet, Alexios smiled grimly. He remembered Poe's old story, "The Cask of Amontillado." What were Fortunato's last words? *"For the love of God, Montresor!"* And Montresor replied, as he put the last brick in place and sealed his former friend into a lingering death, "Yes, for the love of God!"

"Hey!" Molina called. "I really need some help here."

"I'm sure you do," Alexios said calmly.

And he pictured himself bringing the sad news back to the base. Telling Yamagata how the noted astrobiologist had killed himself out on the surface of Mercury, nobly searching for evidence of life. I tried to help him, Alexios saw himself explaining, but by the time I reached him he was gone. He just pushed it too far. I warned him, but he paid no attention to the safety regs.

Then I'll have to tell his widow. Lara, your husband is dead. No, I couldn't say it like that. Not so abruptly, so brutally. Lara, I'm afraid I have very bad news for you. . . .

He could see the shock in her soft gold-flecked eyes. The pain.

"I'm really stuck here," Molina called, a hint of desperation in his voice. "I need you to help me. What are you doing up there?"

Alexios heard himself say, "I'm coming down. It'll take a few minutes. Hang in there."

"Well for Christ's sake don't dawdle! I'm sloshing in my own sweat inside this frigging suit."

Alexios smiled again. You're not helping yourself, Victor. You're not making it easier for me to come to your aid.

But he pushed the door of the tractor's cab open and jumped to the ground, almost hoping that he'd snap an ankle or twist a knee and be unable to save Victor's self-centered butt. Angry with himself, furious with Victor, irritated at the world in general, Alexios marched to the winch and wrapped the cable around both his gloved hands. Slowly he began lowering himself down the steep side of the gully.

"What are you doing?" Molina demanded. "Are you coming?"

"I'll be there in a few minutes," Alexios said between gritted teeth.

I'll save your ass, Victor, he thought. I'll save your body. I won't let you die. I'll bring you back and let you destroy yourself. That's just as good as killing you. Better, even. Destroy yourself, Victor. With my help.

TORCH SHIP *BRUDNOY*

ad a bit of a scrape out there, eh?" asked Professor McFergusen as he poured a stiff whisky for himself.

Molina was sitting on the curved couch of the *Brudnoy*'s well-stocked lounge, his wife close beside him. Two tall glasses of fruit juice stood on the low table before them. No one else was in the lounge; McFergusen had seen to it that this meeting would be private.

McFergusen kept a fatherly smile on his weather-seamed face as he sat down in the plush faux-leather chair at the end of the cocktail table. He and the chair sighed in harmony.

"You're all right, I trust?" he asked Molina. "No broken bones, as far as I can see."

"I'm fine," Molina said. "It was just a little accident. Nothing to fuss over."

Mrs. Molina looked to McFergusen as if she thought otherwise, but she said nothing and hid her emotions by picking up her glass and sipping at it. Fruit juice. McFergusen suppressed a shudder of distaste.

"I think the entire affair has been exaggerated," said Lara. "From what Victor tells me, he was never in any real danger."

McFergusen nodded. "I suppose not. Good thing that Alexios fellow was there to help out, though."

"That's why the safety regulations require that no one goes out onto the surface alone," Molina said, a bit stiffly.

"Yes. Of course. The important thing, though—the vital question—is: Did you find any more specimens while you were out there?"

Now Molina grabbed for his glass. "No," he admitted, then took a gulp of the juice.

McFergusen's bearded face settled into a worried frown. "You see, the problem is that we still have nothing but those specimens you collected your very first day on the planet."

"There must be more," Molina insisted. "We simply haven't found them yet."

"We've searched for weeks, lad."

"We'll have to search further. And more extensively."

The tumbler of whisky had never left McFergusen's hand. He took a deep draft from it, then finally put it down on the table. Shaking his head, he said firmly, "Yamagata's putting pressure on the IAA. And, frankly, I'm running out of excuses to send back to headquarters. Do you realize how much it costs to keep this ship here? And my committee?"

Molina looked obviously irritated. "How much is the discovery of life on Mercury worth? Can you put a dollar figure on new knowledge?"

"Is there life on Mercury?"

"That's the question, isn't it?"

"Some of my committee members think we're here on a fool's errand," McFergusen admitted.

"They're the fools, then," Molina snapped.

"Are they?"

Molina started to reply, but his wife put a hand on his arm. Just a feather-light touch, but it was enough to silence him.

"Wasn't it Sagan" she asked, in a soft voice, "who said that absence of proof is not proof of absence?"

McFergusen beamed at her. "Yes, Sagan. And I agree! I truly do! I'm not your enemy, lad. I want you to succeed."

Lara immediately understood what he had not said. "You want Victor to succeed, but you have doubts."

"Worse than that," McFergusen said, his tone sinking. "There's a consensus among my committee that your evidence, Dr. Molina, is not conclusive. It may not even be pertinent."

Molina nearly dropped his glass. "Not pertinent! What do you mean?"

Decidedly unhappy, McFergusen said, "I've called a meeting for tomorrow morning at ten. I intend to review all the evidence that we've uncovered."

"We've gone over the evidence time and again."

"There's something new," McFergusen said. "Something that's changed the entire situation here."

"What is it?" Lara asked.

"I prefer to wait until the entire committee is assembled," said McFergusen.

"Then why did you ask us to join you here this evening?"

Looking squarely at Molina, the professor said grimly, "I wanted to give you a chance to think about what you've done and consider its implications."

Molina's brow wrinkled in puzzlement. "I don't understand what you're talking about."

"All to the good, then," said McFergusen. "If you're telling the truth."

"Telling the truth! What the hell do you mean?"

Raising his hands almost defensively, McFergusen said, "Now, now, there's no sense losing your temper."

"Is somebody calling me a liar? Are any of those academic drones saying my evidence isn't valid?"

"Tomorrow," McFergusen said. "We'll thrash all this out tomorrow, when everyone's present." He gulped down the rest of his whisky and got to his feet.

Molina and his wife stood up, too.

"I don't understand any of this," Lara said.

McFergusen realized she was just as tall as he was. "Perhaps I shouldn't have met with you this evening. I merely wanted to give you a fair warning about what to expect tomorrow."

Molina's face was red with anger. His wife clutched at his arm and he choked back whatever he was going to say.

"I'll see you tomorrow at ten, in the conference room," McFergusen said, clearly embarrassed. "Good evening."

He hurried out of the lounge and ducked through the hatch into the ship's central passageway.

Lara turned to her husband. "At least he didn't have the effrontery to wish us pleasant dreams."

Molina was too furious to smile at her attempted humor.

TRIBUNAL

Molina could see from the expressions on their faces that this was going to be bad. McFergusen sat at the head of the conference table, his team of scientists along its sides. What bothered Molina most was that Danvers and his two young acolytes were also present, seated together toward the end of the table. The only empty chair, waiting for Molina, was at the absolute foot of the table.

They all looked up as Molina entered the conference room at precisely ten o'clock. A few of them smiled at him, but it was perfunctory, pasted on, phony. Obviously McFergusen had ordered them to come in earlier, most likely because he wanted to go over their testimony with them. *Testimony.* Molina grimaced at the word he had automatically used. This was going to be a trial, he knew. Like a court martial. Like a kangaroo court.

The conference room fell into complete silence as soon as he opened the door from the passageway and entered. In silence Molina took his chair and slipped his data chip into the slot built into the faux mahogany table.

"Dr. Molina," said McFergusen, "I presume you know everyone here."

Molina nodded. He had met most of the scientists and knew of their reputations. Danvers was an old friend, at least an old acquaintance. The two other ministers with him were nonentities, as far as Molina was concerned, but that didn't matter.

The conference room was stark. The narrow table that lined one of its walls was bare; no refreshments, not even an urn of coffee or a pitcher of water. The wall screens were blank. The room felt uncomfortably warm, stuffy, but Molina was ice-cold inside. This is going to be a battle, he told himself. They're all against me, for some reason. Why? Jealousy? Disbelief? Refusal to accept the facts? It doesn't matter. I have the evidence. They can't take that away from me. I've already published my findings on the nets. Maybe that's it. Maybe they're pissed off because I didn't send my findings through the regular academic channels to be refereed before putting them out for all the world to see.

McFergusen ostentatiously pressed the keypad on the board built into the head of the table. "I hereby call this meeting to order. It is being recorded, as is the usual practice."

Molina cleared his throat and spoke up. "I wish to submit my findings as proof that evidence of biological activity has been discovered on Mercury."

McFergusen nodded. "Your evidence is entered into the record of this meeting."

"Good."

"Any comments?"

A plump, grandmotherly woman with graying hair neatly pulled back off her roundish face spoke up. "I have a comment."

"Dr. Paula Kantrowitz," said McFergusen, for the benefit of the recording. "Geobiologist, Cornell University."

You're overdue for a regeneration treatment, Molina sneered silently at Dr. Kantrowitz. And a month or two in an exercise center.

She tapped at the keypad before her and Molina's data sprang up on the wall screens on both sides of the room.

"The evidence that Dr. Molina has found is incontrovertible," she said. "It clearly shows a range of signatures that are indicative of biological activity."

Molina felt his entire body relax. Maybe this isn't going to be so bad after all, he thought.

"There is no question that the rocks Dr. Molina tested bear high levels of biomarkers."

A few nods around the table.

"The question is," Kantrowitz went on, "did those rocks originate on Mercury?"

"What do you mean?" Molina snapped.

Avoiding his suddenly angry eyes, Kantrowitz went on, "When I tested the rock samples that Dr. Molina so kindly lent to us, I was bothered by the results I saw. They reminded me of something I had seen elsewhere."

"And what is that?" McFergusen asked, like the straight man in a well-rehearsed routine.

Kantrowitz touched another keypad and a new set of data curves sprang up on the wall screens alongside Molina's data. They looked so similar they were almost identical.

"This second data set is from Mars," she said. "Dr. Molina's rocks bear biomarkers that are indistinguishable from the Martian samples."

"What of it?" Molina challenged. "So the earliest biological activity on Mercury produces signatures similar to the earliest biological activity on Mars. That in itself is an important discovery."

"It would be," Kantrowitz replied, still not looking at Molina, "if your samples actually came from Mercury."

"Actually came from Mercury?" Molina was too stunned to be angry. "What do you mean?"

Kantrowitz looked sad, as if disappointed with the behavior of a child.

"Once I realized the similarity to Martian rocks, I tested the morphology of Dr. Molina's samples."

The data sets on the walls winked off, replaced by a new set of curves.

"The upper curves, in red, are from well-established data on Martian rocks. The lower curves, in yellow, are from Dr.

Molina's samples. As you can see, they are so parallel as to be virtually identical."

Molina stared at the wall screen. No, he said to himself. Something is wrong here.

"The third set of curves, in red at the bottom, is from random samples of rocks I personally picked up from the surface of Mercury. They are very different in mineral content and in isotope ratios from the acknowledged Martian rocks. And from Dr. Molina's samples."

Molina sagged back in his chair, speechless.

Relentlessly, Kantrowitz went on, "I then used the tunneling microscope to search for inclusions in the samples."

Another graph appeared on the wall screen.

"I found several, which held gasses trapped within the rock. The ratio of noble gases in the inclusions match the composition of the Martian atmosphere, down to the limits of the measurement capabilities. If these samples had been on the surface of Mercury for any reasonable length of time, the gases would have been baked out of the rock by the planet's high daytime temperatures."

"Are you saying," McFergusen asked, "that Dr. Molina's samples are actually rocks from Mars?"

"They're not from Mercury at all?" Danvers asked, unable to hide a delighted smile.

"That's right," Kantrowitz replied, nodding somberly. At last she turned to look directly at Molina. "I'm very sorry, Dr. Molina, but your samples are Martian in origin."

"But I found them here," Molina said, his voice a timid whine. "On Mercury."

McFergusen said coolly, "That raises the question of how they got to Mercury."

A deadly silence fell across the conference table. After several moments, one of the younger men sitting across from Kantrowitz, raised his hand. An Asian of some sort, Molina saw. Or perhaps an Asian-American.

"Dr. Abel Lee," pronounced McFergusen. "Astronomy department, Melbourne University."

Lee got to his feet. Molina was surprised to see that he was quite tall. "It's well known that some meteorites found on Earth originated from Mars. They were blasted off the planet by the impact of a much more energetic meteor, achieved escape velocity, and wandered through interplanetary space until they fell into Earth's gravity well."

"In fact," McFergusen added, "the first evidence that life existed on Mars was found in a meteorite that had landed in Antarctica—although the evidence was hotly debated for many years."

Lee made a little bow toward the professor, then continued, "So it is possible that a rock that originated on or even beneath the surface of Mars can be blasted free of the planet and eventually impact on another planet."

Molina nodded vigorously.

"But is it likely that such a rock would land on Mercury?" asked one of the other scientists. "After all, Mercury's gravity well is considerably smaller than Earth's."

"And with its being so close to the Sun," said another, "wouldn't the chances be overwhelming that the rock would fall into the Sun, instead?"

Lee replied, "I'd have to do the statistics, but I think both points are valid. The chances of a Martian rock landing on Mercury are vanishingly small, I would think."

"There's more to it than that," said McFergusen, his bearded face looking grim.

Molina felt as if he were the accused at a trial being run by Torquemada.

"First," said McFergusen, raising a long callused finger, "Dr. Molina did not find merely one Martian rock, but a total of eight, all at the same site."

"It might have been a single meteor that broke up when it hit the ground," Molina said.

McFergusen's frown showed what he thought of that possibility. "Second," he went on, "is the fact that although we have searched an admittedly small area of the planet's surface, no other such samples have been found."

"But you've only scratched the surface of the problem!" Molina cried, feeling more and more desperate.

McFergusen nodded like a judge about to pronounce a death sentence. "I agree that we have searched only a small fraction of the planet's surface. Still . . . ," he sighed, then, staring squarely down the table at Molina, he went on, "There is such a thing as Occam's razor. When faced with several possible answers to a question, the simplest answer is generally the correct one."

"What do you mean?" Molina whispered, although he knew what the answer would be.

"The simplest answer," McFergusen said, his voice a low deadly rumble, "is that the site at which you discovered those rocks was deliberately seeded with samples brought to that location from Mars."

"No!" Molina shouted. "That's not true!"

"You worked on Mars, did you not?"

"Four years ago!"

"You had ample opportunity to collect rocks from Mars and eventually bring them to Mercury."

"No, they were already here! Some of the construction people found them! They sent a message to me!"

"That could all have been prearranged," McFergusen said.

"But it wasn't! I didn't—"

McFergusen sighed again, even more heavily. "This committee will make no judgment on how your samples arrived on Mercury, Dr. Molina. Nor will we accuse you or anyone else of wrongdoing. But we must conclude that the samples you claimed as evidence of biological activity on Mercury originated on Mars."

Molina wanted to cry. I'm ruined, he thought. My career as a scientist is finished. Ended. Absolutely ruined.

SCAPEGOAT

Bishop Danvers felt almost gleeful as he composed a message of triumph for New Morality headquarters in Atlanta.

The scientists themselves had disproved Molina's claim of finding life on Mercury! That was a victory for Believers everywhere. The entire thing was a sham, a hoax. It just shows how far these godless secularists will go in their efforts to destroy people's faith, Danvers said to himself.

He was saddened to see Molina's credibility shattered. Victor was a friend, an acquaintance of long standing. He could be boorish and overbearing at times, but now he was a broken man. He brought it on himself, though, Danvers thought. The sin of pride. Now he's going to pay the price for it.

Yet Danvers felt sorry for the man. They had known each other for almost a decade and a half, and although they were far removed from one another for most of that time, still he felt a bond with Victor Molina. Danvers had even performed the ceremony when Victor married Lara Tierney. It's wrong for me to rejoice in his mistake, he thought.

Deeper still, Danvers knew that the real bond between them had been forged in the destruction of another man, Mance Bracknell. Danvers and Victor had both played their part in the aftermath of that terrible tragedy in Ecuador. They had both helped to send Bracknell into exile. Well, Danvers said to himself, it could have been worse. After all, we saved the man from being torn apart by an angry mob.

With a heavy sigh, Danvers pushed those memories out of the forefront of his mind. Concentrate on the task at hand, he told himself. Send your report to Atlanta. The archbishop and his staff will be delighted to hear the good news. They can trumpet this tale as proof of how scientists try to undermine our faith in God. I'll probably be promoted higher up the hierarchy.

He finished dictating his report, then read it carefully as it scrolled on the wall screen in his quarters aboard the *Himawari,* adding a line here, changing an emphasis there, polishing his prose until it was fit to be seen by the archbishop. Yamagata must be pleased, he realized as he edited his words. He can resume his construction work, or whatever it is the engineers are supposed to be doing down on the planet's surface.

Nanomachines, he remembered. They want to begin using nanomachines on Mercury. What can I do to prevent that? If I could stop them, this mission to Mercury would become a double triumph for me.

When he was finally satisfied with his report, Danvers transmitted it to Earth. As an afterthought he sent courtesy copies to the two young ministers that Atlanta had sent to assist him. They'll be heading back to Earth now, he thought. He got to his feet and rubbed his tired eyes. In all probability I'll be heading back to Earth myself soon. He smiled at the prospects of a promotion and a better assignment as a reward for his work here. His smile turned wry. I hardly had to lift a finger, he thought. The scientists did all the work for me.

Then his thoughts returned to Molina. Poor Victor. He must be beside himself with grief. And anger, too, I suppose. Knowing Victor, the anger must be there. Perhaps suppressed right now, he's feeling so low. But sooner or later the anger will come out.

Bishop Danvers knew what he had to do. Squaring his shoulders, he left his quarters and marched down the ship's passageway toward the compartment that housed Victor Molina and his wife.

Molina was close to tears, Lara realized. He had burst into their compartment like a drunken man, staggering, wild-eyed. He frightened her, those first few moments.

Then he blubbered, "They think I falsified it! They think I'm a cheat, a liar!" And he nearly collapsed into her arms.

More than an hour had passed. Lara still held her husband in her arms as they sat on the couch. He was still shuddering, his face buried in her breast, his arms wrapped around her, mumbling incoherently. Lara patted his disheveled hair soothingly. Haltingly, little by little, he had told her what had transpired at the meeting with McFergusen and the other scientists. She had murmured consoling words, but she knew that nothing she could say would help her husband. He had been accused of cheating, and even if he eventually proved he hadn't, the stigma would remain with him all his life.

"I'm ruined," he whimpered. "Destroyed."

"No, it's not that bad," she cooed.

"Yes it is."

"It will pass," she said, trying to ease his pain.

Abruptly, he pushed away from her. "You don't understand! You just don't understand!" His eyes were red, his hair wild and matted with perspiration. "I'm done! Finished! They've destroyed me. It would've been kinder if they'd blown my brains out."

Lara sat up straighter. "You are *not* finished, Victor," she said firmly. "Not if you fight back."

His expression went from despair to disgust. "Fight back," he growled. "You can't fight them."

"You can if you have the courage to do it," she snapped, feeling angry with her husband's self-pity, angry at the vicious fools who did this to him, angry at whoever caused this disaster. "You don't have to let them walk all over you. You can stand up and fight."

"You don't know—"

"Someone sent you a message, didn't they?"

"Yes, but—"

"You have a record of that message?"

"In my files, yes."

Lara said, "Whoever sent that message to you probably put those Martian rocks at the site you found."

Molina blinked several times. "Yes, but McFergusen and the others think that I set that up using a stooge."

"Prove that they're wrong."

"How in hell—"

"Find the man who set you up," Lara said. "He had to come to Mercury to plant those rocks at the site. He's probably still here."

"Do you think . . ." Molina fell silent. Lara studied his face. He wasn't bleating any more. She could see the change in his eyes.

"I don't think anybody's left Mercury since I arrived here. Certainly none of the team down at the base on the surface. None of Yamagata's people, I'm pretty sure."

"Then whoever set you up is probably still here."

"But how can we find him?"

Before Lara could think of an answer, they heard a soft rap at their door.

"I'll get it," she said, jumping to her feet. "You go wash up and comb your hair."

She slid the door open. Bishop Danvers's big, blocky body nearly filled the doorway.

"Hello, Lara," he said softly. "I've come to do what I can to solace Victor and help him in his hour of need."

Lara almost smiled. "Come right in, Elliott. We're going to need all the help we can get."

In his bare little office at Goethe base, Dante Alexios heard the news directly from Yamagata.

"It was all a hoax!" Yamagata was grinning from ear to ear. "The rocks were planted here. They actually came from Mars."

"Molina salted the site?" Alexios asked, trying to look astonished.

"Either he or a confederate."

"That's . . . shocking."

"Perhaps so, but it means that the blasted scientists have withdrawn their interdict on our operations."

"So soon?"

Yamagata shrugged. "They will, in a day or so. In the meantime, I want you to come up here to *Himawari* first thing tomorrow morning. We must plan the next phase of our operation."

"Building powersats here, out of materials from Mercury itself."

"Yes. Using nanomachines."

Alexios nodded. "We'll have to plan this very carefully."

"I realize that," Yamagata said, his grin fading only slightly. "That's why I want you here first thing in the morning."

"I'll be there."

"Good." Yamagata's image winked out.

Alexios leaned back in his chair and clasped his hands behind his head. Victor's finished, he said to himself. Now to get Danvers. And then my dear employer, Mr. Saito Yamagata, the murderer.

BOOK II

TEN YEARS EARLIER

And much of Madness, and more of Sin,
And Horror the soul of the plot.

THE SKYTOWER

ara Tierney couldn't catch her breath. It wasn't merely the altitude, although at more than three thousand meters the air was almost painfully thin. What really took her breath away, though, was the sight of the tower splitting the sky as the ancient Humvee rattled and jounced along the rutted, climbing road. Mance, sitting beside her, handed her a lightweight pair of electronic binoculars.

"They'll lock onto the tower," he shouted over the grinding roar of the Humvee's diesel engine. "Keep it in focus for you."

Lara put the binoculars to her eyes and found that they really did make up for some of the bumps in the Humvee's punishing ride. The skytower wavered briefly, then clicked into sharp focus, a thick dark column of what looked in the twin eyepieces like intertwined cables spiraling up, up, higher and higher, through the soft clouds and into the blue sky beyond, up into infinity.

"It's like a banyan tree," she gasped, resting the binoculars on her lap.

"What?" Mance Bracknell yelled from beside her. They were sitting together on the bench behind the driver, a short, stocky, dark-skinned mestizo who had inherited this rusting, dilapidated four-wheel-drive from his father, the senior taxi entrepreneur of the Quito airport.

Lara took several deep breaths, trying to get enough air into her lungs to raise her voice above the noise of the Humvee's clattering diesel engine.

"It's like a banyan tree," she shouted back, turning toward

him. "All those strands . . . woven together . . . like a . . . banyan." She had to pull in more air.

"Right! That's exactly right!" Mance yelled, his dark brown eyes gleaming excitedly. "Like a banyan tree. It's organic! Nanotubes spun into filaments and then wrapped into coils; the coils are wound into those cables you're looking at."

She had never seen him so tanned, so athletically fit, so indestructibly cheerful. He looks more handsome than ever, she thought.

"Just like a banyan tree," he repeated, straining to make himself heard. "Damned near a hundred thousand individual buckyball fibers wound into those strands. Strongest structure on the face of the Earth."

"It's magnificent!"

Bracknell's smile grew wider. "We're still almost thirty kilometers away. Wait'll you get up close."

Like the beanstalk of the old fairy tale, the skytower rose up into the heavens. Lara spent the jouncing, dusty ride alternately staring at it and then glancing at Mance, sitting there as happy as a little boy on Christmas morning opening his presents. He's doing something that no one else has been able to do, she thought, and he's succeeding. He has what he wants. And that includes me.

All during the long flight from Denver to Quito she had wondered about her impulsive promise to marry Mance Bracknell. For the past three years all she'd seen of him was his quick visits back to the States and his occasional video messages. He had gone to Ecuador, asked her to marry him, and she had agreed. She had flown to Quito once before, when Mance was just starting on the project. He was so busy, so happily buried in his work that she had quietly returned home to Colorado. He didn't need her underfoot, and he barely raised more than a perfunctory objection when she told him she was going back home.

That was more than three years ago. I have a rival for his attentions, Lara realized. This tower he's building. She wondered if her rival would always stand between them. But when Mance called this latest time and asked her to come to Ecuador and stay with him, she had agreed immediately even though he hadn't mentioned a word about marriage.

Once she saw him, though, waiting for her at the airport terminal in Quito, the way his whole face lit up when he caught sight of her, the frenetic way he waved to her from the other side of the glass security partition as she went through the tiresome lines at customs, the way he smiled and took her in his arms and kissed her right there in the middle of the crowded airport terminal—she knew she loved him and she would follow him wherever he went, rival and marriage and everything else fading into trivia.

". . . if it works," he was hollering over the rumble of the truck's groaning engine, "we'll be able to provide electricity for the whole blinking country. Maybe for Colombia, Peru, parts of Brazil, the whole blasted northwestern bloc of South America!"

"If what works?" she asked.

"Tapping the ionosphere," he answered. Gesturing with both hands as he spoke, he shouted, "Enormous electrical energy up there, megawatts per cubic meter. At first we were worried that the tower would be like a big lightning rod, conducting down to the ground. Zap! Melt the bedrock, maybe."

"My god," Lara said.

"But we insulated the outer shell so that's not a problem."

Before Lara could think of something to say, Mance went on, "Then I started thinking about how we might tap some of that energy and use it to power the elevators."

"Tap the ionosphere?"

"Right. It's replenished by the solar wind. Earth's magnetic field traps solar protons and electrons."

"That's what causes the northern lights," Lara said, straining to raise her voice above the laboring diesel's growl.

"Yep. If we work it right, we can generate enough electricity to run the blinking tower and still have enough to sell to users on the ground. We can recoup all the costs of construction by selling electrical power!"

"How much electricity can you generate?" she asked.

"What?" he yelled.

She repeated her question, louder.

He waggled his right hand. "Theoretically, the numbers are staggering. Lots of gigawatts. I've got Mitchell working on it."

That's a benefit no one thought about, Lara said to herself. The original idea of the skytower was to build an elevator that could lift people and cargo into space cheaply, for the cost of the electrical energy it takes to carry them. Pennies per pound, instead of the hundreds of dollars per pound that rocket launchings cost. Now Mance is talking about using the tower to generate electricity, as well. How wonderful!

Then a new thought struck her. "Isn't this earthquake territory?" she shouted into Mance's ear.

His grin didn't fade even as much as a millimeter. He nodded vigorously. "You bet. We've had two pretty serious tremors already, Richter sixes. The world's highest active volcano is only a couple hundred kilometers or so from our site."

"Isn't that dangerous?"

"Not for us. That's one of the reasons we used the banyan tree design. The ground can sway or ripple all it wants to—the tower's not anchored to the ground, just tethered lightly. It won't move much."

Lara realized she looked unconvinced because Mance added, "Besides, we're not on a fault line. Nowhere near one. I got solid geological data before picking the site. The ground's not going to open up beneath us, and even if it did the tower would just stand there, solid as the Rock of Gibraltar."

"But if it should fall . . . all that weight . . ."

Mance's smile turned almost smug. "It won't fall, honey. It can't. The laws of physics are on our side."

DATA BANK

Skyhook. Beanstalk. Space elevator. Skytower. All these names and more have been applied to the idea of building an elevator that can carry people and cargo from the Earth's surface into orbital space.

Like many other basic concepts for space transportation, the idea of a skytower originated in the fertile mind of Konstantin Tsiolkovsky, the Russian pioneer who theorized about rocketry and astronautics in relative obscurity around the turn of the twentieth century. His idea for a "celestial castle" that could rise from the equator into orbital space, published in 1895, may have been inspired by the newly built Eiffel Tower, in Paris.

In 1960, the Russian engineer Yuri Artsutanov revived the concept of the space elevator. Six years later an American oceanographer, John Isaacs, became the first outside of Russia to write about the idea. In 1975, Jerome Pearson, of the U.S. Air Force Research Laboratory, brought the space elevator concept to the attention of the world's scientific community through a more detailed technical paper.

The British author Arthur C. Clarke popularized the sky-hook notion in several of his science fiction novels.

Although it sounds outlandish, the basic concept of a space elevator is well within the realm of physical possibility. As Clarke himself originally pointed out, a satellite in geostationary orbit, slightly more than thirty-five thousand kilometers above the equator, circles the Earth in precisely the same time it takes for the Earth to revolve about its axis. Thus such a satellite remains constantly above the same spot on the equator. Communications satellites are placed in geostationary *Clarke orbits* so that ground-based antennas may be permanently locked onto them.

To build a skytower, start at geostationary orbit. Drop a line down to the Earth's surface and unreel another line in the opposite direction, another thirty-five thousand kilometers into space. Simple tension will keep both lines in place. Make the line strong enough to carry freight and passenger elevators. *Voila!* A skyhook. A beanstalk. A skytower.

However, in the real world of practical engineering, the skytower concept lacked a suitable construction material. All known materials strong enough to serve were too heavy for the job. The tower would collapse of its own weight. A material with a much better strength-to-weight ratio was needed.

Buckyball fibers were the answer. Buckminsterfullerene is a molecule of sixty carbon atoms arranged in a sphere that reminded the chemists who first produced them of a geodesic dome, the type invented by the American designer R. Buckminster Fuller. Quickly dubbed buckyballs, it was found that fibers built of such molecules had the strength-to-weight ratio needed for a practical space elevator—with a considerable margin of error to spare. Where materials such as graphite, alumina, and quartz offer tensile strengths in the order of twenty gigapascals (a unit of measurement for tensile strength) the requirements for a space elevator are more than sixty gigapascals. Buckyball fibers have tensile strengths of more than one hundred gigapascals.

By the middle of the twenty-first century all the basic technical demands of a skytower could be met. What was needed was the capital and the engineering skill to build such a structure: a tower that rises more than seventy thousand kilometers from the equator, an elevator that can carry payloads into space for the price of the electricity used to lift them.

Backed by the nation of Ecuador and an international consortium of financiers, Skytower Corporation hired Mance Bracknell to head the engineering team that built the skytower a scant hundred kilometers from Quito. People in the streets of the Ecuadorian capital could see the tower rising to the heavens, growing thicker and stronger before their eyes.

Many glowed with pride as the tower project moved toward completion. Some shook their heads, however, speaking in worried whispers about the biblical Tower of Babel. Even in the university, philosophers spoke of man's hubris while engineers discussed moduli of elasticity. In Quito's high-rise business towers, men and women who dealt in international trade looked forward to the quantum leap that the tower would produce for the Ecuadorian economy. They saw their futures rising as high as the sky, and quietly began buying real estate rights to all the land between Quito and the base of the tower.

None of them realized that the skytower would be turned into a killing machine.

CIUDAD DE CIELO

t's *huge*," Lara said, as she stepped down from the Humvee. Inwardly she thought of all the phallic jokes the men must be making about this immense tower.

"A hundred meters across at the base," Bracknell said, heading for the back of the truck where her luggage was stored. "The size of a football field."

The driver stayed behind his wheel, anxious to get his pay and head back to the airport.

"It tapers outward slightly as it rises," Bracknell went on. "The station up at geosynch is a little more than a kilometer across."

The numbers were becoming meaningless to her. Everything was so huge. This close, she could see that each of the interwound cables making up the thick column must be a good five meters in diameter. And there were cables angling off to the sides, like the roots of a banyan, except that there were buildings where the cables reached the ground. They must be the tethers that Mance told me about, Lara thought.

"Well," he said, grinning proudly as he spread his arms, "this is it. Sky City. *Ciudad de Cielo.*"

It was hard to take her eyes off the skytower, but Lara made the effort and looked around her. At Mance's instruction, the taxi had parked in front of a two-story building constructed of corrugated metal walls. It reminded her of an airplane hangar or an oversized work shed. Looking around, she saw rows of such buildings laid out along straight paved streets, a neat gridwork of almost identical structures, a prefabricated little city. Sky City. It was busy, she saw. Trucks and minivans bustled about the streets, men and women strode purposively along the concrete sidewalks. Very little noise, though, she realized. None of the banging and thumping that usually accompanied construction projects. Of course, Lara thought: all the vehicles are powered by electrical engines. This city was quietly intense, humming with energy and purpose.

Then she smiled. Somewhere down one of those streets someone was playing a guitar. Or perhaps it was a recording. A softly lyrical native folk song, she guessed. Its gentle notes drifted through the air almost languidly.

Bracknell pointed. "The music's coming from the restaurant. Some of our people have formed groups; they entertain in the evenings. Must be rehearsing now."

He picked up both her travel bags and led her from the parking lot up along the sidewalk toward the building's entrance.

"This is where my office is. And my living quarters, up on the second floor." He hesitated, his tanned face flushing slightly. "Uh, I could set you up in a separate apartment if you want. . . ."

Both his hands were full with her luggage, so she stepped to him and wrapped her arms around his neck and kissed him soundly. "I didn't come all this way to sleep alone."

Bracknell's face went even redder. But he grinned like a schoolboy. "Well, okay," he said, hefting her travel bags. "Great."

Lara had brought only the two bags with her. They were close enough to Quito for her to buy whatever she lacked, she had reasoned.

Bracknell's apartment was small, utilitarian, and so gleamingly neat that she knew he had cleaned it for her. Through the screened windows she could see the streets of the little city and, beyond them, the green-clad mountains. The skytower was not in view from here.

"No air conditioning?" she asked as he plopped her bags onto the double-sized bed.

"Don't need it. Climate's very mild; it's always springtime here."

"But we're on the equator, aren't we?"

"And nearly four kilometers high."

She nodded. Like Santa Fe, she thought. Even Denver had a much milder climate than most people realized.

As she opened the larger of her two bags, Lara asked, "So the weather's not a problem for the skytower?"

"Even the rainy season isn't all that bad. That's one of the reasons we picked this site," Bracknell said as he peered into the waist-high refrigerator in his kitchen alcove. He pulled out an odd-shaped bottle. "Some wine? I've got this local stuff that's pretty bad, and a decent bottle of Chilean—"

"Just cold water, Mance," she said. "We can celebrate later."

He nearly dropped the bottle he was holding.

Bracknell had a surprise for her at dinner: Victor Molina, whom they had both known at university.

"I had no idea you were part of this project," Lara said, as they sat at a small square table in the corner of the city's only restaurant. A quartet of musicians was tuning up across the way. Lara noticed that their amplifiers were no bigger than tissue boxes, not the man-tall monsters that could collapse your lungs when they were amped up full blast.

The restaurant was hardly half filled, Lara saw. Either most of the people eat at home or they come in much later than this, she reasoned. It was a bright, clean little establishment. No tablecloths, but someone had painted cheerful outdoor scenes of jungle greenery and colorful birds on the tabletops.

"Victor's the reason we're moving ahead so rapidly," Bracknell said.

Lara refocused her attention on the two men. "I thought you were into biology back at school," she said.

"I still am," Molina replied, his striking blue eyes fastened on her. He was as good-looking as ever, she thought, in an intense, urgent way. Lara remembered how, at school, Molina had pursued the best-looking women on campus. She had dated him a few times, until she met Mance. Then she stopped dating anyone else.

Before she could ask another question, the robot waiter rolled up to their table. Its flat top was a display screen that showed the evening's menu and wine list.

"May I bring you a cocktail before you order dinner?" the robot asked, in a mellow baritone voice that bore just a hint of an upper-class British accent. "I am programmed for voice recognition. Simply state the cocktail of your choice in a clear tone."

Lara asked for sparkling water and Bracknell did the same. Molina said, "Dry vodka martini, please."

"Olives or a twist?" she asked the robot.

"Twist."

The little machine pivoted neatly and rolled off toward the service bar by the kitchen.

Lara leaned slightly toward Molina. "I still don't understand what a biologist is doing on this skytower project."

Before Molina could reply, Bracknell answered, "Victor's our secret weapon. He's the one who's allowed us to move ahead so rapidly."

"A biologist?"

Molina's eyes were still riveted on her. "You've heard of nanotechnology, haven't you?"

"Yes. It's banned, forbidden."

"True enough," he said. "But do you realize there's

nanotechnology going on inside your body at this very instant?"

"Nanotech?"

"Inside the cells of your body. The ribosomes in your cells are building proteins. And what are they other than tiny little nanomachines?"

"Oh. But that's natural."

"Sure it is. So is the way we build buckyball fibers."

"With nanomachines?"

"Natural nanomachines," Bracknell said, trying to get back into the conversation. "Viruses."

The robot brought their drinks and, later, they selected their dinner choices from the machine's touch screen. Molina and Bracknell explained how Molina had used genetically engineered viruses to produce buckyball molecules and engineered microbial cells to put the bucky-balls together into nanotubes.

"Once we have sets of nanotubes," Molina explained, "I turn them over to the regular engineers, and they string them together into the fibers that make up the tower."

"And you're allowed to do this in spite of the ban on nano-technology?" Lara asked.

"There's nothing illegal about it," Molina said lightly.

"But we're not shouting the news from the rooftops," Bracknell added. "We want to keep this strictly under wraps."

"It's a new construction technique that'll be worth billions," Molina said, his eyes glowing. "Trillions!"

"Once we get it patented," Bracknell added.

Lara nodded, absently taking a forkful of salad and chewing contemplatively. Natural nanotechnology, she thought. Genetically engineered viruses. There are a lot of people who're going to get very upset when they hear about this.

"I can see why you want to keep it under wraps," she said.

PUBLISH OR PERISH

W hat I really want," Molina was saying, "is to get into astrobiology."

"Really?" Lara felt surprised. In all the weeks she had been at Ciudad de Cielo, this was the first time he'd broached the subject with her.

She was walking with the biologist along the base city's main street, wearing a colorful wool poncho that she'd bought from one of the street vendors that Mance allowed into town on the weekends. The wind off the mountains was cool, and it had drizzled for a half hour earlier in the morning. The thick wool poncho was just the right weight for this high-altitude weather. Molina had pulled a worn old leather jacket over his shirt and jeans.

"Astrobiology's the hot area in biology," he said. "That's where a man can make a name for himself."

"But you're doing such marvelous things here."

He looked over his shoulder at the skytower looming over them. Gray clouds scudded past it. With a discontented shrug, Molina said, "What I'm doing here is done. I've trained some bugs to make buckyball fibers for Mance. Big deal. I can't publish my work; he's keeping the whole process secret."

"Only until the patent comes through."

Molina frowned at her. "Do you have any idea of how long it takes to get an international patent? Years! And then the Skytower Corporation'll probably want to keep the process to themselves. I could waste the best years of my career sitting around here and getting no credit for my work."

Lara saw the impatience in his face, in his rigidly

clenched fists, as they walked down the street. "So what do you intend to do?"

Molina hesitated for a heartbeat, then replied, "I've sent an application to several of the top astrobiology schools. It looks like Melbourne will accept me."

"Australia?"

"Yes. They've just gotten a grant to search for more Martian ruins and they're looking for people."

"To go to Mars?"

He made a bitter smile. "Australia first, then maybe Mars. If I do well enough for them here on Earth."

"I suppose that would be a good career move for you, Victor."

"Ought to be. Astrobiology. The field's wide open, with all the discoveries they're making on the moons of Jupiter and all."

"Then you'll be leaving us?"

"I've got to!" His voice took on a pained note. "I mean, Mance won't let me publish my work here until that fucking patent comes through. I'll be dead meat unless I can get into an area where I can make a name for myself."

"You and Mance work so well together, though," Lara said. "I know he'll be shocked when you tell him."

"He doesn't need me around here anymore. He's milked my brain and gotten what he wants."

Lara was surprised at the bitterness in his voice. "Mance will miss you," she said.

"Will *you?*"

"Of course I'll miss you, Victor."

He licked his lips, then blurted, "Then come to Melbourne with me, Lara! Let's get away from here together!"

Stunned, Lara staggered a few steps away from him.

"I'm in love with you, Lara. I really am. The past couple of months . . . it's been so . . ." He hesitated, as though gasping for breath. "I want to marry you."

He looked so forlorn, so despairing, yet at the same time so intense, so burning with urgency that Lara didn't know what to reply, how to react.

"I'm so sorry, Victor," she heard herself say gently. "I really am. I love Mance. You know that."

He hung his head, mumbling, "I know. I'm sorry, too. I shouldn't have told you."

"It's very sweet of you, Victor," she said, trying to soften his anguish. "I'm really very flattered that you feel this way. But it can't be."

"I know," he repeated. "I know." But what he heard in her words was, *If it weren't for Mance I could fall in love with you, Victor.*

Elliott Danvers knew that the elders of the New Morality were testing him. He had sweated and struggled through divinity school, accepting the snickers and snide jokes about a punch-drunk ex-prizefighter trying to become a minister of God. He had kept his temper, even when some of his fellow students' practical jokes turned vicious. *I can't get into a fight,* he would tell himself. *I'd be accused of attempted manslaughter if I hit one of them, and they know it. That's why they feel free to torment me. And I'm not clever enough to outwit them. Be silent. Be patient with those who persecute you. Turn the other cheek. This nonsense of theirs is a small price to pay for setting my life on a better path.*

He graduated near the bottom of his class, but he graduated. Danvers was a man who drove doggedly onward to complete whatever task he was burdened with. He had learned as a child in the filth-littered back alleys of Detroit that you took what came and you dealt with it, whether it was the punches of a faster, harder-hitting opponent or the thinly veiled contempt of a teacher who'd be happy to flunk you.

His reward for graduating without getting into any trouble was a ministry. He was now the Reverend Elliott Danvers, D.D. His faculty advisor congratulated him on bearing all the crosses that his playful classmates and vindictive teachers had hung on his broad shoulders.

"You've done well, Elliott," said his advisor, a pleased smile on his gray, sagging face. "There were times when I didn't think you'd make it, but you persevered and won the final victory."

Danvers knew that his academic grades had been marginal, at best. He bowed his head humbly and murmured, "I couldn't have made it without your help, sir. And God's."

His advisor laid a liver-spotted hand on Danvers's bowed head. "My blessings on you, my son. Wherever the New Morality sends you, remember that you are doing God's work. May He shower His grace upon you."

"Amen," said Danvers, with true conviction.

So they sent him to this strange, outlandish place in the mountains of Ecuador. It's a test, Danvers kept telling himself. The elders are testing my resolve, my dedication, my ability to win converts to God.

Ciudad de Cielo was a little prefab nest of unbelievers, scientists and engineers who were at best agnostics, together with local workers and clerks who practiced a Catholic faith underlain with native superstitions and idol worship.

Worst of all, though, they were all engaged in an enormous project that smacked of blasphemy. A tower that reached into the sky. A modern, high-technology Tower of Babel. Danvers was certain it was doomed to fail. God would not permit mortal men to succeed in such a work.

Then he remembered that he had been placed here to do God's work. If this tower is to fail, I must be the agent of its destruction. God wills it. That's why the New Morality sent me here.

Danvers knew that his ostensible task was to take care of people's souls. But hardly anyone wanted his help. The natives seemed quite content with their hodge-podge of tribal rituals and Catholic rites. Most of the scientists and engineers simply ignored him or regarded him as a spy sent by the New Morality to snoop on them. A few actively baited him, but their slings and barbs were nothing compared to the cruelty of his laughing classmates.

One man, though, seemed troubled enough to at least put up with him: Victor Molina, a close assistant of the chief of this tremendous project. Danvers watched him for weeks, certain that Molina was showing the classic signs of depression: moodiness, snapping at his coworkers, almost always taking his meals alone. He looked distinctly unhappy. The only time he seemed to smile was on those rare occasions when he had dinner in the restaurant with the project chief and the woman he was living with.

Living in sin, Danvers thought darkly. He himself had given up all thought of sex, except for the fiendish dreams that were sent to tempt him. No, he told himself during his waking hours. It was the desire for women and money that almost led you to your destruction in the ring. They broke your hand, they nearly destroyed your soul because of your indecent desires. Better to pluck out your eye if it offends you. Instead, Danvers used modern pharmacology to keep his libido stifled.

He approached Molina carefully, gradually, knowing that the man would reject or even ridicule an overt offer of help.

During lunchtime the city's only restaurant offered a buffet. After thinking about it for weeks, Danvers used it as an opening ploy with Molina.

"Do you mind if I sit with you?" he asked, holding his lunch-laden tray in both hands. "I hate to eat alone."

Molina looked up sourly, but then seemed to recognize

the minister. Danvers did not use clerical garb; he wore no collar. But he always dressed in a black shirt and slacks.

"Yeah, why not?" Molina said. He was already halfway through his limp sandwich, Danvers saw.

Suppressing an urge to compliment the scientist on his gracious manners, Danvers sat down and silently, unobtrusively said grace as he began unloading his tray. They talked about inconsequential things, the weather, the status of the project, the sad plight of the refugees driven from coastal cities such as Boston by the greenhouse flooding.

"It's their own frigging fault. They had plenty of warning," Molina grumbled, finishing his sandwich. "Years of warning. Nobody listened."

Danvers nodded silently. No contradictions, he told himself. You're here to win his confidence, not to debate his convictions.

Over the next several weeks Danvers bumped into Molina often enough so that they started to be regular luncheon partners. Their conversations grew less guarded, more open.

"Astrobiology?" Danvers asked at one point. "That's what you want to do?"

Molina grinned wickedly at him. "Does that shock you?"

"Not at all," Danvers replied, trying to hide his uneasiness. "There's no denying that scientists have found living organisms on other worlds."

"Even intelligent creatures," Molina jabbed.

"If you mean those extinct beings on Mars, they might have been connected in some way with us, mightn't they?"

"At the cellular level, maybe. The DNA of the extant Martian microbial life is different from ours, though, even though it has a similar helical structure."

Danvers wasn't entirely sure of what his luncheon companion was saying, but that didn't matter. He said, "It doesn't seem likely that God would create an intelligent species and then destroy it."

"That's what happened."

"Don't you think that the Martians were a branch of ourselves? After all, the two planets are—"

"About sixty million kilometers apart, at their closest," Molina snapped.

"Yes, but Martian meteorites have been found on Earth."

"So?"

"So Mars and Earth have had exchanges in the past. Perhaps the human race began on Mars and moved to Earth."

Molina guffawed so loudly that people at other tables turned toward them. Danvers sat silently, trying to keep a pleasant face.

"Is that what you believe?" Molina asked at last, between chuckles.

"Isn't it possible?" Danvers asked softly.

"Possible for creatures with a stone age culture to build spacecraft to take them from Mars to Earth? No way!"

Molina was still chuckling when they left the restaurant. No matter, Danvers thought. Let him laugh. I'm winning his trust. Soon he'll be unburdening his soul to me.

As the weeks flowed into one another, Danvers began to understand that winning Molina's trust would not be that easy. Beneath his smug exterior Victor Molina was a desperately unhappy man. Despite his high standing in the skytower project, he was worried about his career, his future. And something else. Something he never spoke of. Danvers thought he knew what it was: Lara Tierney, the woman who was living with Bracknell.

Danvers felt truly sorry for Molina. By this time he regarded the biologist as a friend, the only friend he had in this den of idolaters and atheists. Their relationship was adversarial, to be sure, but he was certain that Molina enjoyed their barbed exchanges as much as he himself did. *Sooner or later he'll break down and tell me what's truly troubling him.*

Many, many weeks passed before Danvers realized there was something about Molina that was jarringly out of place. *What's Victor doing here, on this damnable project? Why is a biologist involved in building the skytower?*

NEW KYOTO

Nobuhiko Yamagata stood at his office window gazing out at the city spread out far below him. Lake Biwa glittered in the distance. A flock of large birds flapped by, so close that Nobu inadvertently twitched back, away from the window.

He was glad no one was in the office to see his momentary reaction. It might look like cowardice to someone; unworthy weakness, at least.

The birds were black gulls, returning from their summer grounds far to the north. *A sign that winter is approaching,* Nobuhiko knew. *Winter.* He grunted to himself. *There hasn't been enough natural snow to ski on since my father died.*

Nobu looked almost like a clone of his illustrious father: a few centimeters taller than Saito, but stocky, short-limbed, his face round and flat, his brown eyes hooded, unfathomable. The main difference between father and son was that while Saito's face was lined from frequent laughter, the lines on Nobu's face came from worry.

He hadn't heard from his father for more than a year now. The elder Yamagata had gone into a fit of regret over the killings out in the Asteroid Belt and become a true lama, full of holy remorse and repentance. It's as if he's died again, Nobu thought. He's cut off all contact with the world outside his lamasery, even with his only son.

The clock chimed once. No matter, Nobuhiko thought as he turned from the window. I can carry my burdens without Father's help. Squaring his shoulders, he said to the phone on his desk, "Call them in."

The double doors to his office swung inward and a half-dozen men in nearly identical dark business suits came in, each bearing a tiny gold flying crane pin in his lapel, each bowing respectfully to the head of Yamagata Corporation. They took their places at the long table abutting Nobu's desk like the stem of the letter T. No women served on this committee. There were several women on Yamagata's board of directors, but the executive committee was a completely male domain.

There was only one item on their agenda: the skytower.

Nobuhiko sat in his high-backed leather desk chair and called the meeting to order. They swiftly dispensed with formalities such as reading the minutes of the previous meeting. They all knew why they were here.

Swiveling slightly to his right, Nobu nodded to the committee's chairman. Officially, Nobuhiko was an ex-officio member of the executive committee, present at their meetings but without a vote in their deliberations. It was a necessary arrangement, to keep outsiders from accusing that Yamagata Corporation was a one-man dictatorship. Which it very nearly was. Nobu might not have had a vote on this committee, but the committee never voted against his known wishes.

"We are here to decide what to do about the skytower project," said the chairman, his eyes on Nobuhiko.

"It is progressing satisfactorily?" Nobu asked, knowing full well the answer.

"They are ahead of schedule," said the youngest member of the committee, down at the end of the conference table.

Nobuhiko let out a patient sigh.

"When that tower goes into operation," fumed one of the older men, "it will knock the bottom out of the launch services market."

One of Nobu's coups, once he took the reins of the corporation from his father, had been to acquire the American firm Masterson Aerospace Corporation. Masterson had developed the Clippership launch vehicle, the rocket that reduced launch costs from thousands of dollars per pound to hundreds, the doughty little, completely reusable vehicle that not only opened up orbital space to industrial development, but also served—in a modified version—as a hypersonic transport that carried passengers to any destination on Earth in less than an hour.

By acquiring Masterson, Yamagata gained a major share not only of the world's space launching market, but of long-distance air travel, as well.

"One tower?" scoffed one of the other elder members from across the conference table. "How badly can one tower cut into the launch services market? How much capacity can it have?"

The other man closed his eyes briefly, as if seeking strength to deal with a fool. "It is not merely the one tower. It is the *first* skytower. If it succeeds, there will be others."

Nobu agreed. "And why pay for Clipperships to go into orbit when you can ride a skytower for a fraction of the cost?"

"Exactly so, sir."

"The skytower is a threat, then?"

"Not an immediate threat. But if it is successful, within a few years such towers will spring up all along the equator."

"Fortunate for us," said another, smiling, "that most of the equator is over deep ocean instead of land."

No one laughed.

"How much of our profit comes from Clippership operations?" Nobuhiko asked.

"Not as much from space launch services as from air transportation here on Earth," said the comptroller, seated on Yamagata's left.

Nobu said softly, "The numbers, please."

The comptroller tapped hurriedly on the palmcomp in his hand. "It's about eight percent. Eight point four, so far this year. Last fiscal year, eight point two."

"It's pretty constant."

"Rising slightly."

Nobu folded his hands across his vest, a gesture he remembered his father using often.

"Can we afford to lose eight percent of our profits?" asked the youngster.

"Not if we don't have to," said the comptroller.

"We own part of this skytower project, don't we?" Nobu asked.

"We bought into it, yes. We have a contract to supply engineers and other technical staff and services. But it's only a minor share of their operation, less than five percent. And the contract will terminate once they begin operations."

Nobu felt his brows rise. "We won't share in their operating profits?"

The comptroller hesitated. "Not unless we negotiate a new contract for maintenance or other services, of course."

"Of course," Nobuhiko muttered darkly. Sweat broke out on the comptroller's forehead.

The office fell silent. Then the director of the corporation's aerospace division cleared his throat and said, "May I point out that all of our discussion is based on the premise that the skytower will be successful? There is no guarantee of that."

Nobuhiko understood him perfectly. The skytower could be a failure if we take action to make certain it fails. Looking around the conference table, he saw that each and every member of the executive committee understood the unspoken decision.

CIUDAD DE CIELO

Elliott Danvers was not brilliant, but he was not stupid, either. And he possessed a stubborn determination that allowed him to push doggedly onward toward a goal when others would find easier things to do.

Why is a biologist working on the skytower project? When he asked Molina directly, the man became reticent and evasive.

"What's a New Morality minister doing here, in Ecuador?" Molina would counter.

When Danvers frankly explained that his mission was to provide spiritual comfort to all who sought it, Molina cocked an eyebrow at him.

"Aren't you here to snoop on us, Elliott?" Molina asked, good-naturedly. "Aren't your superiors in Atlanta worried that this project is a modern Tower of Babel?"

"Nonsense," Danvers sputtered.

"Is it? My take on the New Morality is that they don't like change. They've arranged North America just the way they like it, with themselves in control of the government—"

"Control of the government!" Danvers was truly shocked at that. "We're a religious organization, not a secular one."

"So was the Spanish Inquisition," Molina murmured.

Despite their differences, they remained friends of a sort. Bantering, challenging friends. Danvers knew quite well that the only other man in Sky City that Molina regarded as a friend was the project director, Mance Bracknell. But something had come between them. No, not some*thing,* Danvers thought. Some*one.* Lara Tierney.

Molina invited Danvers to have dinner with him from time to time. Once, they joined Bracknell and Lara on a quick jaunt to Quito and dined in the best restaurant Danvers had ever seen. It didn't take long for Danvers to understand Molina's problem. Before the main courses were served he realized that Molina was in love with her, but she loved Bracknell. The eternal triangle, Danvers thought. It has caused the ruin of many a dream.

For himself, Danvers treasured Molina's company. Despite his atheistic barbs, Molina was the only close friend Danvers had made in this city of godless technicians and dark-skinned mestizos who worshiped their old blood-soaked gods in secret.

Yet the question nagged at him. Why is Molina here? What can a biologist do for this mammoth project?

After many weeks of asking everyone he knew, even men and women he had barely been introduced to, the path to understanding suddenly came to him, like a revelation from on high.

The woman. Lara Tierney. She is the key to Molina's presence here. To get him to tell the truth, Danvers realized, to open up his inner secrets, I must use his love for this woman. That's his vulnerable spot. Still, he wavered, reluctant to cause the pain that he knew Molina would feel. Danvers prayed long hours kneeling by his bedside, seeking guidance. Do I have the right to do this? he asked. The only answer he received was a memory of his mentor's words: *Remember that you are doing God's work.*

And then the revelation came to him. The way to promotion, the path to advancement within the New Morality, was by stopping this godless project. That's why they sent me here, he realized. To see if I can prevent these secularists from succeeding in their blasphemous project. That's how they're testing me.

Danvers rose from his knees, his heart filled with determination. The hour was late, but he told the phone to call Molina. He got the man's answering machine, of course, but made a date with him for dinner the following night. Not lunch. What he had to do would take more time than a lunch break. Better to do it after the working day is finished, in the dark of night. Be hard, he advised himself. Show no mercy. Drive out all doubts, all qualms. Be a man of steel.

Dinner wasn't much, and afterward Danvers and Molina walked slowly up the gently rising street toward the building where they both were quartered. The skytower was outlined by safety lights, flashing on and off like fireflies, trailing upward until they disappeared into the starry sky. A sliver of a Moon was riding over the mountains to the east. The sky was clear, hardly a cloud in sight, the night air crisp and chill.

All through dinner Danvers had avoided starting this probe into his friend's heart. But as they approached their building, he realized he could delay no longer.

"Victor," he began softly, "you and Bracknell and Ms. Tierney seem to be old friends."

"We all went to university together," Molina replied evenly.

The lamps along the street were spaced fairly widely, far

apart enough for the two men to stroll through pools of shadow as they walked along. Danvers saw that Molina kept his eyes down, watching where he was stepping rather than gazing up at the skytower looming above them.

"You studied biology there?"

"Yes," said Molina. "Mance bounced around from one department to another in the school of engineering."

"And Ms. Tierney?"

Through the shadows he could hear Molina's sudden intake of breath. "Lara? She started out in sociology, I think. But then she switched to engineering. Aerospace engineering, can you believe it?"

"That was after she'd met Bracknell."

"Yeah, right. After she met Mance. She went so goofy over him that she switched her major just to be closer to him."

"You were attracted to her yourself, weren't you?"

"Fucking lot of good it did me once she met Mance."

Danvers walked on for a few steps in silence. He heard the bitterness in Molina's voice, and now that he had touched on the sore spot he had to open up that wound again.

"Did you love her then?" he asked.

Molina did not answer.

"You still love her, don't you?"

"That's none of your damned business, Elliott."

"I think it is, Victor. You're my friend, and I want to help you."

"How the hell can you help me? You want to pray for a miracle, maybe?"

"Prayer has its powers."

"Bullshit!"

Danvers nodded in the darkness. Victor's in pain, no doubt of it. My task is to use his pain, channel it into a productive course.

"Why did you come here, then? If you knew that Bracknell

was heading this project, didn't you expect her to show up, sooner or later?"

"I suppose I did, subconsciously. Maybe I thought she wouldn't, that they were finished. I don't know!"

"But you came here, to this project. Did you volunteer or did Bracknell ask you to come?"

"Mance called me when he got the go-ahead for the project. All excited. Said he needed me to make it work."

"He needed you?"

"Like an idiot I agreed to take a look at his plans. Next thing I knew I was on a plane to Quito."

"Why did he need you?"

"I didn't think Lara would come down here," Molina went on, ignoring the question. "I figured Mance would be so fucking busy with this crazy scheme of his that he wouldn't have time for her. Maybe he'd even forgotten her. Damned fool me."

"But why did he need you?" Danvers insisted.

"To make the buckyball fibers," Molina snapped, "what the fuck do you think?"

Ignoring Molina's deliberate crudities, Danvers pressed, "A biologist to build the fibers?"

"A biologist, yeah. Somebody who can engineer viruses to assemble buckyballs for you. You need a damned smart biologist to work down at the nanometer scale."

Danvers sucked in his breath. "Nanomachines?"

They were under a streetlamp now and Danvers could see the pain and anguish in Molina's face. For several long moments the biologist struggled for self-control. At last he said calmly, coldly:

"Not nanomachines, Elliott. Viruses. Living creatures. Is this what you're after? Trying to find out if we're using nanotech so you can turn us in to the authorities?"

"No, Victor, not at all," Danvers half-lied. "I'm trying to find out what's troubling you. I want to help you, I truly do."

"Great. You want to help me? Find some way to get Mance out of the picture. Get him away from Lara. That's the kind of help I need."

ATLANTA

The headquarters building of the New Morality was not as large as the capitol of a secular government, nor as ornate as a cathedral. But it was, in fact, the seat of a power that stretched across all of the North American continent north of the Rio Grande and extended its influence into Mexico and Central America.

In the days before the greenhouse floods, the New Morality was little more than a fundamentalist Christian sect, sterner than most others, that concentrated its work in the rundown cores of cities such as Atlanta, Philadelphia, Detroit, and other urban blights. It did good works: rescuing lost souls, driving drug dealers out of slum neighborhoods, rebuilding decaying houses, making certain that children learned to read and write in the schools it had installed in abandoned storefronts. In return for these good works, the New Morality insisted on iron discipline and obedience. Above all, obedience.

Then the Earth's climate tumbled over the greenhouse cliff. After half a century of warnings from climatologists that were ignored by temporizing politicians and ridiculed by disbelieving pundits, the global climate abruptly switched from postglacial to the kind of semitropical environment that had ruled the Earth in earlier eons. Icecaps melted. Sea levels rose by twenty meters over a few years. Coastal cities everywhere were flooded. The electrical power grid that sustained modern civilization collapsed. Killer storms raged while farmlands eroded into dust. Hundreds of millions of men, women, and children were driven from their homes, their jobs, their lives, all of them hungry, frightened, desperate.

The New Morality rejoiced. "This is the wrath of God that has been called down upon us!" thundered the Reverend Harold Carnaby. "This is our just punishment for generations of sinful licentiousness."

Governments across the world turned authoritarian, backed by fundamentalist organizations such as the Holy Disciples in Europe and the Flower Dragon in the Far East. Even the fractious Muslims came together under the banner of the Sword of Islam once Israel was obliterated.

After decades of authoritarian rule, however, people all across the Earth were growing restive. The climate had stabilized, although once again scientists were issuing dire warnings, this time of a coming Ice Age. They were ignored once again as the average family moved toward economic well-being and a better life. Prosperity was creeping across the world once more. Church attendance was slipping.

Carnaby, now a self-appointed archbishop, mulled these factors in his mind as he sat in his powered wheelchair and gazed out across the skyline of Atlanta's high-rise towers.

"We saved this city," he grumbled.

"Yes, sir," said one of the aides standing behind him respectfully. "We surely did."

"We saved the nation when it was sinking into crime and depravity," Carnaby added. "Now that the people are growing richer, they're turning away from God. They're more interested in buying the latest virtual reality games than in saving their souls."

"Too true," said the second aide.

Carnaby pivoted his wheelchair to face them. They were

standing before his desk, arms at their sides, eyes focused on the archbishop.

"Sir, about the medical report . . ."

"I'm not interested in saving my mortal body," Carnaby said, frowning up at them through his dead-white eyebrows.

"But you must, sir! The Movement needs your guidance, your leadership!"

"I'm ready to meet my Maker whenever He calls me."

The one aide glanced at the other, obviously seeking support. The two of them were as alike as peas in a pod in their dark suits and starched white shirts. Carnaby wondered if they were twins.

"Sir," said the other one, his voice slightly deeper than his companion's, "the physicians are unanimous in their diagnosis. You must accept a heart implant. Otherwise . . ." He left the conclusion unspoken.

"Put a man-made pump into my chest and remove the heart that God gave me? Never!"

"No, sir, that isn't it at all. It's merely a booster pump, an auxiliary device to assist your heart. Your natural heart will be untouched," the deeper-voiced aide coaxed. "It's really rather minor surgery, sir. They insert it through an artery in the thigh."

"They won't open my chest?"

"No, sir," both aides said in chorus.

Carnaby huffed. He had accepted other medical devices. One day, he'd been told, he would have to get artificial kidneys. Ninety-two years old, he told himself, and I've never taken a rejuvenation treatment. Not many my age can say that. God is watching over me.

"An auxiliary pump, is it?"

"Yes, sir."

"You need it, sir. With all the burdens of work and the pressures you face every day, it's a miracle that your heart has lasted this long without assistance."

Carnaby huffed again to make sure that they understood that he didn't like the idea. But then he lowered his head and said humbly, "God's will be done."

The aides scampered out of his office, delighted that he had acquiesced, and more than a little awed at the archbishop's willingness to sacrifice his obvious distaste of medical procedures for the good of the Movement.

Alone at his desk, Carnaby called up the latest computer figures on church attendance. The New Morality was officially a nonsectarian organization. The bar graph that sprang up on his smart wall screen showed attendance reports for nearly every denomination in North and South America. The numbers were down—not by much, but the trend was clear. Even the Catholics were falling away from God.

His desktop intercom chimed. "Deacon Gillette calling, Archbishop," said the phone's angel-sweet voice. "Urgent."

"Urgent? What's so urgent?"

The phone remained silent for a moment, then repeated, "Deacon Gillette calling—"

"All right," Carnaby interrupted the synthesized voice, irked at its limited abilities. "Put him through."

Gillette's face replaced the attendance statistics. He was an African-American, his skin so dark it seemed to shine as if he were perspiring. His deepset brown eyes always looked wary, as if he expected some enemy to spring upon him.

"Deacon," said Carnaby, by way of greeting.

"Archbishop. I've received a disturbing report from our man in Ecuador."

"We have a man in Ecuador?"

"At the skytower project, sir," said Gillette.

"Ah, yes. A disturbing report, you say?"

"According to Rev. Danvers, the scientists of the skytower project are using a form of nanotechnology to build their structure."

"Nanotechnology!" Carnaby felt a pang of alarm. "Nanomachines are outlawed, even in South America."

Gillette closed his heavy-lidded eyes briefly, then explained, "They are not using nanomachines, exactly. Instead, they have developed genetically engineered viruses to work as nanomachines would, assembling the structural components of their tower."

Carnaby felt the cords at the back of his neck tense and knew he would soon be suffering a headache.

"Tell Danvers to notify the authorities down there."

"What they're doing is not illegal, Archbishop. They're using natural creatures, not artificial machines."

"But you said these creatures have been genetically engineered, didn't you?"

"Genetic engineering is not outlawed, sir," Gillette replied, then quickly added, "Unfortunately."

Carnaby sucked in a breath. "Then what can we do about it?"

With a sad shake of his head, Gillette answered, "I don't know, sir. I was hoping that you would think of a solution."

Fumbling for the oxygen mask in the compartment built into the wheelchair's side, Carnaby groused, "All right, let me think about it." He abruptly cut the phone connection and his wall returned to its underlying restful shade of pastel blue.

Carnaby held the plastic mask over his face for several silent moments. The flow of cool oxygen eased the tension that was racking his body.

Sudden thunder shook the building, startling Carnaby so badly that he dropped his oxygen mask. Then he realized it was another of those damnable rockets taking off from the old Hartsfield Airport.

He spun his chair to the window once again and craned his dewlapped neck, but there was nothing to see. No trail of smoke. No pillar of fire. The rockets used some kind of clean fuel: hydrogen, he'd been told. Doesn't hurt the environment.

He slumped back in his wheelchair, feeling old and tired. I've spent my life trying to save their souls. I've rescued them from sin and the palpable wrath of God. And what do they do as soon as things begin to go smoothly again? They complain about our strict laws. They want more freedom, more license to grow fat and prosperous and sinful.

Then he looked out at the empty sky again. They're getting richer because those rockets are bringing in metals and stuff from the asteroids. And they've built those infernal solar satellites up in orbit to beam electrical power to the ground.

Those space people. Scientists and engineers. Godless secularists, all of 'em. Poking around on other worlds. Claiming they've found living creatures. Contradicting Genesis every chance they get.

And now, Carnaby thought, those space people are building a high-tech Tower of Babel. They're going to make it *easier* to get into space, easier to make money out there. And using nanotechnology to do it. Devil's tools. Evil, through and through.

They're building their blasphemous tower in South America someplace, right in the middle of all those Catholics.

They've got to be stopped, Carnaby told himself, clenching his blue-veined hands into bony fists. But how? How?

RIDING THE ELEVATOR

How high are we?" Lara asked, her eyes wide with excitement.

Bracknell glanced at the readout screen set next to the elevator's double doors, where Victor Molina was standing. "Eighty-two kilometers, no, now it's eighty-three."

"I don't feel anything," she said. "No sense of motion at all."

For nearly a month Bracknell had resisted Lara's pleas for a ride in the space elevator. The instant he had told her the first elevator tube had completed all its tests and was officially operational, she had begged him for a ride. Bracknell had temporized, delayed, tried to put her off. To his surprise, he found that he was worried about the elevator's safety. *All these years I've drafted the plans, laid out the schematics, overseen the construction,* he castigated himself, *and when we get right down to it, I don't trust my own work. Not with Lara's life. I'm afraid to let her ride the elevator.*

That realization stunned him. *All the number crunching, all the tests, and I don't trust my own work. I'm willing to let others ride the elevator, I'm even willing to ride it myself, but when it comes to Lara—I'm afraid. Superstition, pure and simple,* he told himself. Yet he found excuses to keep her from his skytower.

The elevator worked fine, day after day, week after week, hauling technicians and cargo up to the stations at the various levels of the tower. Bracknell's confidence in the system grew, and Lara's importunings did not abate. If anything, she became even more insistent.

"You've been up and down a dozen times," she whispered to him as they lay together in the shadows of their darkened bedroom, her head on his naked chest. "It's not fair for you to keep me from going with you. Just once, at least."

Despite his inner tension, he grinned in the darkness. "It's not fair? You're starting to sound like a kid arguing with his parents."

"Was I whining?" she asked.

"No," he had to admit. "I've never heard you whine."

She lay silent for several moments. He could feel her breathing slowly, rhythmically, as she lay against him.

"Okay," he heard himself say. "We'll go up to the LEO deck," he conceded.

Lara knew the Low Earth Orbit station was five hundred kilometers up. Her elation was immediately tinged with disappointment.

"Not all the way?" she asked. "Not to the geostationary level?"

Bracknell shook his head. "That's up on the edge of the Van Allen Belt radiation. The crew hasn't installed the shielding yet. They work up there in armored suits."

"But if they—"

"No," he said firmly, grasping her bare shoulders. "Some day we're going to have children. I'm not exposing you to a high-radiation environment, even in a shielded spacesuit."

He sensed her smiling at him. "The ultimate argument," she said. "It's for the good of our unborn children."

"Well, it is."

"Yes dear," she teased. Then she kissed him.

They made love slowly, languorously. Afterward, as they lay spent and sticky in their sweaty sheets, Bracknell thought: This is the real test. Do you trust your work enough to risk her life on it?

And Lara understood: He worries about me so. He lets others ride the elevator but he's worried about me.

The next day was a Sunday, and although a full team of technicians was at work, as usual, Bracknell walked over to the operations office and told the woman on duty there that he and Lara would be riding up to the LEO platform.

The operations chief that Sunday morning was a portly woman who wore her ash-blonde hair pulled back in a tight bun, and a square gold ring on her left middle finger.

"I'll tell Jakosky," she said, grinning. "He's won the lottery."

"What lottery?" Bracknell asked, surprised.

"We've been making book about when you'd let your lady take a ride up," said the operations chief. "Jackpot's up to damn near a thousand Yankee dollars."

Bracknell grinned weakly to cover his surprise and a pang of embarrassment. As he left the building and started back up toward his quarters, he saw Molina coming down the street, heading toward him. Victor's going to be leaving, Bracknell knew. Going to Australia to start a new career in astrobiology. And he's sore at me for not letting him publish the work he's done here.

"Hello, Victor," he called as the biologist neared. He knew that Molina despised being called Vic.

"Hi, Mance," Molina replied, without slowing his pace.

Bracknell grasped his arm, stopping him. "Lara and I are riding up to the LEO deck. Want to come with us?"

Molina's eyes widened. "You're taking her up?"

"Just to the lowest level."

"But the safety certification . . ."

"Came through a week ago. For the LEO platform."

"Oh."

"Come with us," Bracknell urged. "You're not doing anything vital this morning, are you?"

Molina stiffened. "I'm finishing up my final report."

"You can do that later. You don't want to head off to Australia without riding in the tower you helped to build, do you? Come on with us."

With a shake of his head, Molina said, "No, I've got so much to do before I leave. . . ."

Bracknell teased, "You're not scared, are you?"

"Scared? Hell no!"

"Then come on along. The three of us. Like old times."

"Like old times," Molina echoed, his face grim.

Bracknell knew that he himself was frightened, a little. *If we bring Victor along I'll have him to talk to, to keep me from worrying about Lara's safety.* But he knew that was an excuse. Superstition again: *nothing bad will happen if it isn't just Lara and me riding the tube.*

Molina, who hadn't been alone with Lara since he'd confessed that he was in love with her, allowed Bracknell to turn him around and lead him back to their apartment building. *What the fuck,* he said to himself. *This may be the last time I see her.*

"It's like we're standing still," Lara said as the elevator rose smoothly past the hundred-kilometer mark.

"Like Einstein's old thought experiment about the equivalence of gravity and acceleration," Bracknell said.

The elevator cab was big enough to handle freight and new enough to still look sparkling and shiny. An upholstered bench ran along its rear wall, but Lara and the two men remained standing. The walls and floor of the cab were buckyball sheets, hard as diamond but not as brittle, coated with scuff-resistant epoxy. The ceiling was a grillwork through which Lara could see the shining inner walls of the tube speeding smoothly by.

No cables, she knew. No pulleys or reels like an ordinary elevator. The entire tube was a vertical electric rail gun; the elevator cab was being lifted by electromagnetic forces, like a particle in a physics lab's accelerator or a payload launched off the Moon by an electric mass driver. Pretty slow for a bullet, Lara thought, but they were accelerating all the way up to the halfway point, where they would start decelerating until the cab braked to a stop at the LEO level.

Molina stayed tensely silent. He hadn't said more than two words to either of them since Lara had joined them for this brief trip into space.

LEO PLATFORM

"You should have windows," Lara said as she walked to the bench along the cab's rear wall and sat down. "It's boring without a view."

Bracknell sat beside her and glanced at his wristwatch. "Another twenty minutes."

Molina had not spoken a word since they'd boarded the elevator, more than a half hour earlier. He remained standing, pecking away at his palmcomp.

"You need a window," Lara repeated. "The view would be spectacular."

"If you didn't get nauseous watching the Earth fall away from you. Some people are afraid of glass elevators in hotels, you know."

"They wouldn't have to look," Lara replied primly. "I think the view would be a marvelous attraction, especially for tourists."

Conceding her point with a nod, Bracknell said, "We'll be adding several more elevator tubes. I'll look into the possibilities of glassing in at least one of them."

"Are we slowing down?" Lara asked.

"Should be."

"I get no sensation of movement at all."

"That's because we've kept the cab's acceleration down to a minimum. We could go a lot faster if we need to."

"No," she said, with a slight shake of her head. "This is fine. I'm not complaining."

As he sat next to Lara, Bracknell got a sudden urge to take her in his arms and kiss her. But there was Molina standing a few meters away, like a dour-faced duenna, his nose almost touching his handheld's screen.

"Victor," he called, "come and sit down. You don't have to work *all* the time."

"Yes, I do," Molina snapped.

Turning back to Lara, "Tell him to put away that digital taskmaster of his and come over here and join us."

To his surprise, Lara responded, "Leave Victor alone. He's doing what he feels he has to do."

Feeling a little puzzled, Bracknell clasped his hands behind his head and leaned back against the cab's rear wall. It felt cool and very hard. We ought to put some cushioning along here, he thought, making a mental note to suggest it to the people who were handling interior design. And look into glassing in one of the outer tubes, he added silently.

When the cab finally stopped, a chime sounded and a synthesized female voice announced, "Level one: Low Earth Orbit."

Bracknell got to his feet, Lara beside him. She looked puzzled.

"I thought we'd be in zero gravity," Lara said.

With a shake of his head, Bracknell said, "We're five hundred klicks up, but the tower isn't moving at orbital velocity. It's moving at the same rate as the Earth."

"Oh." Lara looked slightly disappointed, he thought.

The elevator doors slid open and the din of work teams

immediately assailed their ears as they stepped out of the
elevator cab. Lara saw a wide expanse of bare decking
topped by a dome that looked hazy in the dust-filled air.
A drill was screeching annoyingly off somewhere and
the high-pitched whine of an electrical power generator
made her teeth ache. Sparks from welding torches hissed
off to her right. The dust-laden air smelled of burnt insulation and stranger odors she could not place. Men and
women in coveralls were putting up partitions, most of them
working in small groups along the deck; she spotted several clambering along the scaffolding, high above. An
electrically-powered cart scurried past on a rail fastened
to the deck plates, its cargo bed piled high with bouncing
sheets of what looked like honeycomb metal. Everyone
seemed to be yelling at everyone else:

"Hold it there! That's it!"

"I need more light up here; it's darker than a five-star
restaurant, fer chrissakes!"

"When the hell were you ever in a five-star restaurant,
bozo?"

"I've got it. Ease up on your line."

Bracknell made a sweeping gesture and hollered over the
din, "Welcome to level one."

Moline scowled out at the noisy activity. Lara clapped
her hands over her ears. Bracknell grinned at them.

Pointing off to their left, Bracknell led them carefully
past a gaggle of workers gathered around a small table that
held a large stainless steel urn of coffee. At least, Lara assumed it was coffee. Several of the workers raised their
covered plastic mugs to Bracknell as he led them past.
Mance nodded and grinned at them in return.

"Sippy cups," Lara said, with a giggle. "Like babies use."

"Keeps the dust out of the coffee," Bracknell said.

There were curved partitions in place here, and the noise
abated a little. As they walked onward, the partitions became

roofed over like an arched tunnel and the din diminished considerably.

"As you can see—and hear," Bracknell said, "level one is still very much under construction."

"My ears are ringing," Lara said.

"They're a noisy bunch, all right," Bracknell conceded. "But if they were quiet they wouldn't be getting any work done."

Moline gave a half-hearted nod.

Pointing to the curved metal overhead, Bracknell said with a hint of pride in his voice, "These partitions were scavenged from the heavy-lift boosters that brought most of the materials up here."

Lara grinned at him. "Waste not, want not."

"In spades. Nothing of the boosters was returned to Earth except their rocket engines."

She pointed to the open gridwork of the floor. "There aren't any floor tiles."

With a nod, Bracknell said, "The crew hasn't gotten this far yet. We've got to gandydance the rest of the way."

"Gandydance?"

"Just step along the girders and don't get your foot caught in the open space. Be careful." Then Bracknell saw Molina's grim expression. "Victor, will you be okay?"

"I think so," Molina said, without much conviction.

As they inched along the bare gridwork of the corridor, holding their arms out for balance, Bracknell explained, "Back there where we came in, the biggest area will be a preparation center for launching satellites."

Lara said, "You'll carry them up here on the elevators and then launch them at this altitude."

"It'll be a lot cheaper than launching them from the ground with rockets," Bracknell said, "even though we'll still need a kick booster to place the satellite in the orbit its owners want."

"You'll launch geostationary satellites from the platform up at that level, right?" Lara asked.

"Right. Up at that level all we'll need is a little maneuvering thrust to place them in their proper slots."

"Masterson Aerospace and the other rocket companies aren't going to like you," she said.

"I guess not. The buggywhip makers must have hated Henry Ford."

Lara laughed.

The noise was far behind them now, still discernable, but down to a background level. They came to a heavy-looking hatch set into a wall. Bracknell tapped out the proper code on the keypad set into the wall and the hatch sighed open. Lara felt a slight whisper of air brush past her from behind.

"You wanted a window?" Bracknell said to her. "Here's a window for you."

They stepped through and Lara's breath caught in her throat. They were in a narrow darkened compartment. One entire wall was transparent. Beyond it curved the gigantic bulk of Earth, sparkling blue oceans gleaming in the sunlight, brilliant white clouds hugging the surface, wrinkles of brown mountains.

"Oh my god," Lara gasped, gliding to the long window.

Molina hung back.

Bracknell rapped his knuckles against the window. "Glassteel," he said. "Imported from Selene."

"It's so *beautiful!*" Lara exclaimed. "Look! I think I can see the Panama Canal."

"That's Central America, all right," Bracknell said. Pointing to a wide swirl of clouds, "And that looks like a tropical storm off in the Pacific."

Molina pushed up behind him and peered at the curling swath of clouds. "Will it affect the tower?"

"Not likely. Tropical storms don't come down to the equator, and we're well away from the coast anyway."

"But still . . ."

"The tower can take winds of a thousand kilometers per hour, Victor. More than three times the most powerful hurricane on record."

"I can't see straight down," Lara said, almost like a disappointed child. "I can't see the base of the tower."

"Look out to the horizon," said Bracknell. "That's the Yucatan peninsula, where the ancient Mayas built their temples."

"And those mountains to our right, they must be the Andes," she said. The peaks were bare, gray granite, snowless since the greenhouse warming had struck.

"Mance," said Lara, "you could use glassteel to build a transparent elevator tube."

He snorted. "Not at the prices Selene charges for the stuff."

Molina glided back toward the open hatch. "This door is an airtight seal, isn't it?"

"That's right," Bracknell answered. "If the outside wall of this compartment is punctured and there's a loss of air pressure, that hatch automatically closes and seals off the leak."

"And traps anybody in this compartment," Molina said.

"That's right," Bracknell replied gravely.

Lara said, "But you have spacesuits in here so they can save themselves. Don't you?"

Bracknell shook his head. "It would take too long to get into the suits. Even the new nanofiber soft suits would take too long."

"What you're telling us," Molina said, "is that we're in danger in here."

"Only if the outer shell is penetrated."

"How likely is that?" said Lara.

Smiling tightly, Bracknell said, "The tower's been dinged

by micrometeorites thousands of times. Mostly up at higher altitudes. No penetrations, though."

"Wasn't there a satellite collision?" Molina asked.

"Every satellite launch is planned so that the bird's orbit doesn't come closer than a hundred kilometers of the tower. The IAA's been very strict about that."

"But a satellite actually hit the tower?" Lara looked more curious than afraid.

With a nod, Bracknell replied, "Some damnfool paramilitary outfit launched a spy satellite without clearing it with the IAA. It smacked into the tower on its second orbit."

"And?"

"Hardly scratched the buckyball cables, but it wrecked the spysat completely. Most of the junk fell down and burned up in the atmosphere. We had to send a team outside to clean off the remaining debris and inspect the area where it hit. The damage was very superficial."

"When you stop to think about it," Lara said, "the impact of even a big satellite hitting this tower would be like a mosquito ramming an elephant."

Bracknell laughed as he turned back toward the open hatch.

"The only way to hurt this beanstalk," said Molina, "would be to somehow disconnect it up at the geostationary level."

Bracknell looked over his shoulder at the biologist. "That's right, Victor. Do that, and the lower half of the tower collapses to the ground, while the upper half goes spinning off into deep space."

"The tower would collapse?" Lara asked. "It would fall down to the ground?"

Bracknell nodded. "Only if it's disconnected from the geostationary platform."

"That would destroy everything?" Lara asked.

"Quite completely," said Bracknell. "But don't worry, we've built that section with a two-hundred-percent overload capacity. It can't happen."

YAMAGATA ESTATE

Nobuhiko Yamagata's knees ached as he sat on the tatami mat facing this, this . . . fanatic. There was no other way to describe the leader of the Flower Dragon movement. Like a ninja of old, he thought, this man is a fanatic.

Yoshijiro Umetsu was named after a shamed ancestor, a general who had surrendered his army rather than fight to the death. From earliest childhood his stern father and uncles had drilled into him their expectation that he would grow up to erase this century-old stain on the family's honor. While upstarts like Saito Yamagata made vast fortunes in business and Japanese scientists earned world recognition for their research work, Umetsu knew that only blood could bring true respect. Respect is based on fear, he was told endlessly. Nothing less.

By the time he was a teenager, the world was racked with terrorism. The poor peoples of the world struck almost blindly against the rich, attempting to destroy the wealth that they themselves could never attain. Japan was the target of many terrorist attacks: poison gas killed thousands in Tokyo; biological weapons slaughtered tens of thousands in Osaka. The nanomachine plague that nearly destroyed the entire island of Kyushu, killing millions, led directly to the international treaty banning nanotechnology everywhere on Earth.

When the greenhouse cliff toppled the world's climate, coastal cities everywhere were drowned by the suddenly rising seas. But an even worse fate befell Japan: in addition to the devastating floods, earthquakes demolished the home islands.

Out of the ashes, though, rose a new Japan. The century-long experiment in democracy was swept aside and a new government, strong and unyielding, came to power. The true strength of that government was the Flower Dragon movement, a strange mix of religion and zeal, of Buddhist acceptance and disciplined political action. Like other fundamentalist movements elsewhere in the world, the Flower Dragon movement spread beyond its place of origin: Korea, China, Thailand, Indochina. On the vast and miserable Indian subcontinent, decimated by biowar and decades-long droughts brought on by the collapse of the monsoons, followers of the Flower Dragon clashed bloodily with the Sword of Islam.

Now the leader of the Flower Dragon movement sat on the other side of the exquisite tea set from Nobuhiko. Umetzu wore a modern business suit, as did Yamagata. The leader of the Flower Dragon movement had the lean, parched face of an ascetic, his head shaved bald, a thin dark moustache drooping down the corners of his mouth almost to his jawline. The expression on his face was severe, disapproving. Nobuhiko felt distinctly uneasy in his presence, almost ashamed of his well-fed girth.

Yet Nobu understood that Umetzu had come to him. I called and he came, Yamagata told himself. I'm not without power here. The fact that Umetzu was apparently a few years younger than he should have made Nobu feel even more in command of this meeting. But it didn't.

Umetzu had arrived at the Yamagata family estate in an unmarked helicopter, accompanied by four younger men. Nobu had chosen his family's home for this meeting so that they would be safe from the prying eyes and news media snoops that were unavoidable in the corporate offices in New Kyoto. Here, on his spacious estate up in the hills, surrounded by servants who had been with the family for generations, he could have airtight security.

They sat in a small room paneled in polished oak, the tea set between them. The wall to Nobu's right was a sliding shoji screen; to his left a window looked out on a small, enclosed courtyard and raked stone garden. The kimono-clad women who had served the tea had left the room. Umetzu's aides were being fed in another room, far enough away so that they could not overhear their master's discussion with Yamagata, close enough so that they could reach him quickly if they had to. Nobu understood without being told that those young men were bodyguards.

"What do you want of me?" Umetzu asked, dropping all pretense of polite conversation. He had not touched the lacquered cup before him.

Nobu took a sip of the hot, soothing tea before answering. "There is a task that must be done in complete secrecy."

Umetzu said nothing.

"I had thought of negotiating with one of the Islamic groups," Nobu went on. "They are accustomed to the concept of martyrdom."

"Yet you have asked to speak with me. In private."

"It is a very delicate matter."

Umetzu took in a long, slow breath. "A matter that involves death."

"Many deaths, most likely."

"The followers of the Flower Dragon's way do not fear death. Many of them believe in reincarnation."

"You do not?" Nobuhiko asked.

"My beliefs are not the subject of this meeting."

Nobu bowed his head a centimeter or so.

"Just what is it that you require?" asked Umetzu.

Now Nobuhiko hesitated, trying to fathom what lay behind his guest's hooded eyes. Can I trust him? Is this the best way for me to go? He wished he had his father here to advise him, but the elder Yamagata was still locked away in the Himalayas, playing at being a lama.

"What I require," Nobu said at last, "must never be traced back to me or to Yamagata Corporation. Is that clear? Never."

Umetzu almost smiled. "It must be truly horrible, for you to be so afraid."

"Horrible enough," said Nobu. "Horrible enough."

"Then what is it?"

"The skytower. It must be destroyed."

Umetzu drew in a breath. "I have been informed that the skytower is being built by nanomachines."

Surprised, Nobuhiko blurted, "Where did you hear that?"

Allowing himself a thin smile, Umetzu replied, "Flower Dragon has contacts in many places, including the New Morality."

"I did not realize that they are using nanomachines."

"Of a sort. They are within the law, apparently, but just barely."

"Perhaps we could stop them legally, through the international courts."

Umetzu shook his head the barest fraction of a centimeter. "Do not put your faith in the courts. Direct action is better."

"Then you are willing to help me?" Nobuhiko asked.

"Of course. The skytower must be destroyed."

"Yes. And it must be destroyed in a manner that will discredit the very idea of building such towers. It must be brought down in a disaster so stunning that no one will ever dare to bring up the idea of building another."

Nobuhiko felt his cheeks flushing and realized that he

was squeezing his miniature teacup so hard its edge was cutting into the flesh of his palm.

Umetzu seemed unmoved. "How do you intend to accomplish this tremendous feat?"

Regaining his self-control, Nobuhiko put the lacquered cup back on its tray as he answered, "My technical people know how to bring it down. They have all the information we require. What I need is men who will do the task."

"Men who will become martyrs."

Nobuhiko bowed his head once again.

"That is not terribly difficult," said Umetzu. "There are those who welcome death, especially if they believe they will accomplish something of worth in their dying."

"But it must be kept absolutely secret," Nobuhiko repeated in an urgent hiss. "It must never be traced back to Yamagata Corporation."

Umetzu closed his eyes briefly. "We can recruit martyrs from elsewhere: even the fat Americans have fanatics among their New Morality groups."

"Truly?" Nobuhiko asked.

"But what of your own technicians? Will they be martyred also?"

"That will not be necessary."

"Yet they will have the knowledge that you wish kept secret. Once the tower falls, they will know that you have done it."

"They will be far from Earth when that happens," Nobuhiko said. "I have already had them transferred to Yamagata operations in the Asteroid Belt."

Umetzu considered this for a moment. "I have heard that the Asteroid Belt is a very dangerous place."

"It can be."

"Wars have been fought there. Many were killed."

"I have heard that the Flower Dragon has followers even in the Belt. Loyal followers."

Umetzu understood Nobu's unspoken request. This time he did smile thinly. "So your people will not be martyrs. Instead they will fall victims to accidents."

"As you said," Nobu replied, "the Belt is a very dangerous place."

CIUDAD DE CIELO

Elliott Danvers was lonely after Molina left for Australia. He missed their meals together, their adversarial chats, the verbal cut and parry that kept his mind stimulated.

Over the weeks that followed Molina's departure, Danvers tried to forget his own needs and buried himself in his work. No, he reminded himself time and again. Not my work. God's work.

He felt puzzled that Atlanta had shown no visible reaction to his report that nanotechnology was being used to build the skytower. He had expected some action, or at least an acknowledgement of his intelligence. Nothing. Not a word of thanks or congratulations on a job well done. Well, he told himself, a good conscience is our only sure reward. And he plunged himself deeper into his work. Still, he felt nettled, disappointed, ignored.

He went to Bracknell and asked permission to convert one of the warehouse buildings into a nondenominational chapel. As the skytower neared completion, some of the buildings fell into disuse, some of the workers departed for their homes. Danvers noted that there seemed to be fewer Yankee and Latino construction workers in the streets, and more Asian computer and electronics technicians.

"A chapel?" Bracknell looked surprised when Danvers raised the question.

Standing in front of Bracknell's desk, Danvers nodded. "You have several empty buildings available. I won't need much in way of—"

"You mean you've been working here all this time without a church building?" Bracknell looked genuinely surprised. "Where do you hold your services?"

"Outdoors, mostly. Sometimes in my quarters, for smaller groups."

Bracknell's office was far from imposing. Nothing more than a corner room in the corrugated-metal operations building. He sat at a scuffed and dented steel desk. One wall held a smart screen that nearly reached the low ceiling. Another had photos of the tower at various stages of its construction pasted to it. Two windows looked out on the streets and, beyond one of them, the dark trunk of the tower, rising above the distant green hills and into the heavens.

Gesturing to the plain plastic chair in front of his desk, Bracknell said, "I thought we already had a church here, someplace."

Danvers smiled bitterly as he settled his bulk in the creaking little chair. "You're not a churchgoer."

With an almost sheepish grin, Bracknell admitted, "You've got me there."

"Are you a Believer?"

Bracknell thought it over for a moment, his head cocked slightly. "Yes, I think I can truthfully say that I am. Not in any organized religion, understand. But—well, the universe is so blasted *orderly*. I guess I do believe there's some kind of presence overseeing everything. Childhood upbringing, I suppose. It's hard to overcome."

"You don't have to apologize about it," Danvers said, a little testily. He was thinking, Not in any organized religion, the man says. He's one of those intellectual esthetes who rationalizes everything and thinks that that's religion. Nothing more than a damnable Deist, at best.

Bracknell called up a map of the city and told his computer to highlight the unused buildings. The wall screen showed four of them in red.

"Take your pick," he said to Danvers, gesturing to the screen.

Danvers stood up and walked to the map, studying it for several moments. "This one," he said at last, rapping his knuckles against the screen.

"That's the smallest one," said Bracknell.

"My congregations have not been overwhelming. Besides, the location is good, close to the city's center. More people will see their friends and associates going to services. It's a proven fact that people tend to follow a crowd."

"It's the curious monkey in our genes," Bracknell said easily.

Danvers tried to erase the frown that immediately came over him.

"Was that too Darwinian for you?"

"We are far more than monkeys," Danvers said tightly.

"I suppose we are. But we're mammals; we enjoy the companionship of others. We need it."

"That's true enough, I suppose."

"So why don't you join Lara and me at dinner tonight? We can talk over the details of your new chapel."

Danvers was surprised at the invitation. He knew, in his mind, that a man could be a non-Believer and still be a decent human being. But this man Bracknell, he's leading this nearly blasphemous skytower project. I mustn't let him lull me into friendship, Danvers told himself. He may be a pleasant enough fellow, but he is the enemy. You either do God's work or the devil's. There is no neutrality in the struggle between good and evil.

* * *

The restaurant was only half full, Bracknell saw as he came through the wide-open double doors with Lara. A lot of the construction people had already left. Once the geostationary platform was finished, they would shift entirely to operational status.

He saw that Rev. Danvers was already seated at a table, chatting with the restaurant's owner and host, a tall suave Albanian who towered over his mestizo kitchen staff. As soon as the host saw Bracknell and Lara enter, he left Danvers in midsentence and rushed to them.

"Slow night tonight," he said by way of greeting.

Bracknell said, "Not for much longer. Lots of people heading here. By this time next year you'll have to double the size of this place."

The host smiled and pointed out new paintings, all by local artists, hanging on the corrugated metal walls. Village scenes. Cityscapes of Quito. One showed the mountains and the skytower in Dayglo orange. Bracknell thought they were pretty ordinary and said nothing, while Lara commented cheerfully on their bright colors.

The dinner with Rev. Danvers started off rather awkwardly. For some reason the minister seemed guarded, tight-lipped. But then Lara got him to talking about his childhood, his early days in the slums of Detroit.

"You have no idea of what it was like growing up in that cesspool of sin and violence. If it weren't for the New Morality, Lord knows where I'd be," Danvers said over a good-sized ribeye steak. "They worked hard to clean up the streets, get rid of the crooks and drug pushers. They worked hard to clean *me* up."

Lara asked lightly, "Were you all that dirty?"

Danvers paled slightly. "I was a prizefighter back then," he said, his voice sinking low. "People actually paid money to see two men try to hurt each other, try to pound one another into unconsciousness."

"Really?"

"Women, too. Women fought in the ring and the crowds cheered and screamed, like animals."

Bracknell saw that Danvers's hands were trembling. But Lara pushed further, asking, "And the New Morality changed all that?"

"Yes, praise God. Thanks to their workers, cities like Detroit became safer, more orderly. Criminals were jailed."

"And their lawyers, too, from what I hear," Bracknell said. He meant it as a joke, but Danvers did not laugh and Lara shot him a disapproving glance.

"Many lawyers went to jail," Danvers said, totally serious, "or to retraining centers. They were protecting the criminals instead of the innocent victims! They deserved whatever they got."

"With your size," Lara said, "I'll bet you were a very good prizefighter."

Danvers smiled ruefully. "They could always find someone bigger."

"But you beat them, didn't you?"

"No," he answered truthfully. "Not very many of them."

"And now you fight for people's souls," Lara said.

"Yes."

"That's much better, isn't it?"

"Yes."

Bracknell looked around the restaurant. Only about half the tables were taken. "Looks like a slow night," he said, trying to change the subject.

"Mondays are always slow," said Lara.

"Not for us," Bracknell said. "We topped off the LEO platform today. It's all finished and ready to open for business."

"Really!" Lara beamed at him. "That's ahead of schedule, isn't it?"

Bracknell nodded happily. "Skytower Corporation's going to make a public announcement about it at their board meeting next month. Big news push. I'm going to be on the nets."

"That's wonderful!"

Danvers was less enthusiastic. "Does this mean that you're ready to launch satellites from the LEO platform?"

"We already have contracts for four launches."

"But the geostationary platform isn't finished yet, is it?"

"We're ahead of schedule there, too."

"But it's not finished."

"Not for another six months," Bracknell said, feeling almost as if he were admitting a wrongdoing. Somehow Danvers had let the air out of his balloon.

By the time they finished their desserts and coffee, theirs was the only occupied table in the restaurant. The robot waiter was already sweeping the floor and two of the guys from the kitchen were stacking chairs atop tables to give the robot leeway for its chore.

Danvers bade them good night out on the sidewalk and headed for his quarters. Bracknell walked with Lara, arm in arm.

As they passed through the pools of light and shadow cast by the streetlamps, Lara said, "Rev. Danvers seems a little uncomfortable with the idea that we're living in sin."

Bracknell grinned down at her. "Best place to live, all things considered."

"Really? Is that what you think?"

Looking up at the glowing lights of the tower that split the night in half, Bracknell murmured, "Um . . . Paris is probably better."

"That's where the board meeting's going to be, isn't it?"

"Right," said Bracknell. "That's where Skytower Corporation turns me into a news media star."

"My handsome hero."

"Want to come with me?" he asked.

"To Paris?"

"Sure. You can do some clothes shopping there."

"Are you saying I need new clothes?"

He stopped in the darkness between streetlamps and slipped his arms around her waist. "You'll need a new dress for the wedding, won't you?"

"Wedding?" Even in the shadows he could see her eyes go wide with surprise.

Bracknell said, "With the tower almost finished and all this publicity the corporation's going to generate, I figure I ought to make an honest woman of you."

"You chauvinist pig!"

"Besides," he went on, "it'll make Danvers feel better."

"You're serious?" Lara asked. "This isn't a joke?"

He kissed her lightly. "Dead serious, darling. Will you marry me?"

"In Paris?"

"If that's what you want."

Lara flung her arms around his neck and kissed him as hard as she could.

GEOSTATIONARY PLATFORM

ook on my works, ye mighty," quoted Ralph Waldo Emerson, the chief engineer, "and despair."

In a moment of whimsy brought on by their joy at his birth, his parents had named him after the poet. Emerson suspected their euphoria was helped along by the recreational drugs they used; certainly he saw enough evidence of that while he was growing up in the caravan city that trundled through the drought-dessicated former wheat belt of Midwestern America.

His father was a mechanic, his mother a nurse: both highly prized skills in the nomadic community. And both of them loved poetry. Hence his name.

Everybody called him Waldo. He learned to love things mechanical from his father and studied mechanical engineering through the computer webs and satellite links that sometimes worked and sometimes didn't. Once he grew into manhood Emerson left the caravan and entered a real, bricks-and-mortar engineering college. All he wanted was a genuine degree so that he would have real credentials to show prospective employers. No caravan life for Waldo. He wanted to settle down, get rich (or at least moderately prosperous), be respectable, and build new things for people.

His life didn't quite work out that way. There was plenty of work for a bright young engineer, rebuilding the shattered electrical power grid, erecting whole new cities to house the refugees driven from their homes by the greenhouse floods, designing solar power farms in the clear desert skies of the Southwest. But the various jobs took him from one place to another. He was still a nomad; he just stayed in one place a bit longer than his gypsying parents did.

He never got rich, or even very prosperous. Much of the work he did was commissioned by the federal or state government at minimum wage. Often enough he was conscripted by local chapters of the New Morality and he was paid nothing more than room, board, and a pious sermon or two about doing God's work. He married twice, divorced twice, and then gave up the idea of marriage.

Until a guy named Bracknell came to him with a wild idea and a gleam in his eye. Ralph Waldo Emerson fell in love with the skytower project.

Now that it was nearly finished he almost felt sad. He had spent more years in Ecuador than anywhere else in his whole life. He was becoming fond of Spanish poetry. He no longer got nauseous in zero gravity. He gloried in this monumental piece of architecture, this tower stretching toward heaven. He had even emblazoned his name into one of the outside panels that sheathed the tower up here at the geostationary level, insulating the tower from the tremendous electrical flux of the Van Allen belt. Working in an armored spacesuit and using an electron gun, he laboriously wrote his full name on one of the buckyball panels.

He laughed at his private joke. Someday some maintenance dweeb is going to see it, he thought, and wonder who the hell wrote the name of a poet on this tower's insulation skin.

Now he stood at the control board in the compact oval chamber that would soon be the geosynch level's operations center. His feet were ensconced in plastic floor loops so that he wouldn't float off weightlessly in the zero gravity of the station. Surrounding him were display screens that lined the walls like the multifaceted eyes of some giant insect. Technicians in gray coveralls bobbed in midair as they labored to connect the screens and get them running. One by one, the colored lights on the control board winked on and a new screen lit up. Emerson could see a dozen different sections of the mammoth geostationary structure. There was still a considerable amount of work to do, of course, but it was mostly just a matter of bringing in equipment and setting it up. Furnishing the hotel built into the platform's upper level. Checking out the radiation shielding and the electrical insulation and the airlocks. Making certain the zero-g toilets worked. Monkey work. Not creative. Not challenging.

There was talk of starting a new skytower in Borneo or central Africa.

"'Tis not too late to seek a newer world," he muttered to himself. "To sail beyond the sunset."

"Hey, Waldo," the voice of one of his assistants grated annoyingly in the communication plug in his right ear, "the supply ship is coming in."

"It's early," Emerson said, without needing to look at the digital clock set into the control board.

"Early or late, they're here and they want a docking port."

Emerson glanced up at the working screens, then played his fingers across the keyboard on the panel. One of the screens flicked from an interior view of the bare and empty hotel level upstairs to an outside camera view of a conical Masterson Clippership hovering in co-orbit a few hundred meters from the platform. He frowned at the image.

"We were expecting an uncrewed supply module," he said into his lip mike.

"And we got a nice shiny Clippership," his assistant replied. "They got our cargo and they want to offload it and go home."

Shaking his head slightly, Emerson checked the manifest that the Clippership automatically relayed to the platform's logistics program. It matched what they were expecting.

"Why'd they use a Clipper?" he wondered aloud.

"They said the freight booster had a malf and they swapped out the supply module with the Clippership's passenger module."

It didn't make sense to Emerson, but there was the Clippership waiting to dock and offload its cargo, and the manifest was exactly what they expected.

"Ours not to reason why," Emerson misquoted. "Hook 'em to docking port three; it's closest to them."

"Will do."

* * *

Franklin Zachariah hummed a cheerful tune to himself as he sat shoehorned into the cramped cockpit of the Clippership. The pilot, a Japanese or Vietnamese or some kind of Asian gook, shot an annoyed glance over his shoulder. Hard to tell his nationality, Zach thought, with those black shades he's wearing. Like a mask or some macho android out of a banned terminator flick.

Zachariah stopped his humming but continued to play the tune in his head. It helped to pass the boring time. He had expected to get spacesick when the rocket went into orbit, but the medication they'd given him was working fine. Zero gravity didn't bother him at all. No upchucks, not even dizziness.

Zachariah was an American. He did not belong to the New Morality or the Flower Dragon or any other fundamentalist movement. He did not even follow the religion of his forefathers. He found that he couldn't believe in a god who made so many mistakes. He himself was a very clever young man—everyone who had ever met him said so. What they didn't know was that he was also a very destructive fellow.

Although he'd been born in Brooklyn, when he was six years old and the rising sea level caused by the greenhouse warming finally overwhelmed the city's flood control dams, Zachariah's family fled to distant cousins in the mountains near Charleston, West Virginia. There young Zach, as everyone called him, learned what it meant to be a Jew. At school, the other young boys alternately beat him up and demanded help with their classwork from him. His father, a professor in New York, had to settle for a job as a bookkeeper for his younger cousin, a jeweler in downtown Charleston who was ultimately shot to death in a holdup.

Zach learned how to avoid beatings by hiring the toughest thugs in school to be his bodyguards. He paid them with money he made from selling illicit drugs that he cooked up in the moldy basement of the house they shared with four other families.

By the time Zach was a teenager he had become a very accomplished computer hacker. Unlike his acne-ridden friends, who delved into illegal pornographic sites or shut down the entire public school system with a computer virus, Zach used his computer finesse in more secretive and lucrative ways. He pilfered bank accounts. He jiggered police records. He even got the oafish schoolmate who'd been his worst tormentor years earlier arrested by the state police for abetting an abortion. The kid went to jail protesting his innocence, but his own computer files proved his guilt. Cool, Zach said to himself as the bewildered lout was hauled off to a New Morality work camp.

Zach disdained college. He was having too much fun tweaking the rest of the world. He was the lone genius behind the smallpox scare that forced the head of the Center for Disease Control to resign. He even reached into the files of a careless White House speechwriter and leaked the contents of a whole sheaf of confidential memos, causing mad panic among the president's closest advisors. Way cool.

Then he discovered the thrill of true destruction. It happened while he was watching a pirated video of the as-yet-unreleased Hollywood re-re-remake of *Phantom of the Opera*. Zach sat in open-mouthed awe as the Phantom sawed through the chain supporting the opera house's massive chandelier. Cooler than cool! he thought as the ornate collection of crystal crashed into the audience, splattering fat old ladies in their gowns and jewels and fatter old men in black tuxes.

Franklin Zachariah learned the sheer beauty, the sexual rush, of real destruction. Using acid to weaken a highway bridge so that it collapsed when the morning's traffic of overloaded semis rolled over it. Shorting out an airport's electrical power supply—and its backup emergency generator—in the midst of the evening's busiest hour. Quietly disconnecting the motors that moved the floodgates along a stretch of the lower Potomac so that the storm surge from the approaching hurricane flooded the capital's streets and sent those self-important politicians screaming to pin the blame on someone. Coolissimo.

Most of the time he worked alone, living off bank accounts here and there that he nibbled at, electronically. For some of the bigger jobs, like the Potomac floodgates, he needed accomplices, of course. But he always kept his identity a secret, meeting his accomplices only through carefully buffered computer links that could not, he was sure, be traced back to him.

It was a shock, then, when a representative of the Flower Dragon movement contacted him about the skytower. But Zach got over his shock when they described to him the coolest project of them all. He quickly asked for the detailed schematics of the skytower and began to study hard.

THE APPROACH

Lara and Bracknell were driving one of the project's electric-powered minivans to the Quito airport. Bracknell planned to attend Skytower Corporation's board meeting and the news conference at which they would make the announcement that the tower was ready for operations. Then they would stay for a weekend of interviews and publicity events and return to Quito the following Monday.

"You sure you don't want to get married in Paris?" he

asked her, grinning happily as he drove the quiet minivan down the steep, gravel-surfaced road. "We could have the ceremony at the top of the Eiffel Tower. Be kind of symbolic."

Trucks and buses ground by in the opposite direction, raising clouds of gritty gray dust as they headed uphill toward Sky City.

Lara shook her head. "I tried to get through all the red tape on the computer link, Mance, but it's hopeless. We'd have to stay two weeks, at least."

"The French want our tourist dollars."

"And they want to do their own blood tests, their own searches of our citizenship data. I think they even check Interpol for criminal records."

"So we'll get married when we come back," he said easily.

"And we can invite our families and friends."

"I'll ask Victor if he can come back for the occasion and be my best man."

Lara made no reply.

"Hey! Why don't we ask Rev. Danvers to perform the ceremony?"

"At his new chapel?"

"Unless you'd rather do it in the cathedral in Quito."

"No," Lara said. "Let's do it at the base of the tower. Rev. Danvers will be fine."

He wanted to kiss her; he even considered pulling off on the shoulder of the road to do it. Instead, he drove in silence for a while, grinning happily. The road became paved as they neared Quito's airport. Traffic built up. Lara turned in her seat and looked out the rear window.

"It's going to feel strange not seeing the tower in the sky," she said.

"It'll be there when we get back," Bracknell said easily.

"For the next few days you'll just have to settle for the Eiffel Tower."

"Docking confirmed," said the Clippership's copilot. He was wearing dark glasses, too, like the pilot. Zach thought he looked kind of like an Asian, but his accent sounded California or some other part of the States.

"Tell the tower crew they can begin unloading," the pilot replied.

Zach knew what that meant. The Clipper was attached to the skytower now by a docking adaptor, a short piece of insulated tunnel that linked the tower's airlock to the Clipper's cargo hatch. A team of technicians from the skytower would come through the adaptor and begin unloading the Clipper's cargo bay. Zach thought of them as chimps doing stupid monkey tasks.

Unseen by the tower personnel, a dozen men and women recruited from god knows where would exit one of the Clippership's other airlocks, in spacesuits, of course, carrying the Clipper's *real* cargo: fifty tiny capsules of nanomachines, gobblers programmed to tear apart carbon molecules such as buckyballs. Zach had spent months studying the schematics of the skytower that the Flower Dragon people had supplied him, calculating just how to bring the tower down. They had balked at first when he suggested gobblers; nanotechnology was anathema to them. But someone higher up in the organization had overridden their objections and provided the highly dangerous gobblers for Zach's project of destruction.

Now twelve religious fanatics were out there playing with nanomachines that could kill them if they weren't careful. Each of the EVA team bore a minicam attached to his or her helmet, so Zach could direct their actions from the safety of the cockpit, securely linked to the outside crew by hair-thin optical fibers that carried his radio commands with no chance that they'd be overheard by the guys in the tower.

Now comes the fun part, Zach thought as he powered up the laptop he would use for communicating with the EVA team.

Ralph Waldo Emerson was also remotely watching the unloading, still wondering why the supply contractor had gone to the expense of hiring a shiny new Clippership instead of sending up another automated freighter.

"In faith, 'twas strange," he murmured as he stood in the control center, "'twas passing strange."

"You spouting poetry again?" his assistant asked.

Emerson considered yanking the comm plug out of his ear, but knew that would be the wrong thing to do. Instead he asked, "How's it going?"

"It's going. Riley and his guys are pushin' the packages through the hatch and I'm checkin' 'em off as they come in. Nothing much to it. Just a lot of muscle work. Trained chimps could do this."

Emerson could see the bored team on one of the working screens, gliding the weightless big crates along through the adaptor tunnel.

"Well just be careful in there," he said. "Just because we're in zero-g doesn't mean those packages don't have mass. Get caught between a crate and a wall and you'll get your ribs caved in, just like on Earth."

"I know that." His assistant sounded impatient, waspish.

"Just make sure your chimpanzees know it."

"What? No poetry for the occasion?"

Emerson immediately snapped, "A fool and his ribcage are soon parted."

Zach was humming tunelessly to himself as he called up the schematics and matched them with the camera views from his EVA team. The connection between the geostationary platform and the tower's main cables was the crucial point. Sever that link and some thirty-five thousand kilometers of skytower go crashing down to Earth. And the other thirty-five thou, on the other side of the platform, goes spinning off into space, carrying the platform with it.

He suppressed the urge to giggle, knowing it would annoy the sour-faced pilots sitting as immobile as statues an arm's reach in front of him. I'm going to wipe out the biggest structure anybody's ever built! *Wham!* And down it goes.

It'll probably fall onto Quito, Zach reasoned. Kill a million people, maybe. Like the hammer of god slamming them flat. Like a big boot squishing bugs.

The culmination of my career, Zach thought. But nobody will know that I did it. Nobody really knows who I am. Not anybody who counts. But they will after this. I'm going to stand up and tell the world that *I* did this. Me. Franklin Zachariah. The terror of terrors. Dr. Destruction.

Lara was wearing open-weave huaraches instead of regular shoes, Bracknell realized as they inched along the line at the airport's security site. He frowned as he thought that they'd probably want him to take off his boots before going through the metal detector.

Damned foolishness, he said to himself. There hasn't been a terrorist threat at an airport in more than twenty years but they still go through this goddamned nonsense.

Sure enough, the stocky, stern-faced security guard pointed silently to Bracknell's boots as Lara sailed unbothered through the metal detector's arch. Grumbling, Bracknell tugged the boots off and thumped them down on the conveyor belt that ran through the X-ray machine.

He set off the metal detector's alarm anyway and had to be searched by a pair of grim-looking guards. He had forgotten the handheld computer/phone he was carrying in his shirt pocket.

"No, no," Zach said sharply into his laptop's microphone. "Just open the capsule and wedge it into the cable. That's all you have to do, the nanobugs'll do the rest."

The job was taking much longer than he'd expected. Fifty cables, that's all we have to break, Zach grumbled silently, and these chimps are taking all fucking day to do it.

The underside of the geostationary platform looked like an immense spiderweb to Zach as he peered at it through the cameras of his EVA team. It matched the specs in his files almost exactly; there were always slight deviations between the blueprints and the actual construction. Nobody can build anything this big without straying from the plans here and there, at least a little bit.

Zach knew that the tower's main support came from these cables, stretched taught by centrifugal force as the whole gigantic assembly swung through space in synchrony with the Earth's daily spin. Break that connection here at the geostationary level and the stretching force disappears. The tower will collapse to the ground while the equally-long upper section goes spinning out into space.

Fifty cables, he repeated to himself. Let those nanobugs eat through fifty cables and the others won't have the strength to hold the rig together. Fifty cables.

Emerson's ear plug chimed softly with the tone he knew came from the safety officer.

"Go ahead," he said into his lip mike.

"Got something strange goin' on here."

"What?"

"That Clipper you've got docked. It's venting gases."

"Venting?"

"Hydrogen and oxygen, from what the laser spectrometer tells me."

Emerson thought a moment. "Bleeding a nearly-empty tank, maybe?"

The safety officer's voice sounded troubled. "This isn't a bleed. They're pumpin' out a lot of gas. Like the propellant they'd be using for their return trip."

"Curiouser and curiouser," Emerson quoted.

Zach licked his lips. The fifty cables were now being eaten away by the gobblers. He had calculated that blowing thirty of the cables would be enough to do the job, but he'd gone for fifty as an extra precaution. Okay, we've got fifty and we're all set.

He looked up at the two Asian pilots, still wearing those cool dark shades. "The nanomachines are in place."

"Good."

"All the EVA guys are back inside?"

"That is not your responsibility."

Zach felt the pilot was being snotty. "Okay," he said, "if any of them get eaten by the bugs, you write the condolence letters."

"Start the nanomachines working," the pilot said, without turning to look at Zach.

"They are working."

"Very well."

"Shouldn't we disconnect from the dock now?"

"No. Not yet."

THE COLLAPSE

Zach thought it was a little weird to stay connected to the tower's geostationary docking tunnel while the nano-machines were chewing away at the cables, but he figured the pilot knew what he was doing. The bugs won't get the chance to damage the Clippership; we'll disconnect before we're in any danger, he was pretty certain.

Besides, these two black-goggled pilots aren't going to kill themselves, Zach further assured himself. Not knowingly.

Outside the ship there was no sound. No vibration. Nothing.

For the first time, the pilot turned in his seat and lifted his glasses to glare directly at Zach. "Well? Have you done it?"

"Yeah," Zach replied, feeling nettled. "It's done. Now get us the hell out of here before the upper half of the tower starts spinning off to Alpha Centauri."

"That won't be necessary," said the pilot.

In the geostationary operations center, Emerson felt a slight tremor, a barely sensed vibration, as if a subway train had passed below the floor he stood on.

"What was that?" he wondered aloud.

His assistant's voice responded, "Yeah, I felt it too."

Tremors and vibrations were not good. In all the hours he'd spent in the tower at its various levels, it had always been as solid and unmoving as a mountain. What the hell could cause it to shake?

"Whatever it was," his assistant said, "it stopped."

But Emerson was busy flicking his fingers along his keyboard, checking the safety program. No leaks, no loss of air pressure. Electrical systems in the green. Power systems functioning normally. Structural integrity—

His eyes goggled at the screen. Red lights cluttered the screen. Forty, no fifty of the one hundred and twenty main cables had been severed. For long moments he could not speak, could hardly breathe. His brain refused to function. Fifty cables. We're going to die.

As he stared at the screen's display, another cable tore loose. And another. He could feel the deck beneath his feet shuddering.

"Hey, what's going on?" one of the technicians yelled from across the chamber.

"Let's to it, pell mell," Emerson whispered, more to himself than anyone who might hear him. "If not to heaven, then hand in hand to hell."

Bracknell was standing by the ceiling-high window at the Quito airport terminal gate, waiting for the Clippership for Paris to begin boarding. It sat out on its blast-scarred concrete pad, a squat cone constructed of diamond panels, manufactured by lunar nanomachines at Selene. They can use nanomachines up there but we can't here, Bracknell thought. Well, we've gotten around that stupid law. Once we get the patent—

A flash of light caught his eye. It was bright, brilliant even, but so quick that he wasn't certain if he'd actually seen anything real. Like a bolt of lightning. It seemed to come from the skytower, standing straight and slim, rising from the mountains and through the white clouds that swept over their peaks.

Lara came up beside him, complaining, "They can fly from Quito to Paris in less than an hour, but it takes longer than that to board the Clipper."

Bracknell smiled at her. "Patience is a virtue, as Rev. Danvers would say."

"I don't care. I'm getting—" Her words broke off. She was staring at the skytower. "Mance . . . look!"

He saw it, too. The tower was no longer a straight line bisecting the sky. It seemed to be rippling, like a rope that is flicked back and forth at one end.

His mind racing, Bracknell stared at the tower. It can't fall! It can't! But if it does . . .

He grabbed Lara around the shoulders and began running, dragging her, away from the big windows. "Get away from the windows!" he bellowed. "*Quitarse las ventanas! Run! Vamos!*"

"Nothing is happening," said the pilot accusingly.

"Yes it is," Zach answered. He was getting tired of the Asian's stupidity. These guys are supposed to be patient; didn't anybody ever give them Zen lessons? "Give it a few minutes. Those cables are popping, one by one. The more that snap, the faster the rest of 'em go."

"I see nothing," insisted the pilot, pointing toward the cockpit window.

Maybe if you took off those flicking glasses you could see better, creep, Zach grumbled silently. Aloud, he snapped, "You're gonna see plenty in two-three minutes. Now get us the flick outta here or else we're gonna go flipping out into deep space!"

"So you say."

A blinding flash of light seared Zach's eyes. He heard both pilots shriek. What the fuck was that? Zach wondered, pawing at his eyes. Through burning tears he saw the Clippership's cockpit, blurred, darkened, everything tinged in red. Rubbing his eyes again Zach squinted down at his laptop. The screen was dark, dead.

Then he realized that both pilots were jabbering in their Asian language.

"What happened?" he screeched.

"Electrical discharge." The pilot's voice sounded edgy for the first time. "An enormous electrical discharge."

"Even though we expected it," said the copilot, "it was a helluva jolt."

"Are we okay?" Zach demanded.

"Checking . . ."

"Get us out of here!" Zach screamed.

"All systems are down," the copilot said. "Complete power failure."

"Do something!"

"There is nothing to be done."

"But we'll die!"

"Of course."

Zach began blubbering, babbling incoherently at these two lunatics.

Removing his glasses and rubbing at his burning eyes, the pilot turned to his copilot and said in Japanese, "The American genius doesn't want to be a martyr."

The copilot's lean face was sheened with perspiration. "No one told him he would be."

"Will that affect his next life, I wonder? Will he be reborn as another human being or something less? A cockroach, perhaps."

"He doesn't believe in reincarnation. He doesn't believe in anything except destruction and his own ego."

The pilot said, "In that case, he has succeeded admirably. He has destroyed his own ego."

Neither man laughed. They sat strapped into their seats awaiting their fate with tense resignation while Zach screamed at them to no avail.

The massive electrical discharge released when some of the skytower's insulating panels were eaten away completed the destruction of the connectors that held the tower's two segments together at the geostationary level.

Although buckyball fibers are lighter in weight than any material that is even half their tensile strength, a structure of more than thirty-five thousand kilometers' length weighs millions of metric tons.

The skytower wavered as it tore loose from the geostationary platform, disconnected from the centrifugal force that had pulled it taut. One end suddenly free of its mooring, its other end still tethered to the ground, the lower half of the tower staggered like a prizefighter suddenly struck by a knockout blow, then began its long, slow-motion catastrophic collapse.

The upper end of the tower, equally as long as the lower, was also suddenly released from the force that held it taut. It reacted to the inertia that made it spin around the Earth each twenty-four hours. It continued to spin, but now free of its anchor it swung slowly, inexorably, unstoppably, away from Earth and into the black silent depths of space.

In the geostationary ops center Emerson saw every damned screen suddenly go dark; his control panel went dead. He felt himself sliding out of his foot restraints and sailing in slow motion across the operations center while the technicians who had been working on installing the new equipment were yanked to the ends of their tethers, hanging in midair, more shocked and surprised than frightened.

"What the shit is going on, Waldo?" one of them hollered.

He banged his shoulder painfully against the wall and slid to the floor. Soon enough, he knew, the immense structure would swing around and we'll all be slung in the opposite direction.

"Waldo, what the fuck's happening?" He heard panic creeping into their voices now.

We're dead, he knew. There's not a thing that anybody can do. Nor all thy tears wash out a word of it.

"Waldo! What's goin' on?"

They were screaming now, horror-struck, aware now that something had gone terribly wrong. Emerson tried to blank out their yammering, demanding, terrified screams.

"Fear death?" he quoted Browning:

"To feel the fog in my throat,
    The mist in my face,
When the snows begin, and the blasts denote
    I am nearing the place . . .
    The post of the foe;
Where he stands, the Arch Fear in a visible form,
    Yet the strong man must go . . ."

And the upper half of the skytower spun out and away from the Earth forever.

The lower half of the skytower slowly, slowly tumbled like a majestic tree suddenly turned to putty. Its base, attached to the rotating Earth, was moving more than a thousand kilometers per hour from west to east. Its enormous length, unsupported now, collapsed westward in a long, long, *long* plunge to Earth.

The operations crew on duty at Sky City saw their screens glare with baleful red lights. Some of them rushed out into the open, unwilling to believe what their sensors were telling them unless they saw it with their own fear-widened eyes. The skytower was collapsing. They could see it! It was wavering and toppling over like a reed blown by the wind.

People on the streets in Quito looked up and screamed. Villagers in the mountains stared and crossed themselves.

At the Quito airport, Mance Bracknell dragged Lara by the arm as he ran down the terminal's central corridor, screaming, "Keep away from the windows! *Quitarse las ventanas!*"

He pulled Lara into the first restroom he saw, a men's room. Two men, an elderly maintenance worker in wrinkled coveralls and a businessman in a linen suit, stood side by side at urinals. They both looked shocked at the sight of a wild-eyed gringo dragging a woman into this place. They began to object but Mance yelled at them, "Down on the floor! Get down on the floor! There's going to an explosion! An eruption!"

"*Erupción?*" asked the old man, hastily zipping his fly.

"*Erupción grande!*" Mance said "*Temblor de tierra!* Earthquake!"

The businessman rushed for the exit while the older man stood there, petrified with sudden fear.

Mance pushed Lara onto the cold tiles and dropped down beside her, his arm wrapped protectively around her.

"Mance, how can—"

"There's no place to run to," he hissed in her ear. "If it hits here we're pulverized."

Slowly at first, but then with ever-increasing speed, the sky-tower's lower half collapsed to the Earth. Its immense bulk smashed into Ciudad de Cielo, the tethers at its base snapping like strings, the shock wave from its impact blowing down those buildings it did not hit directly. The thunder of its fall shattered the air like the blast of every volcano on Earth exploding at once. Seconds later the falling tower smashed down on the northern suburbs of Quito like a gigantic tree crushing an ant hill. The city's modern high-rise glass and steel towers, built to withstand earthquakes, wavered and shuddered. Their safety-glass facades blew out in showers of pellets. Ordinary windows shattered into razor-sharp shards that slashed to bloody ribbons the people who crowded the streets, screaming in terror. Older buildings were torn from their foundations as if a nuclear explosion had ripped through the city. The old cathedral's thick masonry walls cracked and its stained glass windows shattered, each and every one of them. Water pipes ruptured and gas mains broke. Fire and flood took up their deadly work where the sheer explosive impact of the collapse left off.

And still the tower fell.

Down the slope that led to the sea, villages and roads and farms and open fields and trees were smashed flat, pulverized, while the shock wave from the impact blew down woodlands and buildings for a hundred kilometers and more in either direction, as if a giant meteor had struck out of the sky. A fishing village fell under the shadow of sudden doom, its inhabitants looking up to see this immense arm of God swinging down on them like the mighty bludgeon of the angel of death.

And still the tower fell.

Its length splashed into the Pacific Ocean with a roar that broke eardrums and ruptured the innards of men, beasts, birds, and fish. Across the coastal shelf it plunged and out beyond into the abyssal depths. Whales migrating hundreds of kilometers out to sea were pulped to jelly by the shock wave that raced through the water. The tsunami it raised washed away shoreline settlements up and down the coast and rushed across the Pacific, flooding the Galapagos Islands, already half-drowned by the greenhouse warming. The Pacific coast of Central America was devastated. Hawaii and Japan were struck before their warning systems could get people to move inland. Samoa and Tahiti were hit by a wall of water nearly fifteen meters high that tore away villages and whole cities. People in Los Angeles and Sydney heard the mighty thunderclap and wondered if it was a sonic boom.

And still the tower fell, splashing all the way across the Pacific, groaning as part of its globe-girdling length sank slowly into the dark abyssal depths. When it hit the spiny tree-covered mountain backbone of Borneo it snapped in two, one part sliding down the rugged slopes, tearing away forests and villages and plantations as it slithered snake-like across the island.

The other part plunged across Sumatra and into the Indian Ocean, narrowly missing the long green finger of Malaysia but sending a tsunami washing across the drowned ruins of Singapore. Along the breadth of equatorial Africa it fell, smashing across Kenya, ploughed into the northern reaches of Lake Victoria, drowning the city of Kampala with a tidal wave, and continued westward, crushing cities and forests alike, igniting mammoth forest fires, driving vast herds of animals into panicked, screaming stampedes. Its upper end, still smoking from the titanic electrical discharge that had severed it, plunged hissing into the Atlantic, sinking deep down into the jagged rift where hot magma from the Earth's core embraced the man-made structure that had, mere minutes earlier, stood among the stars.

Across the world the once-proud skytower lay amidst a swath of death and desolation and smoking ruin, crushing the life from people, animals, plants, crushing human ambition, human dreams, crushing hope itself.

Lying flat on the tiles of the airport men's room, Bracknell felt the floor jump as a roll of thunder boomed over them, so loud that his ears rang. Even so, he heard screams and terrified cries.

"Are you all right?" he asked Lara, his voice sounding strange, muffled, inside his head.

She nodded weakly. He saw that her nose was bleeding slightly. Bracknell climbed slowly to his feet. The old man was still lying on the floor, facedown. Bracknell called to him, then nudged his shoulder. The man did not move. Rolling him over, Bracknell saw his soft brown eyes staring out sightlessly.

"He's dead," Lara said. Bracknell could barely hear her over the buzzing in his head.

Feeling stunned, thick-witted, Bracknell gazed around the windowless men's room. One of the tiled walls had cracked. Or had it been that way when they had rushed in here?

"Dead?" he echoed numbly.

"A heart attack, maybe," Lara said. She clung close to Bracknell. He could feel her trembling.

"He's lucky," said Bracknell.

THE RUINS

It took three days before they arrested Bracknell. He had made his way back to the shattered ruins of the Sky City, fighting through the panicked crowd at the airport, holding Lara close to him. The vast parking lot outside the airport seemed undamaged, except for the gritty dust that covered everything and crunched under their feet as they walked, tottering, for what seemed like hours until they found the minivan sitting there where they'd left it. Other people were milling around the parking lot, looking dazed, shocked.

A pall of smoke was rising from the city. Soon enough the looting would begin, Bracknell realized. For the moment they're too stunned to do much of anything, but that'll pass and they'll start looting and stealing. And raping.

The minivan looked as if it had gone a thousand klicks without being washed. Bracknell helped Lara into the right-hand seat, then went around and got in himself. The car started smoothly enough. He used the windshield wipers to clear away enough of the dust so he could see to drive, then started slowly out toward the road that led back up into the hills. A few people waved pathetically to him, seeking a ride. To where? Bracknell asked himself silently as he drove past them, accelerating now. A couple of young men trotted toward the minivan and he pushed the accelerator harder. The toll gate at the exit was unoccupied, its arm raised, so he drove right through. In the rear mirror he saw a uniformed guard or policeman or something waving angrily at him. He drove on.

When they finally reached Ciudad de Cielo, they saw that most of it was flattened. Buildings were crushed beneath the skytower's fallen bulk or blown flat by the shock wave of its collapse. Trucks overturned, lampposts bent and twisted. Dust hung in the air and the stench of death was everywhere, inescapable.

For three days Bracknell and Lara did nothing but dig bodies out of the collapsed buildings of the base city. The tower lay across the ruins like an immense black worm, dead and still, strangely warm to the touch. It had ripped out of all but one of its base tethers. In a distant corner of his mind Bracknell thought that they had designed the tethers pretty well to stand up even partially to the stress.

He worked blindly, numbly, side by side with the few surviving technicians, clerks, maintenance people, cooks, and others who had once been a proud team of builders. Lara worked alongside him, never complaining, like Bracknell and all the others too tired and shocked and disheartened to do much of anything except scrabble in the debris, eat whatever meager rations they could find, and sleep when they were too tired to stand any longer. Grimy, her face smeared with soot, her fingers bloody from digging, her clothes sodden with perspiration, Lara still worked doggedly at rescuing the few who were still alive and dragging out the mangled bodies of the dead.

The third night they saw torches lining the road from Quito, heading toward them.

"Volunteers?" Lara asked, her voice ragged with exhaustion.

"More likely a lynch mob," said Bracknell, getting up from the rubble he'd been digging in.

"Can you blame them?" said Danvers who was working beside them. "They're coming to kill everyone here."

"No," Bracknell replied, standing up straighter. "It's me they want. I'm the one responsible for this."

Lara, her weariness suddenly forgotten, turned her smudged face to Danvers. "You're a man of god! Do something! Talk to them! Stop them!"

Danvers looked terrified. "Me?"

"There's no one else," Lara insisted.

"I'll go," Bracknell said grimly. "I'm the one they want."

"I'll . . . I'll go with you," Danvers stammered.

"You stay here," Bracknell said to Lara.

"The hell I will!"

"This is going to be ugly."

"I'm going where you go, Mance."

The three of them walked—tottered, really—down the rubble-strewn street to the main road, where the torch-waving mob was marching toward them. Farther down the road, Bracknell could see the headlights of approaching trucks.

The crowd was mainly young men, all of them looking tired and grimy, clothes torn, faces blackened with soot and dirt. They carried shovels, picks, planks of wood. Christ, they look like us, Bracknell said to himself. They've been digging for survivors, too.

Danvers fished a small silver crucifix out of his pocket and held it up. In the flickering torchlight it gleamed fitfully. The mob stopped uncertainly.

"My sons," he began.

One of the men, taller than the others, his eyes glittering with anger and hatred, spat out a string of rapid Spanish. Bracknell caught his drift: We want the men who killed our families. We want justice.

Danvers raised his voice, "Do any of you speak English?"

"We want justice!" a voice yelled from the crowd.

"Justice is the Lord's," Danvers bellowed. "God will avenge."

The crowd surged forward dangerously. Danvers backed up several steps. Bracknell saw that it was going to be no use. The trucks were inching through the rear of the mob now. Bringing reinforcements, he thought. He stepped forward. "I'm the one you want," he said in Spanish. "I'm the man responsible."

An older man scurried up to Bracknell and peered at him. Turning back to the others, he shouted, "This is he! This is the chief of the skytower!"

The mob flowed forward, surrounding Bracknell. Lara screamed as Danvers dragged her back into the shadows, toward safety. The leader of the mob spat in Bracknell's face and raised his shovel high in the air.

A shot cracked through the night. Everyone froze into immobility. Bracknell could feel his heart pounding against his ribs. Then he saw soldiers pouring out of the trucks, each of them armed with assault rifles. An officer waved a pistol angrily and told the men of the mob to back away.

"This man is under arrest," the officer announced loudly. "He is going to jail."

Bracknell's knees nearly gave way. Jail seemed much better than having his brains splattered with a shovel.

THE TRIAL

As the crisply uniformed soldiers with their polished helmets and loaded guns bundled Bracknell into one of the trucks, he thought, Of course. They need to blame someone for this catastrophe. Who else? I'm the one in charge. I'm the one at fault.

He was treated with careful respect, as if he were a vial of nitroglycerine that might explode if mishandled. They placed him in the prison hospital, where a team of physicians and psychologists diagnosed Bracknell as suffering from physical exhaustion and severe emotional depression. He was dosed with psychotropic drugs for five of the six months between his arrest and his trial. During those five months, he was allowed no visitors, no television, nor any contact with the outside world, although police investigators questioned him for hours each day.

Skytower Corporation declared bankruptcy. Its board of directors issued a statement blaming the tower's collapse on the technical director who headed the construction project in Ecuador, the American engineer Mance Bracknell. Several of the board members fled to the lunar city of Selene, where Earthly legal jurisdiction could not reach them.

After five months of imprisonment Bracknell's interrogators flushed his body of the drugs they had used on him and showed him the written record of his confession. He signed it without argument. Only then was he allowed to speak to an attorney whom the government of Ecuador had appointed to represent him. When Lara was at last allowed to visit him, he had only the haziest of notions about what had happened to him since his arrest. Physically he was in good condition, except that he had lost more than five kilos in weight, his deep tan had faded, and his voice had withered to a whisper. Emotionally he was a wreck.

"I'll get you the best lawyers on Earth," Lara told him urgently.

Bracknell shrugged listlessly. "What difference does it make?"

The whole world watched his trial, in the high court in what was left of Quito. The court building had escaped major damage, although there were still engineers who had been brought in from Brazil poking around the building's foundations; most of the court's high stately windows, blown out by the shock of the tower's collapse, had been replaced by sheets of clear plastic.

Skytower Corporation dissolved itself in the face of trillions of dollars of damage claims. Bracknell was too guilt-ridden even to attempt to find himself a lawyer other than the government-appointed lackey. Lara coaxed a family friend to help represent him. The old man came out of retirement reluctantly and told Bracknell at their first meeting that his highest hope was to avoid the death penalty.

Lara was shocked. "I thought international law forbids the death penalty."

"More than four million deaths are being blamed on you," the old man said, frowning disapprovingly at Bracknell. "Mass murder, they're calling it. They want to make an example of you."

"Why not?" Bracknell whispered.

Although the trial took place in Quito, it was held under the international legal regime. Years earlier, Lara's lawyer had helped to write the international legal regime's guiding rules. That did not help much. Nor did Bracknell do much to help himself.

"It's my fault," he kept repeating. "My fault."

"No, it isn't," Lara insisted.

"The structure failed," he told Lara and her lawyer, time and again. "I was in charge of the project, so it's my responsibility."

"But you're not to blame," Lara insisted each time. "You didn't deliberately destroy the tower."

"I'm the only one left to blame," Bracknell pointed out morosely. "All the others were killed in the collapse."

"No, that's not true," said Lara. "Victor is in Melbourne. He'll help you."

At Lara's importuning Molina flew in from Melbourne. Sitting between his two lawyers on the opening day of the trial, dressed in a state-provided suit and a stiffly starched shirt that smelled of detergent, Bracknell felt a flicker of hope when he saw his old friend enter the courtroom and sit directly behind him, beside Lara. But once the trial began, it became clear that nothing on Earth could save him.

The first witness called by the three-judge panel was the Reverend Elliott Danvers.

The prosecuting attorney was a slim, dark-haired Ecuadorian of smoldering intensity, dressed in a white three-piece suit that fit him without a wrinkle. The video cameras loved his handsome face with its dark moustache, and he knew how to play to the vast global audience watching this trial. To Bracknell he looked like a mustachioed avenging angel. He started by establishing Danvers's position as spiritual advisor to the people of Ciudad de Cielo.

"Most of them are dead now, are they not?" asked the prosecutor. Since the trial was being held under the international legal regime, and being broadcast even to Selene and the mining center at Ceres, it was conducted in English.

Danvers answered with a low "Yes."

The prosecutor smoothed his moustache as he gazed up at the cracks in the courtroom's coffered ceiling, preparing dramatically for his next question. "You were troubled by what you learned about this construction projection, were you not?"

Bit by bit, the prosecutor got Danvers to tell the judges that Bracknell had been using genetically engineered microbes as nanomachines to produce the tower's structural elements.

The state-appointed defense attorney said nothing, but the lawyer that Lara had hired rose slowly to his feet and called in a tired, aged voice, "Objection. There is nothing illegal about employing genetically engineered microbes. And referring to them as 'nanomachines' is prejudicial."

The judges conferred in hurried whispers, then upheld the objection.

The prosecutor smiled thinly and bowed his head, accepting their decision, knowing that the dreaded term would be remembered by everyone.

"Have such genetically engineered microbes been used in any other construction projects?"

Danvers shrugged his heavy shoulders. "I'm not an engineer. . . ."

"To the best of your knowledge."

"To the best of my knowledge: no, they have not. The project's biologist, Dr. Molina, seemed quite proud of the originality of his work. He had applied for a patent."

The prosecutor turned toward Bracknell with a thin smile. "Thank you, Rev. Danvers."

Bracknell's defense attorney got to his feet, glanced at the state-appointed attorney, then said, "I have no questions for this witness at this time."

Lara, sitting behind Bracknell, touched his shoulder. He turned to her, saw the worried look on her face. And said nothing. Molina, sitting beside her, looked impatient, uncomfortable.

"I call Dr. Victor Molina to the stand," said the prosecutor, with the air of a magician pulling a rabbit out of his hat.

Molina got to his feet and walked slowly to the witness chair; he tried to make a smile for Bracknell but grimaced instead.

Once again, the prosecutor spent several minutes establishing Molina's credentials and his position on the project. Then he asked:

"You left the skytower project before it was completed, did you not?"

"Yes, I did," said Molina.

"Why is that?"

Molina hesitated a moment, his eyes flicking toward Bracknell and Lara, sitting behind him.

"Personal reasons," he answered.

"Could you be more specific?"

Again Molina hesitated. Then, drawing in a breath, he replied, "I wasn't certain that the structures produced by my gengineered microbes were sufficiently strong to stand the stresses imposed by the tower."

Bracknell blinked and stirred like a man coming out of a coma. "That's not true," he whispered, more to himself than to his lawyers.

But Molina was going on, "I wanted more testing, more checking to make sure that the structure would be safe. But the project director wouldn't do it."

"The project director was Mr. Mance Bracknell," asked the prosecuting attorney needlessly. "The accused?"

"Yes," said Molina. "He insisted that we push ahead before the necessary tests could be done."

Bracknell said to his attorney, "That's not true!" Turning to Lara, he said, "That isn't what happened!"

The chief judge, sitting flanked by his two robed associates at the high banc of polished mahogany, tapped his stylus on the desktop. "The accused will remain silent," he said sternly. "I will tolerate no disruptions in this court."

"Thank you, Your Honor," said the prosecutor. Then he turned back to Molina, in the witness chair.

"So the accused disregarded your warnings about the safety problems of the tower?"

Molina glanced toward Bracknell, then looked away. "Yes, he did."

"He's lying!" Bracknell said to his lawyer. Jumping to his feet, he shouted to Molina, "Victor, why are you lying?"

His lawyer pulled him back down onto his chair while the chief judge leveled an accusatory stare at Bracknell. "I warn you, sir: another such outburst and you will be removed from this courtroom."

"What difference would that make?" Bracknell snapped. "You've convicted me already."

The judge nodded to the pair of burly soldiers standing to one side of the banc. They pushed past the attorney on Bracknell's left and grabbed him by his arms, hauling him to his feet.

He turned to glance back at Lara as they dragged him out of the courtroom. She was smiling. Smiling! Bracknell felt his guts churn with sudden hatred.

Lara watched them hustle Mance out of the courtroom, smiling as she thought, At least he's waking up. He's not just sitting there and accepting all the blame. He's starting to defend himself. Or trying to.

THE VERDICT

The trial proceeded swiftly. With Bracknell watching the proceedings on video from a locked and guarded room on the other side of the courthouse, the prosecuting attorney called in a long line of engineers and other technical experts who testified that the skytower was inherently dangerous.

"No matter what safety precautions may or may not have been taken," declared the somber, gray-haired dean of the technology ethics department of Heidelberg University, "such a structure poses an unacceptable danger to the global environment, as we can all see from this terrible tragedy. Its very existence is a menace to the world."

Bracknell's attorney called in technical witnesses, also, who testified that all the specifications and engineering details of the skytower showed that the structure had been built well within tolerable limits.

"I personally reviewed the plans before construction ever started," said the grizzled, square-faced professor of engineering from Caltech. "The plan for that tower was sound."

"Yet it fell!" snapped the prosecutor, on cross-examination. "It collapsed and killed millions."

"That shouldn't have happened," said the Caltech professor.

"It shouldn't have happened," the prosecutor repeated, "*if* the actual construction followed the plans."

"I'm sure it did," the professor replied.

"Did the plans call for nanotechnology to be employed in manufacturing the structural elements?"

"No, but—"

"Thank you. I have no further questions."

As Bracknell sat and seethed in his locked room, the prosecution built its case swiftly and surely. There were hardly any of the skytower crew left alive to testify to the soundness of the tower's construction. And when they did the prosecutor harped back to the use of nanotechnology.

"Call Victor back to the stand," Bracknell urged his attorney with white-hot fury. "Cross-examine him. Make him tell the truth!"

"That wouldn't be wise," the old man said. "There's no sense reminding the judges that you used nanomachines."

"I didn't! They were natural organisms!"

"Genetically modified."

"But that doesn't make any difference!"

The attorney shook his head sadly. "If I put Molina back in the witness stand and he sticks to his story, it will destroy you."

"If you don't, I'm destroyed anyway."

The hardest part of the trial, for Bracknell, was the fact that the judges would not let him see anyone except his attorneys. Every day he sat in that stuffy little isolation room and watched Lara in the courtroom, with Molina now at her side. She would leave with Victor. On the morning that the verdict was to be announced she arrived with Victor.

On that morning, before the proceedings began, the chief judge stepped into Bracknell's isolation room, flanked by two soldiers armed with heavy black pistols at their hips. After weeks of viewing him only in his black robe up on his high banc, Bracknell was mildly surprised to see that the man was very short and stocky. His skin was light, but he was built like a typical mestizo. His face bore the heavy, sad features of a man about to do something unpleasant.

Bracknell got to his feet as the judge entered the little room.

Without preamble, the judge said in barely accented

English, "I am to pass sentence on you this morning. Can you restrain yourself if I allow you back into the courtroom?"

"Yes," said Bracknell.

"I have your word of honor on that?"

Almost smiling, Bracknell replied, "If you believe that I have any honor, yes, you have my word."

The judge did not smile back. He nodded wearily. "Very well, then." Turning, he told the soldiers in rapid Spanish to escort the prisoner into the courtroom.

The courtroom was jammed, Bracknell saw as he came in, escorted by the soldiers. From the video screen in his isolation room he'd been unable to see how many people attended the trial. Now he realized there were reporters and camerapersons from all over the world wedged along both side walls. The benches were packed with people, most of them dour, dark Ecuadorians who stared at him with loathing. Looking for my blood, Bracknell realized.

Lara jumped to her feet as he entered; Molina rose more slowly. Both of Bracknell's attorneys stood up, too, looking as if they were attending a funeral. They are, Bracknell thought. Once he got to his chair Lara leaned across the mahogany railing separating them and threw her arms around his neck.

"I'm with you, darling," she whispered into his ear. "No matter what happens, I'm with you."

Bracknell drank in the warmth of her body, the scent of her. But his eyes bore into Molina's, who glared back angrily at him.

Why is Victor sore at me? Bracknell asked himself. What's he got to be pissed about? *He* betrayed *me*; I haven't done anything to *him*.

"Everyone stand," called the court announcer.

The judges filed in, their robes looking newer and darker than Bracknell remembered them. Their faces were dark, too.

Once everyone was properly seated, the chief judge picked up a single sheet of paper from the desk before him. Bracknell noted that his hand trembled slightly.

"The prisoner will stand."

Bracknell got to his feet, feeling as if he were about to face a firing squad.

"It is the judgment of this court that you, Mance Bracknell, are responsible for the deaths of more than four million human souls, and the destruction of many hundreds of billions of dollars in property."

Bracknell felt nothing. It was as if he were outside his own body, watching this foreordained drama from a far distance.

"Since your crime was not willful murder, the death sentence will not be considered."

A stir rippled through the packed courtroom. "He killed my whole family!" a woman's voice screeched in Spanish.

"Silence!" roared the judge, with a power in his voice that stilled the crowd. "This is a court of justice. The law will prevail."

The courtroom went absolutely silent.

"Mance Bracknell, you have been found guilty of more than four million counts of negligent homicide. It is the decision of this court that you be exiled from this planet Earth forever, so that you can never again threaten the lives of innocent men, women, and children."

Bracknell's knees sagged beneath him. He leaned on the tabletop for support.

"This case is closed," said the judge.

BOOK III

EXILED

Beware the fury of a patient man.

LEAVING EARTH

They wasted no time hustling Bracknell off the planet. Within two days of his trial's inevitable conclusion, a squad of hard-faced soldiers took him from his prison cell to a van and out to the Quito airport, where a Clippership was waiting to carry him into orbit.

The airport looked relatively undamaged, Bracknell saw from the window of the van, except for the big plywood sheets where the sweeping windows had been. It's a wonder the crash didn't trigger earthquakes, he thought.

The soldiers marched him through the terminal building, people turning to stare at him as they strode to the Clippership gate. Bracknell was not shackled, not even handcuffed, but everyone recognized him. He saw the look in their eyes, the expressions on their faces: hatred, anger, even fear—as if he were a monster that terrified their nightmares.

Lara was waiting at the terminal gate, wearing black, as if she were attending a funeral. She is, Bracknell thought. Mine.

She rushed to him and leaned her head against his chest. Bracknell felt awkward, with the grim-faced soldiers flanking him. He slid his arms around her waist hesitantly, tentatively, then suddenly clung to her like a drowning man clutching a life preserver.

"Darling, I'll go out to the Belt with you," Lara said, all in a gush. "Wherever they send you, I'll go there too."

He pushed her back away from him. "No! You can't throw away your life. They're putting me in some sort of a penal colony; you won't be allowed there."

"But I—"

"Go back home. Live your life. Forget about me. I'm a dead man. Dead and gone. Don't throw away your life on a corpse."

"No, Mance, I won't let you—"

He shoved her roughly and turned to the soldier on his left. "Let's go. *Andale!*"

Lara looked shocked, her eyes wide, her mouth open in protest.

"Andale!" he repeated to the soldiers, louder, and started walking toward the gate. They rushed to catch up with him. He did not dare look back at Lara as the soldiers marched him into the access tunnel that led to the Clippership's hatch. His last sight of her was the stunned look on her face. He didn't want to see the tears filling her eyes, the hopelessness. He felt wretched enough for both of them.

The access tunnel was smooth windowless plastic. A birth canal, Bracknell thought. I'm being born into another life. Everything I had, everything and everyone I knew, is behind me now. I'm leaving my life behind me and entering hell.

And then he saw the bulky form of Rev. Danvers standing at the end of the tunnel, blocking the Clippership hatch. The minister was also in black, he looked downcast, sorrowful, almost guilty.

Bracknell felt a wave of fury burn through his guts. Damned ignorant viper. Frightened of anything new, anything different. He's happy that the tower failed, but he's trying to put on a sympathetic face.

Bracknell walked right up to Danvers. "Don't tell me you're going out to the Belt with me."

Danver's face reddened. "No, I hadn't intended to. But if you feel the need for spiritual consolation, perhaps I—"

With a bitter laugh, Bracknell said, "Don't worry, I was only joking."

"I can contact the New Morality office at Ceres on your behalf," Danvers suggested.

Bracknell wanted to spit out, "Go to hell," but he bit his lip and said nothing.

"You'll need spiritual comfort out there," Danvers said, his voice low, almost trembling. "You don't have to be alone in your time of tribulation."

"Is that what you came here to tell me? That I can have some pious psalm singer drone in my ear? Some consolation!"

"No," Danvers said, his heavy head sinking slightly. "I came to . . . to tell you how sorry I am that things have worked out the way they have."

"Sure you are."

"I am. Truly I am. When I reported to my superiors about your using nanotechnology, I was merely doing my duty. I had no personal animosity toward you. Quite the opposite."

Despite his anger Bracknell could see the distress in Danvers's flushed face. Some of the fury leached out of him.

"I had no idea it would lead to this," Danvers was going on, almost blubbering. "You must believe me, I never wanted to cause harm to you or anyone else."

"Of course not," Bracknell said tightly.

"I was merely doing my duty."

"Sure."

One of the soldiers prodded Bracknell's back.

"I've got to get aboard," he said to Danvers.

"I'll pray for you."

"Yeah. Do that."

They left Danvers at the hatch and entered the Clippership. Its circular passenger compartment was empty:

twenty rows of seats arranged two by two with an aisle down the middle. Instead of flight attendants, two marshals with stun wands strapped to their hips were standing just inside the hatch.

"Take any seat you like, Mr. Bracknell," said the taller of the two men.

"This flight is exclusively for you," said the other, with a smirk. "Courtesy of Masterson Aerospace Corporation and the International Court of Justice."

Bracknell fought down an urge to punch him in his smug face. He looked around the circular compartment, then chose one of the few seats that was next to a window. One of the soldiers sat next to him, the other directly behind him.

It took nearly half an hour before the Clippership was ready for launch. Bracknell saw there was a video screen on the seat back in front of him. He ignored its bland presentation of a Masterson Aerospace documentary and peered out the little window at the workers moving around the blast-blackened concrete pad on which the rocket vehicle stood. He heard thumps and clangs, the gurgling of what he took to be rocket propellant, then the screen showed a brief video about safety and takeoff procedures.

Bracknell braced himself for the rocket engines' ignition. They lit off with a demon's roar and he felt an invisible hand pressing him down into the thickly cushioned seat. The ground fell away and he could see the whole airport, then the towers and squares of Quito, and finally the long black snake of the fallen skytower lying across the hilly land like a dead and blasted dream.

It was only then that he burst into tears.

IN TRANSIT

Although Bracknell's Clippership ride from Quito to orbit was exclusively for him, the vehicle they transferred him to held many other convicts.

It was not a torch ship, the kind of fusion-driven vessel that could accelerate all the way out to the Belt and make it to Ceres in less than a week. Bracknell was put aboard a freighter named *Alhambra,* an old, slow bucket that spent months coasting from Earth out to the Belt.

His fellow prisoners were mostly men exiled for one crime or another, heading for a life of mining the asteroids. Bracknell counted three murderers (one of them a sullen, drug-raddled woman), four thieves of various accomplishments, six embezzlers and other white-collar crooks, and an even dozen others who had been convicted of sexual crimes or violations of religious authority.

The captain of the freighter obviously did not like ferrying convicts to the Belt, but it paid more than going out empty to pick up ores. The prisoners were marched into the unused cargo hold, which had been fitted out with old, rusting cots and a row of portable toilets. It was a big, bare metal womb with walls scuffed and scratched by years worth of heavy wear. The narrow, sagging metal-framed cots were bolted to the floor, the row of toilet cubicles lined one wall. As soon as the *Alhambra* broke orbit and started on its long, coasting journey to the Belt, the captain addressed his "passengers" over the ship's video intercom.

"I am Captain Farad," he announced. In the lone screen fixed high overhead in the hold, Bracknell and the others could see that the captain's lean, sallow face was set in a sour, stubbly scowl that clearly showed his contempt for his "passengers."

"I give the orders aboard this vessel and you obey them," he went on. "If you don't give me any trouble I won't give you any trouble. But if you start any trouble, if you're part of any trouble, if you're just only *near* trouble when it happens, I'll have you jammed into a spacesuit and put outside on the end of a tether and that's the way you'll ride out to Ceres."

The convicts mumbled and glowered up at the screen. Bracknell thought that the captain meant every word of what he'd said quite literally.

Even with that warning, the journey was not entirely peaceful. There were no private accommodations for the convicts aboard the freighter; they were simply locked into the empty cargo hold. Within a day, the hold stank of urine and vomit.

Alhambra's living module rotated slowly at the end of a five-kilometer tether, with its logistics and smelting modules on the other end, so that there was a feeling of nearly Earth-level gravity inside. Meals were served by simple-minded robots that could neither be bribed nor coerced. Bracknell did his best to stay apart from all the others, including the women convicted of prostitution, who went unashamedly from cot to cot once the overhead lights had been turned down for the night.

Still, it was impossible to live in peace. His mind buzzed constantly with the memory of all he'd lost: Lara, especially. His dreams were filled with visions of the skytower collapsing, of the millions who had been killed, all of them rising from their graves and pointing accusing skeletal fingers at him. Where did it go wrong? Bracknell asked himself, over and over and over again. The questions tortured him. The structure was sound, he knew it was. Yet it had failed. Why? Had some unusually powerful electrical current in the ionosphere snapped the connector links at the geostationary level? Should I have put more insulation up at that level? What did I do wrong? What did I do?

It was his dreams—nightmares, really—that got him into trouble. More than once he was awakened roughly by one of the other convicts, angry that his moaning was keeping all those around his cot from sleeping.

"You sound like a fuckin' baby," snarled one of the angry men, "cryin' and yellin'."

"Yeah," said another. "Shut your mouth or we'll shut it for you."

For several nights Bracknell tried to force himself to stay awake, but eventually he fell asleep and once he did his haunting dreams returned.

Suddenly he was being yanked off his cot, punched and kicked by a trio of angry men. Bracknell tried to defend himself, he fought back and unexpectedly found himself enjoying the pain and the blood and the fury as he smashed their snarling faces, grabbed a man by the hair and banged his head off the metal rail of his cot, kneed another in the groin and pounded him in the kidneys. More men swarmed over him and he went down, but he was hitting, kicking, biting, until he blacked out.

When he awoke he was strapped down in a bunk. Through swollen, blood-encrusted eyes he realized that this must be the ship's infirmary. It smelled like a hospital: disinfectant and crisply clean sheets. No one else was in sight. Medical monitors beeped softly above his head. Every part of his body ached miserably. When he tried to lift his head a shock of pain ran the length of his spine.

"You've got a couple of broken ribs," said a rough voice from behind him.

The captain stepped into his view. "You're Bracknell, eh? You put up a good fight, I'll say that much for you." He was a small man, lean and lithe, his skin an ashen light tan, the stubble on his unshaved face mostly gray. A scar marred his upper lip, making him look as if he were perpetually snarling. His hair was pulled back off his face and tied into a little queue.

Bracknell tried to ask what happened, but his lips were so swollen his words were terribly slurred.

"I reviewed the fight on the video monitor," the captain said, frowning down at him. "Infrared images. Not as clear as visible light, but good enough for the likes of you scum."

"I'm not scum," Bracknell said thickly.

"No? You killed more people than the guys who were pounding you ever did."

Bracknell turned his head away from the captain's accusing eyes.

"I was an investor in Skytower Corporation," the captain went on. "I was going to retire and live off my profits. Now I'm broke. A lifetime's savings wiped out because you screwed up the engineering. What'd you do, shave a few megabucks on the structure so you could skim the money for yourself?"

It was all Bracknell could do to murmur, "No."

"Not much, I'll bet." The captain stared down at Bracknell, unconcealed loathing in his eyes. "The guys who jumped you are riding outside, just as I promised trouble-makers would. You'd be out there, too, except I don't have enough suits."

Bracknell said nothing.

"You'll spend the rest of the flight here, in the infirmary," said the captain. "Think of it as solitary confinement."

"Thanks," Bracknell muttered.

"I'm not doing this for you," the captain snapped. "Long as you're in the hold with the rest of those savages you're going to be a lightning rod. It'll be a quieter ride with you in here."

"You could have let them kill me."

"Yeah, I could have. But I get paid for every live body I deliver at Ceres. Corpses don't make money for me."

With that, the captain left. Bracknell lay alone, strapped into the bunk. When his nightmares came there was no one to be bothered by his screams.

CERES

As the weeks dragged by, Bracknell's ribs and other injuries slowly healed. The ship's physician—an exotic-looking, dark-skinned young Hindu woman—allowed him to get up from the bunk and walk stiffly around the narrow confines of the infirmary. She brought him his meals, staring at him through lowered lashes with her big liquid eyes.

Once, when he woke up screaming in the middle of the night, the physician and the captain both burst into the tiny infirmary and sedated him with a hypospray. He slept dreamlessly for a day and a half.

After weeks of being tended by this silent physician with her almond eyes and subtle perfume, Bracknell realized, My god, even in a wrinkled, faded set of sloppy coveralls she looks sexy. He thought of Lara and wondered what she was doing now, how she was putting together the shattered pieces of her life. The physician never spoke a word to him and Bracknell said nothing to her beyond a half-whispered "Thank you" when she'd bring in a tray of food. The young woman was obviously wary of him, almost frightened. If I touch her and she screams I'll end up outside in a space-suit, trying to stay alive on liquids and canned air, he told himself.

At last one day, when he was walking normally again, he blurted, "May I ask you something?"

She looked startled for a moment, then nodded wordlessly.

"Why put the troublemakers outside?" Bracknell asked. "Wouldn't it be easier to dope them with psychotropics?"

The young woman hesitated a heartbeat, then said, "Such drugs are very expensive."

"But I should think the government would provide them for security purposes, to keep the prisoners quiet."

A longer hesitation this time, then, "Yes, they do. My father sells the drugs at Ceres. They fetch a good price there."

"Your father?"

"The captain. He is my father."

Holy lord! Bracknell thought. Good thing I haven't touched her. I'd arrive in Ceres in a body bag.

The next morning the captain himself carried in his food tray and stayed to talk.

"She told you I'm her father," he said, standing by the bunk as Bracknell picked at the tray on his lap.

"She reports everything to you, doesn't she?" Bracknell replied.

"She doesn't have to. I watch you on the monitor when she's in here."

"Oh. I see."

"So do I. Every breath you draw. Remember that."

"She doesn't look like you."

The captain's scarred lip curled into a cold sneer. "Her mother was a Hindu. Met her in Delhi when I was running Clipperships there from the States. Once her parents found out she had married a Muslim they threw her out of their home."

"You're a Muslim?"

"All my life. My father and his father, too."

"And you married a Hindu."

"In India. Very tight situation. I wanted to take her back to the States but she was trying to get her parents to approve of our marriage. They wouldn't budge. I knew that, but she kept on trying."

"Is your wife on the ship, too?"

Without even an eyeblink's hesitation the captain answered, "She was killed in the food riots back in 'sixty-four. That's where I got this lip."

Bracknell didn't know what to say. He stared down at his tray.

"My daughter says I shouldn't be so hard on you."

Looking up into the captain's cold stone gray eyes, Bracknell said, "I think you've been treating me pretty well."

"Do you."

"You could have let them kill me, back in the hold."

"And lost the money I get when I deliver you? No way."

There didn't seem to be anything else to say. Bracknell picked up his plastic fork. Then a question arose in his mind.

"How did you break up the fight? I mean, how'd you stop them from killing me?"

With a sardonic huff, the captain said, "Soon's the automated alarm woke me up and I looked at the monitor, I turned down the air pressure in the hold until you all passed out. Brought it down to about four thousand meters' equivalent, Earth value."

Bracknell couldn't help grinning at him. "Good thing none of those guys were from the Andes."

"I'd've just lowered the pressure until everybody dropped," the captain evenly. "Might cause some brain damage, but I get paid to deliver live bodies, regardless of their mental capacities."

Alhambra arrived at Ceres at last and Bracknell was marched with the other convicts through the ship's airlock and into the *Chrysalis II* habitat.

The mining community that had grown at Ceres had built the habitat that orbited the asteroid. It was a mammoth ring-shaped structure that rotated so that there was a feeling of gravity inside: the same level as the Moon's, one-sixth of Earth normal.

Stumbling, walking haltingly in the unaccustomedly low gravity, the twenty-six men and women were led by a quartet of guards in coral-red coveralls into what looked to Bracknell like an auditorium. There was a raised platform at one end and rows of seats along the carpeted floor. The guards motioned with their stun wands for the prisoners to sit down. Most of them took seats toward the rear of the auditorium while the guards stationed themselves at the exits. Bracknell went down to the third row; no one else had chosen to sit so close to the stage.

For a few minutes nothing happened. Bracknell could hear half-whispered conversations behind him. The auditorium looked clean, sparkling, even though its walls and ceiling were bare tile. It even smelled new and fresh, although he realized the scent could be piped in through the air circulation system.

Just as the pitch of the chatter behind started to rise to the level of impatience, a huge mountain of a shaggy, red-haired man strode out onto the stage. Bracknell expected to see the stage's floorboards sag under his weight, even in the lunar-level gravity.

"My name's George Ambrose," he said, in a surprisingly sweet tenor voice. "For some obscure reason folks 'round here call me Big George."

A few wary laughs from the convicts.

"For my sins I've been elected chief administrator of this habitat. It's like bein' the mayor or the governor. Top dog. Which means everybody drops their fookin' problems in my lap."

Like the guards, George Ambrose wore coral-red coveralls, although his looked old and more than slightly faded. His brick-red hair was a wild thatch that merged with an equally thick beard.

Pointing at his audience, Ambrose continued, "You blokes've been sent here because you were found guilty of crimes. Each of you has been sentenced to a certain length of what they call penal servitude. That means you work for peanuts or less. Okay. I don't like havin' my home serve as a penal colony, but the powers-that-be back Earthside don't know what else to do with you. They sure don't want you anywhere near them!"

No one laughed.

"Okay. Here's the way we work it here in the Belt. We don't give a shit about your past. What's done is done. You're here and you're gonna work for the length of your sentence. Some of you got life, so you're gonna stay here in the Belt. The rest of you, if you work hard and keep your arses clean, you'll be able to go home with a clear file once you've served your time. You can't get rejuvenation treatments while you're serving time, of course, but we can rejuve you soon's your time's been served, if you can afford it. Fair enough?"

Bracknell heard muttering behind him. Then someone called out, "Do we get any choice in the jobs we get?"

Ambrose's shaggy brows rose slightly. "Some. We've got miners and other employers all across the Belt reviewin' your files. Some of 'em will make requests for you. If you get more'n one request you can take your choice. Only one, then you're stuck with it."

A deep, heavy voice asked, "Suppose I don't get any?"

"Then *I'll* have to deal with you," Ambrose replied. "Don't worry, there's plenty of work to be done out here. You won't sit around doin' nothing."

I'm here for life, Bracknell said to himself. I'll have to make a life for myself out here in the Belt. Maybe it's a good thing that I won't be allowed any rejuvenation treatments. I'll just get old and die out here.

JOB OFFER

The rest of the day, the convicts were led through medical exams and psychological interviews, then shown to the quarters they would live in until assigned to a job. Bracknell noted that each of the prisoners obeyed the guards' instructions without objection. This is all new to them, and they don't know what to make of it, he thought. There's no sense making trouble and there's no place for them to run to. We're millions of klicks from Earth now; tens of millions of kilometers.

They were served a decent meal in a cafeteria that had been cleared of all its regular customers. No mixing with the local population, Bracknell realized. Not yet, at least.

At the end of the long, strangely tense day, the guards led them down a long corridor faced with blank doors and assigned them to their sleeping quarters, two to a compartment. Bracknell was paired with a frail-looking older man, white haired and with skin that looked like creased and crumpled parchment.

The door closed behind them. He heard the lock click. Surveying the compartment, Bracknell saw a pair of bunks, a built-in desk and bureau, a folding door that opened onto the lavatory.

"Not bad," said his companion. He went to the lower

bunk and sat on it possessively. "Kinda plush, after that bucket we rode here in."

Bracknell nodded tightly. "I'll take the upper bunk."

"Good. I got a fear of heights." The older man got up and went to the bureau. Opening the top drawer he exclaimed, "Look! They even got jammies for us!"

Trying to place the man's accent, Bracknell asked, "You're British?"

Frowning, the man replied, "Boston Irish. My name's Fennelly."

Bracknell extended his hand. "I'm—"

"I know who you are. You're the screamer."

Feeling embarrassed, Bracknell admitted, "I have nightmares."

"I'm a pretty heavy sleeper. Maybe that's why they put us in together."

"Maybe," Bracknell said.

"You're the guy from the skytower, ain'tcha."

"That's right."

"They arrested me for lewd and lascivious behavior," said Fennelly, with an exaggerated wink. "I'm gay."

"Homosexual?"

"That's right, kiddo. Watch your ass!" And Fennelly cackled as he walked to the lavatory, nearly stumbling in the light gravity.

In the top bunk with the lights out and the faintly glowing ceiling a bare meter above his head, Bracknell suddenly realized the ludicrousness of it all. Fennelly's down there wondering if I'm going to keep him up all night with my nightmares and I'm up here worried that he might try to make a pass at me. It was almost laughable.

If he did dream, Bracknell remembered nothing of it in the morning. They were awakened by a synthesized voice calling through the intercom, "Breakfast in thirty minutes in the cafeteria. Directions are posted on the display screens in the corridor."

The scrambled eggs were mediocre, but better than the fare they had gotten on the *Alhambra*. After breakfast the same quartet of guards took the convicts, one by one, to job interviews. Bracknell watched them leave the cafeteria until he was the only person left sitting at the long tables.

No one wants to take me on, he thought. I'm a pariah. Sitting alone with nothing to do, his mind drifted back to the skytower and its collapse, and the mockery of a trial that had condemned him to a life of exile. And Victor's betrayal. It was Victor's testimony that convicted me, he thought. Then he told himself, No, you were judged and sentenced before the first minute of the trial. But Victor did betray you, insisted a voice in his mind. He sat there and lied. Deliberately.

Why? Why? He was my friend. Why did he turn on me?

And Danvers. He reported to his New Morality superiors that we were using nanotechnology. In league with the devil, as far as he's concerned. Did the New Morality have something to do with the tower's collapse? Did they sabotage the skytower? No, they couldn't have. They wouldn't have. But somebody did. Suddenly Bracknell was convinced of it. Somebody deliberately sabotaged the tower! It couldn't have collapsed by itself. The construction was sound. Somebody sabotaged it.

One of the guards reappeared at the cafeteria's double doors and crooked a finger at him. Bracknell got to his feet and followed the guard down another corridor—or maybe it was merely an extension of the passageway he'd gone through earlier. It was impossible to get a feeling for the size or scope of this habitat from the inside, and he and his fellow convicts had not been allowed an outside view.

There were other people moving along this corridor, men

in shirts and trousers, women wearing skirted dresses or blouses and slacks. He saw only a few in coveralls. They all looked as if they had someplace to go, some task to accomplish. That's what I must have looked like, back before the accident, Bracknell thought. Back when I had a life.

But it wasn't an accident, whispered a voice in his head. It wasn't your fault. The tower was deliberately destroyed.

He saw names on the doors lining both sides of the corridors. Some of the doors were open, revealing offices or conference rooms. This is where they run this habitat, he realized. Why is this guard bringing me here?

They stopped at a door marked CHIEF ADMINISTRATOR. The guard opened it without knocking. Inside was a sizable office: several desks with young men and women busily whispering into lip mikes. Their display screens showed charts and graphs in vivid colors. They glanced up at him and the guard, then quickly returned their attention to their work.

Gesturing for him to follow, the guard led Bracknell past their desks and to an inner door. No name on it. Again the guard opened it without knocking. It was obviously an anteroom. A matronly looking woman with short-cropped silver hair sat at the only desk, holding a conversation in low tones with another woman's image in her display screen. Beyond her desk was still another door, also unmarked.

She looked up and, without missing a beat of her conversation, touched a button on her phone console. The inner door popped open a few centimeters. The guard shooed Bracknell to it.

Pushing the door all the way open, Bracknell saw George Ambrose sitting behind a desk that looked too small for his bulk, like a man sitting at a child's play desk. He was speaking to his desktop screen.

"Come on in and sit down," Ambrose said. "Be with you

in a sec." Turning his gaze to his desktop screen he said, "Save file. Clear screen."

The display went dark as Bracknell took the contoured chair in front of the desk. It gave slightly under his weight. Ambrose swiveled his high-backed chair to face Bracknell squarely.

"I've got a message for you," Ambrose said.

"From Lara?"

Shaking his shaggy head, Ambrose said, "Convicts aren't allowed messages from Earthside, normally. But this one is from some New Morality bloke, the Reverend Elliott Danvers."

"Oh." The surge of hope that Bracknell felt faded away.

"D'you want to see it in privacy?"

"No, it doesn't matter."

Pointing to the wall on Bracknell's right, Ambrose said, "Okay, then, here it is."

Danvers's slightly bloated, slightly flushed face appeared on the wall screen. Bracknell felt his innards tighten.

"Mance—if you don't mind me calling you by your first name—I hope this message finds you well and healthy after your long journey to Ceres. I know this is a time of turmoil and anguish for you, but I want you to realize that you are not alone, not forgotten. In your hour of need, you may call on me. Whenever you feel the need of council, or prayer, or even just the need to hear a familiar voice, call me. The New Morality will pay the charges. Call me whenever you wish."

Danvers's image disappeared, replaced by the cross-and-scroll logo of the New Morality.

Bracknell stared at the screen for a few heartbeats, then turned back to Ambrose. "That's the entire message?"

Nodding, "Looks it. I di'n't open it till you got here."

Bracknell said nothing.

"D'you want to send an answer? It'll take about an hour to reach Earth."

"No. No answer."

"You sure?"

"That man's testimony helped convict me."

Ambrose shook his red-maned head. "Way it looks to me, you were convicted before the trial even started. They needed a scapegoat. Can't have four million deaths and chalk it up as an act of god."

Bracknell stared at the man. It was difficult to tell the color of his eyes beneath those bushy red brows.

"Well, anyway," Ambrose said more cheerfully, "I got a job offer for you."

"A job offer?"

"Only one. You're not a really popular fella, y'know."

"That means I'll have to take the job whether I want to or not."

"'Fraid so."

Taking in a breath, Bracknell asked, "What is it?"

"Skipper of the ship you came in on. Says he needs a new third mate."

Blinking with surprise, Bracknell said, "I don't know much about spacecraft."

"You'll learn on the job. It's a good offer, a lot better than spendin' half your life in a suit runnin' nanobugs on some chunk o' rock."

"The captain of the *Alhambra* asked for me? Me, specifically?"

"That he did."

"Why on Earth would he do that?" Bracknell wondered.

"You're not on Earth, mate. Take the job and be glad of it. You got no choice."

THE BELT

At first Bracknell half-thought, half-feared, that he'd been brought to the *Alhambra* to become a husband for the captain's daughter. His first day aboard the ship disabused him of that notion.

Bracknell was taken from the habitat by one of the coral-uniformed guards to an airlock, where he retraced his steps of a few days earlier and returned to the *Alhambra*. The captain was standing at the other end of the connector tunnel with his hands clasped behind his back, waiting for him with a sour expression on his lean, pallid face.

"I'm taking you on against my better judgment," said the captain as he walked with Bracknell toward the ship's bridge. Bracknell saw that he gripped a stun wand in his right hand. "Only the fact that my third man jumped his contract and took off for Earthside has made me desperate enough to do this."

Bracknell began, "I appreciate—"

"You will address me as Sir or Captain," the captain interrupted. "The computers do most of the brainwork aboard ship, but you will still have to learn astrogation, logistics, communications, propulsion, and life support. If you goof off or prove too stupid to master these subjects I'll sell you off to the first work gang on the first rock we rendezvous with. Is that clear?"

"Perfectly clear," said Bracknell. Then, seeing the captain's eyes flare, he hastily added, "Sir."

Captain Farad stopped at a door in the corridor. "This is your quarters. You will maintain it in shipshape condition

at all times. You'll find clothing in there. It should fit you;
if it doesn't, alter it. I'll expect you on the bridge, ready to
begin your duties, in half an hour."

"Yes, sir," said Bracknell.

Alhambra departed Ceres that day, heading deeper into
the Belt to begin picking up metals and minerals from mining crews at various asteroids. For the next several weeks
Bracknell studied the computer's files on all he was supposed to learn, and took regular stints of duty on the bridge,
always under the sternly watchful eyes of Captain Farad. He
saw nothing of the captain's daughter.

He spent virtually all of his spare time learning about
the ship and its systems. Like most deep-space vessels, *Alhambra* consisted of two modules balanced on either side
of a five-kilometer-long buckyball tether, rotating to produce an artificial gravity inside them. One module held the
crew's quarters and the cargo hold that was often used to
hold convicts outward bound to the Belt. The other module contained supplies and what had once been a smelter
facility. The smelter had become useless since the introduc-
tion of nanomachines to reduce asteroids to purified metals and minerals.

The captain assigned Bracknell to the communications
console at first. It was highly automated; all Bracknell had
to do was watch the screens and make certain that there
was always a steaming mug of coffee in the receptacle built
into the left arm of the captain's command chair.

Through the round ports set into the bridge's bulkhead
Bracknell could see outside: nothing but dark emptiness
out there. The deeply tinted quartz windows cut out all
but the brightest stars. There were plenty of them to see,
but somehow they seemed to accentuate the cold darkness out there rather than alleviate it. No Moon in that empty
sky. No warmth or comfort. For days on end he didn't even

see an asteroid, despite being in the thick of the so-called Belt.

Bracknell didn't see the captain's daughter either until the day one of the crew's family got injured.

He was gazing morosely through the port at the endless emptiness out there when an alarm started hooting, startling him like a sudden electric shock.

"What's going on there, Number Three?" the captain growled.

Bracknell saw that one of the keys on his console was blinking red. He leaned a thumb on it and his center screen showed two women kneeling beside the unconscious body of what appeared to be a teenaged boy. His face was covered with blood.

"We've had an accident!" one of the women was shouting, looking up into the camera set far above her. "Emergency! We need help down here!"

"What the hell's going on over there?" the captain growled. Pointing at Bracknell, he commanded, "Get into a suit and go across to them."

"Me?" he piped.

"No, Jesus Christ and the twelve apostles. You, dammit! Get moving! Take a medical kit and a VR rig. Addie will handle whatever medical aid the kid needs."

That was how Bracknell learned the name of the captain's daughter: Addie.

He jumped from his comm console chair and loped to the main airlock. It took several minutes for him to wriggle into one of the nanofabric spacesuits stored in the lockers there, and minutes more for him to locate the medical kit and virtual reality rig stored nearby. Through the ship's intercom the captain swore and yelled at him every microsecond of the time.

"The kid could bleed to death by the time you get your dumb ass there!"

It was scary riding the trolley along the five-kilometer-long tether that connected the ship's two rotating units. The trolley was nothing more than a platform with a minuscule electric motor propelling it. With nothing protecting him except the flimsy nanofiber suit, Bracknell felt like a turkey wrapped in a plastic bag inside a microwave oven. He knew that high-energy radiation was sleeting down on him from the pale, distant Sun and the still-more-distant stars. He hoped that the suit's radiation protection was as good as its manufacturer claimed.

At last he reached the smelter unit and clambered through its airlock hatch. He felt much safer inside.

Despite its being unused for several years, the smelter bay was still gritty and smeared with dark swaths of sooty dust. As Bracknell pulled down the hood of his monomolecular-thin suit, a heavy, pungent odor filled his nostrils. The boy was semiconscious by the time Bracknell reached him. The two women were still kneeling by him. They had cleaned most of the blood from his face.

Clamping the VR rig around his head so that its camera was positioned just above his eyes, Bracknell asked, "What happened?"

One of the women pointed to the catwalk that circled high above the smelting ovens. "He fell."

"How in the world could he fall from up there?"

The woman snapped, "He's a teenaged boy. He was playing a game with his brother."

"Thank the Lord we're running at one-sixth g," said the other woman.

Then Bracknell heard the captain's daughter's voice in his earplug. "The bleeding seems stopped. We must test to see if he has a concussion."

For the better part of an hour Bracknell followed Addie's instructions. The boy had a concussion, all right, and a bad laceration on his scalp. Probably not a fractured skull, but they would X-ray him once they had him safely in the infirmary. No other bones seemed to be broken, although his right knee was badly swollen.

At Addie's direction he sprayed a bandage over the laceration and inflated a temporary splint onto the leg. With the women's help he got the still-groggy kid into a nanosuit. All three of them carried him to the airlock and strapped him onto the trolley.

Clinging to the trolley by a handhold, Bracknell again rode the length of the ship's connecting tether, surrounded by swarms of stars that gazed unblinkingly down at him. And invisible radiation that could kill him in an instant if his suit's protection failed. He tried not to think about that. He gazed at the stars and wished he could appreciate their beauty. One of them was Earth, he knew, but he couldn't tell which one it was.

Addie and the captain were waiting for him at the airlock on the other end of the tether. Together they carried the boy to the infirmary that had once been Bracknell's isolation cell and left him in Addie's care.

"What's a teenaged boy doing aboard the ship, captain?" Bracknell asked as he peeled himself out of the nanosuit, back at the airlock.

"My number one sails with his family. They make their quarters in the old smelter. Cheaper for him than paying rent at Ceres, and his wife's aboard to keep him company."

A cozy arrangement, Bracknell thought. But boys can get themselves into trouble. I'll bet they don't sail with us on the next trip from Ceres.

"Your shift on the bridge is just about finished," the captain said gruffly, as they headed back toward the bridge. "You might as well go back to your quarters. I can get along on the bridge without you."

It wasn't until he was back in his quarters, after a quick stop at the galley for some hot soup, that Bracknell realized his duty shift still had more than two hours to run.

Was the captain being kind to me? he wondered.

PURGATORY

His life had no purpose, Bracknell realized. He breathed, he ate, he slept, he worked on the bridge of *Alhambra* under the baleful scrutiny of Captain Farad. But why? What was the point of it? He lived for no reason, no goal, drifting through the cold dark emptiness of the Belt, sailing from one nameless chunk of rock to another, meaninglessly. He was like an automaton, working his brain-numbingly dull tasks as if under remote control while his mind churned the same agonizing visions over and over again: the tower, the collapse, the crushed and bleeding bodies.

Sometimes he thought of Lara and wondered what she was doing. Then he would tell himself that he wanted her to forget him, to build a new life for herself. One of the terms of his exile was that neither Lara nor anyone else he'd known on Earth would be told where he was. He was cut off from all communication with his former friends and associates; he was totally banished. For all those who once knew him on Earth, Mance Bracknell was dead and gone forever.

Except for Rev. Danvers. He got a message through to me; maybe he'll accept a message from me. Bracknell tried to put that out of his mind. What good would it do to talk to the minister? Besides, Danvers had helped to convict him. Maybe his call was in response to a guilty conscience, Bracknell thought. Damn the man! Better to be totally cut off than to have this slim hope of some communication, some link with his old life. Danvers was torturing him, holding out that meaningless thread of hope.

Now and then, between duty shifts and always with the captain's permission, Bracknell would pull on one of the nanofabric spacesuits and go outside the ship. Hanging at the end of a tether he would gaze out at the stars, an infinite universe of stars and worlds beyond counting. It made him feel small, insignificant, a meaningless mote in the vast spinning galaxy. He learned to find the blue dot that was Earth. It made him feel worse than ever. It reminded him of how alone he was, how far from warmth and love and hope. In time, he stopped his outside excursions. He feared that one day he would open his suit and let the universe end his existence.

The only glimmer of sunshine in his new life was the captain's daughter, Addie. Although *Alhambra* was a sizable ship, most of its volume was taken up by cargo holds and the smelting facility where the first mate's family lived. The crew numbered only twelve, at most, and often Farad sailed without a full complement of crew. The habitation module was small, almost intimate. Bracknell knew there were liaisons between crew members; he himself had been propositioned more than once, by men as well as women. He had always refused. None of them tempted him at all. He saw relationships form among crew members, both hetero and homosexual. He saw them break apart, too, sometimes in bitterness and sorrow, more than once in violence that the captain had to suppress with force.

Once in a while he bumped into Addie, quite literally, as they squeezed past one another in the ship's narrow passageways or happened to be in the galley at the same time. She always had a bright smile for him on her dark, almond-eyed face. Her figure was enticingly full and supple. Yet he never spoke more than a few words of polite conversation to her, never let himself react to the urgings of his glands.

One day, as he left the bridge after another tediously boring stint of duty, Bracknell ducked into the galley for a cup of coffee. Addie was sitting at the little square table, sipping from a steaming mug.

"How's the coffee today?" Bracknell asked.

"It's tea."

"Oh." He picked out a mug and poured from the ceramic urn, then pulled a chair out and sat next to her. Addie's eyes flicked to the open hatch and for an instant Bracknell thought she was going to jump to her feet and flee.

Instead, she seemed to relax, at least a little.

"Life on this ship isn't terribly exciting, is it?" he said.

"No, I suppose it isn't."

For long moments neither one of them knew what to say. At last Bracknell asked, "Your name—Addie. Is it short for Adelaide?"

She broke into an amused smile. "No, certainly not. My full name is Aditi."

"Aditi?"

"It is a Hindu name. It means 'free and unbounded.' It is the name of the mother of the gods."

Hindu, Bracknell thought. Of course. The captain told me she's from India. That explains the lilt in her accent.

"Free and unbounded," he echoed. "Kind of ironic, here on this nutshell of a ship."

"Yes," she agreed forlornly. Then she brightened. "But my father is making arrangements for me to marry. He has amassed a large dowry for me. In another few years I will be wed to a wealthy man and live in comfort back on Earth."

"You're engaged?"

"Oh, no, not yet. My father hasn't found the proper man for me. But he is seeking one out."

"And you'll marry whoever he picks?"

"Yes, of course."

"Don't you want to pick your husband for yourself?"

Her smile turned slightly remorseful. "What chance do I have for that, aboard this ship?"

Bracknell had to admit she was right.

He went back to his quarters, but before he could close the door, the captain pushed against it, glowering at him.

"I told you to keep away from my daughter."

"She was in the galley," Bracknell explained. "We spoke a few words together."

"About marriage."

"Yes." Bracknell felt his temper rising. "She's waiting for you to find her a husband."

"She'll have to wait a few more years. Fifteen's too young for marriage. Maybe it's old enough in India, but where I come from—"

"Fifteen? She's only fifteen?"

"That's right."

"How can she be a doctor . . . ?"

The captain's twisted lip sneered at him. "She's smart enough to run the computer's medical diagnostics. Like most doctors, she lets the computer program make the decisions."

"But—"

"You keep your distance from her."

"Yes, *sir*," Bracknell said fervently. Fifteen, he was thinking. That voluptuous body is only fifteen years old.

"Remember, I watch everything you do," the captain said. "Stay away from her."

He left Bracknell's quarters as abruptly as he'd entered. Bracknell stood there alone, shaking inside at the thought that a fifteen-year-old could look so alluring.

YAMAGATA ESTATE

He was the family's oldest retainer, a wizened, wrinkled man with a flowing white mane that swept past the shoulders of his modest sky-blue kimono. Nobuhiko remembered riding on those shoulders when he'd been a tot. The man had never accepted rejuvenation treatments, but his shoulders were still broad and only slightly sagging.

They walked together along the gravel path that wound through the carefully tended rock garden just inside the high wall that sheltered the Yamagata estate in the hills above New Kyoto. A cutting, clammy wind was blowing low gray clouds across the sky; Nobuhiko suppressed the urge to shiver beneath his light gray business suit. He had never shown such a weakness before his servant and he never willingly would.

Never show a weakness to anyone, he reminded himself. Not even yourself. He had been shocked when he learned that four million had been killed by the skytower's collapse. Four million! Nobu had known there would be deaths, that was unavoidable. It was what the military called "collateral damage." But four million! It had taken years to overcome the sense of guilt that had risen inside him like a tidal wave, threatening to engulf him. What difference does it make? he argued against his own conscience. Four hundred or four thousand or four million? They would have died anyway, sooner or later. The world goes on. I did what I had to do. For the good of the family, for the good of the corporation. For the good of Japan, even. What's done is done.

It hadn't been finished easily, he knew. There were still

more lives that had to be snuffed out, loyal men and women whose only offense had been to carry out Nobuhiko's wishes. They were repaid with death, the ultimate silencer. But now it's done, Nobuhiko thought. It's finished at last. That's what this old man has come to tell me.

Once they were too far from the house to be overheard, Nobu said politely, "The years have been very kind to you."

The old man dipped his chin slightly. "You are very gracious, sir."

With a wry grin, Nobu patted his belly. "I wish I could be as fit as you are."

The man said nothing. They both knew that Yamagata's tastes in food and wine, and his distaste for exercise, caused the difference between their figures.

Delicately changing the subject, the old man asked, "May I inquire as to your father's well-being?"

Nobu looked up at the sky. This man had served his father since he'd been a teenager. He still regards Saito as the head of the family, Nobu thought, no matter that Father has been retired in that lamasery for so many years.

"My father is well," he said at last. It was not a lie, although Nobu had not heard from his father for many months.

"I am pleased to hear it. He has great strength of character to abandon this world and take the hard path toward enlightenment."

And I do not have strength of character? Nobu snarled inwardly. Is this old assassin throwing an insult into my teeth?

Aloud, however, he said merely, "Yet some of us must remain in this world and carry its burdens."

"Most true, sir."

"How many years has it been since the skytower fell?" Nobuhiko asked.

"Not enough for anyone to dare suggest building another."

"So. That is good."

The old man dipped his chin again in acknowledgement.

"Have all the people who participated in the event been properly disposed of?"

"They have been tracked down and accounted for." Both men knew what that meant.

"All of them?"

The old man hesitated only a fraction of a second. "All but one."

"One?" Nobu snapped, suddenly angry. "After all this time, one of them still lives?"

"He is either very clever or very lucky."

"Who is he? Where is he?"

"He is the nanotechnology expert that we recruited from Selene."

Nobu could feel his pulse thundering in his ears. Before he could respond to his servant's words the old man added:

"He has changed his identity and his appearance several times. Even his retinal patterns have been altered, my agents report. The man is something of a genius."

"He must be found," Nobu said firmly. "And dealt with."

"He will be, I assure you."

"I don't want assurances. I want results!"

"Sir, please do not alarm yourself. The man is neutralized. He cannot tell anyone of his part in the skytower project without revealing his true identity. If he should dare to do that, we would locate him and deal with him. He is intelligent enough to understand that, so he maintains his silence."

"Not good enough," said Nobu. "I will not be held dependent on this fugitive's decisions."

"So I understand, sir. We are tracking him down."

"No one must know *why* are tracking him!"

"No one does, sir, except you and me."

Nobuhiko took a deep breath, trying to calm himself.

The old man added, "And once he is found and disposed of, I too will leave this world. Then only you will have the knowledge of the skytower program."

"You?"

"I have lived long enough. Once this obligation to you is filled, my master, I will join my honorable ancestors."

Nobu stood on the gravel path and stared at this relic from the ancient past. The chill wind blew the man's long white hair across his face, hiding his expression from Nobu. Still, Yamagata could see the implacable determination in those unblinking eyes.

BETRAYAL

Months slipped into years. *Alhambra* plied its slow, silent way through the Belt and then back toward Earth at least once a year. Bracknell saw the blue and white splendor of his home world, close enough almost to touch, bright clouds and sparkling seas and land covered with green. All his life was there, all his hopes and love and dreams. But he never reached it. The captain and other crew members shuttled down to the surface for a few days each time they visited Earth, but Bracknell stayed aboard the ship, knowing that no port of entry would accept an exile, not even for a day or two of ship's liberty. Nor would Selene or any of the other lunar settlements.

Each time, once *Alhambra*'s crew unloaded the refined metals it had carried in its hold and taken a few days' liberty, Captain Farad headed back to the dark silence of the Belt once more.

Like a vision of heaven, Bracknell said to himself as the

glowing blue and white sphere dwindled in the distance. It grew blurry as his eyes teared.

He grew a beard, then shaved it off. He had a brief affair with a woman who signed aboard as a crew member to pay for her passage on a one-way trip from Earth to Ceres, feeling almost ashamed of himself whenever he saw Addie. By the time his erstwhile lover left the ship he was glad to be rid of her.

The captain never relaxed his vigilance over his daughter, although he seemed to grow more tolerant of Bracknell holding casual conversations with her. He even invited Bracknell to have dinner with himself and his daughter, at rare intervals. The captain was sensitive enough never to talk about Earth nor to ask Bracknell about his former life.

Addie began to explain Buddhism to him, trying to help him accept the life that had been forced upon him.

"It is only temporary," she would tell him. "This life will wither away and a new life will begin. The great wheel turns slowly, but it does turn. You must be patient."

Bracknell listened and watched her animated face as she earnestly explained the path toward enlightenment. He never believed a word of it, but it helped to pass the time.

On some visits to Earth, *Alhambra* picked up other groups of convicts exiled to the Belt. The captain forbade Bracknell and the other crew members to have anything to do with them beyond what was absolutely necessary.

When fights broke out among the prisoners in the hold, the captain lowered their air pressure until everyone passed out. Then Bracknell and other crew members crammed the troublemakers into old-fashioned hard-shell spacesuits and tethered them outside the ship until they learned their lesson. It had happened many times, but Bracknell never became inured to it. Always he thought, There but for the grace of god go I.

Then he would ask himself, God? If there is a god he

must be as callous and capricious as the most sadistic tyrant in history. At least the Buddha that Addie tells me about doesn't pretend to control the world; he just sought a way to get out of it.

There is a way, Bracknell would remind himself late at night as he lay in his bunk, afraid to close his eyes and see again in his nightmares the skytower toppling, crushing the life out of so many millions, crushing the life he had once known. I can get out of this, he thought. Slice my wrists, swallow a bottle of pills from Addie's infirmary, seal myself in an airlock and pop the outer hatch. There are lots of ways to end this existence.

Yet he kept on living. Like a man on an endless treadmill he kept going through the paces of a pointless life, condemning himself for a coward because he lacked the guts to get off the wheel of life and find oblivion.

Except for Addie he had no friends, no companions. The captain tolerated him, even socialized with him now and then, but always kept a clear line of separation between them. The women that occasionally joined the crew hardly appealed to him, except when his needs overcame his reluctance. And even in the throes of sexual passion he thought of Lara.

If I could only see her, he thought. Talk to her. Even if it's only a few words.

In the midst of his tortured fantasies he remembered the old message from Rev. Danvers, back when he'd just started this miserable banishment. Call me, the minister had said. Despite the fact that he was supposed to be held incommunicado with everyone back on Earth, Danvers had held out that slim hope.

Bracknell was wise enough in the ways of his captain to ask Farad's permission before attempting to contact Danvers.

The captain snorted disdainfully. "Call somebody Earthside? Won't do you any good, they won't put the call through."

Desperate enough to overcome his fears, Bracknell replied, "You could put the call through for me, sir."

The captain scowled at him and said nothing. Bracknell returned to his duties, defeated.

Yet the next day, as Bracknell took up his station on the bridge, the captain said, "Take the comm console, Mr. Bracknell."

Feeling more curiosity than hope, Bracknell relieved the communications officer. The captain told him to put through a call for him to the Reverend Danvers, routing it through New Morality headquarters in Atlanta. His fingers trembling, Bracknell wormed the speaker plug into his ear and got to work.

With more than an hour's transit time for messages, there was no hope of a normal conversation. It took half his duty shift for Bracknell to get through to the communications program at Atlanta and learn that Danvers was now a bishop serving in Gabon, on Africa's west coast.

When Danvers's ruddy face finally came up on Bracknell's screen, the captain called from his command chair, "Go ahead and see if he'll talk to you."

Danvers was sitting at a polished ebony desk, wearing an open-necked black shirt with some sort of insignia pinned to the points of his collar. Behind him a window looked down on the busy streets and buildings of Libreville and, beyond, the blue Atlantic's white-frothed combers rolling up on a beach. A dark cylindrical form snaked through the greenery beyond the city and disappeared in the frothing surf. Bracknell's heart clutched inside him: it was the remains of the fallen skytower, still lying there after all these years.

It took more hours of one-way messages and long waits between them before Danvers realized who was calling him.

"Mance!" Surprise opened his eyes wide. "After so many years! I'm delighted to hear from you." The bishop turned slightly in his high-backed chair. "You can probably see the remains of the skytower. It's a tourist attraction here. People come from all over Africa to see it."

Bracknell's insides smoldered. A tourist attraction.

"The locals have stripped a lot from it. Filthy scavengers. We've had to post guards to protect the ruins, but still they sneak in and rip off parts."

Bracknell closed his eyes, trying to keep his temper under control. No sense getting angry with Danvers; he can't help the situation. Get to the point, tell him why you've contacted him.

He took a breath, then plunged in. "I was wondering, hoping, that you might get a message to Lara Tierney for me," he said, embarrassed at how much it sounded like begging. "I don't know where she is now, but I thought perhaps you could find her and give her a message for me."

Then he waited. His shift on the bridge ended and his replacement arrived at the comm console but the captain silently waved the woman away. Bracknell sat there attending to the ship's normal communications while his eyes constantly flicked back to the screen where Bishop Danvers's image sat frozen.

At last the attention light beneath that screen went from orange to green. The bishop's image shimmered slightly and became animated. But his expression looked doubtful, uncertain.

"Mance, she's Lara Molina now. She and Victor married more than eighteen months ago. I performed the ceremony."

Bracknell felt his face redden with sudden anger.

"Under the circumstances," Bishop Danvers continued,

"I don't think it would be wise for you to contact her. After all, it would be illegal, wouldn't it? And there's no sense bringing up old heartaches, opening old wounds. After all, it's taken her all this time to get you out of her mind and begin her life again. Don't you agree that it would be better if you—"

Bracknell cut the connection with a vicious stab of his thumb on the keyboard.

Married, his mind echoed. She married Victor. The man who betrayed me. And that pompous idiot performed the ceremony. He betrayed me, too. They've all betrayed me!

REVELATION

For weeks Bracknell stormed through his duties aboard *Alhambra,* raging inwardly at Molina and Danvers. He wanted to be angry with Lara, too; he wanted to be furious with her. Yet he found he couldn't be. He couldn't expect her to live out the rest of her life alone. But with Victor? She married that lying, backstabbing son of a bitch?

She doesn't realize that Victor betrayed me, Bracknell told himself; Lara doesn't know that Victor lied in his testimony at the trial. But Victor knew, and so did Danvers. Of that Bracknell was certain. They had combined to put him out of the way so that Victor could have Lara for himself.

Bracknell understood it all now. Victor betrayed him because he wanted Lara for himself. Once the skytower collapsed, Victor had the perfect opportunity to get me out of his way forever. And Danvers helped him, of that Bracknell was certain.

Once the skytower collapsed, he repeated to himself. Could they have *made* the tower collapse? Caused it? Sabotaged it? Bracknell wrestled with that idea for weeks on end. No. How could they? Victor didn't know enough about the tower's construction to bring it down. He's a biologist, not a structural engineer. It would take a team of trained saboteurs, demolition experts. It would take money and planning and a ruthless cold-bloodedness that was frighteningly beyond Victor's capability. Or Danvers's. He doubted that even the New Morality at its most fanatical had the viciousness to deliberately bring the tower down. Or the competence.

No, Bracknell concluded. Victor simply took advantage of his opportunity. Took advantage of me. And Danvers helped him.

Still, his rage boiled inside him, made him morose and curt with everyone around him, even Addie. The captain watched his new attitude and said nothing, except once, when Bracknell was assigned to escorting a new group of convicts into their makeshift quarters down in the hold. One of the prisoners started a scuffle with another one. Bracknell dove into them swinging his stun wand like a club and beat them both unconscious.

"You're starting to come back to life," the captain said after a pair of husky crewmen had pulled him off the bleeding prisoners. He made a strange, twisted smile. "You're starting to feel pain again."

"I've felt pain before," Bracknell muttered as they trudged up the passageway toward the bridge.

"Maybe," said the captain. "But now you can feel the demon gnawing at your guts. Now you know how I felt when they killed my wife. How I still feel."

Bracknell stared at him with new understanding.

Back and forth through the Belt sailed *Alhambra,* and then set out on the long, tedious journey to Earth to deliver refined metals and pick up convicts. It seemed to Bracknell, when he thought about it, that there were always more convicts waiting to be sent out to the Belt, always more men and women who'd run afoul of the law. Teenagers, too. The governments of Earth had found a convenient way to get rid of troublemakers: dump them out in the Asteroid Belt. They must be making the laws tighter all the time, more restrictive, he thought. Or maybe they're just using banishment to the Belt instead of other punishments.

On one of *Alhambra*'s stops at Earth, still another set of convicts was herded into the empty cargo hold—sixteen men and eleven women, most of them looking too frightened to cause any trouble. Only two of the bunch had been guilty of violent crimes: a strong-arm mugger and a murderer who had stabbed her boyfriend to death.

Bracknell was surprised, then, when the alarm hooted shortly after they had locked the prisoners in the hold. From his duty station on the bridge he looked over at the intercom screen. Two men were beating up a third, a tall, skinny scarecrow of a man. He saw their hapless victim trying to defend himself by wrapping his long arms around his head, but his two attackers knocked him to the metal deck with a rain of vicious body blows, then began kicking him.

"Get down there!" the captain snapped to Bracknell as he tapped on the controls set into the armrest of his command chair. Bracknell jumped up from his own seat, ducked through the hatch and sprinted toward the hold. He knew that the captain was dropping the air pressure in there hard enough to pop eardrums. They'll all be unconscious by the time I get to the hold, he thought.

He could hear the footfalls of two other crewmen following him down the passageway. Stopping at the hatch only long enough to slip on the oxygen masks hanging on the wall, the three of them opened the hatch and pulled out three of the unconscious bodies: the bloodied scarecrow

and his two attackers. Leaving the other crewmen to deal
with the attackers, Bracknell picked up the victim and
started running toward the infirmary. The man was as light
as a bird, nothing but skin and bones.

Addie was waiting at the infirmary. She allowed Bracknell to lay the unconscious man on one of the two beds
there as she powered up the diagnostic sensors built into
the bulkhead.

"You should get back to the bridge," she said to Bracknell as she began strapping the man down.

"As soon as he's secure," Bracknell said, fastening a strap
across the man's frail chest. "He's a prisoner, after all."

The man moaned wretchedly but did not open his eyes.
Bracknell saw that they were both swollen shut, and his
nose appeared to be broken. Blood covered most of his face
and was spattered over his gray prison-issue coveralls.

"Go!" Addie said in an urgent whisper. "I can take care
of him now."

Bracknell headed back to the bridge. By the time he slid
back into the chair before his console, he could see that the
other convicts were stirring in the hold, regaining consciousness as the air pressure returned to normal. The two
attackers were already sealed into hard-shell space-suits
and being dragged to an airlock.

"What started the fight?" he wondered aloud.

"What difference does it make?" the captain retorted. "It
wasn't much of a fight, anyway. Looked to me like those two
gorillas wanted to beat the scarecrow to death. He probably tried to proposition them."

Half an hour later Bracknell punched up the outside
camera view. One of the spacesuited figures was floating
inertly at the end of a buckyball tether. The other had
crawled along the length of his tether and was pounding at
the airlock hatch with a gloved fist.

"Too bad there's no radio in his suit," the captain remarked sourly. "I imagine we'd pick up some choice vocabulary."

Once his shift was finished, Bracknell headed for his quarters. As he passed the open door of the infirmary, though, Addie called to him.

He stopped at the doorway and saw that she was at the minuscule desk in the infirmary's anteroom, the glow from the desktop screen casting an eerie greenish light on her face.

"You were the chief of the skytower project, weren't you," Addie said. It was not a question.

His insides twitched, but Bracknell answered evenly, "Yes. And this is where it got me."

"Permanently exiled from Earth."

He nodded wordlessly.

Glancing over her shoulder at the open doorway to the infirmary's beds, Addie said, "The man you brought in, he keeps mumbling something about the skytower."

"Lots of people remember the skytower," Bracknell said bitterly. "It was the biggest disaster in history."

She shook her head. "But this man is not who he claims to be in his prison file."

"What do you mean?"

"The patient in the infirmary," she said, "keeps babbling about the skytower. He says they want to kill him because he knows about the skytower."

"Knows what?"

Addie's almond eyes were steady, somber. "I don't know. But I thought that you would want to speak with him."

"You're damned right I do."

She got up from the desk and Bracknell followed her into the infirmary. Her patient was asleep or unconscious as they squeezed into the cramped compartment. The other bed was unoccupied. Medical monitors beeped softly. The place had that sterile smell of antiseptics overlaying the metallic tang of blood.

Bracknell saw a tall, very slim, long-limbed man stretched out on the narrow infirmary bed. He was still in the clothes he'd been wearing when he'd been hurt: a pair of gray coveralls, wrinkled and dark with perspiration, spattered with his own blood. His face was battered, swollen, a bandage sprayed over one lacerated brow, another along the length of his broken nose. His body was immobilized by the restraining straps, and a slim plastic intravenous tube was inserted in his left forearm.

Addie called up the diagnostic computer and scans of the man's body sprang up on the wall beside his bed.

"He has severe internal injuries," she said, in a whisper. "They did a thorough job of beating him. A few more minutes and he would have died."

"Will he make it?"

"The computer's prognosis is not favorable. I have called back to Selene to ask for a medevac flight, but I doubt that they will go to the trouble for a prisoner."

Bracknell asked, "What's his name?"

"That's just it," she said, with a tiny frown that creased the bridge of her nose. "I'm not certain. His prison file shows him as Jorge Quintana, but when I ran a scan of his DNA profile the Earthside records came up with the name Toshikazu Koga."

"Japanese?"

"Japanese descent, third generation American. Raised in Selene, where he graduated with honors in molecular engineering."

Bracknell gaped at her. "Nanotechnology?"

"I believe so."

Bracknell stared down at the unconscious convict. He did not look Asian, there were no epicanthic folds in his closed eyes. Yet there was an odd, unsettling quality about his face. The skin was stretched tight over prominent cheekbones and a square jaw that somehow looked subtly wrong for the rest of his face, as if someone had roughed it out and pasted it onto him. The color of his skin was strange, too, a mottled gray. Bracknell had never seen a skin tone like it.

He looked back at Addie. "Can you wake him up?"

THE PRISONER'S TALE

"They'll kill me sooner or later," said Toshikazu Koga, his voice little more than a painfully labored whisper. "There's no place left that I can run to."

Bracknell was bending over his infirmary bed to hear him better. Addie sat on the other, unused bed.

"Who wants to kill you?" she asked. "Why?"

"The skytower—"

"What do you know about the skytower?" Bracknell demanded.

"I was a loyal follower, a Believer . . ."

"What about the skytower?"

"I didn't know. I should have guessed." Toshikazu coughed. "Truth is, I didn't want to know."

It took all of Bracknell's self-control to keep from grabbing the man by the shoulders and shaking his story out of him.

"What was it that you didn't want to know?" Addie asked gently.

"All that money. They wouldn't pay all that money for something legitimate. I should have refused. I should have . . ." His voice faded away.

"Damn!" Bracknell snapped. "He's passed out again."

Addie's eyes flicked to the monitors on the wall. "We must let him rest."

"But he knows something about the skytower! Something to do with nanotechnology and the tower."

Getting up from the bed and looking him squarely in the eyes, Addie said, "We'll learn nothing from him if he dies. Let him rest. Let me try to save his life."

Knowing she was right despite his desperate desire to wring the truth out of the unconscious patient, Bracknell nodded tightly. "Let me know when he comes to."

He got as far as the doorway to the anteroom, then turned. "And don't let anyone else near him. No one!"

She looked alarmed at the vehemence of his command.

Little by little, in bits and pieces over the next two days, they wormed Toshikazu's story out of him while Addie repeatedly called to Selene to beg for a medevac mission before *Alhambra* coasted too far from the Moon.

"The best I can do is stabilize him. He'll die unless he gets proper medical help."

Bracknell hoped he'd stay alive long enough to reveal what he knew about the skytower.

Toshikazu Koga had been an engineer in Selene's nanotechnology laboratory, working mainly on nanomachines designed to separate pure metals out of the ores in asteroids. Instead of the rock rats digging out the ores and smelting them the old-fashioned way, nanomachines could pull out individual atoms of a selected metal while the human miners waited and watched from the comforts of their spacecraft.

Toshikazu was also a Believer, a devout, churchgoing member of the New Morality. Although his fellow churchgoers disapproved of nanotechnology, he saw nothing wrong with its practice on the Moon or elsewhere in space.

"It's not like we're on Earth, with ten billion people

jammed in cheek by jowl," he would tell those who scowled at his profession. "Here on the Moon nanomachines produce the air we breathe and the water we drink. They separate helium three from the regolith sands to power the fusion generators. And now I'm helping the miners in the Asteroid Belt, making their lives safer and more profitable."

But there was another side to his nanotech work. His brother Takeo ran a lucrative clinic at the Hell Crater complex, where he used Toshikazu's knowledge of nanotechnology for medical purposes. Because of his religious beliefs, Toshikazu felt uneasy about his brother's using nanomachines to help rejuvenate aging men and women. Or for the trivial purposes of cosmetic surgery.

"Why use a scalpel or liposuction," his brother would ask him, "when you can produce nanobugs that will tighten a sagging jawline or trim a bulging belly?"

Toshikazu knew that his brother was doing more than lifting breasts and buttocks. Men would come to him furtively, asking to have their faces completely changed. Takeo accepted their money and never asked why they wanted to alter their appearance. Toshikazu knew they were criminals trying to escape the law.

He was surprised, then, when a pair of churchmen visited him in his laboratory in Selene.

"At first I thought they wanted me to give them evidence against my brother," he whispered painfully to Bracknell from his infirmary bed. "But no . . . it was worse than that . . ."

One of the churchmen was a high official of the New Morality. The other was a Chinese member of the Flower Dragon movement. What they wanted was a set of nanomachines that could destroy buckyball fibers.

Bracknell clutched at the injured man's arm when he heard that, making him yowl so loud that Addie rushed in to see what had happened.

"You'll kill him!" she screamed at Bracknell.

"I . . . I'm sorry," he stammered. "I didn't mean to hurt him."

Toshikazu lay on the bed, his eyes glazed with pain. Addie demanded that Bracknell leave the infirmary.

"I'll tell you when you can come back," she said.

For a moment he thought he'd push her out of his way and get the rest of the story from the injured man. Then he took a deep breath and wordlessly left the infirmary.

All that night his mind seethed with what Toshikazu was telling him. He checked in at the infirmary on his way to the bridge the next morning, but Addie would not let him past the anteroom. "Let him rest," she said. "He'll be no use to you dead."

Bracknell could hardly keep his attention on his duties. The captain snarled at him several times for his mental lapses. Then a message came in from another vessel, a Yamagata torch ship named *Hiryu*. Bracknell saw on the comm console's main screen an aged Japanese man with long snow-white hair flowing past his shoulders.

"We have heard your call for a medical evacuation," said the white-haired man. "We can reach you in six hours and evacuate your injured prisoner."

Bracknell was tempted to tell the man not to bother; he didn't want Toshikazu removed from *Alhambra* until he'd gotten his full story out of him. But, feeling the captain's eyes on his back, he dutifully switched the call to the captain's screen. In two minutes they had agreed for *Hiryu* to pick up the convict and ferry him back to Selene's medical center.

"*Hiryu*," the captain muttered after the call was terminated. "That means 'flying dragon' in Japanese, I think."

As soon as his shift was finished, Bracknell hurried down the passageway to the infirmary. Addie wasn't in the anteroom; he saw her bending over Toshikazu's bed. He could see from the tortured look on her face that something was very wrong.

"He's dying," she said.

"A ship is on its way to pick him up," Bracknell said, torn between his need to hear Toshikazu's full story and a humanitarian instinct to get proper medical care for the man. "It'll be here in less than four hours."

"Thank the gods," breathed Addie.

"Is he awake?"

She nodded. Bracknell pushed past her to the injured man's bedside. Toshikazu's eyes were open, but they looked unfocused, dazed from the analgesics Addie had been pumping into him.

"I've got to know," Bracknell said, bending over him. "What did those church people want from you? What did you do for them?"

"Gobblers," Toshikazu whispered.

Bracknell heard Addie, behind him, draw in her breath. She knew what gobblers were. Nanomachines that disassembled molecules, tore them apart atom by atom. Gobblers had been used as murder weapons, ripping apart protein molecules.

"To break up the buckyball fibers of the skytower?" Bracknell asked urgently.

Toshikazu nodded and closed his eyes.

"Gobblers are illegal," said Addie. "Even in Selene . . ."

"But you made them, didn't you?" Bracknell said to Toshikazu.

He understood it all now. Gobblers tore apart the skytower's structure at the geostationary level. That's why the lower half of the tower collapsed while the upper half went spinning off into deep space. And the evidence was at the bottom of the Atlantic's midocean ridge, being melted away by the hot magma boiling into the ocean water.

"I made . . . gobblers . . . for them," Toshikazu admitted, his eyes still closed.

"You made the gobblers for the Flower Dragon people?" Bracknell asked. "Or for the New Morality?"

With a weary shake of his head, Toshikazu replied, "Neither. They were . . . merely the agents . . . for . . ."

"For who?"

"Yamagata."

Bracknell gaped at the dying man. Yamagata Corporation. Of course! It would take a powerful interplanetary corporation to plan and execute the destruction of the skytower.

"Yamagata," Toshikazu repeated. "I was the last . . . the last one to know . . ."

Addie looked up at Bracknell. "Now we know."

"No!" said Toshikazu. "I've told you . . . nothing. Nothing. I died . . . without telling you . . . anything. If they thought you knew . . ."

His eyes closed. His head slumped to one side.

And Bracknell said, "Yamagata."

CRIME AND PUNISHMENT

Bracknell was still in the infirmary with Addie and the unconscious Toshikazu when the rescue team from *Hiryu* came in, led by Captain Farad. The elderly Japanese man was accompanied by two young muscular types, also Asian, who gently lifted Toshikazu onto a stretcher and carried him away.

The old man stayed and asked Addie for Toshikazu's

medical file. She popped the chip from the computer storage and handed it to him.

With a sibilant hiss of thanks, the old man pushed his long hair back away from his face and asked her, "Does this chip include audio data, perhaps?"

"Audio data?" asked Addie.

"You must have spoken to him extensively while he was under your care," said the old man. "Are your conversations included in this chip?"

She glanced at Bracknell, who said, "He was unconscious most of the time. When he did talk, it was mostly rambling, incomprehensible."

"I see." The old man looked from Bracknell's face to Addie's and then back again. "I see," he repeated.

Captain Farad, impatient as usual, asked, "Is there anything else you need?"

The old man stroked his chin for a moment, as though thinking it over. "No," he said at last. "I believe I have everything I need."

He left with the captain.

Addie broke into a pleased smile. "I think we saved his life, Mance."

"Maybe," Bracknell said, still gazing at the open hatch where the captain and the Japanese elder had left.

"There's nothing more to do here," said Addie. "I'm going to my quarters and take a good long shower."

Bracknell nodded.

"Will you walk me home?" she asked, smiling up at him.

Her quarters were down the passageway; his own a dozen meters farther. When they got to her door, Addie clutched at his arm and tugged him into her compartment.

He began to protest, "Your father—"

"—Is busy seeing off the rescue team," Addie interrupted.

"And there are no cameras in my quarters; I've made certain of that."

"But I shouldn't be in here alone with you."

"Are you afraid?" She grinned impishly.

"Damned right!"

The compartment was much like his own quarters: a bunk, a built-in desk and dresser, accordion-pleat doors for the closet and lavatory.

Addie touched the control panel on the wall and the overhead lights turned off, leaving only the lamp on the bedside table.

"Addie, this is wrong." But he heard the blood pulsing through his body, felt his heart pounding.

She stood before him, smiling knowingly. "Don't you like me, Mance? Not even a little?"

"It's not that—"

"Today is my seventeenth birthday, Mance. I am legally an adult now. And rather wealthy, you know. I can control my own dowry now. I can make my own decisions."

She reached up to the tab at the throat of her coveralls and slid the zipper all the way down to her crotch. She wasn't wearing a bra, he saw. Her body was young and full and beckoning.

"I love you, Mance," Addie murmured, stepping up to him and sliding her arms around his neck.

He clutched her and pulled her close and kissed her upturned face.

And heard the door behind him burst open with a furious roar from Captain Farad. Before Bracknell could turn to face her father, he felt the searing pain of a stun wand at full charge and blacked out as he slumped to the floor.

Aboard *Hiryu* the elderly Japanese assassin composed a final message to Nobuhiko Yamagata. He encrypted the video himself, a task which took no little time, even with the aid of the ship's computer:

"Most illustrious master: The last individual is now in our care. He will be treated as required. Unfortunately, he has probably contaminated the vessel in which we found him. Therefore that vessel will be dealt with. This will be my last transmission to you or anyone in this life. Sayonara."

When Bracknell came back to consciousness he was already in a hard-shell suit, its helmet sealed to the neck ring. The captain was glaring at him, his eyes raging with fury.

"I told you to keep away from her!" he screamed at Bracknell, loud enough to penetrate the helmet's thick insulation. "I *warned* you!"

"Where is she? What have you done—"

"She's in her quarters, crying. She'll get over it. I'll have to marry her off sooner than I planned, but it'll be better than having her throw herself at scum like you."

Bracknell felt himself being hauled to his feet and realized there were at least two other crewmen behind him. His legs wouldn't function properly; the stun wand's charge was still scrambling his nervous system.

"Drag him down to the auxiliary airlock," the captain snarled. "That goddamn *Hiryu* is still connected to the main lock."

"But I didn't do anything!" Bracknell protested.

"The hell you didn't!"

Like a sack of limp laundry Bracknell was hauled along the passageway and into the airlock. The captain clipped a tether to the waist of his spacesuit and handed him the loose end.

"You can find a cleat for yourself and clip onto it. Otherwise you can float out to infinity, for all I care."

Bracknell tottered uncertainly in the hard-shell suit. His legs tingled as if they'd been asleep. He's going to kill me! he thought. I'm going to die out there! There's no way I can survive in a suit all the way out to the Belt. Even if he sends out more air and food how can I—

The inner airlock hatch slammed shut and Bracknell felt through the thick soles of his boots the pump starting to chug the air out of the darkened metal chamber. In less than a minute the pump stopped and the outer hatch swung open silently.

Bracknell saw the cold distant stars staring at him. On unsteady legs still twitching from the stun charge, he clumped to the lip of the hatch. Peering out along the ship's skin, he saw a set of cleats within arm's reach. For a moment he thought of refusing to go outside. I'll just stay here in the airlock, he told himself. Then he realized that the captain would simply have a few men suit up and throw him out, maybe without even the tether. So, like a man going through the motions of a nightmare, he attached the end of his tether to the nearest cleat and then stepped out into nothingness. The airlock hatch slid shut behind him.

He glided silently as the tether unreeled, then was pulled up short. A sardonic voice in his head mocked, You're at the end of your tether. A helluva way to die. He realized that despite his contemplation of suicide, despite Addie's tutoring him in the desirelessness of the Buddhist path, he very much wanted to live.

Why? Why not just open the seal of this helmet and end it all here and now? The answer rose in his mind like the fireball of a nuclear explosion: Vengeance. Victor and Danvers had betrayed him. And Yamagata was the biggest bastard of them all. Yamagata had brought down the sky-tower, and that had given Victor the opportunity to steal Lara from him.

Molina. Danvers. Yamagata. He would live to work his

vengeance on them. But you won't live long enough to succeed, that mocking inner voice told him.

Looking around as he floated in the emptiness he saw,
on the far side of *Alhambra*'s curving hull, that the other
ship was still linked. What was its name? *Hiryu,* the captain had said. Flying dragon. Why would it still be connected? If they intend to bring Toshikazu back to Selene
they ought to light off as quickly as they can.

Then Bracknell remembered that *Hiryu* was a Yamagata
vessel. And Yamagata certainly wasn't here to help Toshikazu recover from his wounds.

The silent explosion blinded him, but it did not surprise
him.

DEATH AND TRANSFIGURATION

Whirling blindly through space, Bracknell knew for
certain that he was a dead man now.

He could feel himself spinning giddily. The explosion must have torn my tether free of *Alhambra,* I
thought. I'll twirl like this forever. I'll probably be the first
man to reach Alpha Centauri, even though I'll be too dead
to know it.

Then the realization hit him. Addie! The captain. All the
people on *Alhambra.* Did the bastards kill everybody?
Madly he tried to paw at his tear-filled eyes; his gloved
hands bumped into the thick quartz visor of his helmet.
Blinking furiously, he tried to force his vision to return. All
he saw was the searing after-image of the explosion's fireball.

They wouldn't have blown up the whole ship, he said to

himself. Why would they? They wanted Toshikazu and they got him. Why the explosion? An accident?

No, he realized. They suspected that Toshikazu had been talking to us. They wanted no witnesses, nobody left alive. Dead men tell no tales. Neither do dead women, even if they're only seventeen years old. His eyes filled with tears again, but now he was sobbing for Addie, killed because of me. The final casualty of the skytower. They killed her and everybody else because of me.

Then he thought of Yamagata. I didn't kill them, Bracknell reminded himself. He did. Yamagata. He's back on Earth, living in luxury, with the blood of millions on his hands.

Slowly his vision returned. Eventually he could see the wreckage of *Alhambra* spreading outward like dandelion seeds puffed by the wind. It was dwindling, dwindling as he himself spiraled away through space.

Yamagata did this. Bracknell kept the image of Saito Yamagata in the forefront of his mind. It kept him alive, gave him a reason to keep on breathing. He had never met the mighty founder of Yamagata Corporation, but he had seen vids of the man on the news net. Yamagata was supposed to have retreated to some monastery in Tibet, Bracknell remembered, but the newscasters smugly reported that this was just a ruse. The old man was still running his interplanetary corporate maneuvers, they assured their watchers.

Saito Yamagata, Bracknell told himself as he tumbled endlessly through space. Saito Yamagata. When he finally lapsed into unconsciousness he was still burning with hatred of Saito Yamagata.

He opened his eyes and almost smiled. Bracknell found himself lying on an infirmary bed, safe and warm, with a crisp sheet over his naked body. It was all a dream, he thought. A nightmare.

But the dark-skinned, slightly plump nurse who stepped into his view was a stranger. And she wore a white uniform with the crescent logo of Selene on her left breast, just above a name tag that identified her as NORRIS, G.

Bracknell blinked at her, then croaked, "Where am I?"

She smiled pleasantly at him, white teeth gleaming in her dark face. "A classic question."

"But where—"

"You're in the hospital at Selene. A salvage team picked you up when they went out to claim the wreck of *Alhambra*."

"*Alhambra*?"

The nurse fussed over the intravenous drip inserted in Bracknell's arm as she replied, "From what I hear, *Alhambra* collided with some Yamagata ship and they both blew up. You're lucky to be alive."

Raising his head anxiously, Bracknell asked, "Did anybody else . . . are there are any other . . ."

"No, you're the only one who survived. What were you doing outside in a spacesuit?" Without waiting for an answer the nurse went on, "Whatever, it saved your life. Were you outside doing some repairs, or what?"

He sank back onto the pillow. "I don't remember," he lied.

The nurse cast him a doubtful glance. "There wasn't any ID on you when they brought you in. What's your name?"

Bracknell started to reply, then caught himself. "I . . . I don't remember," he said.

"You don't remember your own name?"

Trying to look upset about it, Bracknell said, "I can't remember *anything*. It's all a blank."

"Posttraumatic shock," muttered the nurse. "We'll have to run some scans on you, then, and check them against the files."

She left Bracknell's bedside. He raised himself up on his elbows and looked around. He was in a cubicle created by portable plastic partitions. His clothes were nowhere in sight. And he knew he had to get out of this hospital before the computer scans identified him as Mance Bracknell, the criminal who'd been sentenced to lifelong exile.

In his office in New Kyoto, Nobuhiko Yamagata watched the image of the white-haired servant as he delivered his final message. It's finished, then, he said to himself. At last it's finished. I can breathe freely again.

Within an hour the news came that a corporation ship named *Hiryu* had been destroyed in an accident that also wiped out the freighter *Alhambra*. No survivors were reported.

Nobu's first instinct was to uncork a bottle of champagne, but he knew that would be incorrect. Besides, he found that he didn't feel like celebrating. Instead, a profound sense of gloom settled upon him like a massive weight.

It's finished, he repeated to himself. This terrible business is finished at last.

BOOK IV

VENGEANCE

Vengeance is in my heart, death in my hand,
Blood and revenge are hammering in my head.

SELENE HOSPITAL

After a bland meal, Bracknell pushed his tray aside and got out of the hospital bed. The floor tiles felt comfortably warm to his bare feet. He seemed strong enough, no wobbles or shakes. The cubicle was barely large enough to hold his bed. Portable plastic partitions, he saw. No closet. Not even a lavatory. And this damned IV hooked into my arm.

He cracked the accordion door a centimeter and peeped out. The same nurse was striding down the corridor in his direction.

Bracknell hopped back into the bed and pulled the sheet over his naked body.

She pushed the door back and gave him an accusing look. "I saw you peeking out the door. Feeling better, huh?"

"Yes," said Bracknell.

"Long as you're taking solid food we can disconnect this drip," she said, gripping his arm and gently pulling the IV tube out of him. Even so, Bracknell winced.

As she sprayed a bandage over his punctured arm, Nurse Norris said happily, "You're going to have a pair of visitors, Mr. X."

"Visitors?" He felt immediately alarmed.

"Yep. Psychotechnician to talk to you about your amnesia, and some suit from the corporate world. Don't know what he wants."

"Can I get some clothes?" Bracknell asked. "It's kind of awkward like this."

Norris looked at one of the monitors on the wall behind the bed and fiddled with her handheld remote. "The coveralls you came in with were pretty raw. I sent 'em to the laundry. I'll see if I can find them for you. Otherwise it's hospital issue."

"Before the visitors arrive?"

She gave him that unhappy look again. "For a charity case you make a lot of demands."

Before he could answer, though, she ducked back outside and slid the partition closed.

Once I get my clothes back I can make a run for it, Bracknell said to himself. I can't let them scan me; I've got to get out of here before they find out who I am.

And go where? I'm in Selene, on the Moon. As soon as they find out who I am they'll slap me into another ship and send me back to the Belt. Where can I hide?

He thought about escaping back to Earth, to Lara. But he knew that was ridiculous. How can I get to Earth from here? Besides, she's Victor's wife now. Even if she wanted to hide me, she wouldn't be able to. Then he realized that he hadn't the faintest idea of where on Earth Lara might be. Shaking his head morosely, he decided that going back to Earth would be impossible.

Toshikazu said he had a brother, he remembered. What was his name? Takeo. Takeo Koga. And he's here, on the Moon. Somewhere in the Hell Crater complex. Maybe I can get to him. Maybe—

The partition slid open again and somebody, he couldn't see who, tossed a flapping pair of gray coveralls at him. In the soft lunar gravity they arched languidly through the air and landed softly on his bed. By then the door had slid shut again. A new set of underwear was tucked into one of his coverall sleeves.

He was sealing the Velcro seam up his torso when someone rapped politely on his door frame. They can see me, Bracknell realized, looking up toward the ceiling. They must have a camera in here somewhere.

He sat on the bed and swung his legs up onto the sheet. "Come in," he called. Then he realized that his feet were bare. They hadn't brought any shoes.

Two men entered his cubicle as Bracknell touched the control stud that raised the bed to a sitting position. One of the men wore a white hospital smock over what looked like a sports shirt and corduroy slacks. He was round-faced and a little pudgy, but his eyes seemed aware and alert. The other was in a gray business suit and white turtleneck, hawk-nosed, his baggy-eyed expression morose.

"I'm Dr. DaSilva," said the medic. "I understand you're having a little trouble remembering things."

Bracknell nodded warily.

"My name is Pratt," said the suit. "I represent United Life and Accident Assurance, Limited." His accent sounded vaguely British.

"Insurance?" Bracknell asked.

DaSilva grinned. "Well, you remember insurance, at least."

Bracknell fell back on a pretense of confusion. "I don't understand. . . ."

Pratt said, "We have an awkward situation here. Like many ship's crews, the crew of *Alhambra* was covered by a shared-beneficiary accident policy."

"Shared beneficiary?"

"It's rather like an old-fashioned tontine. In case of a fatal accident, the policy's principal is paid to the survivors among the crew—after the deceaseds' beneficiaries have been paid, of course."

"What does that mean?" Bracknell asked, feeling nervous at being under DaSilva's penetrating gaze.

"It means, sir," said Pratt, "that as the sole survivor of *Alhambra*'s fatal accident, you are the secondary beneficiary of each member of the crew; you stand to gain in excess of ten million New International Dollars."

Bracknell gasped. "Ten million?"

"Yes," Pratt replied, quite matter-of-factly. "Of course, we must pay out to the families of the deceased; they *are* the primary beneficiaries. But there will still be some ten million or so remaining in the policy's fund."

"And it goes to me?"

Pratt cleared his throat before answering, "It goes to you, providing you can identify yourself. The company has a regulation against paying to anonymous persons or John Does. International laws are involved, you know."

"I . . . don't remember . . . very much," Bracknell temporized.

"Perhaps I can help," said DaSilva.

"I hope so," Bracknell said.

"Before we start scanning your brain to see if there's any physical trauma, let me try a simple test."

"What is it?"

DaSilva pulled a handheld from the breast pocket of his smock. Smiling cheerfully, he said, "This is what I call the ring-a-bell test. I'm going to read off the names of *Alhambra*'s crew and you tell me if any of them ring a bell."

Bracknell nodded, thinking furiously. Ten million dollars! If I can get my hands on that money—

"Wallace Farad," DaSilva called out.

Bracknell blinked at him. "The captain's name was Farad."

"Good! Your memory isn't a total blank."

"You couldn't forget the captain," said Bracknell fervently. Then he remembered that the captain was dead. And Addie. And all the rest of them. Dead. Killed by Yamagata.

"I'll skip the women's names," DaSilva was saying. "I don't think you had a sex-change procedure before they picked you up."

Pratt chuckled politely. Bracknell thought of Addie and said nothing.

DaSilva read off several more names of the crew while Bracknell tried to figure out what he should do.

Finally DaSilva said, ". . . and Dante Alexios. That's the last of them."

Dante Alexios had been the vessel's second mate, Bracknell knew. He didn't know much about him except that he wasn't a convict and he didn't have a wife or children.

"Dante Alexios," he repeated. "Dante Alexios."

"Ring a bell?" DaSilva asked hopefully.

Bracknell looked up at the psychotechnician. "Dante Alexios! That's who I am!"

Pratt looked less than pleased. "All well and good. But I'm afraid you're going to have to prove your identity before I can allow the release of the policy's payout."

HELL CRATER

atch-22, Bracknell thought as he sat on his bed. I can get ten million dollars if I can prove I'm Dante Alexios, so I need to let them scan my body. But as soon as they do they'll find out I'm Mance Bracknell and ship me back out to the Belt as a convict.

A different nurse breezed into his cubicle and shoved a data tablet onto his lap. "Press your right thumb on the square at the bottom," she said.

Bracknell looked up at her. She was young, with frizzy red hair, rather pretty.

"What's this?" he asked, almost growling.

"Standard permission form for a full-spectrum body scan. We need your thumbprint."

I don't want a scan, Bracknell said to himself, and I don't

want to give them a thumbprint; they could compare it with Alexios's real print.

He handed the tablet back to the nurse. "No."

She looked stunned. "Whattaya mean, no? You've got to do it or we can't do the scan on you."

"I don't want a scan. Not yet."

"You've got to have a body scan," the nurse said, somewhere between confused and angry at his refusal. "It says so in your chart."

"Not now," Bracknell said. "Maybe tomorrow."

"They can *make* you take a scan, whether you want to or not."

"The hell they can!" Bracknell snapped. The nurse flinched back half a step. "I'm not some criminal or lunatic. I'm a free citizen and I won't be coerced into doing something I don't want to do."

She stared at him, bewildered. "But it's for your own good."

"I'll decide what's good for me, thank you." And Bracknell felt a surge of satisfaction well up in him. He hadn't asserted himself for years, he realized. I used to be an important man, he told himself. I gave orders and people hopped to follow them. I'm not some convict or pervert. I didn't kill all those people. Yamagata did.

The redheaded nurse was fidgeting uncertainly by his bed, shifting the tablet from one hand to the other.

"Listen," Bracknell said, more gently, "I've been through a lot. I'm not up to getting poked and prodded—"

"The scan is completely nonintrusive," the nurse said hopefully.

"Okay, tell you what. Find me a pair of shoes and let me walk around a bit, stretch my legs. Then tomorrow morning I'll sign for the scan. Okay?"

She seemed relieved, but doubtful. "I'll hafta ask my supervisor."

"Do that. But first, get some shoes for me."

Less than half an hour later Mance Bracknell walked out of Selene Hospital's busy lobby, wearing his old gray coveralls and a crinkled pair of hospital-issue paper shoes. No one tried to stop him. No one even noticed him. There was only one guard in the lobby, and when Bracknell brazenly waved at him the guard gave him a half-hearted wave in return. He wasn't in hospital-issue clothes; as far as the guard was concerned, Bracknell was a visitor leaving the hospital. Or maybe one of the maintenance crew going home.

Most of Selene was underground, and the hospital was two levels down. Bracknell's first move was to call up a map on the information screen across the corridor from the hospital's entrance. He found the transportation center, up in the Main Plaza, and headed for it.

I'm free! he marveled as he strode along the spacious corridor, passing people walking the other way. Not a thing in my pockets and the hospital authorities might call Selene's security people to search for me, but for the moment I'm free to go where I want to.

The place he wanted to go to was Hell Crater.

He located a powered stairway and rode it up to Selene's Main Plaza, built on the surface of the great crater Alphonsus. Its concrete dome projected out from the ringwall mountains and onto the crater floor. Bracknell saw that the Plaza was green with grass and shrubbery; there were even trees planted along the winding walkways. An Olympic-sized swimming pool. A bandshell and stage for performances. Shops and little bistros where people sat and chatted and sipped drinks. Music and laughter floated through the air. Tourists flitted overhead, flying on their own muscle power with colorful rented plastic wings. Bracknell smelled flowers and the aroma of sizzling food.

It's marvelous, he thought as he headed for the transportation center. This is what they cut me off from: real life, real people enjoying themselves. Freedom. Then he realized that he had neither cash nor credit. *How can I get to Hell Crater? Freedom doesn't mean much when you are penniless.*

As he approached the transportation center, an eager-looking young man in a splashy sports shirt and a sparkling smile fell in step beside him. "Going to Hell?" he asked brightly.

Bracknell looked him over. Blond crew cut, smile plastered in place, perfect teeth. A glad-handing salesman, he realized.

"I'm thinking about it," Bracknell said.

"Don't miss Sam Gunn's Inferno Casino," said the smiling young man. "It's got the best action."

"Action?" Bracknell played naïve.

"Roulette, blackjack, low-grav craps tables, championship karate competition." The smile grew even wider. "Beautiful women and free champagne. Dirty minds in clean bodies. What more could you ask for?"

Bracknell looked up at the transportation center's huge display of departures and arrivals.

The young pitchman gripped his arm. "Don't worry about that! There's an Inferno Special leaving in fifteen minutes. Direct to the casino! You'll be there in less than two hours and they'll even serve you a meal in transit!"

"The fare must be—"

"It's free!" the blond proclaimed. "And your first hundred dollars' worth of chips is on the house!"

"Really?"

"As long as you buy a thousand dollars' worth. That's a ten percent discount, right off the bat."

Bracknell allowed himself to be chivvied into a cable car painted with lurid red flames across its silver body. Fourteen other men and women were already sitting inside, most of them middle-aged and looking impatient.

As he took the empty seat up front, by the forward window, one of the dowdyish women called out, "When are we leaving? We've been waiting here almost an hour!"

The blond gave her the full wattage of his smile. "I'm supposed to fill up the bus before I let it go, but since you've been so patient, I'll send you off just as soon as I get one more passenger."

It took another quarter hour, but at last the car was sealed up. It rode on an overhead cable to the massive airlock built into the side of the Main Plaza's dome. Within minutes they were climbing across Alphonsus's worn old ringwall mountains and then down onto the plain of Mare Nubium. The cable car rocked slightly as it whizzed twenty meters above the bleak, pockmarked regolith. It smelled old and used; too many bodies have been riding in this bucket for too long, Bracknell thought. But he smiled to himself as the car raced along and the overhead speakers gave an automated lecture about the scenic wonders they were rushing past.

There was no pilot or crew in the cable car; everything was automated. The free meal consisted of a thin sandwich and a bottle of "genuine lunar water" obtained from the vending machine at the rear of the car. Bracknell chewed contentedly and watched the Straight Wall flash by.

True to the blond pitchman's word, the cable car went directly inside the Inferno Casino. The other passengers hurried out, eager to spend their money. Bracknell left the car last, looking for the nearest exit from the casino. It wasn't easy to find; all he could see was an ocean of people lapping up against islands of gaming tables, looking either frenzied or grim as they gambled away their money. Raucous music poured from overhead speakers, drowning out any laughter or conversation. No exits in sight; the casino management wanted their customers to stay at the gaming tables or restaurants. There were plenty of sexy young women sauntering around, too, many in spray-paint costumes, but none of them gave Bracknell more than a cursory glance: in his gray coveralls he looked more like a maintenance man than a high roller.

When he finally found the casino's main entrance, Bracknell saw that the entire Hell Crater complex of casinos, hotels, restaurants, and shops was built inside one massive dome. Like Selene, the complex's living quarters and offices were tunneled underground. Bracknell studied a map display, then headed on foot to the rejuvenation clinic of Takeo Koga. It was one of six such clinics in the complex.

Down two levels and then a ten-minute walk along the softly lit, thickly carpeted corridor to Koga's clinic. It was blessedly quiet down here, and there were only a few other people in sight. No one paid attention to Bracknell, for which he was thankful. It meant that there was no alarm yet from the hospital about his absence.

The sign on the door was tastefully small, yet Bracknell found it almost ludicrously boastful: IDEAL RENEWAL CENTER. KOGA TAKEO, M.D., D.C.S.

Hoping he didn't look too disreputable, Bracknell opened the door and stepped into the small waiting room. Two brittle-looking women sitting in comfortable armchairs looked up at him briefly, then turned their attention back to the screen on the far wall, which was showing some sort of documentary about wild animals. Silky music purred from hidden speakers. There were two empty armchairs and a low table with another screen built into its surface. The table's screen glowed softly.

Bracknell went to the table and bent over it slightly.

"Welcome to Ideal Renewal Center," said a woman's pleasant voice. "How may I help you?"

"I need to see Dr. Koga."

"Do you have an appointment?"

"This is about his brother, Toshikazu," Bracknell replied.

A moment's hesitation, then a different voice said, "Please take a seat. Someone will be with you in a moment."

KOGA CLINIC

A young Asian woman opened the door on the far end of the waiting room and crooked a finger at Bracknell. Wordlessly she led him to a small examination room, gestured to the chair next to the examination table, and softly closed the door behind her as she left.

Bracknell suddenly felt uncomfortable. What if they're calling security? But no, how would they know who I am? Still, he felt trapped in this tiny, utterly quiet room.

He stood up and reached for the door just as it swung open and a stocky, grim-faced Asian stepped in. He looked young, but his handsome face did not seem to go with his chunky build. His cheekbones were sculptured, his jawline firm, his throat slim and unlined. He wore a trim, dark moustache, and his hair was cut short and combed straight back off his forehead.

"I am Toshikazu's brother, Takeo," he said as he firmly closed the door behind him. Takeo looked suspicious, almost angry. He took in Bracknell's unimpressive coveralls and paper shoes at a glance. He must be a good diagnostician, Bracknell thought.

"Well, what's he done now?"

Bracknell took in a breath, then said, "I'm afraid he's dead."

Takeo's eyes widened. He tottered to the examination couch and sagged against it. "Dead? How did it happen?"

"He died in an explosion aboard the freighter *Alhambra*. He was a convict, being shipped out to the Belt."

"They finally got him, then."

"You know about it," Bracknell said.

Rubbing at his eyes, Takeo replied, "Only that he was running from something, someone. He was frightened for his life. He wouldn't tell me what it was about; he said then I'd be marked for murder, too."

Bracknell sat in the chair in the corner. "Did he ever mention Yamagata to you?"

"No," Takeo answered, so sharply that Bracknell knew it was a lie. "He never told me anything about why he was being pursued. I only knew that he was in desperate trouble. I changed his appearance, his whole identity, twice."

"And they still found him."

"Poor Toshi." Takeo's chin sank to his chest.

"He told me about your ability to change people's identities," said Bracknell.

Takeo's head snapped up. He glared at Bracknell.

"I need my identity changed."

"You said Toshi was a convict? You're one also, eh?"

Bracknell almost smiled. "The less you know, the safer you are."

Shaking his head, Takeo said, "I helped my brother because he's my brother. I'm not going to stick my neck out for you."

"You've helped other people who wanted to start new lives. Toshikazu told me about your work."

"Those people could afford my fees. Can you?"

With a rueful grin, Bracknell admitted, "I don't have a penny."

"Then why should I help you?"

"Because if you don't, I'll tell you your brother's whole story. Who was after him, and why. Then you'll know, and then I'll let Yamagata's people know that you know. The people who killed him will come here to kill you."

Takeo was silent for several long moments. He stared into Bracknell's eyes, obviously trying to calculate just how desperate or determined this stranger was.

At last he said, "You want a complete makeover, then?"

"I want to become a certain individual, a man named Dante Alexios."

"I presume this Alexios is dead. It would be embarrassing if he showed up after you claim his identity."

"He died in the same explosion your brother did."

Takeo nodded. "I'll need his complete medical records."

"They should be available from the International Astronautical Authority. They keep duplicates of all ship's crews."

"And they keep those records private."

"You've done this sort of thing before," said Bracknell.

"For people who provided me with what I needed."

"You're a doctor. Tell the IAA you've got to identify a body for United Life and Accident Assurance, Limited. They carried the policy for *Alhambra*."

Takeo said, "I don't like getting involved in this."

"You've done worse, from what Toshikazu told me. Besides, you don't have much of a choice."

"You're blackmailing me!"

Bracknell sighed theatrically. "I'm afraid I am."

The makeover took weeks, and it wasn't anything like what Bracknell had expected. Takeo obtained Alexios's medical files from the IAA easily enough; a little money was transferred electronically and he received the dead man's body scans in less than a day. Then began the hard, painful work.

Takeo kept Bracknell in one of the small but luxuriously appointed suites behind his medical offices. For the first ten days he didn't see Takeo, except through the intercom phone. Bracknell grew increasingly impatient, increasingly fearful. Any moment he expected security guards to burst into the little suite and drag him back to a ship headed outward to the Belt.

He paced the suite: sitting room, bedroom, a closet-sized kitchen in which he prepared bland microwaved meals from the fully stocked pantry. No liquor, no drugs, no visitors. His only entertainment was video, and he constantly scanned the news nets from Selene and Earth for any hint that he was being hunted. Nothing. He wanted to phone the Selene hospital to see what their files showed about him, but found that he could not place outgoing calls. He was a prisoner again. His jail cell was comfortable, even plush, but still he felt penned in.

When he complained to Takeo, the physician's artificially handsome image on the phone screen smiled at him. "You're free to leave whenever you want."

"You haven't even started my treatment yet!"

"Yes I have."

Bracknell stared at the face on the screen.

"The most difficult part of this process," Takeo explained, with ill-concealed annoyance, "is programming the nanomachines. They've got to alter your face, your skin, your bone structure. Once I've got them programmed, the rest is easy."

It wasn't easy.

One ordinary morning, as Bracknell flicked from one news channel to another, thinking that even being arrested again would be better than this utter boredom, a young Asian nurse entered his sitting room bearing a silver tray with a single glass of what looked like orange juice.

"This is your first treatment, sir."

"This?" Bracknell asked dubiously as he picked up the glass.

"You should go to bed for a nap as soon as you drink it," the nurse said. "It contains a sedative."

"And nanomachines?"

She nodded solemnly. "Oh, yes, sir. Many nanomachines. Hundreds of millions of them."

"Good," said Bracknell. He drained the glass, then put it back on her tray with a clink.

"You should go to bed now, sir."

Bracknell thought of asking her if she would accompany him, but decided against it. She left the suite and he walked into his bedroom. The bed was still unmade from the previous night's sleep.

This is ridiculous, he thought. I'm not sleepy and there's no—

A wave of giddiness made his knees sag. He plopped onto the bed, heart thumping. His face tingled, itched. He felt as if something was crawling under his skin. It's only psychosomatic, he told himself. But as he stretched out on the rumpled bed he felt as if some alien parasites had invaded his body. He wanted to scratch his face, his ribs, everywhere. He writhed on the bed, filled with blind dread, moaning in his terror. He squeezed his eyes shut and hoped that sleep would come before he began screaming like a lunatic.

Each morning for six days, the same nurse brought him a glass filled with fruit juice. And nanomachines. For six mornings Bracknell took it with a trembling hand, then went to bed and waited for the sedative to knock him out while his body twitched and writhed. Each day the pain grew sharper, deeper. It was as if his bones were being sawn apart, the flesh of his face and body flayed by a sadistic torturer. He thought of insects infected with the eggs of parasitic wasps that ate out their host's insides. He lived in writhing agony and horror as the nanomachines did their work inside his body.

But he saw no difference in his face. Every morning he staggered to the lavatory and studied himself in the mirror above the sink. He looked the same, except that his beard did not grow. After three days of the nanotherapy he stopped shaving altogether. There was no need. Besides, his frightened hands shook too much.

He phoned Takeo every day, and received only a computer's synthesized, "Dr. Koga will return your call at the appropriate time."

Maybe he's killing me, Bracknell thought. Using nanomachines to eat out my guts and get rid of me. Still, despite his fears each morning he swallowed down the juice and the invisible devices swarming in it. And suffered the agonies of hell until he passed thankfully into unconsciousness.

One week to the day after Bracknell had started taking the nanotherapy, Koga showed up in his suite.

"How do you feel?" the physician asked, peering at Bracknell intently.

"Like I'm being eaten inside," Bracknell snapped.

Takeo tilted his head slightly. "Can't be helped. Normally we go more slowly, but both of us are in a hurry so I've given you some pretty heavy dosages."

"I don't see any change," said Bracknell.

"Don't you?" Takeo smiled condescendingly. "I do."

"My face is the same."

Walking over to the desktop phone, Takeo said, "The day-to-day change is minuscule, true enough." He spoke a command in Japanese to the phone. "But a week's worth of change is significant."

Bracknell saw his own image on the phone's display.

"Take a look in the mirror," said Takeo.

Bracknell went to the bathroom. He stared, then ducked back into the living room. The difference was subtle, but clear.

Takeo smiled at his handiwork. "In another week not even United Life and Accident Assurance will be able to tell you from the original Dante Alexios."

"It's painful," Bracknell said.

"Having your bones remolded involves some discomfort," Takeo replied, unconcerned. "But you're getting a side benefit: you'll never have to shave again. I've eliminated the hair follicles on your face."

"It still hurts like hell."

Takeo shrugged. "That's the price you must pay."

Another week, thought Bracknell. I can put up with this for another week.

DANTE ALEXIOS

Marvin Pratt frowned at the dark-haired man sitting in front of his desk. The expression on the stranger's face was utterly serious, determined.

"You're not the man I saw in the hospital," he said.

"I am Dante Alexios," said Bracknell. "I've come to claim my money as the sole beneficiary of the *Alhambra*'s accident policy."

"Then who was the man in the hospital?" Pratt demanded.

Alexios shrugged his shoulders. They were slimmer than Bracknell's had been. "Some derelict, I suppose."

"He disappeared," Pratt said, suspicion etched onto his face. "Walked out of the hospital and disappeared."

"As I said, a derelict. I understand there's an underground community of sorts here in Selene. Criminals, homeless people, all sorts of oddballs hiding away in the tunnels."

Pratt leaned back in his swivel chair and let air whistle softly between his teeth as he compared the face of the man sitting before him with the image of Dante Alexios on his desktop screen. Both had pale skin and dark hair; the image on the screen had a shadow of stubble along his jaw while the man facing him was perfectly clean-shaven. His face seemed just a trifle out of kilter, as if the two halves of it did not quite match. His smile seemed forced, twisted. But the retinal patterns of his dark brown eyes matched those on file in the computer. So did his fingerprints and the convolutions of his ears.

"How did you survive the explosion?" Pratt asked, trying to keep his tone neutral, nonaccusative.

Smoothly, Alexios replied, "I was outside doing routine maintenance on the attitude thrusters when the two ships blew up. I went spinning off into space for several days. I nearly died."

"Someone picked you up?"

"Another freighter, the *Dubai,* outbound for the Belt. After eight days they transferred me to an inbound ship, the *Seitz,* and I arrived here in Selene yesterday. That's when I called your office."

Pratt looked as if he didn't believe a word of it, but he went through the motions of checking Alexios's story. Alexios had paid the captains of the two vessels handsomely for their little lies, using Takeo's money on the promise that he'd repay the physician once he got the insurance payout into his hands.

"This other man, the amnesiac," said Pratt warily. "He was rescued from the *Alhambra* also."

Smoothly, Bracknell answered, "Then he must have been a convict. Captain Farad had the pleasant little trick of putting troublemakers outside, in spacesuits, until they learned to behave themselves."

"I see." At last Pratt said, "You're a very fortunate man, Mr. Alexios."

"Don't I know it!"

With a look of utter distaste, Pratt commanded his phone to authorize payment to Dante Alexios.

Alexios asked, "May I ask, how much is the, uh, benefit?"

Pratt glanced at his display screen. "Twelve point seven million New International Dollars."

Alexios's brows lifted. "That much?"

"What do you intend to do with your money?"

Taking a deep breath, Alexios said, "Well, there are some debts I have to pay. After that . . . I don't know . . . I just might start my own engineering firm."

He surprised Takeo by paying the physician's normal fee for a cosmetic remake. Then Dante Alexios opened a small consulting engineering office in Selene. He started by taking on charity work and performing community services, such as designing a new water processing plant for Selene's growing population of retirees from Earth. His first paying assignment was as a consultant on the new mass driver being built out on Mare Nubium to catapult cargos of lunar helium three to the hungry fusion power plants on Earth. He began to learn how to use nanotechnology. With a derisive grin he would tell himself, Damned useful, these little nanomachines.

In two years he was well known in Selene for his community services. In four he was wealthy in his own right, with enough contracts to hire a small but growing staff of engineers and office personnel. Often he thought about returning to Earth and looking up Lara, but he resisted the temptation. That part of his life was finished. Even his hatred of Victor and Danvers had abated. There was nothing to be done. The desire for vengeance cooled, although he still felt angry whenever he thought of their betrayal.

Instead of traveling to Earth, Dante Alexios won a contract to build a complete research station on Mars, a new base in the giant circular basin in the southern hemisphere called Hellas. He flew to Mars to personally supervise the construction.

He lived at the construction site, surrounded by nanotech

engineers and some of the scientists who would live and work at the base once it was finished. He walked the iron sands of the red planet and watched the distant, pale Sun set in the cloudless caramel-colored sky. He felt the peace and harmony of this empty world, with its craggy mountains and rugged canyons and winding ancient river beds.

We haven't corrupted this world, Alexios told himself. There are only a handful of humans here, not enough to tear the place apart and rebuild it the way we've done to Earth, the way we're doing to the Moon.

Yet he knew he was a part of that process; he had helped to extend human habitation across the dead and battered face of the Moon. Mars was different, though. Life dwelled here. Once, a race of intelligent creatures built their homes and temples into the high crevasses in the cliffs. Alexios got permission from the scientists running the exploration effort to visit the ruins of their cliff dwellings.

Gone. Whoever built these villages, whoever farmed those valleys, they were all wiped out by an impersonal planetwide catastrophe that snuffed out virtually all life on the red planet, blew away most of its atmosphere, flash-froze this world into a dusty, dry global desert. The scientists thought the plain of Hellas held the key to the disaster that sterilized Mars sixty-five million years ago, the same disaster that wiped out the dinosaurs and half of all living species on Earth.

Alexios felt very humble when he stared through his spacesuit visor at the crumbling ruins of a Martian cliff dwelling. Life can be snuffed out so easily. Like a skytower falling, crushing the life out of millions, ending a lifetime of hope and work with a snap of destiny's fingers.

He was mulling his own destiny when he returned to the base nearing completion at Hellas. As the rocket glider that carried him soared over the vast circular depression,

Alexios looked through the thick quartz window with some pride. The base spread across several square kilometers of the immense crater's floor, domes and tunnels and the tangled tracks of many vehicles. The work of my mind, he said to himself. The base is almost finished, and I did it. I created it. With a little help from my nanofriends. Like the skytower, taunted a voice in his mind.

That night, he lay in his bunk and watched the Earthside news broadcasts while the Martian wind moaned softly past the plastic dome that housed the construction crew. Then he saw an item that made him sit straight up in bed.

Saito Yamagata was going to start a project to build solar power satellites in orbit around the planet Mercury.

Yamagata! He's come out of his so-called retreat in Tibet and he's heading for Mercury.

Without a moment's hesitation, without a heartbeat of reflection, Alexios decided he would go to Mercury, too. He owed Yamagata a death. And as he sat in his darkened bedroom, the flickering light from the video screen playing across his transformed features, he realized that he could pay back both Victor and Danvers, too.

All the old hatred, all the old fury, all the old seething acid boiled up anew in his guts. Alexios felt his teeth grinding together. I'll make them pay, he promised himself. I had almost forgotten about them, about what they did to me and all those millions of others. Almost forgotten Addie and her father and the others aboard *Alhambra*. How easy it is to let a comfortable life swallow you up. How easy to let the blade's edge go dull.

He threw back the bed covers and strode naked to his desktop phone. Yamagata. Molina. Danvers. I'll get all three of them on that hellhole of a world, Mercury.

GOETHE BASE

itting in his bare little office, Dante Alexios smiled bitterly to himself as the memories of his ten lost years came flooding back to him. He finished reading the report issued by McFergusen and his ICU committee and leaned back in his desk chair. They've worded it very diplomatically, Alexios thought as he read the final paragraph, but their meaning is clear.

> The aforementioned tests unequivocally show that the rocks in question originated on Mars. While there is a vanishingly small chance that they were deposited on Mercury's surface by natural processes, the overwhelming likelihood is that they were transported to Mercury by human hands. The discovery of biomarkers in these samples by V. Molina is not, therefore, indicative of biological activity on the planet Mercury.

Victor is wiped out, Alexios said to himself, with satisfaction. McFergusen won't come right out and say it, but the implication is crystal clear: either Victor planted those rocks here himself, or he fell dupe to some prankster who did it. Either way, Victor's reputation as a scientist is permanently demolished.

Laughing out loud, Alexios thought, Now it's your turn, Danvers.

He put in a call to Molina, to start the process of destroying Bishop Elliott Danvers.

* * *

As he strode down the central corridor of the orbiting *Himawari,* heading toward Molina's quarters, Alexios began to feel nervous. Lara will be there, he knew. She lives with him. Sleeps with him. They have an eight-year-old son. He worried that sooner or later she would see through his nano-therapy and recognize Mance Bracknell. Then he realized that even if she did it wouldn't change anything.

Still, he hesitated once he arrived at the door to their stateroom, his fist in midair poised to knock. What will I do if she does recognize me? he asked himself. What will you do if she doesn't? replied the scornful voice in his head.

He took a breath, then knocked. Lara opened the door immediately, as if she had been standing behind it waiting anxiously for him.

He had to swallow before he could say, "Hello, Mrs. Molina."

"Mr. Alexios." Her voice was hushed, apprehensive. "Won't you come in?"

Feeling every fiber of his body quivering nervously, Alexios stepped into their compartment. Victor was sitting on the two-place sofa set against the far bulkhead, his head in his hands. The bed was neatly made up; everything in the stateroom seemed in fastidious order. Except for Molina: he looked a wreck, hair mussed, face ashen, a two-day stubble on his jaw, dark rings under his eyes.

Alexios relaxed somewhat. This isn't going to be difficult at all. He's ready to clutch at any straw I can offer.

Lara asked, "Can I get you something, Mr. Alexios?"

"Dante," he said. "Please call me Dante."

With a nod, she said, "Very well, Dante. A drink, maybe?"

His memory flashed a picture of all the times he and Lara had drunk together. She'd been partial to margaritas in the old days; Mance Bracknell had a taste for wine.

"Just some water, please," he said.

"Fruit juice?" she suggested.

He almost shuddered with the recollection of the nanomachine-laden juice he had drunk in Koga's clinic. "Water will be fine, thank you."

Lara went to the kitchenette built behind a short bar next to the sofa. Alexios pulled up one of the plush chairs and sat across the coffee table from Molina.

"As I said on the phone, Dr. Molina, I'm here to help you in any way I can."

Molina shook his head. "There isn't anything you can do," he said in a hoarse whisper.

"Someone set you up for this," Alexios said gently. "If we can find out who did it, that would show everyone that you're not at fault."

Lara placed a tray of glasses on the coffee table and sat next to her husband. "That's what I've been telling him. We can't just take this lying down. We've got to find out who's responsible for this."

"What can you do?" Molina asked morosely.

Alexios tilted his head slightly, as if thinking about the problem. "Well . . . you said you received an anonymous call about the rocks."

"Yes. Somebody left a message for me at my office on campus. No name. No return address."

"And on the strength of that one call you came out here to Mercury?"

Anger flared in Molina's eyes. "Don't you start, too! Yes, I came here on the strength of that one call. It sounded too good to be ignored."

Lara laid a placating hand on his knee. "Victor, he's trying to help you," she said soothingly.

Molina visibly choked back his anger. "I figured that if it's a blind alley I could be back home in a couple of weeks. But if it is was real, it would be a terrific discovery."

"But it was a deliberate hoax," Alexios said, as sympathetically as he could manage.

"That's right. And they all think I did it. They think I'm a fraud, a cheat, a—"

"The thing to do," Alexios said, cutting through Molina's rising bitterness, "is to track down who made that call."

"I don't see how—"

"Whoever it was had access to Martian rocks," Alexios went on. "And he probably knew you."

"What makes you think that?" Lara asked, surprise showing clearly in her amber eyes.

With a small shrug, Alexios replied, "He called you, no one else. He wanted you, specifically you, to come here and be his victim."

"Who would do such a thing?" Lara wondered. "And why?"

"That's what we've got to find out."

EVIDENCE

Alexios knew he had to work fast, because Lara and Victor were due to leave Mercury in a few days. Yet he couldn't be too swift; that might show his hand to them. Besides, now that the IAA's interdict on his work on the planet's surface was lifted, he had plenty of tasks to accomplish: resume scooping raw materials from the regolith, hire a nanotech team and bring them to Mercury, lay out plans for building a mass driver and the components for solar power satellites that would be catapulted into orbit and assembled in space.

He waited for two days. Then he rode the shuttle back to *Himawari* with the evidence in his tunic pocket.

Lara and Victor eagerly greeted him at the airlock. They hurried down the passageway together toward the Molinas' stateroom, Victor in a sweat to see what Alexios had uncovered, Lara just as eager but more controlled.

As soon as the stateroom door closed Molina demanded, "Well? What did you find?"

"Quite a bit," said Alexios. "Is McFergusen still here? He should see—"

"He left two days ago," Molina snapped. "What did you find out?"

Alexios pulled two thin sheets of plastic from his tunic and unfolded them on the coffee table as Molina and his wife sat together on the little sofa. He tapped the one on top.

"Is this the anonymous message you received?" he asked Molina.

The astrobiologist scanned it. "Yes, that's it."

Alexios knew it was. He had sent it. He turned that sheet over to show the one beneath it.

"What's this?" Lara asked.

"A copy of a requisition from the International Consortium of Universities, selling eleven Martian rocks to a private research facility on Earth."

"My rocks!" Molina blurted.

"How did they get from Earth to Mercury?" Lara asked.

Alexios knew perfectly well, but he said, "That part of it we'll have to deduce from the available evidence."

"Who sent this message to me?" Molina demanded, tapping the first sheet.

"It wasn't easy tracking down the sender. He was very careful to cover his tracks."

"Who was it?"

"And he had a large, well-financed organization behind him, as well," Alexios added.

"Who was it?" Molina fairly screamed.

Alexios glanced at Lara. She was obviously on tenterhooks, her lips parted slightly, her eyes wide with anticipation.

"Bishop Danvers," said Alexios.

"Elliott?" Molina gasped.

"I can't believe it," said Lara. "He's a man of god—he wouldn't stoop to such chicanery."

"He's my friend," Molina said, looking bewildered. "At least, I thought he was."

Alexios said, "The New Morality hates the discoveries you astrobiologists have made, you know that. What better way to discredit the entire field than by showing a prominent astrobiologist to be a fraud, a liar?"

Molina sank back in the sofa. "Elliott did this? To me?"

"What proof do you have?" Lara asked.

Alexios looked into her gold-flecked eyes. "The people who traced this message used highly irregular methods—"

"Illegal, you mean," she said flatly.

"Extralegal," Alexios countered.

"Then this so-called evidence won't hold up in a court of law."

"No, but there must be a record of this message in Danvers's computer files. Even if he erased the message, a scan of his memory core might find a trace of it."

Lara stared hard at him. "The bishop could claim that someone planted the message in his computer."

Alexios knew she was perfectly correct. But he said, "And why would anyone do that?"

Impatiently, Molina argued, "We can't examine Elliott's computer files without his permission. And if he really did this he won't give permission. So where are we?"

"You're forgetting this invoice," said Alexios. "It can be traced to the New Morality school in Gabon, in west Africa."

Lara looked at her husband. "Elliott was stationed in Libreville."

"For almost ten years," Molina said.

She turned back to Alexios. "You're certain of all this?"

He nodded and lied, "Absolutely. I paid a good deal of money to obtain this information."

"Elliott?" Molina was still finding it difficult to accept the idea. "Elliott deliberately tried to destroy me?"

"I'm afraid he *has* destroyed you," Alexios said grimly. "Your reputation is permanently tainted."

Molina nodded ruefully. Then his expression changed, hardened. "Then I'm taking that pompous sonofabitch down with me!"

CONFRONTATION

t's utterly ridiculous!" cried Bishop Danvers.

Molina was standing in Danvers's stateroom, too furious to sit down. He paced the little room like a prowling animal. Lara sat on one of the upholstered chairs, Alexios on the other one. Danvers was on the sofa between them, staring bewilderedly at the two flimsy sheets that Alexios had brought.

"We have the proof," Molina said, jabbing a finger toward the message and the invoice.

"It's not true, Victor," said Danvers. "Believe me, it's not true."

"You deliberately ruined me, Elliott."

"No, I—"

"Why?" Molina shouted. "Why did you do this to me?"

"I didn't!" Danvers howled back, his face reddening. "It's

a pack of lies." Desperately, he turned to Lara. "Lara, you believe me, don't you? You know I wouldn't have done this. I couldn't have!"

Lara's eyes flicked from her husband to the bishop and back again.

"Someone has deliberately ruined Victor's reputation," she said evenly, fixing her gaze on Alexios. "No matter who did this, Victor's career is destroyed."

"But it wasn't me!" Danvers pleaded.

"Wasn't it?" Molina snapped. "When I think of all the talks we've had, over the years, all the arguments—"

"Discussions!" Danvers corrected. "Philosophical discussions."

"You've had it in for me ever since you found out that I was using those gengineered viruses to help build the skytower," Molina accused. "You and your kind hate everything that science stands for, don't you?"

"No, it's not true." Danvers seemed almost in tears.

Molina stopped his pacing to face the bishop. "When I told you about what I was doing at the skytower, you reported it to your New Morality superiors, didn't you?"

"Of course. It was important information."

"You were a spy back in Ecuador. You were sent to the skytower project to snoop, not to pray for people's souls."

"Victor, please believe me—"

"And now they've sent you here to Mercury to destroy my work, my career. You've ruined my life, Elliott! You might as well have taken a knife and stabbed me through the heart!"

Danvers sank his face in his hands and started blubbering. Lara stared at him, her own eyes growing misty. Then she looked up at her husband.

"Victor, I don't think he did this," she said calmly.

"Then who did?" Molina demanded. "Who would have any reason to?"

Lara focused again squarely on Alexios. "Are you certain of this information?" she asked. "Absolutely certain?"

Alexios fought down the urge to squirm uncomfortably under her gaze. As smoothly as he could, he replied, "As your husband said, who else would have a motive for doing this to him? The New Morality must have marked Victor years ago, when they learned what he was doing for the skytower."

"And they'd wait all this time to get back at him?"

Shrugging, Alexios said, "Apparently so. That's what the evidence suggests."

Abruptly, Molina bent over the coffee table and snatched the two flimsy sheets. "I'm calling McFergusen. I've been the victim of a hoax, a scam. And then I'm calling the news nets. The New Morality is going to pay for this! I'll expose them for the psalm-singing hypocrites that they are!"

Exactly what I thought you'd do, Alexios said to himself. Aloud, however, he tried to sound more reasonable. "I agree that a call to McFergusen is in order. But a news conference? Do you really want to attack the New Morality?"

"Why not?" Molina snapped. "What do I have to lose?"

Lara got to her feet. "Victor, Mr. Alexios is right. Don't be too hasty. Talk with McFergusen first. He might be able to salvage something out of this situation."

"Salvage what? Even if I can prove that I've been scammed, I still look like an idiot. Nobody will ever believe me again. My career is finished!"

"But perhaps—"

"Perhaps nothing! They've destroyed me; I'm going to do my damnedest to destroy them. And you in particular, Elliott, you goddamned lying bastard!"

Danvers looked up at the astrobiologist, his face white with shock, his eyes filled with tears.

Molina took his wife by the wrist and slammed out of the stateroom, leaving Alexios alone with the bishop.

"I didn't do it," Danvers mewed, bewildered. "As God is my witness, I never did any of this."

Alexios scratched his chin, trying to prevent himself from gloating. "Would you allow me to check your computer? I presume you brought your memory core with you when you came to Mercury."

Danvers nodded glumly and gestured toward the desk, where the palm-sized computer rested. Alexios spent a half hour fiddling with it while the bishop sat on the sofa in miserable silence. Alexios found the trace of the message he had paid to have planted in the computer's core. It looked as if it had been erased from the active memory, but still existed deep in the core.

Getting up from the desk at last, Alexios lied, "Well, if it's in your machine's memory it would take a better expert than me to find it."

"It doesn't matter," Danvers said, his heavy head drooping.

"I should think it would be important."

His voice deep and low with despair, Danvers said, "You don't understand. A scandal like this will ruin me. The New Morality doesn't permit even a suspicion of wrongdoing among its hierarchy. We must all be above evil, above even accusations of evil. This . . . once Victor tells people about this . . . I'll be finished in the New Morality. Finished."

Alexios took a breath, then replied, "Maybe you can get a position as chaplain on a prison ship, or out in the Asteroid Belt. They could use your consolations there."

Danvers looked up at him, blinking. He seemed to have aged ten years in the past half hour.

Alexios smiled, thinking, You wouldn't last a month out there, you fat old fraud. Somebody would strangle you in the middle of your hymns.

OBSERVATION LOUNGE

A lexios fidgeted nervously as he stood in *Himawari*'s dimmed observation lounge, gazing through the glassteel blister as the star-flecked depths of infinite space spun slowly, inexorably past his altered eyes. The eyes of heaven, he said to himself, half-remembering a poem from his school days. The army of unalterable law, that's what the poet called the stars.

I should feel triumphant, he thought. Victor's career is in tatters, and Danvers is in disgrace. All that's left is Yamagata and I'll be taking care of him shortly. Yet he felt no delight in his victory over them. No triumph. He was dead inside, cold and numb. Ten years I've waited to get even with them and now that I have . . . so what? So Victor will spend the rest of his life in some obscure university trying to live down his mistake here on Mercury. And Danvers will be defrocked, or whatever they do in the New Morality. What of it? How does that change my life?

Lara, he said to himself. It all depends on Lara. She's the one I did this for. She's the one who kept me alive through all those long years out in the Belt. My only glimmer of hope when I was a prisoner, a miserable exile.

As the torch ship rotated, the surface of Mercury slid into view, barren, heat-blasted, pitted with craters and seamed with cracks and fault lines. Like the face of an old, old man, Alexios thought, a man who's lived too long. He saw a line of cliffs and the worn, tired mountains ringing an ancient crater. He knew where Goethe base was, but he could not see the modest mound of rubble covering its dome from the distance of the ship's orbit, nor the tracks of the vehicles that churned up the thin layer of dust on the ground down there.

Once we've built the mass driver you'll be able to see it from orbit, he thought. Five kilometers long. We'll see it, all right.

The door behind him slid open, spilling light from the passageway into the darkened compartment. Alexios's heart constricted in his chest. He did not dare to turn around, but in the reflection off the glassteel bubble he saw that it was Lara.

He slowly turned toward her as she slid the door shut. The compartment became dim and shadowed again, but he could see her lovely face, see the curiosity in her eyes.

"You asked me to meet you here?" she said, her voice soft and low.

He realized he'd been holding his breath. He nodded, then managed to get out, "It's one of the few places aboard ship where we can meet privately."

"You have some further information about my husband?"

"No . . . not really . . ." It took all his self-control to keep from reaching out and clasping her in his arms. Surely she could hear his heart thundering.

"I don't understand," Lara said with a little frown. "You asked me to see you, to come alone, without Victor."

"Lara, it's me," he blurted. "Mance."

Her mouth dropped open.

"I know I look different," he said, the words coming in a rush now. "I had to change my appearance, my background, I came here to Mercury but I had no idea you'd come out here too and now that you're here I can't keep up the masquerade any longer, I want to—"

"Mance?" she whispered, unbelieving.

"Yes, it's me, darling."

She staggered back several steps, dropped onto the bench

running along the compartment's rear bulkhead. "It can't be," she said, her voice hollow.

He went to her, knelt before her, grasped both her hands in his own. "Lara, I've gone through hell to find you again. I love you. I've always loved you."

She was staring at him, searching for the Mance Bracknell she had known. He could see the play of starlight in her eyes and then the harsh glare reflected from Mercury casting her face into stark light and shadow.

"I know I don't look the same, Lara. But it really is me, Mance. I have a new identity. I'm a free man now. The old Mance Bracknell is dead, as far as the officials are concerned. But we can begin our lives again, Lara, we can take up where we left off."

She shuddered, like a woman coming out of a trance. "Begin our lives again?"

"Yes! I love you, dearest. I want to marry you and—"

"I'm already married. I have an eight-year-old son. Victor's son."

"You can divorce Victor. Nobody will blame you for leaving him."

Recognition lit her eyes. "*You* did this to Victor! It wasn't Elliott, it was you!"

"I did it for you," he said.

"You destroyed my husband's career and ruined Elliott."

"Because I love you."

"What kind of love is that?"

Alexios saw the disgust in her eyes. "You don't understand," he said. "They destroyed me. Victor deliberately lied at my trial. He wanted me out of the way so he could have you. He stole you from me. He stole my entire life!"

"And now you've stolen his."

"Yes! And I want you back. You're the reason I've done all this."

"Oh, my god," she moaned.

"You loved me, you know you did. You said you wanted to be with me. Well, now we can—"

"And Elliott, too? What do you have against him?"

Anger rising inside him, Alexios said, "He's the one who started the scheme to destroy the skytower. Him and his New Morality hatred for nanotechnology or anything else that they can't find in the Old Testament."

"Destroy the skytower?"

"It was sabotaged. Deliberately knocked down. They didn't care how many people they killed, they just wanted the tower destroyed. And me with it."

She stared at him. "You're saying that Victor helped to bring the tower down?"

"No, I don't think so. I don't know. But he lied at my trial. He was perfectly willing to lie so that the blame would all be dumped on me. So that I'd be sent off Earth and he'd have you to himself."

Lara shook her head, just the slightest of movements, as she said, "I can't believe that. I don't believe any of this!"

"But it's true! It's all true! Victor is a lying thief and Danvers helped him."

She sagged back on the padded bulkhead. Alexios climbed to his feet and sat beside her.

"I know it's a lot to accept all at once. But I really am Mance Bracknell. At least I was, once. Now I'm Dante Alexios. I'm fairly prosperous; I can offer you a fine life back on Earth. Victor stole you from me. I want you back."

"He's my husband," Lara repeated weakly.

He looked directly into her eyes. In the dim lighting of the compartment he could not see any tears in them.

"Lara, you can't tell me that you love Victor the way you loved me."

She said nothing.

"We were perfect for each other," he said. "The minute I first saw you, back in that dull statistics class with the

Chinese T.A. who could barely speak English, I fell hopelessly in love with you."

For long moments she remained silent. Then, "You certainly didn't show it."

"I was too shy. It didn't seem possible that anyone as wonderful as you would have the slightest interest in me."

Lara smiled faintly.

"We belong together, Lara. They've separated us for so many years, but we can be together again now."

Again that slight shake of her head. "So many years have gone by."

"But we can start again," he urged.

"It's not that simple."

"It can be, if you want it to be. Victor got what's coming to him. He's finished, out of the picture."

"He's my husband," she said, still again.

"He stole you from me!"

She looked away for a moment, then turned back to him. "Look, Mance or Alexios or whoever you are. I am married to Victor Molina. He's the father of my child. You've tried to ruin him—"

"Nothing less than he deserves," Alexios growled, feeling his anger simmering inside him again. "In fact, he deserves a lot worse."

"What you've told me might save him," Lara said.

Alexios was thunderstruck. He felt a wave of nausea wash over him. "You'd take him over me?"

"Mance Bracknell is dead," Lara said, her voice flat and cold. "So be it. We could never recapture what we had all those years ago. Do you think I could leave Victor and go with you, knowing what you've done to him?"

"But he *deserves* it!"

"No, he doesn't. And even if he did, his wife should be by his side, protecting and supporting him. For the sake of our child, if for no other reason."

"You belong with me!"

"No. My place is with my husband and son, no matter what happened in the past."

"That's . . ." Alexios ran out of words. This has gone all wrong, he said to himself. All wrong.

Lara got to her feet. "I'm going to tell Victor about this, and then McFergusen. I won't mention Mance Bracknell. I'll simply tell them that you confessed to me that you planted the false evidence."

"They'll find out who I am!" Alexios pleaded. "They'll send me back to the Belt!"

"Not if you can prove that the skytower was sabotaged. Not if you can lead the authorities to the people who are really responsible for all those deaths."

He stood up beside her, his knees unsteady, and watched as she abruptly turned away from him and left the observation lounge. He stood frozen, watching as the door slid closed. Then he felt the glare from Mercury's surface blaze through the heavily tinted blister of glassteel. It felt like the hot breath of doom.

GOETHE BASE

I t's all gone wrong, Alexios said to himself as he sat miserably alone in his sparely furnished office at the construction base. Horribly wrong.

Lara, Victor, and Danvers had left for Earth on the ship that had shepherded the six new power satellites from Selene. She must be telling Victor everything, Alexios thought. It's only a matter of time before the IAA or some other group sends investigators here to check me out. If they suspect I'm not who I say I am, they'll want to do DNA scans on me. If I refuse they'll get a court order.

It's finished, he told himself. Over. She's not the same Lara I knew. The years have changed her.

He stood up and studied his reflection in the blank wall screen. They've changed me, too, he realized. He paced across the little office, thinking that he was still all alone in the universe. Lara doesn't love me anymore. No one in the entire solar system cares about me. There's only one thing left to do. Get Yamagata down here and finish the job. Make him pay before they come after me. After that, it doesn't matter what happens.

Yet he hesitated. When the investigators come I could tell them the whole story, tell them how Yamagata sabotaged the skytower, how *he's* the one who's really responsible for all those deaths.

But the mocking voice in his head sneered, And they'll believe you? Against Yamagata? Where's your evidence? He's murdered everyone connected with the sabotage. Toshikazu was the last one, and his assassins even killed themselves so there'd be no possible witnesses remaining.

Alexios knew the severed end of the skytower lay more than four thousand meters beneath the surface of the Atlantic, near the fracture zone where hot magma wells up from deep beneath the Earth's crust. No one would send an expedition to search for the remains of nanomachines that had probably been dissolved by now, he knew.

He also knew that Saito Yamagata maintained the convenient fiction that his son ran Yamagata Corporation. He was in a lamasery in Tibet when the skytower went down, Alexios remembered. Yes, of course, the voice in his mind taunted. He pulled all the strings for this vast murderous conspiracy from his retreat in the Himalayas. Try getting the authorities to buy that.

Alexios shook his head slowly. No, I'm not going to try

to get the authorities to do anything. I'm going to take care of Yamagata myself. I'm going to end this thing once and for all.

He told the phone to call Saito Yamagata.

Yamagata was clearly uncomfortable about being out on the surface; Alexios could see the unhappy frown on his face through the visor of his helmet. Don't worry, he said silently, you won't be out here long. Only for the rest of your life.

The two men were riding a slow, bumping tractor across the bleak surface of Mercury, dipping down into shallow craters and then laboring up the other side, moving farther and farther from the base. It was night; the Sun would not rise for another hour, but the glow of starlight and the pale glitter of the zodiacal light bathed the bleak landscape in a cold, silvery radiance.

Despite all the months he'd been on Mercury, Alexios still could not get accustomed to the little planet's short horizon. It was like the brink of a cliff looming too close; the edge of the world. In the airless vacuum the horizon was sharp and clear, no blurring or softening with distance, a knife edge: the solid world ended and the black infinity of space lay beyond.

"You'll be out of camera range in two more minutes," the base controller's calm flat voice said in Alexios's helmet earphones.

"You have a satellite track on us, don't you?" he asked.

"Affirmative. Two of 'em, as a matter of fact."

"Our beacon's coming through all right?"

"Loud and clear."

"Good enough."

Even though the tractor's glassteel cabin was pressurized, both Yamagata and Alexios were wearing full spacesuits, their helmet visors closed and sealed. Safety regulations, Alexios had told Yamagata when the older man had grumbled about getting into the uncomfortable suit.

"How far are we going to go?" Yamagata asked as the tractor slewed around a house-sized boulder.

Taking one gloved hand off the steering controls to point out toward the horizon, Alexios said, "We've got to get to the other side of that fault line. Then we'll double back."

Yamagata grunted, and the frown on his face relaxed, but only slightly.

It had been easy enough to get him down to the planet's surface.

"I'd like to show you the site we're considering for the mass driver," Alexios had told Yamagata. "Naturally, we can't make the final decision. That's up to you."

Yamagata's image in Alexios's wall screen had turned thoughtful. "Is it necessary for me to inspect this location personally?"

Choosing his words carefully, Alexios had replied, "I understand, sir, that it's inconvenient and uncomfortable to come down here to the surface. Even a little dangerous, to be truthful."

Yamagata had stiffened at that. Drawing himself up to his full height, he'd told Alexios, "I will come to the base tomorrow. My transportation coordinator will inform you of when you may expect me."

Alexios had smiled. Touch the man on his Japanese brand of machismo and you've got him. The old samurai tradition. He doesn't want to lose face in front of his employees.

"I received a report from my son's technical experts in Japan," Yamagata said, staring straight ahead as he sat alongside Alexios in the lumbering tractor. "They believe your numbers on the solar cell degradation problem are exaggerated."

Alexios knew perfectly well that they were. "Exaggerated?" he asked.

"Overstated," said Yamagata, his voice muffled slightly by the spacesuit helmet.

It was impossible to shrug inside the heavy suit. Alexios said smoothly, "I admit that I showed you the worst-case numbers. I thought it best that way."

Yamagata grunted. "We may not have to harden the power satellites after all."

"That's good news, then," Alexios replied. It didn't matter now, he thought. None of it mattered any more.

Yamagata was silent for several kilometers. Then, "What makes you think this is the best site for the catapult launcher?" he demanded. "If it takes this long to get there, why is this site so preferable?"

Alexios smiled behind his visor. "It's that blasted fault line. If you approve the site, we'll bridge over it. But right now we have to go all the way around it. Won't be long now, though."

Yamagata nodded and seemed to settle down inside his suit.

It won't be long now, Alexios repeated silently.

FREIGHTER *XENOBIA*

Lara Tierney Molina could not sleep. Victor lay beside her, dead to the world on the sedatives and tranquilizers he'd been taking ever since boarding the creaking old freighter, coasting now on a four-month trajectory back to Selene.

The clock's digits glowing in the darkness read 12:53. She slipped out of bed, groped in the shadows of the darkened stateroom for the first dress she could find in her travel bag, and pulled it on. Victor would sleep for hours more, she knew. She tiptoed to the door, opened it as softly as she could, and stepped out into the passageway. As she slid the door closed and heard the faint click of its lock, she wondered which way led to the galley.

I have to think, she told herself as she walked slowly along the passageway. Its plastic walls were scuffed and dulled from long use, the floor tiles even worse. *Xenobia* had ferried a set of solar power satellites to Mercury for Yamagata's project; now its only cargo was a disgraced New Morality bishop, a humiliated astrobiologist, and herself. The IAA was paying Victor's fare and her own. The New Morality had refused to pay for Danvers's return; Saito Yamagata had graciously taken care of it.

Victor had demanded a hearing before the IAA's disciplinary board. McFergusen will chair that meeting, Lara thought. I'll have to tell them what Mance confessed to me. No, not Mance. He's a different man, this Dante Alexios. He's no longer Mance Bracknell.

Deep inside her she wondered why she hadn't told Victor about Alexios's confession. Victor was dazed and thick-witted from the tranquilizers that Yamagata's medical people had dosed him with, but she knew that wasn't the reason. Could she believe this Alexios person? Is he really Mance? How else would he know about how we met? He must be Mance. But that makes it even worse, even more complicated. Mance deliberately ruined Victor, revenged himself on poor Victor like some savage out of the dark ages. I'll *have* to tell Victor, I can't keep this from him. It might save his career, save his life.

Yet she hesitated, wondering, uncertain of herself or anything. Victor had lied at Mance's trial? Perjured himself to get rid of Mance? For me? How can I believe that? How can I believe any of this?

She saw a phone screen on the passageway wall and called up a schematic of the ship's interior layout. She'd been heading in the wrong direction, she saw. Turning, she started more confidently toward the galley. No one else was in the passageway at this time of night. There's probably a crew on duty in the bridge, Lara thought. Otherwise they're all sleeping.

All but me. I can save Victor. I'll go to the meeting and tell them that he was deliberately duped by false evidence planted by Dante Alexios. I can clear Victor's name. Elliott's, too.

And what happens to Dante Alexios? she asked herself. She thought she knew. McFergusen and his committee would not take her unsupported word. They'd want corroboration. They would send investigators to Mercury to question Mance—Alexios. And what if he claims innocence? What if he tells them my story is a total fabrication, a desperate attempt to save my husband?

The galley was empty. Nothing more than a small metal table and four swivel chairs bolted to the deck, with a row of food and drink dispensers lining one wall. Lara poured herself a mug of tepid coffee and sat wearily in one of the chairs.

I'll have to tell them that Alexios is really Mance Bracknell, she realized. They'll run tests on him to settle his identity. Once they find that he's Mance they'll send him back to the Belt, back to exile.

Can I do that to him? He said Victor stole me from him, said that he still loves me and wants me. Can I reward him by sending him back into exile? She wanted to cry. It would be such a relief to simply dissolve into tears and wait for someone else to solve this problem for her.

But there is no one else, she told herself. Except Victor, Jr. That made her sit up straighter. Her son. Hers and Victor's.

He has a stake in this, too. I can't allow McFergusen or Mance or anyone else to ruin little Victor's future. He needs my protection.

A shadow fell across her and she turned to see Elliott Danvers's hulking form filling the hatchway.

"You couldn't sleep either?" Danvers said, going to the coffee dispenser.

"No."

Danvers settled his bulk in the chair opposite Lara. It groaned as he sat on it, and the bishop sighed heavily.

"I've sent half a dozen messages to my superiors in Atlanta and they haven't seen fit to reply to any of them."

Lara saw that his fleshy face was pale, creased with lines she'd never noticed before. "What will happen to you once we get back to Earth?" she asked.

Danvers shrugged his massive shoulders. "I wish I knew. A reassignment, at least. They'll want to strip me of my title, I'm sure. Perhaps they'll throw me out altogether."

"I know you didn't do it," Lara said.

Danvers's eyes flared briefly. Then he murmured, "Thank you."

"I'm not merely being kind, Elliott. I know who actually duped Victor and planted the evidence that puts the blame on you."

Now his eyes stayed wide. "You . . . you do?"

"But if I tell who it really is, it will ruin his life."

"But he's trying to ruin my life!"

"I don't know what I should do," Lara said plaintively.

"Yes, you do," said the bishop. "You must do what is right. You can't cover up a lie. Forget about me—your husband's career is at stake."

"I know," said Lara.

"And what about your son? This affects him, too."

"I know," she repeated.

Danvers stared at her as if trying to pry the information

out of her by sheer willpower. At last he asked, "Why wouldn't you name the wrongdoer?"

"Because it will hurt him. Because he's been terribly hurt already and I'm not sure that I can do this to him, hurt him again."

"But . . . your husband! Your son! Me!"

Lara gripped her cup with both hands and stared down into it. "Maybe if I simply tell the committee that the man told me he did it, that he cleared you entirely, maybe that would be enough."

"Without naming him, so they can check? They'd think you're nothing but a wife who's willing to lie to protect her husband."

She nodded dejectedly. "I can't help one without hurting the other."

The bishop waited a heartbeat, then reached across the table to take her hands in his massive paws. "Lara, morality doesn't come in shades of gray. It's black and white. You either do the right thing or you do the wrong thing. There's no middle ground."

She looked into his soft gray eyes, red with sleeplessness, and thought that morality was simple when doing the right thing would save your own neck.

"It's more complicated than that," she said quietly.

"Then think of this," Danvers said, almost gently. "What is the greatest good for the greatest number of people? You have your husband and son to think of, as opposed to this mysterious wrongdoer."

She nodded. "My husband and son—and you."

BOREALIS PLANITIA

Wrapped in their cumbersome spacesuits, Alexios and Yamagata sat side by side in the tractor's transparent cab as it slowly trundled along the pitted, rock-strewn landscape.

"Borealis Planitia," Yamagata muttered. "The northern plain."

He sounded slightly nervous to Alexios, a little edgy. Inside the pressurized glassteel cabin they could hear one another without using the suits' radios, although their voices were muffled by the heavy helmets.

"This region is an ancient lava flow," Yamagata went on, as much to himself as to his companion. "Planetologists claim that this entire area was once a lake of molten lava, billions of years ago."

Alexios contented himself with steering the tractor through the maze of boulders that lay scattered across the ground. Now and again he rolled right over a smaller rock, making the tractor pitch and sway. To their right, the yawning crack of the fault line was narrowing. They would reach the end of it soon, Alexios knew.

Yamagata continued, "From orbit you can see the outlines of even older craters, ghost craters, drowned by the lava when it flowed across this region."

Alexios nodded inside his helmet. The man's talking just to hear himself talk, he thought. Trying to hide his fear at being out here. Grimly, Alexios added, He has a lot to be afraid of.

They drove on in silence. The time stretched. Alexios could feel in his bones the vibrating hum of the tractor's electric motors, hear his own breathing inside the helmet. He drove like an automaton; there seemed to be no emotion left inside him.

"You are very quiet," Yamagata said at last.

"Yes," replied Alexios.

"What are you thinking about?"

Alexios turned his head inside the fishbowl helmet to look squarely at the older man. "I've been thinking," he said, "about the skytower."

"The skytower?" Yamagata looked surprised. "That was years ago."

"Many years. Many lives."

"Technological hubris," said Yamagata. "The people who built it paid no attention to the danger it might pose."

"Part of it is still spinning outward, in deep space."

"Carrying the bodies of dozens of dead men and women."

"Murdered men and women," said Alexios.

Yamagata grunted. "That's one way to look at it, I suppose."

"The tower was sabotaged. All those who died were murdered."

"Sabotaged?"

"By agents of Yamagata Corporation."

Yamagata's jaw dropped open. "That's not true! It's impossible!"

Without taking his gloved hands from the steering controls, Alexios said, "We both know that it *is* possible and it did happen."

"Paranoid fantasy," Yamagata snapped.

"Is it? I was told the full story by the last surviving member of the plot. Just before your hired killers closed his mouth forever."

"My hired killers?" Yamagata scoffed. "I was in Chota Lamasery in the Himalayas when the skytower fell. We didn't even hear about it until a week or more after the tragedy."

"Yes, I know. That's your cover story."

Yamagata stared at this coldly intent man sitting beside him. He's insane, he thought. Alexios's eyes glittered with something beyond anger, beyond fury. For the first time since he'd been diagnosed with brain cancer, back in his first life, Yamagata felt fear gripping his innards.

"I was the director of the skytower project," Alexios told him, all the while wondering at the glacial calm that had settled upon him, as if he were sheathed in ice.

"The director of the skytower project was exiled," said Yamagata.

Alexios made a wan smile. "Like you, I've led more than one life."

"I had nothing to do with the skytower," Yamagata insisted.

"It was sabotaged by Yamagata Corporation people, using nanomachines to snap the tower at its most vulnerable point. The man who produced the nanobugs for you told me the entire story just before your assassins caught up with him."

"And you believed him?"

"He was terrified for his life," said Alexios. "Your assassins got him. They also blew up the ship we were in, to make sure that anyone he talked to would be killed, too."

"But you survived."

"I survived. To seek justice for all those you killed. To gain vengeance for having my own life destroyed."

"But I—" Yamagata caught himself and shut his mouth. He's a madman, he told himself. I had nothing to do with this; I was in the lamasery. Nobuhiko was running the corporation, just as he is now.

Suddenly his pulse began thudding in his ears. Nobu! If

Yamagata Corporation was involved in destroying the sky-tower, it was under Nobu's direction!

No, that couldn't be, Yamagata said to himself. Shaking his head, he thought, Nobu wouldn't do such a thing. He couldn't be that ruthless, that . . . murderous.

Or could he? Yamagata recalled those years when his advice to his son had led to the slaughters of the second Asteroid War, the massacre of the *Chrysalis* habitat. Nobu learned to be ruthless from me, he realized. The blood drained from his face. I have turned my son into a monster.

Alexios misread the ashen expression on Yamagata's face. "You admit it, then? You admit that the skytower was destroyed on your orders. Four million men, women, and children murdered—by you."

Yamagata realized there was nothing else to do. If I tell him that it was Nobuhiko's doing this madman will want to kill Nobu. Better to let him think it was me. Nobu is my son, my responsibility. Whatever he has done is my fault as much as his. Better for me to take the blame and the punishment. Let my son live.

"Well?" Alexios demanded.

Yamagata seemed to draw himself up straighter inside the bulky spacesuit. "I accept full responsibility," he said, his voice flat, lifeless.

"Good," said Alexios. He turned the steering wheel and the tractor veered slowly toward the yawning fault line, grinding slowly but inexorably toward the rift in Mercury's bleak ground as the first blazing edge of the Sun peeped above the horizon.

FREIGHTER *XENOBIA*

Bishop Danvers's mind was churning as he made his way back to his compartment. Is Lara telling the truth? he asked himself. She must be. She *must* be! She wouldn't make up a story like that, she couldn't. But the other side of his mind argued, Why wouldn't she? She's desperate to save her husband and protect her son. She might say anything if she thought it would help Victor.

As he slid back the door to his compartment he saw that the phone's yellow message light was blinking in the darkness. A message! His heart began thumping. From Atlanta. It must be an answer to my calls to Atlanta. Flicking on the ceiling lights, Danvers rushed to the compartment's flimsy little desk and told the phone to display the message.

It was indeed from Atlanta. From the archbishop himself!

Carnaby's wrinkled, bald, gnomish features took form in the phone's small display screen. He was unsmiling, his eyes flinty.

"Bishop Danvers, I am replying to your messages personally because your case is one of extreme importance to the New Morality movement."

Danvers felt immensely grateful. The archbishop is replying to me personally! Even though he knew it would take half an hour, at least, to get a reply back to Earth he automatically started to frame his message of gratitude to the archbishop.

Carnaby was going on, however, "A great American once said that extremism in the defense of our values is no vice. I can appreciate the extreme measures you took to discredit the godless scientists you've been battling against. But in our battle against these secularists, the movement must be seen by the general public as being beyond reproach, above suspicion. Your methods, once exposed to the public, will bring suspicion and discredit upon us all."

But I didn't do it! Danvers screamed silently at Carnaby's implacable image. I haven't done anything discreditable! Lara can prove it!

"Therefore," the archbishop continued, "I have no choice but to ask you for your resignation from the New Morality. One man must not be allowed to throw doubt upon our entire movement. I know this seems harsh to you, but it is for the higher good. Remember that a man may serve God in many ways, and your way will be to resign your office and your ordination in the movement. If you refuse you will be put on public trial as soon as you return to Earth and found guilty. I'm truly sorry it has to be this way, but you have become a liability to the New Morality and no individual, no matter who he is, can be allowed to threaten our work. May God be merciful to you."

The screen went blank.

Danvers stared at it for long, wordless minutes. His mind seemed unable to function. His chest felt constricted; it was an effort just to breathe.

At last, blinking with disbelief, lungs rasping painfully, Danvers realized that he had been drummed out of the New Morality movement. Thrown out into the gutter, just as the gamblers had done to him all those long years ago. All my work, all my years of service, they mean nothing, he thought. Lara's claim to know who actually planted the false evidence won't move them. I've been tainted, and they will be merciless with me.

I'm ruined. Destroyed. I have nowhere to go! No one to

turn to. Even if I could prove my innocence they wouldn't take me back. I'm tainted! Unclean!

My life is over, he told himself.

Lara returned to her compartment, where Victor was still tossing fitfully in their bed. She sat at the desk and sent a message to Victor, Jr., smiling reassuringly for her son and telling him she and his father would be back home in a few weeks.

Then she sat, wide awake, until Victor rose groggily from the roiled bedclothes and blinked sleep-fogged eyes at her.

"You're up?" he asked dully.

"I couldn't sleep."

He padded barefoot to the lavatory. She heard him urinate, then wash his face. He came back, hair still tousled, but looking reasonably alert.

"Victor," Lara heard herself ask him, "at Mance's trial, did you tell the truth about the skytower's construction?"

He looked instantly wary. "Why do you ask that?"

"Did you tell the truth?"

"It was so many years ago. . . ."

"Did you deliberately lie to put the blame on Mance?"

Molina stood next to the lavatory doorway, wearing nothing but his wrinkled underpants, staring at his wife.

"I've got to know, Victor," said Lara. "You've got to tell me the truth now."

He shuffled to the bed and sat wearily on it. "The tower collapsed," Molina said. "There was nothing any of us could do about that. They were going to blame it on Mance anyway—he didn't have a chance in hell of getting out of that trial alive. I wanted you, Lara! I've always wanted you! But as long as Mance was around you wouldn't even look at me!"

Lara said nothing. She didn't know what she could say.

"I wanted Mance out of the way," he admitted, his voice so low she could barely hear him. "I was so crazy in love with you. I still am."

He burst into tears.

Lara got up from the desk chair and went to the bed. Cradling her husband's head in her arms she crooned soothingly, "I understand, darling. I understand."

"I shouldn't have done it, I know," Molina blubbered. "I ruined Mance's life. But I did it for you. For you."

Lara was quite dry-eyed. "What's done is done," she said. "Mance is dead now. We've got to live the rest of our lives."

As she held him, Lara did not think of Mance Bracknell, nor of the strangely vicious man who called himself Dante Alexios. She did not think of Bishop Danvers or her husband, really, or even of herself. She thought of their son. Only Victor, Jr. He was the only one who mattered now.

SUNRISE

The rim of the slowly rising Sun was like molten lava pouring heat into the tractor's little bubble of a cab. Yamagata saw that Alexios was steering directly toward the sunrise and the yawning rift.

"What are you doing?" he demanded.

Turning the lumbering vehicle just before it reached the edge of the fault line, Alexios leaned on the brakes. The tractor ground to a halt.

"We get off here," he said.

"I thought—"

"Let's stretch our legs a little," said Alexios, popping the hatch on his side of the glassteel bubble.

Although he felt nothing inside his spacesuit, Yamagata realized that all the air in the cabin immediately rushed into the vacuum outside. Alexios turned back toward him and tapped the keypad on the wrist of his spacesuit. Yamagata heard the man's voice in his helmet earphones, "We'll have to use the suit radios to speak to one another now."

"You intend to kill me, then?" Yamagata asked as he opened the hatch on his side.

"You murdered four million people," Alexios said, his voice strangely soft, almost amused. "I think executing you is a simple act of justice."

"I see." Yamagata clambered slowly down from his seat to the hard, rock-strewn, airless ground. I'm in the hands of a madman, he thought.

"In case you're wondering," Alexios said as he walked around the tractor toward Yamagata, "your suit radio won't reach the base. Not without the tractor's relay, and I've disabled the tractor's outgoing frequency."

"I can't call for help, then," said Yamagata.

"Neither can I." With that, Alexios touched a control stud on his suit and the tractor started up again, silently churning up puffs of dust from the ground, and started trundling away from them.

"You're not going with it?" Yamagata asked, surprised.

"No, I'll stay here with you. We'll die together. Back at the base they'll see the tractor's beacon and think everything is normal. Until it's too late."

Yamagata almost laughed. "This is a simple act of justice?"

"Maybe not so simple, after all," Alexios agreed. "I've been dispensing justice for several days, but I don't quite seem to have the proper knack for it."

Alexios stepped closer to him. Yamagata backed away a

few steps, then realized the edge of the fault rift was close behind him.

"Dispensing justice?" he asked, stalling for time to think. "What do you mean?"

"Molina and Danvers," Alexios answered easily. "I'm the one who brought those Martian rocks here. I led Molina to them and he took the bait like the fool that he is."

"And Danvers?"

"I put the blame on him. Now they're both heading back to Earth in disgrace."

"You've deliberately ruined their careers."

"They deserve it. They destroyed my life, the two of them. They took everything I had."

He's insane, Yamagata told himself. The tractor was dwindling slowly, lumbering off toward the disturbing close edge of the horizon.

"Message for Mr. Yamagata." He heard the voice of the base controller in his helmet's earphones. "From the captain of the freighter *Xenobia*."

Alexios spread his gloved hands. "We can't reply to them."

"Then what—"

The controller didn't wait for an acknowledgement. "Here's the incoming message, sir."

Yamagata heard a soft click and then a different voice spoke. "Sir! I apologize for interrupting whatever you are doing, illustrious sir. The captain thought you would want to know that one of the passengers aboard ship has committed suicide. Bishop Danvers slit his throat in the lavatory of his cabin. The place is a bloody mess."

Yamagata stared hard at Alexios, but only saw his own reflection in the heavily tinted visor of the spacesuit's helmet.

"Thank you for the information," he said, in a near whisper.

"They can't hear you," Alexios reminded him.

The base controller's voice returned. "Is there any reply to the message, Mr. Yamagata? Sir? Can you hear me?"

Alexios walked to the rim of the rift. Damn! he said to himself. If they don't hear anything back they'll start worrying about us.

"Mr. Yamagata? Mr. Alexios? Reply, please."

If they send out a rescue team they'll go after the tractor, Alexios thought. It won't be until they find that we're not on it that they'll start hunting for us.

He gripped the arm of Yamagata's suit. "Come on, we're going to take a little walk."

Yamagata resisted. "Where do you want to take me?"

Pointing with his free hand, Alexios said, "Down there, to the bottom of the rift. With the Sun coming up you'll be more comfortable sheltered from direct sunlight. It'll be cooler down there, only a couple of hundred degrees Celsius in the shade."

"You wish to prolong my execution?"

"I wish to prevent our being rescued," Alexios replied.

Yamagata stepped to the edge of the rift. Inside the spacesuit it was difficult to see straight down, but the chasm's slope didn't seem terribly steep. Rugged, though, he saw. A slip of the foot could send me tumbling down to the bottom. If that didn't rupture my suit and kill me quickly, it might damage my radiators and life support pack enough to let me boil in my own juices.

He looked back at Alexios, standing implacably next to him. "After you," Alexios said, gesturing toward the edge of the rift.

Yamagata hesitated. Even with only the slimmest arc of the Sun's huge disk above the nearby horizon a flood of heat was sweeping across the barren ground. Dust motes sparkled and jumped like fireflies, suddenly electrified by the Sun's powerful ionizing radiance. Both men stared at the barren dusty ground suddenly turned manic as the particles danced and jittered in the newly risen Sun. Slowly they fell to the ground again, as if exhausted, their electrical charges neutralized at last.

They looked out to the horizon and gazed briefly at the blazing edge of the Sun; even through the deeply tinted visors of their helmets its overpowering brilliance made their eyes water. The Sun's rim was dancing with flaming prominences that writhed like tortured spirits in hell.

Yamagata heard his spacesuit groan and ping in the surging, all-encompassing heat. He looked down into the chasm again, and the after-image of the Sun burned in his vision. Turning around slowly in the cumbersome suit, he started down the pebbly, cracked slope backwards. Alexios followed him. It was hard, exhausting work. Yamagata's booted foot slipped on a loose stone and he went skittering down the pebbly slope several meters before grinding to a stop. Alexios came skidding down beside him.

"Are you all right?"

It took Yamagata several panting breaths before he could reply, "What difference does it make?"

Alexios grunted. "You're all right, then."

Yamagata nodded inside his helmet. The suit seemed intact; its life support equipment still functioned.

Both men were soaked with perspiration by the time they reached the bottom of the rift. Yamagata looked up and saw that the edge of the chasm was ablaze with harsh light.

"Sunrise," said Alexios. "You come from the land of the rising sun, don't you?"

Yamagata decided he wouldn't dignify that snide remark with a reply. Instead he said, "The message for me was that Bishop Danvers has committed suicide."

Silence for several heartbeats. Then Alexios said, "I didn't expect that."

"He slit his throat. Very bloody, from the description."

"I imagine it would be."

"You are responsible for his death."

Again a long wait before Alexios replied, "I suppose I am, in a way."

"In a way?" Yamagata jeered. "You planted false evidence and accused him falsely. As a result he killed himself. Murder, it seems to me. Or was that an execution, too?"

"He was a weak man," Alexios said. His voice sounded tight, brittle, in Yamagata's earphones.

"Weak or strong, he is dead because of you."

No reply.

Yamagata decided to twist the knife. "I am not a Christian, of course, but isn't it true that in your religion killing one man is just as hideous a sin as killing millions?"

Alexios immediately snapped, "I'm not a Christian, either."

"Ah, no? But do you feel any guilt for the death of Bishop Danvers?"

"He destroyed my life! Him and Molina. He got what he deserved."

Yamagata nodded inside his helmet. "You feel the guilt, don't you?"

"No," Alexios snapped. Then he raised his hand and pointed to the steep wall of the chasm. Yamagata saw that the slim line of glaring sunlight made the rift's edge look molten, so brilliant that it hurt his eyes to look up there.

"In five or six hours we'll be in the direct sun. A few hours after that our life support systems will run out of air. Then all the guilts, all the debts, they'll be paid. For both of us."

VALLEY OF DEATH

Alexios could not see Yamagata's face as they stood together in the bottom of the fault rift. I might as well be looking at a statue, he thought. A faceless, silent statue.

But then Yamagata stirred, came to life. He began walking down the rough uneven floor of the chasm, heading in the direction opposite to the path of the unoccupied tractor. Alexios realized he was heading back toward the base.

"You'll never make it," he said. "The base is more than thirty klicks from here. You'll run out of air long before then."

"Perhaps so," Yamagata replied, sounding almost cheerful in Alexios's helmet earphones. "However, I find it easier on my nerves to be active, rather than standing by passively waiting to die."

Despite himself, Alexios started after him. "You don't expect to be rescued, I hope."

"When I was in Chota Lamasery the lamas tried to teach me to accept my fate. I was a great disappointment to them."

"I imagine you were."

They walked along the broken, stony ground for several minutes. The walls of the rift rose steeply on both sides higher than their heads, higher even than the fins of the radiators that projected from their life support packs. The ground was hard, cracked here and there. Pebbles and larger rocks were strewn along the bottom, although not as plentifully as they were up on the surface. The planetologists would have a field day here, Alexios thought. Then he grinned at his inadvertent pun.

Yamagata stumbled up ahead of him and Alexios automatically grabbed him in both gloved hands, steadying him.

"Thank you," said Yamagata.

Alexios muttered, *"De nada."* Sweat dripped into his eyes, stinging. He felt perspiration dripping along his ribs. "I forgot to put on a sweatband," he said, wishing he could rub his eyes, mop his brow.

Yamagata made no reply, but Alexios could hear the man's steady breathing through the suit radio.

"I think the lamas made some impression on you," Alexios said, after almost half an hour of silent, steady, sweaty walking.

"Ah so?"

"You're taking this all very stoically."

"Not at all," Yamagata replied. "I am walking toward the base. I am doing what I can to get myself rescued. I have no intention of dying without a struggle."

"It won't do you any good."

"Perhaps not. But still, one must try. You didn't accept your fate when you were exiled, did you?"

That brought a flash of anger back from Alexios's memory. "No, I guess I didn't."

"Yet now you are committing suicide," Yamagata said. "You could have thrown me out of the tractor and returned to the base alone. Why give up your own life?"

"I have nothing left to live for."

"Nonsense! You are still a young man. You have many productive years ahead of you."

Thinking of Lara, of the skytower, of Danvers lying slumped in a ship's lavatory splattered with his own blood, Alexios repeated, "I have nothing left to live for."

"Not even the stars?" Yamagata asked.

"What's that supposed to mean?"

"The reason I came to Mercury, the real purpose behind building these power satellites, is to use them to propel a starship. Perhaps many starships."

Without a heartbeat's pause Alexios countered, "The reason I lived, the real purpose behind *my* life, was to build a tower that gave the human race cheap and easy access to space. You destroyed that. Finished it forever. They'll never build another skytower. They're too frightened of what happened to the first one."

"And for this you would deny the stars to humankind?"

"I'm not interested in humankind anymore. The stars will still be there a hundred years from now. A thousand."

"But we could do it now!" Yamagata insisted. "In a few years!"

"We could have been riding the skytower to orbit for pennies per pound by now."

Yamagata grunted. "I believe you have a saying about two wrongs?"

"You're a murderer."

"So are you."

"No, I'm an executioner," Alexios insisted.

"A convenient excuse." Yamagata wondered what Alexios would say if he revealed that Nobuhiko had destroyed the skytower. He shook his head inside the bubble helmet. Never, he told himself. Nobu must be protected at all costs. Even at the cost of my own life. My son has done a great wrong, but killing him will not make things right.

On they walked. With each step it seemed to grow hotter. Down at the bottom of the fault rift they were in shadow, yet the Sun's glaring brilliance crept inexorably down the chasm's wall, as slow and inescapable as fate. They could see the glaring line of sunlit rock inching down toward them; it made the rock face look almost molten hot. The heat increased steadily, boiling the juices out of them. Alexios heard his suit fans notch up to a higher pitch, and then a few minutes later go still higher. Even so he was drenched with perspiration, blinking constantly to keep the stinging sweat out of his eyes. He licked his lips and tasted salt. Wish I had a margarita, he thought. Then he realized how foolish that was. Maybe I'm getting delirious.

Yamagata kept moving doggedly along.

"Let's rest a couple of minutes," Alexios said to him.

"You rest, if you wish. I'm not tired."

Not tired? Alexios thought that Yamagata was simply being macho, unwilling or perhaps unable to show weakness to a man he took to be an inferior. He's older than I am, Alexios told himself. A lot older. Of course, he must have had all sorts of rejuve therapies. Or maybe he's just too damned stubborn to admit he's tired, too.

The heat was getting bad. Despite the suit's insulation and internal air conditioning, Alexios was sloshing. His legs felt shaky, his vision blurred from the damned sweat. He could *feel* the Sun's heat pressing him down, like the breath of a blast furnace, like a torrent of molten steel pouring over him. Still Yamagata plowed ahead steadily, as if nothing at all was bothering him. Blast it all, Alexios thought. If he can do it, so can I. And he trudged along behind the older man.

Until, hours later, the harsh unfiltered rays of the Sun reached the fins of his suit's radiator.

DEATH WISHES

Yamagata stumbled, up ahead of him. Alexios reached for the spacesuited figure but he was too slow. Yamagata pitched forward and, in the dreamlike slow-motion of Mercury's low gravity, hit the ground: knees first, then his outstretched hands, finally his body and helmeted head.

Alexios heard him grunt as if he'd been hit by a body blow. The rift was narrow here; there was barely room for him to step beside the fallen man without scraping his radiator fins on the steep rocky wall of the chasm.

"Are you all right?"

"If I were all right I'd be on my feet," Yamagata retorted, "instead of lying here on my belly."

The bottom of the rift was half in sunlight now, the huge rim of the Sun peering down at them now like a giant unblinking eye, like the mouth of a red-hot oven. Alexios was so hot inside his suit that he felt giddy, weak. Blinking away sweat, he peered at Yamagata's backpack. It looked okay. Radiator fins undamaged. No loose hoses.

"I can't seem to move my legs," Yamagata said.

"I'll help you up."

It was difficult to bend in the hard-shell suit. Alexios tried to reach down and grasp Yamagata by the arm.

"Put your hands beneath you and push up," he said. "I'll help."

They both tried, grunting, moaning with strain. After several minutes Yamagata was still on his belly and Alexios sank down to a sitting position beside him, exhausted, totally drained.

"It's . . . not going to . . . work," he panted.

Yamagata said. "My nose is bleeding. I must have bumped it on the visor when I fell."

"Let's rest a few minutes, then try again."

"I have no strength left."

Alexios turned his head slightly and sucked on the water nipple inside his helmet. Nothing. Either it was blocked or he'd drunk the last of his suit's water supply. It's all coming out as sweat, he said to himself.

"There ought to be some way to recondense our sweat and recycle it back into drinkable water," he mused.

"An engineer's mind never stops working," said Yamagata.

"Fat lot of good it does us."

"You should record the idea, however," said Yamagata, "so that whoever finds us will be able to act on it."

"A tycoon's mind never stops working," Alexios muttered.

"This tycoon's mind will stop soon enough."

Alexios was too hot and tired to argue the point. We're being baked alive, he thought. The suits' life support systems are running down.

"What do you think will kill us," Yamagata asked, "dehydration or suffocation, when our air runs out?"

Squeezing his eyes shut to block out the stinging sweat, Alexios replied, "I think we'll be parboiled by this blasted heat."

Yamagata was silent for a few moments. Then, "Do you think the base has sent out a search team?"

"Probably, by now. They'll follow the tractor's beacon, though."

"But when they find the tractor is empty . . . ?"

Alexios desperately wanted to lean back against the rock wall, but was afraid it would damage his radiators. "Then they'll start looking for us. They'll have to do that on foot, or in tractors. We'll be dead by the time they find us."

"Hmm," Yamagata murmured. "Don't you think they could hear our suit radios?"

"Down in this rift? Not likely."

"Then we will die here."

"That's about the size of it."

After several silent minutes Yamagata asked, "Is your sense of justice satisfied?"

Alexios thought it over briefly. "All I really feel right now is hot. And tired. Bone tired. Tired of everything, tired of it all."

"I too."

"Vengeance isn't much consolation for a man," Alexios admitted.

"Better to have built the starship."

"Better to have built the skytower."

"Yes," said Yamagata. "It is better to create than destroy."

"I'll drink to that."

Yamagata chuckled weakly. "A bottle of good champagne would be very fine right now."

"Well chilled."

"Yes, ice cold and sparkling with bubbles."

"That's not going to happen."

"No, I fear not."

"Maybe we should just open the suits and get it over with. I'm broiling in here."

Yamagata said, "First I want to record my last will and testament, but I can't reach the keypad on my wrist. Can you assist me?"

Alexios let out a weary breath, then slowly rolled over onto all fours and crawled over the gritty ground to Yamagata's extended left hand. It took all his strength to move less than two meters. At last he reached his outstretched arm and pressed the RECORD tab on the wrist keypad. In his earphones he heard a faint click and then a deadness as Yamagata's suit-to-suit frequency shut off.

Lying there on his own belly now, head to helmeted head with Yamagata, Alexios thought, Last will and testament. Not a bad idea. With his last iota of strength, he turned his own suit radio to the recording frequency and began speaking, slowly, his throat dry, his voice rasping, offering his final words to the woman he had loved.

When the rescue team finally found them, some twelve hours later, Alexios and Yamagata were still lying head to head. Their gloved hands were clasped, Alexios's right with Yamagata's left. It was impossible to tell if their hands were locked in a final grasp of friendship or a last, desperate grip of struggle. Some of the rescuers thought the former, some the latter.

The team argued about it as they tenderly carried their spacesuited bodies back to Goethe base. From there they were flown up to *Himawari,* still in orbit around Mercury. The medical team there determined that both men had died of dehydration. They were only five kilometers from Goethe base when they died.

The recording found on Yamagata's suit radio was sent to his son, Nobuhiko, in New Kyoto. Alexios's recording was sent to Lara Tierney Molina, in her family's home in Colorado.

EPILOGUE:
LAST WILLS

Lara sat alone in her old bedroom in her family's house in Colorado, listening to Mance's grating, bone-dry voice forcing out the words that would clear her husband. He confessed to everything: to assuming the identity of Dante Alexios, to spiriting the rocks from Mars and planting them on Mercury, to luring Victor to Mercury and making him the victim of the hoax.

Victor can clear his name with this, she thought. He'll never outlive the stigma entirely, but at least he can show that he was deliberately duped, that he's not a cheat. He can rebuild his career.

She looked out the bedroom window and saw that evening shadows were draping the distant mountains in shades of purple. Victor would be coming home soon, she knew. She briefly wondered why she felt no joy, not even a sense of relief that Victor's ordeal was at last finished. But she knew why: Mance. Mance is dead. That's finished, too.

Tears misted her eyes as she thought of all the things that might have been. But a chill ran through her. Victor was willing to send Mance to hell because he loved me and wanted me. And Mance fought his way out of exile and died on Mercury because he loved me. He gave up his revenge on Victor, he even gave up his life, because he loved me.

She began sobbing softly, wondering what she should do now, what she could do. She felt surrounded by death.

Then she heard footsteps pounding up the stairs and before she could dab at her eyes with a tissue the bedroom door flung open and Victor, Jr., burst in.

"Daddy's home!" the eight-year-old announced, as if it was the most glorious event in history. "He's parking his car in the driveway."

Lara got to her feet and smiled for her son. Life goes on, she told herself. Life goes on.

Sitting alone in the dim shadows of the small, teak-paneled office of his privacy suite, where not even the oldest family retainer dared to interrupt him, Nobuhiko Yamagata listened in stony silence to his father's gasping, grating final words.

He knows that I caused the skytower to fall, Nobuhiko said to himself. He blames himself for teaching me to be ruthless. How like my father: credit or blame, he takes it all for himself.

". . . four million deaths," the elder Yamagata's voice was rasping. "That is a heavy burden to bear, my son."

Nobu nodded. Unbidden, a childhood memory rushed upon him. He was six years old, and he had run down one of the house's cats with his electric go-cart. His father loomed before him, his face stern. Young Nobu admitted he'd killed the cat, and even confessed that it was no accident; he'd deliberately tried to hit the animal.

"I thought it would get out of my way," he said. "It was too fat and lazy to save itself."

Father's face showed surprise for an instant, then he regained his self-control. "That creature's life was in your hands," he said. "It was your responsibility to protect it, not to kill it. The world is filled with fat and lazy creatures. You have no right to kill them simply because they get in your way." And he walked away from his son. No punishment, although Nobu drove his go-cart with greater care afterward. For a while.

"Four million deaths," his father's voice rasped from the

audio speaker. "And mine, too. I'm dying because of the skytower."

Nobu's eyes widened. Father! I've murdered you!

Aloud, he cried, "What have I done? What have I done?"

As if he could hear his son's sudden anguish, Saito Yamagata gasped, "If you have any . . . feelings for me . . . come to Mercury. Finish . . . my work. Please, Nobu. Give us . . . the stars."

His father's voice went silent. Nobuhiko sank back against his desk chair. The intimate office was lit only by the lamp on his desk, a single pool of light against the shadows.

Nobu fingered the controls in his chair's armrest that turned the office ceiling transparent. Leaning his head back, he saw the stars glittering in the dark night sky.

Father went to Mercury to atone for his sins, Nobuhiko thought. Now he expects me to do the same to atone for my own.

His lips curled into an ironic smile. Leave everything and traipse off to Mercury to build power satellites that will propel a starship. How like Father. Always trying to make me live up to my responsibilities.

Nobu got to his feet. I suppose I could direct the star project from here, he thought. I can visit Mercury but I don't have to remain there permanently.

He knew he was fooling himself. As he left his office and rejoined his family, he wondered how long it would take to travel to Alpha Centauri.

ACKNOWLEDGMENTS

My thanks once again to Jeff Mitchell, who really is a rocket scientist from MIT; to Steven Howe, as bright and innovative a physicist as I ever met; and to David Gerrold, whose description of a "beanstalk" in his novel *Jumping Off the Planet* is the best I have seen—true friends in need, each one of them.

The epigraphs heading the prologue and main sections of this novel are from William Shakespeare, Sonnets 29 and 123; Edgar Allan Poe, "The Conqueror Worm"; John Dryden, "Absalom and Achitophel"; and Shakespeare again, *Titus Andronicus,* Act II, Scene 3.

PROMETHEANS

To Ray Bradbury,
a Promethean if ever there was one.

INTRODUCTION

There are two kinds of people in the world: Luddites and Prometheans. This book is about Prometheans.

But first let me tell you what a Luddite is, and then what a Promethean is, so that you can decide for yourself which type of person you are.

History has not been kind to Ned Ludd, the unwitting founder of the Luddite movement of the early nineteenth century. Webster's *New World Dictionary* describes Ludd as feeble-minded. The *Encyclopaedia Britannica* says he was probably mythical.

The Luddites were very real, however. They were English craftsmen who tried to stop the young Industrial Revolution by destroying the textile mills that were taking away their jobs. Starting in 1811, the Luddites rioted, wrecked factories, and even killed at least one employer who had ordered his guards to shoot at a band of rioting workmen. After five years of such violence, the British government took harsh steps to suppress the Luddites, hanging dozens and transporting others to prison colonies in far-off Australia. That broke the back of the movement, but did not put an end to the underlying causes that had created the movement. Slowly, painfully, over many generations, the original Luddite violence evolved into more peaceful political and legal activities. The labor movement grew out of the ashes of the Luddites' terror. Marxism arose in reaction to capitalist exploitation of workers. The Labour Party in Britain, and socialist governments elsewhere in the world, are the descendants of that early resistance against machinery.

Today the progeny of those angry craftsmen live in

greater comfort and wealth than their embattled forebears could have dreamed in their wildest fantasies. Not because employers and factory owners suddenly turned beneficent. Not because the labor movement and socialist governments have eliminated human greed and selfishness. But because the machines—the machines that the Luddites feared and tried to destroy—have generated enough wealth to give common laborers houses of their own, plentiful food, excellent medical care, education for their children, personally owned automobiles, television sets, refrigerators, stereos, all the accouterments of modern life which we take so much for granted that we almost disdain them, but which would have seemed miracles beyond imagination to the original Luddites.

We still have the Luddite mentality with us today: people who distrust or even fear the machines that we use to create wealth for ourselves. The modern Luddites are most conspicuous in their resistance to high technology such as computers and automated machinery, nuclear reactors, high-voltage power lines, airports, fertilizers and food additives. To today's Luddites, any program involving high technology is under immediate and intense suspicion. In their view, technology is either dangerous or evil or both, and must be stopped. Their automatic response is negative; their most often used word is *no*.

Opposing the Luddite point of view stands a group of people who fear neither technology nor the future. Instead, they rush forward to try to build tomorrow. They are the Prometheans, named so after the demigod of Greek legend who gave humankind the gift of fire.

Every human culture throughout history has created a Prometheus myth, a legend that goes back to the very beginnings of human consciousness. In this legend, the first humans are poor, weak, starving, freezing creatures, little

better than the animals of the forest. A godling—
Prometheus to the Greeks, Loki to the Norse, Coyote to
the Plains Indians of America—takes pity on the miserable humans and brings down from the heavens the gift of
fire. The other gods are furious, because they fear that with
fire the humans will exceed the gods themselves in power.
So they punish the gift-giver, eternally.

And, sure enough, with fire the human race does indeed
become the master of the world.

The myth is fantastic in detail, yet absolutely correct in
spirit. Fire was indeed a gift from the sky. Undoubtedly a
bolt of lightning set a tree or bush afire, and an especially
curious or courageous member of our ancestors overcame
the very natural fear of the flames to reach out for the bright
warm energy. No telling how many times our ancestors got
nothing for their troubles except burned fingers and yowls
of pain. But eventually they learned to handle fire safely, to
use it. And with fire, technology became the main force in
human development.

Technology is our way of dealing with the world, our
path for survival. We do not grow wings like the eagle, or
claws like the bear, or fleet-running legs like the deer. We
make tools. We build planes, we make clothing, we manufacture automobiles. The English biologist J. B. S. Haldane
said, "The chemical or physical inventor is always a Prometheus. There is no great invention, from fire to flying,
that has not been hailed as an insult to some god."

In a broader context, we might say that the basic difference between the Luddites and the Private is the
difference between an optimist and a pessimist. Is the glass
half full of water or half empty?

Many human beings see themselves, and the entire human race, through the weary eyes of ancient pessimism.
They see humankind as a race of failed angels, inherently

flawed, destined for eternal frustration. Thus we get the myth of Sisyphus, whose punishment in Hades was to eternally struggle to roll a huge stone up a hill, only to have it always roll back down again as soon as he got it to the summit. It sounds very intellectual to be a pessimist, to adopt a world-weary attitude; at the very least, no one can accuse you of enthusiasm or youthful vigor.

The optimists tend to see the human race as a species evolving toward immortality. We are perfectible creatures, they believe. Optimists can be accused of naïveté, but they can also point to recent history and show that human thought has improved the human condition immensely within the few short centuries in which science has come into play. Certainly there are shortcomings, pitfalls, drawbacks, to every advance the human race makes. But the optimists look to the future with the confidence that humankind can use its brains, its hands and its heart to constantly improve the world.

Incidentally, it is this difference between the pessimists and optimists that causes a fundamental resistance among the pessimists to science fiction. Especially among those who specialize in the literature of the past, the optimistic literature of a brighter tomorrow is anathema. They simply cannot fathom it; they are blind to what science fiction says. Even *within* the science fiction field, its practitioners often fall prey to this ancient schism, regarding darkly pessimistic stories as somehow more "literary" than brightly optimistic ones.

There is a bit of the pessimistic Luddite in each of us, and each of us is something of an optimistic Promethean. This book, though, deals exclusively with Prometheans, men and women who do not fear technology but rather embrace it and use it to build the future.

About half of this book is fiction, short stories of the relatively near future. The other half is nonfiction, speculative essays and articles that relate to the fictional pieces in a general way. Fact and fiction both deal with Prometheans, real and imagined, the kind of people who call down the lightning from the sky—and then use it to make a better world.

—Ben Bova
West Hartford, Connecticut

SAM GUNN

The basic idea for this story occurred to me back in the years when I was an editor. For the better part of a decade I tried to get one writer after another to write a story for *Analog* or, later, *Omni* around this idea. All I ever got for my troubles was a series of blank stares and muttered promises to "give it a shot."

When I finally stopped being an editor and began to write short fiction again, I tackled the idea myself. *Sam Gunn* is the result. Sam is a true Promethean—inventive and irreverent, feisty and tough, good-hearted and crafty. Ed Ferman, editor and publisher of *The Magazine of Fantasy and Science Fiction* not only bought the story, he published it in his magazine's 34th anniversary issue, which pleased me no end.

By the time I was finished with the story, it occurred to me that Sam is too good a character to drop. There will be more tales about Sam Gunn, and maybe even a novel about him. But that's for the future. Here's what Sam looked like when I first set my inner eye on him.

■

The spring-wheeled truck rolled to a silent stop on the Sea of Clouds. The fine dust kicked up by its six wheels floated lazily back to the mare's soil. The hatch to the truck cab swung upward, and a space-suited figure climbed slowly down to the lunar surface, clumped a dozen ponderously careful steps, then turned back toward the truck.

"Yeah, this is the spot. The transponder's beeping away, all right."

Two more figures clambered down from the cab, bulbous and awkward-looking in the bulky space suits. One of them turned a full three hundred sixty degrees, scanning the scene through the gold-tinted visor of the suit's bubble helmet. There was nothing to be seen except the monotonous gray plain, pockmarked by craters like an ancient, savage battlefield that had been petrified into solid stone long eons ago.

"Christ, you can't even see the ringwall from here!"

"That's what he wanted—to be out in the open, without a sign of civilization in sight. He picked this spot himself, you know."

"Helluva place to want to be buried."

"That's what he specified in his will. Come on, let's get to work. I want to get back to Selene City before the sun sets."

It was a local joke: the three space-suited workers had more than two hundred hours before sunset.

Grunting even in the general lunar gravity, they slid the coffin from the back of the truck and placed it gently on the roiled, dusty ground. Then they winched the four-meter-high crate from the truck and put it down softly next to the coffin. While one of them scoured out a coffin-sized hole in the ground with the blue-white flame of a plasma torch, the other two uncrated the big package.

"Ready for the coffin," said the worker with the torch.

The leader of the trio inspected the grave. The hot plasma had polished the stony ground. The two workers heard him muttering over their helmet earphones as he used a hand laser to check the grave's dimensions. Satisfied, he helped them drag the gold-filagreed coffin to the hole and slide it in.

"A lot of work to do for a dead man."

"He wasn't just any ordinary man."

"It's still a lot of work. Why in hell couldn't he be recycled like everybody else?"

"Sam Gunn," said the leader, "never did things like everybody else. Not in his whole cussed long life. Why should he be like the rest of us in death?"

They chattered back and forth through their suit radios as they uncrated the big package. Once they had removed all the plastic and the bigger-than-life statue stood sparkling in the sunlight, they stepped back and gaped at it.

"It's glass!"

"Christ, I never saw anything so damned big."

"Must have cost a fortune to get it here. Two fortunes!"

"He had it done at Island One, I hear. Brought the sculptor up from Earthside and paid him enough to keep him at L-4 for two whole years. God knows how many times he tried to cast a statue this big and failed."

"I didn't know you could make a glass statue so big."

"In zero gee you can. It's hollow. If we were in air, I could ping it with my finger and you'd hear it ring."

"Crystal."

"That's right."

One of the workers, the young man, laughed softly.

"What's so funny?" the leader asked.

"Who else but Sam Gunn would have the gall to erect a crystal statue to himself and then have it put out in the middle of this godforsaken emptiness, where nobody's ever going to see it. It's a monument to himself, for himself. What ego! What monumental ego."

The leader chuckled, too. "Yeah. Sam had an ego, all right. But he was a smart little guy, too."

"You knew him?" the young woman asked.

"Sure. Knew him well enough to tell you that he didn't pick this spot for his tomb just for the sake of his ego. He was smarter than that."

"What was he like?"

"When did you know him?"

"Come on, we've still got work to do. He wants the statue positioned exactly as he stated in his will, with its back toward Selene and the face looking up toward Earth."

"Yeah, okay, but when did you know him, huh?"

"Oh golly, years ago. Decades ago. When the two of us were just young pups. The first time either of us came here, back in—Lord, it's thirty years ago. More."

"Tell us about it. Was he really the hero that the history tapes say he was? Did he really do all the things they say?" asked the young woman.

"He was a phony!" the young man snapped. "Everybody knows that. A helluva showman, sure, but he never did half the stuff he took credit for. Nobody could have, not in one lifetime."

"He lived a pretty intense life," said the leader. "If it hadn't been for a faulty suit valve he'd still be running his show from here to Titan."

"A showman. That's what he was. No hero."

"What was he like?" the young woman repeated.

So, while the two youngsters struggled with the huge, fragile crystal statue, the older man sat himself on the lip of the truck's cab hatch and told them what he knew about the first time Sam Gunn came to the Moon.

The skipper used the time-honored cliché. He said, "Houston, we have a problem here."

There were eight of us, the whole crew of Artemis IV, huddled together in the command module. After six weeks of living on the Moon, the module smelled like a pair of unwashed gym socks. With a woman President, the space agency figured it would be smart to name the second round of lunar explorations after a female: Artemis was Apollo's sister. Get it?

But it had just happened that the computer who picked the crew selections for Artemis IV picked all men. Six weeks without even the sight of a woman, and now our blessed-be-to-god return module refused to light up. We were stranded. No way to get back home.

As usual, capcom in Houston was the soul of tranquility. "Ah, A-IV, we read you and copy that the return module is no-go. The analysis team is checking the telemetry. We will get back to you soonest."

It didn't help that capcom, that shift, was Sandi Hemmings, the woman we all lusted after. Among the eight of us, we must have spent enough energy dreaming about cornering Sandi in zero gravity to propel each of us right back to Houston. Unfortunately, dreams have a very low specific impulse, and we were still stuck on the Moon, a quarter-million miles from the nearest woman.

Sandi played her capcom duties strictly by the book, especially since all our transmissions were taped for later review. She kept the traditional Houston poker face, but managed to say, "Don't worry, boys. We'll figure it out and get you home."

Praise God for small favors.

We had spent hours checking and rechecking the cursed return module. It was engineer's hell: everything checked but nothing worked. The thing just sat there like a lump of dead metal. No electrical power. None. Zero. The control board just stared at us as cold and glassy-eyed as a banker listening to your request for an unsecured loan. We had pounded it. We had kicked it. In our desperation we had even gone through the instruction manual, page by page, line by line. Zip. Zilch. The bird was dead.

When Houston got back to us, six hours after the skipper's call, it was the stony, unsmiling image of the mission coordinator who glowered at us as if we had deliberately screwed up the return module. He told us:

"We have identified the problem, Artemis IV. The return module's main electrical power supply has malfunctioned."

That was like telling Othello that he was a Moor.

"We're checking out bypasses and other possible fixes," Old Stone Face went on. "Sit tight, we'll get back to you."

The skipper gave him a patient sigh. "Yes, sir."

"We're not going anywhere," said a whispered voice. Sam Gunn's, I was certain.

The problem, we finally discovered, was caused by a micrometeoroid, no less. A little grain of sand that just happened to roam through the solar system for four and a half billion years and then decided to crash-dive itself right into the main fuel cell of our return module's power supply. It was so tiny that it didn't do any visible damage to the fuel cell; just hurt it enough to let it discharge electrically for most of the six weeks we had been on the Moon. And the other two fuel cells, sensing the discharge through the module's idiot computer, tried to recharge their partner for six weeks. The result: all three of them were dead and gone by the time we needed them.

It was Sam who discovered the pinhole in the fuel cell, the eighteenth time we checked out the power supply. I can remember his exact words, once he realized what had happened: "Shit!"

Sam was a feisty little guy who would have been too short for astronaut duty if the agency hadn't lowered the height requirements so that women could join the corps. He was a good man, a whiz with a computer and a born tinkerer who liked to rebuild old automobiles and then race them on the abandoned freeways whenever he could scrounge up enough old-fashioned petrol to run them. The Terror of Clear Lake, we used to call him. The Texas Highway Patrol had other names for him. So did the agency administrators; they cussed near threw him out of the astronaut corps at least half a dozen times.

But we all loved Sam, back in those days, as we went through training and then blasted off for our first mission to the Moon. He was funny, he kept us laughing. And he did the things and said the things that none of us had the guts to do or say.

The skipper loved Sam a little less than the rest of us, especially after six weeks of living in each other's dirty laundry. Sam had a way of *almost* defying any order he received; he reacted very poorly to authority figures. Our skipper, Lord love him, was as stiff-backed an old-school authority figure as any of them. He was basically a good Joe, and I'm cursed if I can remember his real name. But his big problem was that he had memorized the rule book and tried never to deviate from it.

Well, anyway, there we were, stranded on the lunar surface after six weeks of hard work. Our task had been to make a semi-permanent underground base out of the prefabricated modules that had been, as the agency quaintly phrased it, "landed remotely on the lunar regolith in a series of carefully-coordinated unmanned logistics missions." In other words, they had dropped nine different module packages over a fifty-square-kilometer area of Mare Nubium and we had to find them all, drag them to the site that Houston had picked for Base Gamma, set them up properly, scoop up enough of the top layers of soil to cover each module and the connecting tunnels to a depth of 0.3048 meter (that's one foot, in English), and then link in the electric power reactor and all the wiring, plumbing, heating and air circulation units. Which we had done, adroitly and efficiently, and now that our labors were finished and we were ready to leave—no go. Too bad we couldn't have covered the return module with 0.3048 meter of lunar soil; that would have protected the fuel cells from that sharpshooting micrometeoroid.

The skipper decided it would be bad procedure to let us mope around and brood.

"I want each of you to run a thorough inventory of all your personal supplies: the special foods you've brought with you, your spare clothing, entertainment kits, the works."

"That'll take four minutes," Sam muttered, loud enough for us all to hear him. The eight of us were crammed into the command module, eight guys squeezed into a space built for three, at most. It was barely high enough to stand in, and the metal walls and ceiling always felt cold to the touch. Sam was pressed in with the guys behind me; I was practically touching noses with the skipper. The guys in back giggled at his wisecrack. The skipper scowled.

"Goddammit, Gunn, can't you behave seriously for even a minute? We've got a real problem here."

"Yessir," Sam replied. If he hadn't been squeezed in so tightly, I'm sure he would have saluted. "I'm merely attempting to keep morale high, sir."

The skipper made an unhappy snorting noise, and then told us that we would spend the rest of the shift checking out *all* the supplies that were left: not just our personal stuff, but the mission's supplies of food, the nuclear reactor, the water recirculation system, equipment of all sorts, air. . . .

We knew it was busywork, but we had nothing else to do. So we wormed our way out of the command module and crawled through the tunnels toward the other modules that we had laid out and then covered with bulldozed soil. It was a neat little buried base we had set up, for later explorers to use. I got a sort of claustrophobic feeling, just then, that this buried base might turn into a mass grave for eight astronauts.

I was dutifully heading back for barracks module A, where four of us had our bunks and personal gear, to check out my supplies as the skipper had ordered. Sam snaked up beside me. Those tunnels, back in those days, were prefabricated Earthside to be laid out once we got to the construction site. I think they were designed by midgets. You couldn't stand up in them; they were too low. You had to really crawl along on hands and knees if you were my size. Sam was able to shuffle through them with bent knees, knuckle-walking like a miniature gorilla. He loved the tunnels.

"Hey, wait up," he hissed to me.

I stopped.

"Whattaya think will get us first, the air giving out or we starve to death?"

He was grinning cheerfully. I said, "I think we're going to poison our air with methane. We'll fart ourselves to death in another couple of days."

Sam's grin widened. "C'mon . . . I'm setting up a pool on the computer. I hadn't thought of air pollution. You wanna make a bet on that?" He started to King-Kong down the shaft to the right, toward the computer and life-support module. If I had had the space, I would have shrugged. Anyway, I followed him there.

Three of the other guys were in the computer module, huddled around the display screen like Boy Scouts around a campfire.

"Why aren't you checking out the base's supplies, like the skipper said?" I asked them.

"We are, Straight Arrow," replied Mickey Lee, our refugee from Chinatown. He tapped the computer screen. "Why go sorting through all that junk when the computer has it already listed in alphabetical order for us?"

That wasn't what the skipper wanted, and we all knew it, but Mickey was right. Why bother with busywork? We wrote down lists that would keep the skipper happy. By hand. If we had let the computer print out the lists, Skip would have gotten wise to us right away.

While we scribbled away, copying what was on the screen, we talked over our basic situation.

"Why the hell can't we use the nuke to recharge the fuel cells?" Julio Marx asked. He was our token Puerto Rican Jew, a tribute to the agency's Equal Opportunity policy. Julio was also a crackerjack structural engineer who had saved my life the day I had started to unfasten my helmet in the barracks module just when one of those blessed prefab tunnels had cracked its airlock seal. But that's another story.

Sam gave Julio a sorrowful stare. "The two systems are incompatible, Jules." Then, with a grin, Sam launched into the phoniest Latin accent you ever heard. "The nuclear theeng, man, it got too many volts for the fuel cells. Like, you plug the nukie to the fuel cells, man, you make a beeg boom and we all go to dat big San Juan in thee sky. You better steek to plucking chickens, man, an' leave the electreecity alone."

Julio, who towered a good inch and a half over Sam, grinned back at him and answered, "Okay, Shorty, I dig."

"Shorty! Shorty!" Sam's face went red. "All right, that's it. The hell with the betting pool. I'm gonna let you guys all die of boredom. Serve you right."

We made a big fuss and soothed his feathers and cajoled him into setting up the pool. With a great show of hurt feelings and reluctant but utterly selfless nobility, Sam pushed Mickey Lee out of the chair in front of the computer terminal and began playing the keyboard like a virtuoso pianist. Within a few minutes the screen was displaying a list of possible ways for us to die, with Sam's swiftly calculated odds next to each entry. At the touch of a button, the screen displayed a graph, showing how the odds for each mode of dying changed as time went on.

Suffocation, for example, started off as less than a one percent possibility. But within a month the chances began to rise fairly steeply. "The air scrubbers need replacement filters," Sam explained, "and we'll be out of them inside of two more weeks."

"They'll have us out of here in two weeks, for Christ's sake," Julio said.

"Or drop fresh supplies for us," said Ron Avery, the taciturn pilot whom we called Cowboy because of his lean, lanky build and his slow Western drawl.

"Those are the odds," Sam snapped. "The computer does not lie. Pick your poison and place your bets."

I put fifty bucks down on Air Contamination, not telling the other guys about my earlier conversation with Sam. Julio took Starvation, Mickey settled on Dehydration (Lack of Water), and Ron picked Murder—which made me shudder.

"What about you, Sam?" I asked.

"I'll wait 'til the other guys have a chance," he said.

"You gonna let the skipper in on this?" Julio asked.

Sam shook his head. "If I tell him . . ."

"I'll tell him," Ron volunteered, with a grim smile. "I'll even let him have Murder, if he wants it. I can always switch to Suicide."

"Droll fellow," said Sam.

Well, you probably read about the mission in your history tapes. Houston was supporting three separate operations on the Moon at the same time, and they were stretched to the limit down there. Old Stone Face promised us a rescue flight in a week. But they had a problem with the booster when they tried to rush things on the pad too much, and the blessed launch had to be pushed back a week, and then another week. They sent an unmanned supply craft to us, but the descent stage got gummed up, so our fresh food, air filters, water supply and other stuff just orbited over us about fifty miles up.

Sam calculated the odds of all these foul-ups and came to the conclusion that Houston was working overtime to kill us. "Must be some sort of an experiment," he told me. "Maybe they need some martyrs to make people more aware of the space program."

We learned afterward that Houston was in deep trouble because of us. The White House was firing people left and right, Congressional committees were gearing up to investigate the fiasco, and the CIA was checking out somebody's crackbrained idea that the Russians were behind all our troubles.

Meanwhile, we were stranded on the Mare Nubium with nothing much to do but let our beards grow and hope for sinus troubles that would cut off our ability to sense odors.

Old Stone Face was magnificent, in his unflinching way. He was on the line to us every day, despite the fact that his superiors in Houston and Washington were either being fired directly by the President himself or roasted over the simmering coals of media criticism. There must have been a zillion reporters at Mission Control by the second week of our marooning; we could *feel* the hubbub and tension whenever we talked with Stony.

"The countdown for your rescue flight is proceeding on an accelerated schedule," he told us. It would never occur to him to say *We're hurrying as fast as we can.* "Liftoff is now scheduled for 0700 hours on the twenty-fifth."

None of us needed to look at a calendar to know that the twenty-fifth was seventeen days away. Sam's betting pool was looking more serious every hour. Even the skipper had finally taken a plunge: Suffocation.

If it weren't for Sandi Hemmings we might have all gone crazy. She took over as capcom during the night shift, when most of the reporters and the agency brass were asleep. She gave us courage and the desire to pull through, partly just by smiling at us and looking female enough to make us *want* to survive, but mainly by giving us the straight info with no nonsense.

"They're in deep trouble over at Canaveral," she would tell us. "They've had to go to triple shifts and call up boosters that they didn't think they would need until next year. Some senator in Washington is yelling that we ought to ask the Russians or the Japanese to help out."

"As if either of them had upper stages that could make it to the Moon and back," one of our guys muttered.

"Well," Sandi said, with her brightest smile, "you'll all be heroes when you finally get back here. The girls will be standing in line to admire you."

"You won't have to stand in line, Sandi," Ron Avery answered, in a rare burst of words. "You'll always be first with us."

The others crowded into the command module added their heartfelt agreement.

Sandi laughed, undaunted by the prospect of the eight of us grabbing for her. "I hope you shave first," she said.

A night or two later she spent hours reading to us the suggestions made by the Houston medical team on how to stretch out our dwindling supplies of food, water and air. They boiled down to one basic rule: lie down and don't exert yourselves. Great advice, especially when you're beginning to really worry that you're not going to make it through this mess. Just what we needed to do, lie back in our bunks and do nothing but think.

I caught a gleam in Sam's eye, though, as Sandi waded through the medics' report. The skipper asked her to send the report through our computer printer. She did, and he spent the next day reading and digesting it. Sam spent that day—well, I couldn't figure out where he'd gotten to. I just didn't see him all day long, and Base Gamma really wasn't big enough to hide in, even for somebody as small as Sam.

After going through the medics' recommendations,

the skipper ordered us to take tranquilizers. We had a scanty supply of downers in the base pharmaceutical stores, and Skip divided them equally among us. At the rate of three a day, they would last four days, with four pills left over. About as useful as a cigaret lighter in hell, but the skipper played it by the book and ordered us to start gobbling tranquilizers.

"They will ease our anxieties and help us to remain as quiet as possible while we wait for the rescue mission," he told us.

He didn't bother to add that the rescue mission, according to Sandi's unofficial word, was still twelve days off. We would be out of food in three more days, and the recycled water was starting to taste as if it hadn't been recycled, if you know what I mean. The air was getting foul, too, but that was probably just our imaginations.

Sam appeared blithely unconcerned, even happy. He whistled cheerfully as Skip rationed out the tranquilizers, then scuttled off down the tunnel that led toward our barracks module. By the time I got to my bunk, Sam was nowhere in sight. His whistling was gone. So was his pressure suit.

He had gone out on the surface? For what? To increase his radiation dose? To get away from the rest of us? That was probably it. Underneath his wise-guy shell, Sam was probably as worried and tense as any of us, and he just didn't want us to know it. He needed some solitude, and what better place to get it than the airless rocky expanse of Mare Nubium?

That's what I thought, so I didn't go out after him.

The same thing happened the next "morning" (by which I mean the time immediately after our sleep shift), and the next. The skipper would gather us together in the command module, we would each take our ceremonial tranquilizer pill and a sip of increasingly bad water, and then we would crawl back to our bunks and try to do nothing that would use up body energy or air. I found myself resenting it whenever I had to go to the toilet; I kept imagining my urine flowing straight into our water tank without reprocessing. I guess I was beginning to go crazy.

But Sam was as happy as could be: chipper, joking, laughing it up. He would disappear each morning for several hours, and then show up again with a lopsided grin on his face, telling jokes and making us all feel a little better.

Until Julio suddenly sat up in his bunk, the second or third morning after we had run out of tranquilizers, and shouted:

"Booze!"

Sam had been sitting on the edge of Julio's bunk, telling an outrageous story of what he planned to do with Sandi once we got back to Houston.

"Booze!" Julio repeated. "I smell booze! I'm cracking up. I'm losing my marbles."

For once in his life, Sam looked apologetic, almost ashamed.

"No you're not," he said to Julio, in as quiet a voice as I've ever heard Sam speak. "I was going to tell you about it tomorrow—the stuff is almost ready for human consumption."

You never saw three grown men so suddenly attentive.

With a self-deprecating little grin, Sam explained, "I've been tinkering with the propellants and other junk out in the return module. They're not doing us any good, just sitting out there. So I made a small still. Seems to be working okay. I tasted a couple sips today. It'll take the enamel off your teeth, but it's not all that bad. By tomorrow . . ."

He never got any further. We did a Keystone Kops routine, rushing for our space suits, jamming ourselves through the airlock and running out to the inert, idle, cussedly useless return module.

Sam was not kidding us. He had jury-rigged an honest-to-backwoods still inside the return module, fueling it with propellants from the module's tanks. The basic alcohol also came from the propellant, with water from the fuel cells, and a few other ingredients that Sam had scrounged from miscellaneous supplies.

We lost no time pressurizing the module, lifting our helmet visors, and sampling his concoction. It was *terrible*. We loved it.

By the time we had staggered back to our barracks module, laughing and belching, we had made up our minds to let the other three guys in barracks B share in Sam's juice. But the skipper was a problem. Once he found out about it, he'd have Sam up on charges and drummed out of the agency, even before the rescue mission reached us. Old Stone Face would vote to leave Sam behind, I knew, if he found out about it.

"Have no fear," Sam told us, with a giggle. "I will, myself, reveal my activities to our noble skipper."

And before we could stop him, he had tottered off toward the command module, whistling in a horribly sour off-key way.

An hour went by. Then two. We could hear Skip's voice yelling from the command module, although we couldn't make out the words. None of us had the guts to go down the tunnel and try to help Sam. After a while the tumult and the shouting died. Mickey Lee gave me a questioning glance. Silence; ominous silence.

"You think Skip's killed him?" he asked.

"More likely," said Julio, "that Sam's talked the skipper to death."

Timidly, we slunk down the tunnel to the command module. The other three guys were there with Sam and the skipper; they were all quaffing Sam's rocket juice and grinning at each other.

We were shocked, but we joined right in. Six days later, when the guys from Base Alpha landed their return module crammed with food and fresh water for us, we invited them to join the party. A week after that, when the rescue mission from Canaveral finally showed up, we had been under the influence for so long that we told them to go away.

I had never realized before then what a lawyer Sam was. He had convinced the skipper to read the medics' report carefully, especially the part where they recommended using tranquilizers to keep us calm and minimize our energy consumption. Sam had then gotten the skipper to punch up the medical definition of alcohol's effects on the body, out of Houston's medical files. Sure enough, if you squinted the right way, you could claim that alcohol was a sort of tranquilizer. That was enough justification for the skipper, and we just about pickled ourselves until we got rescued.

The crystal statue glittered under the harsh rays of the unfiltered sun. The work leader, still sitting on the lip of the truck's hatch, said:

"It looks beautiful. You guys did a good job. Is the epoxy set?"

"Needs another few minutes," said the young man, tapping the toe of his boot against the base that they had poured on the lunar plain.

"What happened when you got back to Houston?" the young woman asked. "Didn't they get angry at you for being drunk?"

"Sure," said the leader. "But what could they do? Sam's booze pulled us through, and we could show that we were merely following the recommendations of the medics. Old Stone Face hushed it all up and we became heroes, just like Sandi told us we would be—for about a week."

"And Sam?"

"He left the astronaut corps for a while and started his

own business. The rest you know about from the history books. Hero, showman, scoundrel, patriot. It's all true. He was all those things."

"Did he and Sandi ever, uh . . . get together?" the young man asked.

"She was too smart to let him corner her. She used one of the other guys to protect her; married him, finally. Cowboy, I think it was. They eloped and spent their honeymoon in orbit. Zero gee and all that. Sam pretended to be very upset about it, but by that time he was surrounded by women, all of them taller than he was."

The three of them walked slowly around the gleaming statue.

"Look at the rainbows it makes where the sun hits it," said the young woman. "It's marvelous."

"But if he was so smart," said the young man, "why'd he pick this spot way out here for his grave? It's miles from Selene City. You can't even see the statue from the city."

"Silly. This is the place where Base Gamma was," said the young woman. "Isn't that right?"

"No," the leader said. "Gamma was all the way over on the other side of Nubium. It's still there. Abandoned, but still there. Even the blasted return module is still sitting there, as dumb as ever."

"Then why put the statue here?"

The leader chuckled. "Sam was a pretty shrewd guy. He set up, in his will, a tourist agency that will guide people to the important sites on the Moon. They start at Selene City and go along the surface in those big cruisers that're being built back at the city. Sam's tomb is going to be a major tourist attraction, and he wanted it far enough out in the mare so that people wouldn't be able to see it from Selene; they have to buy tickets and take the bus."

Both the young people laughed tolerantly.

"I guess he was pretty smart, at that," the young man confessed.

"And he had a long memory, too," said the leader. "He left this tourist agency to me and the other guys from Artemis IV, in his will. We own it. I figure it'll keep me comfortable for the rest of my life."

"Why did he do that?"

The leader shrugged inside his cumbersome suit. "Why did he build that still? Sam always did what he darned well felt like doing. No matter what you think of him, he always remembered his friends."

The three of them gave the crystal statue a final admiring glance, then clumped back to the truck and started the hourlong drive to Selene City.

PRIVATE ENTERPRISE
GOES INTO ORBIT

While Sam Gunn can set himself up in the distillery business, albeit briefly, on the Moon, other entrepreneurs are going into the space business right here on Earth. For more than two decades, space was the almost exclusive preserve of government agencies; no private enterprise allowed. But that is changing, and rapidly. This article was published in Continental Airlines' magazines, largely because the editor recognized that Continental's business travelers would be interested in the opportunities of moving industry into space.

■

A new industrial revolution is beginning, a hundred miles from where you are right now—straight up. Private companies, large and small, are taking the first experimental steps that will lead to factories in space that manufacture ultrapure medicines, new metal alloys, electronics components and materials that cannot possibly be made on the surface of the Earth.

Before the end of this decade, for example, we may have an entire new line of medicines that are more powerful, yet safer to use, than anything on Earth today. These new pharmaceutical products will be manufactured in orbit.

It is called the EOS Program: EOS standing for Electrophoresis Operations in Space.

"*Eos* is also the name of the Greek goddess of dawn,"

says David W. Richman, "and we like to think that this program is the dawn of a new era."

Richman is the EOS deputy program manager at McDonnell Douglas Astronautics Company, in St. Louis, Missouri. In partnership with the Ortho Pharmaceutical Division of Johnson & Johnson (the Band-Aid company), and with the help of NASA, McDonnell Douglas has already completed two flight tests of experimental EOS hardware, aboard the sixth and seventh space shuttle flights in April and June 1983.

Under the zero-gravity conditions in orbit, the EOS automated minilab equipment used the phenomenon of electrophoresis to separate complex protein molecules from one another, the first step toward developing new and better pharmaceuticals to treat disease. The EOS hardware separated some seven hundred times more proteins than would have been possible in the same time on Earth, where gravity hampers the process. And the separated materials were more than four times purer than they would have been if they had been produced on Earth.

Ortho Pharmaceuticals, of Raritan, N.J., is revealing very little about exactly which proteins are being studied in space, and what the medical applications of zero-gravity drugs will eventually be. The pharmaceutical industry is so competitive that Ortho, a subsidiary of Johnson & Johnson, is keeping its purposes veiled in deep secrecy.

But McDonnell Douglas's Richman points out that many human diseases are caused by lack of specific proteins, such as hormones and enzymes. If a zero-gravity pharmaceutical laboratory in orbit can produce such vitally-needed proteins in greater abundance and purity than it is possible to obtain on Earth, the pharmaceutical industry may go literally "out of this world" to treat protein-deficiency diseases.

A McDonnell Douglas engineer, Charles D. Walker, joined five other astronauts on the twelfth space shuttle mission in early 1984. He was the first payload specialist to fly in the shuttle for a purely commercial project.

Pharmaceuticals, though, are not the only products that can be manufactured in space. Several companies are studying the possibilities of zero-gravity manufacturing of metals, crystals and materials for electronics equipment. Other companies are getting into the business of launching rockets. They expect to make profits from boosting satellites into orbit within the next few years.

Since the first Sputnik went up, in 1957, space operations have been the work of national governments: the Soviet Union, the United States, a group of Western European nations now called the European Space Agency (ESA), China, Japan and India have all launched their own satellites. But now, here in America, private enterprise is going into orbit, with the help of NASA.

The space agency is working with more than half a dozen private firms, providing technical expertise and facilities that range from a "drop tube" at NASA's Marshall Space Flight Center, near Huntsville, Alabama, to flights aboard the space shuttle.

"We're acting as a sort of marriage broker," says Bob Marshall, Director of Program Development at Marshall Space Flight Center, where the space manufacturing program is based.

Starting in the mid-1970s, Marshall and his NASA colleagues began to identify areas in space research that might be turned into commercial products someday. They contacted more than 400 private firms and began showing them how space operations could benefit them.

"We tried to go in at the highest level in each company," Marshall explained, "and talk to the president or the vice president for research or marketing."

NASA set up regional meetings where space engineers discussed these new ideas with area industrial firms. Then

NASA helped the interested companies to "marry" with an experienced aerospace firm. Once that was done, NASA stepped out of the picture—except to provide the technical facilities that each project required.

"We've never turned away a company that showed interest," Marshall says. Some firms have dropped out of the program after an initial investigation. "But I expect most of them will return, sooner or later," states Marshall confidently.

Why try to manufacture things in space? At first the idea sounds strange, even wild. Do these people actually believe that someday there will be factories in orbit?

Yes. The environment of space is new, and can be dangerous. But it is far from useless. The space environment offers four advantages that are extremely valuable for many industrial operations: free energy, controllable temperature extremes, very high vacuum and controllable gravity.

Energy is abundant in space. The Sun shines constantly, and solar energy can be used either directly as heat, or converted into electricity by the same kind of solarvoltaic cells that have powered satellites since the first Vanguard went into orbit in 1958.

The Sun's heat can be used for a wide range of industrial processes. With simple mirrors it is possible to focus sunlight and attain temperatures of many thousands of degrees. Smelting, metalworking, chemical processing, boiling and heating can be done in an orbital factory with direct or concentrated sunlight.

A space factory can easily attain very low temperatures as well, simply by shielding an area from sunlight. A wellshadowed region could be cooled down close to absolute zero. Because vacuum is an excellent thermal insulator (the secret of the Thermos bottle), a space factory could be smelting metals in one place and, only a few yards away, could simultaneously be freezing nitrogen or hydrogen into liquids.

Temperatures can be manipulated up and down the scale,

over thousands of degrees, merely by manipulating the amount of sunlight or shade—without burning an ounce of any fuel, without building heaters or refrigerators, without separating the hot work from the cold work by more than a few yards.

Free solar energy means freedom from the heavy and continuous fuel bills of Earthside factories, plus freedom from the pollution that inevitaby accompanies power plants on Earth.

It costs a lot of time and money to make nothing—a vacuum—on Earth. Many industrial processes require vacuum chambers at some stage of their operation; a considerable part of the cost of electronics components, pharmaceuticals, metals and other industrial products stems from the need to pump air out of a chamber and produce nothingness.

Just a hundred or so miles overhead is a better vacuum *for free* than any that can be bought on Earth, regardless of price. The combination of this excellent vacuum with the zero gravity* of orbit yields the possibility of "containerless" processing, which can lead to the routine manufacture of ultrapure materials.

On Earth, when you want to mix liquids you must put them into a container, whether you are mixing a salad dressing or a white-hot molten steel alloy. No matter how well you stir the ingredients, the heavier ones tend to sink toward the bottom of the bowl. And there are always microscopic bits of the container mixed in, too. This contamination does not matter much for most processes, but in areas such as pharmaceuticals, purity is supremely important.

---

*Purists point out that the condition found in orbit is not exactly *zero* gravity, since the mass of the spacecraft itself exerts a minuscule gravitational force, It is called, therefore, *microgravity* by the experts . . . and zero gravity by everyone else.

In space everything changes for the better. There are no heavier ingredients in orbit; everything is weightless. There is no "bottom" under weightless conditions. So you do not need a bowl. The materials to be mixed can hang in vacuum, containerless, unsullied by impurities. Space factory technicians could melt down a slab of iron, without fear of drips. The molten metal would simply hang there weightlessly and slowly take on a spherical shape, because of internal tension forces.

These four advantages of the space environment are already attracting industrialists and researchers. Even though it costs thousands of dollars to place a pound of material in orbit, space manufacturing offers the promise of highly profitable new products. This means new industries and new jobs—most of them on Earth.

Would you believe that one of the world's leading manufacturers of farm equipment is working with NASA? The John Deere Company, of Moline, Illinois, has used NASA airplanes to simulate zero gravity in a study of new ways to produce cast iron. About 25 percent of the material this $5-billion-per-year company produces is cast iron. Deere ranks among the largest iron foundry operators in the U.S.

Larry L. Fosbinder, a Deere senior engineer, points out that one of the key factors determining the properties of cast iron is the way graphite particles mix within the iron. One way to study how gravity affects the mixture is to eliminate gravity while various samples of mixtures are prepared. Deere has flown experiments aboard NASA F-104 and KC-135 aircraft. The planes achieve weightless conditions for a few seconds to a few minutes by flying a parabolic arc; zero gravity comes when the plane soars through the top of the arc.

James Graham, a senior research associate at Deere, points out that the company has also utilized many other NASA technologies, including new adhesives and computer programs. NASA and the American Foundry Society are also investigating the use of ultrasonic technology to probe the inner details of the composition of various cast iron alloys.

Small companies are working with NASA in space manufacturing, too.

Microgravity Research Associates (MRA), of Coral Gables, Florida, will conduct a series of experiments aboard the space shuttle aimed at developing electronic crystal materials in space. Crystals can be grown larger and purer under zero-gravity conditions than they can be on Earth. Richard L. Randolph, president of MRA, says that the company's experiments aboard the shuttle will be aimed at growing crystals of gallium arsenide, a material that he believes will replace the commonplace silicon chip for many future electronics applications.

"Space-produced gallium arsenide will be making considerable inroads in new applications in electronics and electro-optics," says Mr. Randolph. "The space-produced materials will have superior crystal properties and with that will have superior electronic performance and reliability. [Electronic] equipment that demands the very best performance and reliability will demand space-produced materials."

Seven shuttle flights are planned, in a program that will move from proof-of-concept to demonstration of a full-scale commercial production facility in orbit. Randolph expects to have "meaningful quantities of space-produced crystals" available for evaluation by commercial customers before the end of the 1980s.

Union Carbide Corporation, at Oak Ridge, Tennessee, is studying containerless solidification of metallic "glasses," materials that may someday be used to construct extremely efficient electrical power equipment.

Two companies in Cleveland, TRW and Eaton Corporation, are also working with NASA on various aspects of developing metal alloys under conditions of weightlessness. The DuPont Corporation, Wilmington, Delaware, is engaged in a study of how zero gravity would affect the formation of metals to be used as catalysts—such as the platinum catalytic converters installed to control pollution emissions from automobile engines.

NASA's Marshall Space Flight Center works with the individual private companies in these pioneering efforts. Studies often begin with simple experiments in drop tubes, where a fleeting few seconds of zero gravity are attained while the test object is falling along the length of the tube. The next step is usually to fly experiments aboard the jet aircraft, which can provide up to three minutes of weightlessness as they soar through their parabolic arcs.

Only after these relatively inexpensive tests have proved successful is the experiment packaged for a flight on the space shuttle, where it may be in orbit for anywhere from a few days to two weeks.

Private enterprise is also moving into the business of launching payloads into space.

Since the mid-1960s, the communications satellite industry has blossomed into a multi-billion-dollar global business. Communications companies such as AT&T, RCA, Western Union, Comsat Corporation and many others regularly pay NASA to launch satellites for them. Even at $50 million or more per launch, the satellites are far cheaper than stringing relay stations across a continent or laying cable across an ocean.

So profitable are these communications satellites that the biggest sale ever made by the famous auction house of Sotheby Park Bernet was in 1981, for seven-year leases on seven channels in a new communications satellite. The leases were auctioned for a total of $90.1 million—in a single afternoon.

There are other customers for launch vehicles, as well. The petroleum industry, for example, spends billions of dollars per year exploring remote areas of the world for possible new oil deposits. Satellites are a vital part of such explorations.

When NASA began the space shuttle program in the early 1970s, the agency planned to phase out all its older-type expendable rocket boosters once the shuttle went into operation. NASA's reasoning was that expendable boosters, which can be used only once, would give way to the shuttle, which is reusable, more efficient, and therefore should bring down the costs of launching payloads into orbit.

But private industry sees it differently. While the shuttle is the best vehicle in the world for large and very sophisticated payloads, there are many kinds of satellites that can be placed in orbit with "old-fashioned" throwaway boosters. In fact, NASA's chief competition for commercial customers is the European Space Agency's *Ariane* booster, which is an expendable, one-time rocket rather like the Deltas, Titans and Atlases that were the standbys of the American space program before the shuttle flew.

So while NASA is placing all its payloads in the shuttle, private entrepreneurs are developing their plans for launching satellites aboard expendable boosters—for profit. President Reagan announced his support for this move in May 1983, stating that "the government fully endorses and will facilitate the commercialization of expendable launch vehicles."

The first company to get into the space-launching business was Space Services, Inc., of Houston. Operating from a base they established on Matagorda Island, off the Gulf coast of Texas, SSI successfully launched their Conestoga I rocket on a suborbital test in September 1982. An earlier launch attempt, the company's first, ended abruptly when the rocket blew up on the launch stand.

David Hannah, Jr., president of SSI, expects the company's first orbital launch to take place in 1987. "We're getting our funding in order and designing our launching system," Hannah says. He expects to purchase solid-fuel rocket engines from manufacturers such as United Technologies Corporation or Thiokol and to be able to boost satellites of 900 pounds into 500-mile-high orbits.

Hannah sees a market for at least five orbital launches per year, each of which should cost about $10 million. Most of the satellites will carry Earth-sensing equipment for geological exploration of remote areas. Many of the oil companies based in Houston could become customers of SSI.

Space Projects Company, of Princeton, New Jersey, has an even grander vision. The company has proposed to the government that it will raise a billion dollars for the construction of a fifth space shuttle (NASA has been allowed to build only four, to date). This fifth shuttle would be devoted entirely to commercial flights.

Dr. Klaus Heiss founded the firm, which was originally called Space Transportation Company, in conjunction with William Sword, a Princeton financier. Heiss was the econometrician who did the original economic studies, ten years ago, for NASA on the "market" for the space shuttle's launching services. The studies convinced him that there is a vast commercial market for the shuttle.

Space Transportation also intended to develop a business line in expendable rocket boosters, and started a program with Martin Marietta Corporation, which builds the Titan booster at its Denver, Colorado, plant. But in May 1983, Space Transportation sold off this part of its business to Federal Express Corporation. The new company was called Fedex Spacetran.

Someday, when you have a satellite payload that "absolutely, positively, has to get there," you will be able to call Federal Express.

The original Space Transportation Company changed its

name to Space Projects, and Dr. Heiss left, while Sword remained as chairman of the company.

It was an amicable parting, Dr. Heiss says. "We had a difference of opinion. They took a short-range view, while I want to look at the longer range."

Dr. Heiss believes it will be another two to three years before a commercial space shuttle program can become a reality. But once it does, he foresees "six to eight commercial shuttle flights per year, and a total U.S. market for commercial launch services of one to two billion dollars per year," with a total world market reaching almost three billion dollars per year.

His main intention now is to "broaden the base of investor support," for the plan to build a commercial space shuttle, most likely through a combination of Space Projects and other investors—including the general public. "Broad public participation [will be] appropriate" in the commercialization of space, Dr. Heiss believes.

Space Projects, meanwhile, is proceeding with its original proposal to NASA. James Scott Hill, general counsel for the company, says that the proposal to build a fifth shuttle orbiter "is important for the country, and for science, and for space exploration. We would like to see it come to fruition."

While the government has not yet decided on Space Projects' proposal, Hill says, "We're most optimistic. The concept is sound. Private enterprise should be in space. It should not be an exclusively governmental program."

The advent of private launching services, and the success of the shuttle, raises new problems for NASA. Should the agency operate its four-shuttle fleet as a sort of semicommercial transportation line into space? Or should NASA relinquish control of the shuttle, once all four vehicles have been satisfactorily tested, and allow another government agency or a private firm to operate the shuttle? NASA, after all, is at its best developing new technology and exploring the universe. It was not set up to be a transportation company.

As private enterprise moves into the business of launching payloads into space, as well as developing industrial operations in orbit, what role should NASA play?

Dr. Jerry Grey, publisher of *Aeronautics and Astronautics* magazine and author of the book *Beachheads in Space*, says, "I believe commercial operation of the shuttle is on the way. The shuttle, or its derivatives, will eventually become a private operation." Citing the greater flexibility that private operators would have over a government agency, Dr. Grey believes, "My view is that NASA feels the shuttle isn't ready yet to be turned over to private enterprise," but in "two or three years" it will be. Pointing out that the shuttle program is still in a testing, experimental phase, he adds, "It doesn't make sense for NASA to operate the shuttle once it becomes an operational system. And I think NASA agrees with that."

President Reagan also wants to turn over to private operators the Landsat satellites, which monitor the Earth for natural resources, and the weather observations satellites now under the control of National Oceanic and Atmospheric Administration (NOAA).

While this proposal has been attacked by some members of the Congress and by many scientists, it seems inevitable that private companies will take over more and more functions in space that are now operated by government agencies.

Back in 1979, *Fortune* magazine writer Gene Bylinsky said, "In the wide and starry band of near-earth space . . . [there is] the possibility of an industrial bonanza. . . . No corporation affected by changes in technology can afford to ignore the new era of innovation that is about to begin."

Today, that era *has* begun. For many American companies, large and small, new and old, business is definitely looking up.

VISION

We can talk about the practical benefits of going into space, the fortunes to be made in zero-gravity manufacturing, the benefits of new medicines and materials produced in orbit. But there is the human aspect to consider, also. Don Arnold is a Promethean of a slightly different stripe, a reluctant leader who pioneers into a new domain almost in spite of himself. Philosophers have long argued over whether human history is molded by the daring actions of extraordinary men and women, or whether history responds to implacable, inevitable natural forces which individual human actions can do little to bend or shape. *Vision* might help you to decide which side of that argument you are on; then again, it might just add a little weight to both sides of the argument.

Vision, by the way, was originally published in *Analog* magazine's 50th anniversary issue, and marked my return to that venerable magazine's pages as a writer. My first sale to *Analog* was in May 1962, a short story titled *The Next Logical Step* (see *Escape Plus Ten,* published by Tor Books in 1983). When John W. Campbell, Jr., died in 1971 and I was tapped to become *Analog's* editor, I decided not to write for the science fiction magazines as long as I was an editor of one of them; it would have been too much of a conflict of interest, I felt. Although I continued to write science fiction novels, I also withdrew them from consideration for the Hugo and Nebula awards, for the same reason. Once I left *Analog*, however, I was pleased to submit stories and articles to the science fiction magazines once again, and was very happy when Stanley Schmidt picked it for *Analog*'s 50th anniversary.

■

B ut if you live in orbit, you can live forever!"

Don Arnold said it in sheer frustration and immediately regretted opening his mouth.

Picture the situation. Don was sitting under the glaring lights of a TV studio, in a deep fake-leather couch that looked comfortable but wasn't. His genial talk-show host had ignored him totally since introducing him as "one of NASA's key scientists." (Don was a NASA engineer, and pretty far from the top.)

On one side of Don sat a UFOlogist, a balding, owlishly-bespectacled man with a facial tic and a bulging briefcase clutched in his lap, full of Important Documents.

On Don's other side sat a self-proclaimed Mystic of indeterminate age, a benign smile on his face, his head shaved and a tiny gem in his left earlobe.

They had done all the talking since the show had started, nearly an hour earlier.

"The government has all sorts of data about UFOs," the UFOlogist was saying, hugging his battered briefcase. "NASA has *tons* of information about how the saucers are built and where they're coming from, but they won't release any of this to the people."

Before Don could reply, the Mystic raised both his hands, palms outward. The cameras zoomed in on him.

"All of the universe is a single entity, and all of time is the same," he said in a voice like a snake charmer's reed flute. "Governments, institutions, all forms of society are merely illusions. The human mind is capable of anything, merely by thinking transcendentally. The soul is immortal—"

That's when Don burst out, "But if you live in orbit, you can live forever!"

It surprised them all, especially Don. The Mystic blinked, his mouth still silently shaped for his next pronouncement. The UFOlogist seemed to curl around his briefcase even tighter. The studio audience out there beyond the blinding glare of the overhead lights surged forward in their chairs and uttered a collective murmur of wonderment.

Even the talk show's host seemed stunned for just a moment. He was the best-dressed man on the set, in a deep blue cashmere sports jacket and precisely-creased pearl gray slacks. He was the only man on camera in makeup. His hairpiece gave him a youthful-yet-reliable look.

The host swallowed visibly as Don wished he could call back the words he had just blurted.

"They live forever?" the host asked, so honestly intrigued that he forgot to smile.

How in hell can I backtrack out of this? Don asked himself desperately.

Then the Mystic started to raise his hands again, his cue to the cameras that he wanted their attention on him.

"Our studies have shown that it's possible," Don said, leaning forward slightly to stare right into the host's baby-blue eyes.

"How long have people lived in orbit, anyway?" the host asked.

"The record is held by two Russian cosmonauts, aboard their space station. They were up there for almost nine months. Our Skylab team was up for 83 days, back in '73-'74."

Don could sense the UFOlogist fidgeting beside him, but

the host asked, "And they did experiments up there that showed you could live longer if you stayed in space?"

"Lots of experiments have been done," Don answered before anyone else could upstage him, "both in orbit and on the ground."

"On . . . immortality."

"We tend to call it life extension," he said truthfully. "But it's quite clear that in orbit, where you can live under conditions of very low gravity, your heart doesn't have to work so hard, your internal organs are under much less stress . . ."

"But don't your muscles atrophy? Isn't there calcium loss from the bones?"

"No," Don said flatly. All three cameras were aimed squarely at him. Normally he was a shy man, but nearly an hour of listening to the other two making a shambles of organized thought had made him sore enough to be bold.

"It doesn't?"

"It takes a lot of hard work to move around in low gravity," Don answered. "With a normal work routine, plus a few minutes of planned exercise each day, there's no big muscle-tone loss. In fact, you'd probably be in better condition if you lived in a space station than you are here on Earth."

"Fascinating!" said the host.

"As for calcium loss, that levels off eventually. It's no real problem."

"And then you just go on living," the host said, "forever?"

"For a long, long time," Don hedged. "In a space station, of course, your air is pure, your water's pure, the environment is very carefully controlled. There are no carcinogens lousing up the ecology. And you have all the benefits of low gravity."

"I never knew that! Why hasn't NASA told us about this?"

As Don fished around in his mind for a reply, the host turned on his smile and fixed his gaze on camera one.

"Well, it always seems that we run out of time just when things are *really* interesting." Glancing back along his guests on the couch, he said, "Dr. Arnold, that was fascinating. I hope you can come back and talk with us again, real soon."

Before Don could answer, the host said farewell to the two other guests, mispronouncing both their names.

Don sat up in bed, his back propped by pillows, the sheet pulled up to his navel. It was hot in the upstairs bedroom now that they had to keep the air-conditioner off, but he stayed covered because of the twins. They were nine now, and starting to ask pointed questions.

Judy was putting them into their bunk beds for the night, but they had a habit of wandering around before they finally fell asleep. And Judy, good mother that she was, didn't have the heart to lock the master bedroom door. Besides, on a sultry night like this, the only way to catch a breath of breeze was to keep all the doors and windows open.

Don played a game as he sat up watching television, the remote-control wand in his sweating hand. He found the situation comedies, police shows, doctor shows, even the science fiction shows, on TV so boring that he couldn't bear to watch them for their own sake.

But they were tolerable—almost—if he watched to see how much space-inspired technology he could identify in each show. The remote monitors in the surgeon's intensive-care unit. The sophisticated sensors used by the coroner's hot-tempered pathologist. The pressure-sensitive switch on the terrorists' bomb planted in the cargo bay of the threatened 747.

Judy finally came in and began undressing. The bedroom lights were out, but there was plenty of light coming from the TV screen.

"Better close the door, hon," Don told her as she wriggled her skirt down past her hips. "The twins . . ."

"They're both knocked out," she said. "They spent all day in the Cramers' pool."

"Still . . ." He clicked off the TV sound and listened for the patter of nine-year-old feet.

His wife's body still turned him on. Judy was short, a petite dark-haired beauty with flashing deep-brown eyes and a figure that Don thought of as voluptuous. She stripped off her panties and crawled into the bed beside Don.

Grinning at him, she said, "You worry too much."

"Yeah, maybe I do."

"I thought you were terrific on the show this afternoon. I got so mad when those other two clowns kept hogging the camera!"

"Maybe I should have let them hog it for the whole show," he said.

"No you shouldn't! I sat here for nearly an hour waiting for you to open your mouth."

"Maybe I should've kept it closed."

"You were terrific," she said, snuggling closer to him.

"I was lying," he answered. "Or, at least, stretching the truth until it damn near snapped."

"You looked so handsome on television."

"I just hope nobody at Headquarters saw the show."

"It's a local talk show," Judy said. "Nobody watches it but housewives."

"Yeah . . ."

He started to feel better, especially with Judy cuddling next to him, until almost the very end of the eleven o'clock news. Then they showed a film clip of him staring earnestly into the camera—*I thought I was looking at the host*, Don thought—and explaining how people who live in orbit will live forever.

Don saw his whole career passing in front of his eyes.

* * *

He made sure to get to his office bright and early the next morning, taking a bus that arrived on Independence Avenue before the morning traffic buildup. Don was at his desk, jacket neatly hung behind the door and shirt sleeves rolled up, going over the cost figures for yet another study of possible future options for the Office of Space Transportation Systems, when his phone buzzed.

"Uncle Sam wants *you*," rasped Jack Hardesty's voice in the phone receiver.

He saw the show! was Don's first panicked thought.

"You there, Mr. Personality?" Hardesty demanded.

"Yeah, Jack, I'm here."

"Meet me in Klugie's office in five minutes." The phone clicked dead.

Don broke into a sweat.

Otto von Kluge was as American as the Brooklyn Bridge, but many and various were the jokes around NASA Headquarters about his name, his heritage and his abilities. He was an indifferent engineer, a terrible public speaker, and a barely adequate administrator. But he was one of the few people in the office who had a knack for handling other people—from engineers to congressmen, from White House Whiz Kids to crusty old accountants from the Office of Budget and Management.

Despite the low setting of the building's air-conditioning, von Kluge wore his suit jacket and even a little bow tie under his ample chin. Don always thought of him as a smiling, pudgy used-car salesman. But once in a great while he came across as a smiling, pudgy Junker land baron.

Hardesty—bone-thin, lantern-jawed, permanently harried—was already perched on the front half-inch of a chair at one side of von Kluge's broad desk, puffing intensely on a cigaret. Don entered the carpeted office hesitantly, feeling a little like the prisoner on his way to the guillotine.

Von Kluge grinned at him and waved a hand in the general direction of the only other available chair.

"Come on in, Don. Sit down. Relax."

Just like the dentist says, Don thought.

"The TV station is sending me a tape of your show," von Kluge said, with no further preliminaries.

"Oh," Don said, feeling his guts sink. "That."

Laughing, von Kluge said, "Sounds to me like you're bucking for a job in the PR department."

"Uh, no, I'm not . . . I mean . . ."

"Sounds to *me*"—Hardesty ground his cigaret butt into von Kluge's immaculate stainless steel ashtray—"like you're bucking for a job selling brushes door-to-door!"

"Now don't get your blood pressure up, Jack," von Kluge said easily. "Most of the crimes of this world come out of overreacting to an innocent little mistake."

An overwhelming sense of gratitude flooded through Don. "I really didn't mean to do it," he said. "It's just—"

"I know, I know. Your first time on television. The thrill of show business. The excitement. Takes your breath away, doesn't it?"

Don nodded. Hardesty glowered at him.

"Let's just see the tapes and find out what you really said," von Kluge went on. "I'll bet you don't remember yourself, do you, Don?"

"No . . ."

Shrugging, von Kluge said, "It's probably no big deal. We'll just play it cool until it all blows over."

His office door opened slightly and Ms. Tucker, a black secretary of such sweetness and lithe form that she could make bigots vote pro-bussing, said softly:

"Phone for you, Dr. von Kluge."

"I can't be disturbed now, Alma."

"It's Senator Buford," she said, in an awed whisper.

Von Kluge's eyes widened. "Excuse me," he said to Don and Hardesty as he picked up the phone.

He smiled broadly and said, "Senator Buford, sir! Good morning! How are you—"

And that was all he said for the next twenty-two minutes. Von Kluge nodded, grunted, closed his eyes, gazed at the ceiling, stared at Don. As he listened.

Finally he put the phone down, slowly, wearily, like a very tired man at last letting go of an enormous weight. His ear was red.

Looking sadly at Don, von Kluge said, "Well, son, the Senator wants you to appear at his Appropriations Committee hearing. Tomorrow morning."

Don had expected the hearing chamber to be packed with newsmen, cameras, lights, crowds, people grabbing at him for interviews or comments.

Instead, the ornate old chamber was practically empty, except for the few senators who had shown up for their committee's session and their unctuous aides. Even the senators themselves seemed bored and fidgety as a series of experts from various parts of NASA and the Office of Management and Budget gave conflicting testimony on how much money should be appropriated for the space program.

But flinty old Senator Buford, the committee's chairman, sat unflinchingly through it all. His crafty gray eyes drilled holes through every witness; even when he said nothing, he made the witnesses squirm in their seats.

Don was the last scheduled witness before the lunch break, and he kept hoping that they would run out of time before they called on him. Hardesty and von Kluge had drilled him all night in every aspect of the space agency's programs and budget requests. Don's head hadn't felt so burstingly full of facts since his senior year in college, when he had crammed for three days to get past a Shakespeare final exam.

By the time Don sat himself cautiously in the witness chair, only four senators were left at the long baize-covered table facing him. It was a few minutes past noon, but Senator Buford showed no inclination to recess the hearing.

"Mistah Arnold," Buford drawled, "have you prepared a statement for this committee?"

"Yes, sir, I have." Don leaned forward to speak into the microphone on the table before him, even though there was no need to amplify his voice in the nearly-empty, quiet room.

"In view of the hour"—Buford turned *hour* into a two-syllable word—"we will dispense with your reading your statement and have it inserted into th' record as 'tis. With youh permission, of course."

Don felt sweat beading on his forehead and upper lip. "Certainly, sir." His statement was merely the regular public relations pamphlet the agency put out, extolling its current operations and promising wonders for the future.

Senator Buford smiled coldly. Don thought of a rattle-snake coiled to strike.

"Now what's this I heah," the Senator said, "'bout livin' in space prolongin' youh life?"

Don coughed. "Well, sir, if you're referring to . . . ah, to the remarks I made on television . . ."

"I am, suh."

"Yes, well, you see . . . I had to oversimplify some very complex matters, because . . . you realize . . . the TV audience isn't prepared . . . I mean, there aren't very many scientists watching daytime television talk shows . . ."

Buford's eyes bored into Don. "Ah'm not a scientist either, Mr. Arnold. I'm jest a simple ol' country lawyer tryin' to understand what in the world you're talkin' about."

And in a flash of revelation, Don saw that Senator Buford

was well into his seventies. His skin was creased and dry and dead-gray. The little hair left on his head was wispy and white. Liver spots covered his frail, trembling hands. Only his eyes and his voice had any spark or strength to them.

A phrase from the old Army Air Corps song of Don's childhood skipped through his memory: *We live in fame or go down in flames.*

Taking a deep breath and sitting up straighter in the witness chair, Don said, "Well, sir: there are two ways to look at any piece of information—optimistically or pessimistically. What I'm about to tell you is the optimistic view. I want you to understand that clearly, sir. I will be interpreting the information we have on hand in its most optimistic light."

"You go right ahead and do that," said Senator Buford.

They lunched in the Senate dining room: dry sherry, mock turtle soup, softshell crabs. Just the two of them at a small table, Don and Senator Buford.

"I finally got me a NASA scientist who can talk sense!" Buford was saying as he cut through one of the little crabs.

Don's head was still reeling. "You know, Senator, that there will be lots of experts inside NASA and outside who'll make some pretty strong arguments against me."

Buford fixed him with a baleful eye. "Mebbe so. But they won't get away with any arguments 'gainst *me*, boy."

"I can't guarantee anything, you realize," Don hedged. "I could be completely wrong."

"Ah know. But like you said, if we don't *try*, we'll never know for sure."

This has got to be a dream, Don told himself. *I'm home in bed and I'll have to get up soon and go testify before Buford's committee.*

"Now lessee what we got heah," Buford said as the liveried black waiter cleared their dishes from the table. "You need the permanent space station—with a major medical facility in it."

"Yessir. And the all-reusable shuttle."

Buford looked at Don sharply. "What's wrong with th' space shuttle we got? Cost enough, didn't it?"

"Yessir, it did. But it takes off like a rocket. Passengers pull three or four gees at launch. Too much for . . . er, for . . ."

"For old geezers like me!" Buford laughed, a sound halfway between a wheeze and a cackle.

Don made his lips smile, then said, "An advanced shuttle would take off like an airplane, nice and smooth. Anybody could ride in it."

"Uh-huh. How long'll it take to get it flyin'?"

Don thought a moment, considered the state of his soul, and decided, *What the hell, go for broke.*

"Money buys time, Senator," he said craftily. "Money buys time."

Senator Buford nodded and muttered, mostly to himself, "I finally got a NASA scientist who tells me the truth."

"Sir, I want you to realize the *whole* truth about what I've been telling you—"

But Buford wasn't listening. "Senator Petty will be our major obstacle. Scrawny little Yankee—thinks he's God's chosen apostle to watch out over the federal budget. He'll give us trouble."

The name of Senator Petty was known to make scientists weep. NASA administrators raced to the bathroom at the sound of it.

Buford waggled a lean, liver-spotted hand in Don's general direction. "But don't you worry none 'bout Petty. Ah'll take care o' him! You just concentrate on gettin' NASA to bring me a detailed program for that space station—with th' medical center in it."

"And the advanced shuttle," Don added, in a near whisper.

"Yeh, of course. The advanced shuttle, too. Cain't ride up there to your geriatrics ward in th' sky on a broomstick, now can I?"

"The twins were twelve years old today."

Don looked up from the report he was writing. It had been nearly midnight by the time he'd gotten home, and now it was well past one.

"I forgot all about their birthday," he confessed.

Judy was standing in the doorway of his study, wrapped in a fuzzy pink housecoat. There were lines in her face that Don hadn't noticed before. Her voice was sharper than he'd remembered.

"They could both be in jail for all you think about them!" she snapped. "Or me, for that matter."

"Look, honey, I've got responsibilities. . . ."

"Sure! The big-shot executive. All day long he's running NASA and all night long he's out at parties."

"Meetings," Don said defensively. "It's tough to deal with congressmen and senators in their offices—"

"Meetings with disco bands and champagne and lots of half-naked secretaries prancing around!"

"Judy, for God's sake, I'm juggling a million and one details! The space station, the flyback shuttle booster, and now Senator Buford's in the hospital. . . ."

"I hope he drops dead and Petty cuts your balls off!" Judy looked shocked that the words could have come from her mouth. She turned and fled from the room.

Don gave out a long, agonized sigh and leaned back in his desk chair. For a moment he wanted to toss the report he was writing into the wastebasket and go up to bed with his wife.

But he knew he had to face Senator Petty the next morn-

ing, and he had to be armed for the encounter. He went
back to his writing.

"I think you're pulling the biggest boondoggle this nation's
ever seen since the Apollo project," said Senator Petty,
smiling.

Don was sitting tensely in a big leather chair in front of
the Senator's massive oak desk. On Don's left, in an equally
sumptuous chair, sat Reed McCormack, NASA's chief administrator, the space agency's boss and a childhood chum
of the President.

McCormack looked like a studious, middle-aged banker
who kept trim playing tennis and sailing racing yachts.
Which was almost entirely true. He was not studious. He had
learned early in life that you can usually buy expertise—for
a song. His special talent was making people trust him.

Senator Petty didn't trust anyone.

From the neck up the Senator looked like a movie idol:
brilliant white, straight teeth (capped); tanned, taut handsome face (lifted, twice); thick, curly, reddish-brown hair
(implanted and dyed). Below the neck, however, his body
betrayed him. Despite excruciating hours of jogging and
handball, his stomach bulged and his chest was sunken.

"A boondoggle?" McCormack asked easily. "Your colleagues in the Senate don't seem to think so."

Petty's smile turned acid. "Funny thing about my fellow
senators. The older they are, the more money they want to
appropriate for your gold-plated space station. Why do you
think that is?"

"Age brings wisdom," said McCormack.

"Does it?" Petty turned his mud-brown eyes on Don. "Or
is it that you keep telling them they can live forever, once
they're up in your orbital old-age home?"

"I've never said that," Don snapped. His nerves were

frayed, he realized, as much by Senator Buford's hospitalization as by Judy's growing unhappiness.

"Oh, you've been very careful about what you've said, and to whom, and with what qualifications," Petty replied. "But they all get the same impression: Live in space and you live forever. NASA can give you immortality—if you vote the funds for it."

"That is *not* our policy," McCormack said firmly.

"The hell it isn't," Petty snapped. "But old Bufe's terminal, they tell me. You won't have him to steer your outrageous funding requests through the Senate. You'll have to deal with me."

Don knew it was true, and saw the future slipping away from his grasp.

"That's why we're here," McCormack said. "To deal."

Petty nodded curtly.

"If you try to halt construction of the space station, your colleagues will outvote you overwhelmingly," said McCormack.

"Same thing applies to the new shuttle," Don added.

Petty leaned back in his chair and steepled his fingers. "I know that. But I can slow you down. OMB isn't very happy with your cost overruns, you know. And I can always start an investigation into this so-called science of life extension. I can pick a panel of experts that will blow your immortality story out of the water."

For the first time, McCormack looked uneasy.

"There's no immortality 'story,'" Don said testily. "We've simply reported the conclusions of various studies and experiments. We've been absolutely truthful."

"And you've allowed the senators to believe that if they live in orbit they can all become Methuselahs." Petty laughed. "Well, a couple of biologists from Harvard and Berkeley can shoot you down inside a week—with the proper press coverage. And I can see to it that they get the coverage."

Don gripped the arms of his chair and tried to hold onto his temper. "Senator Buford is dying and you're already trying to tear down everything he worked to achieve."

Petty grinned mischievously. "You bet I am."

"What do you want from us?" McCormack asked.

The Senator's grin faded slowly.

"I said we're here to deal with you," McCormack added, speaking softly. "The President is very anxious to keep this program going. Its effect on the national economy has been very beneficial, you realize."

"So you say."

"What do you want?" McCormack repeated.

"The ground-based medical center that's going to be built as part of your life-extension program . . ."

"In your state?"

"Yes."

McCormack nodded. "I see no reason why that can't be done. It would be rather close to the Mayo Clinic, then, wouldn't it?"

"And one other thing," Petty said.

"What is it?"

He pointed at Don. "I want this man—Senator Buford's dear friend—to personally head up the space station operation."

Don felt his incipient ulcer stab him as McCormack's face clouded over.

"Mr. Arnold is program manager for the space station program already," McCormack said, "and also serves as liaison to the advanced shuttle program office."

"I know that," Petty snapped. "But I want him *up there*, in the space station, with the first permanent crew.

Don stared at the Senator. "Why . . . ?"

Petty gave him a smirk. "You think living up in space is such a hot idea, let's see *you* try it!"

* * *

Senator Buford's intensive-care bed looked more like a spacecraft command module than a hospital room. Electronics surrounded the bed, monitoring the dying old man. Oscilloscope traces wriggled fitfully; lights blinked in rhythm to his sinking heartrate; tubes of nutrients and fresh blood fed into his arteries.

Don had to lean close to the old man's toothless sunken mouth to hear his wheeze:

"'Preciate your comin' to see me . . . got no family left, y'know."

Don nodded and said nothing.

"Looks like I cain't hold out much longer," the Senator whispered. "How's the space station comin' along?"

"We've got Petty behind it," Don answered. "For a price."

Buford smiled wanly. "Good. Good. You'll get th' whole Senate behind you. They're all gettin' older. They'll all want to go . . . up there."

"I'm only sorry that we're not ready to take you."

Cackling thinly, Buford said, "But I'm goin'! Ah made all the arrangements. They're gonna freeze me soon's I'm clinically dead. And then I'm gonna be sent up to your space station. I'll stay froze until the science fellas figure out how to cure this cancer I got. Then they'll thaw me out and I'll live in orbit. I'll outlive all o' you!" He laughed again.

"I hope you do," Don said softly. "You deserve to."

"Only trouble is, once I'm froze I won't need that advanced shuttle to boost me into orbit. Coulda saved th' taxpayers all that money if I'd known. I can ride the regular ol' shuttle, once I'm dipped in that liquid nitrogen stuff."

He was still cackling to himself as Don tiptoed out of his room.

"I'm coming home, honey! For once, I'll be home in time for the twins' birthday."

Don was floating easily in his "office": a semicircular

desk welded into a bulkhead in the zero-gee section of the space station. There was no need for chairs; a few looped straps sufficed to keep one from drifting too far from one's work.

Don took a good look at his wife's face as it appeared in the telephone screen of his desk. Her mouth was a thin, tight line. There were crow's feet at the corners of her eyes. Her hair was totally gray.

"What happened to your hair?" he asked. "It wasn't like that the last time we talked, was it?"

"I've been dyeing it for years and *you* never noticed," Judy said, her voice harsh, strained. "The style is gray this year . . . now I dye it so it's all gray."

"That's the style?" Don glanced at his own reflection in the darkened window above his desk. His hair was still dark and thick.

"How would you know anything about fashion?" Judy snapped, "—living up in that tin can in the sky."

"But I'm coming home early this year," Don said. "Things are going well enough so I can get away a whole month earlier than I thought. I'll be there in time for the twins' birthday."

"Don't bother," Judy said.

"What? But the kids . . ."

"The kids are nineteen and they don't want their Mommy and Daddy embarrassing them, *especially* on their birthday. They want to be with their friends, out on the farm they've set up."

"Farm?"

"In Utah. They've joined the Church of the Latter Day Saints."

"Mormons? Our kids?"

"Yes."

Don felt confused, almost scared. "I've got to talk with them. They're too young to—"

But Judy was shaking her gray head. "They won't be here to talk with. And neither will I."

He felt it like a body blow as he hung there weightlessly, defenselessly, staring into the screen.

"I'm getting a divorce, Don," Judy said. "You're not a husband to me. Not two months out of every twelve. That's no marriage."

"But I *asked* you to come up here with me!"

"I've been living with Jack Hardesty the past six months," she said, almost tonelessly, it was so matter-of-fact. "He's asked me to marry him. That's what I'm going to do."

"Jack Hardesty? Jack?"

"You can live up there and float around forever," Judy said. "I'm going to get what happiness I can while I'm still young enough to enjoy it."

"Judy, you don't understand—"

But he was talking to a blank screen.

Don had to return to Earth for the official opening ceremonies of Space Station Alpha. It was a tremendous international media event, with special ceremonies in Washington, Cape Canaveral, Houston and the new life-extension medical center in Senator Petty's home state.

It was at the medical center ceremonies that Petty pulled Don aside and walked him briskly, urgently, into an immaculate, new, unused men's room.

Leaning on the rim of a sparkling stainless steel sink, Petty gave Don a nervous little half-smile.

"Well, you got what you wanted," the Senator said. "How do you feel about it?"

Don shrugged. "Kind of numb, I guess. After all these years, it's hard to realize that the job is done."

"Cost a whale of a lot of the taxpayers' money," Petty said.

Gesturing at the lavish toilet facility, Don riposted, "You didn't pinch any pennies here, I notice."

Petty laughed, almost like a little boy caught doing something naughty. "Home-state contractors. You know how it is."

"Sure."

"I guess you'll want to start living here on the ground full-time again," Petty said.

Don glared at him. "Oh? Am I allowed to? Is our deal completed?"

With an apologetic spread of his hands, Senator Petty said, "Look, I admit that it was a spiteful thing for me to do. . . ."

"It wrecked my marriage. My kids are total strangers to me now. I don't even have any friends down here anymore."

"I'm . . . sorry."

"Stuff it."

"Listen . . ." The Senator licked his thin lips. "I . . . I've been thinking . . . maybe I won't run for re-election next time around. Maybe . . . maybe I'll come up and see what it's like living up there for a while."

Don stared at him for a long, hard moment. And saw that there was a single light-brown spot about the size of a dime on the back of one of the Senator's hands.

"You want to live in the space station?"

Petty tried to make a nonchalant shrug. "I've . . . been thinking about it."

"Afraid of old age?" Don asked coldly. "Or is it something more specific?"

Petty's face went gray. "Heart," he said. "The doctors tell me I'll be in real trouble in another few years. Thanks to the technology you guys have developed, they can spot it coming that far in advance now."

Don wanted to laugh. Instead, he said, "If that's the case, you'd better spend your last year or two in the Senate pushing through enough funding to enlarge the living quarters in the space station."

Petty nodded. Grimly.

"And you should introduce a resolution," Don added, "to give the station an official name: the Senator Robert E. Buford Space Center."

"Now that's too much!"

Don grinned at him. "Tell it to your doctors."

There was no reason for him to stay on Earth. Too many memories. Too few friends. He felt better in orbit. Even in the living sections of the Buford Space Center, where the spin-induced gee forces were close to Earth-normal gravity, Don felt more alive and happier. His friends were there, and so was his work.

Don had been wrong to think that his job was finished once the space station was officially opened. In reality, his work had merely begun.

A year after the station was officially opened, von Kluge came aboard as a retiree. His secretary, Alma Tucker, still lithe and wonderful despite the added years, came up to work for Don. They were married, a year later. Among the witnesses was Senator Petty, the latest permanent arrival.

The Buford Space Center grew and grew and grew. Its official name was forgotten after a few decades. It was known everywhere as Sky City.

Sky City became the commercial hub of the thriving space industries that reached out across the solar system. Sky City's biomedical labs became system-famous as they took the lead in producing cures for the various genetic diseases known collectively as cancer.

Ex-Senator Petty organized the first zero-gee Olympics,

and participated personally in the Sky City-Tranquility Base yacht race.

Von Kluge, restless with retirement, became an industrial magnate and acquired huge holdings in the asteroid belt: a Junker land baron at last.

Alma Tucker Arnold became a mother—and a prominent low-gravity ballerina.

Don stayed in administration and eventually became the first mayor of Sky City. The election was held on his ninety-ninth birthday, and he celebrated it by leading a bicycle race all around the city's perimeter.

The next morning, his first official act as mayor was to order the thawing of Senator Buford. The two of them spent their declining centuries in fast friendship.

METEORITES

I don't believe in omens from the gods, but when a meteorite fell into a suburban house in a town near my Connecticut home, and conservative old *Yankee* magazine asked me to write a piece about the event, I took it as a signal that it was time to tell the average New Englander about mining the asteroids. After all, these are the descendants of those intrepid whalers and clipper ship crews who have been described as "iron men in wooden ships." Their children, some of whom are in their teens today, will have the opportunity to set sail for the dark depths of interplanetary space, spend two or three years "before the mast" in a mining vessel that will travel out to the asteroids and come back with enough precious ores to make every crew member rich. They'll be Prometheans for sure!

■

Contrary to folk wisdom, lightning often strikes more than once in the same place. But Wethersfield, Connecticut, is only the second community in all of recorded history to be hit on two separate occasions by meteorites.

It was nearly 9:20 p.m. on Monday, November 8, 1982, when a six-pound chunk of rock dropped out of the skies and through the roof of the Donahue home in Wethersfield. Wanda and Robert Donahue were watching *M*A*S*H* on television when the meteorite smashed through their roof at some 500 miles per hour, tore through the second- and firstfloor ceilings, and into their living room. It bounced through the doorway into the dining room, where it hit a chair and finally rolled under the dinner table, leaving a trail of shattered plaster, splintered wood and a badly dented piece of oak flooring behind it.

The Donahues were in the family room, less than twenty feet from the living room, when the falling star struck. Mrs. Donahue told reporters that it sounded like an explosion. Neither she nor her husband were hurt, though the living room seemed to be filled with smoke, which they later learned was only plaster dust. They called the police, who arrived in moments along with the volunteer fire brigade. Only then did the Donahues discover their celestial visitor resting under their dining-room table.

Eleven years earlier, on April 8, 1971, another meteorite had crashed into the Wethersfield home of Mr. and Mrs. Paul J. Cassarino, a scant mile from the Donahue residence. The only other community in the world known to have been hit twice by meteorites is Honolulu, and the two falls there were a century apart.

The Cassarinos' insurance did not cover being struck by a meteorite, but the Donahues' home insurance policy did cover being struck by objects from the sky. Robert Donahue says his career in the life insurance business had nothing to do with getting that clause into their homeowner's policy.

"Wethersfield 1982," as astronomers immediately dubbed the stone, came a long way to reach New England. While meteorites found by scientists recently in Antarctica appear to have originated on the Moon and even on the distant planet Mars, Wethersfield 1982 probably came from the still-farther Asteroid Belt, a zone of the solar system more than 100 million miles from Earth's orbit where thousands of millions of small chunks of rock and metal float through space.

The word asteroid means "little star," because that is how they appear in astronomers' telescopes: tiny points of faint light. The first asteroid was discovered on the night of January 1, 1801, by Father Giuseppe Piazzi, a monk who was then director of a small astronomical observatory at Palermo, Sicily. Since then, thousands have been observed, and calculations show that there must be myriads more, too small and distant to be easily seen from Earth.

They really should be called "planetoids," because they are actually not stars, but minor planets—pieces of rock and metal that might have once been parts of a larger planet that broke up, or the building blocks for a planet that somehow never came together.

The largest of the asteroids is the one Fr. Piazzi discovered, Ceres. It is some 450 miles in diameter. Compared to the Earth's nearly 8000-mile diameter or even the Moon's 2000-odd-mile width, Ceres is indeed a minor planet. Yet most of the asteroids are much, much smaller—the size of a mountain, or a football field, or a boulder.

While the Asteroid Belt lies beyond the orbit of Mars, many asteroids swing in orbits that loop close to the Earth. Some of them are caught by the Earth's powerful gravity and pulled to our planet. Every twenty-four hours, some 20,000 tons worth of asteroids strike our world. Most of them are no larger than a grain of sand, but still, if it were not for the protective blanket of our atmosphere, the Earth would look as battered and dead as the Moon.

Almost all of the asteroids that fall toward Earth are burned up completely when they enter the atmosphere. In the vacuum of space these bodies can travel at tremendous speeds with no harm to themselves. But once they enter our atmosphere, traveling at Mach 20 or faster, friction with the air heats them to the point where they glow. Most of them are burned up completely long before they reach the surface.

Wethersfield 1982, for example, must have weighed several hundred pounds when it hit the top of the atmosphere. By the time it rolled under the Donahues' dining-room table, it had been boiled down to slightly less than six pounds. The meteorite weighed precisely 2704 grams, in the metric measurement that astronomers use. That is 5.9488 pounds, to be precise. Another 50 grams (1.63 ounces) of stone chips were found, which had broken off the main body of the meteorite as it banged around the Donahue house. Wethersfield 1982 is 12 centimeters wide (4.72 inches). Its outer crust is a thin smooth layer of charred stone, visible proof of its fiery trip through the atmosphere.

For centuries, learned men refused to believe that meteorites came from beyond the Earth. Thomas Jefferson, who was widely respected as a naturalist as well as a revolutionary philosopher and politician, was among the skeptics. When told that two Yale professors had reported that a meteorite had fallen in Weston, Connecticut, President Jefferson is said to have remarked, "It is easier to believe that two Yankee professors would lie than that stones would fall from heaven." Jefferson the Virginian had his doubts about Yankees, apparently.

However, when a shower of meteorites pelted the French village of L'Aigle in 1803, the *Académie Française* investigated thoroughly and found that stones really do fall from heaven. Today we know that more than 75 million of them hit the Earth every day, although only a few hundred each year survive their blazing passage through the air to reach the surface.

What we call a "shooting star" or a "falling star," astronomers call a meteor. The word "meteor" comes from a Greek root that means "something high up in the air, lofty." Originally, "meteor" was used in English to denote almost anything that happened overhead; hence our word for the study of the weather is *meteorology*, which has nothing to do with falling stars and meteorites.

When an asteroid begins its long slide down Earth's gravity well, astronomers begin to term it a meteoroid. It is still the same object, a chunk of rock or metal that was born billions of years ago and has been floating in space ever since. But now it is heading for a rendezvous with our planet, drawn by the invisible force of gravity toward its destiny.

As the meteoroid ploughs through the upper fringes of our atmosphere, more than fifty miles above Earth's surface, friction from the air heats it until it glows. We see a "shooting star." It is this streak of light in the sky that astronomers call a meteor. If the meteoroid survives its incandescent passage through the air and reaches the ground, it is then known as a meteorite.

So one and the same body can at different stages be called an:

Asteroid, when it is in space;

Meteoroid, when it is falling toward Earth;

Meteor, when it becomes a blazing light in the sky; and

Meteorite, when what's left of it reaches the ground.

Wethersfield 1982 was seen as a brilliant falling star by observers as far away as Albany, New York. Anyone can see meteors on any clear night of the year, with a little patience. On the average, some five to ten meteors will streak across the sky each hour. The best time to watch for them is between midnight and dawn, for reasons of orbital mechanics that need not be explained here, but which can be found in any good astronomy text.

Nothing can compare with the sudden thrill of seeing a falling star. One moment it's there, the next it has winked out, probably completely burned up high in the atmosphere. Usually the meteor streaks through the sky in total silence, giving the impression that it's in a hurry to get to wherever it's going. Most such meteors are caused by meteoroids that are no bigger than a grain of sand.

But larger meteors can be absolutely startling, lighting up the sky for a few brief moments and rumbling like an express train. The noise is a sonic boom caused by the meteoroid's multi-Mach flight through the air. The head of such a meteor, called the fireball, or bolide, is tear-shaped and followed by a long, scintillating trail that sometimes shows spectacular colors. The fireball of Wethersfield 1982 was reported by at least one observer to have broken into two brilliant, flaming pieces. The second meteorite has not yet been found. Presumably, it fell into the woods nearby.

Often a large meteoroid will explode as it gets close to the Earth, blown apart by the heating it experiences as it drives down into the lowest, thickest layers of our atmosphere. Then its fragments pelt a wide area, like celestial shrapnel. Many areas of Earth have been hit by dozens or even hundreds of meteorites from a single such fall.

Some meteorites are truly huge. The largest one ever found, called Hoba West, is estimated to weigh 60 tons. It landed in South West Africa eons ago. The largest meteorite on public display is the 34-ton Ahnighito, which was discovered in Greenland by polar explorer Robert Peary in 1894 and transported (painfully) to the American Museum of Natural History in New York City, where it still rests.

Every schoolchild in America has seen a photograph of the Meteor Crater in Arizona. Some 20,000 years ago a meteoroid that weighed at least 50,000 tons blasted out this milewide hole in the ground. Known variously as the Winslow Crater, the Barringer Crater, and even as Canyon Diablo, this 650-foot-deep scar in the ground is one of the most prominent reminders that our planet has been bombarded by meteoroids in the past and is still under bombardment today.

In 1908 a heavenly object streaked across the skies of

Europe, heading eastward, and exploded close to the ground in Tunguska, Siberia. The sound of the explosion was heard a thousand miles away. A nearby witness was deafened by it. A herd of 1500 reindeer was incinerated and trees were knocked flat for an area of several miles around the impact site. Seismographs located thousands of miles from Siberia recorded the tremors caused by the event. When scientists finally got to the remote area where the object hit, they found more than a hundred craters, some of them a hundred feet across. But no fragments of meteorite!

Most astronomers believe the Tunguska meteoroid was actually a small comet that exploded in midair, close to the frozen Siberian ground. Comets are believed to be little more than frozen gases and ices, with perhaps a smattering of stones imbedded in the slush. If such an object exploded at a low altitude, very little solid material would be found afterward.

But other scientists (and laymen) have speculated that the Tunguska fireball was something much more exotic. An alien spacecraft, perhaps, damaged and desperately seeking a safe landing on planet Earth; its nuclear engines exploded just before it could reach the ground. Or, even weirder, a microscopic black hole that bored right through the solid mass of our planet and popped out again in the middle of the Atlantic Ocean and headed back into space.

Whatever caused the Tunguska fireball, if it had arrived in Earth's vicinity just a few minutes later than it did, it could have hit somewhere in Europe with the devastating force of a nuclear explosion. If a similar object should strike a civilized part of the world today, it might easily be mistaken for a nuclear attack and trigger World War III.

Considering how many meteorites hit the ground each year, it is something of a wonder that they have not caused more damage than they have. In 1948 a shower of stones peppered Norton County, Kansas. More than a hundred of them were located afterward, the largest one weighing a ton.

The only person known to be injured by a meteorite was a woman in Alabama who was struck a glancing blow while in bed, in 1954. She was bruised, but appeared more worried about the hole in her roof than her own injury.

There are certain times of the year when meteor showers occur, sprinkling hundreds or even thousands of meteors across the night sky withing a few hours. On rare occasions, the sky can be filled with flaming meteors. In a 1966 shower, a thousand meteors per minute were seen!

The meteors that fall in such showers are believed to be the remnants of comets, rather than refugees from the Asteroid Belt. Comets do not live forever. Each time they travel around the Sun they lose more of their substance, gases and ices evaporating away into the long, beautiful cometary tail. Eventually, all these volatile materials are boiled off, leaving nothing but a huge collection of stones rambling through space along the comet's old orbit like a crowd of marathon runners doggedly following their interminable track.

Some of these orbits intersect the orbit of the Earth, and when they do, some of those stones fall into our atmosphere to blaze briefly and then dissipate into harmless dust.

There are more than a dozen annual meteor showers, returning each year like celestial clockwork. The most prominent of them are the Perseids, which occur over several nights around August 12, and the Leonids, which come around November 16. The names of the showers refer to the area of the sky that the meteors seem to stream out of: the constellation Perseus, in the case of the Perseids, and Leo for the Leonids.

The meteors appear in all parts of the sky. But if you track their trails backward, they all seem to intersect in one area. This was the first clue that such meteor showers were being caused by a single cluster of objects traveling through space.

Meteor showers are the spawn of comets. Individual meteoroids were once asteroids. And asteroids may be the miner's bonanza of the twenty-first century. For these minor bodies of the solar system contain all the raw materials, the metals and minerals, that civilization needs for a new age of space-born industries that can enrich all the people of Earth.

Among the thousands of millions of asteroids in space there are at least thirty or forty that are more than a hundred miles across, say, the size of Massachusetts minus Cape Cod. There are thousands that are more than ten miles across, and millions that are a mile or so wide. The rule of thumb is that for every asteroid of a given size, there are ten more that are one-third smaller.

From the evidence of meteorites, astronomers conclude that some asteroids are basically metallic in composition, mostly iron and nickel alloyed naturally into high-grade steel. Most asteroids, though, are rocky, as is Wethersfield 1982, which is composed of stony *chondrules,* or spheres.

A single rocky asteroid of the type astronomers call a *carbonaceous chondrite*, no larger than the length of a football field, could contain some $15 million in gold—as an impurity. The real value of such an asteroid would be in the organic chemicals it contained. A 100-yard-wide asteroid of the nickel-iron variety contains nearly four million tons of high-grade nickel steel, worth more than a billion dollars in today's steel industry. One asteroid. There are uncounted myriads of them.

For eons, asteroids have pelted the Earth, giving us the evidence that these resources exist in space. Soon now, as history counts time, human miners and prospectors will head outward to the Asteroid Belt, armed with electronic gear and lasers, riding nuclear-powered rockets. They will be followed by huge factory ships, sailing the silent sea of vacuum for years at a time, scooping in thousands of millions of tons of rock and metals, and processing them into finished products during the long voyage home.

Like the whalers of New Bedford and the iron men who crewed the wooden ships of old, the men and women who journey out to the asteroids will be prepared to spend several years "before the mast." And like the whalers and sailors of those earlier centuries, they will share in the profits of their voyages and return to Earth richer than any corsair who ever waylaid a treasure galleon.

ZERO GEE

If you've read the novels *Kinsman* and *Millennium* you have met Chet Kinsman. In this short story, Chet is still a cocky youth who believes that nothing in the world can really hurt him, and that flying— especially into the euphoria of zero gravity—is the biggest kick in life. He learns better. As we all do, sooner or later. Kinsman is a Promethean, and later in his life takes on the burden of Prometheus himself, in a way. At the stage of his life depicted in *Zero Gee,* however, he is just beginning to learn that the Second Law of Thermodynamics applies to every- thing in the universe, even personal relationships: You always have to pay more than you receive in return. Only in the rare instances of deeply human love do individuals willingly and gladly pay this price; only in those precious relationships does the Second Law yield to the synergy of true love.

■

Joe Tenny looked like a middle linebacker for the Pitts- burgh Steelers. Sitting in the cool shadows of the Astro Motel's bar, swarthy, barrel-built, scowling face clamped on a smoldering cigar, he would never be taken for that rar- est of all birds, a good engineer who is also a good mili- tary officer.

"Afternoon, Major."

Tenny turned on his stool to see old Cy Calder, the dean of the press-service reporters covering the base.

"Hi. Whatcha drinking?"

"I'm working," Calder answered with dignity. But he settled his once-lanky frame onto the next stool.

"Double scotch," Tenny called to the bartender. "And refill mine."

"An officer and a gentleman," murmured Calder. His voice was gravelly, matching his face.

As the bartender slid the drinks to them, Tenny said, "You wanna know who got the assignment."

"I told you I'm working."

Tenny grinned. "Keep your mouth shut 'til tomorrow? Murdock'll make the official announcement then, at his press conference."

"If you can save me the tedium of listening to the good colonel for two hours to get a single name out of him, I'll buy the next round, shine your shoes for a month, and arrange to lose an occasional poker pot to you."

"The hell you will!"

Calder shrugged. Tenny took a long pull on his drink. Calder did likewise.

"Okay. You'll find out anyway. But keep it quiet until Murdock's announcement. It's going to be Kinsman."

Calder put his glass down on the bar carefully. "Chester A. Kinsman, the pride of the Air Force? That's hard to believe."

"Murdock picked him."

"I know this mission is strictly for publicity," Calder said, "but Kinsman? In orbit for three days with *Photo Day* magazine's prettiest female? Does Murdock want publicity or a paternity suit?"

"Come on, Chet's not that bad. . . ."

"Oh no? From the stories I hear about your few weeks up at the NASA Ames Center, Kinsman cut a swath from Berkeley to North Beach."

Tenny countered, "He's young and good-looking. And

the girls haven't had many single astronauts to play with. NASA's gang is a bunch of old farts compared to my kids. But Chet's the best of the bunch, no fooling."

Calder looked unconvinced.

"Listen. When we were training at Edwards, know what Kinsman did? Built a biplane, an honest-to-God replica of a Spad fighter. From the ground up. He's a solid citizen."

"Yes, and then he played Red Baron for six weeks. Didn't he get into trouble for buzzing an airliner?"

Tenny's reply was cut off by a burst of talk and laughter. Half a dozen lean, lithe young men in Air Force blues—captains, all of them—trotted down the carpeted stairs that led into the bar.

"There they are," said Tenny. "You can ask Chet about it yourself."

Kinsman looked no different from the other Air Force astronauts. Slightly under six feet tall, thin with the lean-ness of youth, dark hair cut in the short, flat military style, blue-gray eyes, long bony face. He was grinning broadly at the moment, as he and the other five astronauts grabbed chairs in one corner of the bar and called their orders to the lone bartender.

Calder took his drink and headed for their table, followed by Major Tenny.

"Hold it," one of the captains called out. "Here comes the press."

"Tight security."

"Why, boys," Calder tried to make his rasping voice sound hurt, "don't you trust me?"

Tenny pushed a chair toward the newsman and took an-other one for himself. Straddling it, he told the captain, "It's okay. I spilled it to him."

"How much he pay you, boss?"

"That's between him and me."

As the bartender brought a tray of drinks, Calder said,

"Let the Fourth Estate pay for this round, gentlemen. I want to pump some information out of you."

"That might take a lot of rounds."

To Kinsman, Calder said, "Congratulations, my boy. Colonel Murdock must think very highly of you."

Kinsman burst out laughing. "Murdock? You should've seen his face when he told me it was going to be me."

"Looked like he was sucking on lemons."

Tenny explained. "The choice for this flight was made mostly by computer. Murdock wanted to be absolutely fair, so he put everybody's performance ratings into the computer and out came Kinsman's name. If he hadn't made so much noise about being impartial, he could've reshuffled the cards and tried again. But I was right there when the machine finished its run, so he couldn't back out of it."

Calder grinned. "All right then, the computer thinks highly of you, Chet. I suppose that's still something of an honor."

"More like a privilege. I've been watching that *Photo Day* chick all through her training. She's ripe."

"She'll look even better up in orbit."

"Once she takes off the pressure suit . . . et cetera."

"Hey, y'know, nobody's ever done it in orbit."

"Yeah . . . free fall, zero gravity."

Kinsman looked thoughtful. "Adds a new dimension to the problem, doesn't it?"

"Three-dimensional." Tenny took the cigar butt from his mouth and laughed.

Calder got up slowly from his chair and silenced the others. Looking down fondly on Kinsman, he said:

"My boy—back in 1915, in London, I became a charter member of the Mile High Club. At an altitude of exactly 5,280 feet, while circling St. Paul's, I successfully penetrated an Army nurse in an open cockpit . . . despite fogged goggles, cramped working quarters and a severe case of windburn.

"Since then, there's been damned little to look forward to. The skin-divers claimed a new frontier, but in fact they are retrogressing. Any silly-ass dolphin can do it in the water.

"But you've got something new going for you: weightlessness. Floating around in free fall, chasing tail in three dimensions. It beggars the imagination!

"Kinsman, I pass the torch to you. To the founder of the Zero Gee Club!"

As one man, they rose and solemnly toasted Captain Kinsman.

As they sat down again, Major Tenny burst the balloon. "You guys haven't given Murdock credit for much brains. You don't think he's gonna let Chet go up with that broad all alone, do you?"

Kinsman's face fell, but the others lit up.

"It'll be a three-man mission!"

"Two men and the chick."

Tenny warned, "Now don't start drooling. Murdock wants a chaperon, not an assistant rapist."

It was Kinsman who got it first. Slouching back in his chair, chin sinking to his chest, he muttered, "Sonofabitch . . . he's sending Jill along."

A collective groan.

"Murdock made up his mind an hour ago," Tenny said. "He was stuck with you, Chet, so he hit on the chaperon idea. He's also giving you some real chores to do, to keep you busy. Like mating the power pod."

"Jill Meyers," said one of the captains disgustedly.

"She's qualified, and she's been taking the *Photo Day* girl through her training. I'll bet she knows more about the mission than any of you guys do."

"She would."

"In fact," Tenny added maliciously, "I think she's the senior captain among you satellite-jockeys."

Kinsman had only one comment: "Shit."

The bone-rattling roar and vibration of liftoff suddenly died away. Sitting in his contour seat, scanning the banks of dials and gauges a few centimeters before his eyes, Kinsman could feel the pressure and tension slacken. Not back to normal. To zero. He was no longer plastered up against his seat, but touching it only lightly, almost floating in it, restrained only by his harness.

It was the fourth time he had felt weightlessness. It still made him smile inside the cumbersome helmet.

Without thinking about it, he touched a control stud on the chair's armrest. A maneuvering jet fired briefly, and the ponderous, lovely bulk of planet Earth slid into view through the port in front of Kinsman. It curved huge and serene, blue, mostly, but tightly wrapped in the purest, dazzling white of clouds, beautiful, peaceful, shining.

Kinsman could have watched it forever, but he heard sounds of motion in his earphones. The two girls were sitting behind him, side by side. The spacecraft cabin made a submarine look roomy: the three seats were shoehorned in among racks of instruments and equipment.

Jill Meyers, who came to the astronaut program from the Aerospace Medical Division, was officially second pilot and biomedical officer. *And chaperon,* Kinsman knew. The photographer, Linda Symmes, was simply a passenger.

Kinsman's earphones crackled with a disembodied link from Earth. "AF-9, this is ground control. We have you confirmed in orbit. Trajectory nominal. All systems go."

"Check," Kinsman said into his helmet mike.

The voice, already starting to fade, switched to ordinary conversational speech. "Looks like you're right on the money, Chet. We'll get the orbital parameters out of the computer and have 'em for you by the time you pass Ascension. You probably won't need much maneuvering to make rendezvous with the lab."

"Good. Everything here on the board looks green."

"Okay. Ground control out." Faintly. "And hey . . . good luck, Founding Father."

Kinsman grinned at that. He slid his faceplate up, loosened his harness and turned in his seat. "Okay, girls, you can take off your helmets if you want to."

Jill Meyers snapped her faceplate open and started unlocking the helmet's neck seal.

"I'll go first," she said, "and then I can help Linda with hers."

"Sure you won't need any help?" Kinsman offered.

Jill pulled her helmet off. "I've had more time in orbit than you. And shouldn't you be paying attention to the instruments?"

So this is how it's going to be, Kinsman thought.

Jill's face was round and plain and bright as a new penny. Snub nose, wide mouth, short hair of undistinguished brown. Kinsman knew that under the pressure suit was a figure that could most charitably be described as ordinary.

Linda Symmes was entirely another matter. She had lifted her faceplate and was staring out at him with wide, blue eyes that combined feminine curiosity with a hint of helplessness. She was tall, nearly Kinsman's own height, with thick honey-colored hair and a body that he had already memorized down to the last curve.

In her sweet, high voice she said, "I think I'm going to be sick."

"Oh for . . ."

Jill reached into the compartment between their two seats. "I'll take care of this. You stick to the controls." And she whipped open a white plastic bag and stuck it over Linda's face.

Shuddering at the thought of what could happen in zero gravity, Kinsman turned back to the control panel. He pulled his faceplate shut and turned up the air blower in his suit, trying to cut off the obscene sound of Linda's struggles.

"For Chrissake," he yelled, "unplug her radio! You want me chucking all over, too?"

"AF-9, this is Ascension."

Trying to blank his mind to what was going on behind him, Kinsman thumbed the switch on his communications panel. "Go ahead, Ascension."

For the next hour Kinsman thanked the gods that he had plenty of work to do. He matched the orbit of their three-man spacecraft to that of the Air Force orbiting laboratory, which had been up for more than a year now, and intermittently occupied by two- or three-man crews.

The lab was a fat, cylindrical shape, silhouetted against the brilliant white of the cloud-decked Earth. As he pulled the spacecraft close, Kinsman could see the antennas and airlock and other odd pieces of gear that had accumulated on it. *Looking more like a junkheap every trip.* Riding behind it, unconnected in any way, was the massive cone of the new power pod.

Kinsman circled the lab once, using judicious squeezes of his maneuvering jets. He touched a command-signal switch, and the lab's rendezvous-radar-beacon came to life, announced by a light on his control panel.

"All systems green," he said to ground control. "Everything looks okay."

"Roger, Niner. You are cleared for docking."

This was a bit more delicate. *Be helpful if Jill could read off the computer . . .*

"Distance, eighty-eight meters," Jill's voice pronounced firmly in his earphones. "Approach angle—"

Kinsman instinctively turned, but his helmet cut off any possible sight of her. "Hey, how's your patient?"

"Empty. I gave her a sedative. She's out."

"Okay," Kinsman said. "Let's get docked."

He inched the spacecraft into the docking-collar on one end of the lab, locked on and saw the panel lights confirm that the docking was secure.

"Better get Sleeping Beauty zipped up," he told Jill as he touched the buttons that extended the flexible access-tunnel from the hatch over their heads to the main hatch of the lab. The lights on the panel turned from amber to green when the tunnel locked its fittings around the lab's hatch.

Jill said, "I'm supposed to check the tunnel."

"Stay put. I'll do it." Sealing his faceplate shut, Kinsman unbuckled and rose effortlessly out of the seat to bump his helmet lightly against the overhead hatch.

"You two both buttoned tight?"

"Yes."

"Keep an eye on the air gauge." He cracked the hatch open a few millimeters.

"Pressure's okay. No red lights."

Nodding, Kinsman pushed the hatch open all the way. He pulled himself easily up and into the shoulder-wide tunnel, propelling himself down its curving length by a few flicks of his fingers against the ribbed walls.

Light and easy, he reminded himself. *No big motions, no sudden moves.*

When he reached the laboratory hatch he slowly rotated, like a swimmer doing a lazy rollover, and inspected every inch of the tunnel seal in the light of his helmet lamp. Satisfied that it was locked in place, he opened the lab hatch and pushed himself inside. Carefully, he touched his slightly adhesive boots to the plastic flooring and stood upright. His arms tended to float out, but they touched the equipment racks on either side of the narrow central passageway. Kinsman turned on the lab's interior lights, checked the air supply, pressure and temperature gauges, then shuffled back to the hatch and pushed himself through the tunnel again.

He reentered the spacecraft upside-down and had to contort himself in slow motion around the pilot's seat to regain a "normal" attitude.

"Lab's okay," he said finally. "Now how the hell do we get her through the tunnel?"

Jill had already unbuckled the harness over Linda's shoulders. "You pull, I'll push. She ought to bend around the corners all right."

And she did.

The laboratory was about the size and shape of the interior of a small transport plane. On one side, nearly its entire length was taken up by instrument racks, control equipment and the computer, humming almost inaudibly behind light plastic panels. Across the narrow separating aisle were the crew stations: control desk, two observation ports, biology and astrophysics benches. At the far end, behind a discreet curtain, was the head and a single hammock.

Kinsman sat at the control desk, in his fatigues now, one leg hooked around the webbed chair's single supporting column to keep him from floating off. He was running through a formal check of all the lab's life systems: air, water, heat, electrical power. All green lights on the main panel. Communications gear. Green. The radar screen to his left showed a single large blip close by—the power pod.

He looked up as Jill came through the curtain from the bunkroom. She was still in her pressure suit, with only the helmet removed.

"How is she?"

Looking tired, Jill answered, "Okay. Still sleeping. I think she'll be all right when she wakes up."

"She'd better be. I'm not going to have a wilting flower around here. I'll abort the mission."

"Give her a chance, Chet. She just lost her cookies when

free-fall hit her. All the training in the world can't prepare you for those first few minutes."

Kinsman recalled his first orbital flight. *It doesn't shut off. You're falling. Like skiing, or skydiving. Only better.*

Jill shuffled toward him, keeping a firm grip on the chairs in front of the work benches and the handholds set into the equipment racks.

Kinsman got up and pushed toward her. "Here, let me help you out of the suit."

"I can do it myself."

"Shut up."

After several minutes, Jill was free of the bulky suit and sitting in one of the webbed chairs in her coverall-fatigues. Ducking slightly because of the curving overhead, Kinsman glided into the galley. It was about half the width of a phone booth, and not as deep nor as tall.

"Coffee, tea or milk?"

Jill grinned at him. "Orange juice."

He reached for a concentrate bag. "You're a hard girl to satisfy."

"No I'm not. I'm easy to get along with. Just one of the fellas."

Feeling slightly puzzled, Kinsman handed her the orange juice container.

For the next couple of hours they checked out the lab's equipment in detail. Kinsman was reassembling a highres-olution camera after cleaning it, parts hanging in midair all around him as he sat intently working, while Jill was nursing a straggly-looking philodendron that had been smuggled aboard and was inching from the biology bench toward the ceiling light panels. Linda pushed back the curtain from the sleeping area and stepped, uncertainly, into the main compartment.

Jill noticed her first. "Hi, how're you feeling?"

Kinsman looked up. She was in tight-fitting coveralls. He

bounced out of his web-chair toward her, scattering camera parts in every direction.

"Are you all right?" he asked.

Smiling sheepishly, "I think so. I'm rather embarrassed. . . ." Her voice was high and soft.

"Oh, that's all right," Kinsman said eagerly. "It happens to practically everybody. I got sick myself my first time in orbit."

"That," said Jill as she dodged a slowly-tumbling lens that ricocheted gently off the ceiling, "is a little white lie, meant to make you feel at home."

Kinsman forced himself not to frown. *Why'd Jill want to cross me?*

Jill said, "Chet, you'd better pick up those camera pieces before they get so scattered you won't be able to find them all."

He wanted to snap an answer, thought better of it, and replied simply, "Right."

As he finished the job on the camera, he took a good look at Linda. The color was back in her face. She looked steady, clear-eyed, not frightened or upset. *Maybe she'll be* okay *after all*. Jill made her a cup of tea, which she sipped from the lid's plastic spout.

Kinsman went to the control desk and scanned the mission schedule sheet.

"Hey, Jill, it's past your bedtime."

"I'm not really very sleepy," she said.

"Maybe. But you've had a busy day, little girl. And tomorrow will be busier. Now you get your four hours, and then I'll get mine. Got to be fresh for the mating."

"Mating?" Linda asked from her seat at the far end of the aisle, a good five strides from Kinsman. Then she remembered, "Oh . . . you mean linking the pod to the laboratory."

Suppressing a half-dozen possible jokes, Kinsman nodded. "Extra-vehicular activity."

Jill reluctantly drifted off her web-chair. "Okay, I'll sack in. I am tired, but I never seem to get really sleepy up here."

Wonder how much Murdock's told her? She's sure acting like a chaperon.

Jill shuffled into the sleeping area and pulled the curtain firmly shut. After a few moments of silence, Kinsman turned to Linda.

"Alone at last."

She smiled back.

"Uh, you just happen to be sitting where I've got to install this camera." He nudged the finished hardware so that it floated gently toward her.

She got up slowly, carefully, and stood behind the chair, holding its back with both hands as if she were afraid of falling. Kinsman slid into the web-chair and stopped the camera's slow-motion flight with one hand. Working on the fixture in the bulkhead that it fit into, he asked:

"You really feel okay?"

"Yes, honestly."

"Think you'll be up to EVA tomorrow?"

"I hope so . . . I want to go outside with you."

I'd rather be inside with you. Kinsman grinned as he worked.

An hour later they were sitting side by side in front of one of the observation ports, looking out at the curving bulk of Earth, the blue and white splendor of the cloud-spangled Pacific. Kinsman had just reported to the Hawaii ground station. The mission flight plan was floating on a clipboard between the two of them. He was trying to study it, comparing the time when Jill would be sleeping with the long stretches between ground stations, when there would be no possibility of being interrupted.

"Is that land?" Linda asked, pointing to a thick band of clouds wrapping the horizon.

Looking up from the clipboard, Kinsman said, "South American coast. Chile."

"There's another tracking station there."

"NASA station. Not part of our network. We only use Air Force stations."

"Why is that?"

He felt his face frowning. "Murdock's playing soldier. This is supposed to be a strictly military operation. Not that we do anything warlike. But we run as though there weren't any civilian stations around to help us. The usual hup-two-three crap."

She laughed. "You don't agree with the colonel?"

"There's only one thing he's done lately that I'm in complete agreement with."

"What's that?"

"Bringing you up here."

The smile stayed on her face but her eyes moved away from him. "Now you sound like a soldier."

"Not an officer and a gentleman?"

She looked straight at him again. "Let's change the subject."

Kinsman shrugged. "Sure. Okay. You're here to get a story. Murdock wants to get the Air Force as much publicity as NASA gets. And the Pentagon wants to show the world that we don't have any weapons on board. We're military, all right, but *nice* military."

"And you?" Linda asked, serious now. "What do you want? How does an Air Force captain get into the space cadets?"

"The same way everything happens—you're in a certain place at a certain time. They told me I was going to be an astronaut. It was all part of the job . . . until my first orbital flight. Now it's a way of life."

"Really? Why is that?"

Grinning, he answered, "Wait'll we go outside. You'll find out."

Jill came back into the main cabin precisely on schedule, and it was Kinsman's turn to sleep. He seldom had difficulty sleeping on Earth, never in orbit. But he wondered about Linda's reaction to being outside while he strapped on the pressure-cuffs to his arms and legs. The medics insisted on them, claimed they exercised the cardiovascular system while you slept.

Damned stupid nuisance, Kinsman grumbled to himself. *Some ground-based MD's idea of how to make a name for himself.*

Finally he zippered himself into the gossamer cocoonlike hammock and shut his eyes. He could feel the cuffs pumping gently. His last conscious thought was a nagging worry that Linda would be terrified of EVA.

When he awoke, and Linda took her turn in the hammock, he talked it over with Jill.

"I think she'll be all right, Chet. Don't hold that first few minutes against her."

"I don't know. There's only two kinds of people up here: you either love it or you're scared sh—witless. And you can't fake it. If she goes ape outside . . ."

"She won't," Jill said firmly. "And anyway, you'll be there to help her. I've told her that she won't be going outside until you're finished with the mating job. She wanted to get pictures of you actually at work, but she'll settle for a few posed shots."

Kinsman nodded. But the worry persisted. *I wonder if Calder's Army nurse was scared of flying?*

He was pulling on his boots, wedging his free foot against an equipment rack to keep from floating off, when Linda returned from her sleep.

"Ready for a walk around the block?" he asked her.

She smiled and nodded without the slightest hesitation.

"I'm looking forward to it. Can I get a few shots of you while you zipper up your suit?"

Maybe she'll be okay.

At last he was sealed into the pressure suit. Linda and Jill stood back as Kinsman shuffled to the airlock-hatch. It was set into the floor at the end of the cabin where the spacecraft was docked. With Jill helping him, he eased down into the airlock and shut the hatch. The airlock chamber itself was coffin-sized. Kinsman had to half-bend to move around in it. He checked out his suit, then pumped the air out of the chamber. Then he was ready to open the outer hatch.

It was beneath his feet, but as it slid open to reveal the stars, Kinsman's weightless orientation flip-flopped, like an optical illusion, and he suddenly felt that he was standing on his head and looking up.

"Going out now," he said into the helmet's mike.

"Okay," Jill's voice responded.

Carefully, he eased himself through the open hatch, holding onto its edge with one gloved hand once he was fully outside, the way a swimmer holds the rail for a moment when he first slides into the deep water. Outside. Swinging his body around slowly, he took in the immense beauty of Earth, dazzlingly bright even through his tinted visor. Beyond its curving limb was the darkness of infinity, with the beckoning stars watching him in unblinking solemnity.

Alone now. His own tight, self-contained universe, independent of everything and everybody. He could cut the lifegiving umbilical line that linked him with the laboratory and float off by himself, forever. And be dead in two minutes. *Ay, there's the rub.*

Instead, he unhooked the tiny gas gun from his waist and, trailing the umbilical, squirted himself over toward the power pod. It was riding smoothly behind the lab, a squat truncated cone, shorter, but fatter, than the lab itself, one edge brilliantly lit by the sun; the rest of it bathed in the softer light reflected from the dayside of Earth below.

Kinsman's job was to inspect the power pod, check its equipment, and then mate it to the electrical system of the laboratory. There was no need to physically connect the two bodies, except to link a pair of power lines between them. Everything necessary for the task—tools, power lines, checkout instruments—had been built into the pod, waiting for a man to use them.

It would have been simple work on Earth. In zero gee, it was complicated. The slightest motion of any part of your body started you drifting. You had to fight against all the built-in mannerisms of a lifetime; had to work constantly to keep in place. It was easy to get exhausted in zero gee.

Kinsman accepted all this with hardly a conscious thought. He worked slowly, methodically, using as little motion as possible, letting himself drift slightly until a more-or-less natural body motion counteracted and pulled him back in the opposite direction. *Ride the waves, slow and easy.* There was a rhythm to his work, the natural dream-like rhythm of weightlessness.

His earphones were silent; he said nothing. All he heard was the purring of the suit's air blowers and his own steady breathing. All he saw was his work.

Finally he jetted back to the laboratory, towing the pair of thick cables. He found the connectors waiting for them on the side wall of the lab and inserted the cable plugs. *I pronounce you lab and power source.* He inspected the checkout lights alongside the connectors. All green. *May you produce many kilowatts.*

Swinging from handhold to handhold along the length of the lab, he made his way back toward the airlock.

"Okay, it's finished. How's Linda doing?"

Jill answered, "She's all set."

"Send her out."

She came out slowly, uncertain wavering feet sliding out first from the bulbous airlock. It reminded Kinsman of a film he had seen of a whale giving birth.

"Welcome to the real world," he said when her head cleared the airlock-hatch.

She turned to answer him and he heard her gasp and he knew that now he liked her.

"It's . . . it's . . ."

"Staggering," Kinsman suggested. "And look at you—no hands."

She was floating freely, pressure suit laden with camera gear, umbilical flexing easily behind her. Kinsman couldn't see her face through the tinted visor, but he could hear the awe in her voice, even in her breathing.

"I've never seen anything so absolutely overwhelming. . . ."

And then, suddenly, she was all business, reaching for a camera, snapping away at the Earth and stars and distant Moon, rapidfire. She moved too fast and started to tumble. Kinsman jetted over and steadied her, holding her by the shoulders.

"Hey, take it easy. They're not going away. You've got lots of time."

"I want to get some shots of you, and the lab. Can you get over by the pod and go through some of the motions of your work on it?"

Kinsman posed for her, answered her questions, rescued a camera when she fumbled it out of her hands and couldn't reach it as it drifted away from her.

"Judging distances gets a little wacky out here," he said, handing the camera back to her.

Jill called them twice and ordered them back inside. "Chet, you're already fifteen minutes over the limit!"

"There's plenty slop in the schedule; we can stay out a while longer."

"You're going to get her exhausted."

"I really feel fine," Linda said, her voice lyrical.

"How much more film do you have?" Kinsman asked her.

She peered at the camera. "Six more shots."

"Okay, we'll be in when the film runs out, Jill."

"You're going to be in darkness in another five minutes!"

Turning to Linda, who was floating upside-down with the cloud-laced Earth behind her, he said, "Save your film for the sunset, then shoot like hell when it comes."

"The sunset? What'll I focus on?"

"You'll know when it happens. Just watch."

It came fast, but Linda was equal to it. As the lab swung in its orbit toward the Earth's night-shadow, the sun dropped to the horizon and shot off a spectacular few moments of the purest reds and oranges and finally a heart-catching blue. Kinsman watched in silence, hearing Linda's breath going faster and faster as she worked the camera.

Then they were in darkness. Kinsman flicked on his helmet lamp. Linda was just hanging there, camera still in hand.

"It's . . . impossible to describe." Her voice sounded empty, drained. "If I hadn't seen it . . . if I didn't get it on film, I don't think I'd be able to convince myself that I wasn't dreaming."

Jill's voice rasped in his earphones. "Chet, get inside! This is against every safety reg, being outside in the dark."

He looked over toward the lab. Lights were visible along its length and the ports were lighted from within. Otherwise, he could barely make it out, even though it was only a few meters away.

"Okay, okay. Turn on the airlock-light so we can see the hatch."

Linda was still bubbling about the view outside, long

after they had pulled off their pressure suits and eaten sandwiches and cookies.

"Have you ever been out there?" she asked Jill.

Perched on the biology bench's edge, near the mice colony, Jill nodded curtly. "Twice."

"Isn't it spectacular? I hope the pictures come out; some of the settings on the camera . . ."

"They'll be all right," Jill said. "And if they're not, we've got a backlog of photos you can use."

"Oh, but they wouldn't have the shots of Chet working on the power pod."

Jill shrugged. "Aren't you going to take more photos in here? If you want to get some pictures of real space veterans, you ought to snap the mice here. They've been up for months now, living fine and raising families. And they don't make such a fuss about it, either."

"Well, some of us do exciting things," Kinsman said, "and some of us tend mice."

Jill glowered at him.

Glancing at his wristwatch, Kinsman said, "Girls, it's my sack time. I've had a trying day: mechanic, tourist guide, and cover boy for *Photo Day*. Work, work, work."

He glided past Linda with a smile, kept it for Jill as he went by her. She was still glaring.

When he woke up again and went back into the main cabin, Jill was talking pleasantly with Linda as the two of them stood over the microscope and specimen-rack of the biology bench.

Linda saw him first. "Oh, hi. Jill's been showing me the spores she's studying. And I photographed the mice. Maybe they'll go on the cover instead of you."

Kinsman grinned. "She been poisoning your mind against me." But to himself he wondered, *What the hell has Jill been telling her about me?*

Jill drifted over to the control desk, picked up the clipboard with the mission log on it and tossed it lightly toward Kinsman.

"Ground control says the power pod checks out all green," she said. "You did a good job."

"Thanks." He caught the clipboard. "Who's turn in the sack is it?"

"Mine," Jill answered.

"Okay. Anything special cooking?"

"No. Everything's on schedule. Next data transmission comes up in twelve minutes. Kodiak station."

Kinsman nodded. "Sleep tight."

Once Jill had shut the curtain to the bunkroom, Kinsman carried the mission log to the control desk and sat down. Linda stayed at the biology bench, about three paces away.

He checked the instrument board with a quick glance, then turned to Linda. "Well, now do you know what I meant about this being a way of life?"

"I think so. It's so different . . ."

"It's the real thing. Complete freedom. Brave new world. After ten minutes of EVA, everything else is just toothpaste."

"It was certainly exciting."

"More than that. It's living. Being on the ground is a drag, even flying a plane is dull now. This is where the fun is . . . out here in orbit and on the Moon. It's as close to heaven as anybody's gotten."

"You're really serious?"

"Damned right. I've even been thinking of asking Murdock for a transfer to NASA duty. Air Force missions don't include the Moon, and I'd like to walk around on the new world, see the sights."

She smiled at him. "I'm afraid I'm not that enthusiastic."

"Well, think about it for a minute. Up here, you're free. Really free, for the first time in your life. All the laws and rules and prejudices they've been dumping on you all your life . . . they're all *down there*. Up here it's a new start. You can be yourself and do your own thing . . . and nobody can tell you different."

"As long as somebody provides you with air and food and water and . . ."

"That's the physical end of it, sure. We're living in a microcosm, courtesy of the aerospace industry and AFSC. But there're no strings on us. The brass can't make us follow their rules. We're writing the rule books ourselves. . . . For the first time since 1776, we're writing new rules."

Linda looked thoughtful now. Kinsman couldn't tell if she was genuinely impressed by his line, or if she knew what he was trying to lead up to. He turned back to the control desk and studied the mission flight plan again.

He had carefully considered all the possible opportunities, and narrowed them down to two. *Both of them tomorrow, over the Indian Ocean. Forty to fifty minutes between ground stations, and Jill's asleep both times.*

"AF-9, this is Kodiak."

He reached for the radio switch. "AF-9 here, Kodiak. Go ahead."

"We are receiving your automatic data transmission loud and clear."

"Roger, Kodiak. Everything normal here; mission profile unchanged."

"Okay, Niner. We have nothing new for you. Oh wait . . . Chet, Lew Regneson is here and he says he's betting on you to uphold the Air Force's honor. Keep 'em flying."

Keeping his face as straight as possible, Kinsman answered, "Roger, Kodiak. Mission profile unchanged."

"Good luck!"

Linda's thoughtful expression had deepened. "What was that all about?"

He looked straight into those cool blue eyes and answered, "Damned if I know. Regneson's one of the astronaut team; been assigned to Kodiak for the past six weeks. He must be going ice-happy. Thought it'd be best just to humor him."

"Oh. I see." But she looked unconvinced.

"Have you checked any of your pictures in the film processor?"

Shaking her head, Linda said, "No, I don't want to risk them on your automatic equipment. I'll process them myself when we get back."

"Damned good equipment," said Kinsman.

"I'm fussy."

He shrugged and let it go.

"Chet?"

"What?"

"That power pod . . . what's it for? Colonel Murdock got awfully coy when I asked him."

"Nobody's supposed to know until the announcement's made in Washington . . . probably when we get back. I can't tell you officially," he grinned, "but generally reliable sources believe that it's going to power a radar set that'll be orbited next month. The radar will be part of our ABM warning system."

"Antiballistic missile?"

With a nod, Kinsman explained, "From orbit you can spot missile launches farther away, give the States a longer warning time."

"So your brave new world is involved in war, too."

"Sort of." Kinsman frowned. "Radars won't kill anybody, of course. They might save lives."

"But this *is* a military satellite."

"Unarmed. Two things this brave new world doesn't have yet: death and love."

"Men have died. . . ."

"Not in orbit. On reentry. In ground or air accidents. No one's died up here. And no one's made love, either."

Despite herself, it seemed to Kinsman, she smiled. "Have there been any chances for it?"

"Well, the Russians have had women cosmonauts. Jill's been the first American girl in orbit. You're the second."

She thought it over for a moment. "This isn't exactly the bridal suite of the Waldorf . . . in fact, I've seen better motel rooms along the Jersey Turnpike."

"Pioneers have to rough it."

"I'm a photographer, Chet, not a pioneer."

Kinsman hunched his shoulders and spread his hands helplessly, a motion that made him bob slightly on the chair. "Strike three, I'm out."

"Better luck next time."

"Thanks." He returned his attention to the mission flight plan. *Next time will be in exactly sixteen hours, chickie.*

When Jill came out of the sack it was Linda's turn to sleep. Kinsman stayed at the control desk, sucking on a container of lukewarm coffee. All the panel lights were green. Jill was taking a blood specimen from one of the white mice.

"How're they doing?"

Without looking up, she answered, "Fine. They've adapted to weightlessness beautifully. Calcium level's evened off, muscle tone is good. . . ."

"Then there's hope for us two-legged types?"

Jill returned the mouse to the colony entrance and snapped the lid shut. It scampered through to rejoin its clan in the transparent plastic maze of tunnels.

"I can't see any physical reason why humans can't live in orbit indefinitely," she answered.

Kinsman caught a slight but definite stress on the word *physical*. "You think there might be emotional problems over the long run?"

"Chet, I can see emotional problems on a three-day mission." Jill forced the blood specimen into a stoppered test tube.

"What do you mean?"

"Come on," she said, her face a mixture of disappointment and distaste. "It's obvious what you're trying to do. Your tail's been wagging like a puppy's whenever she's in sight."

"You haven't been sleeping much, have you?"

"I haven't been eavesdropping, if that's what you mean. I've simply been watching you watching her. And some of the messages from the ground . . . is the whole Air Force in on this? How much money's being bet?"

"I'm not involved in any betting. I'm just—"

"You're just taking a risk on fouling up this mission and maybe killing the three of us, just to prove you're Tarzan and she's Jane."

"Goddammit, Jill, now you sound like Murdock."

The sour look on her face deepened. "Okay. You're a big boy. If you want to play Tarzan while you're on duty, that's your business. I won't get in your way. I'll take a sleeping pill and stay in the sack."

"You will?"

"That's right. You can have your blonde Barbie doll, and good luck to you. But I'll tell you this—she's a phony. I've talked to her long enough to dig that. You're trying to use her, but she's using us, too. She was pumping me about the power pod while you were sleeping. She's here for her own reasons, Chet, and if she plays along with you it won't be for the romance and adventure of it all."

My God Almighty, Jill's jealous!

It was tense and quiet when Linda returned from the bunkroom. The three of them worked separately: Jill fuss-

ing over the algae colony on the shelf above the biology
bench; Kinsman methodically taking film from the observation cameras for return to Earth and reloading them;
Linda efficiently clicking away at both of them.

Ground control called up to ask how things were going.
Both Jill and Linda threw sharp glances at Kinsman. He
replied merely:

"Following mission profile. All systems green."

They shared a meal of pastes and squeeze-tubes together,
still mostly in silence, and then it was Kinsman's turn in
the sack. But not before he checked the mission flight plan.
*Jill goes in next, and we'll have four hours alone, includ-
ing a stretch over the Indian Ocean.*

Once Jill retired, Kinsman immediately called Linda
over to the control desk under the pretext of showing her
the radar image of a Russian satellite.

"We're coming close now." They hunched side by side
at the desk to peer at the orange-glowing radar screen, close
enough for Kinsman to scent a hint of very feminine perfume. "Only a thousand kilometers away."

"Why don't you blink our lights at them?"

"It's unmanned."

"Oh."

"It *is* a little like World War I up here," Kinsman realized, straightening up. "Just being here is more important
than which nation you're from."

"Do the Russians feel that way, too?"

Kinsman nodded. "I think so."

She stood in front of him, so close that they were almost
touching.

"You know," Kinsman said, "when I first saw you on the
base, I thought you were a photographer's model . . . not the
photographer."

Gliding slightly away from him, she answered, "I started
out as a model. . . ." Her voice trailed off.

"Don't stop. What were you going to say?"

Something about her had changed, Kinsman realized. She was still coolly friendly, but alert now, wary, and . . . sad?

Shrugging, she said, "Modeling is a dead end. I finally figured out that there's more of a future on the other side of the camera."

"You had too much brains for modeling."

"Don't flatter me."

"Why on earth should I flatter you?"

"We're not on Earth."

"Touché."

She drifted over toward the galley. Kinsman followed her.

"How long have you been on the other side of the camera?" he asked.

Turning back toward him, "I'm supposed to be getting your life story, not vice versa."

"Okay . . . ask me some questions."

"How many people know you're supposed to lay me up here?"

Kinsman felt his face smiling, an automatic delaying action. *What the hell,* he thought. Aloud, he replied, "I don't know. It started as a little joke among a few of the guys . . . apparently the word has spread."

"And how much money do you stand to win or lose?" She wasn't smiling.

"Money?" Kinsman was genuinely surprised. "Money doesn't enter into it."

"Oh no?"

"No, not with me," he insisted.

The tenseness in her body seemed to relax a little. "Then why . . . I mean . . . what's it all about?"

Kinsman brought his smile back and pulled himself down into the nearest chair. "Why not? You're damned pretty, neither one of us has any strings, nobody's tried it in zero gee before. . . . Why the hell not?"

"But why should I?"

"That's the big question. That's what makes an adventure out of it."

She looked at him thoughtfully, leaning her tall frame against the galley paneling. "Just like that. An adventure. There's nothing more to it than that?"

"Depends," Kinsman answered. "Hard to tell ahead of time."

"You live in a very simple world, Chet."

"I try to. Don't you?"

She shook her head. "No, my world's very complex."

"But it includes sex."

Now she smiled, but there was no pleasure in it. "Does it?"

"You mean never?" Kinsman's voice sounded incredulous, even to himself.

She didn't answer.

"Never at all? I can't believe that. . . ."

"No," she said, "not never at all. But never for . . . for an adventure. For job security, yes. For getting the good assignments; for teaching me how to use a camera, in the first place. But never for fun . . . at least, not for a long, long time has it been for fun."

Kinsman looked into those ice-blue eyes and saw that they were completely dry and aimed straight back at him. His insides felt odd. He put a hand out toward her, but she didn't move a muscle.

"That's . . . that's a damned lonely way to live," he said.

"Yes, it is." Her voice was a steel knifeblade, without a trace of self-pity in it.

"But . . . how'd it happen? Why . . . ?"

She leaned her head back against the galley paneling, her eyes looking away, into the past. "I had a baby. He didn't want it. I had to give it up for adoption—either that or have it aborted. The kid should be five years old now. . . . I don't know where she is." She straightened up, looked back at Kinsman. "But I found out that sex is either for making babies or making careers; not for fun."

Kinsman sat there, feeling like he had just taken a low blow. The only sound in the cabin was the faint hum of electrical machinery, the whisper of the air fans.

Linda broke into a grin. "I wish you could see your face: Tarzan, the Ape-Man, trying to figure out a nuclear reactor."

"The only trouble with zero gee," he mumbled, "is that you can't hang yourself."

Jill sensed something was wrong, it seemed to Kinsman. From the moment she came out of the sack, she sniffed around, giving quizzical looks. Finally, when Linda retired for her final rest period before their return, Jill asked him:

"How're you two getting along?"

"Okay."

"Really?"

"Really. We're going to open a Playboy Club in here. Want to be a bunny?"

Her nose wrinkled. "You've got enough of those."

For more than an hour they worked their separate tasks in silence. Kinsman was concentrating on recalibrating the radar mapper when Jill handed him a container of hot coffee.

He turned in the chair. She was standing beside him, not much taller than his own seated height.

"Thanks."

Her face was very serious. "Something's bothering you, Chet. What did she do to you?"

"Nothing."

"Really?"

"For Chrissake, don't start that again! Nothing, absolutely nothing happened. Maybe that's what's bothering me."

Shaking her head, "No, you're worried about something, and it's not about yourself."

"Don't be so damned dramatic, Jill."

She put a hand on his shoulder. "Chet . . . I know this is all a game to you, but people can get hurt at this kind of game, and . . . well . . . nothing in life is ever as good as you expect it will be."

Looking up at her intent brown eyes, Kinsman felt his irritation vanish. "Okay, kid. Thanks for the philosophy. I'm a big boy, though, and I know what it's all about. . . ."

"You just think you do."

Shrugging, "Okay, I think I do. Maybe nothing is as good as it ought to be, but a man's innocent until proven guilty, and everything new is as good as gold until you find some tarnish on it. That's *my* philosophy for the day!"

"All right, slugger," Jill smiled, ruefully. "Be the ape-man. Fight it out for yourself. I just don't want to see her hurt you."

"I won't get hurt."

Jill said, "You hope. Okay, if there's anything I can do . . ."

"Yeah, there is something."

"What?"

"When you sack in again, make sure Linda sees you take a sleeping pill. Will you do that?"

Jill's face went expressionless. "Sure," she answered flatly. "Anything for a fellow officer."

She made a great show, several hours later, of taking a sleeping pill so that she could rest well on her final nap before reentry. It seemed to Kinsman that Jill deliberately layed it on too thickly.

"Do you always take sleeping pills on the final time

around?" Linda asked, after Jill had gone into the bunk-room.

"Got to be fully alert and rested for the return flight," Kinsman replied. "Reentry's the trickiest part of the operation."

"Oh. I see."

"Nothing to worry about, though," Kinsman added.

He went to the control desk and busied himself with the tasks that the mission profile called for. Linda sat lightly in the next chair, within arm's reach. Kinsman chatted briefly with Kodiak station, on schedule, and made an entry in the log.

Three more ground stations and then we're over the Indian Ocean, with world enough and time.

But he didn't look up from the control panel; he tested each system aboard the lab, fingers flicking over control buttons, eyes focused on the red, amber and green lights that told him how the laboratory's mechanical and electrical machinery was functioning.

"Chet?"

"Yes."

"Are you . . . sore at me?"

Still not looking at her, "No, I'm busy. Why should I be sore at you?"

"Well, not sore maybe, but . . ."

"Puzzled?"

"Puzzled, hurt, something like that."

He punched an entry on the computer's keyboard at his side, then turned to face her. "Linda, I haven't really had time to figure out what I feel. You're a complicated girl; maybe too complicated for me. Life's got enough twists in it."

Her mouth drooped a little.

"On the other hand," he added, "we WASPS ought to stick together. Not many of us left."

That brought a faint smile. "I'm not a WASP. My real name's Szymanski. . . . I changed it when I started modeling."

"Oh. Another complication."

She was about to reply when the radio speaker crackled, "AF-9, this is Cheyenne. Cheyenne to AF-9."

Kinsman leaned over and thumbed the transmitter switch. "AF-9 to Cheyenne. You're coming through faint but clear."

"Roger, Nine. We're receiving your telemetry. All systems look green from here."

"Manual check of systems also green," Kinsman said. "Mission profile okay, no deviations. Tasks about ninety percent complete."

"Roger. Ground control suggests you begin checking out your spacecraft on the next orbit. You are scheduled for reentry in ten hours."

"Right. Will do."

"Okay, Chet. Everything looks good from here. Anything else to report, ol' Founding Father?"

"Mind your own business." He turned the transmitter off. Linda was smiling at him.

"What's so funny?"

"You are. You're getting very touchy about this whole business."

"It's going to stay touchy for a long time to come. Those guys'll hound me for years about this."

"You could always tell lies."

"About you? No, I don't think I could do that. If the girl was anonymous, that's one thing. But they all know you, know where you work . . ."

"You're a gallant officer. I suppose that kind of rumor would get back to New York."

Kinsman grinned. "You could even make the front page of *the National Enquirer*."

She laughed at that. "I'll bet they'd pull out some of my old bikini pictures."

"Careful now," Kinsman put up a warning hand. "Don't stir up my imagination any more than it already is. I'm having a hard enough time being gallant right now."

They remained apart, silent, Kinsman sitting at the control desk, Linda drifting back toward the galley, nearly touching the curtain that screened off the sleeping area.

The ground control center called in and Kinsman gave a terse report. When he looked up at Linda again, she was sitting in front of the observation port across the aisle from the galley. Looking back at Kinsman, her face was troubled now, her eyes . . . he wasn't sure what was in her eyes. They looked different: no longer ice-cool, no longer calculating; they looked aware, concerned, almost frightened.

Still Kinsman stayed silent. He checked and double-checked the control board, making absolutely certain that every valve and transistor aboard the lab was working perfectly. Glancing at his watch: *Five more minutes before Ascension calls.* He checked the lighted board again.

Ascension called in exactly on schedule. Feeling his innards tightening, Kinsman gave his standard report in a deliberately calm and mechanical way. Ascension signed off.

With a long last look at the controls, Kinsman pushed himself out of the seat and drifted, hands faintly touching the grips along the aisle, toward Linda.

"You've been awfully quiet," he said, standing over her.

"I've been thinking about what you said a while ago." What was it in her eyes? Anticipation? Fear? "It . . . it has been a damned lonely life, Chet."

He took her arm and lifted her gently from the chair and kissed her.

"But . . ."

"It's all right," he whispered. "No one will bother us. No one will know."

She shook her head. "It's not that easy, Chet. It's not that simple."

"Why not? We're here together . . . what's so complicated?"

"But—doesn't anything bother you? You're floating around in a dream. You're surrounded by war machines; you're living every minute with danger. If a pump fails or a meteor hits . . ."

"You think it's any safer down there?"

"But life is complex, Chet. And love . . . well, there's more to it than just having fun."

"Sure there is. But it's meant to be enjoyed, too. What's wrong with taking an opportunity when you have it? What's so damned complicated or important? We're above the cares and worries of Earth. Maybe it's only for a few hours, but it's here and now, it's us. They can't touch us, they can't force us to do anything or stop us from doing what we want to. We're on our own. Understand? Completely on our own."

She nodded, her eyes still wide with the look of a frightened animal. But her hands slid around him, and together they drifted back toward the control desk. Wordlessly, Kinsman turned off all the overhead lights, so that all they saw was the glow of the control board and the flickering of the computer as it murmured to itself.

They were in their own world now, their private cosmos, floating freely and softly in the darkness. Touching, drifting, coupling, searching the new seas and continents, they explored their world.

Jill stayed in the hammock until Linda entered the bunkroom, quietly, to see if she had awakened yet. Kinsman sat at the control desk feeling . . . not tired, but strangely numb.

The rest of the flight was strictly routine. Jill and Kinsman did their jobs, spoke to each other when they had to. Linda took a brief nap, then returned to snap a few last pictures.

Finally, they crawled back into the spacecraft, disengaged from the laboratory, and started the long curving flight back to Earth.

Kinsman took a last look at the majestic beauty of the planet, serene and incompatible among the stars, before touching the button that slid the heat-shield over his viewport. Then they felt the surge of rocket thrust, dipped into the atmosphere, knew that air heated beyond endurance surrounded them in a fiery grip and made their tiny craft into a flaming, falling star. Pressed into his seat by the acceleration, Kinsman let the automatic controls bring them through reentry, through the heat and buffeting turbulence, down to an altitude where their finned craft could fly like a rocketplane.

He took control and steered the craft back toward Patrick Air Force Base, back to the world of men, of weather, of cities, of hierarchies and official regulations. He did this alone, silently; he didn't need Jill's help or anyone else's. He flew the craft from inside his buttoned-tight pressure suit, frowning at the panel displays through his helmet's faceplate.

Automatically, he checked with ground control and received permission to slide the heat-shield back. The viewport showed him a stretch of darkening clouds spreading from the sea across the beach and well inland. His earphones were alive with other men's voices now: wind conditions, altitude checks, speed estimates. He knew, but could not see, that two jet planes were trailing along behind him, cameras focused on the returning spacecraft. *To provide evidence if I crash.*

They dipped into the clouds and a wave of gray mist hurtled up and covered the viewport. Kinsman's eyes flicked to the radar screen slightly off to his right. The craft shuddered briefly, then they broke below the clouds and he could see the long, black gouge of the runway looming before him. He pulled back slightly on the controls, hands and feet working instinctively, flashed over some scrubby vegetation, and flared the craft onto the runway. The landing skids touched once, bounced them up momentarily, then touched again with a grinding shriek. They skidded for more than a mile before stopping.

He leaned back in the seat and felt his body oozing sweat.

"Good landing," Jill said.

"Thanks." He turned off all the craft's systems, hands moving automatically in response to long training. Then he slid his faceplate up, reached overhead and popped the hatch open.

"End of the line," he said tiredly. "Everybody out."

He clambered up through the hatch, feeling his own weight with a sullen resentment, then helped Linda and finally Jill out of the spacecraft. They hopped down onto the blacktop runway. Two vans, an ambulance and two fire trucks were rolling toward them from their parking stations at the end of the runway, a half-mile ahead.

Kinsman slowly took off his helmet. The Florida heat and humidity annoyed him now. Jill walked a few paces away from him, toward the approaching trucks.

He stepped toward Linda. Her helmet was off, and she was carrying a bag full of film.

"I've been thinking," he said to her. "That business about having a lonely life . . . You know, you're not the only one. And it doesn't have to be that way. I can get to New York whenever . . ."

"Now who's taking things seriously?" Her face looked calm again, cool, despite the glaring heat.

"But I mean—"

"Listen, Chet. We had our kicks. Now you can tell your friends about it, and I can tell mine. We'll both get a lot of mileage out of it. It'll help our careers."

"I never intended to . . . I didn't . . ."

But she was already turning away from him, walking toward the men who were running up to meet them from the trucks. One of them, a civilian, had a camera in his hands. He dropped to one knee and took a picture of Linda holding the film out and smiling broadly.

Kinsman stood there with his mouth open.

Jill came back to him. "Well? Did you get what you were after?"

"No," he said slowly. "I guess I didn't."

She started to put her hand out to him. "We never do, do we?"

LIVING AND LOVING IN ZERO GRAVITY

This is obviously a companion piece to *Zero Gee*, even though they were written more than fifteen years apart. When I left the world of magazine editing to become a full-time writer, I set myself the challenge of selling pieces to all the major magazines that might conceivably publish either fact or fiction about science, high technology and the future. I tried a few ideas with the articles editor of *Playboy* with no success. It was my agent, bless her, who shrewdly suggested that I ask if *Playboy* would be interested in a piece about the physiology of weightlessness. Of course, I didn't quite phrase my query to the magazine in exactly those terms. . . .

■

Nearly fifteen years ago I wrote a short story about a man and a woman making love in the weightlessness of an orbiting space station. It was science fiction then; it will be history long before another fifteen years have passed.

If you like waterbeds, you're going to love orbital space. The floating sensation of weightlessness has made every astronaut who's gone into space euphoric. Even those who suffered at first from disorientation and nausea quickly became acclimatized to zero gravity and enjoyed it tremendously. The American astronauts who spent months in Skylab back in 1973–74 learned to fly through their commodious space station, weightlessly gliding through a world that had neither "up" nor "down."

Sooner than most people realize, tourists are going to begin riding into orbit. NASA is already selecting ordinary citizens to ride on the space shuttle. Private entrepreneurs are getting into the business of launching rockets. Inevitably, today's Jet Set will become tomorrow's Rocket Set, heading into orbit for zero-gravity fun and games.

We take gravity quite for granted, the one "gee" force that we experience here on Earth. It shapes our bodies, our lives, even the way we think and play. We leave the comfortable floating dark world of the womb and start fighting gravity from the instant of birth. Our bones, our muscles, our blood circulation systems must all work against gravity every moment of our lives. Gravity pulls us down, bends our spines and gives us backaches, makes our faces and breasts sag, hurts us when we fall.

But in zero gravity the body undergoes some marvelous changes. You become wasp-waisted. Your legs thin down. Your face becomes somewhat puffier for the first few days. Skylab astronaut William Pogue thought his face had taken on an oriental cast, with higher cheekbones and narrower eyes than he had on Earth. All this happens because the body's internal fluids are no longer being pulled downward by gravity. Even the placement of the internal organs shifts a little in zero gee. After a few days of weightlessness, the facial puffiness goes away as the body begins to adjust its fluid production to meet the conditions of zero gee.

Dieting is easier in space. You tend to eat less because you are doing less physical work under zero-gee conditions, and the body demands less fuel.

And you tend to grow a couple of inches taller when in orbit because the spine unbends and lengthens. All our lives our spines have been pressed into an ess-shape by the downward-pulling force of gravity. In zero gee, the spine unbends and you gain an inch or two in height. Unfortunately for all the unhappy short people of the world, that added height is taken away once you return to Earth and its one-gee environment. If you want to stay two inches taller, you must stay in orbit.

In 1961, when Yuri Gagarin became the first man to fly in orbit, medical doctors feared that the human mind and body could not stand up to the conditions of space flight: the enormous stresses of a high-gee "blastoff," then zero gravity and all its attendant physical and psychological changes, and finally the strain of returning to Earth and a one-gee environment again. In particular, the medics worried about three major problems of space flight.

First, zero gravity affects the delicate balancing mechanisms in the inner ear. Ever since the first lungfish crawled out of the sea, land-dwelling creatures have developed internal systems for telling them which end is up. For two-legged critters such as we are, who move around the surface of our world by teetering our weight on one foot while we swing the other forward, the balancing devices built into our inner ears are crucially important. When they go awry, we fall on our faces; we can't walk straight and in some cases we can't even stand up at all.

The inner ear's mechanisms are very sensitive to gravity; it's their job to be. It is their message to the brain that gives us that sick-in-the-stomach feeling we have when we are falling.

In orbit, we are "falling" all the time. Weightlessness has often been called "free fall" by scientists and astronauts. In effect, a satellite is falling as it hurtles around the Earth, but its forward speed is so huge—18,000 miles per hour for a low orbit—that the curve of its fall is wider than the size of the Earth. So the satellite, and everyone in it, continues to fall endlessly as long as it is in orbit.

The inner ear's balancing system does not like this. It is

built to warn you when you are falling, to get your attention by making you feel queasy and panicky. NASA medics knew that this would happen when astronauts went into orbit. They trained the astronauts aboard planes that flew special maneuvers which produced a few precious seconds of zero-gee conditions. Such training flights are still called "whoopee missions." Still, most of the astronauts (and cosmonauts) who have gone into orbit have felt queasy, sensitive, and even downright sick for the first few hours or days of their missions.

"Space sickness" is somewhat like sea sickness. You get over it after a while. Training and knowledge of what to expect can help. So can medication, such as Dramamine. Space tourists won't get the kind of intensive training that the astronauts receive, but they will have a full panoply of pharmaceutical products, from improved anti-vertigo drugs to tranquilizers, to help them ward off the physical and psychological impact of "space sickness."

The two other problems that worried space medics were the loss of muscle tone and the loss of bone calcium that come from long exposure to weightlessness. After twenty-two years of space flight, we know that these fears were not groundless, but they were exaggerated. The experiences of our Skylab astronauts and the many Russian cosmonauts show that living in space for months at a time has positive medical benefits.

The Russians are far ahead of us in long-term experience with weightlessness; they have had cosmonauts aboard their Salyut space stations for more than six months at a time. Their current record is 237 days in orbit, and they will probably shatter their own record before very long.

What the medics have learned from these man-years of orbital experience is that the human body adapts to the disappearance of gravity quite nicely. Muscle tone can deteriorate, but exercise can make up for that. The Skylab astronauts had an exercycle in their space station and often pedaled around the world in 80-some minutes. Such exercise keeps up the muscle tone not only of the legs, but of the heart as well, which is equally important. In zero gee, the heart's workload is reduced because the blood it is pumping through the circulatory system is weightless. So it is important to maintain the heart muscle's tone—in anticipation of returning to Earth and its one-gravity environment.

Calcium loss caused more worry among the medics than anything else. The longer an astronaut remained in orbit, it appeared, the less calcium the body produced. This could make the bones so weak that the astronauts could not stand up on Earth once they returned. But the Russians, thanks to their longer-term missions, learned that calcium production levels off after about four months of weightlessness. And the calcium production in the body never gets low enough to cause a serious medical problem. What is happening is *adaptation:* the wonderfully plastic nature of our bodies allows us to adapt to the zero-gravity environment. The bones are not experiencing the kinds of stresses they feel on Earth, so they do not need to be as rigid. Therefore, calcium levels are automatically decreased by the body's internal feedback controls. Once one returns to Earth, calcium levels go back to normal within a few days.

The body adapts to zero gravity. Even the queasiness of "space sickness" disappears after a while. The problems that worried the medics years ago were mainly problems of how the astronauts would fare when they returned to Earth. As long as a person stays in orbit, his or her body will adapt to weightlessness automatically. Almost all our internal bodily functions operate independently of gravity—a heritage of those primeval ages when our ancient ancestors lived in the sea, floating in a sort of zero-gee world underwater.

In orbit, we return to a weightless existence. As our

Skylab and shuttle astronauts have shown, living in zero gee can be fun. You can float effortlessly from one end of the cabin to another, maneuvering with nothing more than fingertip touches against the bulkheads. There are no backaches in zero gee. No post-nasal drips.

Of course, adjusting to life on Earth again after a month or more in orbit presented the Skylab astronauts with a few mental problems, as well as physical ones. Most of them complained of feeling dull, heavy and uncomfortable for days or even weeks after coming back from zero gee. They also had to keep reminding themselves that if they released an object from their hands it would crash to the floor instead of floating obediently in midair, waiting to be picked up again.

Although the first astronauts and cosmonauts were highly-trained jet jockeys from the ranks of military fliers and test pilots, already the space shuttle is carrying nonpilot "payload specialists" into orbit, and scientists who work in the spacelab that the shuttle carries into orbit. NASA is developing plans to build a permanent station in orbit, which the space agency unromantically calls the Space Operations Center (SOC).

The entrepreneurs who today are launching rockets for profit will someday build space stations of their own in orbit, space habitats where ordinary people can live and work for months or even years at a time. Space habitats where tourists can go for zero-gee vacations.

Imagine your very own two-week vacation in orbit. It could happen before the end of this century. The *Love Boat* of 1999 might have wings on it.

At today's prices it would cost more than $100,000 to fly into orbit aboard the space shuttle. But just as engineering improvements made commercial air travel feasible in the 1930s, improvements in shuttle-type craft can bring down the ticket price of a ride into orbit to something like the price of a round-the-world cruise aboard a luxury liner, by the late 1990s. Expensive, yes; but not impossible, especially for the vacation of a lifetime.

The space shuttle of the 1990s will not take off like a rocket. It will look like two airplanes, one riding piggyback on the other, rather like today's shuttle orbiter riding atop its Boeing 747 carrier when it returns to Cape Canaveral after having landed at Edwards AFB in California.

Today's shuttle subjects its crew to three or four gees during the few minutes' liftoff. The all-reusable piggyback shuttle of the 1990s will take off like a commercial airliner. The passengers will sit back and sip their champagne as the orbiter separates from the lifter beneath it, up about 100,000 feet, and accelerates smoothly toward the space station, some two hundreds miles higher.

Once the orbiter's rocket engines shut down, the passengers get their first feel of zero-gee. Under the watchful eyes of the stewards and stewardesses, you can unfasten your safety belt and float out of your seat. You feel as if you are falling, but several weeks of group sessions with the spaceline's psychologist (all part of your fare) have at least prepared you mentally for the stomach-in-your-throat sensation.

Thanks to the experience of the Skylab astronauts, the interior of the space liner's cabin is decorated with strong designs of bright colors, which give you a clear sense of up and down. Even though your inner ear is sending out distress signals, your eyes tell you that the floor is beneath you, the ceiling is overhead, and you are perfectly safe. Still, when the stewardess floats by and offers you an anti-vertigo pill, you take it and slosh it down with champagne.

The cabin attendants are wearing one-piece coverall uniforms of powder blue. The stewardesses are required to wear "comfort bras" of the type designed for NASA's women astronauts. The spaceline company wants no excessive jiggling during the flight. Most of the passengers are wearing equally utilitarian coverall outfits, on the advice of the company, although the clothing locked away in the passengers' luggage is bound to be quite a bit different.

Perhaps it is a coincidence, but the passengers on this flight are divided exactly equally: ten men and ten women. Most of them are your own age, give or take a year. Does the company match tourists by age and sex? Certainly.

By the time the orbiter docks at the space station, all the passengers are feeling fine, although a couple of them have bumped their heads against the softly-padded ceiling of the cabin. It's fun to tow your luggage and float through the cabin's airlock into the reception area of the orbital hotel. Here too, the interior design stresses visual cues that identify which way is up. The hotel lobby looks rather ordinary and Earthlike, with a carpeted floor and a registration desk staffed by smiling young men and women who have their shoes firmly locked into the metal gridwork behind the desk, so that they don't go floating disconcertingly off toward the ceiling.

Other areas of the hotel take full advantage of zero gravity, and have furniture built into the walls and ceiling as well as the floor. What difference does it make, as long as you are weightless?

The bellhop could be a robot, but the hotel management is careful to use human beings—psychology students, mostly—who can spot the symptoms of physical or psychological distress as they guide the tourist through the circular tubes that are the corridors of this hotel. The bellhop chatters pleasantly about "the little things" that make a big difference in weightlessness. You have to be careful about shaving, eating and housecleaning in orbit because whiskers, crumbs and litter do not drop to the floor; they float in the air currents and sooner or later end up sticking to the filter screens over the air vents.

The bellhop tells the story of the Skylab astronauts, who found that small drops of liquid and crumbs from their meals would float around the interior of their space station until they stuck on the wall or the open-grid ceiling just above their dining table. The ceiling became quite dirty, because even though the astronauts could see it, they could not get their hands into the area to clean it. Near the end of the mission it looked like the bottom of a birdcage, and the astronauts took pains not to look at it—especially while they were eating.

Every astronaut who has been in orbit has experienced the heady euphoria that comes with weightlessness. It is as if the body suddenly realizes it is free of a burden it had taken totally for granted, and every nerve begins to tingle with the excitement of this new freedom. Once you realize that you are not going to become nauseated, that weightlessness actually feels wonderful, this excitement begins to grip you. It is a new experience, unlike anything on Earth.

The orbital hotel offers a modest variety of activities for its guests. There are observation bubbles on the outer shell of the hotel, where you can use a small telescope to observe the construction crews at work on other satellites, thousands of miles away, or inspect the surface of the Moon, or gaze out at the stars which stare steadily back at you, without the twinkling effect caused by the Earth's turbulent layers of air.

There is zero-gravity volleyball, with a net that looks like a circular trampoline floating in the middle of a big, heavily-padded gymnasium. There is zero-gee ping-pong, with no net at all, and no table, either. The object is to keep the ball from hitting a wall surface. You quickly get out of the habit of saying "ceiling" or "floor." All six surfaces of any cube-shaped enclosure are called "walls."

Of course, many of the hotel's rooms are not cube-shaped at all. Your bedroom is built like the interior of a padded egg, with no furniture in sight. There is no need for a bed; a simple zip-up webbed bag will hold you in if you're afraid of drifting around the room in your sleep. The closets are built into the walls behind the padding.

Everyone's favorite activity is Earth-watching, and you have chosen to do it from outside the metal shell of the hotel. Along with half a dozen other members of your flight, you are going EVA. Three hotel staffers help you to wriggle into your space suits, which come in small, medium, and large sizes and in garish day-glo colors. You strike up a conversation with your fellow tourists, especially the pretty redhead next to you. But once the hotel staffers lower the space helmets over your heads and seal them to the suits' collars, all you can see of each other is a bulbous helmet with a mirrored visor, riding atop a bulky, cumbersome suit that would weigh at least ninety pounds on Earth. Here, of course, it weighs exactly as much as you do—nothing.

Suit radios, oxygen, heaters, air-circulation fans—and all the joints and seals of the awkward suits—are minutely checked by the hotel people. Then at last they walk you into the big airlock, attach your safety cords and open the outer hatch.

It's like jumping off the highest diving board you can imagine, or stepping out of an airplane. You put out one booted foot and then the other, and you're walking on nothing. Space-walking. You can hear your heart pounding in your ears, but in an instant you forget all about it.

Because you see the Earth. An immense, beautiful, gleaming curve of deepest, richest blue, the jewel of creation, wrapped in dazzling clouds of pure white. The oceans are shot through with colors ranging from aqua and absolute green to surprising browns and reds formed by algal growths that trace out long swirling patterns of ocean currents for hundreds of miles. The land is brown, mostly, wrinkled where mountain chains fold. They look pitifully small from up here. You can see snow on some of the peaks. Your guides tell you where to look, and you see that Dakota's Black Hills really are black.

The panorama of Earth glides before your eyes, land and sea and clouds, and it is so lovely, so endlessly fascinating, that you are shocked when the guides tell you that two hours have gone by and it's time to get back inside.

All of you are surprised, as you struggle out of the space suits, to find that you are thoroughly soaked with perspiration. The space suits that protected you from freezing or broiling in the vacuum outside have also prevented your body's normal moisture from evaporating off your skin. The sweat will not drip off you, of course; it puddles up on your skin like beads of water on a newly-waxed automobile.

You "swim" your way back toward your rooms for a quick shower before dinner. As you glide along the tube-like corridors you make a date for dinner with the redhead. She's from Minnesota, and the farthest above the ground she's been before this has been at the top of the IDS Tower in downtown Minneapolis.

Bathing in zero gee is different from the way it is done on Earth. When you wet a washcloth the water sticks to the fabric like a puddle of jelly. Touch the washcloth to your body and the water sticks to your skin. Spread it around carefully until you are completely wet, then lather in the soap. Don't worry about dripping water; it will not fall, even if you shake it loose from your body. You use a vacuum cleaner attachment to get the soapy water off your skin, then reverse it into a hot air blower to dry yourself.

Fashions in zero gee are quickly evolving away from the strictly utilitarian, such as the coveralls everyone wore on the shuttle. After all, if you've spent enough money to get to this orbital hotel, you're not going to be satisfied with a unisex jumpsuit. Men seem to be going in for uniforms with long vertical design elements that emphasize their new-found height and zero-gee induced slimness. Women prefer wispy, billowing fashions, although most of them want to show off their new wasp-waisted hourglass figures and longer-looking legs. Freed from the need for bras and other gravitationally-required restraints, both women's and men's zero-gee styles are more exotic than anything possible on Earth—where there is always the danger of something falling off.

Hair fashions are also different, for both sexes, because long hair has the tendency to float out wildly from its roots. Zero-gee Afros were popular at first, but short hair styles now are the mark of men and women who have been to space. Of course, snug hair coverings can be made very decorative, too, and there are plenty of those visible as you enter the dining room with your date.

Ever-mindful of their guests' comfort, the hotel has kept its dining room as Earthlike as possible, with a definite floor and no furniture on any other surface. The waiters glide along effortlessly, though, and no one ever drops a tray of food in zero gee. The chairs all have seatbelts, so that you don't inadvertently drift away in the middle of the meal. Burping and other sudden expulsions of gas are not only impolite in zero gee, they can start you moving if you're not strapped down.

Soft candlelight is unlikely, because a candle flame will quickly extinguish itself in zero gravity. Under weightless conditions, the hot carbon dioxide given off by the flame remains right there around the flame itself; hot air is not lighter than cold air in zero gee, and the candle soon dies in its own pollution. But the tables are lit by flickering electric candles, and the mood of the dining room is quite nicely romantic.

Dinner features orbital delicacies such as frog's legs and roasted rabbit: animals that offer a high percentage of meat to bone, and don't need large amounts of feed to fatten them. Hydroponic vegetables, grown in the hotel's own zero-gee garden, are a mainstay of the menu. The *pièce de resistance* is the hotel's special dessert: Sundae *àla* Sky-lab. One of the Skylab astronauts mistakenly put a serving of ice cream into the food warmer; it melted, of course. But being weightless, it melted into a large, sublimely thin, hollow ball. He carefully refroze the ball, then filled it with strawberries: the first ice cream sundae in orbit.

After dinner and an exhilarating round of zero-gee disco, you bring your date back to your room, that intimate dimly-lit ovoid chamber where the wall surfaces are warmly padded so that you can float effortlessly. Sex in zero gee is mind-boggling. Floating weightlessly in your own cozy, private universe, where every slightest touch produces a gentle movement, is the ultimate in sensuousness.

Like almost all other inner functions, the human body is perfectly well adapted to accommodate weightless sex. If anything, the absence of gravity should give a boost to a man's ability to have and maintain an erection, since the blood that engorges the penis's tissue is weightless and can be pumped that much more easily by the heart.

Free of the need to support yourself on a surface of any kind, sexual play can involve the entire body, both arms and legs simultaneously. No cramped limbs from having to support your weight or your partner's. The actual physical act of penetration is more interesting than ever, because you are both floating freely and every movement tends to keep on moving, just as Isaac Newton said it would. In astronautical terms, this becomes a "rendezvous and docking problem." But if astronauts can link multi-ton spacecraft in orbit, a man and a woman should be able to bring themselves together pleasurably. And it's so much fun trying.

Afterward the two of you zip yourselves into the light mesh sleeping bag so that you won't drift around in your sleep and wake yourselves by bumping into a padded wall. You find yourself thinking that living in space all the time might be the kind of lifestyle you would really like. No need for bras or chiropractors up here, and the weightless conditions should be wonderful for the elderly and the infirm—as well as lovers.

Orbital vacations will soon enough replace Niagara Falls, Miami Beach, and even Paris in the springtime. But Apollo 11 astronaut Mike Collins had an even grander vision as he circled the Moon alone while Neil Armstrong and Buzz Aldrin were putting the first footprints on the Moon. Collins imagined:

". . . a spacecraft of the future, with a crew of a thousand ladies, off for Alpha Centauri, with two thousand breasts bobbing beautifully and quivering delightfully in response to their every weightless movement . . . and I am the commander of the craft, and it is Saturday morning and time for inspection . . ."

On to Alpha Centauri!

A SMALL KINDNESS

To this day, I'm not quite certain of how this story originated. I've been to Athens, and found it a big, noisy, dirty city fouled with terrible automobile pollution—and centered on the awe-inspiring Acropolis. The world's most beautiful building, the Parthenon, is truly a symbol of what is best and what is worst in us. Of its beauty, its grace, its simple grandeur I can add nothing to the paeans that have been sung by so many others. But over the millennia, the dark forces of human nature have almost destroyed the Parthenon. It has been blasted by cannon fire, defaced by conquerors and tourists, and now is being eaten away by the acidic outpourings of automobile exhausts.

A Luddite would say, with justice, that this is a case where human technology is obviously working against the human spirit. A Promethean would say that since we recognize the problem, we ought to take steps to solve it. In a way, that's what *A Small Kindness* is about—I think.

■

Jeremy Keating hated the rain. Athens was a dismal enough assignment, but in the windswept rainy night it was cold and black and dangerous.

Everyone pictures Athens in the sunshine, he thought. The Acropolis, the gleaming ancient temples. They don't see the filthy modern city with its endless streams of automobiles spewing out so much pollution that the marble statues are being eaten away and the ancient monuments are in danger of crumbling.

Huddled inside his trench coat, Keating stood in the shadows of a deep doorway across the street from the taverna where his target was eating a relaxed and leisurely dinner—his last, if things went the way Keating planned.

He stood as far back in the doorway as he could, pressed against the cold stones of the building, both to remain unseen in the shadows and to keep the cold rain off himself. Rain or no, the automobile traffic still clogged Filellinon Boulevard, cars inching by bumper to bumper, honking their horns, squealing on the slickened paving. The worst traffic in the world, night and day. A million and a half Greeks, all in cars, all the time. They drove the way they lived—argumentatively.

The man dining across the boulevard in the warm, brightly-lit taverna was Kabete Rungawa, of the Tanzanian delegation to the World Government conference. "The Black Saint of the Third World," he was called. The most revered man since Gandhi. Keating smiled grimly to himself. According to his acquaintances in the Vatican, a man had to be dead before he could be proclaimed a saint.

Keating was a tall man, an inch over six feet. He had the lean, graceful body of a trained athlete, and it had taken him years of constant, painful work to acquire it. The earlier part of his adult life he had spent behind a desk or at embassy parties, like so many other Foreign Service career officers. But that had been a lifetime ago, when he was a minor cog in the Department of State's global machine. When he was a husband and father.

His wife had been killed in the rioting in Tunis, part of the carefully-orchestrated Third World upheaval that had forced the new World Government down the throats of the white, industrialized nations. His son had died of typhus in the besieged embassy, when they were unable to get medical supplies because the U.S. government could not decide whether it should negotiate with the radicals or send in the Marines.

In the end, they negotiated. But by then it was too late. So now Keating served as a roving attaché to U.S. embassies or consulates, serving where his special talents were needed. He had found those talents in the depths of his agony, his despair, his hatred.

Outwardly he was still a minor diplomatic functionary, an interesting dinner companion, a quietly handsome man with brooding eyes who seemed both unattached and unavailable. That made him a magnetic lure for a certain type of woman, a challenge they could not resist. A few of them had gotten close enough to him to trace the hairline scar across his abdomen, all that remained of the surgery he had needed after his first assignment, in Indonesia. After that particular horror, he had never been surprised or injured again.

With an adamant shake of his head, Keating forced himself to concentrate on the job at hand. The damp cold was seeping into him. His feet were already soaked. The cars still crawled along the rainy boulevard, honking impatiently. The noise was making him irritable, jumpy.

"Terminate with extreme prejudice," his boss had told him, that sunny afternoon in Virginia. "Do you understand what that means?"

Sitting in the deep leather chair in front of the section chief's broad walnut desk, Keating nodded. "I may be new to this part of the department, but I've been around. It means to do to Rungawa what the Indonesians tried to do to me."

No one ever used the words *kill* or *assassinate* in these cheerfully lit offices. The men behind the desks, in their pinstripe suits, dealt with computer printouts and satellite photographs and euphemisms. Messy, frightening things like blood were never mentioned here.

The section chief steepled his fingers and gave Keating a long, thoughtful stare. He was a distinguished-looking man with silver hair and smoothly tanned skin. He might be the board chairman you meet at the country club, or the type of well-bred gentry who spends the summer racing yachts.

"Any questions, Jeremy?"

Keating shifted slightly in his chair. "Why Rungawa?"

The section chief made a little smile. "Do you like having the World Government order us around, demand that we disband our armed forces, tax us until we're as poor as the Third World?"

Keating felt emotions burst into flame inside his guts. All the pain of his wife's death, of his son's lingering agony, of his hatred for the gloating, ignorant, sadistic, petty tyrants who had killed them—all erupted in a volcanic tide of lava within him. But he clamped down on his bodily responses, used every ounce of training and willpower at his command to force his voice to remain calm. One thing he had learned about this organization, and about this section chief in particular: never let anyone know where you are vulnerable.

"I've got no great admiration for the World Government," he said.

The section chiefs basilisk smile vanished. There was no need to appear friendly to this man. He was an employee, a tool. Despite his attempt to hide his emotions, it was obvious that all Keating lived for was to avenge his wife and child. It would get him killed, eventually, but for now his thirst for vengeance was a valuable handle for manipulating the man.

"Rungawa is the key to everything," the section chief said, leaning back in his tall swivel chair and rocking slightly.

Keating knew that the World Government, still less than five years old, was meeting in Athens to plan a global economic program. Rungawa would head the Tanzanian delegation.

"The World Government is taking special pains to destroy the United States," the section chief said, as calmly as he might announce a tennis score. "Washington was forced to accept the World Government, and the people went along with the idea because they thought it would put an end to the threat of nuclear war. Well, it's done that—at the cost of taxing our economy for every unemployed black, brown, and yellow man, woman, and child in the entire world."

"And Rungawa?" Keating repeated.

The section chief leaned forward, pressed his palms on his desktop and lowered his voice. "We can't back out of the World Government, for any number of reasons. But we can—with the aid of certain other Western nations—we can take control of it, if we're able to break up the solid voting bloc of the Third World nations."

"Would the Soviets—"

"We can make an accommodation with the Soviets," the section chief said impatiently, waving one hand in the air. "Nobody wants to go back to the old cold-war confrontations. It's the Third World that's got to be brought to terms."

"By eliminating Rungawa."

"Exactly! He's the glue that holds their bloc together. 'The Black Saint.' They practically worship him. Eliminate him and they'll fall back into their old tangle of bickering, selfish politicians, just as OPEC broke up once the oil glut started."

It had all seemed so simple back there in that comfortable sunny office. Terminate Rungawa and then set about taking the leadership of the World Government. Fix up the damage done by the Third World's jealous greed. Get the world's economy back on the right track again.

But here in the rainy black night of Athens, Keating knew it was not that simple at all. His left hand gripped the dart gun in his trench coat pocket. There was enough poison in each dart to kill a man instantly and leave no trace for a coroner to find. The darts themselves dissolved on contact with the air within three minutes. The perfect murder weapon.

Squinting through the rain, Keating saw through the taverna's big plate-glass window that Rungawa was getting up from his table, preparing to leave the restaurant.

Terminate Rungawa. That was his mission: Kill him and make it look as if he'd had a heart attack. It should be easy enough. One old man, walking alone down the boulevard to his hotel. "The Black Saint" never used bodyguards. He was old enough for a heart attack to be beyond suspicion.

But it was not going to be that easy, Keating saw. Rungawa came out of the taverna accompanied by three younger men. And he did not turn toward his hotel. Instead, he started walking down the boulevard in the opposite direction, toward the narrow tangled streets of the most ancient part of the city, walking toward the Acropolis. In the rain. Walking.

Frowning with puzzled aggravation, Keating stepped out of the doorway and into the pelting rain. It was icy cold. He pulled up his collar and tugged his hat down lower. He hated the rain. Maybe the old bastard will catch pneumonia and die naturally, he thought angrily.

As he started across the boulevard a car splashed by, horn bleating, soaking his trousers. Keating jumped back just in time to avoid being hit. The driver's furious face, framed by the rain-streaked car window, glared at him as the auto swept past. Swearing methodically under his breath, Keating found another break in the traffic and sprinted across the boulevard, trying to avoid the puddles even though his feet were already wet through.

He stayed well behind Rungawa and his three companions, glad that they were walking instead of driving, miserable to be out in the chilling rain. As far as he could tell, all three of Rungawa's companions were black, young enough and big enough to be bodyguards. That complicated matters. Had someone warned Rungawa? Was there a leak in the department's operation?

With Keating trailing behind, the old man threaded the ancient winding streets that huddled around the jutting rock of the Acropolis. The four blacks walked around the ancient citadel, striding purposefully, as if they had to be at an exact place at a precise time. Keating had to stay well behind them because the traffic along Theonas Avenue was much thinner, and pedestrians, in this rain, were nowhere in sight except for his quarry. It was quieter here, along the shoulder of the great cliff. The usual nightly *son et lumière* show had been cancelled because of the rain; even the floodlights around the Parthenon and the other temples had been turned off.

For a few minutes Keating wondered if Rungawa was going to the Agora instead, but no, the old man and his friends turned in at the gate to the Acropolis, the Sacred Way of the ancient Athenians.

It was difficult to see through the rain, especially at this distance. Crouching low behind shrubbery, Keating fumbled in his trench coat pocket until he found the miniature "camera" he had brought with him. Among other things, it was an infrared snooperscope. Even in the darkness and rain, he could see the four men as they stopped at the main gate. Their figures looked ghostly gray and eerie against a flickering dark background.

They stopped for a few moments while one of them opened the gate that was usually locked and guarded.

Keating was more impressed than surprised. They had access to everything they wanted. But why do they want to go up to the Parthenon on a rainy wintry night? And how can I make Rungawa's death look natural if I have to fight my way past three bodyguards?

The second question resolved itself almost as soon as Keating asked it. Rungawa left his companions at the gate and started up the steep, rain-slickened marble stairs by himself.

"A man that age, in this weather, could have a heart attack just from climbing those stairs," Keating whispered to himself. But he knew that he could not rely on chance.

He had never liked climbing. Although he felt completely safe and comfortable in a jet plane and had even made parachute jumps calmly, climbing up the slippery rock face of the cliff was something that Keating dreaded. But he did it, nevertheless. It was not as difficult as he had feared. Others had scaled the Acropolis, over the thirty-some centuries since the Greeks had first arrived at it. Keating clambered and scrambled over the rocks, crawling at first on all fours while the cold rain spattered in his face. Then he found a narrow trail. It was steep and slippery, but his soft-soled shoes, required for stealth, gripped the rock well enough.

He reached the top of the flat-surfaced cliff in a broad open area. To his right was the Propylaea and the little temple of Athene Nike. To his left, the Erechtheum, with its Caryatids patiently holding up the roof as they had for twenty-five hundred years. The marble maidens stared blindly at Keating. He glanced at them, then looked across the width of the clifftop to the half-ruined Parthenon, the most beautiful building on Earth, a monument both to man's creative genius and his destructive folly.

The rain had slackened, but the night was still as dark as the deepest pit of hell. Keating brought the snooperscope up to his eyes again and scanned from left to right.

And there stood Rungawa! Directly in front of the Parthenon, standing there with his arms upraised, as if praying.

Too far away for the dart gun, Keating knew. For some reason, his hands started to shake. Slowly, struggling for absolute self-control, Keating put the "camera" back into his trench coat and took out the pistol. He rose to his feet and began walking toward Rungawa with swift but unhurried, measured strides.

The old man's back was to him. All you have to do, Keating told himself, is to get within a few feet, pop the dart into his neck, and then wait a couple of minutes to make certain the dart dissolves. Then go down the way you came and back to the *pensione* for a hot bath and a bracer of cognac.

As he came to within ten feet of Rungawa he raised the dart gun. It worked on air pressure, practically noiseless. No need to cock it. Five feet. He could see the nails on Rungawa's upraised hands, the pinkish palms contrasting with the black skin of the fingers and the backs of his hands. Three feet. Rungawa's suit was perfectly fitted to him, the sleeves creased carefully. Dry. He was wearing only a business suit, and it was untouched by the rain, as well-creased and unwrinkled as if it had just come out of the store.

"Not yet, Mr. Keating," said the old man, without turning to look at Jeremy. "We have a few things to talk about before you kill me."

Keating froze. He could not move his arm. It stood ramrod straight from his left shoulder, the tiny dart gun in his fist a mere two feet from Rungawa's bare neck. But he could not pull the trigger. His fingers would not obey the commands of his mind.

Rungawa turned toward him, smiling, and stroked his chin thoughtfully for a moment.

"You may put the gun down now, Mr. Keating."

Jeremy's arm dropped to his side. His mouth sagged open; his heart thundered in his ears. He wanted to run away, but his legs were like the marble of the statues that watched them.

"Forgive me," said Rungawa. "I should not leave you out in the rain like that."

The rain stopped pelting Jeremy. He felt a gentle warmth enveloping him, as if he were standing next to a welcoming fireplace. The two men stood under a cone of invisible protection. Jeremy could see the raindrops spattering on the stony ground not more than a foot away.

"A small trick. Please don't be alarmed." Rungawa's voice was a deep rumbling bass, like the voice a lion would have if it could speak in human tongue.

Jeremy stared into the black man's eyes and saw no danger in them, no hatred or violence; only a patient amusement at his own consternation. No, more: a tolerance of human failings, a hope for human achievement, an *understanding* born of centuries of toil and pain and striving.

"Who are you?" Jeremy asked in a frightened whisper.

Rungawa smiled, and it was like sunlight breaking through the storm clouds. "Ah, Mr. Keating, you are as intelligent as we had hoped. You cut straight to the heart of the matter."

"You knew I was following you. You set up this . . . meeting."

"Yes. Yes, quite true. Melodramatic of me, I admit. But would you have joined me at dinner if I had sent one of my aides across the street to invite you? I think not."

It's all crazy, Jeremy thought. I must be dreaming this.

"No, Mr. Keating. It is not a dream."

An electric jolt flamed through Jeremy. Jesus Chirst, he can read my mind!

"Of course I can," Rungawa said gently, smiling, the way a doctor tells a child that the needle will hurt only for an instant. "How else would I know that you were stalking me?"

Jeremy's mouth went utterly dry. His voice cracked and

failed him. If he had been able to move his legs he would have fled like a chimpanzee confronted by a leopard.

"Please do not be afraid, Mr. Keating. Fear is an impediment to understanding. If we had wanted to kill you, it would have been most convenient to let you slip while you were climbing up here."

"What . . ." Jeremy had to swallow and lick his lips before he could say, "Just who are you?"

"I am a messenger, Mr. Keating. Like you, I am merely a tool of my superiors. When I was assigned to this task, I thought it appropriate to make my home base in Tanzania." The old man's smile returned, and a hint of self-satisfaction glowed in his eyes. "After all, Tanzania is where the earliest human tribes once lived. What more appropriate place for me to—um, shall we say, *associate* myself with the human race?"

"Associate . . . with the human race." Jeremy felt breathless, weak. His voice was hollow.

"I am not a human being, Mr. Keating. I come from a far-distant world, a world that is nothing like this one."

"No . . . that can't . . ."

Rungawa's smile slowly faded. "Some of your people call me a saint. Actually, compared to your species, I am a god."

Jeremy stared at him, stared into his deep black eyes, and saw eternity in them, whirlpools of galaxies spinning majestically in infinite depths of space, stars exploding and evolving, worlds created out of dust.

He heard his voice, weak and childlike, say, "But you look human."

"Of course! Completely human. Even to your x-ray machines."

An alien. Jeremy's mind reeled. An extraterrestrial. With a sense of humor.

"Why not? Is not humor part of the human psyche? The intelligences who created me made me much more than human, but I have every human attribute—except one. I have no need for vengeance, Mr. Keating."

"Vengeance," Jeremy echoed.

"Yes. A destructive trait. It clouds the perceptions. It is an obstacle in the path of survival."

Jeremy took a deep breath, tried to pull himself together. "You expect me to believe all this?"

"I can see that you do, Mr. Keating. I can see that you now realize that not *all* the UFO stories have been hoaxes. We have never harmed any of your people, but we did require specimens for careful analysis."

"Why?"

"To help you find the correct path to survival. Your species is on the edge of a precipice. It is our duty to help you avoid extinction, if we can."

"Your duty?"

"Of course. Do not your best people feel an obligation to save other species from extinction? Have not these human beings risked their fortunes and their very lives to protect creatures such as the whale and the seal from slaughter?"

Jeremy almost laughed. "You mean you're from some interstellar Greenpeace project?"

"It is much more complex than that," Rungawa said. "We are not merely trying to protect you from a predator, or from an ecological danger. You human beings are your own worst enemy. We must protect you from yourselves—without your knowing it."

Before Jeremy could reply, Rungawa went on, "It would be easy for us to create a million creatures like myself and to land on your planet in great, shining ships and give you all the answers you need for survival. Fusion energy? A toy. World peace? Easily accomplished. Quadruple your global food production? Double your intelligence? Make you immune to every disease? All this we can do."

"Then why . . ." Jeremy hesitated, thinking. "If you did all that for us, it would ruin us, wouldn't it?"

Rungawa beamed at him. "Ah, you truly understand the problem! Yes, it would destroy your species, just as your Europeans destroyed the cultures of the Americas and Polynesia. Your anthropologists are wrong. There are superior cultures and inferior ones. A superior culture always crushes an inferior, even if it has no intention of doing so."

In the back of his mind, Jeremy realized that he had control of his legs again. He flexed the fingers of his left hand slightly, even the index finger that still curled around the trigger of the dart gun. He could move them at will once more.

"What you're saying," he made conversation, "is that if you landed here and gave us everything we want, our culture would be destroyed."

"Yes," Rungawa agreed. "Just as surely as you whites destroyed the black and brown cultures of the world. We have no desire to do that to you."

"So you're trying to lead us to the point where we can solve our own problems."

"Precisely so, Mr. Keating."

"That's why you've started this World Government," Keating said, his hand tightening on the gun.

"You started the World Government yourselves," Rungawa corrected. "We merely encouraged you, here and there."

"Like the riots in Tunis and a hundred other places."

"We did not encourage that."

"But you didn't prevent them, either, did you?"

"No. We did not."

Shifting his weight slightly to the balls of his feet, Keating said, "Without you the World Government will collapse."

The old man shook his head. "No, that is not true. Despite

what your superiors believe, the World Government will endure even the death of 'the Black Saint.'"

"Are you sure?" Keating raised the gun to the black man's eye level. "Are you absolutely certain?"

Rungawa did not blink. His voice became sad as he answered, "Would I have relaxed my control of your limbs if I were not certain?"

Keating hesitated, but held the gun rock-steady.

"You are the test, Mr. Keating. You are the key to your species' future. We know how your wife and son died. Even though we were not directly responsible, we regret their deaths. And the deaths of all the others. They were unavoidable losses."

"Statistics," Keating spat. "Numbers on a list."

"Never! Each of them was an individual whom *we* knew much better than you could, and we regretted each loss of life as much as you do yourself. Perhaps more, because we understand what each of those individuals could have accomplished, had they lived."

"But you let them die."

"It was unavoidable, I say. Now the question is, Can you rise above your own personal tragedy for the good of your fellow humans? Or will you take vengeance upon me and see your species destroy itself?"

"You just said the World Government will survive your death."

"And it will. But it will change. It will become a world dictatorship, in time. It will smother your progress. Your species will die out in an agony of overpopulation, starvation, disease and terrorism. You do not need nuclear bombs to kill yourselves. You can manage it quite well enough merely by producing too many babies."

"Our alternative is to let your people direct us, to become sheep without even knowing it, to jump to your tune."

"No!" Rungawa's deep voice boomed. "The alternative

is to become adults. You are adolescents now. We offer you the chance to grow up and stand on your own feet."

"How can I believe that?" Keating demanded.

The old man's smile showed weariness. "The adolescent always distrusts the parent. That is the painful truth, is it not?"

"You have an answer for everything, don't you?"

"Everything, perhaps, except you. You are the key to your species' future, Mr. Keating. If you can accept what I have told you, and allow us to work with you despite all your inner thirst for vengeance, then the human species will have a chance to survive."

Keating moved his hand a bare centimeter to the left and squeezed the gun's trigger. The dart shot out with a hardly audible puff of compressed air and whizzed past Rungawa's ear. The old man did not flinch.

"You can kill me if you want to," he said to Keating. "That is your decision to make."

"I don't believe you," Jeremy said. "I can't believe you! It's too much, it's too incredible. You can't expect a man to accept everything you've just told me—not all at once!"

"We do expect it," Rungawa said softly. "We expect that and more. We want you working with us, not against us."

Jeremy felt as if his guts were being torn apart. "Work with you?" he screamed. "With the people who murdered my wife and son?"

"There are other children in the world. Do not deny them their birthright. Do not foreclose their future."

"You bastard!" Jeremy seethed. "You don't miss a trick, do you?"

"It all depends on you, Mr. Keating. You are our test case. What you do now will decide the future of the human species."

A thousand emotions raged through Jeremy. He saw Joanna being torn apart by the mob and Jerry in his cot screaming with fever, flames and death everywhere, the filth and poverty of Jakarta and the vicious smile of the interrogator as he sharpened his razor.

He's lying, Jeremy's mind shouted at him. He's got to be lying. All this is some clever set of tricks. It can't be true. It can't be!

In a sudden paroxysm of rage and terror and frustration Jeremy hurled the gun high into the rain-filled night, turned abruptly and walked away from Rungawa. He did not look back, but he knew the old man was smiling at him.

It's a trick, he kept telling himself. A goddamned trick. He knew damned well I couldn't kill him in cold blood, with him standing there looking at me with those damned sad eyes of his. Shoot an old man in the face. I just couldn't do it. All he had to do was keep me talking long enough to lose my nerve. Goddamned clever black man. Must be how he lived to get so old.

Keating stamped down the marble steps of the Sacred Way, pushed past the three raincoated guards who had accompanied Rungawa, and walked alone and miserable back to the *pensione*.

How the hell am I going to explain this back at headquarters? I'll have to resign, tell them that I'm not cut out to be an assassin. They'll never believe that. Maybe I could get a transfer, get back into the political section, join the Peace Corps, anything!

He was still furious with himself when he reached the *pensione*. Still shaking his head, angry that he had let the old man talk him out of his assigned mission. Some form of hypnosis, Keating thought. He must have been a medicine man or a voodoo priest when he was younger.

He pushed through the glassed front door of the *pensione,* muttering to himself. "You let him trick you. You let that old black man hoodwink you."

The room clerk roused himself from his slumber and got

up to reach Jeremy's room key from the rack behind the desk. He was a short, sturdily-built Greek, the kind who would have faced the Persians at Marathon.

"You must have run very fast," he said to Keating in heavily accented English.

"Huh? What? Why do you say that?"

The clerk grinned, revealing tobacco-stained teeth. "You did not get wet."

Keating looked at the sleeve of his trench coat. It was perfectly dry. The whole coat was as clean and dry as if it had just come from a pressing. His feet were dry; his shoes and trousers and hat were dry.

He turned and looked out the front window. The rain was coming down harder than ever, a torrent of water.

"You run so fast you go between raindrops, eh?" The clerk laughed at his own joke.

Jeremy's knees nearly buckled. He leaned against the desk. "Yeah. Something like that."

The clerk, still grinning, handed him his room key. Jeremy gathered his strength and headed for the stairs, his head spinning.

As he went up the first flight, he heard a voice, even though he was quite alone on the carpeted stairs.

"A small kindness, Mr. Keating," said Rungawa, inside his mind. "I thought it would have been a shame to make you get wet all over again. A small kindness. There will be more to come."

Keating could hear Rungawa chuckling as he walked alone up the stairs. By the time he reached his room, he was grinning himself.

GALACTIC GEOPOLITICS

Do the kindly, concerned aliens hinted at in *A Small Kindness* actually exist, somewhere out in the depths of interstellar space? Despite the utter lack of evidence, I firmly believe that intelligent life does exist elsewhere in the universe. But I wonder if the old science fiction dream of intelligent civilizations that are far older, wiser and technologically superior to humankind might not just be dead wrong. In *Galactic Geopolitics* I tried to look at what we know of the laws of physics and chemistry, and the shape of the observable universe, to come to some conclusions about where and when we might find intelligent alien civilizations.

Interestingly, these speculations, originally written more than a dozen years ago, have become an "in" subject among astronomers and cosmologists. Symposia have been held to discuss the problem of where They might be and why They have not visited Earth.

Even here, the participants seems to break down into Luddites and Prometheans, pessimists and optimists. And the argument will continue unless and until we do find Them—or (worse luck) They find us.

■

et's assume that contact with another intelligent race is inevitable. Sooner or later they will come to visit us, or we'll stumble into them once we get our starships cruising across the Milky Way.

It seems almost certain that we won't find another intelligent species among the planets of our own solar system. Mars and Venus have been blasted from our hopes by the pitiless advance of knowledge, thanks to space probes. Mercury, Pluto and our own Moon were never really counted on as habitats for intelligent races. And the Jovian planets—Jupiter, Saturn, Uranus and Neptune—are *too* alien for us. More on them later.

If we find another intelligent race, it will be out among the stars. Assuming that brainy aliens are out there, what are the chances of having any meaningful, fruitful contacts with them? Not just radio chats, not just an occasional awe-inspiring visit. Real, long-term, continuous interaction, the way the United States interacts with the other nations of Earth—trade, cultural interpenetration, tourism, politics, war.

This all depends, of course, on attaining starflight. More than that, it has to be fast, cheap interstellar transportation. Otherwise there can be no large-scale interactions, no politics or trade, between us and them.

Look at a parallel from Earth's history.

Since at least Roman times, Western Europe knew that China and the Orient existed. In the Middle Ages, Marco Polo got there and back, spreading wondrous tales that grew each year. But Europe didn't interact with China in any significant way. True, Europe engaged in trade with the Arab Middle East and obtained goods from China through Arab middlemen. The Middle East was close enough for Europeans to reach on foot if they had no other way to get there. Europe traded with the Middle East, exchanged scholarly works—which is why most of the stars in the sky have Arabic names—and engaged in the pious slaughters called the Crusades.

But there was no direct trade, and no conflict, with China. Once deep-ocean sailing vessels were perfected, though, Europe did indeed contact China directly and treated the Orient to Western technology, trade, disease and war. Today, of course, with intercontinental rockets and instant communications, everybody on the globe can interact politically with everybody else.

The same rules will apply to interstellar politics. There may be glorious civilizations in the Orion complex, or even as close as Alpha Centauri. But we know less about them than Hannibal knew about China. No action.

Yet even today it is possible to visualize starships based on technology that is tantalizingly close to our grasp. If and when we can make trips to the nearest stars within a human lifetime, we'll have reached the Marco Polo stage of interstellar contact—adventure, strange tales and stranger artifacts. But no lasting political relations, for better or worse, with the neighbors.

There would be little tourism, except of a scientific variety, when a person could visit the exotic land only once in a lifetime, and the trip would consume a fair portion of his life span. It is also hard to picture commerce and trade relations based on one ship per human generation. That's more like a cultural exchange. And even the sternest, most fearless and ruthless general might feel a bit foolish about mounting an attack when he knew he could never see the outcome in his own lifetime.

But the real importance of Marco Polo's adventure was the spur it gave to Prince Henry the Navigator and others, including Christopher Columbus. And the importance of the first interstellar contact will be the stimulus it gives to us on Earth.

Now, if you corner a theoretical physicist, the chances

are that you can start him mumbling about tachyons and things that go faster than light. Einstein's light barrier is starting to look—well, not leaky, perhaps, but at least a little translucent. Perhaps one day ships will be able to zip among the stars at speeds far greater than light.

Since we're dealing with improbabilities, let's consider this one. With faster-than-light ships, we can get just as close and chummy with our stellar neighbors as we are today with the Chinese.

But we must realize that there will be many races out among the stars that we simply *cannot* interact with in any useful way, even though we may be able to reach them physically.

We may, for example, find races much younger than our own, with a correspondingly simple technology and social development. Aside from letting them worship us as gods, there's probably little that we could do for them—or they could do for us.

Certainly we would want to study them and learn more about how intelligence and societies evolve. That would be best done from orbit, where we could remain "invisible" and not disturb them in any way. What could they offer us, except for their own artifacts or bodies? The artifacts might be interesting as examples of alien art. And no matter how lopsided or gruesome they appear, there will arise at least one art critic who will explain the hidden aesthetic values that everybody else had missed and sell the stuff at a huge markup.

And their bodies?

We wouldn't use them for meat, for a number of reasons. If their bodies contained some precious chemical substances that couldn't be found elsewhere—the key to immortality or something equally exotic—we would be in a lovely ethical bind. But the chances for that sort of situation are vanishingly small. We certainly would not need muscular slaves in our technological society—electricity is cheaper. And we have laws about such things, anyway.

And what could we offer our younger neighbors? Only the things that would destroy their culture as surely as Western Europe destroyed the American Indians. We hope that by the time we reach such a race, we'll have learned not to interfere with them.

If we should try to meddle with a race that's only slightly younger or technologically weaker than we are, their reaction could very well be the same as the Indians'—they would resist us as strongly as they could, probably with guerrilla warfare. We found out in Vietnam exactly what Custer learned nearly a century ago—that "unsophisticated" and "simple" people can use our own technology very effectively against us. But the Indians were either killed or absorbed into our culture, and the Vietnamese are going through the same process. That part of the world will never again be a simple, unspoiled, isolated Asian backwater. The same thing would probably happen to a younger race that fights against us: the very act of resistance will destroy their native culture.

What happens when we contact a race much more advanced than we are? The same situation, only in reverse. We would have precious little to offer them, except possibly curiosity value. And they would be wise enough not to tamper with us. We hope. Playing Cowboys and Indians is no fun when you're on the foredoomed side.

A really far advanced race would most likely go its own way aloof and serene, even if we tried our hardest to make friends. The picture that comes to mind is a puppydog chasing a monorail train.

That leaves us with races that are more or less at our own stage of development, intellectually, morally and technologically. *That's* where the fun—and the danger—will be.

How much of a range is covered by "more or less" is

rather hard to say. For a thumbnail definition, let's put it this way: We will interact strongly with races that have something to gain from us, and vice versa. Cavemen and angels have so little in common with us that they won't affect us very much, nor will we affect them. But other humans, even if they're purple and have sixteen legs, will provide the interstellar action.

Further, the races we interact with will probably come from planets enough like our own to make this Earth attractive to them. And their home worlds will similarly be attractive—or at least bearable—to us. This is why, even if intelligent Jovians exist under Jupiter's clouds—or Saturn's or Neptune's or Uranus's—we probably will interact with them about as much as we do with the denizens of the Marianas Trench. There's just no common meeting ground. We don't have political relations with dolphins, even if they are as intelligent as we are. We have nothing to trade or fight over.

So it boils down to this: Although we may meet many strange and marvelous races among the stars, if they are physically or intellectually far removed from us we will have little but the most cursory of contacts with them— except for scientific expeditions.

Yet the races that can stand on our planet in their shirtsleeves, or at least a minimum of protective equipment, and have a technology of a roughly similar level to our own, will be the races that we will talk with, laugh with, trade with and fight with. It may be that intelligent life is too thinly scattered through the Milky Way's stars for us to expect to find such a race close enough to us—close enough in distance *and* maturity—to make interstellar politics likely.

Just what are the chances of meeting another intelligent race that is at our own stage of development, give or take 10,000 years? Below that level are cavemen. Much above that level and we're in the realm of highly advanced civilizations that would regard *us* as cavemen.

The chances for meeting neighbors with whom we can truly interact seem mighty slim. But let's look around anyway and see what the real universe holds for us.

There are 37 stars within 5 parsecs of the Sun. Of these 37 stars, 27 are single, 8 are binary, or double, stars and 2 are triples. Four of these stars are known to have "dark companions"—bodies of planetary mass that are too faint and small to be seen. In fact, two of the nearest five stars have planets. Since planets are extremely difficult to detect, we might suspect that there are plenty of them orbiting the farther stars, but we just cannot perceive them from here.

If the population density of stars is about the same as we go farther away from the Sun, then there should be something like 300,000 stars within 100 parsecs of us, and some 300 million stars within 1,000 parsecs. As we have seen, the Milky Way galaxy as a whole contains more than 100 billion stars. Our galaxy is roughly 30,000 parsecs in diameter, and our solar system is some 10,000 parsecs out from the center.

We have no way of knowing how rare intelligence is. But in every cosmological test that has been applied to the Earth and solar system so far, we find absolutely no evidence for our own uniqueness. Quite the opposite. The Sun is a rather average star. It appears that planets form around stars naturally. Planets at our temperature range from their star should turn out to look roughly like Earth, with plenty of liquid water. Life on those planets should be based on carbon, oxygen and water, making use of some of the most abundant materials and most energetic chemical reactions available. Given enough time, the natural forces that led to the evolution of life on Earth would lead to similar results on similar worlds.

The real question is, What are the ages of the stars

around us? If they are about the same age as the Sun, we might expect to find interesting neighbors.

The Sun's age has been pegged at roughly 5 billion years. This is based chiefly on estimates of the amount of the Sun's original hydrogen that has been converted into helium through the hydrogen fusion processes that make the Sun shine. In turn, these estimates are based largely on theory, since no one can look inside the Sun and actually measure the ratio of hydrogen to helium there. In fact, no one knows how much helium, if any, the Sun had when it first began to shine. But 5 billion years is a reasonable guesstimate, and it tallies well with the ages of the oldest rocks of the Earth, the Moon and the meteorites.

Many of the stars around the Sun are clearly much younger. Table 1 shows the classes of typical stars according to their spectra, together with estimates of their stable life spans. By "stable life span" we mean the length of time that the star is on the Main Sequence.

To explain: Stars go through an evolutionary path, a life span, much as do living creatures. In the vastness of the Milky Way, stars are constantly being born and dying. The evolutionary path for an ordinary star, such as the Sun, goes like this:

1. A "protostar" condenses out of interstellar gas and dust. The protostar, a dark clump of mostly hydrogen, is about a light-year wide. It contracts rapidly, falling inward on itself under the gravitational force of its own mass. As it contracts, it naturally gets denser and hotter. Its interior temperature rises sharply.

2. When the density and temperature at the core of the protostar reach a critical value, hydrogen fusion reactions are triggered. The gravitational collapse stops, because now heat and light produced by fusion are making outward-pushing pressures that balance the inward-pulling gravity. The star shines with fusion energy; it becomes a stable

TABLE 1. Spectral Classes and Life spans of Stars

SPECTRAL CLASS	SURFACE TEMPERATURE (°'s KELVIN)	COLOR	STABLE LIFE SPAN	EXAMPLE
B	11,000–25,000	blue	8 to 400 million yrs.	Rigel, Spica
A	7,500–11,000	blue-white	400 million to 4 billion yrs.	Sirius, Vega
F	6,000–7,500	white	4 to 10 billion yrs.	Canopus, Procyon
G	5,000–6,000	yellow	10 to 30 billion yrs.	Sun, Capella, Alpha Centauri A
K	3,500–5,000	orange	30 to 70 billion yrs.	Arcturus, Aldebaran, Alpha Centauri B
M*	below 3,500	red	more than 70 billion yrs.	Alpha Centauri C. Barnard's star

*Red supergiant stars such as Betelgeuse and Antares are not Main Sequence stars, therefore their stable life spans in no way correspond with those of the red M-class dwarfs shown on this table.

member of the great family of stars that astronomers call the Main Sequence. Its size and surface temperature will remain stable as long as hydrogen fusion provides the star's energy source.

3. The bigger and more massive the star is to start with, the hotter it is, and the faster it runs through its hydrogen fuel supply. When the hydrogen runs low, the star begins burning the helium "ash" that is left in its core. Helium fusion, producing oxygen, neon and carbon, runs hotter than hydrogen fusion. The star's central temperature soars, and the outer layers of the star are forced to expand. The star is

no longer a Main Sequence member—astronomers call it a red giant. Soon, in astronomical time scales, the helium runs low, and the star begins burning the heavier elements in its core. The star continues to create, and then burn, constantly heavier elements. All the while, the core is getting hotter and the star's outer envelope is swelling enormously. When the Sun goes into its red giant phase, it may get so large that it swallows its inner planets—including Earth.

4. Eventually the star reaches a critical point. It explodes. There are several different types of stellar explosions, and several courses that the evolutionary track might take from there. For now, we need only realize that the eventual outcome of this stellar violence is a white dwarf star (a fading dim star about the diameter of the Earth or smaller) or an even tinier, denser neutron star. Neutron stars are probably no more than ten kilometers across, yet they contain as much material as the Sun! They are fantastically dense. The pulsars, whose uncannily precise pulses of radio energy led briefly to the "LGM (Little Green Men) theory," are probably fast-spinning neutron stars.

As we can see, a star remains stable for only a certain finite period of time, depending on its mass and temperature. After that, things get pretty dramatic for any planet-dwelling life nearby.

Hot blue giants such as Rigel and Spica won't be stable for more than a few hundred million years. While this is a long time in terms of human life spans, it is an eyeblink in terms of evolution. This means that such stars cannot be more than a few hundred million years old. In all probability, the dinosaurs never saw Rigel. It wasn't there yet.

We know that it took about 5 billion years for intelligent life to develop on Earth. As a rule of thumb, lacking any better evidence, we can say that we shouldn't expect to find intelligent life on planets circling stars that are less than 5 billion years old. So Rigel and the other young blue giants can probably be ruled out as possible abodes for intelligent life.

The stars that are smaller and cooler than the Sun, such as the K and M dwarfs, have much longer life expectancies. But are they older than the Sun? There's no easy way to tell.

We might be able to get some clues to their ages by looking farther afield. Consider the "geography" of the Milky Way.

The Milky Way is, of course, a spiral galaxy very much like the beautiful nebula in Andromeda. The core of our galaxy is presumably thick with stars, but we never see the core because it is hidden behind thick clouds of interstellar dust. Radio and infrared observations have been able to penetrate the clouds to some extent, and observations of the central regions of other galaxies show that they are so rich with stars that these stars are probably no more than a single light-year from each other, at most.

Stars in the core of a galaxy are also presumably much older than the Sun—red giant stars are common there, and astrophysical theory shows that stars become red giants only after they have used up most of their hydrogen fuel and have ended their stable Main Sequence phases. Also, in the cores of galaxies there are no young, hot, blue giants such as Rigel and Spica. These are found only in the spiral arms of galaxies.

Because the core regions of spiral galaxies seem to have different types of stars, predominantly, than the spiral arms, astronomers refer to the two different stellar constituencies as Population I and Population II. And thereby they sometimes cause confusion.

Population I stars are the kind our Sun lives among. These are the youngish stars of the spiral arms. Their brightest members are the blue giants. Population I stars contain a relatively high proportion of elements heavier than hydrogen and helium. Although the proportion of heavy elements hardly ever amounts to more than one percent, the Population I stars are said to be "metal-rich."

Population II stars are those found in the core regions of a galaxy. They are old, their brightest members are red giants, and they are mostly "metal-poor."

The heavy-element content of a star is an important clue to its history. Why are the stars in a galaxy's core metal-poor and the stars in the spiral arms metal-rich? Because the elements heavier than hydrogen have been created inside the stars. It works this way:

Consider the Milky Way before there were any stars. Cosmologists have estimated that the Milky Way is between 10 and 20 billion years old, that is, some two to four times older than the Sun. Presumably, the whole universe is the same age as the Milky Way. But when you are dealing with tens of billions of years, the numbers tend to get imprecise and hazy.

Regardless of the exact age of our galaxy, it began as an immense dark cloud of gas at least 30,000 parsecs across. The gas might have been entirely hydrogen, or it might have been a hydrogen-helium mixture. Where this gas originally came from is a mystery that cosmologists argue about, but no one has been able to prove which side of their argument is right—if either.

The first stars to form had no elements heavier than helium in them. Perhaps nothing more than hydrogen. All the heavier elements, from lithium to iron, were "cooked" inside these stars as they went from hydrogen-burning to helium-burning to heavier-element-burning. Some of these stars exploded, in the last stages of their lives, with the titanic fury of the supernova. In those star-shattering explosions, still heavier elements were created, beyond iron, all the way up to uranium and even beyond that. There's some evidence that the so-called "man-made" element, Californium 254, was present in the supernova of A.D. 1054, which we know today as the Crab nebula.

So the first generation of stars in the Milky Way began with only hydrogen—perhaps laced with a smattering of helium—and eventually produced all the heavier elements. And the stars threw these heavier elements back into space, where they served as the building material for the next generation of stars. The explosions that marked the death throes of the first-generation stars enriched the interstellar clouds with heavy elements. It is from these clouds that new stars are born.

Judging by the heavy-element content in the stars, most astrophysicists estimate that the Sun must be a third-generation star, a grandson of the original stars of the Milky Way. The elements inside the Sun today were once inside other stars. The atoms that make up the solar system were created inside other stars. The atoms of your own body were made in stars. We are truly star children.

Beware of a clash of jargon when we talk about generations of stars and Population I or II. Population I stars are the younger, late-generation stars. Population II stars are the older, early-generation stars. II came before I, historically.

What has all this to do with meeting the neighbors?

Just this: The first-generation stars *could not produce life.* At least, nothing that we would recognize as life. There was no carbon, no oxygen, no nitrogen . . . nothing but hydrogen and perhaps some helium. If those first stars had planets, they would all be frozen ice balls of hydrogen, somewhat like Jupiter but not so colorful, because there would be no ammonia or methane or any other chemical compounds to cause gaudy streaks of colored clouds such as we see on Jupiter and Saturn. There wouldn't even be any water. Not yet.

Second-generation stars? It's possible that they would

have most of the heavier elements, including the carbon, oxygen, nitrogen, potassium, iron and such that we need to develop life. Planets of such stars might be able to support life, even our own kind of life, if these heavier elements were present in sufficient quantities. And if life has appeared on such planets, there's no reason to suppose it wouldn't eventually attain intelligence. Certainly the long-lived red dwarf stars provide plenty of time for intelligence to develop—5 billion years plus.

Let's grant that an intelligent race could arise on the planetary system of a second-generation star. Could such a race develop a high civilization and technology? It all depends on the abundance of natural resources. Fossil fuels such as coal and oil should be plentiful, since they are the result of the biodegrading of plant and animal remains. But what about metals? Our technology here on Earth is built around metals. Even our history rings with the sounds of the Bronze Age, the Iron Age, the Steel Age, the Uranium Age.

Astronomical evidence is indistinct here. Theory shows that second-generation stars should have a lesser abundance of metals than we third-generation types have. But certainly there should be some metals on second-generation planets.

How much metal is enough? There's no way for us to tell. Planets of second-generation stars might have iron mountains and gold nuggets lying on the open ground. Or they might have very little available metal. Our own Jupiter might easily have more iron in it than Earth does. But if it's there, the iron is mixed with 317.4 Earth-masses of hydrogen, helium, methane, ammonia and whatnot. Try to find it! And get at it!

If there are planets of second-generation stars where heavy metals—iron, copper, silver, tin, gold—are abundant and available, those planets could be sites for highly advanced civilizations. But suppose intelligent races arise on planets where heavy metals are not available? What then?

First, we should clearly realize that intelligence per se does not depend on heavy metals. *Life*, though, does, to some extent. There's an atom of iron at the core of every hemoglobin molecule in your body. And hemoglobin is what makes your red blood cells work. So without iron, and certain other heavy metals, we wouldn't be here!

Mankind rose to intelligence before he discovered heavy metals. He used wood, clay, rock and animal bones for his first technology. In a way, man went through a Ceramics Age, working mostly with clay, before he found metals. In fact, it was wood and ceramics that allowed man to handle fire safely and usefully. Only after fire had been tamed could men start to use metals on a large scale.

The history of man shows that once metals became available, we took a giant leap forward. Metals allowed men to build effective plows. And swords. And chariots. Even today our skyscrapers and computers and engines and spacecraft and weapons and household appliances are made mainly from metals. Metals are strong, tough and cheap. They are rather easily found and easily worked, even with low-grade fire.

Could a race build skyscrapers and spacecraft without metals? Well, today there are many "space age" materials such as plastics and boron-fiber composites. But the machinery that produces them is made of stainless steel, copper, brass, etc. Modern technology is showing that there are nonmetallic materials that can outperform metals in strength, weight and many other performance parameters. But these materials couldn't have been developed before an extensive Metal Age technology. Cavemen, or even the ancient Greeks, could not have produced boron-fiber composites or modern plastics. They didn't have the metals to produce them with!

Would a metal-poor second-generation intelligent race be stymied in its attempts at technology? Who can say? All we know for sure is that *our* technology certainly depends on metals, and until metals were available, our ancestors had no civilization or technology higher than Neolithic.

Another vital point. While we have nothing but the history of our own race to go on, it looks very much as if the whole world of electromagnetic forces would never have been discovered without metals such as iron and copper. Man's discovery of magnetism depended on the abundance of iron on this planet. And from the very beginnings of our experiments with electricity, we used lead, zinc, copper, brass, etc. It's hard to see how the entire chain of study and use of electromagnetic forces—from Volta and Faraday and Hertz through to radio telescopes and television and superconducting magnets—could have happened on a metal-poor planet. And where would our technology be without electricity? Back in the early nineteenth century, at best.

So what about the metal-poor second-generation races? It just might be possible to build a complex technology completely out of nonmetals. But tribes on Earth that never had easy access to heavy metals have never developed a high technology. Coincidence? Maybe.

Could a strong technology be built around the lighter metals, such as lithium, beryllium or boron? Ironically (pardon the pun) those metals are much less abundant in the universe than the heavier metals (iron and up). And for good reason. The light metals make excellent "fuel" for the nuclear fusion reactions inside stars. They are used up inside a star before it explodes and spews out its material for later generations. So the chances of having a sophisticated civilization based on light metals seem slim indeed.

If our own history is any guide, it is the heavy metals that lead to high technology. And they also form a natural gateway into the world of electromagnetic forces and the whole concept of "invisible" forces that act over a distance: magnetism, electricity, gravity, nuclear forces. We can trace a direct line from man's use of heavy metals to electromagnetics, nuclear power, and, we hope, beyond.

For second-generation stars the situation is much cloudier. Either they have enough heavy metals to develop a high technology or they don't. If they do, their races are much older and presumably wiser than we are. Which means they probably won't interact with us at all. We would probably bore them to tears, or whatever they have in place of tears.

Second-generation races that don't have metals are no doubt gamboling innocently through some local version of Eden, and we should leave them strictly alone.

There goes the long-standing science-fiction vision of an immense galactic empire, run by the older and wiser races of the Milky Way's ancient core regions. Like the "steaming jungles" of Venus and desert "cities" of Mars, the empire at the center of the galaxy simply doesn't exist. The first-generation stars produced no life. If there are second-generation intelligences around, chances are they're either so far advanced beyond us that empires are meaningless trivialities to them, or they're so metal-starved that they never got past the "Me Tarzan" stage of development.

It's a shame. It would have been pleasant to talk to them—those incredibly ancient, benign and understanding superbeings from the galaxy's core. It's sort of shattering to realize that, if anyone like them does exist, they wouldn't want to be bothered with our chatterings any more than a crotchety grandfather wants to put up with a squalling baby.

On the other hand, science fiction stories abound in which a race only slightly advanced over us—say, a few centuries—does a very ruthless job of conquering Earth. So maybe we should be glad if there's no one older who is interested in us.

Of course, an older race might be benign. If so, it would probably not reveal its presence to us, for fear of damaging irreparably our culture and our spirit. They would prefer to wait until we could meet them on a more equal footing. The "equality" point might be when we've achieved successful starflight for ourselves.

If an older race is not benign, but aggressive, then it might want to gobble us up before we had reached the stage of starflight. That way, we would be alone and defenseless against them.

So if we should be visited by aliens from another solar system *before* we achieve starflight, my hunch is that their intentions will be far from pleasant—no matter what they say.

But the chances of meeting another race that is even within a few centuries of our present stage of development seem rather remote. And remember, the Sun is one of the oldest third-generation stars around this part of the galaxy. There might not be any older races within thousands of parsecs of us.

Could it be that *we* are the oldest, wisest, farthest-advanced race in this neck of the stellar woods?

Now, that's a truly sobering thought!

PRIORITIES

A well-known writer once pontificated that there are only three plots for fiction: 1 Boy meets girl; (2) If this goes on . . . ; and (3) The man who learns better. Well, here's a short-short story about a couple of frustrated Prometheans that might be summarized as a fourth kind of plot: Put the shoe on the other foot.

∎

Dr. Ira Lefko sat rigidly nervous on the edge of the plastic-cushioned chair. He was a slight man, thin, bald, almost timid-looking. Even his voice was gentle and reedy, like the fine thin tone of an English horn.

And just as the English horn is a sadly misnamed woodwind, Dr. Ira Lefko was actually neither timid nor particularly gentle. At this precise moment he was close to mayhem.

"Ten years of work," he was saying, with a barely controlled tremor in his voice. "You're going to wipe out ten years of work with a shake of your head."

The man shaking his head was sitting behind the metal desk that Lefko sat in front of. His name was Harrison Bower. His title and name were prominently displayed on a handsome plate atop the desk. Harrison Bower kept a very neat desktop. All the papers were primly stacked and both the IN and OUT baskets were empty.

"Can't be helped," said Harrison Bower, with a tight smile that was supposed to be sympathetic and understanding. "Everyone's got to tighten the belt. Reordering priorities, you know. There are many research programs going by the boards—New times, new problems, new priorities. You're not the only one to be affected."

With his somber face and dark suit Bower looked like a funeral director—which he was. In the vast apparatus of government, his job was to bury research projects that had run out of money. It was just about the only thing on Earth that made him smile.

The third man in the poorly ventilated little Washington office was Major Robert Shawn, from the Air Force Cambridge Research Laboratories. In uniform, Major Shawn looked an awful lot like Hollywood's idea of a jet pilot. In the casual slacks and sportcoat he was wearing now, he somehow gave the vague impression of being an engineer, or perhaps even a far-eyed scientist.

He was something of all three.

Dr. Lefko was getting red in the face. "But you *can't* cancel the program now! We've tentatively identified six stars within twenty parsecs of us that have—"

"Yes. I know, it's all in the reports," Bower interrupted, "and you've told me about it several times this afternoon. It's interesting, but it's hardly practical, now is it?"

"Practical? Finding evidence of high technology on other planets, not practical?"

Bower raised his eyes toward the cracked ceiling, as if in supplication to the Chief Bureaucrat. "Really, Dr. Lefko. I've admitted that it's interesting. But it's not within our restructured priority rating. You're not going to help ease pollution or solve population problems, now are you?"

Lefko's only answer was a half-strangled growl.

Bower turned to Major Shawn. "Really, Major, I would have thought that you could make Dr. Lefko understand the realities of the funding situation."

Shaking his head, the major answered, "I agree with

Dr. Lefko completely. I think his work is the most important piece of research going on in the world today."

"Honestly!" Bower seemed shocked. "Major, you know that the Department of Defense can't fund research that's not directly related to a military mission."

"But the Air Force owns all the big microwave equipment!" Lefko shouted. "You can't get time on the university facilities, and they're too small anyway!"

Bower waggled a finger at him. "Dr. Lefko, you can't have DOD funds. Even if there were funds for your research available, it's not pertinent work. You must apply for research support from another branch of the government."

"I've tried that every year! None of the other agencies have any money for new programs. Dammit, you've signed the letters rejecting my applications!"

"Regrettable," Bower said stiffly. "Perhaps in a few years, when the foreign situation settles down and the pollution problems are solved."

Lefko was clenching his fists when Major Shawn put a hand on his frail-looking shoulder. "It's no use, Ira. We've lost. Come on, I'll buy you a drink."

Out in the shabby corridor that led to the underground garage, Lefko started to tremble in earnest.

"A chance to find other intelligent races in the heavens. Gone. Wiped out . . . The richest nation in the world . . . Oh my God . . ."

The major took him by the arm and towed him to their rented car. In fifteen minutes they were inside the cool shadows of the airport bar.

"They've reordered the priorities," the major said as he stared into his glass. "For five hundred years and more, Western civilization has made the pursuit of knowledge a respectable goal in its own right. Now it's got to be practical."

Dr. Lefko was already halfway through his second rye and soda. "Nobody asked Galileo to be practical," he muttered. "Or Newton. Or Einstein."

"Yeah, people did. They've always wanted immediate results and practical benefits. But the system was spongy enough to let guys like Newton and Plank and even little fish we never hear about—let 'em tinker around on their own, follow their noses, see what they could find."

" 'Madam, of what use is a newborn baby?' " Lefko quoted thickly.

"What?"

"Faraday."

"Oh."

"Six of them," Lefko whispered. "Six point-sources of intense microwave radiation. Close enough to separate from their parent stars. Six little planets, orbiting around their stars, with higher technology microwave equipment on them."

"Maybe the Astronomical Union will help you get more funding."

Lefko shook his head. "You saw the reception my paper got. They think we're crazy. Not enough evidence. And worse still, I'm associated with the evil Air Force. I'm a pariah . . . and I don't have enough evidence to convince them. It takes more evidence when you're a pariah."

"I'm convinced," Major Shawn said.

"Thank you, my boy. But you are an Air Force officer, a mindless napalmer of Asian babies, by definition—your degrees in astronomy and electronics notwithstanding."

Shawn sighed heavily. "Yeah."

Looking up from the bar, past the clacking color TV, toward the heavily draped windows across the darkened room, Lefko said, "I know they're there. Civilizations like ours. With radios and televisions and radars, turning their planets into microwave beacons. Just as we must be an

anomalously bright microwave object to them. Maybe . . .
maybe they'll find us! Maybe they'll contact us!"

The major started to smile.

"If only it happens in our lifetime, Bob. If only they find
us! Find us . . . and blow us to Hell! We deserve it for being so stupid!"

Tor Kranta stood in the clear night chill, staring at the stars.
From inside the sleeping chamber his wife called, "Tor . . .
stop tormenting yourself."

"The fools," he muttered. "To stop the work because of
the priests' objections. To prevent us from trying to contact another intelligent race, circling another star. Idiocy.
Sheer idiocy."

"Accept what must be accepted, Tor. Come to bed."

He shook his blue-maned head. "I only hope that the
other intelligent races of the universe aren't as blind as
we are."

SETI

Why do men and women engage in scientific research? In particular, why do scientists persist in the search for extraterrestrial life? Not one shred of evidence has been found to confirm the belief that life exists elsewhere than on Earth. In fact, the more we explore the solar system with planetary probing spacecraft, the more doubtful the existence of life on those planets appears to be. The more sophisticated our searches of deep space with radio telescopes, the louder seems the absence of intelligent radio signals. *Psychology Today* was curious about the psychological reasons behind our persistent, but so far fruitless, search for other intelligences. Here is the result. As you might expect, I find myself much more in tune with Prometheans Galileo, Sagan and Morrison than Luddite Proxmire.

■

Sometimes life does imitate art. Several years ago I wrote a novel titled *Voyagers*, in which a radio telescope operated by Harvard University astronomers picked up unmistakable signals from intelligent extraterrestrial creatures. Today, that very radio telescope has become the first instrument to be devoted specifically to the Search for Extraterrestrial Intelligence—SETI.

In my novel, the realization that there are other intelligences in the universe triggered plots and counterplots by the Pentagon, the Kremlin, the Vatican and even certain fundamentalist evangelists. Some people eagerly sought to make meaningful contact with the aliens. Others were terrified of the idea, and actively tried to prevent such contact.

What would happen today, if Harvard's 85-foot radio telescope actually detected a signal from an alien civilization? How would we react to the success of SETI?

When I asked that question of Bruno Bettelheim, the distinguished psychologist, psychiatrist, educator and author, he replied, "There is absolutely no evidence for life in space."

Then why, I asked, are scientists willing to spend their entire careers seeking intelligent life from other worlds? Why is the government spending millions of dollars to fund SETI? Why do tens of millions of people rush to see motion pictures such as *E.T.* and *Close Encounters of the Third Kind?*

Bettelheim chuckled. "People used to believe in gods and demigods. Now they have invented intelligent extraterrestrial life so that they don't have to feel so lonely."

Physicist Philip Morrison, of the Massachusetts Institute of Technology, sees it differently. He believes that every human being carries around in his or her head a "grand internal model" of the universe, a sort of inner map that tells us who and what and where we are in relation to the world around us.

"For me," Morrison said, "exploration is filling in the blank margins of that inner model." He explained that we are constantly trying to fill in the holes in our interior maps, and extending its outermost edges. "This is the essential feature of human exploration, its root cause deep in our minds and in our cultures."

If exploration is a deep-seated drive among human beings, the quest for intelligent creatures beyond the Earth has been an important part of that drive. The search for other creatures equal to us—or even superior to us—has roots that extend far back into prehistory, and deep into the human psyche.

Every human culture has its myths about godlike creatures from realms beyond our own world. When human beings first began studying the skies they quickly saw that there were thousands of stars that remained fixed in their positions against the black bowl of night. But there were others that moved across the heavens. These wandering stars (*planetos* is the Greek word for them) seemed obviously more powerful than the rest. Every culture named the planets after their gods; today we know them by their Romanized names: Mercury, Venus, Mars, Jupiter and Saturn. (Uranus, Neptune and Pluto were so far away that the ancients never knew they existed.)

Spacecraft have visited each of the planets known to the ancients. The Russians have landed spacecraft on the hellish surface of Venus, where the ground is hot enough to melt lead and the air is a choking, thick soup of carbon dioxide laced with clouds of sulfuric acid. American spacecraft have landed on the surface of Mars and found a frozen desert where the air is thinner than Earth's stratosphere and the temperature plummets lower than a hundred degrees below zero every night, even in midsummer.

No trace of life has been found on the Moon or any of the planets. Not a bacterium. Yet the search for life goes on. Astronomers now believe that the giant planet Jupiter, which could swallow a thousand Earths, may be the best place in the solar system to find living organisms. Carl Sagan, the leading scientific figure in the search for extraterrestrial life, believes that Saturn's cloud-covered moon, Titan, may be covered with organic chemicals that are similar to the chemical "soup" in which life arose in Earth's primeval seas.

But not all scientists are equally sanguine about finding life on other worlds. When Harvard biologist George

Gaylord Simpson first learned that the study of extraterrestrial life was being undertaken seriously, and had been titled *exobiology*, he commented, ". . . a curious development in view of the fact that this 'science' has yet to demonstrate that its subject matter exists!"

Many biologists agree with Simpson's point of view; they believe that life itself is so complex, and intelligent life so much more so, that we may very well be the only intelligent creatures in the universe.

Tulane University physicist Frank J. Tipler makes an even stronger point. He claims that if intelligent extraterrestrials existed they would already have visited the Earth. Since there is no evidence that they have (UFO reports aside), then there is a strong inference that there are no intelligent aliens to be found.

Yet, since Galileo first turned a telescope toward the heavens and saw that the Earth is not the only world in space, people have been fascinated by the possibility that life and intelligence may exist elsewhere in the universe.

Although early cultures peopled the sky with gods and the underworld with demons, before the rise of modern science no one expected to find mortal creatures like ourselves anywhere except here on Earth. Then Copernicus showed that the Earth is not the center of creation, and Galileo and later astronomers uncovered a universe so staggeringly vast that it humbled human imagination. Our world shrank to the status of a minor dustmote in a whirlpool galaxy of a hundred billion stars or more, part of an expanding universe of billions upon billions of galaxies.

While the astronomers were downgrading the place of Earth in the cosmos, Charles Darwin and the biologists showed that humankind is not separate and distinct from the rest of the animal kingdom. We were toppled from the pinnacle of self-esteem by the theory of evolution. Later,

Sigmund Freud delivered another hammer-blow to the human ego by revealing the hidden workings of our minds.

By the end of the nineteenth century, humankind had been reduced to a rather bright species of primate ape living on a small planet circling a mediocre star and harboring an oedipal complex. Yet the human spirit, with its enormous capacity for adaptation, still reached out to seek companionship against the cosmic loneliness. In fact, some thinkers began to use the evidence of the universe's vastness and our own littleness to support the idea that there must be other creatures somewhat like ourselves out there in the starry cosmos.

The universe is so large, this argument ran, that it is inconceivable that Earth should be the only place that harbors intelligent life. After all, we are not unique in any other way. Why should the Earth be the only abode for intelligence?

Astronomer Kenneth Franklin, of New York City's Hayden Planetarium, put it this way: "We know that intelligence is 'built into' the universe, because we are intelligent and we're just as much a part of the universe as a tree or a star. So if intelligence is an integral part of the universe, I can't believe that it's arisen only in one place."

While space scientists have spent the past two decades actively probing the planets of our solar system, radio astronomers have used their giant antennas to listen for possible signals from the depths of interstellar space.

This effort began in 1959 when Morrison and Giuseppi Cocconi, who is also a physicist, suggested that the radio telescopes which astronomers use to study the natural radio-wave emissions from stars and interstellar gas clouds might also be able to pick up intelligent signals, if any exist. Admitting that the task would be difficult, and had only a minuscule chance of success, they nevertheless concluded, ". . . but if we never search the chance of success is zero."

Greenbank, West Virginia, became the first place on Earth to host a deliberate search for intelligent extraterrestrial life. Frank Drake, of Cornell University, who then headed the National Radio Astronomy Observatory at Greenbank, used the 85-foot-wide "dish" there to seek radio signals from two relatively nearby stars. Whimsically, Drake called the part-time effort Project Ozma, after the queen of L. Frank Baum's mythical land of Oz. At the cost of a thousand dollars worth of electronic equipment and some two hundred hours of the telescope's heavily-booked time, Drake and his colleagues made the first stab at SETI.

They expected no positive result, and got none. But they were learning how to build the electronic equipment that can sift an intelligent signal out of the constant background of natural radio "noise" emitted by the stars and gas clouds in deep space. Drake and others later used the world's largest radio telescope, the 1000-foot Arecibo dish, which is carved into a hillside in Puerto Rico, to listen and even to send a brief message starward. But these efforts were always on a part-time, very temporary basis. Although a few false alarms temporarily made hearts beat faster, no definite signals were detected.

The biggest alarm came in the summer of 1967, when a group of British astronomers actually thought they might have hit the jackpot. Jocelyn Bell was an undergraduate student at Cambridge University, working on a radio astronomy project that did not involve SETI. She discovered a strange, pulsing signal unlike anything that had ever been picked up before. The signal came in millisecond pulses, bursts that were only 10 to 20 thousandths of a second long, and spaced precisely 1.33730113 seconds apart. It was the precise timing of the pulses, as accurate as any atomic clock, that startled Bell and her colleagues.

For weeks the Cambridge astronomers tried to find a cause for the signals. One of the theories they considered seriously was dubbed LGM—for Little Green Men.

It turned out that the radio pulses were being emitted by entirely natural, though fantastically unusual, astronomical objects. Today they are called pulsars. They are stars like the Sun, but have collapsed down to a size of only a few miles across. A teaspoonful of a pulsar's material would weigh more than the Pacific Ocean.

Musing about those frantic weeks, many years afterward, Bell said, "It is an interesting problem—if one thinks one may have detected life elsewhere in the universe, how does one announce the results responsibly?"

In my novel, when American and Russian astronomers independently detect intelligent radio signals from deep space, both the Pentagon and the Kremlin insist on keeping the information secret. Neither Washington nor Moscow wants the other side to know about the highly advanced technology that might be offered by the aliens. When the Vatican learns of the signals, secrecy is also preferred, because the Church worries how the discovery of intelligent alien creatures would affect the faith of its followers.

The discovery of extraterrestrial life, and intelligence, raises powerful psychological, social and political questions. To begin with, most scientists assume that if we actually do detect intelligent signals from the stars, they will have been sent by a civilization far in advance of our own. After all, we are merely beginning to search for life in the universe. A civilization that is actively transmitting signals over interstellar distances would most likely have been doing so for generations or centuries; its technology would be superior to ours.

What would happen to the human psyche if we suddenly made contact with creatures far advanced over us? Carl Jung once wrote:

"In a direct confrontation with superior creatures from another world, the reins would be torn from our hands and we would, as a tearful old medicine man said to me, find ourselves 'without dreams,' that is, we would find our intellectual and spiritual aspirations so outmoded as to leave us completely paralyzed."

Dr. Warren H. Jones, associate professor of psychology at the University of Tulsa, sees a more active, and more aggressive, human reaction to the discovery of alien-intelligence creatures.

"The basic human reaction to something that shocking and dramatic," he says, "would be fear, anger . . ." If the classic science fiction scenario of aliens landing their flying saucer on the White House lawn ever really happened, Dr. Jones believes, "We would kill them, if we could."

There is a strong and deep xenophobia lurking within the psyche of the average human being, Dr. Jones explains. "There is good evidence that a fundamental principle of human nature is that we don't really like surprises . . . perhaps we enjoy pleasant surprises occasionally, but we really want the world to be predictable and understandable."

Dr. Jones adds that this desire for a predictable, understandable universe, conversely, is one of the reasons why many scientists believe there *must* be intelligent extraterrestrials elsewhere in the cosmos. "It provides understanding and meaning where there doesn't seem to be any."

Certainly there is plenty of evidence of culture shock in human history. Would our discovery of (or rather, *by*) intelligent aliens start the same kind of tragedy as that suffered by the native American and Polynesian cultures, once they were discovered by the Europeans?

Scientists such as Sagan, who is director of Cornell University's Laboratory for Planetary Studies, have no such fears. Instead, they look forward to interstellar communications with creatures who are more highly developed intellectually than we are. How would such a communication be established, though? What language would the people of Earth have in common with alien intelligences from a distant star?

Sagan wrote, "If it is possible to communicate, we think we know what the first communications will be about: They will be about the one thing the two civilizations are guaranteed to share in common . . . science."

If the astronomers are guilty of projecting their own point of view onto the hypothesized extraterrestrials, there is another attitude that sees alien creatures as potential threats to humankind. In science fiction tales, the aliens are often hostile, heartless and gruesome. No less a writer than the redoubtable H. G. Wells described the Martians in his classic *The War of the Worlds* thus:

". . . minds that are to our minds as ours are to those of the beasts that perish, intellects vast and cool and unsympathetic, regarded this earth with envious eyes, and slowly and surely drew their plans against us."

The astronomers may expect to meet angels, or at least college professors, but the fantasists warn that the dark side of intelligence exists side by side with the bright.

People who have reported seeing Unidentified Flying Objects and their crews, however, almost invariably describe the UFO aliens as humanlike in appearance, and utterly benign.

Dr. Janet Jeppson, training and supervising analyst at the William Alanson White Institute of Psychoanalysis in Manhattan, believes that the similarities among all the thousands of UFO "contactee" stories points to the conclusion that these are reports of unconscious wish-fulfillment, rather than descriptions of reality.

"The aliens are always so saintly," Dr. Jeppson remarks. "They always are motivated only by the best interests of the human race." Dr. Jeppson, who is the wife of science fiction writer Isaac Asimov and a writer herself, is in the unique position of seeing the UFO phenomenon from several different points of view.

Tulsa's Dr. Jones agrees that UFO sightings and reports of contacts with alien astronauts are a form of "substitute religion . . . a modernistic, mechanistic modern religion [which] combines the best of science fiction and religion. On the one hand, [the UFO aliens represent] a race of people who are technologically superior, who can solve age-old human frailties and shortcomings: they can stops wars, cure all disease, allow us to live forever . . . and that is fused with the much more ancient notion of a superhuman being out there somewhere in the sky who watches over us, and protects us, and has our best interests at heart."

But to date, no one has found any evidence acceptable to the vast majority of humankind that we have been visited by aliens. Nor has any evidence been found to show that life exists beyond the Earth. Although most scientists are convinced that life should arise wherever the natural conditions for it exist, none of our space probes have found so much as an organic molecule or a fossilized spore, and none of our radio telescopes have yet picked up an intelligible signal.

For years, the federal government supported NASA's planetary exploration programs in the hopes of finding life elsewhere in the solar system. But when the Viking landers showed that Mars was so barren it would make Death Valley look like the Garden of Eden, much of Capitol Hill's enthusiasm for planetary exploration evaporated. NASA's funds for planetary sciences were severely cut, and new probes of the planets were slashed almost entirely out of the space agency's budget.

Meanwhile, the radio astronomy approach to SETI was also under attack in Washington, particularly by Senator William Proxmire (Democrat, Wisconsin). In 1978 Proxmire was chairman of the Senate Committee that controlled NASA's funding. He had won a place for himself in the Washington limelight by giving out each month a Golden Fleece award for "the most ironic or most ridiculous example of wasteful [government] spending."

In February 1978 Proxmire gave his Golden Fleece award to NASA for "riding the wave of popular enthusiasm for *Star Wars* and *Close Encounters of the Third Kind*, [by] proposing to spend $14 to $15 million over the next seven years to try to find intelligent life in outer space. . . . At a time when the country is faced with a $61-billion budget deficit, the attempt to detect radio waves from solar systems should be postponed until right after the federal budget is balanced and income and social security taxes are reduced to zero."

Proxmire succeeded in getting all funding for SETI cut from the NASA budget. Later, when he learned that the space agency was still spending roughly a million dollars a year on research that could be applied to SETI, he got the Congress to prohibit NASA specifically from doing any work connected with the search for extraterrestrial intelligence.

There may have been more afoot than merely an attempt to save the taxpayers' dollars. After all, Proxmire himself always voted in favor of the two-billion-dollar milk subsidy every year. Those who resist the relatively inexpensive research involved in SETI might have psychological motivations for their political stance. They may not want to see the human race displaced even further from the center of the universe's stage. Forced by scientific evidence to accept the fact that the Earth is not unique, and that humans evolved from "lower" animals, many people still unconsciously cling to the faith that life itself—and certainly intelligent life—is singular to our world.

When media pundits, politicians and religious leaders

learned that the spacecraft we have sent to Mars detected no traces of life, Sagan observed, "They were unmistakably *relieved*."

The shock of contact with intelligent extraterrestrials will be very different from its depiction in films such as *E.T.* If and when we meet alien creatures, they will undoubtedly look nothing like human beings; biologists have warned us repeatedly that it would be foolish to expect evolution to follow exactly the same course on a distant, different world. This is why the typical UFO "contact" story is regarded so skeptically by most scientists: such reports almost always depict the UFO aliens as humanlike in appearance. Biologists are more inclined to believe in science fiction's "bug-eyed monsters" than in aliens from a distant star looking more-or-less human.

Thinking about the likelihood that very advanced intelligent aliens will undoubtedly look most un-human, author Arthur C. Clarke pointed out, "The rash assertion that 'God created man in His own image' is ticking like a time bomb at the foundations of many faiths."

Despite these fears and forebodings, the main body of scientists and space enthusiasts chafed unhappily over the cutbacks in planetary exploration and the Proxmire-mandated death of SETI. Once again it was Sagan who spearheaded the counterattack. He wrote a petition calling for a systematic search for extraterrestrial intelligence, which was subsequently signed by 73 scientists from 14 nations, including seven Nobel Prize winners. He and other scientists began meeting with the politicians in Washington, including Proxmire, to "educate" them about the intellectual and practical benefits of SETI. On the practical side, for example, the development of computer technology necessary for SETI will have many other applications in science, business and national defense.

Sagan is also president of the Planetary Society, a grass-roots space activist organization of some 100,000 members. Since 1982, the Planetary Society has been funding an effort at Harvard, directed by physicist Paul Horowitz, to scan 128,000 radio channels simultaneously, using the 85-foot radio telescope at Harvard's Oak Ridge Station. The actual observation work began in March 1983, when Horowitz's compact electronic gear—nicknamed "suitcase SETI" because of its portability—was linked to the radio telescope.

This multi-year program is the first "dedicated" search for intelligent signals. The electronic receiving equipment that Horowitz and his colleagues have devised will enable the radio telescope to make observations within minutes that would have taken Drake and his Project Ozma team thousands of years to perform.

The "moral suasion" by the scientists on Capitol Hill also met with some degree of success, and Proxmire relented in his opposition to SETI enough to allow NASA to spend a total of $12.5 million over the next several years to develop advanced technology to listen for messages from the stars. Proxmire now describes his attitude as "skeptical neutrality," as opposed to his earlier active hostility.

And although NASA's planetary exploration program is still under severe financial constraints, the agency was permitted to develop the Galileo spacecraft to explore Jupiter. The orbiter will fire a probe vehicle down into the giant planet's swirling sea of clouds on a one-way mission to sample the gases there and see if they contain the chemicals of life.

Perhaps Bettelheim is correct, and we are inventing imaginary creatures to protect ourselves against cosmic loneliness. Tipler, who argues forcefully against the existence of extraterrestrials, also points out that there is no certain way to *prove* that they do not exist; no matter how many negative returns we get, the "pro-life" scientists can always hope that ET is waiting to be discovered just beyond the reach of our latest probe.

Typically, Sagan makes a virtue even out of such negativism. If we find no evidence for life or intelligence, he says, it will simply help us to appreciate how rare and precious we ourselves are in the universe.

No matter which argument ultimately turns out to be correct, SETI is now going ahead, at a total cost of a few pennies per taxpayer per year. The benefits of new knowledge that we gain, even if no trace of life is found, will make the effort a fiscal bargain.

Nearly four centuries ago, Galileo wrote, "Astronomers . . . seek to investigate the true constitution of the universe— the most important and most admirable problem that there is." This quest for knowledge, for understanding, this drive to explore, is a fundamental part of the human psyche. We reach out to seek others like ourselves, regardless of the consequences, and in doing so we learn more about the universe—and about ourselves, as well.

Perhaps Lee DuBridge put it best, back when he was President Eisenhower's science advisor. He said, "Either we are alone in the universe or we are not; either way is mind-boggling."

THE GREAT SUPERSONIC ZEPPELIN RACE

Although I count myself among the Prometheans, I do recognize that sometimes Prometheanism can run amok. When the Luddites among us succeeded in stopping the American effort to develop a supersonic transport plane, I found myself writing this story. If nothing else, it shows that a true Promethean is never stopped for long.

The part about the Busemann biplane, incidentally, is true. At least, that's what I heard from these two aerodynamicists one day at lunch in the laboratory cafeteria in Everett.

■

You can make a supersonic aircraft that doesn't produce a sonic boom," said Bob Wisdom.

For an instant the whole cafeteria seemed to go quiet. Bob was sitting at a table by the big picture window that overlooked Everett Aircraft Co.'s parking lot. It was drizzling out there, as it usually did in the spring. Through the haze, Mt. Olympia's snow-topped peak could barely be seen.

Bob smiled quizzically at his lunch pals. He was tall and lanky, round-faced in a handsome sort of way, with dark, thinning hair and dark eyes that were never somber, even in the midst of Everett Aircraft's worst layoffs and cutbacks.

"A supersonic aircraft," mumbled Ray Kurtz from inside his beard.

"With no sonic boom," added Tommy Rohr.

Bob Wisdom smiled and nodded.

"What's the catch?" asked Richard Grand in a slightly Anglified accent.

The cafeteria resumed its clattering, chattering noises. The drizzle outside continued to soak the few scraggly trees and pitiful shrubs planted around the half-empty parking lot.

"Catch?" Bob echoed, trying to look hurt. "Why should there be a catch?"

"Because if someone could build a supersonic aircraft that doesn't shatter people's eardrums, obviously someone would be doing it," Grand answered.

"We could do it," Bob agreed pleasantly, "but we're not."

"Why not?" Kurtz asked.

Bob shrugged elaborately.

Rohr waggled a finger at Bob. "There's something going on in that aerodynamicist's head of yours. This is a gag, isn't it?"

"No gag," Bob replied innocently. "I'm surprised that nobody's thought of the idea before."

"What's the go of it?" Grand asked. He had just read a biography of James Clerk Maxwell and was trying to sound English, despite the fact that Maxwell was a Scot.

"Well," Bob said, with a bigger grin than before, "there's a type of wing that the German aerodynamicist Adolph Busemann invented. Instead of making the wings flat, though, you build your supersonic aircraft with a ringwing. . . ."

"Ringwing?"

"Sure." Leaning forward and propping one elbow on the cafeteria table, Bob pulled a felt-tip pen from his shirt pocket and sketched on the paper placemat.

"See? Here's the fuselage of a supersonic plane." He drew a narrow cigar shape. "Now we wrap the wing around it, like a sleeve. It's actually two wings, one inside the other, and all the shock waves that cause the sonic boom get trapped inside the wings and get canceled out. No sonic boom."

Grand stared at the sketch, then looked up at Bob, then stared at the sketch some more. Rohr looked expectant, waiting for the punch line. Kurtz frowned, looking like a cross between Abe Lincoln and Karl Marx.

"I don't know much about aerodynamics," Rohr said slowly, "but that is a sort of Busemann biplane you're talking about, isn't it?"

Bob nodded.

"Aha . . . and isn't it true that the wings of a Busemann biplane produce no lift?"

"Right," Bob admitted.

"No lift?" Kurtz snapped. "Then how the hell do you get it off the ground?"

Trying to look completely serious, Bob answered, "You can't get it off the ground if it's an ordinary airplane. It's got to be lighter than air. You fill the central body with helium."

"A zeppelin?" Kurtz squeaked.

Rohr started laughing. "You sonofabitch. You had us all going there for a minute."

Grand said, "Interesting."

John Driver sat behind a cloud of blue smoke that he puffed from a reeking pipe. His office always smelled like an opium den gone sour. His secretary, a luscious and sweet-tempered girl of Greek-Italian ancestry, had worn out eight strings of rosary beads in the vain hope that he might give up smoking.

"A supersonic zeppelin?" Driver snapped angrily. "Ridiculous!"

Squinting into the haze in an effort to find his boss, Grand answered, "Don't be too hasty to dismiss the concept. It might have some merit. At the very least, I believe we could talk NASA or the Transportation people into giving us money to investigate the idea."

At the sound of the word "money," Driver took the pipe out of his teeth and waved some of the smoke away. He peered at Grand through reddened eyes. Driver was lean-faced, with hard features and a gaze that he liked to think was piercing. His jaw was slightly overdeveloped from biting through so many pipe stems.

"You have to spend money to make money in this business," Driver said in his most penetrating *Fortune* magazine acumen.

"I realize that," Grand answered stiffly. "But I'm quite willing to put my own time into this. I really believe we may be onto something that can save our jobs."

Driver drummed his slide-rule-calloused fingertips on his desktop. "All right," he said at last. "Do it on your own time. When you've got something worth showing, come to me with it. Not anyone else, you understand. Me."

"Right, Chief." Whenever Grand wanted to flatter Driver, he called him Chief.

After Grand left his office, Driver sat at his desk for a long, silent while. The company's business had been going to hell over the past few years. There was practically no market for high-technology work any more. The military was more interested in sandbags than supersonic planes. NASA was wrapping tourniquets everywhere in an effort to keep from bleeding to death. The newly reorganized Department of Transportation and Urban Renewal hardly understood what a Bunsen burner was.

"A supersonic zeppelin," Driver muttered to himself. It sounded ridiculous. But then, so had air-cushion vehicles and Wankel engines. Yet companies were making millions on those ideas.

"A supersonic zeppelin," he repeated. "SSZ."

Then he noticed that his pipe had gone out. He reached

into his left-top desk drawer for a huge blue-tipped kitchen match and started puffing the pipe alight again. Great clouds of smoke billowed upward as he said: "SSZ . . . no sonic boom . . . might not even cause air pollution."

Driver climbed out of the cab, clamped his pipe in his teeth, and gazed up at the magnificent glass and stainless steel facade of the new office building that housed the Transportation and Urban Renewal Department.

"So this is TURD headquarters," he muttered.

"This is it," replied Tracy Keene, who had just paid off the cabbie and come up to stand beside Driver. Keene was Everett Aircraft's crackerjack Washington representative, a large, round man who always conveyed the impression that he knew things nobody else knew. Keene's job was to find new customers for Everett, placate old customers when Everett inevitably alienated them, and pay off taxicabs. The job involved grotesque amounts of wining and dining, and Keene—who had once been as wiry and agile as a weak-hitting shortstop—seemed to grow larger and rounder every time Driver came to Washington. But what he was gaining in girth, he was losing in hair, Driver noticed.

"Let's go," Keene said. "We don't want to be late." He lumbered up the steps to the magnificent glass doors of the magnificent new building.

The building was in Virginia, not the District of Columbia. Like all new government agencies, it was headquartered outside the city proper. The fact that one of this agency's major responsibilities was to find ways to revitalize the major cities and stop urban sprawl somehow had never entered into consideration when the site for its location was chosen.

Two hours later, Keene was half-dozing in a straight-backed metal chair, and Driver was taking the last of an eight-inch-thick pile of viewgraph slides off the projector.

The projector fan droned hypnotically in the darkened room. They were in the office of Roger K. Memo, Assistant Under Director for Transportation Research of TURD.

Memo and his chief scientific advisor, Dr. Alonzo Pencilbeam, were sitting on one side of the small table, Keene was resting peacefully on the other side. Driver stood up at the head of the table, frowning beside the viewgraph projector. The only light in the room came from the projector, which now threw a blank glare onto the wan, yellow wall that served in place of a screen. Smoke from Driver's pipe sifted through the cone of light.

Driver snapped the projector off. The light and the fan's whirring noise abruptly stopped. Keene jerked fully awake and, without a word, reached up and flicked the wall switch that turned on the overhead lights.

Although the magnificent building was sparkling new, Memo's office somehow looked instant-seedy. There wasn't enough furniture in it for its size: only an ordinary steel desk and swivel chair, a half-empty bookcase, and this little conference table with four chairs that didn't match. The walls and floor were bare, and there was a distinct echo when anyone spoke or even walked across the room. The only window had vertical slats instead of a curtain, and it looked out on an automobile graveyard. The only decoration on the walls was a diploma: Memo's doctorate degree, bought from an obscure Mohawk Valley college for $200 without the need to attend classes.

Driver stood by the projector, frowning through his own smoke.

"Well what do you think?" he asked subtly.

Memo pursed his lips. He was jowly fat, completely bald, wore glasses and rumpled gray suits.

"I don't know," he said firmly. "It sounds . . . unusual . . ."

Dr. Pencilbeam was sitting back in his chair and smiling beautifully. His Ph.D. had been earned during the 1930s, when he had had to work nights and weekends to stay alive and in school. He was still very thin, fragile looking, with the long skinny limbs of a praying mantis.

Pencilbeam dug in his jacket pockets and pulled out a pouch of tobacco and cigarette paper. "It certainly looks interesting," he said in a soft voice. "I think it's technically feasible . . . and lots of fun."

Memo snorted. "We're not here to enjoy ourselves."

Keene leaned across the table and fixed Memo with his best here's-something-from-behind-the-scenes look:

"Do you realize how the Administration would react to a sensible program for a supersonic aircraft? With the Concorde going broke and the Russian SST grounded . . . you could put this country out in front again."

"H'mm," said Memo. "But . . ."

"Balance of payments," Keene intoned knowingly. "Gold outflow . . . aerospace employment . . . national prestige . . . the President would be awfully impressed."

"H'mm," Memo repeated. "I see . . ."

The cocktail party was in full swing. It was nearly impossible to hear your own voice in the swirling babble of chatter and clinking glassware. In the middle of the sumptuous living room, the Vice President was demonstrating his golf swing. Out in the foyer, three senators were comparing fact-finding tours they were arranging for the Riviera, Rio de Janeiro, and American Samoa, respectively. The Cabinet wives held sway in the glittering dining room.

Roger K. Memo never drank anything stronger than ginger ale. He stood in the doorway between the living room and foyer, lip-reading the senators' conversation about travel plans. When the trip broke up and Senator Goodyear (R., Ohio) headed back toward the bar, Memo intercepted him.

"Hello, Senator!" Memo shouted heartily. It was the only way to be heard over the party noise.

"Ah . . . hello." Senator Goodyear obviously knew that he knew Memo, but just as obviously couldn't recall his name, rank or influence rating.

Goodyear was nearly six feet tall, and towered over Memo's paunchy figure. Together they shouldered their way through the crowd around the bar. Goodyear ordered bourbon on the rocks, and therefore so did Memo. But he merely held onto his glass, while the senator immediately began to gulp at his drink.

A statuesque blonde in a spectacular gown sauntered past them. The senator's eyes tracked her like a range finder following a target.

"I hear you're going to Samoa," Memo shouted as they edged away from the bar, following the girl.

"Eh . . . yes," Goodyear answered cautiously, in a tone he usually employed with newspaper reporters.

"Beautiful part of the world," Memo yelled.

The blonde slipped an arm around the waist of a young, long-haired man and they disappeared into another room together. Goodyear turned his attention back to his drink.

"I said," Memo repeated, standing on tiptoes, "that Samoa is a beautiful part of the world."

Nodding, Goodyear said, "I'm going to investigate the ecological conditions there . . . my committee is considering legislation on ecology."

"Of course, of course. You've got to see things firsthand if you're going to enact meaningful laws."

Slightly less guardedly, Goodyear said, "Exactly."

"It's such a long way off, though," Memo said. "It must take considerable thought to decide to make such a long trip."

"Well . . . you know we can't think of our own comforts when we're in public service."

"Yes, of course . . . Will you be taking the SST? I understand Qantas flies it out of San Francisco. . . ."

Suddenly alert again, Goodyear snapped, "Never! I always fly American planes on American airlines."

"Very patriotic," Memo applauded. "And sensible, too. Those Aussies don't know how to run an airline. And any plane made by the British *and* the French . . . well, I don't know. I understand it's financially in trouble."

Goodyear nodded again. "That's what I hear."

"Still—it's a shame that the United States doesn't have a supersonic aircraft. It would cut your travel time in half. Give you twice as much time to stay in Samoa . . . investigating."

The hearing room in the Capitol was jammed with reporters and cameramen. Senator Goodyear sat in the center of the long front table, as befitted the committee chairman.

All through the hot summer morning the committee had listened to witnesses: John Driver, Roger K. Memo, Alonzo Pencilbeam and many others. The concept of the supersonic zeppelin unfolded before the newsmen and started to take on definite solidity right there in the rococo-trimmed hearing room.

Senator Goodyear sat there solemnly all morning, listening to the carefully rehearsed testimony, watching the greenery outside the big sunny window. Whenever he thought about the TV cameras, he sat up straighter and tried to look lean and tough, like Gary Cooper. Goodyear had a drawer full of Gary Cooper movies on video cassettes in his Ohio home.

Now it was his turn to summarize what the witnesses had said. He looked straight at the nearest camera, trying to come across strong and sympathetic, like the sheriff in *High Noon*.

"Gentlemen," he began, immediately antagonizing the

eighteen women in the audience, "I believe that what we have heard here today can mark the beginning of a new program that will revitalize the aerospace industry and put America back in the forefront of international commerce. . . ."

One of the younger senators at the far end of the table interrupted:

"Excuse me, Mr. Chairman, but my earlier question about pollution was never answered. Won't the SSZ use the same kinds of jet engines that the SST was going to use? And won't they cause just as much pollution?"

Goodyear glowered at the junior member's impudence, but controlled his temper well enough to say only, "Em . . . Dr. Pencilbeam, would you care to answer that question?"

Pencilbeam, seated at one of the witness tables, looked startled for a moment. Then he hunched his bony frame around the microphone in front of him and said:

"The pollution arguments about the SST were never substantiated. There were wild claims that if you operated jet engines up in the high stratosphere, you would eventually cause a permanent cloud layer over the whole Earth or destroy the ozone up there and thus let in enough solar ultraviolet radiation to cause millions of cancer deaths. But these claims were never proved."

"But it was never disproved, either, was it?" the junior senator said.

Before Pencilbeam could respond, Senator Goodyear grabbed his own microphone and nearly shouted, "Rest assured that we are all well aware of the possible pollution problems. At the moment, though, there is no problem because there is no SSZ. Our aerospace industry is suffering, employment is way down and the whole economy is in a bad way. The SSZ project will provide jobs and boost the economy. As part of the project, we will consult with the English and French and see what their pollution problems are—if any. And our own American engineers will, I assure you, find ways to eliminate any and all pollution coming from the SSZ engines."

Looking rather disturbed, Pencilbeam started to add something to Goodyear's statement. But Memo put a hand over the scientist's microphone and shook his head in a strong negative.

Mark Sequoia was hiking along a woodland trail in Fairmont Park, Philadelphia, when the news reached him.

Once a flaming crusader for ecological salvation and against pollution, Sequoia had made the mistake of letting the Commonwealth of Pennsylvania hire him as the state ecology director. He had spent the past five years earnestly and honestly trying to clean up Pennsylvania, a job that had driven four generations of the original Penn family into early graves. The deeper that Sequoia buried himself in the solid wastes and politics of Pittsburgh, Philadelphia, Chester, Erie and other hopeless cities, the fewer followers and national headlines he attracted.

Now he led a scraggly handful of sullen high school students through the soot-ravaged woodlands of Fairmont Park on a steaming July afternoon, picking up empty beer cans and loaded prophylactics—and keeping a wary eye out for muggers. Even full daylight was no protection against assault. And the school kids with him wouldn't help. Half of them would jump in and join the fun.

Sequoia was broad-shouldered, almost burly. His face had been seamed by weather and press conferences. He looked strong and fit, but lately his back had been giving him trouble, and his old trick knee . . .

He heard someone pounding up the trail behind him.

"Mark! Mark!"

Sequoia turned to see Larry Helper, his last and therefore most trusted aide, running along the gravel path toward him, waving a copy of the *Evening Bulletin* over his head. Newspaper pages were slipping from his sweaty grasp and fluttering off across the grass.

"Littering," Sequoia mumbled in the tone sometimes used by bishops when faced with a case of heresy.

"Some of you men," Sequoia said in his best Lone Ranger voice, "pick up those newspaper pages."

A couple of kids lackadaisically ambled after the fluttering sheets.

"Mark, look here!" Helper skidded to a stop and breathlessly waved the front page of the newspaper. "Look!"

Sequoia grabbed his aide's wrist and took the newspaper from him. He frowned at Helper, who cringed and stepped back.

"I . . . I thought you'd want to see . . ."

Satisfied that he was in control of things, Sequoia turned his attention to the front page headline.

"Supersonic *zeppelin!*"

By nightfall, Sequoia was meeting with a half-dozen men and women in the basement of a prosperous downtown church that specialized in worthy causes capable of filling the pews upstairs.

Sequoia was pacing across the little room in which they were meeting. There was no table, just a few folding chairs scattered around, and a locked bookcase stuffed with books on sex and marriage.

"No, we've got to do something dramatic!" Sequoia pounded a fist into his open palm. "We can't just drive down to Washington and call a press conference. . . ."

"Automobiles pollute," said one of the women, a comely redhead, whose eyes never left Sequoia's broad, sturdy-looking figure.

"We could take the train; it's electrical."

"Power stations pollute."

"Airplanes pollute, too."

"What about riding down on horseback? Like Paul Revere!"

"Horses pollute."

"They do?"

"Ever been around a stable?"

"Oh."

Sequoia pounded his fist again. "I've got it!" His hand stung; he had hit it too hard.

"What?"

"A balloon! We'll ride down to Washington in a nonpolluting, helium-filled balloon. That's the dramatic way to emphasize our point!"

"Fantastic!"

"Marvelous!"

The redhead was panting with excitement. "Oh, Mark, you're so clever. So dedicated." There were tears in her eyes.

Helper said softly, "Uh . . . does anybody know where we can get a balloon? And how much they cost?"

Sequoia glared at him.

When the meeting finally broke up, Helper had the task of finding a suitable balloon, preferably for free. Sequoia would spearhead the effort to raise money for a knockdown fight against the SSZ. The redhead volunteered to assist him. They left arm in arm.

The auditorium in Foggy Bottom was crammed with newsmen. TV lights were glaring at the empty podium. The reporters and cameramen shuffled, coughed, talked to each other. Then:

"Ladies and gentlemen, the President of the United States."

They all stood up and applauded politely as the President strode across the stage toward the podium in his usual bunched-together, shoulder-first football style. His dark face was somber under its beetling brows.

The President gripped the lectern and nodded, with a perfunctory smile, to a few of his favorites. The newsmen sat down. The cameras started rolling.

"I have a statement to make about the tragic misfortune that has overtaken one of our finest public figures—Mark Sequoia. According to the latest report I have received from the Coast Guard—no more than ten minutes ago—there is still no trace of him or his party. Apparently the balloon they were riding in was blown out to sea two days ago, and nothing has been heard from them since.

"Now let me make this perfectly clear. Mr. Sequoia was frequently on the other side of the political fence from me, your President. He was often a critic of my policies and actions, the policies and actions of your President. He was on his way to Washington to protest our new SSZ project, when this unfortunate accident occurred—to protest the SSZ project despite the fact that it will employ thousands of aerospace engineers who are otherwise unemployable and untrainable. Despite the fact that it will save the American dollar on the international market and salvage American prestige in the technological battleground of the world.

"Now, in spite of the fact that some of us—such as our Vice President, as is well known—feel that Mr. Sequoia carried the constitutional guarantee of free speech a bit too far, despite all this, mind you, I—as your President and Commander-in-Chief-have dispatched every available military, Coast Guard, and Boy Scout plane, ship, and foot patrol to search the entire coastline and coastal waters between Philadelphia and Washington. We will find Mark Sequoia and his brave party of misguided ecology nuts . . . or their remains.

"Are there any questions?"

The Associated Press reporter, a hickory-tough old man with huge, thick glasses and a white goatee, stood up and asked in stentorian tones: "Is it true that Sequoia's balloon was blown off course by a flight of Air Force fighter planes that buzzed it?"

The President made a smile that looked somewhat like a grimace and said: "I'm glad you asked that question. . . ."

Ronald Eames Trafalgar was Her Majesty's Ambassador Plenipotentiary to the Government of the Union of Soviet Socialist Republics.

He sat rather uneasily in the rear seat of the Bentley, watching the white-boled birch trees flash past the car windows. The first snow of autumn was already on the ground, the trees were almost entirely bare, the sky was a pewter gray. Trafalgar shivered with the iron cold of the steppes, even inside his heavy woolen coat.

Next to him sat Sergei Mihailovitch Traktor, Minister of Technology. The two men were old friends, despite their vast differences in outlook, upbringing and appearance. Trafalgar could have posed for Horatio Hornblower illustrations: he was tall, slim, poised, just a touch of gray at his well-brushed temples. Traktor looked like an automobile mechanic (which he once was): stubby, heavy-faced, shifty eyes.

"I can assure you that this car is absolutely clean," Trafalgar said calmly, still watching the melancholy birch forest sliding by. The afternoon sun was an indistinct bright blur behind the trees, trying to burn its way through the gray overcast.

"And let me assure you," Traktor said in flawless English, a startling octave higher than the Englishman's voice, "that *all* your cars are bugged."

Trafalgar laughed lightly. "Dear man. We constantly find your bugs and plant them next to tape recordings of the Beatles."

"You only find the bugs we want you to find."

"Nonsense."

"Truth." Traktor didn't mention the eleven kilos of electronic gear that had been strapped to various parts of his fleshy anatomy before he had been allowed to visit the British embassy.

"Ah, well, no matter . . ." Trafalgar gave up the argument with an airy wave of his hand. "The basic question is quite simple: What are you going to do about this ridiculous supersonic zeppelin idea of the Americans?"

Traktor pursed his lips and studied his friend's face for a moment, like a garage mechanic trying to figure out how much a customer will hold still for.

"Why do you call it ridiculous?" he asked.

"You don't think it's ridiculous?" Trafalgar asked.

They sparred for more than an hour before they both finally admitted that (a) their own supersonic transport planes were financially ruinous, and (b) they were both secretly working on plans to build supersonic zeppelins.

After establishing that confidence, both men were silent for a long, long time. The car drove out to the limit allowed by diplomatic protocol for a British embassy vehicle, then headed back for Moscow. The driver could clearly see the onion-shaped spires of churches before Trafalgar finally broke down and asked quietly:

"Em . . . Sergei, old man, . . . do you suppose that we could work together on this zeppelin thing? It might save us both a good deal of money and time. And it would help us to catch up with the Americans."

"Impossible," said Traktor.

"I'm sure the thought has crossed your mind before this," Trafalgar said.

"Working with a capitalist nation . . ."

"Two capitalist nations," Trafalgar corrected. "The French are in with us."

Traktor said nothing.

"After all, you've worked with the French before. It's difficult, I know. But it can be done. And my own government is now in the hands of the Socialist Party."

"Improbable," said Traktor.

"And you *do* want to overtake the Americans, don't you?"

The President's desk was cleared of papers. Nothing cluttered the broad expanse of redwood except three phones (red, white and black), a memento from an early Latin America tour (a fist-sized rock), and a Ping-Pong paddle.

The President sat back in the elevated chair behind the desk and fired instructions at his personal staff.

"I want to make it absolutely clear," he was saying to his press secretary, "that we are not in a race with the Russians or anybody else. We're building our SSZ for very sound economic and social reasons, not for competition with the Russians."

"Right, Chief," said the press secretary.

He turned to his top congressional liaison man. "And you'd better make darned certain that the Senate Appropriations Committee votes the extra funds for the SSZ. Tell them that if we don't get the extra funding, we'll fall behind the Reds.

"And I want you," he said to the Director of TURD, "to spend every nickel of your existing SSZ money as fast as you can. Otherwise we won't be able to get Congress to put in more money."

"Yes sir."

"But, Chief," the head of Budget Management started to object.

"I know what you're going to say," the President said to the top BUM. "I'm perfectly aware that money doesn't grow on trees. But we've got to make the SSZ a success . . . and before next November. Take money from education, from poverty, from the space program—anything. I want that SSZ flying by next spring, when I'm scheduled to visit Paris, Moscow and Peking."

The whole staff gasped in sudden realization of the President's master plan.

"That's entirely correct," he said, smiling slyly at them. "I want to be the first Chief of State to cross the Atlantic, Europe and Asia in a supersonic aircraft."

The VA hospital in Hagerstown had never seen so many reporters. There were reporters in the lobby, reporters lounging in the halls, reporters bribing nurses, reporters sneaking into elevators and surgical theaters (where they inevitably fainted). The parking lot was a jumble of cars bearing press stickers.

Only two reporters were allowed to see Mark Sequoia on any given day, and they had to share their story with all the other newsmen. Today the two—picked by lot—were a crusty old veteran from UPI and a rather pretty blonde from *Women's Wear Daily*.

"But I've told your colleagues what happened at least a dozen times," Sequoia mumbled from behind a swathing of bandages.

He was hanging by both arms and legs from four traction braces, his backside barely touching the bed. Bandages covered eighty percent of his body.

The two reporters stood by his bed. UPI looked flinty as he scribbled some notes on a rumpled sheet of paper. The blonde had a tiny tape recorder in her hand.

She looked misty-eyed. "Are . . . are you in much pain?"

"Not really," Sequoia answered bravely, with a slight tremor in his voice.

"Why the damned traction?" UPI asked in a tone reminiscent of a cement mixer riding over a gravel road. "The docs said there weren't any broken bones."

"Splinters," Sequoia said weakly.

"Bone splinters? Oh, how awful!" gasped the blonde.

"No—" Sequoia corrected. "Splinters. When the balloon came down, it landed in a clump of trees just outside of Hagerstown. We all suffered from thousands of splinters. It took the surgical staff here three days to pick all the splinters out of us. The chief of surgery said he was going to save the wood and build a scale model of the *Titanic* with it. . . ."

"Oh, how painful!" The blonde insisted on gasping. She gasped very well, Sequoia noted, watching her blouse.

"And what about your hair?" asked UPI gruffly.

Sequoia felt himself blush. "I . . . I must have been very frightened. After all, we were aloft in an open balloon for six days, without food, without anything to drink except a six-pack of beer that one of my aides brought along. We went through a dozen different thunderstorms. . . ."

"With lightning?" the blonde asked.

Nodding painfully, Sequoia added, "We all thought we were going to die."

UPI frowned. "So your hair turned white from fright. There was some talk that cosmic rays might have done it."

"Cosmic rays? We weren't that high. . . . Cosmic rays don't have any effect until you get to very high altitudes . . . isn't that right?"

"How high did you go?"

"I don't know," Sequoia answered. "We didn't have an altimeter with us. Those thunderstorms pushed us pretty high, the air got kind of thin. . . ."

"But not high enough for cosmic-ray damage."

"I doubt it."

"Too bad," said UPI. "Would've made a better story than just being scared. Hair turned white by cosmic rays. Maybe even sterilized."

"Sterilized?"

"Cosmic rays do that, too," UPI said. "I checked."

"Well, we weren't that high."

"You're sure?"

"Yeah . . . well, I don't think we were that high."

"But you could have been."

Shrugging was sheer torture, Sequoia found out.

"Okay, but those thunderstorms could've lifted you pretty damned high. . . ."

The door opened and a horse-faced nurse said firmly, "That's all, please. Mr. Sequoia must rest now."

"Okay, I think I got something to hang a story onto," UPI said with a happy grin on his seamed face.

The blonde looked shocked and terribly upset. "You . . . you don't think you were really sterilized, do you?"

Sequoia tried to make himself sound worried and brave at the same time. "I don't know. I just . . . don't know."

Late that night the blonde snuck back into his room. If she knew the difference between sterilization and impotence, she didn't tell Sequoia about it. On his part, he forgot about his still-tender skin and his traction braces. The day nurse found him the next morning, unconscious, one shoulder dislocated, his skin terribly inflamed, most of his bandages rubbed off and a silly grin on his face.

"Will you look at this!"

Senator Goodyear tossed the morning *Post* across the breakfast table to his wife. She was a handsome woman: nearly as tall as her husband, athletically lean, shoulder-length dark hair with just a wisp of silver. She always dressed for breakfast just as carefully as for dinner. This morning she was going riding, so she wore slacks and a turtleneck sweater that outlined her figure.

But the senator was more interested in the *Post* article. "That Sequoia! He'll stop at nothing to destroy me! Just because the Ohio River melted his houseboat once, years ago . . . he's been out to crucify me ever since."

Mrs. Goodyear looked up from the newspaper. "Sterilized? You mean that people who fly in the SSZ could be sterilized by cosmic rays?"

"Utter nonsense!" Goodyear snapped.

"Of course," his wife murmured soothingly.

But after the senator drove off in his chauffeured limousine, Mrs. Goodyear made three phone calls. One was to the Smithsonian Institution. The second was to a friend in the Zero Population Growth movement. The third was to the underground Washington headquarters of the Women's International Terrorist Conspiracy from Hell. Unbeknownst to her husband or any of her friends or associates, Mrs. Goodyear was an undercover agent for WITCH.

The first snow of Virginia's winter was sifting gently past Roger K. Memo's office window. He was pacing across the plastic-tiled floor, his footsteps faintly echoing in the too-large room. Copies of the *Washington Post, New York Times* and *Aviation Week* were spread across his desk.

Dr. Pencilbeam sat at one of the unmatched conference chairs, all bony limbs and elbows and knees.

"Relax, Roger," he said calmly. "Congress isn't going to stop the SSZ. It means too many jobs, too much international prestige. And besides, the President has staked his credibility on it."

"That's what worries me," Memo mumbled.

"What?"

But Memo's eye was caught by movement outside his window. He waddled past his desk and looked out at the street below.

"Oh, my God."

"What's going on?" Pencilbeam unfolded like a pocket ruler into a six-foot-long human and hurried to the window.

Outside, in the thin mushy snow, a line of somber men was filing down the street past the TURD building. Silently they bore screaming signs:

STOP THE SSZ
DON'T STERILIZE THE HUMAN RACE
SSZ MURDERS UNBORN CHILDREN
ZEPPELINS, GO HOME

"Isn't that one with the sign about unborn children a priest?" Pencilbeam asked.

Memo shrugged. "Your eyes are better than mine."

"Ah-hah! And look at this!"

Pencilbeam pointed further down the street. A swarm of women was advancing on the building. They also carried signs:

SSZ FOR ZPG
ZEPPELINS SI! BABIES NO
ZEPPELINS FOR POPULATION CONTROL
UP THE SSZ

Memo visibly sagged at the window. "This . . . this is awful. . . ."

The women marched through the thin snowfall and straight into the line of picketing men. Instantly the silence was shattered by shouts and taunts. Shrill female voices battled against rumbling baritones and basses. Signs wavered. Bodies pushed. Someone screamed. One sign struck a skull and then bloody war broke out.

Memo and Pencilbeam watched aghast until the helmeted TAC squad police doused the whole scene with riot gas, impartially clubbed men and women and dragged everyone off.

The huge factory assembly bay was filled with the skeleton of a giant dirigible. Great aluminum ribs stretched from titanium nosecap back toward the more intricate cagework of the tail fins. Tiny men with flashing laser welders crawled along the ribbing like maggots cleaning the bones of a noble whale.

Even the jet engines sitting on their loading pallets dwarfed human scale. Some of the welders held clandestine poker games inside them. John Driver and Richard Grand stood beside one of them, craning their necks to watch the welding work going on far overhead. The assembly bay rang to the shouts of working men, the hum of electrical machinery and the occasional clatter of metal against metal.

"It's going to be some Christmas party if Congress cancels the project," Driver said gloomily from behind his inevitable pipe.

"Oh, they wouldn't dare cancel it, now that Women's Liberation is behind it," said Grand with a sardonic little smile.

Driver glared at him. "With those bitches for allies, you don't need any enemies. Half those idiots in Congress will vote against us just to prove that they're not scared of Women's Lib."

"Do you really think so?" Grand asked.

He always acts as if he knows more than I do, Driver thought. It had taken him several years to realize that Grand actually knew rather less than most people—but had a way of hiding this behind protective language.

"Yes, I really think so!" Driver snapped. Then he pulled his pipe out of his mouth and jabbed it in the general direction of Grand's eyeballs. "And listen to me, kiddo. I've been working on that secretary of mine since the last god-damned Christmas party. If this project falls through and the party's a bust, that palpitating hunk of female flesh is going to run home and cry. And so will I!"

Grand blinked several times, then murmured, "Pity."

The banner saying HAPPY HOLIDAYS drooped sadly across one wall of the cafeteria. Outside in the darkness, lights glimmered, cars were moving, and a bright moon lit the snowy peak of Mt. Olympia.

But inside Everett Aircraft's cafeteria there was nothing but gloom. The Christmas party had been a dismal flop, especially so since half the company's employees had received their layoff notices the day before.

The tables had been pushed to one side of the cafeteria to make room for a dance floor. Syrupy music was oozing out of the loudspeakers in the acoustic-tile ceiling. But no one was dancing.

Bob Wisdom sat at one of the tables, propping his aching head on his hands. Ray Kurtz and Tommy Rohr sat with him, equally dejected.

"Why the hell did they have to cancel the project two days before Christmas?" Rohr asked rhetorically.

"Makes for more pathos," Kurtz muttered from inside his beard.

"It's pathetic, all right," Wisdom said. "I've never seen so many secretaries crying at once."

"Even Driver was crying," Rohr said.

"Well," Kurtz said, staring at his half-finished drink on the table before him, "Sequoia did it. He's a big national hero again."

"And we're on the bread line," Rohr said.

"You get laid off?"

"Not yet—but it's coming. This place will be closing its doors before another year is out."

"It's not that bad," said Wisdom. "There's still the Air Force work."

Rohr frowned. "You know what gets me? The way the whole project was scrapped, without giving us a chance to build one of the damned zeps and see how they work. Without a goddam chance!"

Kurtz said, "Congressmen are scared of being sterilized."

"Or castrated by Women's Lib."

"Next time you dream up a project, Bob, make it underground. Something in a lead mine. Then the congressmen won't have to worry about cosmic rays."

Wisdom started to laugh, then held off. "You know," he said slowly, "you just might have something there."

"What?"

"Where?"

"A supersonic transport—in a tunnel."

"Oh, for Chri—"

Wisdom sat up straight in his chair. "No, listen. You could make an air-cushion vehicle go supersonic. If you put it in a tunnel, you get away from the sonic boom and the pollution. . . ."

"Hey, the safety aspects would be a lot better, too."

Kurtz shook his head. "You guys are crazy! Who the hell's going to dig tunnels all over the United States?"

But Wisdom waved him down. "Somebody will. Now, the way I see the design of this . . . SSST, I guess we call it."

"SSST?"

"Sure," he answered, grinning. "Supersonic subway train."

BLESSED BE THE PEACEMAKERS

While the Supersonic Zeppelin is obviously a spoof, the possibility of building defenses in orbit that can protect us against nuclear missile attack is very real. The automatic Luddite reaction to President Reagan's speech of 23 March 1983 was a loud "No!" But this is a case that involves life and death for the entire human race, and it must be examined very carefully, honestly and *openly* by Luddites and Prometheans alike. We may have a chance to remove the terrible threat of nuclear devastation. But like a man defusing a live bomb, we must approach this task with great care and caution.

It is a hopeful sign that at their summit meeting in Geneva in 1985, President Reagan and General Secretary Gorbachev took the first step toward the cooperative program I have advocated.

President Reagan's call for a defense against nuclear attack, using the most scientifically advanced means possible, marks the beginning of a new era in international politics.

In a small way, it is an era I helped to create. I worked at the laboratory where the first breakthrough into truly high-power lasers was made. In February 1966, I helped to arrange the first top secret meeting in the Pentagon to reveal to the Defense Department what our laboratory had accomplished. A group of scientists from our lab, the Avco Everett Research Laboratory, spent more than an hour explaining that lasers of truly enormous power output could now be made. When the last slide was shown, the slide projector turned off and the overhead lights came on, there was a long moment of awed silence—from the best scientists the Pentagon could bring together.

Within months, we were not only developing the technology of high-power lasers, we were also studying how they might be used. Some of the potential uses of such lasers were peaceful: drilling tunnels in hard rock, welding and cutting metal at high speeds, communicating over interplanetary distances.

The most significant weapons application for high-power lasers, however, appeared to be in space—where there is no air to absorb or distort the laser's beam of energy, where the distances between laser and target could be thousands of miles, and where the targets themselves would be moving at thousands of miles per hour.

To give you an idea of the kinds of power outputs these lasers can produce, in 1970 Avco Everett sold a relatively low-power laser to Caterpillar Tractor Company's research laboratory in Muncie, Indiana. This laser produced a mere 10,000 watts output, too low to be of interest to the military. That 10-kilowatt beam cut through three-quarter-inch steel at rates of 50 to 100 inches per minute. Today, Avco sells 100-kilowatt lasers on the commercial marketplace. Military classification begins at higher power levels.

Since the mid-sixties I have been thinking and writing about the technical, political and human implications of using high-power lasers in orbit as a defense against nuclear missile attack. In novels such as *Millennium* and nonfiction books such as *The High Road* I have examined various scenarios dealing with the inevitable time when such weaponry is put in space. It could bring about the end of the threat of nuclear holocaust. But it might also, instead, trigger the very nuclear Armageddon we all fear.

Today all Americans are hostage to the nuclear missiles of the Soviet Union. By deliberate government policy, every American man, woman and child is defenseless against a Soviet missile attack. We have agreed, by the terms of the SALT I accord, not even to attempt to defend our cities and our population. And the Russians have agreed to the same terms.

Since Hiroshima, strategic policy has been based entirely on the idea that there is no visible defense against a determined nuclear attack. Our official policy is literally MAD: Mutual Assured Destruction. We strive to maintain a nuclear attack force that is so strong that even if the Soviets launch a first strike at us, our counterstrike will annihilate the Soviet Union. And the Russians do the same.

This MAD policy has produced the continuing nuclear arms race that has terrified so many people around the world. The nuclear freeze movement is an attempt by people in Europe and America to stop the constant escalation of nuclear weapons. It is a well-intended movement, but it is doomed to failure—unless someone, somewhere, finds a way to assure the leaders in Washington and Moscow that they can actually protect their nations from nuclear annihilation.

Now technology offers the possibility of creating a workable defense against nuclear missiles. Critics of the idea claim that it is impossible, or at least undesirable. Crazy as it may seem, there are some allegedly thoughtful people in America whose instant reaction to the President's suggestion was that it is preferable to live under a nuclear Sword of Damocles than to build a credible defense against nuclear war. This is akin to Neville Chamberlain's hope, when he was Prime Minister of Great Britain in the 1930s, that he could appease Hitler and avert war.

I, for one, do not choose to spend the rest of my life, and the lives of my children, and *their* children, under the constant threat of nuclear holocaust. If there is a way to defend us, it is deadly nonsense to ignore it.

But—and this is the point on which our entire future will turn—we must be prepared not only to open our minds to bold new technological concepts; we must be prepared to consider fairly and openly equally bold new *political* ideas. For just as the technology of gunpowder eventually blew away the political system based on kings and emperors, just as the technology of aircraft ended Britain's snug, smug feeling of safety on their tight little isle, the new technology of space weaponry is going to change international politics forever.

The first political reality we must face is that we no longer live in a bipolarized world of two superpowers, their various allies and satellites, and a scattering of small, poor nations that don't count when it comes to political power. True, our major military concerns all center on the Soviet Union. But the People's Republic of China has nuclear-tipped missiles. So do France and Great Britain. India is launching satellites with its own rockets, and has tested its own nuclear bomb. Pakistan, the most likely target of India's missiles, is undoubtedly trying to produce its own nuclear arsenal so that it, too, can engage in a MAD policy.

What will the world be like in the 1990s, when nations such as Argentina and Libya may have nuclear weapons and missiles to deliver them? Will Iraq finally produce its own nuclear bombs, and if it does, will it use them first against Iran or Israel?

It may be that none of the smaller nations would ever dream of aiming a nuclear-tipped missile at an American city. But would you bet your life on that?

A second fact we must face is that we are not the only nation in the world that might build orbital defenses. Most

American pundits who have come out against what they call "the Star Wars defense" have tacitly assumed that if the United States does not place defensive weapons in orbit, nobody will. That is arrant foolishness. We can decide if *we* will build orbital defense weapons; we cannot decide if the Soviets or other nations will.

Make no mistake: the Soviet Union has been developing this technology for almost as long as we have, and in several key areas of development they are far ahead of us.

In the 1960s, as we at Avco Everett were working on the earliest high-power lasers, we watched the Russian scientific literature carefully. At that time, the Soviets did not classify theoretical work. We saw them developing the same ideas that we ourselves had developed only a year or two earlier. And when those ideas converged on the realization that lasers of virtually unlimited power could be built, all that work disappeared from the open, unclassified scientific journals.

Through the 1970s, as the American space program became moribund after Washington killed the Apollo program, the Soviets sent scores of cosmonauts into orbit aboard a succession of space stations they call Salyuts. Salyut 7 is in orbit today. It is larger than any previous Soviet space station, and may well be the permanent platform from which the Russians will test their own orbital energy weapons.

Soviet scientists have worked hard not only on lasers, but also on particle-beam devices, which fire a stream of subatomic particles such as protons. As a weapon, particle-beam devices may prove to be more effective than lasers. The Soviets have also pushed development of the kinds of electrical power systems that are needed to "drive" high-power lasers and particle-beam weapons.

For nearly twenty years the Soviets have flown military weaponry in space. While both the United States and the

USSR have placed into orbit satellites for military surveillance, communications, early warning, weather observation and mapping, only the Soviets have put actual weapons into space. They have an operational antisatellite weapon system, and unconfirmed leaks from intelligence sources claim that they have blinded American surveillance satellites by firing lasers at them from the ground.

As much as we may want to keep space free of weaponry, the fact is that the military got into space before anyone else did, and that space is already a theater of military operations. The best thing we can do, the wisest thing we can do, is to try to use space in a way that will shield us against nuclear attack.

Is it possible? Technologically, yes. There is no reason why we cannot develop orbital weapons that will find, track and destroy ballistic missiles bearing nuclear warheads. Satellites armed with lasers, particle-beam weapons, or even pellet guns or small missiles could destroy ballistic missiles while their rocket engines are still boosting them, when they are still over their own territory and very vulnerable to attack.

Earlier proposals for defense against ballistic missiles were based on the idea of firing antimissile missiles from the ground at incoming nuclear warheads. Tests proved that you could shoot down a single warhead that way, but that such an antimissile system would be easily overwhelmed by a full-scale attack of hundreds of warheads, decoys and radarjamming techniques.

The idea of defending against missile attack with ground-based antimissile missiles was something like trying to play football by giving your opponent the ball on your own five-yard line, and allowing him five hundred downs in which to score—and in a situation that is truly "sudden death." So the United States agreed to the SALT I treaty provision that limits us—and the USSR—to building only one antimissile system. We soon gave up even on that, convinced that a ground-based system would not work. The Soviets have built their system to protect Moscow, whether it works or not.

Orbital defenses, in which weapons aboard satellites fire at the attacking missiles as soon as they are launched, is more like playing football in midfield, or even on your opponent's five-yard line.

Critics of the idea claim that building an orbital defense system would violate the 1972 ABM treaty. However, the treaty specifically allows *research and development* efforts on missile defense to be carried out. That is what we should be doing. It is undoubtedly what the Soviet Union is already doing. When we are convinced that R&D efforts will lead to an effective defense, it is time to return to the bargaining table.

The loudest argument that critics of orbital defenses make, however, is their claim that such a system will not work. Their forefathers made similar claims against repeating rifles, submarines, airplanes, ballistic missiles and almost every other new idea they ever heard of.

The critics point out that no defense system is perfect, and that some attacking missiles will get through to deliver their nuclear warheads on target. That is quite true. But remember that the goal we pursue is *deterrence*. No one wants to dare the Soviet Union to attack us. We wish to prevent them from deciding that they can or should attack.

If the USSR knows that a substantial portion of its missile force will be destroyed long before the missiles reach their targets, and that a powerful American force will survive a Soviet first strike and be capable of a devastating counterstrike, the decision-makers in the Kremlin will no doubt stay their hand, even though they could inflict considerable damage on the United States. As Admiral Yamamoto reflected after the Japanese attack on Pearl Harbor, it does not pay to enrage a giant.

How would the Soviets respond to such an American buildup of orbital defenses? Perhaps they would respond by producing more ballistic missiles, so that they could overwhelm our defenses and deliver enough warheads on target to demolish our counterstrike missiles, bombers and submarines.

Or, more likely, they would launch a strike when it became clear to them that we are building defenses that will ultimately make their attack forces obsolete and useless. Already the Kremlin has branded Star Wars as a threat against the USSR. In their view, a system that protects the United States against Soviet nuclear attack would lead the U.S. to think that it could attack Russia with impunity. Therefore, Moscow would feel justified in launching a preemptive strike before the U.S. could complete its defensive shield.

All of this reasoning works both ways, of course. What the Soviets are doing in space to defend themselves against our missiles could be seen as a direct threat to America.

It seems clear that orbital defensive systems can be built; if not this year, then certainly in the foreseeable future. Thus the question of whether or not they *should* be built becomes of primary importance now, today.

It will cost tens or even hundreds of billions of dollars to build such an orbiting defensive shield. But what price tag do you place on survival? How much are you willing to pay to prevent nuclear war from happening?

If we match the technological wizardry of high-power lasers and satellite defense systems with equally high-powered political initiatives, we do have a chance—a good chance—of making nuclear war almost impossible.

The key to this is simple in concept, but terribly difficult in practice. It is this: invite the Soviets, the Chinese, the Europeans—everyone in the world—to join us in the effort to build and deploy such defensive satellites.

If we have the moral courage to make this program completely open, and invite the rest of the world to participate in it, sharing our knowledge with them, and placing the orbiting satellites under international control, then we may have found the way to prevent *any* nation from launching a nuclear attack on any other nation.

What we need is a form of Swiss Guard in orbit, an international organization that has the power to destroy any rocket launched from anywhere in the world, if that rocket has not been inspected and found to be carrying only a peaceful payload.

Such an organization would discourage nations from developing nuclear arsenals, or from enlarging the arsenals they already have. And an international program could spread the costs of the system among all the participating nations.

Would the United States voluntarily give up its right to attack its enemies? Would we willingly place our own defense in the hands of some international organization? That *must* be the basis for a full and thorough political dialogue within our own society.

Would the Soviet Union, with its historic fear of invasion and almost-paranoiac insistence on secrecy, be willing to allow such an international organization to control its defenses? I believe the Kremlin would join such an effort, for two reasons:

First, most of the rest of the world would quickly agree to such a global defense system, and the Soviets would find themselves facing not only the U.S. and Western Europe, but almost the whole world. It would be more advantageous to the Soviet Union to join the peace-keeping force than to isolate itself.

Second, by neutralizing the world's nuclear arsenals, the Soviets—with their heavy preponderance of conventional military arms—would feel more secure than they do today. By removing the threat of nuclear war, their advantages in numbers of tanks, guns and planes becomes more important to them. And to us.

Clearly, orbital defenses against nuclear-armed missiles are not the answer to every problem that faces the world. But they can be the answer to nuclear Armageddon, and that is a major step forward for the human race's prospects of survival.

If it is impossible to freeze nuclear weapons, we should at least try to melt them.

THE WEATHERMAKERS

The dream of controlling the weather all around the world is one of the ultimate Promethean fantasies. The Luddite in us warns that we should not even attempt to do it. The practical problems of weather *forecasting,* without even thinking of modifying the weather, are enormous. But when you stop to think that we are just as helpless in the face of the weather as any Stone Age hunter was, you begin to wonder if it wouldn't be a better world where the weather was under firm human control, where, in the words of lyricist Alan Jay Lerner, "The rain may never fall 'til after sundown/By nine p.m. the moonlight must appear. . . ."

∎

Ted Marrett gathered us around the mammoth viewscreen-map that loomed over his desk in the THUNDER control center. The map showed a full-fledged hurricane—Nora—howling up the mid-Atlantic. Four more tropical disturbances, marked by red danger symbols, were strung out along the fifteenth parallel from the Antilles Islands to the Cape Verdes.

"There's the story," Ted told us, prowling impatiently along the foot of the viewscreen. He moved his tall, powerful body with the feline grace of a professional athlete. His stubborn red hair and rough-hewn face made him look more like a football gladiator than "the whiz-kid boss of

Project THUNDER," as the news magazines had called him.

Gesturing toward the map, Ted said, "Nora's no problem; she'll stay out at sea. Won't even bother Bermuda much. But these four lows'll bug us."

Tuli Noyon, Ted's closest buddy and chief of the Air Chemistry Section, said in his calm Oriental way, "This is the day we have all been dreading. There are more disturbances than we can handle. One of them, possibly two, will get past us and form hurricanes."

Ted looked sharply at him, then turned to me. "How about it, Jerry? What's the logistics picture?"

"Tuli's right," I admitted. "The planes and crews have been working around the clock for the past few weeks and we just don't have enough . . ."

"Skip the flute music. How many of these Lows can we hit?"

I shrugged. "Two, I'd say. Maybe three if we really push it."

Barney—Priscilla Barneveldt—said, "The computer just finished an updated statistical analysis on the four disturbances. Their storm tracks all threaten the East Coast. The two closest ones have point-eight probabilities of reaching hurricane strength. The farther pair are only point-five."

"Fifty-fifty," Ted muttered, "for the last two. But they've got the longest time to develop. Chances'll be better for 'em by tomorrow."

Barney was slim and blond as a Dutch jonquil, and had a true Hollander's stubborn spirit. "It's those two closest disturbances that are the most dangerous," she insisted. "They each have an eighty percent chance of turning into hurricanes that will hit the East Coast."

"We can't stop them all," Tuli said. "What will we do, Ted?"

* * *

Project THUNDER: Threatening Hurricane Neutralization, Destruction and Recording. Maybe we were young and daring and slightly fanatical, as the newsmen had said of us. But it took more than knowledge and skill. THUNDER was Ted Marrett's creation, the result of nearly four years of his singleminded determination. None of us would have dared it, even if there were a hundred more of us, without Ted to lead the way. He had brought the Project into being, practically with his own strong hands.

Yet it wasn't enough, not for Ted Marrett. He wasn't satisfied with an experimental program to modify potential hurricanes. Ted wanted to control the weather, fully. Nothing less. To him THUNDER was only a small shadow of what could be done toward controlling the weather. He had said as much to the press, and now the world expected us to prevent all hurricanes from striking the islands of the Caribbean and the North American mainland.

It was an impossible task.

"Where's the analysis?" Ted asked Barney. "I want to go over the numbers."

She looked around absently. "I must have left it on my desk. I'll go get it."

Ted's phone buzzed. He leaned across the desk and flicked the switch. "Dr. Weis calling from Washington," the operator said.

He made a sour face. "Okay, put him on." Sliding into his desk chair, Ted waved us away as Dr. Weis's tanned, well-creased face came on the phone viewscreen.

"I've just seen this morning's weather map," the President's science advisor said with no preliminaries. "It looks to me as though you're in trouble."

"Got our hands full," Ted said.

I started back for my own cubicle. I could hear Dr. Weis's

nasal voice, a little edgier than usual, saying, "The opposition has turned Project THUNDER into a political issue, with only six weeks to the election. If you hadn't made the newsmen think that you could stop every hurricane . . ."

The rest was lost in the chatter and bustle of the control room. THUNDER's nerve center filled the entire second floor of our Miami bayfront building. It was a frenetic conglomeration of people, desks, calculating machines, plotting boards, map printers, cabinets, teletypes, phones, viewscreens and endless piles of paper. Over it all hung Ted's giant electronic plotting screen, showing our battlefield—all of North America and the North Atlantic Ocean. I made my way across the cluttered windowless room and stepped into my glass-walled cubicle.

It was quiet inside, with the door closed. Phone screens lined the walls, and half my desk was covered with a private switchboard that put me in direct contact with a network of THUNDER support stations ranging from New Orleans to ships off the coast of Africa to the Atlantic Satellite Station, in synchronous orbit 23,000 miles above the mouth of the Amazon River.

I looked across the control center again, and saw Ted still talking earnestly into the phone. Dr. Weis called every day. THUNDER was important to him, and to the President. If we failed . . . I didn't like to think of the consequences.

There was work to be done. I began alerting the Navy and Air Force bases that were supporting THUNDER, trying to get ready to hit those hurricane threats as hard and fast as we could.

While I worked, I watched Barney and Ted plowing through the thick sheaf of computer printout sheets that contained the detailed analysis of the storm threats. They made a good-looking couple, and everyone assumed that she was Ted's girl. Including Ted himself. But he never bothered to ask Barney about it. Or me.

As soon as I could, I went down and joined them.

"Okay," he was saying, "if we leave those two fartherout Lows alone, they'll develop into hurricanes overnight. We can knock 'em out now without much sweat, but by tomorrow they'll be too much for us."

"The same applies to the second disturbance," Barney said, "only more so. It's already better developed than the two farther lows."

"We'll have to skip the second one. The first one—off the Leewards—is too close to ignore. So we'll hit Number One, skip the second, and hit Three and Four."

Barney took her glasses off. "That won't work, Ted," she said firmly. "If we don't stop the second one today it certainly will develop into—"

"A walloping big hurricane. I know." He shrugged. "But if we throw enough planes at Number Two to smother it, we'll have to leave Three and Four alone. Then they'll both develop and we'll have *two* brutes on our hands."

"But this one . . ."

"There's a chance that if we knock out the closest Low, Number Two'll change its track and head out to sea."

"That's a terribly slim chance. The numbers show—"

"Okay, it's a slim chance. But it's all we've got to work with. Got any better ideas?"

"Isn't there anything we can do?" she asked. "If a hurricane strikes the coast . . ."

"Weis is already looking through his mail for my resignation," Ted said. "Okay, we're in trouble. Best we can do is hit Number One, skip Two, and wipe out Three and Four before they get strong enough to make waves."

Barney stared at the numbers on the computer sheets. "That means we're going to have a full-grown hurricane heading for Florida within twenty-four hours."

"Look," Ted snapped, "we can sit around here debating

till they *all* turn into hurricanes. Let's scramble. Jerry, you heard the word. Get the planes up."

I headed back to my cubicle and sent out the orders. A few minutes later, Barney came by. Standing dejectedly in the doorway, she asked herself out loud:

"Why did he agree to take on this Project? He knows it's not the best way to handle hurricanes. It's too chancy, too expensive, we're working ourselves to death. . . ."

"So are the aircrews," I answered. "And the season's just starting to hit its peak."

"Then why did he have to make the newsmen think we could run up a perfect score the first year?"

"Because he's Ted Marrett. He not only thinks he can control the weather, he thinks he *owns* it."

"There's no room in him for failure," she said. "If this storm does hit, if the Project is canceled . . . what will it do to him?"

"What will it do to you?" I asked her.

She shook her head. "I don't know, Jerry. But I'm afraid we're going to find out in another day or two."

Tropical storms are built on seemingly slight differences of air temperature. A half-dozen degrees of difference over an area a hundred miles in diameter can power the giant heat engine of a hurricane. Ted's method of smothering tropical disturbances before they reached hurricane strength was to smooth out the temperature difference between the core of the disturbance and its outer fringes.

The nearest disturbance was developing quickly. It had already passed over the Leeward Islands and entered the Caribbean by the time our first planes reached it. The core of the disturbance was a column of warm, rising air, shooting upward from the sea's surface to the tropopause, some ten miles high. Swirling around this warm column was cooler air sliding down from the north into the low-pressure trough created by the warm column.

If the disturbance were left to itself, it would soak up moisture from the warm sea and condense it into raindrops. The heat released by the condensation would power winds of ever-mounting intensity. A cycle would be established: winds bring in moisture, the water vapor condenses into rain, the heat released builds the winds' power. Finally the core would switch over into a cold, clear column of downward-rushing air—the eye of a full-grown hurricane. A thousand megatons of energy would be loose, unstoppable, even by Project THUNDER.

Our job was to prevent that cycle from establishing itself. We had to warm up the air flowing into the disturbance and chill down its core until air temperatures throughout the disturbance were practically the same. A heat engine that has all its parts at the same temperature—or close to it—simply won't work.

We had been doing that job successfully since July. But now, in mid-September, with the hurricane season nearing its peak, there were more disturbances than we could handle simultaneously.

As I started giving out the orders for three missions at once, Tuli stuck his head into my cubicle.

"I'm off to see the dragon firsthand." He was grinning excitedly.

"Which one?"

"Number One dragon; it's in the Caribbean now."

"I know. Good luck. Kill it dead."

He nodded, a round-faced, brown-skinned St. George working against the most destructive menace man had ever faced.

As I parceled out orders over my phones, a battery of gigajoule lasers aboard the Atlantic Station began pumping their energy into the northern peripheries of the storms.

The lasers were part of our project. Similar to the military type mounted in the missle-defense satellites, they had been put aboard the Atlantic Station at Ted's request, and with the personal backing of Dr. Weis and the White House. Only carefully selected Air Force personnel were allowed near them. The entire section of the satellite Station where they were installed was under armed guard, much to the discomfort of the civilians aboard.

Planes from a dozen airfields were circling the northern edges of the disturbances, sowing the air with rain-producing crystals.

"Got to seed for hours at a time," Ted had once told me. "That's a mistake the early experimenters made—never stayed on the job long enough to force an effect on the weather."

And thanks to chemical wizards like Tuli, we had a wide assortment of seeding materials that could squeeze rain from almost any type of air mass. Producing the tonnage of crystals we needed had been a problem, but the Army's Edgewood Arsenal had stepped in with their mass-production facilities to help us.

I was watching the disturbance in the Caribbean. That was the closest threat, and the best-developed of all the four disturbances. Radar plots, mapped on Ted's giant viewscreen, showed rain clouds expanding and showering precipitation over an ever-widening area. As the water vapor in the seeded air condensed into raindrops, the air temperature rose slightly. The satellite-borne lasers were also helping to heat the air feeding into the disturbance.

It looked as though we were just making the disturbance bigger. But Ted and the other technical staff people had figured out the energy balances in the storm. They knew what they were doing . . . but I still found myself frowning worriedly.

Tuli was in an Air Force bomber, part of two squadrons of planes flying at staggered altitudes. From nearly sea level to fifty thousand feet, they roared into the central column of warm air in precise formation and began dumping tons of liquid nitrogen into the rising tropical air.

The effect was spectacular. The TV screen alongside the big plotting screen showed what the planes saw: tremendous plumes of white sprang out behind each plane as the cryogenic liquid flash-froze the water vapor in the warm column. It looked as though some cosmic wind had suddenly spewed its frigid breath through the air. The nitrogen quickly evaporated, soaking up enormous amounts of heat. Most of the frozen vapor simply evaporated again, although radar plots showed that some condensation and actual rainfall occurred.

I made my way to Ted's desk to see the results of the core freezing.

"Looks good," he was saying into a phone.

I checked the teletype chugging nearby. It was printing a report from the observation planes that followed the bombers.

Ted stepped over to me. "Broke up the core okay. Now if she doesn't re-form, we can scratch Number One off the map."

It was early evening before we could tell for sure. The disturbance's source of energy, the differing temperatures of the air masses it contained, had been taken away from it. The plotting screen showed a large swatch of concentric, irregular isobars, like a lopsided bull's-eye, with a sullen red "L" marking its center, just north of Jamaica. The numbers of the screen showed a central pressure of 991 millibars, nowhere near a typical hurricane's. Wind speeds had peaked at fifty-two knots and were dying off now. Kingston and Guantanamo were reporting moderate-to-heavy rain, but at Santo Domingo, six hundred miles to the east, it was already clearing.

The disturbance was just another small tropical storm, and a rapidly weakening one at that. The two farther disturbances, halfway out across the ocean, had been completely wiped out. The planes were on their way home. The laser crews aboard the Atlantic Station were recharging their energy storage coils.

"Shall I see if the planes can reload and fly another mission tonight?" I asked Ted. "Maybe we can still hit the second disturbance."

He shook his head. "Won't do any good. Look at her," he said pointing toward the plotting map. "By the time the planes get to her, she'll be a full-grown hurricane. There's nothing we can do about it now."

So we didn't sleep that night. We stayed at the control center and watched the storm develop on the TV picture being beamed from the Atlantic Station. At night they had to use infrared cameras, of course, but we could still see—in the ghostly IR images—a broad spiral of clouds stretching across four hundred miles of open ocean.

Practically no one had left the control center, but the big room was deathly quiet. Even the chattering, calculating machines and teletypes seemed to have stopped. The numbers on the spotting screen steadily worsened. Barometric pressure sank to 980, 965, 950 millibars. Wind velocity mounted to 50 knots, 60, 80. She was a full-grown hurricane by midnight.

Ted leaned across his desk and tapped out a name for the storm on the viewscreen's keyboard: *Omega*.

"One way or the other, she's the end of THUNDER," he murmured.

The letters glowed out at the top of the plotting screen. Across the vast room, one of the girls broke into sobs.

Through the early hours of the morning, Hurricane Omega grew steadily in size and strength. An immense band of clouds towered from the sea to some sixty thousand feet, pouring two inches of rain per hour over an area of nearly 300,000 square miles. The pressure at her core had plummeted to 942 millibars and central wind speeds were gusting at better than 100 knots, and still rising.

"It's almost as though she's alive," Tuli whispered as we watched the viewscreen intently. "She grows, she feeds, she moves."

By 2:00 a.m. Miami time, dawn was breaking over Hurricane Omega. Six trillion tons of air packing the energy of a hundred hydrogen bombs, a mammoth, mindless heat engine turned loose, aiming for civilization, for us.

Waves lashed by Omega's fury were spreading all across the Atlantic and would show up as dangerous surf on the beaches of four continents. Seabirds were sucked into the storm against their every exertion, to be drenched and battered to exhaustion; their only hope was to make it to the eye, where the air was calm and clear. A tramp steamer on the New York-to-Capetown run, five hundred miles from Omega's center, was calling frantically for help as mountainous waves overpowered the ship's puny pumps.

Omega churned onward, releasing every fifteen minutes as much energy as a ten-megaton bomb.

We watched, we listened, fascinated. The face of our enemy, and it made all of us—even Ted—feel completely helpless. At first Omega's eye, as seen from the satellite cameras, was vague and shifting, covered over by cirrus clouds. But finally it steadied and opened up, a strong column of downward-flowing air, the mighty central pillar of the hurricane, the pivotal anchor around which her furious winds wailed their primeval song of violence and terror.

Barney, Tuli and I sat around Ted's desk, watching his face sink deeper into a scowl as the storm worsened.

We didn't realize it was daylight once more until Dr. Weis phoned again. He looked haggard on the tiny desktop viewscreen.

"I've been watching the storm all night," he said. "The President called me a few minutes ago and asked me what you were going to do about it."

Ted rubbed his eyes. "Can't knock her out, if that's what you mean. Too big now; be like trying to stop a forest fire with a blanket."

"Well, you've got to do something!" Weis snapped. "All our reputations hang on that storm. Do you understand? Yours, mine, even the President's! To say nothing of the future for weather-control work in this country, if that means anything to you."

He might just as easily have asked Beethoven if he cared about music.

"Told you back in Washington when we started this game," Ted countered, "that THUNDER was definitely the wrong way to tackle hurricanes. . . ."

"Yes, and then you announced to the press that no hurricanes would strike the United States! So now, instead of being an act of nature, hurricanes are a political issue."

Ted shook his head. "We've done all we can do."

"No, you haven't. You can try to steer the hurricane . . . change its path so that it won't strike the coast."

"Won't work."

"You haven't tried it!"

"We could throw everything we've got into it and maybe budge it a few degrees. It'll still wind up hitting the coast somewhere. All we'll be doing is fouling up its track so we won't know for sure where it'll hit."

"Well, we've got to do something. We can't just sit here and let it happen to us. Ted, I haven't tried to tell you how to run THUNDER, but now I'm giving an order. You've got to make an attempt to steer the storm away from the coast.

If we fail, at least we'll go down fighting. Maybe we can salvage something from this mess."

"Waste of time," Ted muttered.

Dr. Weis's shoulders moved as though he were wringing his hands, off camera. "Try it anyway. It might work. We might just be lucky . . ."

"Okay," Ted said, shrugging. "You're the boss."

The screen went dark. Ted looked up at us. "You heard the man. We're going to play Pied Piper."

"But we can't do it," Tuli said. "It can't be done."

"Doesn't matter. Weis is trying to save face. You ought to understand that, buddy."

Barney looked up at the plotting screen. Omega was northeast of Puerto Rico and boring in toward Florida. Toward us.

"Why didn't you tell him the truth?" she asked Ted. "Why didn't you tell him that the only way to stop the storm is to control the weather across the whole East Coast."

"Been all through this half a million times," Ted grumbled, slouching back in his chair wearily. "Weis won't buy weather control. Hurricane-killing is what he wants."

"But we can't kill Omega. THUNDER has failed, Ted. You shouldn't have—"

"Shouldn't have what?" he snapped. "Shouldn't have taken THUNDER when Weis offered to let us try it? Think I didn't argue with him? Think I didn't fight it out, right in the White House? I know THUNDER's a shaky way to fight hurricanes. But it's all I could get. I had to take what they were willing to give us."

Barney shook her head. "And what has it got you? A disaster."

"Listen," he said, sitting up erect now and pressing his big hands on the desk. "I spelled it out to the President and to Weis. I told 'em both that chasing tropical disturbances and trying to smother hurricanes before they develop is doing things the hard way. Showed 'em how we could control the weather over the whole country. They wouldn't take the chance. Too risky. Think the President wants to get blamed for every cloudy day in Arizona, or every rainfall in California, or every chill in Chicago?"

He stood up and began pacing. "They wanted something spectacular but safe. So they settled on killing hurricanes—very spectacular. But only by making weather mods out at sea, where nobody would complain about 'em—that's safe, see? I told 'em it was the hard way to do the job. But that's what they wanted. And that's what I took. Because I'd rather do *something*, even if it's not the best something. I wanted to show 'em that we can kill hurricanes. If we had gone through this year okay, maybe they would've tried real weather control next year."

"Then why," she asked, very softly, "did you tell the newsmen that we would stop every hurricane threat? You knew we couldn't do it."

"Why? How should I know? Maybe because Weis was sitting there in front of the cameras looking so blasted sure of himself. Safe and serene. Maybe I was crazy enough to think we could really sneak through a whole hurricane season okay. Maybe I'm just crazy, period. I don't know."

"But what do we do now?" I asked.

He cocked an eye at the plotting-screen. "Try to steer Omega. Try saving Weis's precious face." Pointing to a symbol on the map several hundred miles north of the storm, he said, "This's a Navy sonar picket, isn't it? I'm going to buzz out there, see if I can get a firsthand look at this monster."

"That could be dangerous," Barney countered.

He shrugged.

"Ted, you haven't thought this out," I said. "You can't run the operation from the middle of the ocean."

"Picket's in a good spot to see the storm . . . at least, the edge of it. Maybe I can wangle a plane ride through it. Been fighting hurricanes all season without seeing one. Besides, the ship's part of the Navy's antisubmarine-warning net; loaded with communications gear. Be in touch with you every minute, don't worry."

"But if the storm comes that way . . ."

"Let it come," he snapped. "It's going to finish us anyway." He turned and strode off, leaving us to watch him.

Barney turned to me. "Jerry, he thinks we blame him for everything. We've got to stop him."

"No one can stop him. You know that. Once he gets his mind set on something . . ."

"Then I'll go with him." She got up from her chair. I took her arm.

"No, Jerry," she said. "I can't let him go alone."

"Is it the danger you're afraid of, or the fact that he's leaving?"

"Jerry, in the mood he's in now . . . he's reckless . . ."

"All right," I said, trying to calm her. "All right. I'll go with him. I'll make sure he keeps his feet dry."

"I don't want either one of you in danger!"

"I know. I'll take care of him."

She looked at me with those misty gray-green eyes. "Jerry . . . you won't let him do anything foolish, will you?"

"You know me," I said. "I'm no hero."

"Yes, you are," she said. And I felt my insides do a handspring.

I left her there with Tuli and hurried out to the parking lot. The bright sunshine outdoors was a painful surprise. It was hot and muggy, even though the day was only an hour or so old.

Ted was getting into one of the Project staff cars when I caught up with him.

"A landlubber like you shouldn't be loose on the ocean by himself," I said.

He grinned. "Hop aboard, salt."

The day was sultry. The usual tempering sea breezes had died off. As we drove along the Miami bayfront, the air was oppressive, ominous. The sky was brazen, the water calm. The old-timers along the fishing docks were squinting out at the horizon to the south and nodding to each other. It was coming.

The color of the sea, the shape of the clouds, the sighting of a shark near the coast, the way the sea birds were perching—all these became omens.

It was coming.

We slept for most of the flight out to the sonar picket. The Navy jet landed smoothly in the calm sea and a helicopter from the picket brought us aboard. The ship was similar in style to the deep-sea mining dredges my father operated out in the Pacific. For antisubmarine work, though, the dredging equipment was replaced by a fantastic array of radar and communications antennae.

"Below decks are out of bounds to visitors, I'm afraid," the chunky lieutenant who welcomed us to his ship told us as we walked from the helicopter landing pad toward the bridge. "This bucket's a floating sonar station. Everything below decks is classified except the galley, and the cook won't let even me in there."

He laughed at his own joke. He was a pleasant-faced type, about our own age, square-jawed, solidly built, the kind that stayed in the Navy for life.

We clambered up a ladder to the bridge.

"We're anchored here," the lieutenant said, "with special bottom gear and arresting cables. So the bridge isn't used for navigation as much as a communications center."

Looking around, we could see what he meant. The bridge's aft bulkhead was literally covered with viewscreens, maps, autoplotters and electronics controls.

"I think you'll be able to keep track of your hurricane without much trouble." The lieutenant nodded proudly toward the communications setup.

"If we can't," Ted said, "it won't be your fault."

The lieutenant introduced us to the chief communications technician, a scrappy little sailor who had just received his engineering degree and was putting in two Navy years. Within minutes, we were talking to Tuli back in THUNDER headquarters.

"Omega seems to have slowed down quite a bit," he told us, his face impassive. "She's almost stopped dead in her tracks, about halfway between your position and Puerto Rico."

"Gathering strength," Ted muttered.

They fed the information from Ted's big plotting screen in Miami to the picket's autoplotter, and soon we had a miniature version of the giant map to work with.

Ted studied the map, mumbling to himself. "If we could feed her some warm water . . . give her a shortcut to the outbound leg of the Gulf Stream . . . then maybe she'd stay off the coast."

The lieutenant watched us from a jumpseat that folded out of the port bulkhead.

"Just wishful thinking," Ted muttered on. "Fastest way to move her is to set up a low-pressure cell to the north . . . make her swing more northerly, maybe bypass the coast."

He talked it over with Tuli for the better part of an hour, perching on a swivel chair set into the deck next to the chart table. Their conversation was punctuated with equations and aerodynamics jargon that no one else on the bridge could understand.

"Are they talking about weather?" the ship's executive officer asked the lieutenant. "I know as much about meteorology as most of us do, and I can't make out what they're saying."

I walked over to them. "Standard meteorology is only part of Ted's game. They're looking at the hurricane as an aerodynamics problem—turbulent-boundary-layer theory, I think they call it."

"Oh." The expression on their faces showed that they heard it, but didn't understand it, or even necessarily believe me.

The cook popped through the bridge's starboard hatch with a tray of sandwiches and coffee. Ted absently took a sandwich and mug, still locked in talk with Tuli Noyon.

Finally he said to the viewscreen, "Okay, then we deepen this trough off Long Island and try to make a real storm cell out of it."

Tuli nodded, but he was clearly unhappy.

"Get Barney to run it through the computer as fast as she can, but you'd better get the planes out right now. Don't wait for the computer run. Got to hit while she's still sitting around. Otherwise . . ." His voice trailed off.

"All right," Tuli said. "But we're striking blindly."

"I know. Got any better ideas?"

Tuli shrugged.

"Then let's scramble the planes." He turned to me. "Jerry, we've got a battle plan figured out. Tuli'll give you the details."

Now it was my turn. I spent the better part of the afternoon getting the right planes with the right payloads off to the exact places where their work had to be done. Through it all, I was calling myself an idiot for tracking out to this midocean exile. It took twice as long to process the orders as it would have back at headquarters.

"Don't bother saying it," Ted said when I finished. "So it was kinky coming out here. Okay. Just had to get away from that place before I went over the hill."

"But what good are you going to do here?" I asked.

He gripped the bridge's rail and looked out past the ship's prow to the softly billowing sea and clear horizon.

"We can run the show from here just as well . . . maybe a little tougher than back in Miami, but we can do it. If everything goes okay, we'll get brushed by the storm's edge. I'd like to see that . . . want to feel her, see what she can do. Better than sitting in that windowless cocoon back there."

"And if things don't go well?" I asked. "If the storm doesn't move the way you want it to?"

He turned away. "Probably she won't."

"Then we might miss the whole show."

"Maybe. Or she might march right down here and blow down our throats."

"Omega might . . . we might be caught in the middle of it?"

"Could be," he said easily. "Better get some sleep while you can. Going to be busy later on."

The exec showed us to a tiny stateroom with two bunks in it. Part of the picket's crew was on shore leave, and they had a spare compartment for us. I tried to sleep, but spent most of the late afternoon hours squirming nervously. Around dusk, Ted got up and went to the bridge. I followed him.

"See those clouds, off the southern horizon?" he was saying to the lieutenant. "That's her. Just her outer fringes."

I checked back with THUNDER headquarters. The planes had seeded the low-pressure trough off Long Island without incident. Weather stations along the coast, and automated observation equipment on satellites and planes, were reporting a small storm cell developing.

Barney's face appeared on the viewscreen. She looked very worried. "Is Ted there?"

"Right here," he said, stepping into view.

"The computer run's just finished," she said, pushing a strand of hair from her face. "Omega's going to turn northward, but only temporarily. She'll head inland again late tomorrow. In about forty-eight hours she'll strike the coast somewhere between Cape Hatteras and Washington."

Ted let out a low whistle.

"But that's not all," she continued. "The storm track crosses right over the ship you're on. You're going to be in the center of it!"

"We'll have to get off here right away," I said.

"No rush," Ted said. "We can spend the night here. I want to see her develop firsthand."

Barney said, "Ted, don't be foolish. It's going to be dangerous."

He grinned at her. "Jealous? Don't worry, I just want to get a look at her, then I'll come flying back to you."

"You stubborn—" The blond curl popped back over her eyes again and she pushed it away angrily. "Ted, it's time you stopped acting like a little boy. You bet I'm jealous. I'm tired of competing against the whole twirling atmosphere! You've got responsibilities, and if you don't want to live up to them . . . well, you'd better, that's all!"

"Okay, okay. We'll be back tomorrow morning. Be safer traveling in daylight anyway. Omega's still moving slowly; we'll have plenty of time."

"Not if she starts moving faster. This computer run was just a first-order look at the problem. The storm could move faster than we think."

"We'll get to Miami okay, don't worry."

"No, why should I worry? You're only six hundred miles out at sea with a hurricane bearing down on you."

"Just an hour away. Get some sleep. We'll fly over in the morning."

The wind was picking up as I went back to my bunk, and the ship was starting to rock in the deepening sea. I had sail-boated through storms and slept in worse weather than this. It wasn't the conditions of the moment that bothered me. It was the knowledge of what was coming.

Ted stayed out on the bridge, watching the southern skies darken with the deathly fascination of a general observing the approach of a much stronger army. I dropped off to sleep, telling myself that I'd get Ted off this ship as soon as a plane could pick us up, even if I had to have the sailors wrap him in anchor chains.

By morning, it was raining hard and the ship was bucking severely in the heavy waves. It was an effort to push through the narrow passageway to the bridge, with the deck bobbing beneath my feet and the ship tossing hard enough to slam me into the bulkheads.

Up on the bridge they were wearing slickers and life vests. The wind was already howling evilly. One of the sailors handed me a slicker and vest. As I turned to tug them on, I saw that the helicopter pad out on the stern was empty.

"Chopper took most of the crew out about an hour ago," the sailor hollered into my ear. "Went to meet the seaplane out west of here, where it ain't so rough. When it comes back we're all pulling out."

I nodded and thanked him.

"She's a beauty, isn't she?" Ted shouted at me. "Moving up a lot faster than we thought."

I grabbed a handhold between him and the lieutenant. To the south of us was a solid wall of black. Waves were breaking over the bows and the rain was a battering force against our faces.

"Will the helicopter be able to get back to us?" I asked the lieutenant.

"Certainly," he yelled back. "We've had worse blows than this . . . but I wouldn't want to hang around for another hour or so!"

The communications tech staggered across the bridge to us. "Chopper's on the way, sir. Ought to be here in ten—fifteen minutes."

The lieutenant nodded.

"I'll have to go aft and see that the helicopter's dogged down properly when she lands. You be ready to hop on when the word goes out."

"We'll be ready," I said.

As the lieutenant left the bridge, I asked Ted, "Well, is this doing you any good? Frankly, I would've been just as happy in Miami. . . ."

"She's a real brute," he shouted. "This is a lot different from watching a map."

"But why . . ."

"This is the enemy, Jerry. This is what we're trying to kill. Think how much better you're going to feel after we've learned how to stop hurricanes."

"If we live long enough to learn how!"

The helicopter struggled into view, leaning heavily into the raging wind. I watched, equally fascinated and terrified, as it worked its way to the landing pad, tried to come down, got blown backward by a terrific gust, fought toward the pad again, and finally touched down on the heaving deck. A team of sailors scrambled across the wet square to attach heavy lines to the landing gear, even before the rotor-blades started to slow down. A wave smashed across the ship's stern and one of the sailors went sprawling. Only then did I notice that each man had a stout lifeline around his middle. They finally got the 'copter secured.

I turned back to Ted. "Let's go before it's too late."

We started down the slippery ladder to the main deck. As we inched back toward the stern, a tremendous wave caught the picket amidships and slued her around broadside. The little ship shuddered violently and the deck seemed to drop out from under us. I sagged to my knees.

Ted pulled me up. "Come on, buddy, Omega's breathing down our necks."

Another wave smashed across us. I grabbed for a handhold, and as my eyes cleared, saw the helicopter pitching crazily over to one side, the moorings on her landing gear flapping loosely in the wind.

"It's broken away!"

The deck heaved again and the 'copter careened over on its side, its rotors smashing against the pad. Another wave caught us. The ship bucked terribly. The helicopter slid backward along its side and then, lifted by a solid wall of foaming green, smashed through the gunwale and into the sea.

Groping senselessly on my hands and knees, soaking wet, battered like an overmatched prizefighter, I watched our only link to safety disappear into the raging sea.

From somewhere behind me I heard Ted shouting, "Four years! Four years of killing ourselves and it has to end like this!"

I clambered to my feet on the slippery deck of the Navy picket. The ship shuddered again and slued around. A wave hit the other side and washed across, putting us knee-deep in foaming water until the deck lurched upward again and cleared the waves temporarily.

"Omega's won," Ted roared in my ear, over the screaming wind. "The 'copter's washed overboard. We're trapped."

We stood there, hanging onto the handholds. The sea was impossible to describe—a furious tangle of waves, with no sense or pattern to them, their tops ripped off by the wind, spray mixing with the blinding rain.

The lieutenant groped by, edging along hand over hand on the lifeline that ran along the superstructure bulkhead.

"Are you two all right?"

"No broken bones, if that's what you mean."

"You'd better come back up to the bridge," he shouted.

We were face to face, close enough to nearly touch noses, yet we could hardly hear him. "I've given orders to cast off the anchors and get up steam. We've got to try to ride out this blow under power. If we just sit here, we'll be swamped."

"Is there anything we can do?" I asked.

"Sure. Next time you tinker with a hurricane, make it when I'm on shore leave!"

We followed the lieutenant up to the bridge. I nearly fell off the rain-slicked ladder, but Ted grabbed me with one of his powerful paws.

The bridge was sloshing from the monstrous waves and spray that were drenching the decks. The communications panels seemed to be intact, though. We could see the map that Ted had set up on the autoplotter screen; it was still alight. Omega spread across the screen like an engulfing demon. The tiny pinpoint of light marking the ship's location was well inside the hurricane's swirl.

The lieutenant fought his way to the ship's intercom while Ted and I grabbed for handholds.

"All the horses you've got, Chief," I heard the lieutenant bellow into the intercom mike. "I'll get every available man on the pumps. Keep those engines going. If we lose power we're sunk!"

I realized he meant it literally.

The lieutenant crossed over toward us and hung on to the chart table.

"Is that map accurate?" he yelled at Ted.

The big redhead nodded. "Up to the minute. Why?"

"I'm trying to figure a course that'll take us out of this blow. We can't stand much more of this battering. She's taking on more water than the pumps can handle. Engine room's getting swamped."

"Head southwest then," Ted said at the top of his lungs. "Get out of her quickest that way."

"We can't! I've got to keep the sea on our bows or else we'll capsize!"

"What?"

"He's got to point her into the wind," I yelled. "Just about straight into the waves."

"Right!" The lieutenant agreed.

"But you'll be riding along with the storm. Never get out that way. She'll just carry us along all day!"

"How do you know which way the storm's going to go? She might change course."

"Not a chance." Ted pointed to the plotting screen. "She's heading northwesterly now and she'll stay on that course the rest of the day. Best bet is heading for the eye."

"Toward the center? We'd never make it!"

Ted shook his head. "Never get out of it if you keep heading straight into the wind. But if you can make five knots or so, we can spiral into the eye. Be calm there."

The lieutenant stared at the screen. "Are you sure? Do you know exactly where the storm's moving and how fast she's going to go?"

"We can check it out."

So we called THUNDER headquarters, transmitting up to the Atlantic Station satellite for relay to Miami. Barney was nearly frantic, but we got her off the line quickly. Tuli answered our questions and gave us the exact predictions for Omega's direction and speed.

Ted went inside with a soggy handful of notes to put the information into the ship's course computer. Barney pushed her way on to the viewscreen.

"Jerry . . . are you all right?"

"I've been better, but we'll get through it okay. The ship's in no real trouble," I lied.

"You're sure."

"Certainly. Ted's working out a course with the skipper. We'll be back in Miami in a few hours."

"It looks . . . it looks awful out there."

Another mammoth wave broke across the bow and drenched the bridge with spray.

"It's not picnic weather," I admitted. "But we're not worried, so don't you go getting upset." *No, we're not worried,* I added silently. *We're scared white.*

Reluctantly, the lieutenant agreed to head for the storm's eye. It was either that or face a battering that would split the ship within a few hours. We told Tuli to send a plane to the eye, to try to pick us up.

Time lost all meaning. We just hung on, drenched to the skin, plunging through a wild, watery inferno, the wind shrieking evilly at us, the seas absolutely chaotic. No one remained on the bridge except the lieutenant, Ted and me. The rest of the ship's skeleton crew were below decks, working every pump on board as hard as they could be run. The ship's autopilot and computer-run guidance system kept us heading on the course Ted and Tuli had figured.

Passing into the hurricane's eye was like stepping through a door from bedlam to a peaceful garden. One minute we were being pounded by mountainous waves and merciless winds, the rain and spray making it hard to see even as far as the bow. Then the sun broke through and the wind abruptly died. We limped out into the open, with nothing but a deep swell to mar a tranquil sea.

Towering clouds rose all about us, but this patch of ocean was safe. A vertijet was circling high overhead, sent out by Tuli. The plane made a tight pass over us, then descended onto the helicopter landing pad on the ship's fantail. Her landing gear barely touched the deck and her tail stuck out over the smashed railing where the helicopter had broken through.

We had to duck under the plane's nose and enter from a hatch in her belly because the outer wing jets were still blazing, but the plane took us all aboard. As we huddled in the crammed passenger compartment, the plane hoisted straight up. The jetpods swiveled back for horizontal flight and the wings slid to supersonic sweep. We climbed steeply and headed up for the sky.

As I looked down at the fast-shrinking little picket, I realized the lieutenant was also craning his neck at the port for a last look.

"I'm sorry you had to lose your ship."

"So am I," he said. "But headquarters gave permission to abandon her. We couldn't have stayed in the eye indefinitely, and another hour or so in those seas would have finished us."

"You did a darned good job to get us through," Ted said.

The lieutenant smiled wearily. "We couldn't have done it without your information on the storm. Good thing your numbers were right."

Barney was waiting for us at the Navy airport with dry clothes, the latest charts and forecasts on Omega, and a large share of feminine emotion. I'll never forget the sight of her running toward us as we stepped down from the vertijet's main hatch. She threw her arms around Ted's neck, then around mine, and then around Ted again.

"You had me so worried, the two of you!"

Ted laughed. "We were kind of ruffled ourselves."

It took more than an hour to get out of the Navy's grasp. Debriefing officers, brass hats, press corps men, photographers—they all wanted to hear how Ted and the lieutenant described the situation. We finally got to change our clothes in an officer's wardroom and then battled our way out to the car Barney had come in, leaving the lieutenant and his crew to tell their story in detail.

"Dr. Weis has been on the phone all day," Barney said as the driver pulled out for the main highway leading to the Miami bayfront and THUNDER headquarters.

Ted frowned and spread the reports on Omega across his lap.

Sitting between the two of us, she pointed to the latest chart. "Here's the storm track . . . ninety percent reliability, plus-or-minus two percent."

Ted whistled. "Right smack into Washington and then up the coast. She's going to damage more than reputations."

"I told Dr. Weis you'd phone him as soon as you could."

"Okay," he said reluctantly. "Let's get it over with."

I punched out the Science Advisor's private number on the phone set into the car's forward seat. After a brief word with a secretary, Dr. Weis appeared on the viewscreen.

"You're safe," Dr. Weis said flatly. He looked wearier than we felt.

"Disappointed?" Ted quipped.

"The way this hurricane is coming at us, we could use a martyr or two."

"Steering didn't work. Only thing left to try is what we should've done in the first place. . . ."

"Weather control? Absolutely not! Being hit with a hurricane is bad enough, but if you try tinkering with the weather all across the country, we'll have every farmer, every vacationist, every mayor and governor and traffic cop on our necks!"

Ted fumed. "What else are you going to do? Sit there and take it? Weather control's the only way to stop this beast. . . ."

"Marrett, I'm almost ready to believe that you set up this storm purposely to force us into letting you try your pet idea!"

"If I could do that, I wouldn't be sitting here arguing with you."

"Possibly not. But you listen to me. Weather control is out. If we have to take a hurricane, that's what we'll do. We'll have to admit that THUNDER was too ambitious a project for the first time around. We'll have to back off a little. We'll try something like THUNDER again next year, but without all the publicity. You may have to lead a very quiet life for a year or two, but we'll at least be able to keep going. . . ."

"Why back down when you can go ahead and stop this hurricane?" Ted insisted hotly. "We can push Omega out to sea—I know we can!"

"The way you steered her? That certainly boomeranged on you."

"We tried moving six trillion tons of air with a feather duster! I'm talking about total control of the weather patterns across the whole continent. It'll work!"

"You can't guarantee that it will, and even if you did I wouldn't believe you. Marrett, I want you to go back to THUNDER headquarters and sit there quietly. You can operate on any new disturbances that show up. But you are to leave Omega strictly alone. Is that clear? If you try to touch that storm in any way, I'll see to it that you're finished. For good."

Dr. Weis snapped off the connection. The viewscreen went dark, almost as dark as the scowl on Ted's face. For the rest of the ride back to Project headquarters he said nothing. He simply sat there, slouched over, pulled in on himself, his eyes blazing.

When the car stopped he looked up at me.

"What would you do if I give the word to push Omega off the coast?"

"But Dr. Weis said—"

"I don't care what he said, or what he does afterward. We can stop Omega."

Barney turned and looked at me.

"Ted . . . I can always go back to Hawaii and help my father make his twelfth million. But what about you? Weis can finish your career permanently. And what about Barney and the rest of the Project personnel?"

"It's my responsibility. Weis won't care about the rest of 'em. And I don't care what he does to me . . . I can't sit here like a dumb ape and let that hurricane have its own way. I've got a score to settle with that storm."

"Regardless of what it's going to cost you?"

He nodded gravely. "Regardless of everything. Are you with me?"

"I guess I'm as crazy as you are," I heard myself say. "Let's go do it."

We piled out of the car and strode up to the control center. As people started to cluster around us, Ted raised his arms for silence. Then he said loudly:

"Listen: Project THUNDER is over. We've got a job of weather-making to do. We're going to push that hurricane out to sea."

Then he started rattling off orders as though he had been rehearsing for this moment all his life.

As I started for my glass-walled office, Barney touched my sleeve. "Jerry, whatever happens later, thanks for helping him."

"We're accomplices," I said. "Before, after and during the fact."

"Do you think you could ever look at a cloud in the sky again if you hadn't agreed to help him try this?"

Before I could think of an answer she turned and started toward the computer section.

We had roughly thirty-six hours before Omega would strike the Virginia coast and then head up Chesapeake Bay for Washington. Thirty-six hours to manipulate the existing weather pattern over the entire North American continent.

Within three hours Ted had us around his desk, a thick pack of notes clenched in his right hand. "Not as bad as it could've been," he told us, waving the notes toward the plotting screen. "This big high sitting near the Great

Lakes—good cold, dry air that can make a shield over the East Coast if we can swing it into position. Tuli, that's your job."

Tuli nodded, bright-eyed with excitement.

"Barney, we'll need pinpoint forecasts for every part of the country, even if it takes every computer in the Weather Bureau to wring 'em out."

"Right, Ted."

"Jerry, communications're the key. Got to keep in touch with the whole blinking country. And we're going to need planes, rockets, even slingshots maybe. Get the ball rolling before Weis finds out what we're up to."

"What about the Canadians? You'll be affecting their weather, too."

"Get that liaison guy from the State Department and tell him to have the Canadian Weather Bureau check with us. Don't spill the beans to him, though."

"It's only a matter of time until Washington catches on," I said.

"Most of what we've got to do has to be done tonight. By the time they wake up tomorrow, we'll be on our way."

Omega's central wind speeds had climbed to 120 knots by evening, and were still increasing. As she trundled along toward the coast, her howling fury was nearly matched by the uproar of action at our control center. We didn't eat, we didn't sleep. We worked!

A half-dozen military satellites armed with anti-ICBM lasers started pumping streams of energy into areas pinpointed by Ted's orders. Their crews had been alerted weeks earlier to cooperate with requests from Project THUNDER, and Ted and others from our technical staff had briefed them before the hurricane season began. They didn't question our messages. Squadrons of planes flew out to dump chemicals and seeding materials just off Long Island, where we had created a weak storm cell in the vain atttempt to steer Omega. Ted wanted that low deepened, intensified—a low-pressure trough into which that high on the Great Lakes could slide.

"Intensifying the low will let Omega come in faster, too," Tuli pointed out.

"Know it," Ted answered. "But the numbers're on our side, I think. Besides, the faster Omega moves, the less chance she gets to build up higher wind velocities."

By ten o'clock we had asked for and received a special analysis from the National Meteorological Center in Suitland, Maryland. It showed that we would have to deflect the jet stream slightly, since it controlled the upper-air flow patterns across the country. But how do you divert a river of air that's three hundred miles wide, four miles thick, and racing at better than three hundred miles per hour?

"It would take a hundred-megaton bomb," Barney said, "exploded about fifteen miles up, just over Salt Lake City."

"Forget it!" Ted snapped. "The UN would need a month just to get it on the agenda. Not to mention the sovereign citizens of Utah and points east."

"Then how do we do it?"

Ted grabbed the coffeepot standing on his desk and poured a mug of steaming, black liquid. "Jet stream's a shear layer between the polar and mid-latitude tropopauses," he muttered, more to himself than any of us. "If you reinforce a polar air mass, it can nudge the stream southward. . . ."

He took a cautious sip of the hot coffee. "Tuli, we're already moving a high southward from the Great Lakes. Take a couple of your best people—and Barney, give him top priority on the computers. See if we can drag down a bigger polar air mass from Canada and push the jet stream enough to help us."

"We don't have enough time or equipment to operate in Canada," I said. "And we'd need permission from Ottawa."

"What about reversing the procedure?" Tuli asked. "We could expand the desert high over Arizona and New Mexico until it pushes the jet stream from the south."

Ted raised his eyebrows. "Think you can do it?"

"I'll have to make some calculations."

"Okay, scramble."

In Boston, people who had gone to bed with a weather forecast of "warm, partly cloudy," awoke to a chilly, driving northeast rain. The low we had intensified during the night had surprised the local forecasters. The Boston Weather Bureau office issued corrected predictions through the morning as the little rainstorm moved out, the Great Lakes high slid in and caused a flurry of frontal squalls, and finally the sun broke through. The cool, dry air of the high dropped local temperatures more than ten degrees within an hour. To the unknowing New Englanders it was just another day, slightly more bewildering than most.

Dr. Weis was on the phone at seven-thirty that morning.

"Marrett, have you lost your mind? What do you think you're doing? I told you . . ."

"Can't talk now, we're busy," Ted shot back.

"I'll have your hide for this!"

"Tomorrow you can have my hide. I'll bring it up myself. But first I'm going to find out if I'm right or wrong about this."

The President's Science Advisor turned purple. "I'm going to send out an order to all government installations to stop . . ."

"Better not. Then we'll never find out if it worked. Besides, most of the mods've already been made. Damage's done. Let's see what good it does."

Barney rushed up with a ream of computer printout sheets as Ted cut the phone connection.

"There's going to be a freeze on the central plains and northern Rockies," she said, pushing back her tousled hair. "There'll be some snow. We haven't fixed the exact amount yet."

A harvest-time freeze. Crops ruined, cities paralyzed by unexpected snow, weekend holidays ruined, and, in the mountains, deaths from exertion and exposure.

"Get the forecast out on the main Weather Bureau network," Ted ordered. "Warn 'em fast."

The plotting screen showed the battle clearly. Omega, with central windspeeds of 175 knots now, was still pushing toward Virginia. But her forward progress was slowing, ever so slightly, as the Great Lakes high moved southeastward past Pittsburgh.

By noontime, Ted was staring at the screen and muttering, "Won't be enough. Not unless the jet stream comes around a couple degrees."

It was raining in Washington now, and snow was beginning to fall in Winnipeg. I was trying to handle three phone calls at once when I heard an ear-splitting whoop from Ted. I looked at the plotting screen. There was a slight bend in the jet stream west of the Mississippi that hadn't been there before.

As soon as I could, I collared Tuli for an explanation.

"We used the lasers from the Atlantic Station and every plane and ounce of exothermic catalyst I could find. The effect isn't very spectacular, no noticeable weather change. But the desert high has expanded slightly and pushed the jet stream a little northward, temporarily."

"Will it be enough?" I asked.

He shrugged.

Through the afternoon we watched that little curl travel along the length of the jet stream's course, like a wave snaking down the length of a long, taut rope. Meanwhile, the former Great Lakes high was covering all of Maryland and pushing into Virginia. Its northern extension shielded the coast well into New England.

"But she'll blast right through it," Ted grumbled, watching Omega's glowering system of closely-packed isobars, "unless the jet stream helps to push 'er off."

I asked Barney. "How does the timing look? Which will arrive first, the jet stream change, or the storm?"

She shook her head. "The machines have taken it down to four decimal places and there's still no sure answer."

Norfolk was being drenched with a torrential downpour; gale-force winds were snapping power lines and knocking down trees. Washington was a darkened, windswept city. Most of the federal offices had closed early, and traffic was inching along the rain-slicked streets.

Boatmen from Hatteras to the fishhook angle of Cape Cod—weekend sailors and professionals alike—were making fast extra lines, setting out double anchors, or pulling their craft out of the water altogether. Commercial airlines were juggling their schedules around the storm and whole squadrons of military planes were winging westward, away from the danger, like great flocks of migrating birds. Storm tides were piling up all along the coast, and flood warnings were flashing from Civil Defense centers in a dozen states. The highways were filling up with people moving inland before the approaching fury.

And Omega was still a hundred miles out to sea.

Then she faltered.

You could feel the electricity crackle through our control center. The mammoth hurricane hovered off the coast as the jet stream deflection finally arrived. We all held our breaths. Omega stood off the coast uncertainly for an hour, then turned to the northeast. She began to head out to sea.

We shouted our foolish heads off.

When the furor died down, Ted hopped up on his desk.

"Hold on, heroes. Job's not finished yet. We've got a freeze in the midwest to modify. And I want to throw everything we've got into Omega, weaken her as much as possible. Now *scramble!*"

It was nearly midnight before Ted let us call it quits. Our Project people—real weathermakers now—had weakened Hurricane Omega to the point where she was only a tropical storm, fast losing her punch over the cold waters off the North Atlantic. A light snow was sprinkling much of the upper midwest, but our warning forecasts had been in time, and the weathermakers were able to take most of the snap out of the cold front. The local weather stations were reporting only minor problems from the unexpected freeze, and Barney's final computer run showed that the snow would be less than an inch.

Most of the Project people had left for sleep. There was only a skeleton crew left in the control center. Barney, Tuli and I gravitated to Ted's desk. He had commandeered a typewriter, and was pecking on the keys.

"How do you spell 'resignation'?" he asked me.

Before I could answer, the phone buzzed. It was Dr. Weis.

"You didn't have to call," Ted said. "Game's over. I know it."

Dr. Weis looked utterly exhausted, as though he had personally been battling the storm. "I had a long talk with the President tonight, Marrett. You've put him in a difficult position, and me in an impossible one. To the general public you're a hero. But I wouldn't trust you as far as I could throw a cyclotron."

"Guess I don't blame you," Ted answered calmly. "Don't worry, you won't have to fire me. I'm resigning. You'll be off the hook."

"You can't quit," Dr. Weis said. "You're a national resource, as far as the President's concerned. He spent the night comparing you to nuclear energy: you've got to be tamed and harnessed."

"Harnessed? For weather control?"

Weis nodded wordlessly.

"The President wants to really work on weather control?" Ted broke into a huge grin. "That's a harness I've been trying to get into for four years."

"You're lucky, Marrett. Very lucky. If the weather patterns had been slightly different, if things hadn't worked out so well . . ."

Ted's grin vanished. "Wasn't luck. It was work, a lot of people's work, and brains, and guts. That's where weather control—*real* weather control—wins for you. It doesn't matter what the weather patterns are if you're going to change all of them to suit your needs. You don't need luck, just time and sweat. You can *make* the weather you want. That's what we did. That's why it's got to work, if you just do it on a big enough scale."

"All right, you've won," Dr. Weis said. "Luck or skill or guts, it doesn't matter. Not now. The President wants to see you."

"How about tomorrow . . . I mean later this morning?"

"Fine," Dr. Weis said, although his face was still sullen.

"We've won," Tuli said as Ted shut off the phone. "We've actually won."

Barney sank into the nearest chair. "It's too much happening all at once. I don't think I can believe it all."

"It's real," Ted answered quietly. "Weather control is a fact now. Nobody can say it doesn't work, or that it can't have any important effect on the country."

"So you're seeing the President tomorrow," I said.

"Later today," he corrected, "and I want you three guys with me."

"Guys," Barney echoed.

"Hey, that's right. You're a girl. Come on, Girl, I'll take you home. Looks like you won't have to be playing second fiddle to hurricanes anymore." He took her arm and started for the door. "Think you can stand being the center of my attention?"

Barney looked back at me. I got up and took her other arm. "If you don't mind, she's going to be the center of my attention, too."

Tuli shook his head as he joined us. "You barbarians. No wonder you're nervous wrecks. You never know who's going to marry whom. I've got my future wife all picked out; our families agreed on the match when we were both four."

"That's why you're here in the States," Ted joked.

Barney said, "Tuli, don't do anything to make them change their minds. I haven't had this much attention since *I* was four."

Down the main stairway we went, and out into the street. The sidewalks were puddled from rain, a side effect of Omega, but overhead the stars were shining through tattered, scudding clouds.

"Today the world's going to wake up and discover that man can control the weather," Ted said.

"Not really," Tuli cautioned. "We've only made a beginning. We still have years of learning ahead. Decades. Maybe centuries."

Ted nodded, a contented smile on his face. "Maybe. But we've started, that's the important thing."

"And the political problems this is going to cause?" I asked. "The social and economic changes that weather control will bring? What about them?"

He laughed. "That's for administrators like you and the President to worry about. I've got enough to keep me busy: six quadrillion tons of air . . . and one mathematician."

* * *

It was more than a year later, in October, when the United Nations convened an extraordinary session in Washington to hear an address by the President.

The delegates met at a special outdoor pavilion, built along the banks of the Potomac for their meeting. Ted, Barney, Tuli—most of the key people from the Weather Bureau and Congress and government were in the audience. Beyond the seats set on the grass for the UN delegates and invited guests, a huge thronging crowd looked on, and listened to the President.

". . . For mankind's technology," he was saying, "is both a constant danger and a constant opportunity. Through technology, man has attained the power to destroy himself, or the power to unite this planet in peace and freedom— freedom from war, from hunger, from ignorance.

"Today we meet to mark a new step in the peaceful use of man's growing technical knowledge: the establishment of the United Nations Commission for Planetary Weather Control. . . ."

Like Ted's victory over Hurricane Omega, this was only a first step. Total control of the weather, and total solution of the human problems involved, was still a long way off. But we were started along the right road.

As we sat listening to the President, a gentle breeze wafted by, tossing the flame-colored trees, and tempering the warmth of the sun. It was a crisp, golden October day; bright blue sky, beaming sun, occasional puffs of cottonball cumulus clouds. A perfect day for an outdoor ceremony.

Of course.

MAN CHANGES THE WEATHER

The following excerpts from *Man Changes the Weather* were written more than ten years ago. Sadly (or happily, if you're a Luddite) not very much has happened in the past decade to improve our ability to manipulate the weather deliberately. The biggest improvements have come in the field of electronic computers, where new "fifth-generation" computers of unprecedented capacity and speed just might be able to handle all the data and do all the "number crunching" that is necessary for truly accurate long-range weather forecasts. And perhaps another breakthrough of sorts is on the horizon, as well. If the United States or other nations place gigantic lasers in orbit as defenses against ballistic missile attack, those lasers might be used eventually to pump energy into carefully-selected pinpoint target areas among brewing weather systems. If anti-missile lasers can someday help to modify the weather, the Prometheans will smile and quote Biblical prophecies about swords and plowshares.

■

I. A HANDFUL OF DRY ICE

Year 1946—It was cold and windy on the hill.

Dr. Irving Langmuir stood out there with a pair of binoculars in his hands. At the age of 65, when most men are ready to retire, he was just starting a new career: changing the weather.

It was November 13, 1946. Langmuir was out on the parking lot of the General Electric Company's Research Laboratory, not far from Schenectady, N.Y. With the binoculars he watched a small plane flying over Mt. Greylock, Massachusetts, about 30 miles away.

A long, gray cloud hung over the mountain. The plane circled over it. Suddenly snow began to fall from the cloud.

"This is history!" Langmuir shouted.

For the first time, man had deliberately and predictably made a change in the weather. Six pounds of "dry ice" pellets had caused a man-made snowfall over the mountain.

Born in 1881, Langmuir was a world-known figure in science. He had received a Nobel Prize in 1932.

The man in the plane was Vincent Schaefer, who was then 40 years old. It was he who had discovered that dry ice could cause snow or rain.

Coaxing the Clouds

Deliberately changing the weather is an old, old dream. Ever since our remote ancestors cowered under trees during a rainstorm, they've wanted to be able to control the weather.

They've fired arrows into the sky in an effort to bring rain down from the clouds. In later centuries they switched to cannons. Men have tried dancing, praying, shouting, beating on drums, and all manner of weird gadgets that produced noise and sometimes steam—but seldom produced rain.

Most of man's attempts at changing the weather have been aimed at bringing rainfall. Ever since mankind invented farming—some 10,000 years ago—rainfall has been a crucial factor. Without the right amount of rain, the crops won't grow. But if there's too much rain at the wrong time of the year, that's almost as bad. In most cases, though, the problem is not enough rain. So most of man's efforts to influence the weather have been in the area of rainmaking.

As we'll soon see, there's a modern industry of rainmaking that does millions of dollars' worth of business each year in the United States alone. It's based on the techniques invented by Schaefer, Langmuir, and Bernard Vonnegut when they worked together at the GE Research Laboratory in the late 1940s.

The trick in rainmaking is to coax the clouds into dropping more moisture than they would do naturally. No one knows how to bring rain out of a clear, dry sky. But modern rainmakers can squeeze rainfall from clouds that might not have produced rain unless men tinkered with them.

The key to modern rainmaking is knowing how a cloud produces rain naturally.

A raincloud consists of millions upon millions of tiny water droplets. These droplets are so small and light they actually float on air: air pressure and currents keep them buoyed up. They're too light to fall! In fact, the water droplets are so small that a cubic yard of the darkest, most threatening cloud contains only about a tenth of an ounce of water.

Rainfall only happens when these droplets get big enough and heavy enough to fall out of the cloud. To begin with, the droplets are usually only about one hundredth of a millimeter in diameter (0.01 mm). Under the right conditions in a cloud, they'll start to combine into bigger drops. The usual raindrop that splatters on the ground is about one millimeter in diameter: 1 mm is about the width of the lead in a mechanical pencil.

The drops in a fine drizzle can be as small as 0.1 mm in diameter, while the drops in a heavy summer shower are sometimes as big as 6 mm.

How do the tiny droplets become raindrops? There are two possible ways. First, they can grow fat and heavy by *coalescing*, simply bumping together inside the cloud and merging. Coalescing is something like a tiny droplet inching down a windowpane, merging with other drops on the glass and getting bigger and heavier.

In many clouds there are ice crystals present, as well as droplets, because the air inside the cloud is below the freezing temperature. The water droplets can remain liquid even at temperatures below freezing: this is known as a *supercooled cloud*. The smaller the droplet, the lower the temperature at which it can remain liquid. Large drops can remain liquid down to about 5°F; all droplets, no matter how small, freeze at -40°F.

In a supercooled cloud, the ice crystals tend to grow and get bigger, while the droplets get smaller. The water in the cloud goes mainly into the ice crystals as time moves on, and eventually the crystals become heavy enough to fall out of the cloud. If the air temperature below the cloud is warm enough, the crystals will melt and reach the ground as raindrops.

This ice-crystal system is called the *Bergeron process* of droplet growth, after Tor Bergeron, a Swedish meteorologist.

Whether the raindrops form by coalescence or the Bergeron process, it's important to realize that each tiny droplet needs a speck of dust or sand or salt to form around. If there were no dust in our atmosphere, or no sand or salt from the oceans, there could be no rain or snow. Most of the water in the air exists as water vapor, a gas, which comes from the oceans, lakes and rivers, evaporated by the sun. The vapor cannot condense into even the tiniest of droplets unless there's a particle of some sort for it to condense onto. The particles are called *condensation nuclei*, since each particle forms the nucleus of a droplet.

The Deep-Freeze Laboratory

In 1946, Schaefer was trying to find some way to trigger ice crystal formation in clouds. His "laboratory" was a deep-freeze chest, the kind of freezer that housewives store food in. The freezer holds cold, moist air, under conditions that are very similar to the conditions inside a cloud. The particular freezer that Schaefer was working with was a top loader (a GE model, of course); its lid was on the top.

Schaefer wanted to trigger the Bergeron process in his deep-freeze laboratory. His idea was to throw different materials into the cold, moist air inside the freezer, to see if they would produce ice crystals. He felt that if he could make enough ice crystals form inside the freezer's air, much of the moisture in that air would condense onto the crystals and form a miniature snowfall.

He started by simply blowing his own breath into the freezer. Then he tried hundreds of different substances, from talcum powder to sand. Nothing worked.

On July 12, 1946, he came back from lunch and saw that the freezer had been left open and had warmed up slightly (only slightly, because the cold air in the freezer was denser than the room-temperature air outside, and therefore mixed very little with the room air). To quickly get the freezer's air temperature back down to where he wanted it, Schaefer tossed a handful of dry ice into the freezer.

A tiny snowstorm sprang up!

Dry ice is frozen carbon dioxide (CO_2). Carbon dioxide is one of the gases in our air; we breathe it out as a waste gas, but plants breathe it in—it's as important to them as oxygen is to us. It's called dry ice because frozen carbon dioxide doesn't melt into a liquid, as water ice does. It goes straight from a solid frozen state into a gas, with no liquid phase in between, under ordinary conditions.

Solid carbon dioxide is much colder than water ice. It

freezes at −109.3°F. At this very chilly temperature, it's an excellent material for quickly cooling down a freezer, which is why Schaefer threw it into his freezer chest.

The air in the freezer chest was well below the 32°F temperature at which water freezes. (After all, that's what a freezer is for!) But that doesn't mean that all the water vapor in the air inside the freezer had turned to ice crystals. Just as in a supercooled cloud, the moist air in the freezer had some water droplets in it, as well as ice crystals. It was supercooled.

But at the dry-ice temperature of lower than −100°F even the tiniest droplet freezes instantly. So when Schaefer tossed the dry ice into his freezer, he turned all the microscopic water droplets into ice crystals. Water-ice crystals. Snowflakes.

It took some time for Schaefer and Langmuir to be certain that this was what had happened. They repeated the experiment many times, until they were convinced that they knew what was going on, and why.

Then they decided to try a "real-life" experiment. They needed a supercooled cloud, some dry ice and an airplane. Four months and one day after his semi-accidental discovery, Schaefer tossed six pounds of dry ice into the supercooled cloud over Mt. Greylock while Langmuir, watching from the parking lot of the laboratory, saw the first man-made snowfall in history.

While all this was going on, another GE scientist was methodically working on another way to cause clouds to give up their moisture.

Bernard Vonnegut was trying to find a microscopic crystal that had the same size and shape as an ordinary ice crystal. He reasoned that if water droplets sometimes condense onto ice crystals to form snowflakes or raindrops, then perhaps they could be "fooled" into forming around another type of crystal that has the same size and shape as an ice crystal.

Working systematically to find a crystal that closely resembles natural ice crystals, Vonnegut hit upon silver iodide. A mixture of silver iodide and other chemicals can be put into a special type of burner; the resulting smoke contains crystals of silver iodide, which work just as well as dry ice to cause supercooled clouds to release precipitation.

Moreover, the silver iodide burners—which are also called generators—can stay on the ground. You don't need to carry them aloft in a plane; their smoke wafts upward, bringing the crystals to the clouds.

This technique of putting dry ice or silver iodide crystals into a cloud to cause precipitation is called *cloud seeding*. The "seed" material triggers the cloud's natural mechanisms for making rain or snow. Once started by man's hand, the precipitation continues just as it naturally would. Thus a tiny amount of seeding material can cause billions of gallons of water to drop out of a cloud.

Project Cirrus

By 1947, Langmuir, Schaefer and Vonnegut had proved that it was possible to alter the weather deliberately, to wring rain or snow from a supercooled cloud—sometimes.

This was a startling new idea, and many professional meteorologists refused to believe it. But Langmuir was enthusiastic and insistent. He claimed that *weather modification* was too important an idea to ignore. With his international reputation as a scientist, he was able to convince some people to take weather modification seriously.

Some of the people he convinced were in the Department of Defense. Military men have battled against the weather just as often as they've fought opposing armies and navies.

The men in the Pentagon knew that even small weather "mods"—such as clearing fog from an airport—could save many lives. Moreover, in 1947, with World War II still a very fresh memory and the cold war threatening to plunge the world into destruction once again, the Pentagon had plenty of money for research. After all, research had produced the radars and rockets and nuclear bombs of World War II. Could research now offer a way of taming the weather?

Langmuir was set up in New Mexico, and his work was code-named *Project Cirrus.*

On one of the first Project Cirrus flights, an Air Force plane dropped 15 pounds of dry ice along a path 20 miles long through a heavy layer of cloud. Within minutes, a 20-mile-long clearing had been carved out of the cloud bank. The plane's pilot said, "Its sides were as sharp and steep as though someone had taken a spade and shoveled a path through a snowdrift."

By October 1948, both silver iodide and dry ice were being used. On October 14, four different cloud-seeding flights were made near Albuquerque. Half an inch of rain fell over an area of 4000 square miles.

By July 1949, Langmuir was running silver iodide generators on the ground for hours at a time. On July 21, he ran them for more than ten hours straight. Although the Weather Bureau predicted no rain for that day, an afternoon cloudburst dropped nearly an inch and a half of rain on Langmuir's equipment. Heavy rain also hit other parts of New Mexico. Creeks that were normally dry overflowed with sudden rainwater. Langmuir calculated that Project Cirrus had caused nearly 500 billion gallons of water to fall in New Mexico in just two days.

But how can you tell "man-made" rain from "natural" rain?

In other words, how could Langmuir be certain that it

was Project Cirrus causing the rainfalls? Perhaps it would have rained anyway, without the silver iodide or dry ice. Many people, including scientists and meteorologists, began to dispute Langmuir's claims.

His only defense was in statistics, using numbers to show that the laws of chance were on his side. Langmuir showed that unusually heavy rainfalls almost always happened only when he seeded the clouds. He claimed it happened too often to be just a coincidence.

But statistics are tricky, and they're not as powerful as other forms of evidence—especially when people decide not to believe the numbers that the statistics produce.

The more his claims were doubted, the stronger Langmuir made his claims. He showed—with statistics—that his cloud-seeding operations had changed rainfall patterns clear across the eastern two-thirds of the United States. When he seeded clouds in New Mexico, sudden and unusual rainstorms came a few days later and as far away as Florida. Langmuir insisted that this happened because the prevailing westerly winds across the U.S. carried his cloud-seeding crystals from New Mexico eastward.

The doubters still doubted him. But now other people began to blame Project Cirrus for storms and floods. Some of them went to court to sue Langmuir and the U.S. Government for damaging their property. Others blamed *droughts* on the cloud seedings!

To make matters worse, cloud seeding became a popular activity. Other agencies of the government began cloud-seeding experiments. Universities, newspapers, amateur scientists and self-styled "rainmakers" started seeding clouds all over the country. A host of private companies sprang up and began selling rainmaking services to farmers, especially in the drier midwestern and southwestern regions of the nation.

Many of these private companies were run by reputable,

professional meteorologists who had closely followed the work of Langmuir and his associates. But many others were run by people who only knew that you dumped some chemicals out of an airplane and took in cash.

The result was chaos. Langmuir had wanted to do orderly experiments and lay the scientific foundation for weather modification. But his work was being drowned out in arguments, claims and counterclaims. Instead of a controlled scientific experiment, he had a three-ring circus on his hands.

Worst of all, since there were so many wild claims being made on all sides, the word began to spread that *all* rainmakers were charlatans. Langmuir's evidence came to be regarded as rather weak. "After all," said the nonbelievers, "it's only statistics." The implication was that you could rig statistics any way you wanted to.

The Committee on Weather Control

But all this fuss about rainmaking had attracted the interest of some of the nation's most important people: the farmers.

Most farmers didn't know very much about Langmuir's statistics. But they knew that an extra ten or fifteen percent of rainfall often spelled the difference between a good year and a failure. So congressmen and senators from farm states became interested in weather mods and cloud seeding.

In 1953, with Langmuir still claiming great success and predicting a future when men would control the weather almost completely, while skeptical scientists called the whole business little more than a hoax, Congress established an Advisory Committee on Weather Control. The committee was set up to study the whole question of weather modification and to recommend to the Congress whether or not the government should allow, encourage or support weather modification work.

Government committees have a reputation for being leisurely. In most cases, this reputation isn't deserved. But the Advisory Committee on Weather Control took four years before releasing its report, on the last day of 1957. The report was sober, factual—and cautious.

The committee reported that the only evidence for successful rainmaking was statistical evidence, and the numbers showed that cloud seeding had probably increased rainfall in mountainous areas by ten to fifteen percent. In the flatlands, where most of the farms are, the results were so unclear that the committee couldn't say anything about them, one way or the other.

Rightly or wrongly, this report put a sharp pin into the bubble of hope that men could someday alter or even control the weather. Cloud seeding got a rather bad name in government circles, and even in most research laboratories. (Even science fiction writers, who should have known better, turned their backs on weather control.)

Langmuir died in 1957, shortly before the report was released. But he knew what was in it, and he must have died a very disappointed man.

But on the other hand, he probably knew better than anyone else that his battle was an important one in the long road toward man's eventual control of the weather.

II. TAMING THE CLOUDS

The history of any new idea generally follows a rather predictable pattern. Whether the new idea is a laser, a superconducting magnet, artificial satellites, artificial hearts, weather modifications or what-have-you, it always seems to go the same way.

At first the new idea generates a tremendous burst of excitement and enthusiasm. The enthusiasm builds very quickly to a high peak as predictions are made about the new idea. It will solve everybody's problems faster, better, cheaper than ever before.

Soon, though, it becomes clear that the new idea won't solve *everyone's* problems. In fact, there are problems raised by the new idea itself, and bugs in it that need to be worked out. Disenchantment sets in and many of the original followers drop away. Some of the people who thought that the new idea would help them become rather bitter and suspicious of *all* new ideas.

In time, the new idea will either prove itself or disappear into the dusty shelves of reference libraries.

By 1958, cloud seeding and weather modification work had reached the point of disenchantment. Langmuir, Schaefer and Vonnegut had shown that it worked—sometimes. But the original hopes of being able to change the weather at will had given way to statistics, arguments and the 1957 report by the Advisory Committee on Weather Control.

An Industry Is Born

While most people in Washington and elsewhere turned their backs on weather modification, a few determined men quietly pressed on. Langmuir died, but Schaefer and Vonnegut continued their work, and both of them eventually became teachers and researchers at the State University of New York.

And almost without anyone realizing it, a new industry took shape—rainmaking.

Farmers in the Midwest and Southwest live every year on the edge of failure. The success of their crops depends on the amount of rain they get, and even a ten to fifteen percent increase in rainfall can be critically important to them. Ever since settlers moved into these relatively dry western areas from the rain-rich east coast, they've had to battle against a lack of water, a scarcity of rain. For decades they've failed when the rains were too sparse.

By the mid-1950s, though, there were a handful of men who had followed the work of Langmuir, Schaefer and Vonnegut. They knew the scientific basis for producing rain. So they went into the modern rainmaking business.

There were others who were out-and-out fakes, whose only knowledge of cloud seeding was what they read in the newspapers. But the professional rainmakers included meteorologists of the highest caliber.

Modern rainmakers sell rainfall by the inch. That is, the farmer pays only for the rainfall he gets that's over and above what neighboring areas get. Honest rainmakers never claim they can bring rain from a clear sky; they don't even pretend that they can make every cloud drop moisture. What they can do—under the right circumstances—is squeeze extra rainfall from clouds that would sooner or later drop rain anyway. They can modify a natural weather situation to make it more useful to the farmer. Hence the term *weather modification*, or weather "mods."

Pulling extra rainfall from the clouds or redistributing rainfall that would naturally come, so that it falls on farmlands rather than cities, is a multimillion-dollar business in the United States today.

Science and a New Frontier

Although interest and enthusiasm over weather mods dropped to an all-time low when the report of the Advisory Committee on Weather Control was released, some work went on.

The report itself recommended that the National Science Foundation should conduct basic research into the possibilities of modifying the weather. This approach—quiet, sober, university research—was so much less than the news stories had promised about rainmaking and storm-killing that the public never paid much attention to the recommendation.

But the White House did. In 1958, Congress passed a law that allowed the National Science Foundation to investigate weather modification and weather control. Small-scale studies were started at several universities. The professional rainmakers, meanwhile, continued to sell rainfall by the inch to the American farmers.

And that's where matters stood until 1961, when the Kennedy Administration came to Washington. President John Kennedy's campaign theme had been "New Frontiers"; he wanted to expand America's activities in all areas, to reach for excellence in everything we did.

His science advisor was Jerome Weisner of MIT. Weisner strongly believed that science and technology should be put to work in areas that would encourage international cooperation. Everyone in the world knew that science helped to make weapons; Weisner wanted to show that science could also help to make the world safer, healthier.

Weather modification was one exciting possibility to demonstrate "peaceful" science at its best. Many new technical ideas had been developed in the few years between 1957 and 1961. Weisner and several other scientists believed that practical weather mods might be much closer at hand than most people ever realized.

Among the new ideas were new mathematical techniques that promised more reliable weather forecasts, faster and larger computers that could handle the enormous amounts of data needed to understand weather processes on a large scale, and artificial satellites and other observational tools that could keep the entire world's weather under constant scrutiny.

One of the key people in pushing the "weather frontier" with the Kennedy Administration was Thomas F. Malone, vice president and research director of the Travelers Insurance Company. This company had been a leader in private weather forecasting and research for many years. Malone was also chairman of the Committee on Atmospheric Sciences. In 1963, he appointed a special panel to report to the Academy on the progress in rainmaking and other weather mods. Chairman of this Panel on Weather and Climate Modification was Gordon J. F. MacDonald of the University of California at Santa Barbara.

Although it's not an official arm of the government, the National Academy of Sciences (founded by President Lincoln) represents the nation's foremost scientists and acts as an advisory group to the government on scientific matters.

By October 1964, the MacDonald Panel released a preliminary report. It said that weather mods were possible, given enough time and research money to work out the problems. It also stated that statistical evidence still showed no strong proof that cloud seeding produced rain reliably. In other words, the scientists' conclusions were pretty much the same as they had been seven years earlier, even though the report was phrased in much more optimistic language.

Then a curious thing happened.

The commercial rainmakers, some of whom had been making their living for nearly twenty years from cloud seeding, launched a counterattack.

The National Academy Panel and the earlier Advisory Committee on Weather Control had never seen all the evidence that the commercial rainmakers had amassed. The rainmakers had mainly ignored the Advisory Committee back in the 1950s. But faced with another "official" decision that rainmaking didn't work, the commercial cloud seeders marched on Washington armed with their records—proof of their successes.

This was unexpected. MacDonald had a vacancy to fill

on his panel, and wanted to fill it with someone who could tackle the newly-arrived data from the rainmakers. He picked James C. McDonald of the University of Arizona. McDonald (the "Mc" McDonald, not MacDonald, the panel chairman), a highly respected cloud physicist, was at that time openly skeptical about rainmaking. But he was known to be a fair and impartial scientist. In fact, he had been one of the few professional scientists who had publicly called for a careful investigation of Unidentified Flying Objects, to determine just what the "flying saucers" really were. Most scientists avoided making any comments on controversial subjects such as UFOs and cloud seeding. But not McDonald.

Through all of 1965, McDonald studied the rainmakers' private data. Not satisfied with his own efforts, which included the help of several Arizona graduate students, he called for separate checks of the evidence by experts from Rand Corporation, the University of Chicago and the Weather Bureau.

In January 1966, the panel issued a new report. It said that rainfall can be increased by cloud seeding in mountainous areas by ten to fifteen percent, just as the 1957 report had concluded. But it added that commercial rainmaking operations had apparently increased rainfall by as much as twenty percent—sometimes—in non-mountainous areas. Most important of all, the new report concluded that the evidence was clear that cloud seeding could produce rain under proper conditions.

Today, rainmaking is an accepted part of modern science and technology (even though a few states, such as Maryland, have passed laws against cloud seeding). It's not as reliable as turning on an electric light, and there's a staggering amount of knowledge still to be learned. We simply don't know enough about how the weather works to predict natural weather events more than a few days—or sometimes only a few hours—in advance. And if we can't predict natural weather processes, then deliberate weather mods are going to be hit-or-miss affairs for some time to come.

Still, there's a great deal of work being done: determined men are trying to understand and control some of the damaging and destructive forces of the weather—hurricanes, tornadoes, lightning, hail, fog.

And they're succeeding!

Clouds and Rain, Hail and Lightning

Most of the weather modification work that's been done to date has involved seeding clouds, very much as Schaefer and Vonnegut did more than twenty years ago.

In a way, clouds are like storehouses of energy. Within their water droplets, they've captured the energy that helps to make the weather. It takes energy to evaporate water from the surface of a lake or sea, and when water vapor condenses into a droplet, this energy is released into the air. This give-and-take of energy is the driving force behind our weather. It's still not very well understood by atmospheric scientists, which is why weather forecasts can't be made very far ahead.

For this reason, many research teams are vitally interested in studying clouds, to see how they work. They hope to learn more about the give-and-take of energy from the clouds' mixtures of water vapor, droplets and ice crystals. One way to study these processes in clouds is to deliberately try to alter a cloud by seeding it.

While this kind of research-oriented cloud seeding can help tell scientists quite a lot about the way clouds work, it doesn't really have much of an influence on the weather. A single cloud, or even a small group of clouds, doesn't really affect the weather over much territory. So cloud research doesn't run much risk of causing damaging weather effects such as severe storms or floods.

As we've already seen, many farmers are willing to pay for influencing the weather: they want rain, and they pay professional cloud seeders for it.

For more than twenty years now, professional rainmakers have been making their living from seeding clouds. And for just that long, an argument has raged among meteorologists as to whether the cloud seeding does more harm than good.

The doubters claim that seeding doesn't always produce rain, and in fact may prevent rain that might otherwise have fallen. At best, they feel, all that can be done by cloud seeding is to *redistribute* rainfall that will come down anyway, and make rainfall heavier in one location by causing less rainfall somewhere else. This is "robbing Peter to pay Paul."

But even if cloud seeding does nothing more than redistribute rain and snowfalls, this can still be put to good use. For example, the U.S. Bureau of Reclamation is using cloud seeding techniques to cause extra rain and snow in certain areas of the western United States. The idea is to produce as much precipitation as possible in areas that will help fill water reservoirs serving the growing and thirsty cities and farmlands of the west. Winter storms are seeded in the hope of keeping the reservoirs filled during the dry summer.

Further east, cloud seeding operations on the American side of the Great Lakes are aimed at redistributing the snowfalls that often cripple upper New York State. Under normal conditions, the moist cold air blowing in over the Lakes dumps heavy snowfalls along the shore, crippling cities such as Buffalo and Rochester, while a few miles inland there's no snow at all. By seeding the clouds over the Lakes, it's been possible to slightly redistribute the snowfall: the shoreside cities get less snow, and the inland areas get enough to make winter sports possible.

* * *

Hail Suppression: A strong hailstorm with large hailstones can ruin a farmer's crop. In the Midwest it's not uncommon to find hailstones as big as baseballs. Hailstorms cause some $200 to $300 million of damage to crops each year in the United States—more than the damage tornadoes inflict.

One way to ease the sting of hailstorms is to make the stones small and soft enough so that they won't cause much damage. This can sometimes be done by overseeding the clouds where the hailstorms are being formed. By pouring a huge amount of condensation nuclei into the clouds, many small hailstones form, rather than a smaller number of big ones.

Hail-suppression operations have been going on for many years all over the world. In Russia, France and Italy, men fire rockets or cannon shells loaded with silver iodide or dry ice into clouds that look threatening. In the United States, silver iodide "smoke" generators are more frequently used.

Although it's impossible to say that a particular cloud would have dropped hailstones big enough to cause damage if it hadn't been seeded, the records of many years show that cloud seeding operations have resulted in far fewer destructive hailstorms. At a relatively slight cost, farmers in many nations have saved themselves many millions of dollars in crop damages.

Lightning Suppression: Lightning bolts strike the Earth about a hundred times every second. That's more than five million strokes each day. More people are killed by lightning strokes than by any other aspect of the weather, including hurricanes and tornadoes. And most of the forest fires that destroy valuable timber are caused not by man, but by lightning.

The U.S. Forest Service started Project Skyfire in an attempt to reduce lightning-caused forest fires. The aim of the cloud seeding here was to change the electrical nature of the clouds and reduce the number of lightning strokes that reached the ground. Skyfire didn't show very dramatic results, although some meteorologists believed that the clouds weren't seeded enough.

Another attempt at reducing lightning strikes is being made by scientists of the Environmental Research Laboratories, which are part of the National Oceanographic and Atmospheric Agency (NOAA). Strips of aluminized foil, called chaff, are either dropped into the clouds from airplanes or fired into the clouds by rockets launched from the ground. The chaff strips are electrically charged, and under the proper circumstances can cause the cloud to dissipate its electrical energy without making lightning bolts that strike the ground. Some indications of reduced lightning activity have been found, but much more work needs to be done in this area.

Fog: Nobody likes fog. And many government agencies and private companies have worked at methods of getting rid of fog.

Cloud seeding techniques have been used on fog: after all, fog is merely a cloud that's sitting on or near the ground. Cloud seeding can dissipate cold fog, just as seeding can cause supercooled clouds to release precipitation. The seeding crystals produce precipitation in the fog; the fog melts away and the ground gets wet.

But seeding works only on cool fogs, and ninety-five percent of the fogs that occur in the United States are too warm for seeding to be effective. Some research teams have tried to come up with seeding agents that will work on warm fogs. To date, they haven't been very successful.

There are simpler ways to get rid of fog, though. Simpler, but more expensive than seeding.

One is called FIDO. It dates back to World War II. FIDO stands for Fog Investigation and Dispersal Operations. The problem was to get rid of fog shrouding airfield runways. The solution was to set up large drums of kerosene along the runway and set the kerosene on fire. The currents of hot air created by the fires caused updrafts that lifted the fog off the ground. Also, the heat from the fires helped to "bake out" some of the fog droplets, turning them back into water vapor.

Orly Airport, which serves Paris, now has a series of gas turbine jet engines placed underground alongside the runways. When fog develops, the turbine engines produce hot air, just as FIDO oil fires did, and the fog is blown away.

Several research teams in the United States have considered using high-powered lasers to break up fog. If a laser beam had enough energy in it—many megawatts of continuous power—it could theoretically bake off the fog droplets. It could produce clearings in a fog bank exactly where you wanted them, and very quickly too. A laser "fog knife" would be a very handy tool, if lasers of sufficient power could be built, and if they would be economical enough to operate.

As for economics, officials of the Air Transport Association of America and of United Airlines have reported that fog seeding is definitely a money-saving operation. Flights that are cancelled because of fog, or are re-routed to another airport because fog has "socked in" the airport that the flight was scheduled to land at, cost the airlines more than $75 million each year. United Airlines has for years been involved in seeding cool fogs at the airports it uses in the Pacific Northwest and Alaska. The airline claims that it's saved five dollars for every dollar spent on fog seeding.

Taming Hurricanes

Going from individual clouds or cloud systems to a hurricane is like stepping from a quiet meadow into downtown Manhattan at rush hour.

A hurricane is an organized storm that's often several hundred miles in diameter. It releases a megaton of energy every fifteen minutes or so. Hurricanes have dropped more than a foot of rain per hour over thousands of square miles of territory. Wind speeds of two hundred miles per hour are not uncommon in a full-grown hurricane. These winds blow out windows, knock over electric cables and their poles, uproot trees, tear down signs, rip off roofs and pile up tidal waves that sweep over low-lying coastal lands and cause enormous damage.

Over the five-year period of 1965–1969, hurricanes caused more than $2.4 *billion* worth of damage in the United States alone, and killed nearly 500 people. One hurricane that hit Galveston in 1900 killed 6000 people. Today, better prediction and warnings have cut down the death toll greatly, especially since airplanes and satellites have been used to spot hurricanes while they're still far out at sea.

Hurricanes are a class of *tropical cyclones,* in the language of the meteorologists. The word "cyclone" simply means a revolving, roughly circular mass of low-pressure air. Meteorologists use terms such as *cyclonic depression* and *cyclonic storm.*

Most of the property damage and killing done by a hurricane stems from its enormously powerful winds, which can blow down buildings and pile up waves that sweep everything in their path. It's been estimated that if we could somehow reduce the force of a hurricane's winds by as little as fifteen percent, the damage caused by the storm would be cut in half.

In 1961, Project Stormfury was born. Operated jointly by the Department of Commerce and the Department of Defense, Stormfury saw the cooperative efforts of the National Weather Service, Navy, Air Force and Marines pitted against the fury of the hurricane.

For all of its strength and frightening power, a hurricane is actually a rather delicate balance of forces. Some meteorologists have described it as a heat engine. It works this way: Winds and warm air of the storm sweep up water vapor from the warm ocean. The vapor condenses into droplets, a process that releases heat energy. This heat energy provides the driving force that builds up the wind speeds, and allows the storm to sweep up still more water vapor. Once a hurricane runs onto dry land, or over cold northern waters, it's cut off from its basic supply of energy: warm water. Then it dies, although usually it takes several days to break up completely.

This very rough outline leaves many questions to be answered. The details of just how a hurricane does all this are yet to be understood. And even more puzzling is the fact that, although there are hundreds of tropical disturbances over the ocean in a year, only a few of them develop into hurricanes. Why don't they all? What happens to the disturbances that *don't* become hurricanes? Can we use such knowledge to prevent a hurricane from forming?

Such thoughts of preventing hurricanes from forming, or steering full-grown hurricanes so that they don't hit populated land areas, lie in the future. At present, Project Stormfury's aim is to seed the hurricane's clouds and see if this can help to reduce the wind speeds in the storm. Answer: Yes, it can and does.

The aim of Stormfury's seeding is to smooth out the differences in air pressure around the eye of the hurricane. Air pressure in the relatively calm eye is very low. Just next to it, in the bands of clouds that spiral around the eye, the air pressure is much higher. In these wall clouds are located the strongest winds of the storm.

Seeding the wall clouds causes many of their super-cooled water droplets to freeze into ice crystals. This process releases heat and makes the seeded area of the clouds warmer, more buoyant, lower in pressure. The difference in air pressure between the eye and the wall clouds becomes less and, theoretically, the wind speed should go down.

Hurricanes were first seeded by Stormfury planes in 1961 and 1963. The results looked interesting, but not really clear. The wind speeds in the hurricanes diminished slightly right after the seeding flights, but picked up again almost immediately.

Between 1963 and 1969 several factors combined to keep the Stormfury planes away from hurricanes: For one thing, the Project people had agreed at the outset of their work that they'd seed only hurricanes that showed little likelihood of reaching land areas. This is because no one could predict what long-term effects seeding would have on a storm. If seeding operations turned out to make a storm stronger, or change its course, then it could cause more harm than good.

Secondly, the work on the first hurricanes showed that the meteorologists needed to know a great deal more about the behavior of tropical clouds. So, much of the time was spent seeding individual clouds and learning how they are affected.

Then, in August 1969, along came Hurricane Debbie. It was in the right place at the right time for Stormfury's handful of airplanes and its little group of determined men and women.

A little armada of planes flew into Hurricane Debbie at carefully selected altitudes and along precise flight paths. The planes seeded the hurricane with silver iodide crystals, and took measurements of the storm. Not just once a day, as had been done in earlier years—Debbie was seeded five times within eight hours on August 18 and again on August 20.

The results were perfectly clear. On August 18, the strongest winds in Debbie dropped from 98 knots to 68 knots within a few hours after seeding: a decrease of 31 percent. On August 19 there were no seeding flights and the storm re-intensified. On August 20, maximum wind speeds were 99 knots before seeding and 84 knots afterward, a decrease of 15 percent.

Man can change a hurricane. What's been done to date is only a tiny start on a huge task. But at least we know that we needn't sit helplessly in the face of nature's most furious storms. Someday we may understand how to prevent the storm from causing any damage at all.

Taming Tornadoes

While the prospects of dealing with hurricanes are beginning to look encouraging, tornadoes are still very much an enigma to meteorologists.

Compared to a hurricane, a tornado is a tiny storm. It packs only a ten-thousandth the energy of a hurricane. A tornado funnel forms suddenly under a threatening, thunderstorm filled sky. The funnel streaks across a few miles of landscape and then breaks up as suddenly as it formed. But in its wake, the tornado funnel leaves nothing but pure destruction.

Tornado winds have never been measured accurately. Usually there's nothing left to measure with when a tornado hits. It's been estimated that wind speeds in the "twister's" funnel may reach 400 miles per hour or more. And the air pressure inside the funnel is so low that the funnels have been seen to suck up ponds of water and even pull snow off the ground, like some wild vacuum cleaner. Trucks, roofs, trees—twisters have lifted them all and hurled them around like matchsticks.

This extremely-low-presure air is one of the tornado's most terrifying weapons. When a tornado hits a building, the air pressure inside the funnel is so low that the normal air pressure inside the building blows the windows and sometimes even the walls outward. Whole buildings have exploded themselves this way, when a tornado strikes.

Although meteorologists can generally forecast the weather conditions that will spawn tornadoes, it's still impossible to predict exactly where and when an individual funnel will form. So attempts at controlling tornadoes are aimed at changing the general weather pattern that might produce tornadoes, rather than trying to stop an individual funnel once it's formed. It all happens so fast, and so violently, that there's not much chance for altering the intensity or direction of an individual twister.

Usually "tornado weather" is caused by the movement of a cold air front into a mass of warm, very moist air. Tornadoes are always associated with the severe thunderstorms that mark the advance of such a cold front.

In general, the types of seeding operations that have been aimed at reducing lightning might help to prevent tornadoes from forming. The basic hope is to seed the areas where severe thunderstorms and tornadoes might break out, but to date there's been little success in taming killing "twisters."

Where Do We Stand?

Although men have been seeding clouds for decades, we can see that the work on taming storms has really just begun.

Weather-changing men can coax extra rainfall from clouds with some success. Their attempts at reducing the damage from hailstorms have been successful; attempts at reducing lightning, less so. Hurricanes have been modified, tornadoes have not. Fog can be cleared under some conditions, and work goes on toward clearing it under all conditions.

In 1958, the magazine *Science Newsletter* ran a survey of professional meteorologists, to find out what they thought about weather modification. Among the questions asked was: Do you believe that men will learn to *control* the large-scale features of the weather? The question was not concerned with merely modifying individual clouds or storms, but controlling weather.

Thirty percent of the meteorologists answered that they did believe weather control would be possible by the end of this century.

The work on weather modification that's been done since 1958 gives some evidence that weather control might indeed be possible some day. The real question now is, Should we try to control the weather?

III. SHOULD WE CONTROL THE WEATHER?

It's a long, long way from the weather mods of today to intentional control of the weather.

But the work that's been done so far—and the *unintentional* changes we make in the weather every day—are making weather control more than a possibility. The day might come when we'll *have to* deliberately control the weather.

John von Neumann (1903–1957) was one of the principal geniuses behind the development of modern electronic computers. In addition to many other interests, he was fascinated by the idea of using computers to help predict the weather. One enormous problem in weather forecasting is that there's so much information to be taken into account that it's difficult to make a forecast that's accurate for more than a few hours ahead. Von Neumann once said that he thought it might be easier to control the weather than to predict it. That is, if we take control of all the forces in our atmosphere that make the weather happen, then we'll know exactly what's going on, and forecasting will become simple.

What do we need to know, and what must we do to achieve weather control? Thomas Malone, chairman of the National Academy of Sciences' Committee on Atmospheric Sciences, pointed out in 1966 that four key developments were needed:

One: We need a much better understanding of the basic physical nature of the atmosphere and its behavior.

At present, weather forecasting is done partly by understanding how the atmosphere behaves, but mostly by matching today's weather patterns against old patterns. That is, weather forecasters know that certain patterns produce certain changes in the weather. When they see a major storm coming from the west, for example, they know that it will follow roughly the same track that most storms follow, so they make their forecasts accordingly.

No meteorologist on Earth can predict how much rain a certain storm will produce, or exactly where the storm will hit, or when. No one knows precisely how storm systems are created.

If we could know these things, precisely and in detail, weather forecasts could be made accurate for many days, weeks, perhaps even months, ahead. The amount of information that would be needed to make such forecasts is staggering, of course. But modern computers offer the hope of storing and digesting such mountains of data.

Two: The second need that Malone pointed out was improved computers, which can handle all the data necessary for understanding the weather patterns all around the world. Such computers are being developed.

Three: Malone showed that we need a huge worldwide network of observational instruments to monitor and measure weather conditions around the world continuously, every minute of the day.

Before the first artificial satellites went into orbit, only about five percent of the world's surface was monitored for weather conditions. In the industrial and populated regions of North America and Europe, there were plenty of weather observation stations. But in the other parts of the world, and across the broad oceans and polar ice caps (where the weather is made) there were no observation stations.

Satellites such as TIROS and NIMBUS and the Russian METEOR have changed all that. Orbiting the planet every few hours, or hanging in stationary orbit where they can watch half the world continuously, satellites have given meteorologists their first chance to see the planet's weather on a truly global scale.

And there are other observational systems going into action, too. Huge buoys are being placed in the oceans, with a complex of measuring instruments powered by small nuclear electric generators. These buoys monitor weather and sea conditions around the world, and give valuable information about how the oceans and the air affect each other. Long-range balloons that carry meteorological sensors are "orbiting" the world in the upper atmosphere, measuring weather conditions and automatically radioing the data to ground stations, under a program called Project GHOST (which stands for Global Horizontal Sounding Technique).

Four: New mathematical techniques must be worked out, techniques that will allow long-range forecasts of the weather and show *before the fact* what the effects of possible weather modifications will be.

It would be terribly foolish to try to change the weather in any major way without knowing in detail how this change will affect the world's weather. For example, suppose we learn how to smother a hurricane so completely that the storm dies away altogether before it ever reaches full strength. What effect will this have on the rainfall in the regions that the hurricane would have hit? Would killing the storm cause problems with the weather in other parts of the world?

If and when computers become large and fast enough to handle the job, men will make their weather changes on paper (or magnetic tape) first, and then let the computer tell them what the long-range effects of such changes will be. Only then can we make major weather changes in the real world safely.

There's a fifth item that Malone didn't include in his list, but it's necessary before large-scale weather alterations can be made: *energy sources.*

So far, the only halfway reliable method we've found to change the weather is cloud seeding. In effect, seeding triggers energy changes in the cloud, makes the cloud release the energy it's stored up in its water droplets and/or ice crystals.

If we're going to make any major changes in the weather, we must find better energy sources—more reliable triggers. Think of the energy involved in the weather: a quarter-inch rainfall over a 100-mile-square area (about the size of the District of Columbia) releases some 20 million kilowatts.

Certainly man isn't going to match the energy of the weather on a head-to-head basis. But neither did man match the strength of the mammoths, head-to-head, back in the Ice Age. Still, Ice Age men slaughtered the mammoths. Not by using brute strength, but by using cunning.

Will we be clever enough to control the weather someday? The answer is most likely yes. But this brings us back to the question that started this discussion: Should we try to control the weather?

As we've seen earlier, man is constantly changing the weather around him without even thinking about it. Unless we begin to control the ways we pour heat and pollution into the atmosphere, we may cause disasters much worse than the killing smogs of Donora and London.

When it comes to pollution and the unconscious effects man has on the weather, it seems that we *must* exert some controls. We can control these aspects of the weather mainly by controlling ourselves.

It can be done.

The great city of London has been famous for some of the most impenetrable fogs (and smogs) on record. Up until a few years ago, everyone knew that these fogs were at least partially man-made, but no one did anything about it. Most of the homes in London are heated by coal-burning furnaces, and the coal used most often was rich in sulfur. Coal smoke pouring out of millions of chimneys and factory smokestacks produced countless particles of sulfur-bearing soot, which in turn produced droplets of water and sulfur dioxide.

In the terrible smog of December 1952, about 4000 residents died, most of them from lung ailments brought on by the action of the sulfur dioxide. Trains couldn't run. Birds couldn't see to fly. An opera was cancelled because the singers couldn't see the orchestra conductor. Movies shut down because people couldn't see the screen. Prize cattle, brought into the city for a livestock show, lay down and died on the spot.

Londoners finally decided that they'd had enough. Parliament tackled the problem, and after much argument and investigation, passed the British Clean Air Act of 1956. It was a very mild law. Basically, all it did was to make it illegal to burn smoke-producing fuels in certain parts of the vast city.

But the law was *enforced*. The local London government

paid up to seventy percent of the cost to any homeowner who had to change his heating furnace so that he could burn smokeless fuel. The suppliers where people bought their fuel stopped selling the smoke-producing kind. Police patrolmen simply noted whose chimneys were smoking and asked them to comply with the law. For the most part people cooperated and worked together to save their city—and their own lives.

The result: sunshine!

The amount of sunshine in London during the winter months has increased fifty percent since 1956. The number of dense fogs has gone down by eighty percent. Bird species that hadn't been seen in London's parks for decades have started to reappear. And some of the city's finest stone buildings—from Buckingham Palace to St. Paul's Cathedral—have been cleaned up and had the soot of two centuries scraped off them, revealing lovely warm colors of stone beneath their pollution-gray coats.

What happened in London can be done in other cities. The pollution problems of New York and Los Angeles seem much tougher, but London's success offers hope that even these cities can be saved.

This form of weather control—controlling man's unconscious effects on the weather—can be made to work. What about more deliberate alterations of the natural weather?

For example, Eugene Bollay, one of the nation's leading commercial rainmakers, has proposed a bold scheme for adding a million or more acre-feet of water to the Colorado River. The Colorado and its tributaries provide the water for Southern California, Arizona and part of Mexico. A million acre-feet of additional water each year would help to solve the growing water shortages caused by explosive growth of the area's population and industry.

Bollay's scheme is to set up a "picket fence" of ground-based seeding generators near the snowpack atop the Rockies, where the Colorado River-system begins. The snow on these mountains feeds the river system. During the winter months, approaching storms would be seeded so that they would yield ten to fifteen percent more snowfall than they would normally. Bollay calculated that this would add a million acre-feet of water to the rivers when the snow melted in the spring.

This kind of weather control can be done now. In the future, it might be possible to control most of the large-scale features of the weather around the world. Man may learn to regulate the amount of rainfall that a given section of land receives; control when, where and how much rain and snow falls. Destructive storms might be weakened or steered away from populated areas. Weather might be made perfect for farmers, so that they can grow all the food that's needed to feed the hungry billions of the world.

But—who will control the weather? Who will make the decision? Will weather control be used for good or evil?

During the summer of 1967, riots erupted in many American cities. Detroit and Washington burned. People died in the streets. Two particular riots were very interesting because they did *not* happen.

During one week of that violent summer, in Milwaukee and then a few days later in Washington, riots that were just getting started suddenly broke up when heavy rain showers drenched the streets and made everybody run home. In both cases, the showers were caused by completely natural weather patterns.

But what if a government could control the weather well enough to drown out a street demonstration? What if a government could actually control the weather for its farmers and businessmen and vacationers? Would it be a step toward a police state, where you did what you were told or you didn't get good weather?

Suppose government decided to use weather control as

a weapon against other nations. By causing droughts, or floods, or violent storms, weather control could ruin a nation just as effectively as an invading army. And the nation might not even know it was being attacked!

The United States isn't the only nation working on weather modification and control. Suppose the ability to control weather was mastered by some of the nations that now have nuclear weapons: the U.S., Russia, England, France and China. In such a world, every rainstorm might signal an enemy action.

If half a dozen countries tried to tinker with each other's weather, the resulting chaos might cause a disaster for us all. Because of this, the chances are that weather control might become a subject for international cooperation, instead of conflict.

Some people worry that cloud seeding and rainmaking are merely taking rainfall away from where it would naturally fall and giving it to the area that's been seeded. Perhaps, on the small scale that's been attempted up to now, the cloud seeders really are "robbing Peter to pay Paul."

But, as Secretary of the Interior Stewart Udall pointed out in 1967, there are some 47.5 *billion* acre-feet of water flowing across the United States in "rivers in the sky." If we could learn to squeeze just an extra two percent out of this treasure, it would benefit everyone in the nation without hurting anyone, since most of this moisture would fall into the oceans, anyway.

Our atmosphere is a precious resource, much more vital to us than gold or oil. We're just starting to understand this, and are beginning to learn how to use this resource wisely, rather than use it as a dumping ground. If the nations of the world act together, weather control can help to erase some of the ancient causes for war—hunger and poverty.

Should we try to control the weather? That's for you to

decide. It seems clear that before we can ever hope to really control the weather, we must learn to control ourselves.

If we do, then someday we might have the kind of world where it will never rain until everyone's safely under shelter, where snow will come on schedule and never be allowed in cities (where it's not really appreciated), where there will always be fair winds for sailors and sunshine for us all.

It might be a pleasant world to live in.

THE MAN WHO ...

Of all the new capabilities that science has offered humankind, none are so powerful as genetic engineering. When we take the very material of life itself into our hands and begin to tinker with it, we put ourselves on Nietzsche's tightrope between immortality and oblivion. *The Man Who...* looks into one possible use of "the new biology" in a field that has been quick to adapt for its own purposes such new technologies as television and computers: the field of politics.

■

He doesn't have cancer!"

Les Trotter was a grubby little man. He combed his hair forward to hide his baldness, but now as I drove breakneck through the early Minnesota morning, the wind had blown his thinning hair every which way, leaving him looking bald and moon-faced and aging.

And upset as hell.

"Marie, I'm telling you, he doesn't have cancer." He tried to make it sound sincere. His voice was somewhere between the nasality of an upper-register clarinet and its Moog synthesis.

"Sure," I said sweetly. "That's why he's rushed off to a secret laboratory in the dead of night."

Les's voice went up still another notch. "It's not a secret lab! It's the Wellington Memorial Laboratory. It's worldfamous. And ... goddammit, Marie, you're *enjoying* this!"

"I'm a reporter, Les." Great line. Very impressive. It hadn't kept him from making a grab for my ass, when we had first met. "It's my job."

He said nothing.

"And if your candidate has cancer . . ."

"He doesn't."

"It's news."

We whipped past the dead, bare trees with the windows open to keep me from dozing. It had been a long night, waiting for Halliday at the Twin Cities Airport. A dark horse candidate, sure, but the boss wanted *all* the presidential candidates covered. So we drew lots and I lost. I got James J. Halliday, the obscure. When his private jet finally arrived, he whisked right out to this laboratory in the upstate woods.

I love to drive fast. And the hours around dawn are the best time of the day. The world's clean. And all yours . . . a new day coming. This day was starting with a murky gray as the sun tried to break through a heavy, late-winter overcast.

"There's ice on the road, you know," Les sulked.

I ignored him. Up ahead I could see lighted buildings.

The laboratory was surrounded by a riot-wire fence. The guard at the gate refused to open up and let us through. It took fifteen minutes of arguing and a phone call from the guard shack by Les before the word came back to allow us in.

"What'd you tell them?" I asked Les as I drove down the crunchy gravel driveway to the main laboratory building.

He was still shivering from the cold. "That it was either see you or see some nasty, scare headlines."

The lab building was old and drab, in the dawning light. There were a few other buildings farther down the driveway. I pulled up behind a trio of parked limousines, right in front of the main entrance.

We hurried through the chilly morning into the lobby. It was paneled with light mahogany, thickly carpeted, and *warm*. They had paintings spotted here and there—abstracts that might have been amateurish or priceless. I could never figure them out.

A smart-looking girl in a green pantsuit came through the only other door in the lobby. She gave me a quick, thorough inspection. I had to smile at how well she kept her face straight. My jeans and jacket were for warmth, not looks.

"Governor Halliday would like to know what this is all about," she said tightly. Pure efficiency: all nerves and smooth makeup. Probably screwed to a metronome beat. "He is here on a personal matter; there's no news material in this visit."

"That depends on his x-rays, doesn't it?" I said.

Her eyes widened. "Oh." That's all she said. Nothing more. She turned and made a quick exit.

"Bright," I said to Les. "She picks up right away."

"His whole staff's bright."

"Including his advance publicity man?" *With the over-active paws*, I added silently.

"Yes, including my advance publicity man."

I turned back toward the door. Walking toward me was James J. Halliday, Governor of Montana, would-be President of these United States: tall, cowboy-lean, tanned, good-looking. He was smiling at me, as if he knew my suspicions and was secretly amused by them. The smile was dazzling. He was a magnetic man.

"Hello, Les," Halliday said as he strode across the lobby toward us. "Sorry to cause you so much lost sleep." His voice was strong, rich.

And Les, who had always come on like a lizard, was blooming in the sunshine of that smile. He straightened up and *his* voice deepened. "Perfectly okay, Governor. I'll sleep after your inauguration."

Halliday laughed outright.

He reached out for my hand as Les introduced, "This is Marie Kludjian of—"

"I know," Halliday said. His grip was firm. "Is *Now*'s circulation falling off so badly that you have to invent a cancer case for me?" But he still smiled as he said it.

"Our circulation's fine," I said, trying to sound unimpressed. "How's yours?"

He stayed warm and friendly. "You're afraid I'm here for a secret examination or treatment, is that it?"

I wasn't accustomed to frankness from politicians. And he was just radiating warmth. Like the sun. Like a flame.

"You . . . well . . ." I stammered. "You come straight to the point, at least."

"It saves a lot of time," he said. "But I'm afraid you're wasting yours. I'm here to visit Dr. Corio, the new director of the lab. We went to school together back East. And Les has such a busy schedule arranged for me over the next week that this was the only chance I had to see him."

I nodded, feeling as dumb as a high school groupie.

"Besides," he went on, "I'm interested in science. I think it's one of our most important national resources. Too bad the current administration can't seem to recognize a chromosome from a clavicle."

"Uh-huh." My mind seemed to be stuck in neutral. *Come on!* I scolded myself. *Nobody can have that powerful an effect on you! This isn't a gothic novel.*

He waited a polite moment for me to say something else, then cracked, "The preceding was an unpaid political announcement."

We laughed, all three of us together.

Halliday ushered Les and me inside the lab, and we

stayed with him every minute he was there. He introduced me to Dr. Corio—a compactly built intense man of Halliday's age, with a short, dark beard and worried gray eyes. I spent a yawnprovoking two hours with them, going through a grand tour of the lab's facilities. There were only five of us: Halliday, Corio, the girl in the green suit, Les and me. All the lab's offices and workrooms were dark and unoccupied. Corio spent half the time feeling along the walls for light switches.

Through it all something buzzed in my head. Something was out of place. Then it hit me. *No staff. No flunkies. Just the appointments secretary and Les . . . and I dragged Les here.*

It was a small thing. But it was different. *A politician without pomp?* I wondered.

By seven in the morning, while Corio lectured to us about the search for carcinoma antitoxins or some such, I decided I had been dead wrong about James J. Halliday.

By seven-thirty I was practically in love with him. He was intelligent. And concerned. He had a way of looking right at you and turning on that dazzling smile. Not phony. Kneewatering. *And unattached,* I remembered. *The most available bachelor in the Presidential sweepstakes.*

By eight-thirty I began to realize that he was also as tough as a grizzled mountain man. I was out on my feet, but he was still alert and interested in everything Corio was showing me.

He caught me in mid-yawn, on our way back to the lobby. "Perhaps you'd better ride with us, Marie," he said. "I'll have one of Corio's guards drive your car back to the airport."

I protested, but feebly. I *was* tired. And, after all, it's not every day that a girl gets a lift from a potential President.

Halliday stayed in the lobby for a couple of minutes while Les, the appointment girl and I piled into one of the limousines. Then he came out, jogged to the limo and slid in beside me.

"All set. They'll get your car back to the airport."

I nodded. I was too damned sleepy to wonder what had happened to the people who had filled the other two limousines. And all the way back to Minneapolis, Halliday didn't smile at me once.

Sheila Songard, the managing editor at *Now,* was given to making flat statements, such as: "You'll be back in the office in two weeks, Marie. He won't get past the New Hampshire primary."

You don't argue with the boss. I don't, anyway. Especially not on the phone. But after Halliday grabbed off an impressive 43% of the fractured New Hampshire vote, I sent her a get-well card.

All through those dark, cold days of winter and early spring I stayed with Jim Halliday, got to know him and his staff, watched him grow. The news and media people started to flock in after New Hampshire.

The vitality of the man! Not only did he have sheer animal magnetism in generous globs, he had more energy than a half-dozen flamenco dancers. He was up and active with the sunrise every day and still going strong long after midnight. It wore out most of the older newsmen trying to keep up with him.

When he scored a clear victory in Wisconsin, the Halliday staff had to bring out extra buses and even arrange a separate plane for the media people to travel in, along with The Man's private 707 jet.

I was privileged to see the inside of his private jetliner. I was the only news reporter allowed aboard during the whole campaign, in fact. He never let news or media people fly with him. Superstition, I thought. Or just a desire to have a place that can be really private—even if he had to go 35,000 feet above the ground to get the privacy. Then I'd start daydreaming about what it would be like to be up that high with him. . . .

The day I saw the plane, it was having an engine overhauled at JFK in New York. It was still cold out, early April, and the hangar was even colder inside than the weakly sunlit out-of-doors.

The plane was a flying command post. The Air Force didn't have more elaborate electronics gear. Bunks for fifteen people. *There goes the romantic dream,* I thought. No fancy upholstery or decorations. Strictly utilitarian. But row after row of communication stuff: even picturephones, a whole dozen of them.

I had known that Jim was in constant communication with his people all over the country. But picturephones—it was typical of him. He wanted to be *there,* as close to the action as possible. Ordinary telephones or radios just weren't good enough for him.

"Are you covering an election campaign or writing love letters?" Sheila's voice, over the phone, had that bitchy edge to it.

"What's wrong with the copy I'm sending in?" I yelled back at her.

"It's too damned laudatory, and you know it," she shrilled. "You make it sound as if he's going through West Virginia converting the sinners and curing the lepers."

"He's doing better than that," I said. "And I'm not the only one praising him."

"I've watched his press conferences on TV," Sheila said. "He's a cutie, all right. Never at a loss for an answer."

"And he never contradicts himself. He's saying the same things here that he did in New York . . . and Denver . . . and Los Angeles."

"That doesn't make him a saint."

"Sheila, believe it. He's *good*. I've been with him nearly four months now. He's got it. He's our next President."

She was unimpressed. "You sound more like you're on his payroll than *Now*'s."

Les Trotter had hinted a few days earlier that Jim wanted me to join his staff for the California primary campaign. I held my tongue.

"Marie, listen to Momma," Sheila said, softer, calmer. "No politician is as good as you're painting him. Don't let your hormones get in the way of your judgment."

"That's ridiculous!" I snapped.

"Sure . . . sure. But I've seen enough of Halliday's halo. I want you to find his clay feet. He's got them, honey. They all do. It might hurt when you discover them, but I want to see what The Man's standing on. That's your job."

She meant it. And I knew she was right. But if Jim had clay feet, nobody had been able to discover it yet. Not even the nastiest bastards Hearst had sent out.

And I knew that I didn't want to be the one who did it.

So I joined Jim's staff for the California campaign. Sheila was just as glad to let me go. Officially I took a leave of absence from *Now*. I told her I'd get a better look inside The Man's organization this way. She sent out a lank-haired slouchy kid who couldn't even work a dial telephone, she was that young.

But instead of finding clay feet on The Man, as we went through the California campaign, I kept coming up with gold.

He was beautiful. He was honest. Everyone of the staff loved him and the voters were turning his rallies into victory celebrations.

And he was driving me insane. Some days he'd be warm and friendly and . . . well, it was just difficult to be near him without getting giddy. But then there were times—sometimes the same day, even—when he'd just turn off. He'd be as cold and out of reach as an Antarctic iceberg. I couldn't understand it. The smile was there, his voice and manners and style were unchanged, but the vibrations would be gone. Turned off.

There were a couple of nights when we found ourselves sitting with only one or two other people in a hotel room, planning the next days' moves over unending vats of black coffee. We made contact then. The vibes were good. He wanted me, I know he did, and I certainly wanted him. Yet somehow we never touched each other. The mood would suddenly change. He'd go to the phone and come back . . . different. His mind was on a thousand other things.

He's running for President, I raged at myself. *There's more on his mind than shacking up with an oversexed ex-reporter.*

But while all this was going on, while I was helping to make it happen, I was also quietly digging into the Wellington Memorial Laboratory, back in Minnesota. And its director, Dr. Corio. If Jim did have feet of clay, the evidence was there. And I had to know.

I got a friend of a friend to send me a copy of Corio's doctoral thesis from the Harvard library, and while I waited for it to arrive in the mail, I wanted more than anything to be proved wrong.

Jim was beautiful. He was so much more than the usual politician. His speech in Denver on uniting the rich and poor into a coalition that would solve the problems of the nation brought him as much attention for its style as its content. His position papers on R&D, the economy, tax reform, foreign trade, were all called "brilliant" and "pace-setting." A crusty old economist from Yale, no less, told the press, "That man has the mind of an economist." A compliment, from him. A half-dozen of Nader's Raiders joined the Halliday staff because they felt, "He's the only candidate who gives a damn about the average guy."

A political campaign is really a means for the candidate to show himself to the people. And *vice versa*. He must get to know the people, all the people, their fears, their prides, their voices and touch and smell. If he can't feel for them, can't reach their pulse and match it with his own heartbeat, all the fancy legwork and lovely ghostwriting in the universe can't help him.

Jim had it. He grew stronger every minute. He kept a backbreaking pace with such ease and charm that we would have wondered how he could do it, if we had had time enough to catch our own breaths. He was everywhere, smiling, confident, energetic, *concerned*. He identified with people and they identified with him. It was uncanny. He could be completely at ease with a Missouri farmer and a New York corporation chairman. And it wasn't phony; he could *feel* for people.

And they felt for him.

And I fell for him; thoroughly, completely, hopelessly. He realized it. I was sure he did. There were times when the electric current flowed between us so strongly that I could barely stand it. He'd catch my eye and grin at me, and even though there were ninety other people in the room, for that instant everything else went blank.

But then an hour later, or the next day, he'd be completely cold. As if I didn't exist . . . or worse yet, as if I was just another cog in his machine. He'd still smile, he'd say the same things and look exactly the same. But the spark between us just wouldn't be there.

It was driving me crazy. I put it down to the pressures of the campaign. He couldn't have any kind of private life in this uproar. I scolded myself, *Stop acting like a dumb broad!*

Corio's thesis arrived three days before the California primary. I didn't even get a chance to unwrap it.

Jim took California by such a huge margin that the TV commentators were worriedly looking for something significant to say by ten that evening. It was no contest at all.

As we packed up for the last eastern swing before the national convention, I hefted Corio's bulky thesis. Still unopened. I was going to need a translator, I realized; his doctoral prose would be too technical for me to understand. We were heading for Washington, and there was a science reporter there that I knew would help me.

Besides, I needed to get away from Jim Halliday for a while, a day or so at least. I was on an emotional roller coaster, and I needed some time to straighten out my nerves.

The phone was ringing as the bellman put my bags down in my room at the Park Sheraton. It was Sheila.

"How are you?" she asked.

She never calls for social chatter. "What do you want, Sheila?" I asked wearily. It had been a long, tiring flight from the coast, and I knew my time zones were going to be mixed up thoroughly.

"Have you found anything . . . clay feet, I mean?"

The bellman stood waiting expectantly beside me. I started fumbling with my purse while I wedged the phone against my shoulder.

"Listen, Marie," Sheila was saying. "He's too good to be true. *Nobody* can be a masterful politician *and* a brilliant economist *and* a hero to both the ghetto and the suburbs. It's physically impossible."

I popped a handful of change from my wallet and gave it over to the bellman. He glanced at the coins without smiling and left.

"He's doing it," I said into the phone. "He's putting it all together."

"Marie," she said with great patience, as I flopped on the bed, "he's a puppet. A robot that gets wound up every morn-

ing and goes out spouting whatever they tell him to say.
Find out who's running him, who's making all those brilliant plans, who's making his decisions for him."

"He makes his own decisions," I said, starting to feel a
little desperate. If someone as intelligent as Sheila couldn't
believe in him, if politics had sunk so low in the minds of
the people that they couldn't recognize a knight in brilliant
armor when he paraded across their view . . . then what
would happen to this nation?

"Marie," she said again, with her Momma-knows-best
tone, "listen to me. Find out who's running him. Break the
story in *Now*, and you'll come back on the staff as a full
editor. With a raise. Promise."

I hung up on her.

She was right in a way. Jim was superman. More than
human. *If only he weren't running for President! If only we
could*—I shut off that line of thought. Fantasizing wasn't
going to help either one of us. Lying there on the hotel
bed, I felt a shiver go through me. It wasn't from the air-
conditioning.

Even with translation into language I could understand,
Corio's thesis didn't shed any light on anything. It was all
about genetics and molecular manipulation. I didn't get a
chance to talk with the guy who had digested it for me. We
met at National Airport, he sprinting for one plane and me
for another.

My flight took me to San Francisco, where the national
convention was due to open in less than a week.

The few days before a national convention opens are
crazy in a way nothing else on Earth can match. It's like
knowing you're going to have a nervous breakdown and doing everything you can to make sure it comes off on schedule. You go into a sort of masochistic training, staying up
all night, collaring people for meetings and caucuses,

yelling into phones, generally behaving like the world is going to come to an end within the week—and you've got to help make it happen.

Jim's staff was scattered in a half-dozen hotels around San Francisco. I got placed in the St. Francis, my favorite. But there wasn't any time for enjoying the view.

Jim had a picturephone network set up for the staff. For two solid days before the convention officially convened, I stayed in my hotel room and yet was in immediate face-to-face contact with everyone I had to work with. It was fantastic, and it sure beat trying to drive through those jammed, hilly streets.

Late on the eve of the convention's opening gavel—it was morning, actually, about two-thirty—I was restless and wide awake. The idea wouldn't have struck me, I suppose, if Sheila hadn't needled me in Washington. But it *did hit me*, and I was foolish enough to act on the impulse.

None of Jim's brain-trusters are here, I told myself. *They're all safe in their homes, far from this madhouse. But what happens if we need to pick at one of their mighty intellects at some godawful hour? Can we reach them?*

If I hadn't been alone and nervous and feeling sorry for myself, sitting in that hotel room with nothing but the picturephone to talk to, I wouldn't have done it. I knew I was kidding myself as I punched out the number for Professor Marvin Carlton, down in La Jolla. I could hear Sheila's *listen to Momma* inside my head.

To my surprise, Carlton's image shaped up on the phone's picture-screen.

"Yes?" he asked pleasantly. He was sitting in what looked like a den or study—lots of books and wood. There was a drink in his hand and a book in his lap.

"Professor . . ." I felt distinctly foolish. "I'm with Governor Halliday's staff. . . ."

"Obviously. No one else has the number for this TV phone he gave me."

"Oh."

"What can I do for you . . . or the governor? I was just about to retire for the night."

Thinking with the speed of a dinosaur, I mumbled, "Oh well, we were just . . . um, checking the phone connection . . . to make certain we can reach you when we have to. . . ."

He pursed his lips. "I'm a bit surprised. The governor had no trouble reaching me this afternoon."

"This afternoon?"

"Yes. We went over the details of my urban restructuring program."

"Oh—of course." I tried to cover up my confusion. I had been with Jim most of the afternoon, while he charmed incoming delegates at various caucuses. We had driven together all across town, sitting side by side in the limousine. He had been warm and outgoing and . . . and then he had changed, as abruptly as putting on a new necktie. *Was it something I said? Am I being too obvious with him?*

"Well?" the professor asked, getting a bit testy. "Are you satisfied that I'm at my post and ready for instant service?"

"Oh, yes . . . yes sir. Sorry to have disturbed you."

"Very well."

"Um—Professor? One question? How long did you and the governor talk this afternoon? For our accounting records, you know. The phone bill, things like that."

His expression stayed sour. "Lord, it must have been at least two hours. He dragged every last detail out of me. The man must have an eidetic memory."

"Yes," I said. "Thank you."

"Good night."

I reached out and clicked the phone's off switch. If Jim

had spent two hours talking with Professor Carlton, it couldn't have been that afternoon. He hadn't been out of my sight for more than fifteen minutes between lunch and dinner.

I found myself biting my tongue and punching another number. This time it was Rollie O'Malley, the guy who ran our polling services. He was still in New York.

And sore as hell. "Goin' on five o'clock in the motherin' morning and you wanna ask me what?"

"When's the last time you talked with The Man?"

Rollie's face was puffy from sleep, red-eyed. His skin started turning red, too. "You dizzy broad . . . why in the hell—"

"It's important!" I snapped. "I wouldn't call if it wasn't."

He stopped in mid-flight. "Whassamatter? What's wrong?"

"Nothing major . . . I hope. But I need to know when you talked to him last. And for how long."

"Christ." He was puzzled, but more concerned than angry now. "Lessee . . . I was just about to sit down to dinner here at the apartment . . . musta been eight, eight-thirty. 'Round then."

"New York time?" That would put it around five or so our time. *Right when Jim was greeting the Texas delegation.*

"No! Bangkok time! What the hell is this all about, Marie?"

"Tell you later," and I cut him off.

I got a lot of people riled. I called the heads of every one of Jim's think-tank teams: science, economics, social welfare, foreign policy, taxation, even some of his Montana staff back in Helena. By dawn I had a crazy story: eleven different people had each talked *personally* with The Man that afternoon for an average of an hour and a half apiece, they claimed. Several of them were delighted that Jim would spend so much time with them just before the convention opened.

That was more than sixteen hours of face-to-face conversation on the picturephones. All between noon and 7 p.m., Pacific Daylight Time.

And for most of that impossible time, Jim had been in my presence, close enough to touch me. And never on the phone once.

I watched the sun come up over the city's mushrooming skyline. My hands were shaking. I was sticky damp with a cold sweat.

Phony. I wanted to feel anger, but all I felt was sorrow. And the beginnings of self-pity. *He's a phony. He's using his fancy electronics equipment to con a lot of people into thinking he's giving them his personal attention. And all the while he's just another damned public relations robot.*

And his smiles, his magnetism, the good vibes that he could turn on or off whenever it suited him. *I hate him!*

And then I asked myself the jackpot question: *Who's pulling his strings?* I had to find out.

But I couldn't.

I tried to tell myself that it wasn't just my emotions. I told myself that, puppet or not, he was the best candidate running. And God knows we needed a good President, a man who could handle the job and get the nation back on the right tracks again. But, at that bottom line, was the inescapable fact that I loved him. As wildly as any schoolgirl loved a movie star. But this was real. I wanted Jim Halliday . . . I wanted to be *his* First Lady.

I fussed around for two days, while the convention got started and those thousands of delegates from all over this sprawling nation settled preliminary matters like credentials and platform and voting procedures. There were almost as many TV cameras and news people as there were delegates. The convention hall, the hotels and the streets were all crawling with people asking each other questions.

It was a steamroller. That became clear right at the outset when all the credentials questions got ironed out so easily. Halliday's people were seated with hardly a murmur in every case where an argument came up.

Seeing Jim privately, where I could ask him about the phony picturephone conversations, was impossible. He was surrounded in his hotel suite by everybody from former party chieftains to movie stars.

So I boiled in my own juices for two days, watching helplessly while the convention worked its way toward the inevitable moment when The Man would be nominated. There was betting down on the streets that there wouldn't even be a first ballot: he'd be nominated by acclamation.

I couldn't take it. I bugged out. I packed my bag and headed for the airport.

I arrived at Twin Cities Airport at 10 p.m., local time. I rented a car and started out the road toward the Wellington Lab.

It was summer now, and the trees that had been bare that icy morning, geologic ages ago, were now full-leafed and rustling softly in a warm breeze. The moon was high and full, bathing everything in cool beauty.

I had the car radio on as I pushed the rental Dart up Route 10 toward the laboratory. Pouring from the speaker came a live interview with James J. Halliday, from his hotel suite in San Francisco.

". . . and we're hoping for a first-ballot victory," he was saying smoothly, with that hint of earnestness and boyish enthusiasm in his voice. *I will not let myself get carried away,* I told myself. *Definitely not.*

"On the question of unemployment . . ." the interviewer began.

"I'd rather think of it as a mismatch between—"

I snapped it off. I had written part of that material for him. But dammit, he had dictated most of it, and he never said it the same way twice. He always added something or shaded it a little differently to make it easier to understand. If he was a robot, he was a damnably clever one.

The laboratory gate was coming up, and the guard was already eyeing my car as I slowed down under the big floodlights that lined the outer fence.

I fished in my purse for my Halliday staff ID card. The guard puzzled over it for a second or two, then nodded.

"Right, Ms. Kludjian. Right straight ahead to the reception lobby."

No fuss. No questions. As if they were expecting me.

The parking area was deserted as I pulled up. The lobby was lit up, and there was a girl receptionist sitting at the desk, reading a magazine.

She put the magazine down on the kidney-shaped desk as I pushed the glass door open. I showed her my ID and asked if Dr. Corio was in.

"Yes he is," she said, touching a button on her phone console. Nothing more. Just the touch of a button.

I asked, "Does he always work this late at night?"

She smiled very professionally. "Sometimes."

"And you too?"

"Sometimes."

The speaker on her phone console came to life. "Nora, would you please show Ms. Kludjian to Room A-14?"

She touched the button again, then gestured toward the door that led into the main part of the building. "Straight down the corridor," she said sweetly, "the last door on your right."

I nodded and followed instructions. She went back to her magazine.

Jim Halliday was waiting for me inside Room A-14.

My knees actually went weak. He was sitting on the corner of the desk that was the only furniture in the little, tilepaneled room. There was a mini-TV on the desk. The convention was roaring and huffing through the tiny speaker.

"Hello, Marie." He reached out and took my hand.

I pulled it away, angrily. "So that 'live' interview from your hotel was a fake, too. Like all your taped phone conversations with your think-tank leaders."

He smiled at me. Gravely. "No, Marie. I haven't faked a thing. Not even the way I feel about you."

"Don't try that . . ." But my voice was as shaky as my body.

"That was James J. Halliday being interviewed in San Francisco, live, just a few minutes ago. I watched it on the set here. It went pretty well, I think."

"Then . . . who the hell are you?"

"James J. Halliday," he answered. And the back of my neck started to tingle.

"But—"

He held up a silencing hand. From the TV set, a florid speaker was bellowing, "This party *must* nominate the man who has swept all the primary elections across this great land. The man who can bring together all the elements of our people back into a great, harmonious whole. The man who will lead us to *victory* in November. . . ."— The roar of applause swelled to fill the tiny bare room we were in—". . . The man who will be our next President!" The cheers and applause were a tide of human emotion. The speaker's appleround face filled the little screen: "James J. Halliday, of Montana!"

I watched as the TV camera swept across the thronged convention hall. Everybody was on their feet, waving Halliday signs, jumping up and down. Balloons by the thousands fell from the ceiling. The sound was overpowering. Suddenly the picture cut to a view of James J. Halliday sitting in his hotel room in San Francisco, watching *his* TV set and smiling.

James J. Halliday clicked off the TV in the laboratory room and we faced each other in sudden silence.

"Marie," he said softly, kindly, "I'm sorry. If we had met another time, under another star . . ."

I was feeling dizzy. "How can you be there . . . and here . . ."

"If you had understood Corio's work, you'd have realized that it laid the basis for a practical system of cloning human beings."

"Cloning . . ."

"Making exact replications of a person from a few body cells. I don't know how Corio does it—but it works. He took a few patches of skin from me, years ago, when we were in school together. Now there are seven of us, all together."

"Seven?" My voice sounded like a choked squeak.

He nodded gravely. "I'm the one that fell in love with you. The others . . . well, we're not *exactly* alike, emotionally."

I was glancing around for a chair. There weren't any. He put his arms around me.

"It's too much for one man to handle," he said, urgently, demandingly. "Running a Presidential campaign takes an inhuman effort. You've got to be able to do everything— either that or be a complete fraud and run on slogans and gimmicks. I didn't want that. I want to be the best President this nation can elect."

"So . . . you . . ."

"Corio helped replicate six more of me. Seven exactly similar James J. Hallidays. Each an expert in one aspect of the Presidency such as no Presidential candidate could ever hope to be, by himself."

"Then that's how you could talk on the picturephones to everybody at the same time."

"And that's how I could know so much about so many different fields. Each of us could concentrate on a few separate problem areas. It's been tricky shuffling us back and forth—especially with all the newspeople around. That's why we keep the 707 strictly off-limits. Wouldn't want to let the public see seven of us in conference together. Not yet, anyway."

My stomach started crawling up toward my throat.

"And me . . . us . . . ?"

His arms dropped away from me. "I hadn't planned on something like this happening. I really hadn't. It's been tough keeping you at arm's length."

"What can we do?" I felt like a little child—helpless, scared.

He wouldn't look at me. Not straight-on. "We'll have to keep you here for a while, Marie. Not for long. Just 'til after the Inauguration. 'Til I . . . we . . . are safely in office. Corio and his people will make you comfortable here."

I stood there, stunned. Without another word Jim suddenly got up and strode out of the room, leaving me there alone.

He kept his promises. Corio and his staff made life very comfortable for me here. Maybe they're putting things in my food or something, who can tell? Most likely it's for my own good. I do get bored. And so lonely. And frightened.

I watched his Inauguration on television. They let me see TV. I watch him every chance I get. I try to spot the tiny difference that I might catch among the seven of them. So far, I haven't been able to find any flaw at all.

He said they'd let me go to him after the Inauguration. I hope they remember. His second Inauguration is coming up soon, I know.

Or is it his third?

THE SEEDS OF TOMORROW

This final piece is excerpted from the only book of mine to be cited as a reference in the *Encyclopaedia Britannica*. It shows how the Promethean ideal affects our society. After all, scientific research and new technological developments do not occur in a vacuum. The way we shape our society determines how well we use—or misuse—the products of research and development. While comparatively few men and women in any society become research scientists, it is critically important that every citizen in a democracy understand what science can and cannot do. The only real "enemy of the people" is ignorance. Those who do not understand science and technology inevitably become Luddites, through and through. And the terrible consequence of the Luddite philosophy is that we lose the golden opportunities that science and technology offer us, because we are afraid of the unknown, unsure of our own abilities, unwilling to trust ourselves.

We build our own future, each one of us, day by day. We build it by the things we do and the things we fail to do. Each time we turn away from knowledge, from learning, we take a step backward toward the darkness. Each time we use our brains and our skills to build some new capability, we take a step toward the stars, toward the abode of the gods, toward the citadel where Prometheus waits to welcome us.

■

I. THE REVOLUTIONARIES:
SCIENCE AND TECHNOLOGY

Technology has brought us changes, most of which we should welcome, rather than reject. Wealth is the least important of these changes. Of greater importance is change itself. Those young humanists who think themselves revolutionaries are nothing compared to technology.

—Lewis M. Branscomb

America celebrated its Bicentennial in 1976, commemorating two hundred years of independence, two centuries since the start of the American Revolution. To celebrate our Bicentennial year, we landed a pair of Viking spacecraft on the surface of Mars, and automated laboratories aboard the Viking landers began to search the Martian soil for evidence of life.

Sending spacecraft to another world is a particularly fitting tribute to the revolutionary spirit of America, for science and technology were important ingredients in the American Revolution of 1776.

The seeds of our revolution were actually planted in Europe during the fifteenth and sixteenth centuries. In 1454, in the German city of Mainz, Johann Gutenberg published the first book printed from movable metal type. The printing press was a revolutionary invention. For the first time in history, knowledge could be spread to everyone, instead of being restricted to the elite upper classes of society. Books could be made cheaply enough and in large enough numbers so that even the poorest people could afford them. Knowledge became available to all and was no longer a rare and guarded secret.

In 1492, of course, Columbus discovered the New World, although he didn't realize at the time that he had not reached the East Indies (modern Indonesia), which was his target. The fact that mariners could voyage across the open ocean, instead of hugging the shoreline, was the result of several technological breakthroughs, such as the development of deepwater sailing ships and crude but serviceable navigation instruments.

As small and fragile as Columbus's ships were, they can still be compared to today's spacecraft—technological wonders that could travel into realms where earlier generations of vessels had dared not go.

In 1543, Nicolaus Copernicus, the Polish astronomer, published the most revolutionary book of all time. It was entitled *De Revolutionibus*, and its "inflammatory" contents dealt with the idea that perhaps the Earth was not the center of the universe, but instead was a planet that revolved around the Sun.

Copernicus was so timid about his idea that he didn't allow his book to be published until he was on his deathbed. As a civil employee of the Roman Catholic Church, he could foresee quite clearly the furor that his book would cause.

Copernicus's idea flew in the face of the Church's teachings. It was bad enough that Columbus had given a practical demonstration of the fact that the Earth was not flat. But to believe that it was not the fixed and immovable center of the universe? Heresy!

In the sixteenth century the Church was a powerful political force as well as a spiritual one. The Church was rich in land holdings and gold, and it could command armies when the need arose. But the Church was threatened by the Protestant Reformation, which had thrown all of Europe into turmoil. For the first time since the Roman Empire had adopted Catholicism as its official state religion, Europeans were turning away from the Church, to the new teachings of Martin Luther and other Protestants. The Church responded with force, and even war, in many parts of Europe, to the challenge of its dogma.

Many in the Church, as well as other European intellectuals (including Luther!), wanted Copernicus's book suppressed.

A century earlier that would have been a simple matter. The few painfully reproduced copies of the book could have been quietly taken off the rare library shelves in the universities and either locked up or burned. But by 1543 large numbers of books were being printed and distributed throughout Europe. There was no way for the authorities to prevent people from reading Copernicus's revolutionary ideas.

Not only did Copernicus's ideas fly in the face of the acknowledged authorities of that era, they also ran contrary to the common belief that the Sun and Moon and stars revolved around the Earth.

Men of learning argued about Copernicus's concept for more than half a century. For despite all that the authorities of the day could do to suppress the idea—including burning people at the stake—the Copernican revolution would not die.

In the early summer of 1609, the great Italian physicist and astronomer, Galileo Galilei, made the first astronomical observations using a telescope. The startling things he discovered confirmed Copernicus's concept that the Earth revolves around the Sun. Although the Church forced Galileo to recant his statements about these discoveries, under threat of torture and imprisonment, the world knew by then that the Earth does move and it is not the center of the universe.

Copernicus had won. But what has this to do with the American Revolution? Just this: The Copernican revolution showed the world that new ideas can be developed, tested and confirmed no matter what the authorities of the day say or do. Men began investigating the world around them for themselves, rather than letting the authorities tell them what they should think. The scientific way of thinking, based on evidence and logic, was developed by Roger Bacon and others. During the seventeenth century this scientific attitude led to the Age of Enlightenment, during which thinking men across all of Europe prided themselves on their acceptance and understanding of the scientific method of thought.

England's Isaac Newton uncovered some of the basic principles that govern our universe, such as gravitation and the laws of motion. But equally important, in the eighteenth century, philosophers and social thinkers such as the Frenchmen Voltaire and Rousseau began to apply the scientific method of thought to social problems. Instead of accepting society as they found it, they began to question the rules laid down by the authorities: Why should people be governed by a king and hereditary nobles? Where does the rightful power of government lie? And what rights do the common people have?

Meanwhile, on a completely different level, a technological revolution was taking place. In the early Renaissance years of the fifteenth century, gunpowder and cannons made it possible for kings to overpower their barons and gather all the political power and authority of the land into their own hands. Throughout the Middle Ages, feudal barons had ruled small principalities, and the acknowledged king of each land was merely one of the barons with a grander title—but little more wealth or power—than the rest.

The technology of gunpowder changed all that. As the Middle Ages gave way to the Renaissance, gunpowder was as strange and new as intercontinental missiles are today. Only the richest, most farsighted and powerful could gather and train enough men to create an army proficient in the use of cannons and muskets. The men who were able to bring such armies into existence became kings. They battered down the other barons' castle walls with cannons and shot their armored knights with muskets.

By the time the fledgling American colonies were beginning to grumble about taxation and other grievances against Mother England, the technology of gunpowder had trickled down from the rich into the hands of the common people.

By 1776 even the ragged, embattled farmers who stood against the Redcoats at Lexington and Concord had guns in their hands—guns made by their neighbors, and gunpowder and shot that they had made for themselves. The richest kings of Europe no longer had a technological advantage over the common people. Revolution could succeed. And did.

Scientific thinking, which examines the world around us in a questioning, critical light, allowed people to begin examining their own way of life and to search for better ways of living. Timid Copernicus was the intellectual grandfather of Thomas Jefferson. And you can see the reasoned, scientific mode of thought in every line of the Declaration of Independence.

Technological development, which eventually made the yeoman farmer equal to the professional soldier in firepower, provided the military basis on which the Revolutionary War was won. By 1814, Andrew Jackson's ragtag collection of defenders was able to riddle a strong, professional British Army at New Orleans and send it reeling in flight because the Americans had accurate long-range rifles in their hands, while the British still used old-fashioned muskets.

In the 1960s, the "unsophisticated" guerillas of Southeast Asia often battled the U.S. Army to a standstill, using modern technological devices such as transistorized radios, cheap mortars and mass-produced submachine guns.

Today many Americans complain about the government's use of electronic surveillance techniques and phone taps to pry into the lives of private citizens. Modern electronics technology is in the same stage of development as gunpowder was during the Renaissance: It is new enough, strange enough and expensive enough so that only the very rich and powerful elements of our society can use it. Electronics technology has not yet filtered down to the common people, as gunpowder technology had by 1776. But it will.

The point of all this history is to show that political and social revolutions have never occurred without being accompanied—or preceded—by scientific or technological revolutions. Science and technology have always been revolutionary forces. Most other forces in our society—religion, politics, tradition, law—are essentially conservative. They look backward, not forward. They seek to maintain the status quo, to keep everything exactly the way it was yesterday.

Science and technology, by their very nature, are forwardlooking. Every new idea, every new invention or development, upsets the status quo, changes people and society.

Certainly science and technology are not the only revolutionary forces in human history. Nor are they the only revolutionary forces at work in our world today. The urge to be free, the desire of poor people to gain a fairer share of their national wealth, and new religious and political ideas are all revolutionary forces. But science and technology are crucially important to all of us, now more than at any time in our past.

We live today in a world that has been shaped by science and technology. This world faces enormous problems. Overpopulation threatens to reduce every nation to poverty and starvation. Already there are food shortages in Africa and Asia. In the wealthy nations of Europe and North

America (and in Japan and Australia, too) pollution of the air and water makes it actually dangerous to breathe and eat.

We face energy crises and shortages of such critical raw materials as copper and potassium. Looming behind all these problems is the ever-present threat of nuclear devastation. Each year more nations acquire the means to build and deliver nuclear bombs. Each year the moment when one madman can destroy the world comes closer.

Some people feel that science and technology are to blame for these problems. They would like to somehow stop our modern world, end our reliance on science and technology, and turn back the clock to an earlier, simpler time when these shattering problems did not exist.

But that is no answer. Imagine the situation for yourself. Picture what would happen if today, right *now*, we shut down all the research laboratories in the world, all the science and engineering colleges, all the factories, engineering offices, and electrical power plants, and all the automobiles, trucks, trains, planes and ships that use engines of any sort. Picture a world without electricity, without radio or television, without tractors or chemical fertilizers, computers, telephones, plastics, antibiotics, air-conditioning or central heating.

If all these products of modern science and technology were eliminated today, almost everyone in the world would die within a month. Billions of human beings would starve. Food from the world's farms could not reach most of the people without modern transport vehicles and the electronically assisted intelligence to send the food to the places where it is needed. Four and a half billion human beings cannot all feed themselves on their own little plots of self-sufficient farms. Organic, family-style farms cannot produce enough food to feed everyone in the world. There isn't enough arable land on Earth to feed four billion people that way.

It would not be a case of people going hungry for a while, until they learned how to grow their own food. Most people would starve to death—within a month. And those who did not starve would be attacked by disease within a short time.

A world without science and technology is not the Garden of Eden; it is Death Valley. A human being without science and technology would not be a yeoman farmer or a noble savage; he'd be a dead naked ape.

We are caught on the horns of a painful dilemma. We cannot live without science and technology. That statement is true in the most literal sense: We cannot live, eat, breathe, love, exist, without science and technology. On the other hand, byproducts of science and technology have made our world overcrowded, overpolluted and overly dangerous. Nuclear war is an ever-present threat. Pollution silently kills millions every year and threatens to poison our air and seas to the point where they can no longer sustain life. Our antibiotic medicines and insecticides have led to the rise of bacteria and insects that are stronger and more menacing to our health than the weaker strains we have eliminated.

How can this be? Are science and technology good, or are they evil? The answer is . . . neither, and both. Science is a way of thinking. Technology is a tool. Each can be put to evil uses or good uses. It is *people* who do good and evil. A hammer has no moral sense. Neither does an atom.

It is quite true that science and technology have played an enormous part in shaping the world we live in today, both the good and the bad. And we do face staggering problems. Science and technology can be used to help solve our problems and lead us toward a future that is bright with hope and promise. They are the seeds of tomorrow that we can plant today, seeds that can yield a beautiful harvest of knowledge and wealth for all the world's people.

II. CITIZENS OF THE WORLD

New sources of energy; information systems that can bring new knowledge and wealth to all the world's people: expansion into the solar system's vast domain of new resources; the challenges, dangers, and breathless opportunities of the new biological sciences—these are the seeds of the future that can bring a golden era of peace and plenty to the entire human race. But it is necessary for us to begin planting those seeds now, today, if this bright future is to blossom into reality. Because, as we know, the seeds of our own destruction have already been planted by earlier generations of shortsighted, selfish people.

The harvest that these bad seeds will yield has been outlined in the Club of Rome's study, *The Limits to Growth:* choking pollution, soaring death rate, crumbling cities, exhausted farmlands, chaos, war, the end of civilization and quite possibly the end of humanity. Yet we possess the scientific knowledge and the technological tools not merely to avert the predicted disaster, but to make life better and richer than it has ever been for every member of the human race.

But a basic problem exists. How do we use this knowledge and these wonderful tools? How can we employ our science and technology to solve the problems of overpopulation, starvation, ignorance, and greed? How can you and I, for example, turn the experimental studies of fusion reactors into practical controlled thermonuclear reactors that will supply all the world's energy needs cheaply and efficiently? And how do we get to where we want to be from where we are today?

These questions are largely political and social rather than scientific. But since the days of Copernicus, every advance in scientific thinking and technological capability has involved crucial political and social questions. Galileo faced torture and imprisonment; Einstein's work in nuclear energy resulted in Hiroshima; today's molecular biologists are more worried about social consequences than the ultimate success of their work.

The problems we face today are global ones. The disaster that awaits us will hit everyone. The solutions to global problems must also be global in scope. It will do little good for the United States, alone, to maintain a high standard of living while the rest of the world starves. Our economy is too dependent on the economies of other nations. And we would soon find ourselves attacked by hungry, jealous and frightened nations. And most important, it would be *wrong*—by any reasonable standard of morality.

We must find ways of using our scientific and technological skills on a global scale, to attack and defeat the problems that threaten us. How can this be done?

Ask yourself: Where are the citizens of the world? If you live in Maine, or California, or Montana, or Alabama, you still consider yourself to be an American. But how many Americans—or Englishmen, Chinese, Czechs, New Zealanders or Nigerians—consider themselves to be citizens of the world?

With the exception of a few idealists who have renounced their national citizenship, every human being on Earth gives his highest political allegiance to a nation-state: the United States of America, the Union of Soviet Socialist Republics, India, Libya, Uruguay.

True, there are still a handful of primitive societies in which the individual members give their highest allegiance to their own tribe or clan. In some rural areas of Southeast Asia the true allegiance of most of the people is to their village; the only connection they have with a national government is when a tax collector comes to the village or when soldiers turn their rice paddies into battlefields.

For most of the Earth's four billion people, the strongest political loyalty professed is to a nation. We consider ourselves to be Americans, or Germans, Canadians, Turks, Israelis, Australians, etc. No more than a tiny fraction of the world's population thinks of itself as citizens of the world.

We may say that we think of ourselves as human beings first and as national citizens second, but we *act* as if the citizens of nations other than our own are something less than truly human. Foreigners are *them*, not *us*. Our policies of trade and commerce, finance, politics, even our behavior at the Olympic Games, show the force of nationalism. We're Number One! Buy American! See America First! Don't Sell America Short! America, love it or leave it!

Make no mistake about it: the United States of America is, to me, the finest nation in the world. You have only to travel overseas a little to realize that the rights and freedoms we take for granted here in the United States are very rare and extremely precious. Nor is nationalistic zeal restricted to America. It is not even restricted to the industrialized nations of the West. The newly emerging nations of the Third World burn with fierce nationalistic ambition. In Latin America nations have gone to war over soccer games, so intense is their national rivalry.

If nationalism were entirely stupid, evil or harmful, it would have disappeared centuries ago. Human beings may be shortsighted and greedy, but they seldom cling to something very long, once they realize that it is harming them.

The roots of nationalism go back to the Middle Ages, when royal houses such as the Tudors in England and the Bourbons of France were struggling to increase their power over the power of rival noble families. In time, such European struggles transformed the patchworks of medieval baronies and duchies into modern nations with centralized leadership and government.

Today, in many of the new nations of the Third World,

small, educated groups of leaders are struggling to bring their villagers and tribesmen into the twentieth century. To accomplish this, they must get their peoples' thinking habits to leapfrog from tribalism to the concept of nationalism. This is why so many of the new members of the United Nations display so much pomp and pride of nationalism. It is only this new and exciting idea of a nation that is holding their people together.

So nationalism has its uses. But it also has very real limitations. And, as we said earlier, the global disaster that lurks in our future cannot be solved piecemeal, by individual nations. It requires an international, global response.

How do we go from nationalism to a global community? How can a world divided into nations learn to work together, in a unified way, to meet global problems? How can the United States or Soviet Russia or Zaire surrender any of its national power and authority to an international organization?

Alexander Hamilton, one of the founders of the United States, saw the situation quite clearly almost two hundred years ago: "Do not expect nations to take the initiative in imposing restrictions upon themselves," he said.

In other words, no national government is going to willingly give up any of its power to an international organization. For years people have complained that the United Nations is little more than a debating society, that it has no real power in the arena of international politics. This is very true. But it is true because the nations that created the United Nations built powerlessness into its very foundations. How well would the U.S. government work if one single state in the Union could nullify any piece of federal legislation simply by casting a veto?

Americans fought the bloody Civil War to affirm the supremacy of the federal government over the powers of the individual states. We still have legal wrangles over states' rights. The United Nations is effectively powerless because any member nation of the Security Council can veto almost any action. It was the most powerful nations of the world, including the United States, that wrote the veto into the UN charter.

The few idealistic persons who have proclaimed themselves citizens of the world have not brought about a step forward in international cooperation. In fact, by renouncing their citizenship in any particular nation, they have become legally stateless persons. They have no citizenship anywhere on Earth. They have no legal residence, no voting privileges, no passports, no civil rights. They are literally exiles from every nation on this planet. Without citizenship in a nation, an individual human being has no legal protection from any government. He is as helpless as an Ice Age hunter who belonged to no tribe: a single, frail human being all alone in a cold and dangerous world.

Perhaps, in our increasingly complex and dangerous world, it would be desirable to have a single, unified world government. Perhaps not. Leaving that question aside for the moment, let us see if there are any trends on the world scene today that are moving the separate nations toward more international cooperation.

Clearly, the influence of modern technology is to unite the world socially and culturally, if not politically. Electronic communications has turned the world into a "global village," in the words of Marshall McLuhan. Diplomats can fly from one capital to another at the speed of sound, shuttling back and forth over more miles in a single day than Talleyrand, the nineteenth-century French statesman and diplomat, covered in a lifetime. Rock singers are known instantly all over the world. Western clothing styles, business methods and social attitudes can be found from Tokyo to Timbuktu.

Spearheaded by our science-based technology, Western

culture is homogenizing most of the world. All the industrialized nations and most of the emerging ones have adopted a Western form of society. As *The Limits to Growth* has shown, it is this very industrialization and its resulting population explosion that is causing most of the world's problems today. Can the same high-technology industrialization become part of the solution to these problems?

Western culture may be literally conquering the world socially and economically, but what is happening politically? There has been some movement toward supra-national *(supra*, meaning "beyond, over, more than") groupings of nations. These alliances among nations have been spurred mainly by the military confrontation between the West and the Soviet Bloc. NATO, in the West, and the East's Warsaw Pact are supra-national organizations that are mainly military alliances.

Most of the nations of Western Europe have banded together to form the European Economic Community, the so-called Common Market. But this has done rather little to bring these nations together *politically*.

Economically, socially, culturally and technologically, we are moving toward a unified world, whether we like it or not. But politically we are still divided into separate, suspicious, hostile nations. Many writers and researchers who deal in forecasts have said that it is modern technology that will lead the way toward uniting the world's peoples and nations. "First come the scientists," they say, "then the engineers, the financiers, the businessmen and finally—way behind—come the politicians."

How far behind are the politicians? A few years? A decade? A generation? How far behind can we allow them to be when they have their fingers on the H-bomb buttons? In a world simmering with little wars, with vast nuclear armaments, with growing gaps between the rich and the poor, and with steadily rising population and steadily dwindling resources, how much longer can we remain divided into nation-states and expect to survive?

Look at history. Most historians agree that the most brilliant civilization on Earth prior to our modern age was that of ancient Greece. Many feel that the Greeks, particularly the Athenians, produced the highest civilization humankind has yet achieved.

Yet that beautiful civilization was swept away by people who were barbarians, compared to the Athenians. The Macedonians, and later the Romans, conquered all of Greece and ended the glory of Athens and the other Greek city-states. Greek culture permeated the conquerors, true enough. But the wisdom of the Greeks never advanced an inch further after the Macedonians conquered Greece.

The brilliant and beautiful Greek culture stagnated under Macedonian and Roman rule. Would it have advanced further if it had remained free? Would there had been a scientific revolution fifteen hundred years before Copernicus's time? If Greece had remained free, perhaps we would not have had to wait fifteen centuries between Aristotle and Galileo. Perhaps today, in the twentieth century, our knowledge and abilities would be *fifteen hundred years* ahead of where we are now.

Perhaps.

But this much we do know for certain. No citizen of Athens thought of himself as a Greek. He was an Athenian. There were no Greeks. There were Spartans and Thebans and Corinthians. No citizen of the Greek city-states had a political allegiance higher than that to his city. The Greeks could band together temporarily to fight off invaders. But even when a handful of Athenians, Spartans, *et al.* threw back the full might of the Persian Empire, the victors marched home to the separate cities and resumed squabbling among themselves. They never realized that, united, they were the most powerful force in the world. They destroyed themselves with intercity wars. The Macedonians conquered an exhausted Athens.

To paraphrase the philosopher George Santayana, those who ignore the lessons of history are doomed to repeat the mistakes. The civilization of ancient Greece fell because the Greek people never developed a political loyalty to any entity higher than their city-states. Today we live in a world where our highest political allegiance is given to the nation-state. Yet it seems clear that the global problems that threaten us cannot be solved by individual nations, each working by itself. The problems of nationalism now outweigh the advantages.

Nationalism has served us well in the past. It has provided the framework for the development of nation-states the size of whole continents, and for empires of globe-spanning proportions. But today, nationalism is not part of the solution; it is part of the problem.

In his book *The Story of Man*, anthropologist Carleton S. Coon warns:

> Because it now takes less time to fly around the world than it took President Washington to travel from his home in Virginia to Independence Hall in Philadelphia . . . what prevents the peoples of the world from pooling their efforts . . . is not distance, time, or technology.
>
> It is the retention by twentieth-century, Atom Age men of the Neolithic point of view that says: *You stay in your village, and I will stay in mine. If your sheep eat our grass we will kill you, or we may kill you anyhow to get all the grass for our own sheep. Anyone who tries to make us change our ways is a witch and we will kill him. Keep out of our village.*

This "Neolithic point of view" has been with us since the end of the Ice Age. It must change, if we are to survive.

We are biological creatures, and to some extent so are our societies. Biological forces are extremely conservative. The basic motivating principle among biological creatures seems to be, "Do it today exactly as you did it yesterday." Human societies are very complex biological entities, but they follow the same basic conservative rule. They change slowly, and very reluctantly.

Yet biological organisms do change. If they did not, this planet would be inhabited by nothing more than viruses. People do change. And so do societies. Sooner or later there will be an effective international organization of some sort, and the limitations of today's nationalism will be overcome. The seeds for this tomorrow exist today in our technology, in our growing interdependence with all the peoples of this planet, in our minds and our hopes for a better future.

But we are definitely in a race against time. For if we do not take the necessary steps to solve the problems that threaten us, we will be overwhelmed by them and go down to destruction under a bloody tide of population, pollution, starvation and war.

In 1974 the Club of Rome published a second report, entitled *Mankind at the Turning Point*. The club's first report, *The Limits of Growth,* was devoted to showing the disaster awaiting us within a few decades, in the strongest possible manner. That first report had to catch the attention of the whole world, had to make people realize that we must face tomorrow's problems today. It succeeded in doing that.

In *Mankind at the Turning Point*, the investigators showed that there are ways to avoid the impending disaster, scientific and technological approaches that we can take to solve key problems such as energy, food, information and natural resources. The Club of Rome's second report also stresses the fact that international cooperation will be absolutely indispensable, if we are to succeed in solving these problems.

The final paragraph of *Mankind at the Turning Point* states:

> Mankind cannot afford to wait for change to occur spontaneously and fortuitously. Rather, man must initiate on his own changes of necessary but tolerable magnitude in time to avert intolerably massive [and destructive] change. A strategy for such change can be evolved only in the spirit of truly global cooperation, shaped in free partnership by the world's diverse regional communities and guided by a rational master plan for long-term organic growth. All our computer simulations have shown quite clearly that this is the only sensible and feasible approach to avoid major regional and ultimately global catastrophe, and that the time that can be wasted before developing such a global world system is running out. Clearly *the only alternatives are division and conflict, hate and destruction.*

The problem is clear and real, global in its scope and frightening in its complexity and seriousness. But the human race has struggled through Ice Ages, plagues, wars, famines—and, yes, even the collapse of whole civilizations.

We have the knowledge and the tools to meet the problems of the coming decades. We have the skill and the courage to make the twenty-first century a Golden Age for all the human race, rather than a Dark Age of misery and death.

But do we have the heart and the willpower to change our own ways of living, our own views of the world? Are we willing to act *now,* to plant the seeds of tomorrow that will bring forth a good future?

Science and technology hold the key to our future. We

must all learn as much as we can about what science and technology can do for us, and what they cannot do—where the shortcomings and pitfalls are. Then we must use our knowledge in the political arena, and see to it that our governments use these powerful tools wisely, for the benefit of all the people.

We live in a world brim-full of new energy sources, new information-handling techniques, new scientific capabilities all around us. We can lift the scourge of hunger and fear from all people, everywhere. We can expand outward to new worlds in space, and improve our own minds and bodies to the point where we can challenge immortality itself.

But we must start now. Each one of us. This golden future will never come to be if we do not plant the good seeds of tomorrow in today's waiting ground. The old saying holds for each one of us: "If you're not part of the solution, you're part of the problem."